KURT VONNEGUT

# KURT VONNEGUT

## NOVELS 1976–1985

*Slapstick*
*Jailbird*
*Deadeye Dick*
*Galápagos*

Sidney Offit, editor

THE LIBRARY OF AMERICA

# Contents

# SLAPSTICK

*or Lonesome No More!*

Dedicated to the memory of
Arthur Stanley Jefferson and Norvell Hardy,
two angels of my time.

*"Call me but love, and I'll be new baptiz'd . . ."*
—ROMEO

# Prologue

THIS IS THE CLOSEST I will ever come to writing an autobiography. I have called it "Slapstick" because it is grotesque, situational poetry—like the slapstick film comedies, especially those of Laurel and Hardy, of long ago.

It is about what life *feels* like to me.

There are all these tests of my limited agility and intelligence. They go on and on.

The fundamental joke with Laurel and Hardy, it seems to me, was that they did their best with every test.

They never failed to bargain in good faith with their destinies, and were screamingly adorable and funny on that account.

• • •

There was very little love in their films. There was often the situational poetry of marriage, which was something else again. It was yet another test—with comical possibilities, provided that everybody submitted to it in good faith.

Love was never at issue. And, perhaps because I was so perpetually intoxicated and instructed by Laurel and Hardy during my childhood in the Great Depression, I find it natural to discuss life without ever mentioning love.

It does not seem important to me.

What does seem important? Bargaining in good faith with destiny.

• • •

I have had some experiences with love, or think I have, anyway, although the ones I have liked best could easily be described as "common decency." I treated somebody well for a little while, or maybe even for a tremendously long time, and that person treated me well in turn. Love need not have had anything to do with it.

Also: I cannot distinguish between the love I have for people and the love I have for dogs.

When a child, and not watching comedians on film or listening to comedians on the radio, I used to spend a lot of time rolling around on rugs with uncritically affectionate dogs we had.

And I still do a lot of that. The dogs become tired and confused and embarrassed long before I do. I could go on forever.

Hi ho.

•  •  •

One time, on his twenty-first birthday, one of my three adopted sons, who was about to leave for the Peace Corps in the Amazon Rain Forest, said to me, "You know—you've never hugged me."

So I hugged him. We hugged each other. It was very nice. It was like rolling around on a rug with a Great Dane we used to have.

•  •  •

Love is where you find it. I think it is foolish to go looking for it, and I think it can often be poisonous.

I wish that people who are conventionally supposed to love each other would say to each other, when they fight, "Please—a little less love, and a little more common decency."

•  •  •

My longest experience with common decency, surely, has been with my older brother, my only brother, Bernard, who is an atmospheric scientist in the State University of New York at Albany.

He is a widower, raising two young sons all by himself. He does it well. He has three grown-up sons besides.

We were given very different sorts of minds at birth. Bernard could never be a writer. I could never be a scientist. And, since we make our livings with our minds, we tend to think of them as gadgets—separate from our awarenesses, from our central selves.

•  •  •

We have hugged each other maybe three or four times—on birthdays, very likely, and clumsily. We have never hugged in moments of grief.

• • •

The minds we have been given enjoy the same sorts of jokes, at any rate—Mark Twain stuff, Laurel and Hardy stuff.

They are equally disorderly, too.

Here is an anecdote about my brother, which, with minor variations, could be told truthfully about me:

Bernard worked for the General Electric Research Laboratory in Schenectady, New York, for a while, where he discovered that silver iodide could precipitate certain sorts of clouds as snow or rain. His laboratory was a sensational mess, however, where a clumsy stranger could die in a thousand different ways, depending on where he stumbled.

The company had a safety officer who nearly swooned when he saw this jungle of deadfalls and snares and hair-trigger booby traps. He bawled out my brother.

My brother said this to him, tapping his own forehead with his fingertips: "If you think this laboratory is bad, you should see what it's like in *here*."

And so on.

• • •

I told my brother one time that whenever I did repair work around the house, I lost all my tools before I could finish the job.

"You're lucky," he said. "I always lose whatever I'm working on."

We laughed.

• • •

But, because of the sorts of minds we were given at birth, and in spite of their disorderliness, Bernard and I belong to artificial extended families which allow us to claim relatives all over the world.

He is a brother to scientists everywhere. I am a brother to writers everywhere.

This is amusing and comforting to both of us. It is nice.

It is lucky, too, for human beings need all the relatives they can get—as possible donors or receivers not necessarily of love, but of common decency.

•  •  •

When we were children in Indianapolis, Indiana, it appeared that we would always have an extended family of genuine relatives there. Our parents and grandparents, after all, had grown up there with shoals of siblings and cousins and uncles and aunts. Yes, and their relatives were all cultivated and gentle and prosperous, and spoke German and English gracefully.

•  •  •

They were all religious skeptics, by the way.

•  •  •

They might roam the wide world over when they were young, and often have wonderful adventures. But they were all told sooner or later that it was time for them to come home to Indianapolis, and to settle down. They invariably obeyed—because they had so many relatives there.

There were good things to inherit, too, of course—sane businesses, comfortable homes and faithful servants, growing mountains of china and crystal and silverware, reputations for honest dealing, cottages on Lake Maxinkuckee, along whose eastern shore my family once owned a village of summer homes.

•  •  •

But the delight the family took in itself was permanently crippled, I think, by the sudden American hatred for all things German which unsheathed itself when this country entered the First World War, five years before I was born.

Children in our family were no longer taught German. Neither were they encouraged to admire German music or literature or art or science. My brother and sister and I were raised as though Germany were as foreign to us as Paraguay.

We were deprived of Europe, except for what we might learn of it at school.

We lost thousands of years in a very short time—and then tens of thousands of American dollars after that, and the summer cottages and so on.

And our family became a lot less interesting, especially to itself.

So—by the time the Great Depression and a Second World War were over, it was easy for my brother and my sister and me to wander away from Indianapolis.

And, of all the relatives we left behind, not one could think of a reason why we should come home again.

We didn't belong anywhere in particular any more. We were interchangeable parts in the American machine.

•    •    •

Yes, and Indianapolis, which had once had a way of speaking English all its own, and jokes and legends and poets and villains and heroes all its own, and galleries for its own artists, had itself become an interchangeable part in the American machine.

It was just another someplace where automobiles lived, with a symphony orchestra and all. And a race track.

Hi ho.

•    •    •

My brother and I still go back for funerals, of course. We went back last July for the funeral of our Uncle Alex Vonnegut, the younger brother of our late father—almost the last of our old-style relatives, of the native American patriots who did not fear God, and who had souls that were European.

He was eighty-seven years old. He was childless. He was a graduate of Harvard. He was a retired life insurance agent. He was a co-founder of the Indianapolis Chapter of Alcoholics Anonymous.

•    •    •

His obituary in the *Indianapolis Star* said that he himself was not an alcoholic.

This denial was at least partly a nice-Nellyism from the past, I think. He used to drink, I know, although alcohol never seriously damaged his work or made him wild. And then he stopped cold. And he surely must have introduced himself at meetings of A. A. as all members must, with his name—followed by this brave confession: "I'm an alcoholic."

Yes, and the paper's genteel denial of his ever having had trouble with alcohol had the old-fashioned intent of preserving from taint all the rest of us who had the same last name.

We would all have a harder time making good Indianapolis marriages or getting good Indianapolis jobs, if it were known for certain that we had had relatives who were once drunkards, or who, like my mother and my son, had gone at least temporarily insane.

It was even a secret that my paternal grandmother died of cancer.

Think of that.

•   •   •

At any rate, if Uncle Alex, the atheist, found himself standing before Saint Peter and the Pearly Gates after he died, I am certain he introduced himself as follows:

"My name is Alex Vonnegut. I'm an alcoholic."

Good for him.

•   •   •

I will guess, too, that it was loneliness as much as it was a dread of alcoholic poisoning which shepherded him into A. A. As his relatives died off or wandered away, or simply became interchangeable parts in the American machine, he went looking for new brothers and sisters and nephews and nieces and uncles and aunts, and so on, which he found in A. A.

•   •   •

When I was a child, he used to tell me what to read, and then make sure I'd read it. It used to amuse him to take me on visits to relatives I'd never known I had.

He told me one time that he had been an American spy in Baltimore during the First World War, befriending German-Americans there. His assignment was to detect enemy agents. He detected nothing, for there was nothing to detect.

He told me, too, that he was an investigator of graft in New York City for a little while—before his parents told him it was time to come home and settle down. He uncovered a scandal involving large expenditures for the maintenance of Grant's Tomb, which required very little maintenance indeed.

Hi ho.

•   •   •

I received the news of his death over a white, push-button telephone in my house in that part of Manhattan known as "Turtle Bay." There was a philodendron nearby.

I am still not clear how I got here. There are no turtles. There is no bay.

Perhaps I am the turtle, able to live simply anywhere, even underwater for short periods, with my home on my back.

• • •

So I called my brother in Albany. He was about to turn sixty. I was fifty-two.

We were certainly no spring chickens.

But Bernard still played the part of an older brother. It was he who got us our seats on Trans World Airlines and our car at the Indianapolis airport, and our double room with twin beds at a Ramada Inn.

The funeral itself, like the funerals of our parents and of so many other close relatives, was as blankly secular, as vacant of ideas about God or the afterlife, or even about Indianapolis, as our Ramada Inn.

• • •

So my brother and I strapped ourselves into a jet-propelled airplane bound from New York City to Indianapolis. I sat on the aisle. Bernard took the window seat, since he was an atmospheric scientist, since clouds had so much more to say to him than they did to me.

We were both over six feet tall. We still had most of our hair, which was brown. We had identical mustaches—duplicates of our late father's mustache.

We were harmless looking. We were a couple of nice old Andy Gumps.

There was an empty seat between us, which was spooky poetry. It could have been a seat for our sister Alice, whose age was halfway between mine and Bernard's. She wasn't in that seat and on her way to her beloved Uncle Alex's funeral, for she had died among strangers in New Jersey, of cancer—at the age of forty-one.

"Soap opera!" she said to my brother and me one time, when discussing her own impending death. She would be leaving four young boys behind, without any mother.

"Slapstick," she said.

Hi ho.

•  •  •

She spent the last day of her life in a hospital. The doctors and nurses said she could smoke and drink as much as she pleased, and eat whatever she pleased.

My brother and I paid her a call. It was hard for her to breathe. She had been as tall as we were at one time, which was very embarrassing to her, since she was a woman. Her posture had always been bad, because of her embarrassment. Now she had a posture like a question mark.

She coughed. She laughed. She made a couple of jokes which I don't remember now.

Then she sent us away. "Don't look back," she said.

So we didn't.

She died at about the same time of day that Uncle Alex died—an hour or two after the sun went down.

And hers would have been an unremarkable death statistically, if it were not for one detail, which was this: Her healthy husband, James Carmalt Adams, the editor of a trade journal for purchasing agents, which he put together in a cubicle on Wall Street, had died two mornings before—on "The Brokers' Special," the only train in American railroading history to hurl itself off an open drawbridge.

Think of that.

•  •  •

This really happened.

•  •  •

Bernard and I did not tell Alice about what had happened to her husband, who was supposed to take full charge of the children after she died, but she found out about it anyway. An ambulatory female patient gave her a copy of the New York *Daily News*. The front page headline was about the dive of the train. Yes, and there was a list of the dead and missing inside.

Since Alice had never received any religious instruction, and since she had led a blameless life, she never thought of her awful luck as being anything but accidents in a very busy place.

Good for her.

•   •   •

Exhaustion, yes, and deep money worries, too, made her say toward the end that she guessed that she wasn't really very good at life.

Then again: Neither were Laurel and Hardy.

•   •   •

My brother and I had already taken over her household. After she died, her three oldest sons, who were between the ages of eight and fourteen, held a meeting, which no grownups could attend. Then they came out and asked that we honor their only two requirements: That they remain together, and that they keep their two dogs. The youngest child, who was not at the meeting, was a baby only a year old or so.

From then on, the three oldest were raised by me and my wife, Jane Cox Vonnegut, along with our own three children, on Cape Cod. The baby, who lived with us for a while, was adopted by a first cousin of their father, who is now a judge in Birmingham, Alabama.

So be it.

The three oldest kept their dogs.

•   •   •

I remember now what one of her sons, who is named "Kurt" like my father and me, asked me as we drove from New Jersey to Cape Cod with the two dogs in back. He was about eight.

We were going from south to north, so where we were going was "up" to him. There were just the two of us. His brothers had gone ahead.

"Are the kids up there nice?" he said.

"Yes, they are," I replied.

He is an airline pilot now.

They are all something other than children now.

•   •   •

One of them is a goat farmer on a mountaintop in Jamaica. He has made come true a dream of our sister's: To live far from the madness of cities, with animals for friends. He has no telephone or electricity.

He is desperately dependent on rainfall. He is a ruined man, if it does not rain.

•   •   •

The two dogs have died of old age. I used to roll around with them on rugs for hours on end, until they were all pooped out.

•   •   •

Yes, and our sister's sons are candid now about a creepy business which used to worry them a lot: They cannot find their mother or their father in their memories anywhere—not anywhere.

The goat farmer, whose name is James Carmalt Adams, Jr., said this about it to me, tapping his forehead with his fingertips: "It isn't the museum it should be."

The museums in children's minds, I think, automatically empty themselves in times of utmost horror—to protect the children from eternal grief.

•   •   •

For my own part, though: It would have been catastrophic if I had forgotten my sister at once. I had never told her so, but she was the person I had always written for. She was the secret of whatever artistic unity I had ever achieved. She was the secret of my technique. Any creation which has any wholeness and harmoniousness, I suspect, was made by an artist or inventor with an audience of one in mind.

Yes, and she was nice enough, or Nature was nice enough, to allow me to feel her presence for a number of years after she died—to let me go on writing for her. But then she began to fade away, perhaps because she had more important business elsewhere.

Be that as it may, she had vanished entirely as my audience by the time Uncle Alex died.

So the seat between my brother and me on the airplane seemed especially vacant to me. I filled it as best I could—with that morning's issue of *The New York Times*.

•  •  •

While my brother and I waited for the plane to take off for Indianapolis, he made me a present of a joke by Mark Twain—about an opera Twain had seen in Italy. Twain said that he hadn't heard anything like it ". . . since the orphanage burned down."

We laughed.

•  •  •

He asked me politely how my work was going. I think he respects but is baffled by my work.

I said that I was sick of it, but that I had always been sick of it. I told him a remark which I had heard attributed to the writer Renata Adler, who hates writing, that a writer was a person who hated writing.

I told him, too, what my agent, Max Wilkinson, wrote to me after I complained again about what a disagreeable profession I had. This was it: "Dear Kurt—I never knew a blacksmith who was in love with his anvil."

We laughed again, but I think the joke was partly lost on my brother. His life has been an unending honeymoon with his anvil.

•  •  •

I told him that I had been going to operas recently, and that the set for the first act of *Tosca* had looked exactly like the interior of Union Station in Indianapolis to me. While the actual opera was going on, I said, I daydreamed about putting track numbers in the archways of the set, and passing out bells and whistles to the orchestra, and staging an opera about Indianapolis during the Age of the Iron Horse.

"People from our great-grandfathers' generation would mingle with our own, when we were young—" I said, "and all the generations in between. Arrivals and departures would be announced. Uncle Alex would leave for his job as a spy in Baltimore. You would come home from your freshman year at M.I.T.

"There would be shoals of relatives," I said, "watching the travelers come and go—and black men to carry the luggage and shine the shoes."

•    •    •

"Every so often in my opera," I said, "the stage would turn mud-colored with uniforms. That would be a war.

"And then it would clear up again."

•    •    •

After the plane took off, my brother showed me a piece of scientific apparatus which he had brought along. It was a photo-electric cell connected to a small tape recorder. He aimed the electric eye at clouds. It perceived lightning flashes which were invisible to us in the dazzle of daytime.

The secret flashes were recorded as clicks by the recorder. We could also hear the clicks as they happened—on a tiny earphone.

"There's a hot one," my brother announced. He indicated a distant cumulus cloud, a seeming Pike's Peak of whipped cream.

He let me listen to the clicks. There were two quick ones, then some silence, then three quick ones, then silence again.

"How far away is that cloud?" I asked him.

"Oh—a hundred miles, maybe," he said.

I thought it was beautiful that my big brother could detect secrets so simply from so far away.

•    •    •

I lit a cigarette.

Bernard doesn't smoke any more, because it is so important that he live a good while longer. He still has two little boys to raise.

•    •    •

Yes, and while my big brother meditated about clouds, the mind *I* was given daydreamed the story in this book. It is about desolated cities and spiritual cannibalism and incest and loneliness and lovelessness and death, and so on. It depicts myself and my beautiful sister as monsters, and so on.

This is only natural, since I dreamed it on the way to a funeral.

•   •   •

It is about this terribly old man in the ruins of Manhattan, you see, where almost everyone has been killed by a mysterious disease called "The Green Death."

He lives there with his illiterate, rickety, pregnant little granddaughter, Melody. Who is he really? I guess he is myself—experimenting with being old.

Who is Melody? I thought for a while that she was all that remained of my memory of my sister. I now believe that she is what I feel to be, when I experiment with old age, all that is left of my optimistic imagination, of my creativeness.

Hi ho.

•   •   •

The old man is writing his autobiography. He begins it with words which my late Uncle Alex told me one time should be used by religious skeptics as a prelude to their nightly prayers.

These are the words: "To whom it may concern."

•   •   •

# *Chapter 1*

---

TO WHOM IT MAY CONCERN:
   It is springtime. It is late afternoon.

Smoke from a cooking fire on the terrazzo floor of the lobby of the Empire State Building on the Island of Death floats out over the ailanthus jungle which Thirty-fourth Street has become.

The pavement on the floor of the jungle is all crinkum-crankum—heaved this way and that by frost-heaves and roots.

There is a small clearing in the jungle. A blue-eyed, lantern-jawed old white man, who is two meters tall and one hundred years old, sits in the clearing on what was once the back seat of a taxicab.

I am that man.

My name is Dr. Wilbur Daffodil-11 Swain.

• • •

I am barefoot. I wear a purple toga made from draperies found in the ruins of the Americana Hotel.

I am a former President of the United States of America. I was the final President, the tallest President, and the only one ever to have been divorced while occupying the White House.

I inhabit the first floor of the Empire State Building with my sixteen-year-old granddaughter, who is Melody Oriole-2 von Peterswald, and with her lover, Isadore Raspberry-19 Cohen. The three of us have the building all to ourselves.

Our nearest neighbor is one and one-half kilometers away.

I have just heard one of her roosters crow.

• • •

Our nearest neighbor is Vera Chipmunk-5 Zappa, a woman who loves life and is better at it than anyone I ever knew. She is a strong and warm-hearted and hard-working farmer in her early sixties. She is built like a fireplug. She has slaves whom she treats very well. And she and the slaves raise cattle and pigs and chickens and goats and corn and wheat and vegetables and fruits and grapes along the shores of the East River.

They have built a windmill for grinding grain, and a still for making brandy, and a smokehouse—and on and on.

"Vera—" I told her the other day, "if you would only write us a new Declaration of Independence, you would be the Thomas Jefferson of modern times."

•   •   •

I write this book on the stationery of the Continental Driving School, three boxes of which Melody and Isadore found in a closet on the sixty-fourth floor of our home. They also found a gross of ball-point pens.

•   •   •

Visitors from the mainland are rare. The bridges are down. The tunnels are crushed. And boats will not come near us, for fear of the plague peculiar to this island, which is called "The Green Death."

And it is that plague which has earned Manhattan the sobriquet, "The Island of Death."

Hi ho.

•   •   •

It is a thing I often say these days: "Hi ho." It is a kind of senile hiccup. I have lived too long.

Hi ho.

•   •   •

The gravity is very light today. I have an erection as a result of that. All males have erections on days like this. They are automatic consequences of near-weightlessness. They have little to do with eroticism in most cases, and nothing to do with it in the life of a man my age. They are hydraulic experiences—the results of confused plumbing, and little more.

Hi ho.

•   •   •

The gravity is so light today, that I feel as though I might scamper to the top of the Empire State Building with a manhole cover, and fling it into New Jersey.

That would surely be an improvement on George Washington's sailing a silver dollar across the Rappahannock. And yet some people insist that there is no such thing as progress.

. . .

I am sometimes called "The King of Candlesticks," because I own more than one thousand candlesticks.

But I am fonder of my middle name, which is "Daffodil-II." And I have written this poem about it, and about life itself, of course:

> "I was those seeds,
> "I am this meat,
> "This meat hates pain,
> "This meat must eat.
> "This meat must sleep,
> "This meat must dream,
> "This meat must laugh,
> "This meat must scream.
> "But when, as meat,
> "It's had its fill,
> "Please plant it as
> "A Daffodil."

. . .

And who will read all this? God knows. Not Melody and Isadore, surely. Like all the other young people on the island, they can neither read nor write.

They have no curiosity about the human past, nor about what life may be like on the mainland.

As far as they are concerned, the most glorious accomplishment of the people who inhabited this island so teemingly was to die, so we could have it all to ourselves.

I asked them the other evening to name the three most important human beings in history. They protested that the question made no sense to them.

I insisted that they put their heads together anyway, and give me some sort of answer, which they did. They were very sulky about the exercise. It was painful to them.

They finally came up with an answer. Melody does most of the talking for them, and this is what she said in all seriousness: "You, and Jesus Christ, and Santa Claus."

Hi ho.

• • •

When I do not ask them questions, they are as happy as clams.

• • •

They hope to become slaves of Vera Chipmunk-5 Zappa some day. That is O.K. with me.

• • •

# Chapter 2

A ND I REALLY WILL try to stop writing "Hi ho" all the time.
Hi ho.

• • •

I was born right here in New York City. I was not then a *Daffodil*. I was christened Wilbur *Rockefeller* Swain.

I was not alone, moreover. I had a dizygotic twin, a female. She was named Eliza Mellon Swain.

We were christened in a hospital rather than in a church, and we were not surrounded by relatives and our parents' friends. The thing was: Eliza and I were so ugly that our parents were ashamed.

We were monsters, and we were not expected to live very long. We had six fingers on each little hand, and six toes on each little footsie. We had supernumerary nipples as well—two of them apiece.

We were not mongolian idiots, although we had the coarse black hair typical of mongoloids. We were something new. We were *neanderthaloids*. We had the features of adult, fossil human beings even in infancy—massive brow-ridges, sloping foreheads, and steamshovel jaws.

• • •

We were supposed to have no intelligence, and to die before we were fourteen.

But I am still alive and kicking, thank you. And Eliza would be, too, I'm certain, if she had not been killed at the age of fifty—in an avalanche on the outskirts of the Chinese colony on the planet Mars.

Hi ho.

• • •

Our parents were two silly and pretty and very young people named Caleb Mellon Swain and Letitia Vanderbilt Swain, née Rockefeller. They were fabulously well-to-do, and descended

from Americans who had all but wrecked the planet with a form
of Idiot's Delight—obsessively turning money into power, and
then power back into money again, and then money back into
power again.

But Caleb and Letitia were harmless themselves. Father was
very good at backgammon and so-so at color photography,
they say. Mother was active in the National Association for the
Advancement of Colored People. Neither worked. Neither was
a college graduate, though both had tried.

They wrote and spoke nicely. They adored each other. They
were humble about having done so poorly in schools. They were
kind.

And I cannot fault them for being shattered by having given
birth to monsters. Anyone would have been shattered by giving
birth to Eliza and me.

•    •    •

And Caleb and Letitia were at least as good at parenting as
I was, when my turn rolled around. I was wholly indifferent
to my own children, although they were normal in every way.

Perhaps I would have been more entertained by my children
if they had been monsters like Eliza and me.

Hi ho.

•    •    •

Young Caleb and Letitia were advised not to break their
hearts and risk their furniture by attempting to raise Eliza and
me in Turtle Bay. We were no more true relatives of theirs, their
advisors said, than baby crocodiles.

Caleb's and Letitia's response was humane. It was also expensive and Gothic in the extreme. Our parents did not hide us
in a private hospital for cases such as ours. They entombed us
instead in a spooky old mansion which they had inherited—in
the midst of two hundred acres of apple trees on a mountaintop, near the hamlet of Galen, Vermont.

No one had lived there for thirty years.

•    •    •

Carpenters and electricians and plumbers were brought in to
turn it into a sort of paradise for Eliza and me. Thick rubber

padding was put under all the wall-to-wall carpets, so we would not hurt ourselves in case we fell. Our diningroom was lined with tile, and there were drains in the floor, so we and the room could be hosed off after every meal.

More important, perhaps, were two chain-link fences which went up. They were topped with barbed wire. The first enclosed the orchard. The second separated the mansion from the prying eyes of the workmen who had to be let in through the first from time to time in order to look after the apple trees.

Hi ho.

•   •   •

A staff was recruited from the neighborhood. There was a cook. There were two cleaning women and a cleaning man. There were two practical nurses who fed us and dressed us and undressed us and bathed us. The one I remember best is Withers Witherspoon, a combination guard, chauffeur and handyman.

His mother was a Withers. His father was a Witherspoon.

•   •   •

Yes, and these were simple country people, who, with the exception of Withers Witherspoon, who had been a soldier, had never been outside Vermont. They had rarely ventured more than ten miles from Galen, for that matter—and they were necessarily all related to one another, as inbred as Eskimos.

They were of course distantly related to Eliza and me, too, since our Vermont ancestors had once been content to dog-paddle endlessly, so to speak, in the same tiny genetic pool.

But, in the American scheme of things at that time, they were related to our family as carp were related to eagles, say—for our family had evolved into world-travelers and multimillionaires.

Hi ho.

•   •   •

Yes, and it was easy for our parents to buy the fealty of these living fossils from the family past. They were given modest salaries which seemed enormous to them, since the money-making lobes of their brains were so primitive.

They were given pleasant apartments in the mansion, and color television sets. They were encouraged to eat like emperors, charging whatever they liked to our parents. They had very little work to do.

Better still, they did not have to think much for themselves. They were placed under the command of a young general practitioner who lived in the hamlet, Dr. Stewart Rawlings Mott, who would look in on us every day.

Dr. Mott was a Texan, incidentally, a melancholy and private young man. To this day, I do not know what induced him to move so far from his people and his birthplace—to practice medicine in an Eskimo settlement in Vermont.

As a curious footnote in history, and a probably meaningless one: The grandson of Dr. Mott would become the King of Michigan during my second term as President of the United States.

I must hiccup again: Hi ho.

• • •

I swear: If I live to complete this autobiography, I will go through it again, and cross out all the "Hi ho's."

Hi ho.

• • •

Yes, and there was an automatic sprinkler system in the mansion—and burglar alarms on the windows and doors and skylights.

When we grew older and uglier, and capable of breaking arms or tearing heads off, a great gong was installed in the kitchen. This was connected to cherry red push-buttons in every room and at regular intervals down every corridor. The buttons glowed in the dark.

A button was to be pushed only if Eliza or I began to toy with murder.

Hi ho.

• • •

# Chapter 3

FATHER WENT TO GALEN with a lawyer and a physician and an architect—to oversee the refurbishing of the mansion for Eliza and me, and the hiring of the servants and Dr. Mott. Mother remained here in Manhattan, in their townhouse in Turtle Bay.

Turtles in great profusion, incidentally, have returned to Turtle Bay.

Vera Chipmunk-5 Zappa's slaves like to catch them for soup.

Hi ho.

• • •

It was one of the few occasions, except for Father's death, when Mother and Father were separated for more than a day or two. And Father wrote a graceful letter to Mother from Vermont, which I found in Mother's bedside table after Mother died.

It may have been the whole of their correspondence by mail.

"My dearest Tish—" he wrote, "Our children will be very happy here. We can be proud. Our architect can be proud. The workmen can be proud.

"However short our children's lives may be, we will have given them the gifts of dignity and happiness. We have created a delightful asteroid for them, a little world with only one mansion on it, and otherwise covered with apple trees."

• • •

Then he returned to an asteroid of his own—in Turtle Bay. He and Mother, thereafter, again on the advice of physicians, would visit us once a year, and always on our birthday.

Their brownstone still stands, and it is still snug and weathertight. It is there that our nearest neighbor, Vera Chipmunk-5 Zappa, now quarters her slaves.

• • •

"And when Eliza and Wilbur die and go to Heaven at last," our father's letter went on, "we can lay them to rest among their

Swain ancestors, in the private family cemetery out under the apple trees."

Hi ho.

• • •

As for who was already buried in that cemetery, which was separated from the mansion by a fence: They were mostly Vermont apple farmers and their mates and offspring, people of no distinction. Many of them were no doubt nearly as illiterate and ignorant as Melody and Isadore.

That is to say: They were innocent great apes, with limited means for doing mischief, which, in my opinion as an old, old man, is all that human beings were ever meant to be.

• • •

Many of the tombstones in the cemetery had sunk out of sight or capsized. Weather had dimmed the epitaphs of those which still stood.

But there was one tremendous monument, with thick granite walls, a slate roof, and great doors, which would clearly last past Judgment Day. It was the mausoleum of the founder of the family's fortune and the builder of our mansion, Professor Elihu Roosevelt Swain.

• • •

Professor Swain was by far the most intelligent of all our known ancestors, I would say—Rockefellers, Du Ponts, Mellons, Vanderbilts, Dodges and all. He took a degree from the Massachusetts Institute of Technology at the age of eighteen, and went on to set up the Department of Civil Engineering at Cornell University at the age of twenty-two. By that time, he already had several important patents on railroad bridges and safety devices, which alone would soon have made him a millionaire.

But he was not content. So he created the Swain Bridge Company, which designed and supervised the construction of half the railroad bridges in the entire planet.

• • •

He was a citizen of the world. He spoke many languages, and was the personal friend of many heads of state. But when it came time to build a palace of his own, he placed it among his ignorant ancestors' apple trees.

And he was the only person who loved that barbarous pile until Eliza and I came along. We were so happy there!

•  •  •

And Eliza and I shared a secret with Professor Swain, even though he had been dead for half a century. The servants did not know it. Our parents did not know it. And the workmen who refurbished the place never suspected it, apparently, although they must have punched pipes and wires and heating ducts through all sorts of puzzling spaces.

This was the secret: There was a mansion concealed within the mansion. It could be entered through trap doors and sliding panels. It consisted of secret staircases and listening posts with peepholes, and secret passageways. There were tunnels, too.

It was actually possible for Eliza and me, for example, to vanish into a huge grandfather clock in the ballroom at the top of the northernmost tower, and to emerge almost a kilometer away—through a trap door in the floor of the mausoleum of Professor Elihu Roosevelt Swain.

•  •  •

We shared another secret with the Professor, too—which we learned from going through some of his papers in the mansion. His middle name hadn't actually been *Roosevelt*. He had given himself that middle name in order to seem more aristocratic when he enrolled as a student at M.I.T.

His name on his baptismal certificate was Elihu Witherspoon Swain.

It was from his example, I suppose, that Eliza and I got the idea, eventually, of giving simply everybody new middle names.

•  •  •

# Chapter 4

WHEN PROFESSOR SWAIN died, he was so fat that I do not see how he could have fitted into any of his secret passageways. They were very narrow. Eliza and I were able to fit into them, however, even when we were two meters tall—because the ceilings were so high—

Yes, and Professor Swain died of his fatness in the mansion, at a dinner he gave in honor of Samuel Langhorne Clemens and Thomas Alva Edison.

Those were the days.

Eliza and I found the menu. It began with turtle soup.

• • •

Our servants would tell each other now and then that the mansion was haunted. They heard sneezing and cackling in the walls, and the creaking of stairways where there were no stairways, and the opening and shutting of doors where there were no doors.

Hi ho.

• • •

It would be exciting for me to cry out, as a crazed old centenarian in the ruins of Manhattan, that Eliza and I were subjected to acts of unspeakable cruelty in that spooky old house. But we may have in fact been the two happiest children that history has so far known.

That ecstasy would not end until our fifteenth year.

Think of that.

Yes, and when I became a pediatrician, practicing rural medicine in the mansion where I was raised, I often told myself about this childish patient or that one, remembering my own childhood: "This person has just arrived on this planet, knows nothing about it, has no standards by which to judge it. This person does not care what it becomes. It is eager to become absolutely anything it is supposed to be."

That surely describes the state of mind of Eliza and me, when we were very young. And all the information we received about the planet we were on indicated that idiots were lovely things to be.

So we cultivated idiocy.

We refused to speak coherently in public. "Buh," and, "Duh," we said. We drooled and rolled our eyes. We farted and laughed. We ate library paste.

Hi ho.

•   •   •

Consider: We were at the center of the lives of those who cared for us. They could be heroically Christian in their own eyes only if Eliza and I remained helpless and vile. If we became openly wise and self-reliant, they would become our drab and inferior assistants. If we became capable of going out into the world, they might lose their apartments, their color televisions, their illusions of being sorts of doctors and nurses, and their high-paying jobs.

So, from the very first, and without quite knowing what they were doing, I am sure, they begged us a thousand times a day to go on being helpless and vile.

There was only one small advancement they wished us to make up the ladder of human achievements. They hoped with all their hearts that we would become toilet-trained.

Again: We were glad to comply.

•   •   •

But we could secretly read and write English by the time we were four. We could read and write French, German, Italian, Latin and ancient Greek by the time we were seven, and do calculus, too.

There were thousands of books in the mansion. By the time we were ten, we had read them all by candlelight, at naptime or after bedtime—in secret passageways, or often in the mausoleum of Elihu Roosevelt Swain.

•   •   •

But we continued to drool and babble and so on, whenever grownups were around. It was fun.

We did not itch to display our intelligence in public. We did not think of intelligence as being useful or attractive in any way. We thought of it as being simply one more example of our freakishness, like our extra nipples and fingers and toes.

And we may have been right at that. You know?

Hi ho.

•   •   •

# Chapter 5

AND MEANWHILE the strange young Dr. Stewart Rawlings Mott weighed us and measured us, and peered into our orifices, and took samples of our urine—day after day after day.

"How is everybody today?" he would say.

We would tell him "Bluh" and "Duh," and so on. We called him "Flocka Butt."

And we ourselves did all we could to make each day exactly like the one before. Whenever "Flocka Butt" congratulated us on our healthy appetites and regular bowel movements, for example, I would invariably stick my thumbs in my ears and waggle my fingers, and Eliza would hoist her skirt and snap the elastic at the waist of her pantyhose.

Eliza and I believed then what I believe even now: That life can be painless, provided that there is sufficient peacefulness for a dozen or so rituals to be repeated simply endlessly.

Life, ideally, I think, should be like the Minuet or the Virginia Reel or the Turkey Trot, something easily mastered in a dancing school.

•  •  •

I teeter even now between thinking that Dr. Mott loved Eliza and me, and knew how smart we were, and wished to protect us from the cruelties of the outside world, and thinking that he was comatose.

After Mother died, I discovered that the linen chest at the foot of her bed was crammed with packets of Dr. Mott's bi-weekly reports on the health of Eliza and me. He told of the ever-greater quantities of food being consumed and then excreted. He spoke, too, of our unflagging cheerfulness, and our natural resistance to common diseases of childhood.

The sorts of things he reported, in fact, were the sorts of things a carpenter's helper would have had no trouble detecting—such as that, at the age of nine, Eliza and I were over two meters tall.

No matter how large Eliza and I became, though, one figure remained constant in his reports: Our mental age was between two and three.

Hi ho.

•   •   •

"Flocka Butt," along with my sister, of course, is one of the few people I am really hungry to see in the afterlife.

I am dying to ask him what he really thought of us as children—how much he suspected, how much he really knew.

•   •   •

Eliza and I must have given him thousands of clues as to our intelligence. We weren't the cleverest of deceivers. We were only children, after all.

It seems probable to me that, when we babbled in his presence, we used words from some foreign language which he could recognize. He may have gone into the library of the mansion, which was of no interest to the servants, and found the books somehow disturbed.

He may have discovered the secret passageways himself, through some accident. He used to wander around the house a great deal after he was through with us, I know, explaining to the servants that his father was an architect. He may have actually gone into the secret passageways, and found books we were reading in there, and seen that the floors were spattered with candlewax.

Who knows?

•   •   •

I would like to know, too, what his secret sorrow was. Eliza and I, when we were young, were so wrapped up in each other that we rarely noticed the emotional condition of anybody else. But we were surely impressed by Dr. Mott's sadness. So it must have been profound.

•   •   •

I once asked his grandson, the King of Michigan, Stewart Oriole-2 Mott, if he had any idea why Dr. Mott had found life to be such a crushing affair. "Gravity hadn't yet turned mean,"

I said. "The sky had not yet turned from blue to yellow, never to be blue again. The planet's natural resources had yet to come to an end. The country had not yet been depopulated by Albanian flu and The Green Death.

"Your grandfather had a nice little car and a nice little house and a nice little practice and a nice little wife and a nice little child," I said to the King. "And yet he used to *mope* so!"

My interview with the King took place, incidentally, in his palace on Lake Maxinkuckee, in northern Indiana, where Culver Military Academy had once stood. I was still nominally the President of the United States of America, but I had lost control of everything. There wasn't any Congress any more, or any system of Federal Courts, or any Treasury or Army or any of that.

There were probably only eight hundred people left in all of Washington, D.C. I was down to one employee when I paid my respects to the King.

Hi ho.

•  •  •

He asked me if I regarded him as an enemy, and I said, "Heavens, no, Your Highness—I am delighted that someone of your calibre has brought law and order to the Middle West."

•  •  •

He grew impatient with me when I pressed him to tell me more about his grandfather, Dr. Mott.

"Christ," he said, "what American knows anything about his grandparents?"

•  •  •

He was a skinny and supple and ascetic young soldier-saint in those days. My granddaughter, Melody, would come to know him when he was an obscene voluptuary, a fat old man in robes encrusted with precious stones.

•  •  •

He was wearing a simple soldier's tunic without any badges of rank when I met him.

As for my own costume: It was appropriately clownish—a top hat, a claw-hammer coat and striped pants, a pearl-gray vest with matching spats, a soiled white shirt with a choke collar and tie. The belly of my vest was festooned with a gold watch-chain which had belonged to John D. Rockefeller, the ancestor of mine who had founded Standard Oil.

Dangling from the watch-chain were my Phi Beta Kappa key from Harvard and a miniature plastic daffodil. My middle name had by then been legally changed from *Rockefeller* to *Daffodil-11*.

"There were no murders or embezzlements or suicides or drinking problems or drug problems in Dr. Mott's branch of the family," the King went on, "as far as I know."

He was thirty. I was seventy-nine.

"Maybe Grandfather was just one of those people who was *born* unhappy," he said. "Did you ever think of that?"

•  •  •

# *Chapter 6*

PERHAPS SOME PEOPLE really are born unhappy. I surely hope not.

Speaking for my sister and myself: We were born with the capacity and the determination to be utterly happy all the time.

Perhaps even in this we were freaks.

Hi ho.

•  •  •

What is happiness?

In Eliza's and my case, happiness was being perpetually in each other's company, having plenty of servants and good food, living in a peaceful, book-filled mansion on an asteroid covered with apple trees, and growing up as specialized halves of a single brain.

Although we pawed and embraced each other a great deal, our intentions were purely intellectual. True—Eliza matured sexually at the age of seven. I, however, would not enter puberty until my last year in Harvard Medical School, at the age of twenty-three. Eliza and I used bodily contact only in order to increase the intimacy of our brains.

Thus did we give birth to a single genius, which died as quickly as we were parted, which was reborn the moment we got together again.

•  •  •

We became almost cripplingly specialized as halves of that genius, which was the most important individual in our lives, but which we never named.

When we learned to read and write, for example, it was I who actually did the reading and writing. Eliza remained illiterate until the day she died.

But it was Eliza who did the great intuitive leaping for us both. It was Eliza who guessed that it would be in our best interests to remain speechless, but to become toilet-trained. It was Eliza who guessed what books were, and what the little marks on the pages might mean.

It was Eliza who sensed that there was something cockeyed about the dimensions of some of the mansion's rooms and corridors. And it was I who did the methodical work of taking actual measurements, and then probing the paneling and parquetry with screwdrivers and kitchen knives, seeking doors to an alternate universe, which we found.

Hi ho.

•   •   •

Yes, I did all the reading. And it seems to me now that there is not a single book published in an Indo-European language before the First World War that I have not read aloud.

But it was Eliza who did the memorizing, and who told me what we had to learn next. And it was Eliza who could put seemingly unrelated ideas together in order to get a new one. It was Eliza who *juxtaposed*.

•   •   •

Much of our information was hopelessly out of date, of course, since few new books had been brought into the mansion since 1912. Much of it, too, was timeless. And much of it was downright silly, such as the dances we learned to do.

If I wished, I could do a very presentable and historically accurate version of the Tarantella, here in the ruins of New York.

•   •   •

Were Eliza and I really a genius, when we thought as one?

I have to say yes, especially in view of the fact that we had no instructors. And I am not boasting when I say so, for I am only half of that fine mind.

We criticized Darwin's Theory of Evolution, I remember, on the grounds the creatures would become terribly vulnerable while attempting to improve themselves, while developing wings or armorplate, say. They would be eaten up by more practical animals, before their wonderful new features could be refined.

We made at least one prediction that was so deadly accurate that thinking about it even now leaves me thunderstruck.

Listen: We began with the mystery of how ancient peoples had erected the pyramids of Egypt and Mexico, and the great heads of Easter Island, and the barbaric arches of Stonehenge, without modern power sources and tools.

We concluded there must have been days of light gravity in olden times, when people could play tiddledy winks with huge chunks of stone.

We supposed that it might even be abnormal on earth for gravity to be stable for long periods of time. We predicted that at any moment gravity might become as capricious as winds and heat and cold, as blizzards and rainstorms again.

•   •   •

Yes, and Eliza and I composed a precocious critique of the Constitution of the United States of America, too. We argued that it was as good a scheme for misery as any, since its success in keeping the common people reasonably happy and proud depended on the strength of the people themselves—and yet it described no practical machinery which would tend to make the people, as opposed to their elected representatives, strong.

We said it was possible that the framers of the Constitution were blind to the beauty of persons who were without great wealth or powerful friends or public office, but who were nonetheless genuinely strong.

We thought it was more likely, though, that the framers had not noticed that it was natural, and therefore almost inevitable, that human beings in extraordinary and enduring situations should think of themselves as composing new families. Eliza and I pointed out that this happened no less in democracies than in tyrannies, since human beings were the same the wide world over, and civilized only yesterday.

Elected representatives, hence, could be expected to become members of the famous and powerful family of elected representatives—which would, perfectly naturally, make them wary and squeamish and stingy with respect to all the other sorts of families which, again, perfectly naturally, subdivided mankind.

Eliza and I, thinking as halves of a single genius, proposed that the Constitution be amended so as to guarantee that every citizen, no matter how humble or crazy or incompetent or deformed, somehow be given membership in some family as covertly xenophobic and crafty as the one their public servants formed.

Good for Eliza and me!

•  •  •

Hi ho.

•  •  •

# Chapter 7

How nice it would have been, especially for Eliza, since she was a girl, if we had been ugly ducklings—if we had become beautiful by and by. But we simply grew more preposterous with each passing day.

There were a few advantages to being a male 2 meters tall. I was respected as a basketball player at prep school and college, even though I had very narrow shoulders and a voice like a piccolo, and not the first hints of a beard or pubic hair. Yes, and later on, after my voice had deepened and I ran as a candidate for Senator from Vermont, I was able to say on my billboards, "It takes a Big Man to do a Big Job!"

But Eliza, who was exactly as tall as I was, could not expect to be welcomed anywhere. There was no conceivable conventional role for a female which could be bent so as to accommodate a twelve-fingered, twelve-toed, four-breasted, Neanderthaloid half-genius—weighing one quintal, and two meters tall.

• • •

Even as little children we knew we weren't ever going to win any beauty contests.

Eliza said something prophetic about that, incidentally. She couldn't have been more than eight. She said that maybe she could win a beauty contest on Mars.

She was, of course, destined to *die* on Mars.

Eliza's beauty prize there would be an avalanche of iron pyrite, better known as "Fool's Gold."

Hi ho.

• • •

There was a time in our childhood when we actually agreed that we were *lucky* not to be beautiful. We knew from all the romantic novels I'd read out loud in my squeaky voice, often with gestures, that beautiful people had their privacy destroyed by passionate strangers.

We didn't want that to happen to us, since the two of us alone composed not only a single mind but a thoroughly populated Universe.

•   •   •

This much I must say about our appearance, at least: Our clothing was the finest that money could buy. Our astonishing dimensions, which changed radically almost from month to month, were mailed off regularly, in accordance with our parents' instructions, to some of the finest tailors and cobblers and dressmakers and shirtmakers and haberdashers in the world.

The practical nurses who dressed and undressed us took a childish delight, even though we never went anywhere, in costuming us for imaginary social events for millionaires—for tea dances, for horse shows, for skiing vacations, for attending classes at expensive prep schools, for an evening of theater here in Manhattan and a supper afterwards with lots of champagne.

And so on.

Hi ho.

•   •   •

We were aware of all the comedy in this. But, as brilliant as we were when we put our heads together, we did not guess until we were fifteen that we were also in the midst of a tragedy. We thought that ugliness was simply amusing to people in the outside world. We did not realize that we could actually nauseate strangers who came upon us unexpectedly.

We were so innocent as to the importance of good looks, in fact, that we could see little point to the story of "The Ugly Duckling," which I read out loud to Eliza one day—in the mausoleum of Professor Elihu Roosevelt Swain.

The story, of course, was about a baby bird that was raised by ducks, who thought it was the funniest-looking duck they had ever seen. But then it turned out to be a swan when it grew up.

Eliza, I remember, said she thought it would have been a much better story if the little bird had waddled up on shore and turned into a rhinoceros.

Hi ho.

•   •   •

# Chapter 8

U NTIL THE EVE of our fifteenth birthday, Eliza and I
never heard anything bad about ourselves when we eaves-
dropped from the secret passageways.

The servants were so used to us that they hardly ever mentioned us, even in moments of deepest privacy. Dr. Mott seldom
commented on anything but our appetites and our excretions.
And our parents were so sickened by us that they were tongue-
tied when they made their annual space voyage to our asteroid.
Father, I remember, would talk to Mother rather haltingly
and listlessly about world events he had read about in news
magazines.

They would bring us toys from F.A.O. Schwarz—guaranteed
by that emporium to be educational for three-year-olds.

Hi ho.

• • •

Yes, and I think now about all the secrets about the human
condition I withhold from young Melody and Isadore, for
their own peace of mind—the fact that the human afterlife is
no good, and so on.

And then I am awed yet again by the perfect Lulu of a secret
that was concealed from Eliza and me so long: That our own
parents wished we would hurry up and die.

• • •

We imagined lazily that our fifteenth birthday would be like
all the rest. We put on the show we had always put on. Our parents arrived at our suppertime, which was four in the afternoon.
We would get our presents the next day.

We threw food at each other in our tile-lined diningroom. I
hit Eliza with an avocado. She hit me with a filet mignon. We
bounced Parker House rolls off the maid. We pretended not
to know that our parents had arrived and were watching us
through a crack in the door.

Yes, and then, still not having greeted our parents face-to-
face, we were bathed and talcumed, and dressed in our pajamas

43

and bathrobes and bedroom slippers. Bedtime was at five, for Eliza and I pretended to sleep sixteen hours a day.

Our practical nurses, who were Oveta Cooper and Mary Selwyn Kirk, told us that there was a wonderful surprise waiting for us in the library.

We pretended to be gaga about what that surprise could possibly be.

We were full-grown giants by then.

I carried a rubber tugboat, which was supposedly my favorite toy. Eliza had a red velvet ribbon in the mare's nest of her coal black hair.

•  •  •

As always, there was a large coffee table between Eliza and me and our parents when we were brought in. As always, our parents had brandy to sip. As always, there was a fizzing, popping blaze of pine and sappy apple logs in the fireplace. As always, an oil painting of Professor Elihu Roosevelt Swain over the mantelpiece beamed down on the ritual scene.

As always, our parents stood. They smiled up at us with what we still did not recognize as bittersweet dread.

As always, we pretended to find them adorable, but not to remember who they were at first.

•  •  •

As always, Father did the talking.

"How do you do, Eliza and Wilbur?" he said. "You are looking very well. We are very glad to see you. Do you remember who we are?"

Eliza and I consulted with one another uneasily, drooling, and murmuring in ancient Greek. Eliza said to me in Greek, I remember, that she could not believe that we were related to such pretty dolls.

Father helped us out. He told us the name we had given to him years ago. "I am Bluth-luh," he said.

Eliza and I pretended to be flabbergasted. "Bluth-luh!" we told each other. We could not believe our good fortune. "Bluth-luh! Bluth-luh!" we cried.

"And this," said Father, indicating Mother, "is Mub-lub."

This was even more sensational news to Eliza and me. "Mub-lub! Mub-lub!" we exclaimed.

And now Eliza and I made a great intellectual leap, as always. Without any hints from anybody, we concluded that, if our parents were in the house, then our birthday must be close at hand. We chanted our idiot word for birthday, which was "Fuff-bay."

As always, we pretended to become overexcited. We jumped up and down. We were so big by then that the floor began to go up and down like a trampoline.

But we suddenly stopped, pretending, as always, to have been rendered catatonic by more happiness than was good for us.

That was always the end of the show. After that, we were led away.

Hi ho.

•   •   •

# Chapter 9

W E WERE PUT INTO custom-made cribs—in separate but adjacent bedrooms. The rooms were connected by a secret panel in the wall. The cribs were as big as railroad flatcars. They made a terrible clatter when their sides were raised.

Eliza and I pretended to fall asleep at once. After a half an hour, however, we were reunited in Eliza's room. The servants never looked in on us. Our health was perfect, after all, and we had established a reputation for being, as they said, ". . . as good as gold at bedtime."

Yes, and we went through a trapdoor under Eliza's crib, and were soon taking turns watching our parents in the library—through a tiny hole we ourselves had drilled through the wall, and through the upper corner of the frame around the painting of Professor Elihu Roosevelt Swain.

• • •

Father was telling mother of a thing he had read in a news magazine on the day before. It seemed that scientists in the People's Republic of China were experimenting with making human beings smaller, so they would not need to eat so much and wear such big clothes.

Mother was staring into the fire. Father had to tell her twice about the Chinese rumor. The second time he did it, she replied emptily that she supposed that the Chinese could accomplish just about anything they put their minds to.

Only about a month before, the Chinese had sent two hundred explorers to Mars—without using a space vehicle of any kind.

No scientist in the Western World could guess how the trick was done. The Chinese themselves volunteered no details.

• • •

Mother said that it seemed like such a long time since Americans had discovered anything. "All of a sudden," she said, "everything is being discovered by the Chinese."

• • •

"We used to discover everything," she said.

• • •

It was such a *stupefied* conversation. The level of animation was so low that our beautiful young parents from Manhattan might have been up to their necks in honey. They appeared, as they had always appeared to Eliza and me, to be under some curse which required them to speak only of matters which did not interest them at all.

And indeed they *were* under a malediction. But Eliza and I had not guessed its nature: That they were all but strangled and paralyzed by the wish that their own children would die.

And I promise this about our parents, although the only proof I have is a feeling in my bones: Neither one had ever suggested in any way to the other that he or she wished we would die.

Hi ho.

• • •

But then there was a *bang* in the fireplace. Steam had to escape from a trap in a sappy log.

Yes, and Mother, because she was a symphony of chemical reactions like all other living things, gave a terrified shriek. Her chemicals insisted that she shriek in response to the *bang*.

After the chemicals got her to do that, though, they wanted a lot more from her. They though it was high time she said what she really felt about Eliza and me, which she did. All sorts of other things went haywire when she said it. Her hands closed convulsively. Her spine buckled and her face shriveled to turn her into an old, old witch.

"I hate them, I hate them, I hate them," she said.

• • •

And not many seconds passed before Mother said with spitting explicitness who it was she hated.

"I hate Wilbur Rockefeller Swain and Eliza Mellon Swain," she said.

• • •

# Chapter 10

MOTHER WAS TEMPORARILY INSANE that night.

I got to know her well in later years. And, while I never learned to love her, or to love anyone, for that matter, I did admire her unwavering decency toward one and all. She was not a mistress of insults. When she spoke either in public or in private, no reputations died.

So it was not truly our mother who said on the eve of our fifteenth birthday, "How can I love Count Dracula and his blushing bride?"—meaning Eliza and me.

It was not truly our mother who asked our father, "How on Earth did I ever give birth to a pair of drooling totem poles?"

And so on.

• • •

As for Father: He engulfed her in his arms. He was weeping with love and pity.

"Caleb, oh Caleb—" she said in his arms, "this isn't me."

"Of course not," he said.

"Forgive me," she said.

"Of course," he said.

"Will God ever forgive me?" she said.

"He already has," he said.

"It was as though a devil all of a sudden got inside of me," she said.

"That's what it was, Tish," he said.

Her madness was subsiding now. "Oh, Caleb—" she said.

• • •

Lest I seem to be fishing for sympathy, let me say right now that Eliza and I in those days were about as emotionally vulnerable as the Great Stone Face in New Hampshire.

We needed a mother's and father's love about as much as a fish needs a bicycle, as the saying goes.

So when our mother spoke badly of us, even wished we would die, our response was intellectual. We enjoyed solving

48

problems. Perhaps Mother's problem was one we could solve—short of suicide, of course.

She pulled herself together again eventually. She steeled herself for another hundred birthdays with Eliza and me, in case God wished to test her in that way. But, before she did that, she said this:

"I would give anything, Caleb, for the faintest sign of intelligence, the merest flicker of humanness in the eyes of either twin."

•　　•　　•

This was easily arranged.

Hi ho.

•　　•　　•

So Eliza and I went back to Eliza's room, and we painted a big sign on a bedsheet. Then, after our parents were sound asleep, we stole into their room through the false back in an armoire. We hung the sign on the wall, so it would be the first thing they saw when they woke up.

This is what it said:

DEAR MATER AND PATER: WE CAN NEVER BE PRETTY BUT WE CAN BE AS SMART OR AS DUMB AS THE WORLD REALLY WANTS US TO BE.
                    YOUR FAITHFUL SERVANTS,
                    ELIZA MELLON SWAIN
                    WILBUR ROCKEFELLER SWAIN

Hi ho.

•　　•　　•

# Chapter 11

THUS DID ELIZA AND I destroy our Paradise—our nation of two.

• • •

We arose the next morning before our parents did, before the servants could come to dress us. We sensed no danger. We supposed ourselves still to be in Paradise as we dressed ourselves.

I chose to wear a conservative blue, pinstripe, three-piece suit, I remember. Eliza chose to wear a cashmere sweater, a tweed skirt, and pearls.

We agreed that Eliza should be our spokesman at first, since she had a rich alto voice. My voice did not have the authority to announce calmingly but convincingly that, in effect, the world had just turned upside down.

Remember, please, that almost all that anyone had ever heard us say up to then was "Buh" and "Duh," and so on.

Now we encountered Oveta Cooper, our practical nurse, in the colonnaded green marble foyer. She was startled to see us up and dressed.

Before she could comment on this, though, Eliza and I leaned our heads together, put them in actual contact, just above our ears. The single genius we composed thereby then spoke to Oveta in Eliza's voice, which was as lovely as a viola.

This is what that voice said:

"Good morning, Oveta. A new life begins for all of us today. As you can see and hear, Wilbur and I are no longer idiots. A miracle has taken place overnight. Our parents' dreams have come true. We are healed.

"As for you, Oveta: You will keep your apartment and your color television, and perhaps even receive a salary increase—as a reward for all you did to make this miracle come to pass. No one on the staff will experience any change, except for this one: Life here will become even easier and more pleasant than it was before."

Oveta, a bleak, Yankee dumpling, was hypnotized—like a rabbit who has met a rattlesnake. But Eliza and I were not a rattlesnake. With our heads together, we were one of the gentlest geniuses the world has ever known.

•   •   •

"We will not be using the tiled diningroom any more," said Eliza's voice. "We have lovely manners, as you shall see. Please have our breakfast served in the solarium, and notify us when Mater and Pater are up and around. It would be very nice if, from now on, you would address my brother and me as 'Master Wilbur' and 'Mistress Eliza.'

"You may go now, and tell the others about the miracle."

Oveta remained transfixed. I at last had to snap my fingers under her nose to wake her up.

She curtseyed. "As you wish, Mistress Eliza," she said. And she went to spread the news.

•   •   •

As we settled ourselves in the solarium, the rest of the staff straggled in humbly—to have a look at the young master and the young mistress we had become.

We greeted them by their full names. We asked them friendly questions which indicated that we had a detailed understanding of their lives. We apologized for having perhaps shocked some of them for changing so quickly.

"We simply did not realize," Eliza said, "that anybody *wanted* us to be intelligent."

We were by then so in charge of things that I, too, dared to speak of important matters. My high voice wouldn't be silly any more.

"With your cooperation," I said, "we will make this mansion famous for intelligence as it has been infamous for idiocy in days gone by. Let the fences come down."

"Are there any questions?" said Eliza.

There were none.

•   •   •

Somebody called Dr. Mott.

•   •   •

Our mother did not come down to breakfast. She remained in bed—petrified.

Father came down alone. He was wearing his nightclothes. He had not shaved. Young as he was, he was palsied and drawn.

Eliza and I were puzzled that he did not look happier. We hailed him not only in English, but in several other languages we knew.

It was to one of these foreign salutations that he responded at last. "Bon jour," he said.

"Sit thee doon! Sit thee doon!" said Eliza merrily.

The poor man sat.

•   •   •

He was sick with guilt, of course, over having allowed intelligent human beings, his own flesh and blood, to be treated like idiots for so long.

Worse: His conscience and his advisors had told him before that it was all right if he could not love us, since we were incapable of deep feelings, and since there was nothing about us, objectively, that anyone in his right mind *could* love. But now it was his *duty* to love us, and he did not think he could do it.

He was horrified to discover what our mother knew she would discover, if she came downstairs: That intelligence and sensitivity in monstrous bodies like Eliza's and mine merely made us more repulsive.

This was not Father's fault or Mother's fault. It was not anybody's fault. It was as natural as breathing to all human beings, and to all warm-blooded creatures, for that matter, to wish quick deaths for monsters. This was an instinct.

And now Eliza and I had raised that instinct to intolerable tragedy.

Without knowing what we were doing, Eliza and I were putting the traditional curse of monsters on normal creatures. We were asking for respect.

•   •   •

# Chapter 12

IN THE MIDST of all the excitement, Eliza and I allowed our heads to be separated by several feet—so we were not thinking brilliantly any more.

We became dumb enough to think that Father was merely sleepy. So we made him drink coffee, and we tried to wake him up with some songs and riddles we knew.

I remember I asked him if he knew why cream was so much more expensive than milk.

He mumbled that he didn't know the answer.

So Eliza told him, "It's because the cows hate to squat on the little bottles."

We laughed about that. We rolled on the floor. And then Eliza got up and stood over him, with her hands on her hips, and scolded him affectionately, as though he were a little boy. "Oh, what a sleepy-head!" she said. "Oh, what a sleepy-head!"

At that moment, Dr. Stewart Rawlings Mott arrived.

• • •

Although Dr. Mott had been told on the telephone about Eliza's and my sudden metamorphosis, the day was like any other day to him, seemingly. He said what he always said when he arrived at the mansion: "And how is everybody today?"

I now spoke the first intelligent sentence Dr. Mott had ever heard from me. "Father won't wake up," I said.

"Won't he, now?" he replied. He rewarded the completeness of my sentence with the faintest of smiles.

Dr. Mott was so unbelievably bland, in fact, that he turned away from us to chat with Oveta Cooper, the practical nurse. Her mother had apparently been sick down in the hamlet. "Oveta—" he said, "you'll be pleased to know that your mother's temperature is almost normal."

Father was angered by this casualness, and no doubt glad to find someone with whom he could be openly angry.

"How long has this been going on, Doctor?" he wanted to know. "How long have you known about their intelligence?"

Dr. Mott looked at his watch. "Since about forty-two minutes ago," he said.

"You don't seem in the least surprised," said Father.

Dr. Mott appeared to think this over, then he shrugged. "I'm certainly very *happy* for everybody," he said.

I think it was the fact that Dr. Mott himself did not look at all happy when he said that which caused Eliza and me to put our heads together again. Something very queer was going on that we badly needed to understand.

•   •   •

Our genius did not fail us. It allowed us to understand the truth of the situation—that we were somehow more tragic than ever.

But our genius, like all geniuses, suffered periodic fits of monumental naïveté. It did so now. It told us that all we had to do to make everything all right again was to return to idiocy.

"Buh," said Eliza.

"Duh," I said.

I farted.

Eliza drooled.

I picked up a buttered scone and threw it at the head of Oveta Cooper.

Eliza turned to Father. "Bluth-luh!" she said.

"Fuff-bay!" I cried.

Father cried.

•   •   •

# Chapter 13

SIX DAYS HAVE PASSED since I began to write this memoir. On four of the days, the gravity was medium—what it used to be in olden times. It was so heavy yesterday, that I could hardly get out of bed, out of my nest of rags in the lobby of the Empire State Building. When I had to go to the elevator shaft we use for a toilet, making my way through the thicket of candlesticks I own, I crawled on all fours.

Hi ho.

Well—the gravity was light on the first day, and it is light again today. I have an erection again, and so does Isadore, the lover of my granddaughter Melody. So does every male on the island.

• • •

Yes, and Melody and Isadore have packed a picnic lunch, and have gone bounding up to the intersection of Broadway and Forty-second Street, where, on days of light gravity, they are building a rustic pyramid.

They do not shape the slabs and chunks and boulders they put into it, and neither do they limit their materials to masonry. They throw in I-beams and oil drums and tires and automobile parts and office furniture and theater seats, too, and all manner of junk. But I have seen the results, and what they are building will not be an amorphous trash-pile when it is done. It will clearly be a pyramid.

• • •

Yes, and if archaeologists of the future find this book of mine, they will be spared the fruitless labor of digging through the pyramid in search of its meaning. There are no secret treasure rooms in there, no chambers of any kind.

Its meaning, which is minuscule in any event, lies beneath the manhole cover over which the pyramid is constructed. It is the body of a stillborn male.

The infant is enclosed in an ornate box which was once a humidor for fine cigars. That box was placed on the floor of the manhole four years ago, amid all the cables and pipes down there—by Melody, who was its mother at the age of twelve, and by me, who was its great-grandfather, and by our nearest neighbor and dearest friend, Vera Chipmunk-5 Zappa.

The pyramid itself is entirely the idea of Melody and Isadore, who became her lover later on. It is a monument to a life that was never lived—to a person who was never named.

Hi ho.

·   ·   ·

It is not necessary to dig through the pyramid to reach the box. It can be reached through other manholes.

Beware of rats.

·   ·   ·

Since the infant was an heir of mine, the pyramid might be called this: "The Tomb of the Prince of Candlesticks."

·   ·   ·

The name of the father of the Prince of Candlesticks is unknown. He forced his attentions on Melody on the outskirts of Schenectady. She was on her way from Detroit, in the Kingdom of Michigan, to the Island of Death, where she hoped to find her grandfather, who was the legendary Dr. Wilbur Daffodil-11 Swain.

·   ·   ·

Melody is pregnant again—this time by Isadore.

She is a bow-legged little thing, rickety and snaggle-toothed, but cheerful. She ate very badly as a child—as an orphan in the harem of the King of Michigan.

Melody sometimes looks to me like a merry old Chinese woman, although she is only sixteen. A pregnant girl who looks like that is a sad thing for a pediatrician to see.

But the love that the robust and rosy Isadore gives her counterbalances my sadness with joy. Like almost all the members of his family, the Raspberries, Isadore has nearly all his teeth, and remains upright even when the gravity is most severe. He carries Melody around in his arms on days like that, and has offered to carry me.

The Raspberries are food-gatherers, mainly, living in and around the ruins of the New York Stock Exchange. They fish off docks. They mine for canned goods. They pick fruits and berries they find. They grow their own tomatoes and potatoes, and radishes, and little more.

They trap rats and bats and dogs and cats and birds, and eat them. A Raspberry will eat anything.

• • •

# Chapter 14

I wish Melody what our parents once wished Eliza and me: A short but happy life on an asteroid.

Hi ho.

• • •

Yes, and I have already said, Eliza and I might have had a long and happy life on an asteroid, if we had not showed off our intelligence one day. We might have been in the mansion still, burning the trees and the furniture and the bannisters and the paneling for warmth, and drooling and babbling when strangers came.

We could have raised chickens. We could have had a little vegetable garden. And we could have amused ourselves with our ever-increasing wisdom, caring nothing for its possible usefulness.

• • •

The sun is going down. Thin clouds of bats stream out from the subway—jittering, squeaking, dispersing like gas. As always, I shudder.

I can't think of their noise as a noise. It is a disease of silence instead.

• • •

I write on—in the light of a burning rag in a bowl of animal fat.

I have a thousand candlesticks, but no candles. Melody and Isadore play backgammon—on a board I painted on the lobby floor.

They double and redouble each other, and laugh.

• • •

They are planning a party for my one hundred and first birthday, which is a month away.

I eavesdrop on them sometimes. Old habits are hard to break. Vera Chipmunk-5 Zappa is making new costumes for the occasion—for herself and her slaves. She has mountains of cloth in her storerooms in Turtle Bay. The slaves will wear pink pantaloons and golden slippers, and green silk turbans with ostrich feather plumes, I heard Melody say.

Vera will be borne to the party in a sedan chair, I've heard, surrounded by slaves carrying presents and food and drink and torches, and frightening away wild dogs with the clangor of dinnerbells.

Hi ho.

•   •   •

I must be very careful with my drinking at my birthday party. If I drank too much, I might spill the beans to everybody: That the life that awaits us after death is infinitely more tiresome than this one.

Hi ho.

•   •   •

# Chapter 15

ELIZA AND I were of course not allowed to return to consolations of idiocy. We were bawled out severely whenever we tried. Yes, and the servants and our parents found one by-product of our metamorphosis positively delicious: They were suddenly entitled to bawl us out.

What hell we caught from time to time!

• • •

Yes, and Dr. Mott was fired, and all sorts of experts were brought in.

It was fun for a while. The first doctors to arrive were specialists in hearts and lungs and kidneys and so on. When they studied us organ by organ and body fluid by body fluid, we were masterpieces of health.

They were genial. They were all family employees in a way. They were research people whose work was financed by the Swain Foundation in New York. That was how they had been so easily rounded up and brought to Galen. The family had helped them. Now they would help the family.

They joshed us a lot. One of them, I remember, said to me that it must be fun to be so tall. "What's the weather up there like?" he said, and so on.

The joshing had a soothing effect. It gave us the mistaken impression that it did not matter how ugly we were. I still remember what an ear, nose and throat specialist said when he looked up into Eliza's enormous sinus cavities with a flashlight. "My God, nurse—" he said, "call up the National Geographic Society. We have just discovered a new entrance to Mammoth Cave!"

Eliza laughed. The nurse laughed. I laughed. We all laughed.

Our parents were in another part of the mansion. They kept away from all the fun.

• • •

That early in the game, though, we had our first disturbing tastes of separation. Some of the examinations required that we be several rooms apart. As the distance between Eliza and me increased, I felt as though my head were turning to wood.

I became stupid and insecure.

When I was reunited with Eliza, she said that she had felt very much the same sort of thing. "It was as though my skull was filling up with maple syrup," she said.

And we bravely tried to be amused rather than frightened by the listless children we became when we were parted. We pretended they had nothing to do with us, and we made up names for them. We called them "Betty and Bobby Brown."

• • •

And now is as good a time as any, I think, to say that when we read Eliza's will, after her death in a Martian avalanche, we learned that she wished to be buried wherever she died. Her grave was to be marked with a simple stone, engraved with this information and nothing more:

• • •

Yes, and it was the last specialist to look us over, a psychologist, Dr. Cordelia Swain Cordiner, who decreed that Eliza and I should be separated permanently, should, so to speak, become forever Betty and Bobby Brown.

•   •   •

# Chapter 16

FËDOR MIKHAILOVICH DOSTOEVSKI, the Russian novelist, said one time that, "One sacred memory from childhood is perhaps the best education." I can think of another quickie education for a child, which, in its way, is almost as salutary: Meeting a human being who is tremendously respected by the adult world, and realizing that that person is actually a malicious lunatic.

That was Eliza's and my experience with Dr. Cordelia Swain Cordiner, who was widely believed to be the greatest expert on psychological testing in the world—with the possible exception of China. Nobody knew what was going on in China any more.

• • •

I have an Encyclopaedia Britannica here in the lobby of the Empire State Building, which is the reason I am able to give Dostoevski his middle name.

• • •

Dr. Cordelia Swain Cordiner was invariably impressive and gracious when in the presence of grownups. She was elaborately dressed the whole time she was in the mansion—in high-heeled shoes and fancy dresses and jewelry.

We heard her tell our parents one time: "Just because a woman has three doctor's degrees and heads a testing corporation which bills three million dollars a year, that doesn't mean she can't be feminine."

When she got Eliza and me alone, though, she seethed with paranoia.

"None of your tricks, no more of your snotty little kid millionaire tricks with me," she would say.

And Eliza and I hadn't done *anything* wrong.

• • •

She was so enraged by how much money and power our family had, and so sick, that I don't think she even noticed how

63

huge and ugly Eliza and I were. We were just two more rotten-spoiled little rich kids to her.

"I wasn't born with any silver spoon in my mouth," she told us, not once but many times. "Many was the day we didn't know where the next meal was coming from," she said. "Have you any idea what that's like?"

"No," said Eliza.

"Of course not," said Dr. Cordiner.

And so on.

• • •

Since she was paranoid, it was especially unfortunate that her middle name was the same as our last name.

"I'm not your sweet Aunt Cordelia," she would say. "You needn't worry your little aristocratic brains about that. When my grandfather came from Poland, he changed his name from Stankowitz to Swain." Her eyes were blazing. "Say 'Stankowitz!'"

We said it.

"Now say 'Swain,'" she said.

We did.

• • •

And finally one of us asked her what she was so mad about.

This made her very calm. "I am not mad," she said. "It would be very unprofessional for me to ever get mad about anything. However, let me say that asking a person of my calibre to come all this distance into the wilderness to personally administer tests to only two children is like asking Mozart to tune a piano. It is like asking Albert Einstein to balance a checkbook. Am I getting through to you, 'Mistress Eliza and Master Wilbur,' as I believe you are called?"

"Then why did you come?" I asked her.

Her rage came out into the open again. She said this to me with all possible nastiness: "Because money talks, 'Little Lord Fauntleroy.'"

• • •

We were further shocked when we learned that she meant to administer tests to us separately. We said innocently that we would get many more correct answers if we were allowed to put our heads together.

She became a tower of irony. "Why, of course, Master and Mistress," she said. "And wouldn't you like to have an encyclopaedia in the room with you, too, and maybe the faculty of Harvard University, to tell you the answers, in case you're not sure?"

"That would be *nice*," we said.

"In case nobody has told you," she said, "this is the United States of America, where nobody has a right to rely on anybody else—where everybody learns to make his or her own way.

"I'm here to test you," she said, "but there's a basic rule for life I'd like to teach you, too, and you'll thank me for it in years to come."

This was the lesson: "Paddle your own canoe," she said. "Can you say that and remember it?"

Not only could I say it, but I remember it to this day: "Paddle your own canoe."

Hi ho.

• • •

So we paddled our own canoes. We were tested as individuals at the stainless steel table in the tile-lined diningroom. When one of us was in there with Dr. Cordiner, with "Aunt Cordelia," as we came to call her in private, the other one was taken as far away as possible—to the ballroom at the top of the tower at the north end of the mansion.

Withers Witherspoon had the job of watching whichever one of us was in the ballroom. He was chosen for the job because he had been a soldier at one time. We heard "Aunt Cordelia's" instructions to him. She asked him to be alert to clues that Eliza and I were communicating telepathically.

Western science, with a few clues from the Chinese, had at last acknowledged that some people could communicate with certain others without visible or audible signals. The transmitters and receivers for such spooky messages were on the surfaces of sinus cavities, and those cavities had to be healthy and clear of obstructions.

The chief clue which the Chinese gave the West was this puzzling sentence, delivered in English, which took years to decipher: "I feel so lonesome when I get hay fever or a cold."

Hi ho.

•  •  •

Well, mental telepathy was useless to Eliza and me over distances greater than three meters. With one of us in the dining-room, and the other in the ballroom, our bodies might as well have been on different planets—which is in fact their condition today.

Oh, sure—and I could take written examinations, but Eliza could not. When "Aunt Cordelia" tested Eliza, she had to read each question out loud to her, and then write down her answer.

And it seemed to us that we missed absolutely every question. But we must have answered a few correctly, for Dr. Cordiner reported to our parents that our intelligence was ". . . low normal for their age."

She said further, not knowing that we were eavesdropping, that Eliza would probably never learn to read or write, and hence could never be a voter or hold a driver's license. She tried to soften this some by observing that Eliza was ". . . quite an amusing chatterbox."

She said that I was ". . . a good boy, a serious boy—easily distracted by his scatter-brained sister. He reads and writes, but has a poor comprehension of the meanings of words and sentences. If he were separated from his sister, there is every reason to believe that he could become a fillingstation attendant or a janitor in a village school. His prospects for a happy and useful life in a rural area are fair to good."

•  •  •

The People's Republic of China was at that very moment secretly creating literally millions upon millions of geniuses—by teaching pairs or small groups of congenial, telepathically compatible specialists to think as single minds. And those patchwork minds were the equals of Sir Isaac Newton's or William Shakespeare's, say.

Oh, yes—and long before I became President of the United States of America, the Chinese had begun to combine those synthetic minds into intellects so flabbergasting that the Universe itself seemed to be saying to them, "I await your instructions. You can be anything you want to be. I will be anything you want me to be."

Hi ho.

• • •

I learned about this Chinese scheme long after Eliza died, and long after I lost all my authority as President of the United States of America. There was nothing I could do with such knowledge by then.

One thing amused me, though: I was told that poor old Western Civilization had provided the Chinese the inspiration to put together such synthetic geniuses. The Chinese got the idea from the American and European scientists who put their heads together during the Second World War, with the single-minded intention of creating an atomic bomb.

Hi ho.

• • •

# Chapter 17

O UR POOR PARENTS had first believed that we were idiots. They had tried to adapt to that. Then they believed that we were geniuses. They had tried to adapt to that. Now they were told that we were dull normals, and they were trying to adapt to that.

As Eliza and I watched through peepholes, they made a pitiful and fog-bound plea for help. They asked Dr. Cordelia Swain Cordiner how they were to harmonize our dullness with the fact that we could converse so learnedly on so many subjects in so many languages.

Dr. Cordiner was razor-keen to enlighten them on just this point. "The world is full of people who are very clever at seeming much smarter than they really are," she said. "They dazzle us with facts and quotations and foreign words and so on, whereas the truth is that they know almost nothing of use in life as it is really lived. My purpose is to *detect* such people — so that society can be protected from them, and so they can be protected from themselves.

"Your Eliza is a perfect example," she went on. "She has lectured to me on economics and astronomy and music and every other subject you can think of, and yet she can neither read nor write, nor will she ever be able to."

• • •

She said that our case was not a sad one, since there were no big jobs we wished to hold. "They have almost no ambition at all," she said, "so life can't disappoint them. They want only that life as they have known it should go on forever, which is impossible, of course."

Father nodded sadly. "And the boy is the smarter of the two?"

"To the extent he can read and write," said Dr. Cordiner. "He isn't nearly as socially outgoing as his sister. When he is away from her, he becomes as silent as a tomb.

"I suggest that he be sent to some special school, which won't be too demanding academically or too threatening socially, where he can learn to paddle his own canoe."

"Do what?" said Father.

Dr. Cordiner told him again. "Paddle his own canoe," she said.

•   •   •

Eliza and I should have kicked our way through the wall at that point—should have entered the library ragingly, in an explosion of plaster and laths.

But we had sense enough to know that our power to eavesdrop at will was one of the few advantages we had. So we stole back to our bedrooms, and then burst into the corridor, and came running down the front stairs and across the foyer and into the library, doing something we had never done before. We were sobbing.

We announced that, if anybody tried to part us, we would kill ourselves.

•   •   •

Dr. Cordiner laughed at this. She told our parents that several of the questions in her tests were designed to detect suicidal tendencies. "I absolutely guarantee you," she said, "that the last thing either one of these two would do would be to commit suicide."

Her saying this so jovially was a tactical mistake on her part, for it caused something in Mother to snap. The atmosphere in the room became electrified as Mother stopped being a weak and polite and credulous doll.

Mother did not say anything at first. But she had clearly become subhuman in the finest sense. She was a coiled female panther, suddenly willing to tear the throats out of any number of childrearing experts—in defense of her young.

It was the one and only time that she would ever be irrationally committed to being the mother of Eliza and me.

•   •   •

Eliza and I sensed this sudden jungle alliance telepathically, I think. At any rate, I remember that the damp velvet linings of my sinus cavities were tingling with encouragement.

We left off our crying, which we were no good at doing anyway. Yes, and we made a clear demand which could be satisfied at once. We asked to be tested for intelligence again—as a *pair* this time.

"We want to show you," I said, "how glorious we are when we work together, so that nobody will ever talk about parting us again."

We spoke carefully. I explained who "Betty and Bobby Brown" were. I agreed that they were stupid. I said we had had no experience with hating, and had had trouble understanding that particular human activity whenever we encountered it in books.

"But we are making small beginnings in hating now," said Eliza. "Our hating is strictly limited at this point—to only two people in this Universe: To Betty and Bobby Brown."

•  •  •

Dr. Cordiner, as it turned out, was a coward, among other things. Like so many cowards, she chose to go on bullying at the worst possible time. She jeered at Eliza's and my request.

"What kind of a world do you think this is?" she said, and so on.

So Mother got up and went over to her, not touching her, and not looking her in the eyes, either. Mother spoke to her throat, and, in a tone between a purr and a growl, she called Dr. Cordiner an "overdressed little sparrow-fart."

•  •  •

# Chapter 18

So Eliza and I were retested—as a *pair* this time. We sat side-by-side at the stainless steel table in the tiled diningroom.

We were so happy!

A depersonalized Dr. Cordelia Swain Cordiner administered the tests like a robot, while our parents looked on. She had furnished us with new tests, so that the challenges would all be fresh.

Before we began, Eliza said to Mother and Father, "We promise to answer every question correctly."

Which we did.

• • •

What were the questions like? Well, I was poking around the ruins of a school on Forty-sixth Street yesterday, and I was lucky enough to find a whole batch of intelligence tests, all set to go.

I quote:

"A man purchased 100 shares of stock at five dollars a share. If each share rose ten cents the first month, decreased eight cents the second month, and gained three cents the third month, what was the value of the man's investment at the end of the third month?"

Or try this:

"How many digits are there to the left of the decimal place in the square root of 692038.42753?"

Or this:

"A yellow tulip viewed through a piece of blue glass looks what color?"

Or this:

"Why does the Little Dipper appear to turn about the North Star once a day?"

Or this:

"Astronomy is to geology as steeplejack is to what?"

And so on. Hi ho.

• • •

We made good on Eliza's promise of perfection, as I have said.

The only trouble was that the two of us, in the innocent process of checking and rechecking our answers, wound up under the table—with our legs wrapped around each other's necks in scissors grips, and snorting and snuffling into each other's crotches.

When we regained our chairs, Dr. Cordelia Swain Cordiner had fainted, and our parents were gone.

• • •

At ten o'clock the next morning, I was taken by automobile to a school for severely disturbed children on Cape Cod.

• • •

# *Chapter 19*

IT IS SUNDOWN AGAIN. A bird down around Thirty-first Street and Fifth, where there is an Army tank with a tree growing out of its turret, calls out to me. It asks the same question over and over again with piercing clarity.

"Whip poor Will?" it says.

I never call that bird a "whippoorwill," and neither do Melody and Isadore, who follow my lead in naming things. They seldom call Manhattan "Manhattan," for example, or "The Island of Death," which is its common name on the mainland. They do as I do: They call it "Skyscraper National Park," without knowing what the joke is in that, or, with equal humorlessness, "Angkor Wat."

And what they call the bird that asks about whipping when the sun goes down is what Eliza and I called it when we were children. It was a correct name which we had learned from a dictionary.

We treasured the name for the superstitious dread it inspired. The bird became a nightmare creature in a painting by Hieronymus Bosch when we spoke its name. And, whenever we heard its cry, we spoke its name simultaneously. It was almost the only occasion on which we would speak simultaneously.

"The cry of *The Nocturnal Goatsucker*," we would say.

• • •

And now I hear Melody and Isadore saying that, too, in a part of the lobby where I cannot see them. "The cry of the Nocturnal Goatsucker," they say.

• • •

Eliza and I listened to that bird one evening before my departure for Cape Cod.

We had fled the mansion for the privacy of the dank mausoleum of Professor Elihu Roosevelt Swain.

"Whip poor Will?" came the question, from somewhere out under the apple trees.

73

• • •

Even when we put our heads together, we could think of little to say.

I have heard that condemned prisoners often think of themselves as dead people, long before they die. Perhaps that was how our genius felt, knowing that a cruel axeman, so to speak, was about to split it into two nondescript chunks of meat, into Betty and Bobby Brown.

Be that as it may, our hands were busy—which is often the case with the hands of dying people. We had brought what we thought were the best of our writings with us. We rolled them into a cylinder, which we hid in an empty bronze funerary urn.

The urn had been intended for the ashes of the wife of Professor Swain, who had chosen to be buried here in New York, instead. It was encrusted with verdigris.

Hi ho.

• • •

What was on the papers?

A method for squaring circles, I remember—and a utopian scheme for creating artificial extended families in America by issuing everyone a new middle name. All persons with the same middle name would be relatives.

Yes, and there was our critique of Darwin's Theory of Evolution, and an essay on the nature of gravity, which concluded that gravity had surely been a variable in ancient times.

There was a paper, I remember, which argued that teeth should be washed with hot water, just like dishes and pots and pans.

And so on.

• • •

It was Eliza who had thought of hiding the papers in the urn. It was Eliza who now put the lid in place.

We were not close together when she did it, so what she said was her own invention: "Say goodbye forever to your intelligence, Bobby Brown."

"Goodbye," I said.

• • •

"Eliza—" I said, "so many of the books I've read to you said that love was the most important thing of all. Maybe I should tell you that I love you now."

"Go ahead," she said.

"I love you, Eliza," I said.

She thought about it. "No," she said at last, "I don't like it."

"Why not?" I said.

"It's as though you were pointing a gun at my head," she said. "It's just a way of getting somebody to say something they probably don't mean. What else can I say, or *anybody* say, but, 'I love you, too'?"

"You don't love me?" I said.

"What could anybody love about Bobby Brown?" she said.

•  •  •

Somewhere outside, out under the apple trees, the Nocturnal Goatsucker asked his question again.

•  •  •

# *Chapter 20*

Eliza did not come down to breakfast the next morning. She remained in her room until I was gone.

Our parents came along with me in their chauffeur-driven Mercedes limousine. I was their child with a future. I could read and write.

And, even as we rolled through the lovely countryside, my forgettery set to work.

It was a protective mechanism against unbearable grief, one which I, as a pediatrician, am persuaded all children have.

Somewhere behind me, it seemed, was a twin sister who was not nearly as smart as I was. She had a name. Her name was Eliza Mellon Swain.

* * *

Yes, and the school year was so structured that none of us ever had to go home. I went to England and France and Germany and Italy and Greece. I went to summer camp.

And it was determined that, while I was surely no genius, and was incapable of originality, I had a better than average mind. I was patient and orderly, and could sort out good ideas from heaps of balderdash.

I was the first child in the history of the school to take College Boards. I did so well that I was invited to come to Harvard. I accepted the invitation, although my voice had yet to change.

And I would now and then be reminded by my parents, who became very proud of me, that somewhere I had a twin sister who was little more than a human vegetable. She was in an expensive institution for people of her sort.

She was only a name.

* * *

Father was killed in an automobile accident during my first year in medical school. He had thought enough of me to name me an executor of his will.

And I was visited in Boston soon after that by a fat and shifty-eyed attorney named Norman Mushari, Jr. He told me what seemed at first to be a rambling and irrelevant story about a woman who had been locked away for many years against her will—in an institution for the feeble-minded.

She had hired him, he said, to sue her relatives and the institution for damages, to gain her release at once, and to recover all inheritances which had been wrongly withheld.

She had a name, which, of course, was Eliza Mellon Swain.

•   •   •

# Chapter 21

MOTHER WOULD SAY later of the hospital where we abandoned Eliza to Limbo: "It wasn't a cheap hospital, you know. It cost two hundred dollars a day. And the doctors begged us to stay away, didn't they, Wilbur?"

"I think so, Mother," I said. And then I told the truth: "I forget."

• • •

I was then not only a stupid Bobby Brown, but a conceited one. Though only a first-year medical student with the genitalia of an infant field mouse, I was the master of a great house on Beacon Hill. I was driven to and from school in a Jaguar—and I had already taken to dressing as I would dress when President of the United States, like a medical mountebank during the era of Chester Alan Arthur, say.

There was a party there nearly every night. I would customarily make an appearance of only a few minutes—smoking hashish in a meerschaum pipe, and wearing an emerald-green, watered-silk dressing gown.

A pretty girl came up to me at one of those parties, and she said to me, "You are so ugly, you're the sexiest thing I ever saw."

"I know," I said. "I know, I know."

• • •

Mother visited me a lot on Beacon Hill, where I had a special suite built just for her—and I visited her a lot in Turtle Bay. Yes, and reporters came to question us in both places after Norman Mushari, Jr., got Eliza out of the hospital.

It was a big story.

It was always a big story when multimillionaires mistreated their own relatives.

Hi ho.

• • •

It was embarrassing, and should have been, of course.

78

We had not seen Eliza yet, and had not been able to reach her by telephone. Meanwhile, though, she said justly insulting things about us almost every day in the press.

All we had to show reporters was a copy of a telegram we had sent to Eliza, in care of her lawyer, and Eliza's reply to it.

Our telegram said:

"WE LOVE YOU. YOUR MOTHER AND YOUR BROTHER."

Eliza's telegram said this:

"I LOVE YOU TOO. ELIZA."

• • •

Eliza would not allow herself to be photographed. She had her lawyer buy a confessional booth from a church which was being torn down. She sat inside it when she granted interviews for television.

And Mother and I watched those interviews in agony, holding hands.

And Eliza's rowdy contralto had become so unfamiliar to us that we thought there might be an imposter in the booth, but it was Eliza all right.

I remember a television reporter asked her, "How did you spend your time in the hospital, Miss Swain?"

"Singing," she said.

"Singing anything in particular?" he said.

"The same song—over and over again," she said.

"What song was that?" he said.

"'Some Day My Prince Will Come,'" she told him.

"And did you have some specific prince in mind—as your rescuer?" he said.

"My twin brother," she said. "But he's a swine, of course. He never came."

• • •

# Chapter 22

MOTHER AND I surely did not oppose Eliza and her lawyer in any way, so she easily regained control of her wealth. And nearly the first thing she did was to buy half-interest in The New England Patriots professional football team.

· · ·

This purchase resulted in more publicity. Eliza would still not come out of the booth for cameras, but Mushari promised the world that she was now wearing a New England Patriots blue and gold jersey in there.

She was asked in this particular interview if she kept up with current events, to which she replied: "I certainly don't blame the Chinamen for going home."

This had to do with the Republic of China's closing its embassy in Washington. The miniaturization of human beings in China had progressed so far at that point, that their ambassador was only sixty centimeters tall. His farewell was polite and friendly. He said his country was severing relations simply because there was no longer anything going on in the United States which was of any interest to the Chinese at all.

Eliza was asked to say why the Chinamen had been so right.

"What civilized country could be interested in a hell-hole like America," she said, "where everybody takes such lousy care of their own relatives?"

· · ·

And then, one day, she and Mushari were seen crossing the Massachusetts Avenue Bridge from Cambridge to Boston on foot. It was a warm and sunny day. Eliza was carrying a parasol. She was wearing the jersey of her football team.

· · ·

My God—was that poor girl ever a mess!

She was so bent over that her face was on level with Mushari's—and Mushari was about the size of Napoleon Bonaparte. She was chain smoking. She was coughing her head off.

Mushari was wearing a white suit. He carried a cane. He wore a red rose in his lapel.

And he and his client were soon joined by a friendly crowd, and by newspaper photographers and television crews.

And mother and I watched them on television—in horror, may I say, for the parade was coming ever closer to my house on Beacon Hill.

• • •

"Oh, Wilbur, Wilbur, Wilbur—" said my mother as we watched, "is that really your sister?"

I made a bitter joke—without smiling. "Either your only daughter, Mother, or the sort of anteater known as an *aardvark*," I said.

• • •

# Chapter 23

Mother was not up to a confrontation with Eliza. She retreated to her suite upstairs. Nor did I want the servants to witness whatever grotesque performance Eliza had in mind—so I sent them to their quarters.

When the doorbell rang, I myself answered the door.

I smiled at the aardvark and the cameras and the crowd. "Eliza! Dear sister! What a pleasant surprise. Come in, come in!" I said.

For form's sake, I made a tentative gesture as though I might touch her. She drew back. "You touch me, Lord Fauntleroy, and I'll bite you, and you'll die of rabies," she said.

• • •

Policemen kept the crowd from following Eliza and Mushari into the house, and I closed the drapes on the windows, so no one could see in.

When I was sure we had privacy, I said to her bleakly, "What brings you here?"

"Lust for your perfect body, Wilbur," she said. She coughed and laughed. "Is dear Mater here, or dear Pater?" She corrected herself. "Oh, dear—dear Pater is dead, isn't he? Or is it dear Mater? It's so hard to tell."

"Mother is in Turtle Bay, Eliza," I lied. Inwardly, I was swooning with sorrow and loathing and guilt. I estimated that her crushed ribcage had the capacity of a box of kitchen matches. The room was beginning to smell like a distillery. Eliza had a problem with alcohol as well. Her skin was bad. She had a complexion like our great-grandmother's steamer trunk.

"Turtle Bay, Turtle Bay," she mused. "Did it ever occur to you, dear Brother, that dear Father was not our Father at all?"

"What do you mean?" I said.

"Perhaps Mother stole from the bed and out of the house on a moonlit night," she said, "and mated with a giant sea turtle in Turtle Bay."

Hi ho.

• • •

"Eliza," I said, "if we're going to discuss family matters, per-haps Mr. Mushari should leave us alone."

"Why?" she said. "Normie is the only family I have."

"Now, now—" I said.

"That overdressed sparrow-fart of a mother of yours is surely no relative of mine," she said.

"Now, now—" I said.

"And you don't consider yourself a relative of mine, do you?" she said.

"What can I say?" I said.

"That's why we're visiting you—to hear all the wonderful things you have to say," she said. "You were always the brainy one. I was just some kind of tumor that had to be removed from your side."

• • •

"I never said that," I said.

"Other people said it, and you believed them," she said. "That's worse. You're a Fascist, Wilbur. That's what you are."

"That's absurd," I said.

"Fascists are inferior people who believe it when somebody tells them they're superior," she said.

"Now, now—" I said.

"Then they want everybody else to die," she said.

• • •

"This is getting us nowhere," I said.

"I'm *used* to getting nowhere," she said, "as you may have read in the papers and seen on television."

"Eliza—" I said, "would it help at all for you to know that Mother will be sick for the rest of our lives about that awful thing we did to you?"

"How could that help?" she said. "That's the dumbest ques-tion I ever heard."

• • •

She looped a great arm over the shoulders of Norman Mu-shari, Jr. "Here's who knows how to help people," she said.

I nodded. "We're grateful to him. We really are."

"He's my mother and father and brother and God, all wrapped up in one," she said. "He gave me the gift of life!

"He said to me, 'Money isn't going to make you feel any better, Sweetheart, but we're going to sue the piss out of your relatives anyway.'"

"Um," I said.

"But it sure helps a hell of a lot more than your expressions of guilt, I must say. Those are just boasts about your own wonderful sensibilities."

She laughed unpleasantly. "But I can see where you and Mother might want to boast about your guilt. After all, it's the only thing you two monkeys ever earned."

Hi ho.

•  •  •

# *Chapter 24*

I ASSUMED THAT ELIZA had now assaulted my self-respect with every weapon she had. I had somehow survived.

Without pride, with a clinical and cynical sort of interest, I noted that I had a cast-iron character which would repel attacks, apparently, even if I declined to put up defenses of any other kind.

How wrong I was about Eliza's having expended her fury!

Her opening attacks had been aimed merely at exposing the cast iron in my character. She had merely sent out light patrols to cut down the trees and shrubs in front of my character, to strip it of its vines, so to speak.

And now, without my realizing it, the shell of my character stood before her concealed howitzers at nearly point-blank range, as naked and brittle as a Franklin stove.

Hi ho.

• • •

There was a lull. Eliza prowled about my livingroom, looking at my books, which she couldn't read, of course. Then she returned to me, and she cocked her head, and she said, "People get into Harvard Medical School because they can read and write?"

"I worked very hard, Eliza," I said. "It wasn't easy for me. It isn't easy now."

"If Bobby Brown becomes a doctor," she said, "that will be the strongest argument I ever heard for the Christian Scientists."

"I will not be the best doctor there ever was," I said. "I won't be the worst, either."

"You might be a very good man with a gong," she said. She was alluding to recent rumors that the Chinese had had remarkable successes in treating breast cancer with the music of ancient gongs. "You look like a man," she said, "who could hit a gong almost every time."

"Thank you," I said.

"Touch me," she said.

"Pardon me?" I said.

"I'm your own flesh. I'm your sister. Touch me," she said.

"Yes, of course," I said. But my arms seemed queerly paralyzed.

•   •   •

"Take your time," she said.

"Well—" I said, "since you hate me so—"

"I hate Bobby Brown," she said.

"Since you hate Bobby Brown—" I said.

"And Betty Brown," she said.

"That was so long ago," I said.

"Touch me," she said.

"Oh, Christ, Eliza!" I said. My arms still wouldn't move.

"I'll touch you," she said.

"Whatever you say," I said. I was scared stiff.

"You don't have a heart condition, do you Wilbur?" she said.

"No," I said.

"If I touch you, you promise you won't die?"

"Yes," I said.

"Maybe *I'll* die," she said.

"I hope not," I said.

"Just because I act like I know what's going to happen," she said, "doesn't mean I know what's going to happen. Maybe nothing will happen."

"Maybe," I said.

"I've never seen you so frightened," she said.

"I'm human," I said.

"You want to tell Normie what you're scared about?" she said.

"No," I said.

•   •   •

Eliza, with her fingertips almost brushing my cheek, quoted from a dirty joke Withers Witherspoon had told another servant when we were children. We had heard it through a wall. The joke had to do with a woman who was wildly responsive during sexual intercourse. In the joke, the woman warned a stranger who was beginning to make love to her.

Eliza passed on the sultry warning to me: "Keep your hat on, Buster. We may wind up miles from here."

• • •

Then she touched me.
We became a single genius again.

• • •

# Chapter 25

W E WENT BERSERK. It was only by the Grace of God that we did not tumble out of the house and into the crowd on Beacon Street. Some parts of us, of which I had not been at all aware, of which Eliza had been excruciatingly aware, had been planning a reunion for a long, long time.

I could no longer tell where I stopped and Eliza began, or where Eliza and I stopped and the Universe began. It was gorgeous and it was horrible. Yes, and let this be a measure of the quantity of energy involved: The orgy went on for five whole nights and days.

• • •

Eliza and I slept for three days after that. When I at last woke up, I found myself in my own bed. I was being fed intravenously.

Eliza, as I later found out, had been taken to her own home in a private ambulance.

• • •

As for why nobody broke us up or summoned help: Eliza and I captured Norman Mushari, Jr., and poor Mother and the servants—one by one.

I have no memory of doing this.

We tied them to wooden chairs and gagged them, apparently, and set them neatly around the diningroom table.

• • •

We gave them food and water, thank Heavens, or we would have been murderers. We would not let them go to the toilet, however, and fed them nothing but peanut butter and jelly sandwiches. I apparently left the house several times to get more bread and jelly and peanut butter.

And then the orgy would begin again.

• • •

I remember reading out loud to Eliza from books on pediatrics and child psychology and sociology and anthropology, and so on. I had never thrown away any book from any course I had taken.

I remember writhing embraces which alternated with periods of my sitting at my typewriter, with Eliza beside me. I was typing something with superhuman speed.

Hi ho.

•    •    •

When I came out of my coma, Mushari and my own lawyers had already paid my servants handsomely for the agony they had suffered at the dinner table, and for their silence as to the dreadful things they had seen.

Mother had been released from Massachusetts General Hospital, and was back in bed in Turtle Bay.

•    •    •

Physically, I had suffered from exhaustion and nothing more.

When I was allowed to rise, however, I was so damaged psychologically that I expected to find everything unfamiliar. If gravity had become variable on that day, as it in fact did many years later, if I had had to crawl about my house on my hands and knees, as I often do now, I would have thought it a highly appropriate response by the Universe to all I had been through.

•    •    •

But little had changed. The house was tidy.

The books were back in their shelves. A broken thermostat had been replaced. Three diningroom chairs had been sent out for repairs. The diningroom carpet was somewhat piebald, pale spots indicating where stains had been removed.

The one proof that something extraordinary had happened was itself a paradigm of tidiness. It was a manuscript—on a coffee table in the livingroom, where I had typed so furiously during the nightmare.

Eliza and I had somehow written a manual on childrearing.

•    •    •

Was it any good? Not really. It was only good enough to become, after The Bible and *The Joy of Cooking*, the most popular book of all time.

Hi ho.

•   •   •

I found it so helpful when I began to practice pediatrics in Vermont that I had it published under a pseudonym, Dr. Eli W. Rockmell, M.D., a sort of garbling of Eliza's and my names.

The publisher thought up the title, which was *So You Went and Had a Baby*.

•   •   •

During our orgy, though, Eliza and I gave the manuscript a very different title and sort of authorship, which was this:

THE CRY OF THE NOCTURNAL GOATSUCKER

by

BETTY AND BOBBY BROWN

•   •   •

# *Chapter 26*

AFTER THE ORGY, mutual terror kept us apart. I was told by our go-between, Norman Mushari, Jr., that Eliza was even more shattered by the orgy than I had been.

"I almost had to put her away again—" he said, "for good cause this time."

• • •

Machu Picchu, the old Inca capital on the roof of the Andes in Peru, was then becoming a haven for rich people and their parasites, people fleeing social reforms and economic declines, not just in America, but in all parts of the world. There were even some full-sized Chinese there, who had declined to let their children be miniaturized.

And Eliza moved into a condominium down there, to be as far away as possible from me.

• • •

When Mushari came to my house to tell me about Eliza's prospective move to Peru, a week after the orgy, he confessed that he himself had become severely disoriented while tied to a diningroom chair.

"You looked more and more like Frankenstein monsters to me," he said. "I became convinced that there was a switch somewhere in the house that controlled you. I even figured out which switch it was. The minute I untied myself, I ran to it and tore it out by the roots."

It was Mushari who had ripped the thermostat from the wall.

• • •

To demonstrate to me how changed he was, he admitted that he had been wholly motivated by self-interest when he set Eliza free. "I was a bounty-hunter," he said, "finding rich people in mental hospitals who didn't belong there—and setting them free. I left the poor to rot in their dungeons."

"It was a useful service all the same," I said.

"Christ, I don't think so," he said. "Practically every sane person I ever got out of a hospital went insane almost immediately afterwards.

"Suddenly I feel old," he said. "I can't take that any more."

Hi ho.

• • •

Mushari was so shaken by the orgy, in fact, that he turned Eliza's legal and financial affairs over to the same people that Mother and I used.

He came to my attention only once more, two years later, about the time I graduated from medical school—at the bottom of my class, by the way. He had patented an invention of his own. There was a photograph of him and a description of his patent on a business page in *The New York Times*.

There was a national mania for tap-dancing at the time. Mushari had invented taps which could be glued to the soles of shoes, and then peeled off again. A person could carry the taps in little plastic bags in a pocket or purse, according to Mushari, and put them on only when it was time to tap-dance.

• • •

# Chapter 27

I NEVER SAW Eliza's face again after the orgy. I heard her voice only twice more—once when I graduated from medical school, and again when I was President of the United States of America, and she had been dead for a long, long time.

Hi ho.

• • •

When Mother planned a graduation party for me at the Ritz in Boston, across from the Public Gardens, she and I never dreamed that Eliza would somehow hear of it, and would come all the way from Peru.

My twin never wrote or telephoned. Rumors about her were as vague as those coming from China. She was drinking too much, we had heard. She had taken up golf.

• • •

I was having a wonderful time at my party, when a bellboy came to tell me I was wanted outside—not just in the lobby, but in the balmy, moonlit night outdoors. Eliza was the farthest thing from my mind.

My guess, as I followed the bellboy, was that there was a Rolls-Royce from my mother parked outside.

I was reassured by the servile manner and uniform of my guide. I was also giddy with champagne. I did not hesitate to follow as he led me across Arlington Street and then into the enchanted forest, into the Public Gardens on the other side.

He was a fraud. He was not a bellboy at all.

• • •

Deeper and deeper we went into the trees. And in every clearing we came to, I expected to see my Rolls-Royce.

But he brought me to a statue instead. It depicted an old-fashioned doctor, dressed much as it amused me to dress. He was melancholy but proud. He held a sleeping youth in his arms.

As the inscription in the moonlight told me, this was a monument to the first use of anaesthetics in surgery in the United States, which took place in Boston.

•   •   •

I had been aware of a clattering whir somewhere in the city, over Commonwealth Avenue perhaps. But I had not identified it as a hovering helicopter.

But now the bogus bellhop, who was really an Inca servant of Eliza's, fired a magnesium flare into the air.

Everything touched by that unnatural dazzle became statuary—lifeless and exemplary, and weighing tons.

The helicopter materialized directly over us, itself made allegorical, transformed into a terrible mechanical angel by the glare of the flare.

Eliza was up there with a bullhorn.

•   •   •

It seemed possible to me that she might shoot me from there, or hit me with a bag of excrement. She had traveled all the way from Peru to deliver one-half of a Shakespearean sonnet.

"Listen!" she said. "Listen!" she said. And then she said, "Listen!" again.

The flare was meanwhile dying nearby—its parachute snagged in a treetop.

Here is what Eliza said to me, and to the neighborhood:

"O! how thy worth with manners may I sing,
"When thou art all the better part of me?
"What can mine own praise to mine own self bring?
"And what is't but mine own when I praise thee?
"Even for this let us divided live,
"And our dear love lose name of single one,
"That by this separation I may give
"That due to thee, which thou deserv'st alone."

•   •   •

I called up to her through my cupped hands. "Eliza!" I said. And then I shouted something daring, and something I genuinely felt for the first time in my life.

"Eliza! I love you!" I said.

All was darkness now.

"Did you hear me, Eliza?" I said. "I *love* you! I *really* love you!"

"I heard you," she said. "Nobody should ever say that to anybody."

"I mean it," I said.

"Then I will say in turn something that I really mean, my brother—my twin."

"What is it?" I said.

She said this: "God guide the hand and mind of Dr. Wilbur Rockefeller Swain."

•   •   •

And then the helicopter flew away.

Hi ho.

•   •   •

# Chapter 28

I RETURNED to the Ritz, laughing and crying—a two-meter Neanderthaler in a ruffled shirt and a robin's-egg blue velvet tuxedo.

There was a crowd of people who were curious about the brief supernova in the east, and about the voice which had spoken from Heaven of separation and love. I pressed past them and into the ballroom, leaving it to private detectives stationed at the door to turn back the following crowd.

The guests at my party were only now beginning to hear hints that something marvelous had happened outside. I went to Mother, to tell her what Eliza had done. I was puzzled to find her talking to a nondescript, middle-aged stranger, dressed, like the detectives, in a cheap business suit.

Mother introduced him as "Dr. Mott." He was, of course, the doctor who had looked after Eliza and me for so long in Vermont. He was in Boston on business, and, as luck would have it, staying at the Ritz.

I was so full of news and champagne, though, that I did not know or care who he was. And, having said my bit to Mother, I told Dr. Mott that it had been nice to meet him, and I hurried on to other parts of the room.

• • •

When I got back to Mother in about an hour, Dr. Mott had departed. She told me again who he was. I expressed pro forma regrets at not having spent more time with him. She gave me a note from him, which she said was his graduation present to me.

It was written on Ritz stationery. It said simply this:

"'If you can do no good, at least do no harm.' Hippocrates."

• • •

Yes, and when I converted the mansion in Vermont into a clinic and small children's hospital, and also my permanent home, I had those words chipped in stone over the front door. But they so troubled my patients and their parents that I had them chipped away again. The words seemed a confession of weakness and indecision to them, a suggestion that they might as well have stayed away.

I continued to carry the words in my head, however, and in fact did little harm. And the intellectual center of gravity for my practice was a single volume which I locked into a safe each night—the bound manuscript of the child-rearing manual Eliza and I had written during our orgy on Beacon Hill.

Somehow, we had put *everything* in there.

And the years flew by.

•  •  •

Somewhere in there I married an equally wealthy woman, actually a third cousin of mine, whose maiden name was Rose Aldrich Ford. She was very unhappy, because I did not love her, and because I would never take her anywhere. I have never been good at loving. We had a child, Carter Paley Swain, whom I also failed to love. Carter was normal, and completely uninteresting to me. He was somehow like a summer squash on the vine— featureless and watery, and merely growing larger all the time.

After our divorce, he and his mother bought a condominium in the same building with Eliza, down in Machu Picchu, Peru. I never heard from them again—even when I became President of the United States.

And the time flew.

•  •  •

I woke up one morning to find that I was almost fifty years old! Mother had moved in with me in Vermont. She sold her house in Turtle Bay. She was feeble and afraid.

She talked a good deal about Heaven to me.

I knew nothing at all about the subject then. I assumed that when people were dead they were dead.

"I know your father is waiting for me with open arms," she said, "and my Mommy and Daddy, too."

She was right about that, it turned out. Waiting around for more people is just about all there is for people in Heaven to do.

•  •  •

The way Mother described Heaven, it sounded like a golf course in Hawaii, with manicured fairways and greens running down to a lukewarm ocean.

I twitted her only lightly about wanting that sort of Paradise. "It sounds like a place where people would drink a lot of lemonade," I said.

"I love lemonade," she replied.

•   •   •

# Chapter 29

MOTHER TALKED toward the end, too, about how much she hated unnatural things—synthetic flavors and fibers and plastics and so on. She loved silk and cotton and linen and wool and leather, she said, and clay and glass and stone. She loved horses and sailboats, too, she said.

"They're all coming back, Mother," I said, which was true.

My hospital itself had twenty horses by then—and wagons and carts and carriages and sleighs. I had a horse of my own, a great Clydesdale. Golden feathers hid her hooves. "Budweiser" was her name.

Yes, and the harbors of New York and Boston and San Francisco were forests of masts again, I'd heard. It had been quite some time since I'd seen them.

• • •

Yes, and I found the hospitality of my mind to fantasy pleasantly increased as machinery died and communications from the outside world became more and more vague.

So I was unsurprised one night, after having tucked Mother in bed, to enter my own bedroom with a lighted candle, and to find a Chinese man the size of my thumb sitting on my mantelpiece. He was wearing a quilted blue jacket and trousers and cap.

As far as I was able to determine afterwards, he was the first official emissary from the People's Republic of China to the United States of America in more than twenty-five years.

• • •

During the same period, not a single foreigner who got inside China, so far as I know, ever returned from there.

So "going to China" became a widespread euphemism for committing suicide.

Hi ho.

• • •

My little visitor motioned for me to come closer, so he would not have to shout. I presented one ear to him. It must have been a horrible sight—the tunnel with all the hair and bits of wax inside.

He told me that he was a roving ambassador, and had been chosen for the job because of his visibility to foreigners. He was much, much larger, he said, than an average Chinese.

"I thought you people had no interest in us any more," I said.

He smiled. "That was a foolish thing for us to say, Dr. Swain," he said. "We apologize."

"You mean that we know things that you don't know?" I said.

"Not quite," he said. "I mean that you *used* to know things that we don't know."

"I can't imagine what those things would be," I said.

"Naturally not," he said. "I will give you a hint: I bring you greetings from your twin sister in Machu Picchu, Dr. Swain."

"That's not much of a hint," I said.

"I wish very much to see the papers you and your sister put so many years ago into the funeral urn in the mausoleum of Professor Elihu Roosevelt Swain," he said.

●    ●    ●

It turned out that the Chinese had sent an expedition to Machu Picchu—to recover, if they could, certain lost secrets of the Incas. Like my visitor, they were oversize for Chinese.

Yes, and Eliza approached them with a proposition. She said she knew where there were secrets which were as good or better than anything the Incas had had.

"If what I say turns out to be true," she told them, "I want you to reward me—with a trip to your colony on Mars."

●    ●    ●

He said that his name was Fu Manchu.

●    ●    ●

I asked him how he had got to my mantelpiece.

"The same way we get to Mars," he replied.

●    ●    ●

# *Chapter 30*

I AGREED TO TAKE Fu Manchu out to the mausoleum. I put him in my breast pocket.

I felt very inferior to him. I was sure he had the power of life and death over me, as small as he was. Yes, and he knew so much more than I did—even about medicine, even about myself, perhaps. He made me feel immoral, too. It was greedy for me to be so big. My supper that night could have fed a thousand men his size.

• • •

The exterior doors to the mausoleum had been welded shut. So Fu Manchu and I had to enter the secret passageways, the alternative universe of my childhood, and come up through the mausoleum's floor.

As I made our way through cobwebs, I asked him about the Chinese use of gongs in the treatment of cancer.

"We are way beyond that now," he said.

"Maybe it is something we could still use here," I said.

"I'm sorry—" he said from my pocket, "but your civilization, so-called, is much too primitive. You could never understand."

"Um," I said.

• • •

He answered all my questions that way—saying, in effect, that I was too dumb to understand anything.

• • •

When we got to the underside of the stone trapdoor to the mausoleum, I had trouble heaving it open.

"Put your shoulder into it," he said, and, "Tap it with a brick," and so on.

His advice was so simple-minded, that I concluded that the Chinese knew little more about dealing with gravity than I did at the time.

Hi ho.

•   •   •

The door finally opened, and we ascended into the mausoleum. I must have been even more frightful than usual to look at. I was swaddled in cobwebs from head to toe.

I removed Fu Manchu from my pocket, and, at his request, I placed him on top of the lead casket of Professor Elihu Roosevelt Swain.

I had only one candle for illumination. But Fu Manchu now produced from his attaché case a tiny box. It filled the chamber with a light as brilliant as the flare that had lit Eliza's and my reunion in Boston—so long ago.

He asked me to take the papers from the urn, which I did. They were perfectly preserved.

"This is bound to be trash," I said.

"To you, perhaps," he said. He asked me to flatten out the papers and spread them over the casket, which I did.

"How could we know when we were children something not known even today to the Chinese?" I said.

"Luck," he said. He began to stroll across the papers, in his tiny black and white basketball shoes, pausing here and there to take pictures of something he had read. He seemed especially interested in our essay on gravity—or so it seems to me now, with the benefit of hindsight.

•   •   •

He was satisfied at last. He thanked me for my cooperation, and told me that he would now dematerialize and return to China.

"Did you find anything at all valuable?" I asked him.

He smiled. "A ticket to Mars for a rather large Caucasian lady in Peru," he replied.

Hi ho.

•   •   •

# Chapter 31

THREE WEEKS LATER, on the morning of my fiftieth birthday, I rode my horse Budweiser down into the hamlet—to pick up the mail.

There was a note from Eliza. It said only this: "Happy birthday to us! Going to China!"

That message was two weeks old, according to the postmark. There was fresher news in the same mail. "Regret to inform you that your sister died on Mars in an avalanche." It was signed, "Fu Manchu."

• • •

I read those tragic notes while standing on the old wooden porch of the post office, in the shadow of the little church next door.

An extraordinary feeling came over me, which I first thought to be psychological in origin, the first rush of grief. I seemed to have taken root on the porch. I could not pick up my feet. My features, moreover, were being dragged downward like melting wax.

The truth was that the force of gravity had increased tremendously.

There was a great crash in the church. The steeple had dropped its bell.

Then I went right through the porch, and was slammed to the earth beneath it.

• • •

In other parts of the world, of course, elevator cables were snapping, airplanes were crashing, ships were sinking, motor vehicles were breaking their axles, bridges were collapsing, and on and on.

It was terrible.

• • •

# Chapter 32

THAT FIRST FEROCIOUS JOLT of heavy gravity lasted less than a minute, but the world would never be the same again.

I dazedly climbed out from under the post office porch when it was over. I gathered up my mail.

Budweiser was dead. She had tried to remain standing. Her insides had fallen out.

• • •

I must have suffered something like shell shock. People were crying for help there in the hamlet, and I was the only doctor. But I simply walked away.

I remember wandering under the family apple trees.

I remember stopping at the family cemetery, and gravely opening an envelope from the Eli Lilly Company, a pharmaceutical house. Inside were a dozen sample pills, the color and size of lentils.

The accompanying literature, which I read with great care, explained that the trade name for the pills was "tri-benzo-Deportamil." The "Deport" part of the name had reference to good deportment, to socially acceptable behavior.

The pills were a treatment for the socially unacceptable symptoms of Tourette's Disease, whose sufferers involuntarily spoke obscenities and made insulting gestures no matter where they were.

In my disoriented state, it seemed very important that I take two of the pills immediately, which I did.

Two minutes passed, and then my whole being was flooded with contentment and confidence such as I had never felt before.

Thus began an addiction which was to last for nearly thirty years.

Hi ho.

• • •

It was a miracle that no one in my hospital died. The beds and wheelchairs of some of the heavier children had broken.

One nurse crashed through the trapdoor which had once been hidden by Eliza's bed. She broke both legs.

Mother, thank God, slept through it all.

When she woke up, I was standing at the foot of her bed. She told me again about how much she hated unnatural things. "I know, Mother," I said. "I couldn't agree with you more. Back to Nature," I said.

• • •

I do not know to this day whether that awful jolt of gravity was Nature, or whether it was an experiment by the Chinese.

I thought at the time that there was a connection between the jolt and Fu Manchu's photographing of Eliza's and my essay on gravity.

Yes, and, coked to the ears on tri-benzo-Deportamil, I fetched all our papers from the mausoleum.

• • •

The paper on gravity was incomprehensible to me. Eliza and I were perhaps ten thousand times as smart when we put our heads together as when we were far apart.

Our Utopian scheme for reorganizing America into thousands of artificial extended families, however, was clear. Fu Manchu had found it ridiculous, incidentally.

"This is truly the work of children," he'd said.

• • •

I found it absorbing. It said that there was nothing new about artificial extended families in America. Physicians felt themselves related to other physicians, lawyers to lawyers, writers to writers, athletes to athletes, politicians to politicians, and so on.

Eliza and I said these were bad sorts of extended families, however. They excluded children and old people and housewives, and losers of every description. Also: Their interests were usually so specialized as to seem nearly insane to outsiders.

"An ideal extended family," Eliza and I had written so long ago, "should give proportional representation to all sorts of Americans, according to their numbers. The creation of ten thousand such families, say, would provide America with ten thousand parliaments, so to speak, which would discuss sincerely and expertly what only a few hypocrites now discuss with passion, which is the welfare of all mankind."

•  •  •

My reading was interrupted by my head nurse, who came in to tell me that our frightened young patients had all gotten to sleep at last.

I thanked her for the good news. And then I heard myself tell her casually, "Oh—and I want you to write to the Eli Lilly Company, in Indianapolis, and order two thousand doses of a new drug of theirs called 'tri-benzo-Deportamil.'"

Hi ho.

•  •  •

# Chapter 33

Mother died two weeks after that.

Gravity would not trouble us again for another twenty years.

And time flew. Time was a blurry bird now—made indistinct by ever-increasing dosages of tri-benzo-Deportamil.

•　•　•

Somewhere in there, I closed my hospital, gave up medicine entirely, and was elected United States Senator from Vermont.

And time flew.

I found myself running for President one day. My valet pinned a campaign button to the lapel of my claw-hammer coat. It bore the slogan which would win the election for me:

•　•　•

I appeared here in New York only once during that campaign. I spoke from the steps of the Public Library at Forty-second and Fifth. This island was by then a sleepy seaside resort. It had never recovered from that first jolt of gravity, which had stripped its buildings of their elevators, and had flooded its tunnels, and had buckled all but one bridge, which was the Brooklyn Bridge.

Now gravity had started to turn mean again. It was no longer a jolting experience. If the Chinese were indeed in charge of it, they had learned how to increase or decrease it gradually, wishing to cut down on injuries and property damage, perhaps. It was as majestically graceful as the tides now.

• • •

When I spoke from the library steps, the gravity was heavy. So I chose to sit in a chair while speaking. I was cold sober, but I lolled in the chair like a drunken English squire from olden times.

My audience, which was composed mostly of retired people, actually lay down on Fifth Avenue, which the police had blocked off, but where there would have been hardly any traffic anyway. Somewhere over on Madison Avenue, perhaps, there was a small explosion. The island's useless skyscrapers were being quarried.

• • •

I spoke of American loneliness. It was the only subject I needed for victory, which was lucky. It was the only subject I had.

It was a shame, I said, that I had not come along earlier in American history with my simple and workable anti-loneliness plan. I said that all the damaging excesses of Americans in the past were motivated by loneliness rather than a fondness for sin.

An old man crawled up to me afterwards and told me how he used to buy life insurance and mutual funds and household appliances and automobiles and so on, not because he liked them or needed them, but because the salesman seemed to promise to be his relative, and so on.

"I had no relatives and I needed relatives," he said.

"Everybody does," I said.

He told me he had been a drunk for a while, trying to make relatives out of people in bars. "The bartender would be kind of a father, you know—" he said. "And then all of a sudden it was closing time."

"I know," I said. I told him a half-truth about myself which had proved to be popular on the campaign trail. "I used to be so lonesome," I said, "that the only person I could share my innermost thoughts with was a horse named 'Budweiser.'"

And I told him how Budweiser had died.

• • •

During this conversation, I would bring my hand to my mouth again and again, seeming to stifle exclamations and so on. I was actually popping tiny green pills into my mouth. They were outlawed by then, and no longer manufactured. I had perhaps a bushel of them back in the Senate Office Building.

They accounted for my unflagging courtesy and optimism, and perhaps for my failure to age as quickly as other men. I was seventy years old, but I had the vigor of a man half that age.

I had even picked up a pretty new wife, Sophie Rothschild Swain, who was only twenty-three.

• • •

"If you get elected, and I get issued all these new artificial relatives—" said the man. He paused. "How many did you say?"

"Ten thousand brothers and sisters," I told him. "One-hundred and ninety-thousand cousins."

"Isn't that an awful lot?" he said.

"Didn't we just agree we need all the relatives we can get in a country as big and clumsy as ours?" I said. "If you ever go to Wyoming, say, won't it be a comfort to you to know you have many relatives there?"

He thought that over. "Well, yes—I expect," he said at last.

"As I said in my speech:" I told him, "your new middle name would consist of a noun, the name of a flower or fruit or nut or vegetable or legume, or a bird or a reptile or a fish, or a mollusk, or a gem or a mineral or a chemical element—connected by a hyphen to a number between one and twenty." I asked him what his name was at the present time.

"Elmer Glenville Grasso," he said.

"Well," I said, "you might become Elmer Uranium-3 Grasso, say. Everybody with Uranium as a part of their middle name would be your cousin."

"That brings me back to my first question," he said. "What if I get some artificial relative I absolutely can't stand?"

• • •

"What is so novel about a person's having a relative he can't stand?" I asked him. "Wouldn't you say that sort of thing has been going on now for perhaps a million years, Mr. Grasso?"

And then I said a very obscene thing to him. I am not inclined toward obscenities, as this book itself demonstrates. In all my years of public life, I had never said an off-color thing to the American people.

So it was terrifically effective when I at last spoke coarsely. I did so in order to make memorable how nicely scaled to average human beings my new social scheme would be.

Mr. Grasso was not the first to hear the startling rowdy-isms. I had even used them on radio. There was no such thing as television any more.

"Mr. Grasso," I said, "I personally will be very disappointed, if you do not say to artificial relatives you hate, after I am elected, 'Brother or Sister or Cousin,' as the case may be, 'why don't you take a flying fuck at a rolling doughnut? Why don't you take a flying fuck at the mooooooooooooooon?'"

•   •   •

"You know what relatives you say that to are going to do, Mr. Grasso?" I went on. "They're going to go home and try to figure out how to be better relatives!"

•   •   •

"And consider how much better off you will be, if the reforms go into effect, when a beggar comes up to you and asks for money," I went on.

"I don't understand," said the man.

"Why," I said, "you say to that beggar, 'What's your middle name?' And he will say 'Oyster-19' or 'Chickadee-1,' or 'Hollyhock-13,' or some such thing.

"And you can say to him, 'Buster—I happen to be a Uranium-3. You have one hundred and ninety thousand cousins and ten thousand brothers and sisters. You're not exactly alone in this world. I have relatives of my own to look after. So why don't you take a flying fuck at a rolling doughnut? Why don't you take a flying fuck at the mooooooooooooooon?'"

•   •   •

# Chapter 34

THE FUEL SHORTAGE was so severe when I was elected, that the first stiff problem I faced after my inauguration was where to get enough electricity to power the computers which would issue the new middle names.

I ordered horses and soldiers and wagons of the ramshackle Army I had inherited from my predecessor to haul tons of papers from the National Archives to the powerhouse. These documents were all from the Administration of Richard M. Nixon, the only President who was ever forced to resign.

• • •

I myself went to the Archives to watch. I spoke to the soldiers and a few passers-by from the steps there. I said that Mr. Nixon and his associates had been unbalanced by loneliness of an especially virulent sort.

"He promised to bring us together, but tore us apart instead," I said. "Now, hey presto!, he will bring us together after all."

I posed for photographs beneath the inscription on the facade of the Archives, which said this:

"THE PAST IS PROLOGUE."

"They were not basically criminals," I said. "But they yearned to partake of the brotherhood they saw in Organized Crime."

• • •

"So many crimes committed by lonesome people in Government are concealed in this place," I said, "that the inscription might well read, 'Better a Family of Criminals than No Family at All.'

"I think we are now marking the end of the era of such tragic monkeyshines. The Prologue is over, friends and neighbors and relatives. Let the main body of our noble work begin.

"Thank you," I said.

• • •

There were no large newspapers or national magazines to print my words. The huge printing plants had all shut down—for want of fuel. There were no microphones. There were just the people there.

Hi ho.

.    .    .

I passed out a special decoration to the soldiers, to commemorate the occasion. It consisted of a pale blue ribbon from which depended a plastic button.

I explained, only half-jokingly, that the ribbon represented "The Bluebird of Happiness." And the button was inscribed with these words, of course:

.    .    .

# Chapter 35

IT IS MID-MORNING here in Skyscraper National Park. The gravity is balmy, but Melody and Isadore will not work on the baby's pyramid today. We will have a picnic on top of the building instead. The young people are being so companionable with me because my birthday is only two days away now. What fun!

There is nothing they love more than a birthday!

Melody plucks a chicken which a slave of Vera Chipmunk-17 Zappa brought to us this morning. The slave also brought two loaves of bread and two liters of creamy beer. He pantomimed how nourishing he was being to us. He pressed the bases of the two beer bottles to his nipples, pretending that he had breasts that gave creamy beer.

We laughed. We clapped our hands.

• • •

Melody tosses pinches of feathers skyward. Because of the mild gravity, it appears that she is a white witch. Each snap of her fingers produces butterflies.

I have an erection. So does Isadore. So does every male.

• • •

Isadore sweeps the lobby with a broom he has made of twigs. He sings one of the only two songs he knows. The other song is "Happy Birthday to You." Yes, and he is tone-deaf, too, so he drones.

"Row, row, row your boat," he drones,
"Gently down the stream.
"Merrily, merrily, merrily, merrily—
"Life is but a dream."

• • •

Yes, and I now remember a day in the dream of my life, far upstream from now, in which I received a chatty letter from the President of my country, who happened to be me. Like any other citizen, I had been waiting on pins and needles to learn from the computers what my new middle name would be.

My President congratulated me on my new middle name. He asked me to use it as a regular part of my signature, and on my mailbox and letterheads and in directories, and so on. He said that the name was selected at immaculate random, and was not intended as a comment on my character or my appearance or my past.

He offered deceptively homely, almost inane examples of how I might serve artificial relatives: By watering their houseplants while they were away; by taking care of their babies so they could get out of the house for an hour or two; by telling them the name of a truly painless dentist; by mailing a letter for them; by keeping them company on a scary visit to a doctor; by visiting them in a jail or a hospital; by keeping them company at a scary picture show.

Hi ho.

•  •  •

I was enchanted by my new middle name, by the way. I ordered that the Oval Office of the White House be painted pale yellow immediately, in celebration of my having become a Daffodil.

And, as I was telling my private secretary, Hortense Muskellunge-13 McBundy, to have the place repainted, a dishwasher from the White House kitchen appeared in her office. He was bent on a very shy errand, indeed. He was so embarrassed that he choked every time he tried to speak.

When he at last managed to articulate his message, I embraced him. He had come out of the steamy depths to tell me ever-so-bravely that he, too, was a *Daffodil-11*.

"My brother," I said.

•  •  •

# Chapter 36

WAS THERE NO substantial opposition to the new social scheme? Why, of course there was. And, as Eliza and I had predicted, my enemies were so angered by the idea of artificial extended families that they constituted a polyglot artificial extended family of their own.

They had campaign buttons, too, which they went on wearing long after I was elected. It was inevitable what those buttons said, to wit:

I had to laugh, even when my own wife, the former Sophie Rothschild, took to wearing a button like that.

Hi ho.

• • •

Sophie was furious when she received a form letter from her President, who happened to be me, which instructed her to stop being a *Rothschild*. She was to become a *Peanut-3* instead.

Again: I am sorry, but I had to laugh.

• • •

Sophie smouldered about it for several weeks. And then she came crawling into the Oval Office on an afternoon of particularly heavy gravity—to tell me she hated me.

I was not stung.

As I have already said, I was fully aware that I was not the sort of lumber out of which happy marriages were made.

"I honestly did not think you would go this far, Wilbur," she said. "I knew you were crazy, and that your sister was crazy, too. But I did not believe you would go this far."

• • •

Sophie did not have to look up at me. I, too, was on the floor—prone, with my chin resting on a pillow. I was reading a fascinating report of a thing that had happened in Urbana, Illinois.

I did not give her my undivided attention, so she said, "What is it you're reading that is so much more interesting than me?"

"Well—" I said, "for many years, I was the last American to have spoken to a Chinese. That's not true any more. A delegation of Chinese paid a call to the widow of a physicist in Urbana—about three weeks ago."

Hi ho.

• • •

"I certainly don't want to waste your valuable time," she said. "You're certainly closer to Chinamen than you ever were to me."

I had given her a wheelchair for Christmas—to use around the White House on days of heavy gravity. I asked her why she didn't use it. "It makes me very sad," I said, "to have you go around on all-fours."

"I'm a *Peanut* now," she said. "*Peanuts* live very close to the ground. *Peanuts* are famous for being low. They are the cheapest of the cheap, and the lowest of the low."

• • •

That early in the game, I thought it was crucial the people not be allowed to change their Government-issue middle names. I was wrong to be so rigid about that. All sorts of name-changing goes on now—here on the Island of Death and everywhere. I can't see that any harm is done.

But I was severe with Sophie. "You want to be an *Eagle* or a *Diamond*, I suppose," I said.

"I want to be a *Rothschild*," she said.

"Then perhaps you should go to Machu Picchu," I said. That was where most of her blood relatives had gone.

• • •

"Are you really so sadistic," she said, "that you will make me prove my love by befriending strangers who are now crawling out from damp rocks like earwigs? Like centipedes? Like slugs? Like worms?"

"Now, now," I said.

"When was the last time you took a look at the freak show outside the fence?" she said.

The perimeter of the White House grounds, just outside the fence, was infested daily with persons claiming to be artificial relatives of Sophie or me.

There were twin male midgets out there, I remember, holding a banner that said "Flower Power."

There was a woman, I remember, who wore an Army field jacket over a purple evening dress. On her head was an old-fashioned leather aviator's helmet, goggles and all. She had a placard on the end of a stick. "Peanut Butter," it said.

• • •

"Sophie—" I said, "that is not the general American population out there. And you are not mistaken when you say that they have crawled out from under damp rocks—like centipedes and earwigs and worms. They have never had a friend or a relative. They have had to believe all their lives that they were perhaps sent to the wrong Universe, since no one has ever bid them welcome or given them anything to do."

"I hate them," she said.

"Go ahead," I said. "There's very little harm in that, as far as I know."

"I did not think you would go this far, Wilbur," she said. "I thought you would be satisfied with being President. I did not think you would go this far."

"Well," I said, "I'm glad I did. And I am glad we have those people outside the fence to think about, Sophie. They are frightened hermits who have been tempted out from under their damp rocks by humane new laws. They are dazedly seeking brothers and sisters and cousins which their President has suddenly given to them from their nation's social treasure, which was until now untapped."

"You are insane," she said.

"Very likely," I replied. "But it will not be an hallucination when I see those people outside the fence find each other, if no one else."

"They deserve each other," she said.

"Exactly," I said. "And they deserve something else which is going to happen to them, now that they have the courage to speak to strangers. You watch, Sophie. The simple experience of companionship is going to allow them to climb the evolutionary ladder in a matter of hours or days, or weeks at most.

"It will not be an hallucination, Sophie," I said, "when I see them become human beings, after having been for so many years, as you say, Sophie—centipedes and slugs and earwigs and worms."

Hi ho.

• • •

# Chapter 37

SOPHIE DIVORCED ME, of course, and skeedaddled with her jewelry and furs and paintings and gold bricks, and so on, to a condominium in Machu Picchu, Peru.

Almost the last thing I said to her, I think, was this: "Can't you at least wait until we compile the family directories? You're sure to find out that you're related to many distinguished women and men."

"I already *am* related to many distinguished women and men," she replied. "Goodbye."

• • •

In order to compile and publish the family directories, we had to haul more papers from the National Archives to the power-house. I selected files from the Presidencies of Ulysses Simpson Grant and Warren Gamaliel Harding this time.

We could not provide every citizen with directories of his or her own. It was all we could do to ship a complete set to every State House, town and City Hall, police department, and public library in the land.

• • •

One greedy thing I did: Before Sophie left me, I asked that we be sent Daffodil and Peanut directories all our own. And I have a Daffodil Directory right here in the Empire State Building right now. Vera Chipmunk-5 Zappa gave it to me for my birthday last year. It is a first edition—the only edition ever published.

And I learn from it again that among my new relatives at that time were Clarence Daffodil-11 Johnson, the Chief of Police of Batavia, New York, and Muhammad Daffodil-11 X, the former Light-Heavy-weight Boxing Champion of the World, and Maria Daffodil-11 Tcherkassky, the Prima Ballerina of the Chicago Opera Ballet.

• • •

I am glad, in a way, incidentally, that Sophie never saw her family directory. The Peanuts really did seem to be a ground-hugging bunch.

The most famous Peanut I can now recall was a minor Roller Derby star.

Hi ho.

•  •  •

Yes, and after the Government provided the directories, Free Enterprise produced family newspapers. Mine was *The Daffy-nition*. Sophie's, which continued to arrive at the White House long after she had left me, was *The Goober Gossip*. Vera told me the other day that the *Chipmunk* paper used to be *The Woodpile*.

Relatives asked for work or investment capital, or offered things for sale in the classified ads. The news columns told of triumphs by various relatives, and warned against others who were child molesters or swindlers and so on. There were lists of relatives who could be visited in various hospitals and jails.

There were editorials calling for family health insurance programs and sports teams and so on. There was one interest-ing essay, I remember, either in *The Daffy-nition* or *The Goober Gossip*, which said that families with high moral standards were the best maintainers of law and order, and that police depart-ments could be expected to fade away.

"If you know of a relative who is engaged in criminal acts," it concluded, "don't call the police. Call ten more relatives."

And so on.

•  •  •

Vera told me that the motto of *The Woodpile* used to be this: "A Good Citizen is a Good Family Woman or a Good Family Man."

•  •  •

As the new families began to investigate themselves, some statistical freaks were found. Almost all *Pachysandras*, for exam-ple, could play a musical instrument, or at least sing in tune. Three of them were conductors of major symphony orchestras. The widow in Urbana who had been visited by Chinese was a

*Pachysandra*. She supported herself and her son by giving piano lessons out there.

*Watermelons*, on the average, were a kilogram heavier than members of any other family.

Three-quarters of all *Sulfurs* were female.

And on and on.

As for my own family: There was an extraordinary concentration of Daffodils in and around Indianapolis. My family paper was published out there, and its masthead boasted, "Printed in Daffodil City, U.S.A."

Hi ho.

• • •

Family clubhouses appeared. I personally cut the ribbon at the opening of the Daffodil Club here in Manhattan—on Forty-third Street, right off Fifth Avenue.

This was a thought-provoking experience for me, even though I was sedated by tri-benzo-Deportamil. I had once belonged to another club, and to another sort of artificial extended family, too, on the very same premises. So had my father, and both my grandfathers, and all four of my great grandfathers.

Once the building had been a haven for men of power and wealth, and well-advanced into middle age.

Now it teemed with mothers and children, with old people playing checkers or chess or dreaming, with younger adults taking dancing lessons or bowling on the duckpin alleys, or playing the pinball machines.

I had to laugh.

• • •

# Chapter 38

IT WAS ON THAT particular visit to Manhattan that I saw my first "Thirteen Club." There were dozens of such raffish establishments in Chicago, I had heard. Now Manhattan had one of its own.

Eliza and I had not anticipated that all the people with "13" in their middle names would naturally band together almost immediately, to form the largest family of all.

And I certainly got a taste of my own medicine when I asked a guard on the door of the Manhattan Thirteen Club if I could come in and have a look around. It was very dark in there.

"All due respect, Mr. President," he said to me, "but are you a *Thirteen*, sir?"

"No," I said. "You know I'm not."

"Then I must say to you, sir," he said, "what I have to say to you.

"With all possible respect, sir:" he said, "Why don't you take a flying fuck at a rolling doughnut? Why don't you take a flying fuck at the mooooooooooooooon?"

I was in ecstasy.

• • •

Yes, and it was during that visit here that I first learned of The Church of Jesus Christ the Kidnapped—then a tiny cult in Chicago, but destined to become the most popular American religion of all time.

It was brought to my attention by a leaflet handed to me by a clean and radiant youth, as I crossed the lobby to the staircase of my hotel.

He was jerking his head around in what then seemed an eccentric manner, as though hoping to catch someone peering out at him from behind a potted palm tree or an easy chair, or even from directly overhead, from the crystal chandelier.

He was so absorbed in firing ardent glances this way and that, that it was wholly uninteresting to him that he had just handed a leaflet to the President of the United States.

"May I ask what you're looking for, young man?" I said.
"For our Saviour, sir," he replied.
"You think He's in this hotel?" I said.
"Read the leaflet, sir," he said.

• • •

So I did—in my lonely room, with the radio on.
At the very top of the leaflet was a primitive picture of Jesus, standing and with His Body facing forward, but with His Face in profile—like a one-eyed jack in a deck of playing cards.
He was gagged. He was handcuffed. One ankle was shackled and chained to a ring fixed to the floor. There was a single perfect tear dangling from the lower lid of His Eye.
Beneath the picture was a series of questions and answers, which went as follows:

QUESTION: What is your name?
ANSWER: I am the Right Reverend William Uranium-8 Wainwright, Founder of the Church of Jesus Christ the Kidnapped at 3972 Ellis Avenue, Chicago, Illinois.
QUESTION: When will God send us His Son again?
ANSWER: He already has. Jesus is here among us.
QUESTION: Why haven't we seen or heard anything about Him?
ANSWER: He has been kidnapped by the Forces of Evil.
QUESTION: What must we do?
ANSWER: We must drop whatever we are doing, and spend every waking hour in trying to find Him. If we do not, God will exercise His Option.
QUESTION: What is God's Option?
ANSWER: He can destroy Mankind so easily, any time he chooses to.

Hi ho.

• • •

I saw the young man eating alone in the diningroom that night. I marvelled that he could jerk his head around and still eat without spilling a drop. He even looked under his plate and water glass for Jesus not once, but over and over again.

I had to laugh.

•  •  •

# Chapter 39

B<small>UT THEN</small>, just when everything was going so well, when Americans were happier than they had ever been, even though the country was bankrupt and falling apart, people began to die by the millions of "The Albanian Flu" in most places, and here on Manhattan of "The Green Death."

And that was the end of the Nation. It became families, and nothing more.

Hi ho.

• • •

Oh, there were claims of Dukedoms and Kingdoms and such garbage, and armies were raised and forts were built here and there. But few people admired them. They were just more bad weather and more bad gravity that families endured from time to time.

And somewhere in there a night of actual bad gravity crumbled the foundations of Machu Picchu. The condominiums and boutiques and banks and gold bricks and jewelry and pre-Columbian art collections and the Opera House and the churches, and *all* that, eloped down the Andes, wound up in the sea.

I cried.

• • •

And families painted pictures everywhere of the kidnapped Jesus Christ.

• • •

People continued to send news to us at the White House for a little while. We ourselves were experiencing death and death and death, and expecting to die.

Our personal hygiene deteriorated quickly. We stopped bathing and brushing our teeth regularly. The males grew beards, and let their hair grow down to their shoulders.

We began to cannibalize the White House almost absent-mindedly, burning furniture and bannisters and paneling and picture frames and so on in the fireplaces, to keep warm.

Hortense Muskellunge-13 McBundy, my personal secretary, died of flu. My valet, Edward Strawberry-4 Kleindienst, died of flu. My Vice-President, Mildred Helium-20 Theodorides, died of flu.

My science advisor, Dr. Albert Aquamarine-1 Piatigorsky, actually expired in my arms on the floor of the Oval Office.

He was almost as tall as I was. We must have been quite a sight on the floor.

"What does it all mean?" he said over and over again.

"I don't know, Albert," I said. "And maybe I'm glad I don't know."

"Ask a Chinaman!" he said, and he went to his reward, as the saying goes.

•   •   •

Now and then the telephone would ring. It became such a rare occurrence that I took to answering it personally.

"This is your President speaking," I would say. As like as not, I would find myself talking over a tenuous, crackling circuit to some sort of mythological creature—"The King of Michigan," perhaps, or "The Emergency Governor of Florida," or "The Acting Mayor of Birmingham," or some such thing.

But there were fewer messages with each passing week. At last there were none.

I was forgotten.

Thus did my Presidency end—two thirds of the way through my second term.

And something else crucial was petering out almost as quickly—which was my irreplaceable supply of tri-benzo-Deportamil.

Hi ho.

•   •   •

I dared not count my remaining pills until I could not help but count them, they were so few. I had become so dependent upon them, so grateful for them, that it seemed to me that my life would end when the last one was gone.

I was running out of employees, too. I was soon down to one. Everybody else had died or wandered away, since there weren't any messages any more.

The one person who remained with me was my brother, was faithful Carlos Daffodil-11 Villavicencio, the dishwasher I had embraced on my first day as a Daffodil.

•   •   •

# Chapter 40

BECAUSE EVERYTHING had dwindled so quickly, and because there was no one to behave sanely for any more, I developed a mania for counting things. I counted slats in venetian blinds. I counted the knives and forks and spoons in the kitchen. I counted the tufts of the coverlet on Abraham Lincoln's bed.

And I was counting posts in a bannister one day, on my hands and knees on the staircase, although the gravity was medium-to-light. And then I realized that a man was watching me from below.

He was dressed in buckskins and moccasins and a coon-skin hat, and carried a rifle.

"My God, President Daffodil," I said to myself, "you've really gone crazy this time. That's ol' Daniel Boone down there."

And then another man joined the first one. He was dressed like a military pilot back in the days, long before I was President, when there had been such a thing as a United States Air Force.

"Let me guess:" I said out loud, "It's either Halloween or the Fourth of July."

• • •

The pilot seemed to be shocked by the condition of the White House. "What's happened here?" he said.

"All I can tell you," I said, "is that history has been made."

"This is terrible," he said.

"If you think this is bad," I told him, and I tapped my fore-head with my fingertips, "you should see what it looks like in *here*."

• • •

Neither one of them even suspected that I was the President. I had become quite a mess by then.

They did not even want to talk to me, or to each other, for that matter. They were strangers, it turned out. They had simply happened to arrive at the same time—each one on an urgent mission.

They went into other rooms, and found my Sancho Panza, Carlos Daffodil-11 Villavicencio, who was making a lunch of Navy hardtack and canned smoked oysters, and some other things he'd found. And Carlos brought them back to me, and convinced them that I was indeed the President of what he called, in all sincerity, "the most powerful country in the world."

Carlos was a really stupid man.

•  •  •

The frontiersman had a letter for me—from the widow in Urbana, Illinois, who had been visited a few years before by Chinese. I had been too busy ever to find out what the Chinese had been after out there.

"Dear Dr. Swain," it began—

"I am an undistinguished person, a piano teacher, who is remarkable only for having been married to a very great physicist, to have had a beautiful son by him, and after his death, to have been visited by a delegation of very small Chinese, one of whom said his father had known you. His father's name was 'Fu Manchu.'

"It was the Chinese who told me about the astonishing discovery my husband, Dr. Felix Bauxite-13 von Peterswald, made just before he died. My son, who is incidentally a Daffodil-11, like yourself, and I have kept this discovery a secret ever since, because the light it throws on the situation of human beings in the Universe is very demoralizing, to say the least. It has to do with the true nature of what awaits us all after death. What awaits us, Dr. Swain, is tedious in the extreme.

"I can't bring myself to call it 'Heaven' or 'Our Just Reward,' or any of those sweet things. All I can call it is what my husband came to call it, and what you will call it, too, after you have investigated it, which is 'The Turkey Farm.'

"In short, Dr. Swain, my husband discovered a way to talk to dead people on The Turkey Farm. He never taught the technique to me or my son, or to anybody. But the Chinese, who apparently have spies everywhere, somehow found out about it. They came to study his journals and to see what was left of his apparatus.

"After they had figured it out, they were nice enough to explain to my son and me how we might do the gruesome trick, if we wished to. They themselves were disappointed with the discovery. It was new to them, they said, but could be 'interesting only to participants in what is left of Western Civilization,' whatever that means.

"I am entrusting this letter to a friend who hopes to join a large settlement of his artificial relatives, the Berylliums, in Maryland, which is very near you.

"I address you as 'Dr. Swain' rather than 'Mr. President,' because this letter has nothing to do with the national interest. It is a highly personal letter, informing you that we have spoken to your dead sister Eliza many times on my husband's apparatus. She says that it is of the utmost importance that you come here in order that she may converse directly with you.

"We eagerly await your visit. Please do not be insulted by the behavior of my son and your brother, David Daffodil-11 von Peterswald, who cannot prevent himself from speaking obscenities and making insulting gestures at even the most inappropriate moments. He is a victim of Tourette's Disease.

"Your faithful servant,

"Wilma Pachysandra-17 von Peterswald."

Hi ho.

•  •  •

# Chapter 41

I WAS DEEPLY MOVED, despite tri-benzo-Deportamil.
    I stared out at the frontiersman's sweaty horse, which was grazing in the high grass of the White House lawn. And then I turned to the messenger himself. "How came you by this message?" I said.

He told me that he had accidentally shot a man, apparently Wilma Pachysandra-17 von Peterswald's friend, the Beryllium, on the border between Tennessee and West Virginia. He had mistaken him for an hereditary enemy.

"I thought he was Newton McCoy," he said.

He tried to nurse his innocent victim back to health, but he died of gangrene. But, before he died, the Beryllium made him promise as a Christian to deliver a letter he had himself sworn to hand over to the President of the United States.

• • •

I asked him his name.

"Byron Hatfield," he said.

"What is your Government-issue middle name?" I said.

"We never paid no mind to that," he replied.

It turned out that he belonged to one of the few genuine extended families of blood relatives in the country, which had been at perpetual war with another such family since 1882.

"We never was big for them new-fangled middle names," he said.

• • •

The frontiersman and I were seated on spindly golden ballroom chairs which had supposedly been bought for the White House by Jacqueline Kennedy so long ago. The pilot was similarly supported, alertly awaiting his turn to speak. I glanced at the name-plate over the breast pocket of the pilot. It said this:

## CAPT. BERNARD O'HARE

• • •

"Captain," I said, "you're another one who doesn't seem to go in for the new-fangled middle names." I noticed, too, that he was much too old to be only a captain, even if there had still been such a thing. He was in fact almost sixty.

I concluded that he was a lunatic who had found the costume somewhere. I supposed that he had become so elated and addled by his new appearance, that nothing would do but that he show himself off to his President.

The truth was, though, that he was perfectly sane. He had been stationed for the past eleven years in the bottom of a secret, underground silo in Rock Creek Park. I had never heard of the silo before.

But there was a Presidential helicopter concealed in it, along with thousands of gallons of absolutely priceless gasoline.

• • •

He had come out at last, in violation of his orders, he said, to find out "what on Earth was going on."

I had to laugh.

• • •

"Is the helicopter still ready to fly?" I asked.

"Yes, sir, it is," he said. He had been maintaining it single-handedly for the past two years. His mechanics had wandered off one-by-one.

"Young man," I said, "I'm going to give you a medal for this." I took a button from my own tattered lapel, and I pinned it to his.

It said this, of course:

. . .

# Chapter 42

THE FRONTIERSMAN refused a similar decoration. He asked for food, instead—to sustain him on his long trip back to his native mountains.

We gave him what we had, which was all the hardtack and canned smoked oysters his saddlebags would hold.

• • •

Yes, and Captain Bernard O'Hare and Carlos Daffodil-11 Villavicencio and I took off from the silo on the following dawn. It was a day of such salubrious gravity, that our helicopter expended no more energy than would have an airborne milkweed seed.

As we fluttered over the White House, I waved to it.

"Goodbye," I said.

• • •

My plan was to fly first to Indianapolis, which had become densely populated with Daffodils. They had been flocking there from everywhere.

We would leave Carlos there, to be cared for by his artificial relatives during his sunset years. I was glad to be getting rid of him. He bored me to tears.

• • •

We would go next to Urbana, I told Captain O'Hare—and then to my childhood home in Vermont.

"After that," I promised, "the helicopter is yours, Captain. You can fly like a bird wherever you wish. But you're going to have a rotten time of it, if you don't give yourself a good middle name."

"You're the President," he said. "You give me a name."

"I dub thee 'Eagle-1,'" I said.

He was awfully pleased. He loved the medal, too.

• • •

Yes, and I still had a little tri-benzo-Deportamil left, and I was so delighted to be going simply anywhere, after having been cooped up in Washington, D.C. so long, that I heard myself singing for the first time in years.

I remember the song I sang, too. It was one Eliza and I used to sing a lot in secret, back when we were still believed to be idiots. We would sing it where nobody could hear us—in the mausoleum of Professor Elihu Roosevelt Swain.

And I think now that I will teach it to Melody and Isadore at my birthday party. It is such a good song for them to sing when they set out for new adventures on the Island of Death.

It goes like this:

> "Oh, we're off to see the Wizard,
> "The wonderful Wizard of Oz.
>       ***
> "If ever a whiz of a Wiz there was,
> "It was the Wizard of Oz."[1]

      •  •  •

And so on.

      •  •  •

Hi ho.

      •  •  •

# Chapter 43

MELODY AND ISADORE went down to Wall Street today—to visit Isadore's large family, the Raspberries. I was invited to become a Raspberry at one time. So was Vera Chipmunk-5 Zappa. We both declined.

Yes, and I took a walk of my own—up to the baby's pyramid at Broadway and Forty-second, then across Forty-third Street to the old Daffodil Club, to what had been the Century Association before that; and then eastward across Forty-eighth Street to the townhouse which was slave quarters for Vera's farm, which at one time had been my parents' home.

I encountered Vera herself on the steps of the townhouse. Her slaves were all over in what used to be United Nations Park, planting watermelons and corn and sunflowers. I could hear them singing "Ol' Man River." They were so happy all the time. They considered themselves very lucky to be slaves.

They were all Chipmunk-5's, and about two-thirds of them were former Raspberries. People who wished to become slaves of Vera had to change their middle names to Chipmunk-5.

Hi ho.

• • •

Vera usually labored right along with her slaves. She loved hard work. But now I caught her tinkering idly with a beautiful Zeiss microscope, which one of her slaves had unearthed in the ruins of a hospital only the day before. It had been protected all through the years by its original factory packing case.

Vera had not sensed my approach. She was peering into the instrument and turning knobs with childlike seriousness and ineptitude. It was obvious that she had never used a microscope before.

I stole closer to her, and then I said, "Boo!"

She jerked her head away from the eyepiece.

"Hello," I said.

"You scared me to death," she said.

"Sorry," I said, and I laughed.

These ancient games go on and on. It's nice they do.

• • •

"I can't see anything," she said. She was complaining about the microscope.

"Just squiggly little animals that want to kill and eat us," I said. "You really want to see those?"

"I was looking at an opal," she said. She had draped an opal and diamond bracelet over the stage of the microscope. She had a collection of precious stones which would have been worth millions of dollars in olden times. People gave her all the jewels they found, just as they gave me all the candlesticks.

• • •

Jewels were useless. So were candlesticks, since there weren't such things on Manhattan as candles any more. People lit their homes at night with burning rags stuck in bowls of animal fat.

"There's probably Green Death on the opal," I said. "There's probably Green Death on everything."

The reason that we ourselves did not die of The Green Death, by the way, was that we took an antidote which was discovered by accident by Isadore's family, the Raspberries.

We had only to withhold the antidote from a troublemaker, or from an army of troublemakers, for that matter, and he or she or they would be exiled quickly to the afterlife, to The Turkey Farm.

• • •

There weren't any great scientists among the Raspberries, incidentally. They discovered the antidote through dumb luck. They ate fish without cleaning them, and the antidote, probably pollution left over from olden times, was somewhere in the guts of the fish they ate.

• • •

"Vera," I said, "if you ever got that microscope to work, you would see something that would break your heart."

"What would break my heart?" she said.

"You'd see the organisms that cause The Green Death," I said.

"Why would that make me cry?" she said.

"Because you're a woman of conscience," I said. "Don't you realize that we kill them by the *trillions*—every time we take our antidote?"

I laughed.

She did not laugh.

"The reason I am not laughing," she said, "is that you, coming along so unexpectedly, have spoiled a surprise for your birthday."

"How is that?" I said.

She spoke of one of her slaves. "Donna was going to make a present of this to you. Now you won't be surprised."

"Um," I said.

"She thought it was an extra-fancy kind of candlestick."

·  ·  ·

She confided to me that Melody and Isadore had paid her a call earlier in the week, had told her again how much they hoped to be her slaves someday.

"I tried to tell 'em that slavery wasn't for everybody," she said.

·  ·  ·

"Answer me this," she went on, "What happens to all my slaves when I die?"

"'Take no thought for the morrow,'" I told her, "'for the morrow shall take thought for the things of itself. Sufficient unto the day is the evil thereof.'

"Amen," I said.

·  ·  ·

# Chapter 44

OLD VERA AND I reminisced there on the townhouse steps about the Battle of Lake Maxinkuckee, in northern Indiana. I had seen it from a helicopter on my way to Urbana. Vera had been in the actual thick of it with her alcoholic husband, Lee Razorclam-13 Zappa. They were cooks in one of the King of Michigan's field kitchens on the ground below.

"You all looked like ants to me down there," I said, "or like germs under a microscope." We didn't dare come down close, for fear of being shot.

"That's what we felt like, too," she said.

"If I had known you then, I would have tried to rescue you," I said.

"That would have been like trying to rescue a germ from a million other germs, Wilbur," she said.

• • •

Not only did Vera have to put up with shells and bullets whistling over the kitchen tent. She had to defend herself against her husband, too, who was drunk. He beat her up in the midst of battle.

He blacked both her eyes and broke her jaw. He threw her out through the tent flaps. She landed on her back in the mud. Then he came out to explain to her how she could avoid similar beatings in the future.

He came out just in time to be skewered by the lance of an enemy cavalryman.

"And what's the moral of that story, do you think?" I asked her.

She lay a callused palm on my knee. "Wilbur—don't ever get married," she replied.

• • •

We talked some about Indianapolis, which I had seen on the same trip, and where she and her husband had been a waitress and a bartender for a Thirteen Club—before they joined the army of the King of Michigan.

I asked her what the club was like inside.

"Oh, you know—" she said, "they had stuffed black cats and jack-o-lanterns, and aces of spades stuck to the tables with daggers and all. I used to wear net stockings and spike heels and a mask and all. All the waitresses and the bartenders and the bouncer wore vampire fangs."

"Um," I said.

"We used to call our hamburgers 'Batburgers,'" she said.

"Uh huh," I said.

"We used to call tomato juice with a shot of gin a 'Dracula's Delight,'" she said.

"Right," I said.

"It was just like a Thirteen Club anywhere," she said, "but it never went over. Indianapolis just wasn't a big Thirteen town, even though there were plenty of Thirteens there. It was a Daffodil town. You weren't anything if you weren't a Daffodil."

• • •

# Chapter 45

I TELL YOU—I have been regaled as a multimillionaire, as a pediatrician, as a Senator, and as a President. But nothing can match for sincerity the welcome Indianapolis, Indiana, gave me as a Daffodil!

The people there were poor, and had suffered an awful lot of death, and all the public services had broken down, and they were worried about battles raging not far away. But they put on parades and feasts for me, and for Carlos Daffodil-11 Villavicencio, too, of course, which would have blinded ancient Rome.

• • •

Captain Bernard Eagle-1 O'Hare said to me, "My gosh, Mr. President—if I'd known about this, I would have asked you to make me a Daffodil."

So I said, "I hereby dub thee a Daffodil."

• • •

But the most satisfying and educational thing I saw out there was a weekly family meeting of Daffodils.

Yes, and I got to vote at that meeting, and so did my pilot, and so did Carlos, and so did every man, woman, and every child over the age of nine.

With a little luck, I might even have become Chairperson of the meeting, although I had been in town for less than a day. The Chairperson was chosen by lot from all assembled. And the winner of the drawing that night was an eleven-year-old black girl named Dorothy Daffodil-7 Garland.

She was fully prepared to run the meeting, and so, I suppose, was every person there.

• • •

She marched up to the lectern, which was nearly as tall as she was.

That little cousin of mine stood on a chair, without any apologies or self-mockery. She banged the meeting to order with a yellow gavel, and she told her silenced and respectful relatives,

"The President of the United States is present, as most of you know. With your permission, I will ask him to say a few words to us at the conclusion of our regular business.

"Will somebody put that in the form of a motion?" she said.

"I move that Cousin Wilbur be asked to address the meeting at the conclusion of regular business," said an old man sitting next to me.

This was seconded and put to a voice vote.

The motion carried, but with a scattering of seemingly heart-felt, by-no-means joshing, "Nays" and "Noes."

Hi ho.

•  •  •

The most pressing business had to do with selecting four replacements for fallen Daffodils in the army of the King of Michigan, who was at war simultaneously with Great Lakes pirates and the Duke of Oklahoma.

There was one strapping young man, I remember, a black-smith, in fact, who told the meeting, "Send me. There's nothing I'd rather do than kill me some 'Sooners,' long as they ain't Daffodils." And so on.

To my surprise, he was scolded by several speakers for his military ardor. He was told that war wasn't supposed to be fun, and in fact wasn't fun—that tragedy was being discussed, and that he had better put on a tragic face, or he would be ejected from the meeting.

"Sooners" were people from Oklahoma, and, by exten-sion, anybody in the service of the Duke of Oklahoma, which included "Show Me's" from Missouri and "Jayhawkers" from Kansas and "Hawkeyes" from Iowa, and on and on.

The blacksmith was told that "Sooners" were human beings, too, no better or worse than "Hoosiers," who were people from Indiana.

And the old man who had moved that I be allowed to speak later on got up and said this: "Young man, you're no better than the Albanian influenza or The Green Death, if you can kill for joy."

•  •  •

I was impressed. I realized that nations could never acknowl-edge their own wars as tragedies, but that families not only could but had to.

Bully for them!

•  •  •

The chief reason the blacksmith was not allowed to go to war, though, was that he had so far fathered three illegitimate children by different women, "and had two more in the oven," as someone said.

He wasn't going to be allowed to run away from caring for all those babies.

•  •  •

# Chapter 46

EVEN THE CHILDREN and the drunks and the lunatics at that meeting seemed shrewdly familiar with parliamentary procedures. The little girl behind the lectern kept things moving so briskly and purposefully that she might have been some sort of goddess up there, equipped with an armload of thunderbolts.

I was so filled with respect for these procedures, which had always seemed like such solemn tomfoolery to me before.

• • •

And I am still so respectful, that I have just looked up their inventor in my Encyclopaedia here in the Empire State Building.

His name was Henry Martyn Robert. He was a graduate of West Point. He was an engineer. He became a general by and by. But, just before the Civil War, when he was a lieutenant stationed in New Bedford, Massachusetts, he had to run a church meeting, and he lost control of it.

There were no rules.

So this soldier sat down and wrote some rules, which were the identical rules I saw followed in Indianapolis. They were published as *Robert's Rules of Order*, which I now believe to be one of the four greatest inventions by Americans.

The other three, in my opinion, were The Bill of Rights, the principles of Alcoholics Anonymous, and the artificial extended families envisioned by Eliza and me.

• • •

The three recruits which the Indianapolis Daffodils finally voted to send off to the King of Michigan, incidentally, were all people who could be most easily spared, and who, in the opinion of the voters, had had the most carefree lives so far.

Hi ho.

• • •

The next order of business had to do with feeding and sheltering Daffodil refugees, who were trickling into town from all the fighting in the northern part of the state.

The meeting again discouraged an enthusiast. A young woman, quite beautiful but disorderly, and clearly crazed by altruism, said that she could take at least twenty refugees into her home.

Somebody else got up and said to her that she was such an incompetent housekeeper that her own children had gone to live with other relatives.

Another person pointed out to her that she was so absent-minded that her dog would have starved to death, if it weren't for neighbors, and that she had accidentally set fire to her house three times.

• • •

This sounds as though the people at the meeting were being cruel. But they all called her "Cousin Grace" or "Sister Grace," as the case might be. She was my cousin too, of course. She was a Daffodil-13.

What was more: She was a menace only to herself, so nobody was particularly mad at her. Her children had wandered off to better-run houses almost as soon as they were able to walk, I was told. That was surely one of the most attractive features of Eliza's and my invention, I think: Children had so many homes and parents to choose from.

Cousin Grace, for her part, heard all the bad reports on herself as though they were surprising to her, but no doubt true. She did not flee in tears. She stayed for the rest of the meeting, obeying Robert's Rules of Order, and looking sympathetic and alert.

At one point, under "New Business," Cousin Grace made a motion that any Daffodil who served with the Great Lakes Pirates or in the army of the Duke of Oklahoma should be expelled from the family.

Nobody would second this.

And the little girl running the meeting told her, "Cousin Grace, you know as well as anybody here, 'Once a Daffodil, always a Daffodil.'"

• • •

## Chapter 47

I T WAS AT LAST my turn to speak.

"Brothers and Sisters and Cousins—" I said, "your nation has wasted away. As you can see, your President has also become a shadow of his former shadow. You have nobody but your doddering Cousin Wilbur here."

"You were a damn good President, Brother Billy," somebody called from the back of the room.

"I would have liked to give my country peace as well as brotherhood and sisterhood," I went on. "There is no peace, I'm sorry to say. We find it. We lose it. We find it again. We lose it again. Thank God, at least, that the machines have decided not to fight any more. It's just people now.

"And thank God that there's no such thing as a battle between strangers any more. I don't care who fights who—everybody will have relatives on the other side."

• • •

Most of the people at the meeting were not only *Daffodils*, but also searchers for the kidnapped Jesus. It was a disconcerting sort of audience to address, I found. No matter what I said, they kept jerking their heads this way and that, hoping to catch sight of Jesus.

But I seemed to be getting across, for they applauded or cheered at appropriate moments—so I pressed on.

• • •

"Because we're just families, and not a nation any more," I said, "it's much easier for us to give and receive mercy in war."

"I have just come from observing a battle far to the north of here, in the region of Lake Maxinkuckee. It was horses and spears and rifles and knives and pistols, and a cannon or two. I saw several people killed. I also saw many people embracing, and there seemed to be a great deal of deserting and surrendering going on.

146

"This much news I can bring you from the Battle of Lake Maxinkuckee:" I said—

"It is no massacre."

•  •  •

# Chapter 48

WHILE IN INDIANAPOLIS, I received an invitation by radio from the King of Michigan. It was Napoleonic in tone. It said that the King would be pleased "to hold an audience for the President of the United States in his Summer Palace on Lake Maxinkuckee." It said that his sentinels had been instructed to grant me safe passage. It said that the battle was over. "Victory is ours," it said.

So my pilot and I flew there.

We left my faithful servant, Carlos Daffodil-11 Villavicencio, to spend his declining years among his countless relatives.

"Good luck, Brother Carlos," I said.

"Home at last, Meester President, me Brudder," he replied. "Tanks you and tanks God for everything. Lonesome no more!"

•  •  •

My meeting with the King of Michigan would have been called an "historic occasion" in olden times. There would have been cameras and microphones and reporters there. As it was, there were notetakers there, whom the King called his "scribes."

And he was right to give those people with pens and paper that archaic title. Most of his soldiers could scarcely read or write.

•  •  •

Captain O'Hare and I landed on the manicured lawn before the King's Summer Palace, which had been a private military academy at one time. Soldiers, who had behaved badly in the recent battle, I suppose, were on their knees everywhere, guarded by military policemen. They were cutting grass with bayonets and pocket knives and scissors—as a punishment.

•  •  •

Captain O'Hare and I entered the palace between two lines of soldiers. They were an honor guard of some sort, I suppose. Each one held aloft a banner, which was embroidered with the totem of his artificial extended family—an apple, an alligator, the chemical symbol for lithium, and so on.

It was such a comically trite historical situation, I thought. Aside from battles, the history of nations seemed to consist of nothing but powerless old poops like myself, heavily medicated and vaguely beloved in the long ago, coming to kiss the boots of young psychopaths.

Inside myself, I had to laugh.

• • •

I was ushered alone into the King's spartan private quarters. It was a huge room, where the military academy must have held dances at one time. Now there was only a folding cot in there, a long table covered with maps, and a stack of folding chairs against one wall.

The King himself sat at the map table, ostentatiously reading a book, which turned out to be Thucydides' *History of the Peloponnesian War*.

Behind him, standing, were three male scribes—with pencils and pads.

There was no place for me or anyone else to sit.

I positioned myself before him, my mouldy Homburg in hand. He did not look up from his book immediately, although the doorkeeper had certainly announced me loudly enough.

"Your Majesty," the doorkeeper had said, "Dr. Wilbur Daffodil-11 Swain, the President of the United States!!"

• • •

He looked up at last, and I was amused to see that he was the spit and image of his grandfather, Dr. Stewart Rawlings Mott, the physician who had looked after my sister and me in Vermont so long ago.

• • •

I was not in the least afraid of him. Tri-benzo-Deportamil was making me soigné and blasé, of course. But, also, I had had more than enough of the low comedy of living by then. I would have found it a rather shapely adventure, if the King had elected to hustle me in front of a firing squad.

"We thought you were dead," he said.

"No, your Majesty," I said.

"It's been so long since we heard anything about you," he said.

"Washington, D.C., runs out of ideas from time to time," I said.

• • •

The scribes were taking all this down, all this history that was being made.

He held up the spine of the book so I could read it. "Thucydides," he said.

"Um," I said.

"History is all I read," he said.

"That is wise for a man in your position, your Majesty," I replied.

"Those who fail to learn from history are condemned to repeat it," he said.

The scribes scribbled away.

"Yes," I said. "If our descendents don't study our times closely, they will find that they have again exhausted the planet's fossil fuels, that they have again died by the millions of influenza and The Green Death, that the sky has again been turned yellow by the propellants for underarm deodorants, that they have again elected a senile President two meters tall, and that they are yet again the intellectual and spiritual inferiors of teeny-weeny Chinese."

He did not join my laughter.

I addressed his scribes directly, speaking over his head. "History is merely a list of surprises," I said. "It can only prepare us to be surprised yet again. Please write that down."

• • •

# Chapter 49

IT TURNED OUT that the young King had an historic document he wished me to sign. It was brief. In it, I acknowledged
that I, the President of the United States of America, no longer
exercised any control over that part of the North American
Continent which was sold by Napoleon Bonaparte to my country in 1803, and which was known as "The Louisiana Purchase."

I, therefore, according to the document, sold it for a dollar,
to Stewart Oriole-2 Mott, the King of Michigan.

I signed with the teeny-weeniest signature possible. It looked
like a baby ant. "Enjoy it in good health!" I said.

The territory I had sold him was largely occupied by the Duke
of Oklahoma, and, no doubt, by other potentates and panjan-
drums unknown to me.

After that, we chatted some about his grandfather.

Then Captain O'Hare and I took off for Urbana, Illinois,
and an electronic reunion with my sister, who had been dead
so long.

Hi ho.

•   •   •

Yes, and I write now with a palsied hand and an aching head,
for I drank much too much at my birthday party last night.

Vera Chipmunk-5 Zappa arrived encrusted with diamonds,
borne through the ailanthus forest in a sedan chair, accompanied by an entourage of fourteen slaves. She brought me wine
and beer, which made me drunk. But her most intoxicating gifts
were a thousand candles she and her slaves had made in a colonial candle mold. We fitted them into the empty mouths of my
thousand candlesticks, and deployed them over the lobby floor.

Then we lit them all.

Standing among all those tiny, wavering lights, I felt as
though I were God, up to my knees in the Milky Way.

•   •   •

# Epilogue

D R. SWAIN DIED before he could write any more. He went to his just reward.

There was nobody to read what he had written anyway—to complain about all the loose ends of the yarn he had spun.

He had reached the climax of his story, at any rate, with his reselling of the Louisiana Purchase to a bandit chief—for a dollar he never received.

Yes, and he died proud of what he and his sister had done to reform their society, for he left this poem, perhaps hoping that someone would use it for his epitaph:

> "And how did we then face the odds,
> "Of man's rude slapstick, yes, and God's?
> "Quite at home and unafraid,
> "Thank you,
> "In a game our dreams remade."

• • •

He never got to tell about the electronic device in Urbana, which made it possible for him to reunite his mind with that of his dead sister, to recreate the genius they had been in childhood.

The device, which those few people who knew about it called "The Hooligan," consisted of a seemingly ordinary length of brown clay pipe—two meters long and twenty centimeters in diameter. It was placed just so—atop a steel cabinet containing controls for a huge particle-accelerator. The particle-accelerator was a tubular magnetic race track for subatomic entities which looped through cornfields on the edge of town.

Yes.

And the Hooligan was itself a ghost, in a way, since the particle-accelerator had been dead for a long time, for want of electricity, for want of enthusiasts for all it could do.

A janitor, Francis Iron-7 Hooligan, stored the piece of pipe atop the dead cabinet, rested his lunchpail there, too, for the moment. He heard voices from the pipe.

•   •   •

He fetched the scientist whose apparatus this had been, Dr. Felix Bauxite-13 von Peterswald. But the pipe refused to talk again.

Dr. von Peterswald demonstrated that he was a great scientist, however, with his willingness to believe the ignorant Mr. Hooligan. He made the janitor go over his story again and again.

"The lunchpail," he said at last. "Where is your lunchpail?"

Hooligan had it in his hand.

Dr. von Peterswald instructed him to place it in relation to the pipe exactly as it had been before.

The pipe began promptly to talk again.

•   •   •

The talkers identified themselves as persons in the afterlife. They were backed by a demoralized chorus of persons who complained to each other of tedium and social slights and minor ailments, and so on.

As Dr. von Peterswald said in his secret diary: "It sounded like nothing so much as the other end of a telephone call on a rainy autumn day—to a badly run turkey farm."

Hi ho.

•   •   •

When Dr. Swain talked to his sister Eliza over the Hooligan, he was in the company of the widow of Dr. von Peterswald, Wilma Pachysandra-17 von Peterswald, and her fifteen-year-old son, David Daffodil-11 von Peterswald, a brother of Dr. Swain, and a victim of Tourette's Disease.

•   •   •

Poor David suffered an attack of his disease—just as Dr. Swain was beginning to talk with Eliza across the Great Divide.

David tried to choke down the involuntary stream of obscenities, but succeeded only in raising their pitch an octave. "Shit . . . sputum . . . scrotum . . . cloaca . . . asshole . . . pecker . . . mucous membrane . . . earwax . . . piss," he said.

•   •   •

And Dr. Swain himself went out of control. He climbed involuntarily on top of the cabinet, as tall and old as he was. He crouched over the pipe, to be that much closer to his sister. He hung his head upside-down in front of the business end of the pipe, and knocked the crucial lunchpail to the floor, breaking the connection.

"Hello? Hello?" he said.

"Perineum . . . fuck . . . turd . . . glans . . . mount of Venus . . . afterbirth," said the boy.

•   •   •

The widow von Peterswald was the only stable person on the Urbana end, so it was she who restored the lunchpail to its correct position. She had to jam it rather brutally between the pipe and the knee of the President. Then she found herself trapped in a grotesque position, bent at a right angle across the top of the cabinet, one arm extended, and her feet a few inches off the floor. The President had clamped down not only on the lunchpail, but on her hand.

"Hello? Hello?" said the President, his head upside down.

•   •   •

There were answering gabblings and gobblings and squawks and clucks from the other end.

Somebody sneezed.

"Bugger . . . defecate . . . semen . . . balls," said the boy.

•   •   •

Before Eliza could speak again, dead people in the background sensed that poor David was a kindred spirit, as outraged by the human condition in the Universe as they were. So they egged him on, and contributed obscenities of their own.

"You tell 'em, kid," they said, and so on.

And they doubled everything. "Double cock! Double clit!" they'd say. "Double shit!" and so on.

It was bedlam.

•   •   •

But Dr. Swain and his sister got together anyway, with such convulsive intimacy that Dr. Swain would have crawled into the pipe, if he could.

Yes, and what Eliza wanted from him was that he should die as soon as possible, so that the two of them could put their heads together. She wanted then to figure out ways to improve the utterly unsatisfactory, so-called "Paradise."

•   •   •

"Are you being tortured there?" he asked her.

"No," she said, "we are being bored stiff. Whoever designed this place knew nothing about human beings. Please, brother Wilbur," she said, "this is *Eternity* here. This is *forever!* Where you are now is just nothing in terms of time! It's a joke! Blow your brains out as quick as you can."

And so on.

•   •   •

Dr. Swain told her about the problems the living had been having with incurable diseases. The two of them, thinking as one, made child's play of the mystery.

The explanation was this: The flu germs were Martians, whose invasion had apparently been repelled by anti-bodies in the systems of the survivors, since, for the moment, anyway, there was no more flu.

The Green Death, on the other hand, was caused by microscopic Chinese, who were peace-loving and meant no one any harm. They were nonetheless invariably fatal to normal-sized human beings when inhaled or ingested.

And so on.

•   •   •

Dr. Swain asked his sister what sort of communications apparatus there was on the other end—whether Eliza, too, was squatting over a piece of pipe, or what.

Eliza told him that there was no apparatus, but only a feeling.

"What is the feeling?" he said.

"You would have to be dead to understand my description of it," she said.

"Try it anyway, Eliza," he said.

"It is like being dead," she said.

"A feeling of deadness," he said tentatively, trying to understand.

"Yes—coldness and clamminess—" she said.

"Um," he said.

"But also like being surrounded by a swarm of invisible bees," she said. "Your voice comes from the bees."

Hi ho.

• • •

When Dr. Swain was through with this particular ordeal, he had only eleven tablets left of tri-benzo-Deportamil, which were originally created, of course, not as a narcotic for presidents, but as suppressants for the symptoms of Tourette's Disease.

And the remaining pills, when he displayed them to himself in the palm of his huge hand, inevitably looked to him like the remaining grains in the hourglass of his life.

• • •

Dr. Swain was standing in the sunshine outside the laboratory building containing the Hooligan. With him were the widow and her son. The widow had the lunchpail, so that only she could turn the Hooligan on.

The gravity was light. Dr. Swain had an erection. So did the boy. So did Captain Bernard Daffodil-11 O'Hare, who stood by the helicopter nearby.

Presumably, the erectile tissues in the widow's body were also engorged.

"You know what you looked like on top of that cabinet, Mr. President?" said the boy. He was clearly sickened by what his disease was about to make him say.

"No," said Dr. Swain.

"Like the biggest baboon in the world—trying to fuck a football," blurted the boy.

Dr. Swain, in order to avoid any more insults like that, handed his remaining supply of tri-benzo-Deportamil to the boy.

• • •

The consequences of his withdrawal from tri-benzo-Depor-tamil were spectacular. Dr. Swain had to be tied to a bed in the widow's house for six nights and days.

Somewhere in there he made love to the widow, conceiving a son who would become the father of Melody Oriole-2 von Peterswald.

Yes, and somewhere in there the widow passed on to him what she had learned from the Chinese—that they had become successful manipulators of the Universe by combining harmonious minds.

•   •   •

Yes, and then he had his pilot fly him to Manhattan, the Island of Death. He intended to die there, to join his sister in the afterlife—as a result of inhaling and ingesting invisible Chinese communists.

Captain O'Hare, not wishing to die yet himself, lowered his President by means of a winch and rope and harness to the observation deck of the Empire State Building.

The President spent the remainder of the day up there, enjoying the view. And then, breathing deeply with every few steps, hoping to inhale Chinese communists, he descended the stairs.

It was twilight when he reached the bottom.

•   •   •

There were human skeletons in the lobby—in rotting nests of rags. The walls were zebra-striped with soot from cooking fires of long ago.

There was a painting of Jesus Christ the Kidnapped on one wall.

Dr. Swain for the first time heard the shuddering whir of bats leaving the subway system for the night.

He considered himself to be already a dead man—a brother to the skeletons.

But six members of the Raspberry family, who had observed his arrival by helicopter, suddenly came out of hiding in the lobby. They were armed with spears and knives.

•   •   •

When they understood who they had captured, they were thrilled. He was a treasure to them not because he was President, but because he had been to medical school.

"A doctor! Now we have everything!" said one.

Yes, and they would not hear of his wish to die. They forced him to swallow a small trapezoid of what seemed to be a tasteless sort of peanut-brittle. It was in fact boiled and dried fish guts, which contained the antidote to The Green Death.

Hi ho.

•   •   •

The Raspberries hustled him down to the Financial District at once, for Hiroshi Raspberry-20 Yamashiro, the head of the family, was deathly ill.

•   •   •

The man seemed to have pneumonia. Dr. Swain could do nothing for him but what physicians of a century before would have done, which was to keep his body warm and his forehead cool—and to wait.

Either the fever would break, or the man would die.

•   •   •

The fever broke.

As a reward, the Raspberries brought their most precious possessions to Dr. Swain on the floor of the New York Stock Exchange. There was a clock-radio, an alto saxophone, a fully-fitted toiletries kit, a model of the Eiffel Tower with a thermometer in it—and on and on.

From all this junk, and merely to be polite, Dr. Swain selected a single brass candlestick.

And thus was the legend established that he was crazy about candlesticks.

Thereafter, everybody would give him candlesticks.

•   •   •

He did not like the communal life of the Raspberries, which required him, among other things, to jerk his head around perpetually, in search of the kidnapped Jesus Christ.

So he cleaned up the lobby of the Empire State Building, and moved in there. The Raspberries supplied him with food.

And time flew.

•　•　•

Somewhere in there, Vera Chipmunk-5 Zappa arrived, and was given the antidote by the Raspberries. They hoped she would be Dr. Swain's nurse.

And she was his nurse for a little while, but then she started her model farm.

•　•　•

And little Melody arrived a long time after that, pregnant, and pushing her pathetic worldly goods ahead of her in a dilapidated baby carriage. Among those goods was a Dresden candlestick. Even in the Kingdom of Michigan, it was well known that the legendary King of New York was crazy about candlesticks.

Melody's candlestick depicted a nobleman's flirtation with a shepherdess at the foot of a treetrunk enlaced in flowering vines.

Melody's candlestick was broken on the old man's last birthday. It was kicked over by Wanda Chipmunk-5 Rivera, an intoxicated slave.

•　•　•

When Melody first presented herself at the Empire State Building, and Dr. Swain came out to ask who she was and what she wanted, she went down on her knees to him. Her little hands were extended before her, holding the candlestick.

"Hello, Grandfather," she said.

He hesitated for a moment. But then he helped her to her feet. "Come in," he said. "Come in, come in."

•　•　•

Dr. Swain did not know at that time that he had sired a son during his withdrawal from tri-benzo-Deportamil in Urbana. He supposed that Melody was a random supplicant and fan. Nor did he bring to that first encounter any daydreams of having descendents somewhere. He had never much wanted to reproduce himself.

So, when Melody gave him shy but convincing arguments that she was an actual blood relative, he had a feeling that he, as he later explained to Vera Chipmunk-5 Zappa, "had somehow sprung a huge leak. And out of that sudden, painless opening," he went on, "there crawled a famished child, pregnant and clasping a Dresden candlestick.

"Hi ho."

• • •

Melody's story was this:

Her father, who was the illegitimate child of Dr. Swain and the widow in Urbana, was one of the few survivors of the so-called "Urbana Massacre." He was then pressed into service as a drummer boy in the army of the perpetrator of the massacre, the Duke of Oklahoma.

The boy begat Melody at the age of fourteen. Her mother was a forty-year-old laundress who had attached herself to the army. Melody was given the middle name "Oriole-2," to ensure that she would be treated with maximal mercy, should she be captured by the forces of Stewart Oriole-2 Mott, the King of Michigan, the chief enemy of the Duke.

And she was in fact captured when a six-year-old—after the Battle of Iowa City, in which her father and mother were slain.

Hi ho.

• • •

Yes, and the King of Michigan had become so decadent by then, that he maintained a seraglio of captured children with the same middle name as his—which, of course, was Oriole-2. Little Melody was added to that pitiful zoo.

But, as her ordeals became more disgusting, so did she gain increasing inner strength from her father's dying words to her, which were these:

"You are a princess. You are the granddaughter of the King of Candlesticks, of the King of New York."

Hi ho.

• • •

And then, one night, she stole the Dresden candlestick from the tent of the sleeping King.

Then Melody crawled under the flaps of the tent and into the
moonlit world outside.

• • •

Thus began her incredible journey eastward, ever eastward,
in search of her legendary grandfather. His palace was one of
the tallest buildings in the world.

She would encounter relatives everywhere—if not Orioles,
then at least birds or living things of some kind.

They would feed her and point the way.

One would give her a raincoat. Another would give her a
sweater and a magnetic compass. Another would give her a baby
carriage. Another would give her an alarm clock.

Another would give her a needle and thread, and a gold
thimble, too.

Another would row her across the Harlem River to the Island
of Death, at the risk of his own life.

And so on.

*–Das Ende–*

# JAILBIRD

*For Benjamin D. Hitz,*
*Close friend of my youth,*
*Best man at my wedding.*
*Ben, you used to tell me about*
*Wonderful books you had just read,*
*And then I would imagine that I*
*Had read them, too.*
*You read nothing but the best, Ben,*
*While I studied chemistry.*
*Long time no see.*

Help the weak ones that cry for help, help the prosecuted and the victim, because they are your better friends; they are the comrades that fight and fall as your father and Bartolo fought and fell yesterday for the conquest of the joy of freedom for all the poor workers. In this struggle of life you will find more love and you will be loved.

—NICOLA SACCO (1891–1927)
   *in his last letter to his thirteen-year-old son, Dante, August 18, 1927, three days before his execution in Charlestown Prison, Boston, Massachusetts. "Bartolo" was Bartolomeo Vanzetti (1888–1927), who died the same night in the same electric chair, the invention of a dentist. So did an even more forgotten man, Celestino Madeiros (1894–1927), who confessed to the crime of which Sacco and Vanzetti had been convicted, even while his own conviction for another murder was being appealed. Madeiros was a notorious criminal, who behaved unselfishly at the end.*

# Prologue

YES—KILGORE TROUT is back again. He could not make it on the outside. That is no disgrace. A lot of good people can't make it on the outside.

•  •  •

I received a letter this morning (November 16, 1978) from a young stranger named John Figler, of Crown Point, Indiana. Crown Point is notorious for a jailbreak there by the bank robber John Dillinger, during the depths of the Great Depression. Dillinger escaped by threatening his jailor with a pistol made of soap and shoe polish. His jailor was a woman. God rest his soul, and her soul, too. Dillinger was the Robin Hood of my early youth. He is buried near my parents—and near my sister Alice, who admired him even more than I did—in Crown Hill Cemetery in Indianapolis. Also in there, on the top of Crown Hill, the highest point in the city, is James Whitcomb Riley, "The Hoosier Poet." When my mother was little, she knew Riley well.

Dillinger was summarily executed by agents of the Federal Bureau of Investigation. He was shot down in a public place, although he was not trying to escape or resist arrest. So there is nothing recent in my lack of respect for the F.B.I.

John Figler is a law-abiding high-school student. He says in his letter that he has read almost everything of mine and is now prepared to state the single idea that lies at the core of my life's work so far. The words are his: "Love may fail, but courtesy will prevail."

This seems true to me—and complete. So I am now in the abashed condition, five days after my fifty-sixth birthday, of realizing that I needn't have bothered to write several books. A seven-word telegram would have done the job.

Seriously.

But young Figler's insight reached me too late. I had nearly finished another book—this one.

•  •  •

In it is a minor character, "Kenneth Whistler," inspired by an Indianapolis man of my father's generation. The inspirer's name was Powers Hapgood (1900–1949). He is sometimes mentioned in histories of American labor for his deeds of derring-do in strikes and at the protests about the executions of Sacco and Vanzetti, and so on.

I met him only once. I had lunch with him and Father and my Uncle Alex, my father's younger brother, in Stegemeier's Restaurant in downtown Indianapolis after I came home from the European part of World War Two. That was in July of 1945. The first atomic bomb had not yet been dropped on Japan. That would happen in about a month. Imagine that.

I was twenty-two and still in uniform—a private first class who had flunked out of Cornell University as a student of chemistry before going to war. My prospects did not look good. There was no family business to go into. My father's architecture firm was defunct. He was broke. I had just gotten engaged to be married anyway, thinking, "Who but a wife would sleep with me?"

My mother, as I have said *ad nauseam* in other books, had declined to go on living, since she could no longer be what she had been at the time of her marriage—one of the richest women in town.

• • •

It was Uncle Alex who had arranged the lunch. He and Powers Hapgood had been at Harvard together. Harvard is all through this book, although I myself never went there. I have since taught there, briefly and without distinction—while my own home was going to pieces.

I confided that to one of my students—that my home was going to pieces.

To which he made this reply: "It *shows*."

Uncle Alex was so conservative politically that I do not think he would have eaten lunch with Hapgood gladly if Hapgood had not been a fellow Harvard man. Hapgood was then a labor union officer, a vice-president of the local CIO. His wife Mary had been the Socialist Party's candidate for vice-president of the United States again and again.

In fact, the first time I voted in a national election I voted for Norman Thomas and Mary Hapgood, not even knowing that she was an Indianapolis person. Franklin D. Roosevelt and Harry S. Truman won. I imagined that I was a socialist. I believed that socialism would be good for the common man. As a private first class in the infantry, I was surely a common man.

•  •  •

The meeting with Hapgood came about because I had told Uncle Alex that I might try to get a job with a labor union after the Army let me go. Unions were admirable instruments for extorting something like economic justice from employers then.

Uncle Alex must have thought something like this: "God help us. Against stupidity even the gods contend in vain. Well—at least there is a Harvard man with whom he can discuss this ridiculous dream."

(It was Schiller who first said that about stupidity and the gods. This was Nietzsche's reply: "Against *boredom* even the gods contend in vain.")

So Uncle Alex and I sat down at a front table in Stegemeier's and ordered beers and waited for Father and Hapgood to arrive. They would be coming separately. If they had come together, they would have had nothing to say to each other on the way. Father by then had lost all interest in politics and history and economics and such things. He had taken to saying that people talked too much. Sensations meant more to him than ideas— especially the feel of natural materials at his fingertips. When he was dying about twenty years later, he would say that he wished he had been a potter, making mud pies all day long.

To me that was sad—because he was so well-educated. It seemed to me that he was throwing his knowledge and intelligence away, just as a retreating soldier might throw away his rifle and pack.

Other people found it beautiful. He was a much-beloved man in the city, with wonderfully talented hands. He was invariably courteous and innocent. To him all craftsmen were saints, no matter how mean or stupid they might really be.

Uncle Alex, by the way, could do nothing with his hands. Neither could my mother. She could not even cook a breakfast or sew on a button.

Powers Hapgood could mine coal. That's what he did after he graduated from Harvard, when his classmates were taking jobs in family businesses and brokerages and banks and so on: He mined coal. He believed that a true friend of the working people should be a worker himself—and a good one, too.

So I have to say that my father, when I got to know him, when I myself was something like an adult, was a good man in full retreat from life. My mother had already surrendered and vanished from our table of organization. So an air of defeat has always been a companion of mine. So I have always been enchanted by brave veterans like Powers Hapgood, and some others, who were still eager for information of what was really going on, who were still full of ideas of how victory might yet be snatched from the jaws of defeat. "If I am going to go on living," I have thought, "I had better follow them."

• • •

I tried to write a story about a reunion between my father and myself in heaven one time. An early draft of this book in fact began that way. I hoped in the story to become a really good friend of his. But the story turned out perversely, as stories about real people we have known often do. It seemed that in heaven people could be any age they liked, just so long as they had experienced that age on Earth. Thus, John D. Rockefeller, for example, the founder of Standard Oil, could be any age up to ninety-eight. King Tut could be any age up to nineteen, and so on. As author of the story, I was dismayed that my father in heaven chose to be only nine years old.

I myself had chosen to be forty-four—respectable, but still quite sexy, too. My dismay with Father turned to embarrassment and anger. He was lemurlike as a nine-year-old, all eyes and hands. He had an endless supply of pencils and pads, and was forever tagging after me, drawing pictures of simply everything and insisting that I admire them when they were done. New acquaintances would sometimes ask me who that strange little boy was, and I would have to reply truthfully, since it was impossible to lie in heaven, "It's my father."

Bullies liked to torment him, since he was not like other children. He did not enjoy children's talk and children's games. Bullies would chase him and catch him and take off his pants and underpants and throw them down the mouth of hell. The mouth of hell looked like a sort of wishing well, but without a bucket and windlass. You could lean over its rim and hear ever so faintly the screams of Hitler and Nero and Salome and Judas and people like that far, far below. I could imagine Hitler, already experiencing maximum agony, periodically finding his head draped with my father's underpants.

Whenever Father had his pants stolen, he would come running to me, purple with rage. As like as not, I had just made some new friends and was impressing them with my urbanity—and there my father would be, bawling bloody murder and with his little pecker waving in the breeze.

I complained to my mother about him, but she said she knew nothing about him, or about me, either, since she was only sixteen. So I was stuck with him, and all I could do was yell at him from time to time, "For the love of God, Father, won't you please grow up!"

And so on. It insisted on being a very unfriendly story, so I quit writing it.

• • •

And now, in July of 1945, Father came into Stegemeier's Restaurant, still very much alive. He was about the age that I am now, a widower with no interest in ever being married again and with no evident wish for a lover of any kind. He had a mustache like the one I have today. I was clean-shaven then.

A terrible ordeal was ending—a planetary economic collapse followed by a planetary war. Fighting men were starting to come home everywhere. You might think that Father would comment on that, however fleetingly, and on the new era that was being born. He did not.

He told instead, and perfectly charmingly, about an adventure he had had that morning. While driving into the city, he had seen an old house being torn down. He had stopped and taken a closer look at its skeleton. He noticed that the sill under the front door was an unusual wood, which he finally decided was poplar. I gathered that it was about eight inches square and four feet long. He admired it so much that the wreckers gave it to him. He borrowed a hammer from one of them and pulled out all the nails he could see.

Then he took it to a sawmill—to have it ripped into boards. He would decide later what to do with the boards. Mostly, he wanted to see the grain in this unusual wood. He had to promise the mill that there were no nails left in the timber. This he did. But there was still a nail in there. It had lost its head, and so was invisible. There was an earsplitting shriek from the circular saw when it hit the nail. Smoke came from the belt that was trying to spin the stalled saw.

Now Father had to pay for a new sawblade and a new belt, too, and had been told never to come there with used lumber again. He was delighted somehow. The story was a sort of fairy tale, with a moral in it for everyone.

Uncle Alex and I had no very vivid response to the story. Like all of Father's stories, it was as neatly packaged and self-contained as an egg.

•  •  •

So we ordered more beers. Uncle Alex would later become a cofounder of the Indianapolis chapter of Alcoholics Anonymous, although his wife would say often and pointedly that he himself had never been an alcoholic. He began to talk now about The Columbia Conserve Company, a cannery that Powers Hapgood's father, William, also a Harvard man, had founded in Indianapolis in 1903. It was a famous experiment in industrial democracy, but I had never heard of it before. There was a lot that I had never heard of before.

The Columbia Conserve Company made tomato soup and chili and catsup, and some other things. It was massively dependent on tomatoes. The company did not make a profit until 1916. As soon as it made one, though, Powers Hapgood's father began to give his employees some of the benefits he thought workers everywhere in the world were naturally entitled to. The other principal stockholders were his two brothers, also Harvard men—and they agreed with him.

So he set up a council of seven workers, who were to recommend to the board of directors what the wages and working conditions should be. The board, without any prodding from anybody, had already declared that there would no longer be any seasonal layoffs, even in such a seasonal industry, and that there would be vacations with pay, and that medical care for workers and their dependents would be free, and that there would be sick pay and a retirement plan, and that the ultimate goal of the company was that, through a stock-bonus plan, it become the property of the workers.

"It went bust," said Uncle Alex, with a certain grim, Darwinian satisfaction.

My father said nothing. He may not have been listening.

•  •  •

I now have at hand a copy of *The Hapgoods, Three Earnest Brothers*, by Michael D. Marcaccio (The University Press of Virginia, Charlottesville, 1977). The three brothers in the subtitle were William, the founder of Columbia Conserve, and Norman and Hutchins, also Harvard men, who were both socialistically inclined journalists and editors and book writers in and around New York. According to Mr. Marcaccio, Columbia Conserve was a quite tidy success until 1931, when the Great Depression hit it murderously. Many workers were let go, and those who were kept on had their pay cut by 50 percent. A great deal of money was owed to Continental Can, which insisted that the company behave more conventionally toward its employees—even if they were stockholders, which most of them were. The experiment was over. There wasn't any money to pay for it anymore. Those who had received stock through profit sharing now owned bits of a company that was nearly dead.

It did not go completely bust for a while. In fact it still existed when Uncle Alex and Father and Powers Hapgood and I had lunch. But it was just another cannery, paying not one penny more than any other cannery paid. What was left of it was finally sold off to a stronger company in 1953.

•  •  •

Now Powers Hapgood came into the restaurant, an ordinary-looking Middle Western Anglo-Saxon in a cheap business suit. He wore a union badge in his lapel. He was cheerful. He knew my father slightly. He knew Uncle Alex quite well. He apologized for being late. He had been in court that morning, testifying about violence on a picket line some months before. He personally had had nothing to do with the violence. His days

of derring-do were behind him. Never again would he fight
anybody, or be clubbed to his knees, or be locked up in jail.

He was a talker, with far more wonderful stories than Father
or Uncle Alex had ever told. He was thrown into a lunatic
asylum after he led the pickets at the execution of Sacco and
Vanzetti. He was in fights with organizers for John L. Lewis's
United Mine Workers, which he considered too right wing. In
1936 he was a CIO organizer at a strike against RCA in Camden,
New Jersey. He was put in jail. When several thousand strikers
surrounded the jail, as a sort of reverse lynch mob, the sheriff thought it best to turn him loose again. And on and on. I
have put my recollections of some of the stories he told into the
mouth of, as I say, a fictitious character in this book.

It turned out that he had been telling stories all morning in
court, too. The judge was fascinated, and almost everybody else
in court was, too—presumably by such unselfish high adventures. The judge had encouraged Hapgood, I gathered, to go
on and on. Labor history was pornography of a sort in those
days, and even more so in these days. In public schools and in
the homes of nice people it was and remains pretty much taboo
to tell tales of labor's sufferings and derring-do.

I remember the name of the judge. It was Claycomb. I am
able to remember it so easily because I had been a high-school
classmate of the judge's son, "Moon."

Moon Claycomb's father, according to Powers Hapgood,
asked him this final question just before lunch: "Mr. Hapgood,"
he said, "why would a man from such a distinguished family
and with such a fine education choose to live as you do?"

"Why?" said Hapgood, according to Hapgood. "Because of
the Sermon on the Mount, sir."

And Moon Claycomb's father said this: "Court is adjourned
until two P.M."

•  •  •

What, exactly, was the Sermon on the Mount?

It was the prediction by Jesus Christ that the poor in spirit
would receive the Kingdom of Heaven; that all who mourned
would be comforted; that the meek would inherit the Earth;
that those who hungered for righteousness would find it; that

the merciful would be treated mercifully; that the pure in heart would see God; that the peacemakers would be called the sons of God; that those who were persecuted for righteousness' sake would also receive the Kingdom of Heaven; and on and on.

• • •

The character in this book inspired by Powers Hapgood is unmarried and has problems with alcohol. Powers Hapgood was married and, so far as I know, had no serious problems with alcohol.

• • •

There is another minor character, whom I call "Roy M. Cohn." He is modeled after the famous anticommunist and lawyer and businessman named, straightforwardly enough, one would have to say, Roy M. Cohn. I include him with his kind permission, given yesterday (January 2, 1979) over the telephone. I promised to do him no harm and to present him as an appallingly effective attorney for either the prosecution or the defense of anyone.

• • •

My dear father was silent for a good part of our ride home from that lunch with Powers Hapgood. We were in his Plymouth sedan. He was driving. Some fifteen years later he would be arrested for driving through a red light. It would be discovered that he had not had a driver's license for twenty years—which means that he was not licensed even on the day we had lunch with Powers Hapgood.

His house was out in the country some. When we got to the edge of the city, he said that if we were lucky we would see a very funny dog. It was a German shepherd, he said, who could hardly stand up because he had been hit so often by automobiles. The dog still came tottering out to chase them, his eyes filled with bravery and rage.

But the dog did not appear that day. He really did exist. I would see him another day, when I was driving alone. He was crouched down on the shoulder of the road, ready to sink his teeth into my right front tire. But his charge was a pitiful thing to see. His rear end hardly worked at all anymore. He might as well have been dragging a steamer trunk with the power in his front feet alone.

That was the day on which the atomic bomb was dropped on Hiroshima.

•  •  •

But back to the day on which I lunched with Powers Hapgood:

When Father put the car into his garage, he finally said something about the lunch. He was puzzled by the passionate manner in which Hapgood had discussed the Sacco and Vanzetti case, surely one of the most spectacular, most acrimoniously argued miscarriages of justice in American history.

"You know," said Father, "I had no idea that there was any question about their guilt."

That is how purely an artist my father was.

•  •  •

There is mentioned in this book a violent confrontation between strikers and police and soldiers called the Cuyahoga Massacre. It is an invention, a mosaic composed of bits taken from tales of many such riots in not such olden times.

It is a legend in the mind of the leading character in this book, Walter F. Starbuck, whose life was accidentally shaped by the Massacre, even though it took place on Christmas morning in eighteen hundred ninety-four, long before Starbuck was born.

It goes like this:

In October of 1894 Daniel McCone, the founder and owner of the Cuyahoga Bridge and Iron Company, then the largest single employer in Cleveland, Ohio, informed his factory workers through their foremen that they were to accept a 10 percent cut in pay. There was no union. McCone was a hard-bitten and brilliant little mechanical engineer, self-educated, born of working-class parents in Edinburgh, Scotland.

Half his work force, about a thousand men, under the leadership of an ordinary foundryman with a gift for oratory, Colin Jarvis, walked out, forcing the plant to shut down. They had found it almost impossible to feed and shelter and clothe their families even without the cut in wages. All of them were white. Most of them were native-born.

Nature sympathized that day. The sky and Lake Erie were identical in color, the same dead pewter-gray.

The little homes toward which the strikers trudged were near the factory. Many of them were owned, and their neighborhood grocery stores, too, by Cuyahoga Bridge and Iron.

• • •

Among the trudgers, as bitter and dejected as anyone, seemingly, were spies and agents provocateurs secretly employed and paid very well by the Pinkerton Detective Agency. That agency still exists and prospers, and is now a wholly-owned subsidiary of The RAMJAC Corporation.

Daniel McCone had two sons, Alexander Hamilton McCone, then twenty-two, and John, twenty-five. Alexander had graduated without distinction from Harvard in the previous May. He was soft, he was shy, he was a stammerer. John, the elder son and the company's heir apparent, had flunked out of the Massachusetts Institute of Technology in his freshman year, and had been his father's most trusted aide ever since.

The workers to a man, strikers and nonstrikers alike, hated the father and his son John, but acknowledged that they knew more about shaping iron and steel than anybody else in the world. As for young Alexander: They found him girllike and stupid and too cowardly ever to come near the furnaces and forges and drop hammers, where the most dangerous work was done. Workers would sometimes wave their handkerchiefs at him, as a salute to his futility as a man.

When Walter F. Starbuck, in whose mind this legend is, asked Alexander years later why he had ever gone to work in such an unhospitable place after Harvard, especially since Alexander's father had not insisted on it, he stammered out a reply, which when unscrambled, was this: "I then believed that a rich man should have some understanding of the place from which his riches came. That was very juvenile of me. Great wealth should be accepted unquestioningly, or not at all."

About Alexander's stammers before the Cuyahoga Massacre: They were little more than grace notes expressing excessive modesty. Never had one left him mute for more than three seconds, with all his thoughts held prisoner inside.

And he would not have done much talking in the presence of his dynamic father and brother in any event. But his silence came to conceal a secret that was increasingly pleasant with each passing day: He was coming to understand the business as well as they did. Before they announced a decision, he almost always knew what it would be and should be—and why. Nobody else knew it yet, but he, too, by God, was an industrialist and an engineer.

*   *   *

When the strike came in October, he was able to guess many of the things that should be done, even though he had never been through a strike before. Harvard was a million miles away. Nothing he had ever learned there would get the factory going again. But the Pinkerton Agency would, and the police would—and perhaps the National Guard. Before his father and brother said so, Alexander knew that there were plenty of men in other parts of the country who were desperate enough to take a job at almost any wage. When his father and brother did say this, he learned something else about business: There were companies, often pretending to be labor unions, whose sole business was to recruit such men.

By the end of November the chimneys of the factory were belching smoke again. The strikers had no money left for rent or food or fuel. Every large employer within three hundred miles had been sent their names, so he would know what troublemakers they had been. Their nominal leader, Colin Jarvis, was in jail, awaiting trial on a trumped-up murder charge.

*   *   *

On December fifteenth the wife of Colin Jarvis, called Ma, led a delegation of twenty other strikers' wives to the main gate of the factory, asking to see Daniel McCone. He sent Alexander down to them with a scribbled note, which Alexander found himself able to read out loud to them without any speech impediment at all. It said that Daniel McCone was too busy to give time to strangers who had nothing to do with affairs of the Cuyahoga Bridge and Iron Company anymore. It suggested that they had mistaken the company for a charitable organization. It said that their churches or police precinct stations would be able to give them a list of organizations to which they might more appropriately plead for help—if they really needed help and felt that they deserved it.

Ma Jarvis told Alexander that her own message was even simpler: The strikers would return to work on any terms. Most of them were now being evicted from their homes and had no place to go.

"I am sorry," said Alexander. "I can only read my father's note again, if you would like me to."

Alexander McCone would say many years later that the confrontation did not bother him a bit at the time. He was in fact elated, he said, to find himself such a reliable ". . . muh-muh-muh-machine."

• • •

A police captain now stepped forward. He warned the women that they were in violation of the law, assembling in such great numbers as to impede traffic and constitute a threat to public safety. He ordered them to disperse at once, in the name of the law.

This they did. They retreated across the vast plaza before the main gate. The façade of the factory had been designed to remind cultivated persons of the Piazza San Marco in Venice, Italy. The factory's clocktower was a half-scale replica of San Marco's famous campanile.

It was from the belfry of that tower that Alexander and his father and his brother would watch the Cuyahoga Massacre on Christmas morning. Each would have his own binoculars. Each would have his own little revolver, too.

There were no bells in the belfry. Neither were there cafés and shops around the plaza below. The architect had justified the plaza on strictly utilitarian grounds. It provided any amount of room for wagons and buggies and horse-drawn streetcars as they came and went. The architect had also been matter-of-fact about the virtues of the factory as a fort. Any mob meaning to storm the front gate would first have to cross all that open ground.

A single newspaper reporter, from *The Cleveland Plain Dealer*, now a RAMJAC publication, retreated across the plaza with the women. He asked Ma Jarvis what she planned to do next.

There was nothing much that she could do next, of course. The strikers weren't even strikers anymore, but simply unemployed persons being turned out of their homes.

She gave a brave answer anyway: "We will be back," she said. What else could she say?

He asked her when they would be back.

Her answer was probably no more than the poetry of hopelessness in Christendom, with winter setting in. "On Christmas morning," she said.

•  •  •

This was printed in the paper, whose editors felt that a threatening promise had been made. And the fame of this coming Christmas in Cleveland spread far and wide. Sympathizers with the strikers—preachers, writers, union organizers, populist politicians, and on and on—began to filter into the city as though expecting a miracle of some kind. They were frankly enemies of the economic order as it was constructed then.

A company of National Guard infantrymen was mobilized by Edwin Kincaid, the governor of Ohio, to protect the factory. They were farm boys from the southern part of the state, selected because they had no friends or relatives among the strikers, no reason to see them as anything but unreasonable disturbers of the peace. They represented an American ideal: healthy, cheerful citizen soldiers, who went about their ordinary business until their country suddenly needed an awesome display of weapons and discipline. They were supposed to appear as though from nowhere, to the consternation of America's enemies. When the trouble was over, they would vanish again.

The regular army of the country, which had fought the Indians until the Indians could fight no more, was down to about thirty thousand men. As for the Utopian militias throughout the country: They almost all consisted of farm boys, since the health of the factory workers was so bad and their hours so long. It was about to be discovered, incidentally, in the Spanish-American War, that militiamen were worse than useless on battlefields, they were so poorly trained.

•  •  •

And that was surely the impression young Alexander Hamilton McCone had of the militiamen who arrived at the factory on Christmas Eve: that these were not soldiers. They were brought on a special train to a siding inside the factory's high iron fence. They straggled out of the cars and onto a loading platform as though they were ordinary passengers on various errands. Their uniforms were only partly buttoned, and often mis-buttoned, at that. Several had lost their hats. Almost all carried laughably unmilitary suitcases and parcels.

Their officers? Their captain was the postmaster of Greenfield, Ohio. Their two lieutenants were twin sons of the president of the Greenfield Bank and Trust Company. The postmaster and the banker had both done local favors for the governor. The commissions were their rewards. And the officers, in turn, had rewarded those who had pleased them in some way by making them sergeants or corporals. And the privates, in turn, voters or sons of voters, had it within their power, if they felt like using it, to ruin the lives of their superiors with contempt and ridicule, which could go on for generations.

There on the loading platform at the Cuyahoga Bridge and Iron Company old Daniel McCone finally had to ask one of the many soldiers milling about and eating at the same time, "Who is in charge here?"

As luck would have it, he had put the question to the captain, who told him this: "Well—as much as anybody, I guess I am."

To their credit, and although armed with bayonets and live ammunition, the militiamen would not harm a single soul on the following day.

•   •   •

They were quartered in an idled machine shop. They slept in the aisles. Each one had brought his own food from home. They had hams and roasted chickens and cakes and pies. They ate whatever they pleased and whenever they pleased, and turned the machine shop into a picnic ground. They left the place looking like a village dump. They did not know any better.

Yes, and old Daniel McCone and his two sons spent the night in the factory, too—on camp cots in their offices at the foot of the bell tower, and with loaded revolvers under their pillows.

When would they have their Christmas dinner? At three o'clock on the following afternoon. The trouble would surely be over by then. Young Alexander was to make use of his fine education, his father had told him, by composing and delivering an appropriate prayer of thanksgiving before they ate that meal.

Regular company guards, augmented by Pinkerton agents and city policemen, meanwhile took turns patrolling the company fence all night. The company guards, ordinarily armed only with pistols, had rifles, and shotguns, too, borrowed from friends or brought from home.

Four Pinkerton men were allowed to sleep all through the night. They were master craftsmen of a sort. They were sharpshooters.

It was not bugles that awakened the McCones the next morning. It was the sound of hammering and sawing, which gabbled around the plaza. Carpenters were building a high scaffold by the main gate, just inside the fence. The chief of police of Cleveland was to stand atop it, in plain view of everyone. At an opportune moment he was to read the Ohio Riot Act to the crowd. This public reading was required by law. The act said that any unlawful assembly of twelve persons or more had to disperse within an hour of having the act read to it. If it did not disperse, its members would be guilty of a felony punishable by imprisonment for from ten years to life.

Nature sympathized again—for a gentle snow began to fall.

•  •  •

Yes, and an enclosed carriage drawn by two white horses clattered into the plaza at full speed and stopped by the gate. Into the dawn's early light stepped Colonel George Redfield, the governor's son-in-law, who had been commissioned by the governor, and who had come all the way from Sandusky to take command of the militiamen. He owned a lumber mill and was in the feed and ice businesses besides. He had no military experience, but was costumed as a cavalryman. He wore a saber, which was a gift from his father-in-law.

He went at once to the machine shop to address his troops.

Soon after that wagons carrying riot police arrived. They were ordinary Cleveland policemen, but armed with wooden shields and blunt lances.

An American flag was flown from the top of the bell tower, and another from the pole by the main gate.

It was to be a pageant, young Alexander supposed. There would be no actual killing or wounding. All would be said by the way men posed. The strikers themselves had sent word that they would have their wives and children with them, and that not one of them would have a gun—or even a knife with a blade more than three inches long.

"We wish only," said their letter, "to take one last look at the factory to which we gave the best years of our lives, and to show our faces to all who may care to look upon them, to show them to God Almighty alone, if only He will look, and to ask, as we stand mute and motionless, 'Does any American deserve misery and heartbreak such as we now know?'"

Alexander was not insensitive to the beauty of the letter. It had, in fact, been written by the poet Henry Niles Whistler, then in the city to hearten the strikers—a fellow Harvard man. It deserved a majestic reply, thought Alexander. He believed that the flags and the ranks of citizen soldiers and the solemn, steady presence of the police would surely do the job.

The law would be read out loud, and all would hear it, and all would go home. Peace should not be broken for any cause.

Alexander meant to say in his prayer that afternoon that God should protect the working people from leaders like Colin Jarvis, who had encouraged them to bring such misery and heartbreak on themselves.

"Amen," he said to himself.

•  •  •

And the people came as promised. They came on foot. In order to discourage them, the city fathers had canceled all street-car service in that part of the city that day.

There were many children among them, and even infants in arms. One infant would be shot to death and inspire the poem by Henry Niles Whistler, later put to music and still sung today, "Bonnie Failey."

Where were the soldiers? They had been standing in front of the factory fence since eight o'clock, with bayonets already fixed, with full packs on their backs. Those packs weighed fifty pounds and more. They were Colonel Redfield's idea of how to make his men more fearsome. They were in a single rank, which stretched the width of the plaza. The battle plan was this: If the crowd would not disperse when told to, the soldiers were to level their bayonets and to clear the plaza slowly but irresistibly, glacially—maintaining a perfectly straight rank that bristled with cold steel, and advancing, always on command, one step, then two, then three, then four . . .

Only the soldiers had been outside the fence since eight. The snow had kept on falling. So when the first members of the crowd appeared at the far end of the plaza, they gazed at the factory over an expanse of virgin snow. The only footprints were those they themselves had just made.

And many more people came than had spiritual business to conduct specifically with Cuyahoga Bridge and Iron. The strikers themselves were mystified as to who all these other ragged strangers might be—who also, often, had brought their families along. These outsiders, too, wished to demonstrate to simply anybody their misery and heartbreak at Christmastide. Young Alexander, peering through his binoculars, read a sign a man was carrying that said, "Erie Coal and Iron unfair to workers." Erie Coal and Iron wasn't even an Ohio firm. It was in Buffalo, New York.

So it was against considerable odds that Bonnie Failey, the infant killed in the Massacre, was actually the child of a striker against Cuyahoga Bridge and Iron, that Henry Niles Whistler was able to say in the refrain of his poem about her:

> *Damn you, damn you, Dan McCone,*
> *With a soul of pig iron and a heart of stone . . .*

Young Alexander read the sign about Erie Coal and Iron while standing at a second-story window in an office wing abutting the north wall of the bell tower. He was in a long gallery, also of Venetian inspiration, which had a window every ten feet and a mirror at its far end. The mirror made its length appear to be infinite. The windows looked out over the plaza. It was in this gallery that the four sharpshooters supplied by Pinkerton set up their places of business. Each installed a table at his chosen window and set a comfortable chair behind that. There was a rifle rest on each table.

The sharpshooter nearest Alexander had put a sandbag on his table and had hammered a groove into it with the edge of his hairy hand. There his rifle would rest, with its butt tucked into his shoulder, as he squinted down his sights at this face or that face in the crowd from his easy chair. The sharpshooter farther down the corridor was a machinist by trade, and had built a squat tripod with a swiveling oarlock on top. This squatted on his table. It was into this oarlock that he would slip his rifle if trouble came.

"Patent applied for," he had told Alexander of his tripod, and he had patted the thing.

Each man had his ammunition and his cleaning rod and his cleaning patches and his oil laid out on the table, as though they might be for sale.

All the windows were still closed now. At some of the others were far angrier and less orderly men. These were regular company guards, who had been up most of the night. Several had been drinking, so they said, ". . . to stay awake." They had been stationed at the windows with their rifles or shotguns—in case the mob should attack the factory at all costs, and nothing but withering fire would turn them away.

They had persuaded themselves by now that this attack would surely come. Their alarm and bravado were the first strong hints young Alexander received, as he would tell young Walter F. Starbuck decades afterward, again stammering, that there were "certain instabilities inherent in the pageant."

He himself, of course, was carrying a loaded revolver in his overcoat pocket—and so were his father and brother, who now came into the corridor to approve of the arrangements one last time. It was ten o'clock in the morning. It was time to open the windows, they said. The plaza was full.

• • •

It was time to go up to the top of the tower, they told Alexander, for the best view of all.

So the windows were opened and the sharpshooters laid their rifles in their cradles of different kinds.

Who were the four sharpshooters, really—and was there really such a trade? There was less work for sharpshooters than there was for hangmen at the time. Not one of the four had ever been hired in this capacity before, nor was he likely, unless war came, to be paid for such work ever again. One was a part-time Pinkerton agent, and the other three were his friends. The four of them hunted together regularly, and had for years praised one another for what unbelievably good shots they were. So when the Pinkerton Agency let it be known that it could use four sharpshooters, they materialized almost instantly, like the company of citizen soldiers.

The man with the tripod had invented the device for the occasion. Nor had the man with the sandbag ever couched his rifle on a sandbag before. So it was, too, with the chairs and tables and the tidy displays of ammunition and all that: They had agreed among themselves as to how truly professional sharpshooters should comport themselves.

Years later Alexander McCone, when asked by Starbuck what he thought the principal cause of the Cuyahoga Massacre had been, would reply: "American am-am-am-amateurism in muh-muh-matters of luh-life and duh-duh-duh-death."

●   ●   ●

When the windows were opened, the oceanic murmurs of the crowd came in with the cold air. The crowd wished to be silent, and imagined itself to be silent—but this person had to whisper a little something, and that one had to reply, and so on. Hence, sounds like a sea.

It was mainly this seeming surf that Alexander heard as he stood with his father and brother in the belfry. The defenders of the factory were quiet. Except for the rattles and bumps of the opening of the windows on the second floor, they had made no reply.

Alexander's father said this as they waited: "It is no dainty thing to shape iron and steel to human needs, my boys. No man in his right mind would do such work, if it were not for fear of cold and hunger. The question is, my boys—how much does the world need iron and steel products? In case anybody wants some, Dan McCone knows how they're made."

Now there was a tiny quickening of life inside the fence. The chief of police of Cleveland, carrying a piece of paper on which the Riot Act was written, climbed the steps to the top of the scaffold. This was to be the climax of the pageant, young Alexander supposed, a moment of terrible beauty.

But then he sneezed up there in the belfry. Not only were his lungs emptied of air, but his romantic vision was destroyed. What was about to happen below, he realized, was not majestic. It would be insane. There was no such thing as magic, and yet his father and his brother and the governor, and probably even President Grover Cleveland, expected this police chief to become a wizard, a Merlin—to make a crowd vanish with a magic spell.

"It will not work," he thought. "It cannot work."

It did not work.

The chief cast his spell. His shouted words bounced off the buildings, warred with their own echoes, and sounded like Babylonian by the time they reached Alexander's ears.

Absolutely nothing happened.

The chief climbed down from the scaffold. His manner indicated that he had not expected much of anything to happen, that there were simply too many people out there. It was with great modesty that he rejoined his own shock troops, who were armed with shields and lances, but safe inside the fence. He was not about to ask them to arrest anyone, or to do anything provocative against a crowd so large.

But Colonel Redfield was enraged. He had the gate opened a crack, to let him out so he could join his half-frozen troops. He took his place between two farm boys at the center of the long line. He ordered his men to level their bayonets at those in front of them. Next, he ordered them to take one step forward. This they did.

•  •  •

Looking down on the plaza, young Alexander could see the people at the front of the crowd backing into those behind them as they shrank from the naked steel. People at the back of the crowd, meanwhile, had no idea what was going on, and were not about to depart, to relieve the pressure some.

The soldiers advanced yet another pace and the people retreating put pressure not only on those behind them, but on those beside them, too. Those at either end found themselves squashed against the buildings. The soldiers facing them had no heart for skewering someone so hopelessly immobilized, so they averted their bayonets, opening a space between the blade tips and the unyielding walls.

When the soldiers took yet another step forward, according to Alexander when old, people began ". . . to squh-squh-squirt around the ends of the luh-luh-line like wuh-wuh-water." The squirts became torrents, crumpling the flanks of the line and delivering hundreds of people to the space between the factory fence and the undefended rears of the soldiers.

Colonel Redfield, his eyes blazing straight ahead, had no idea what was happening on either side. He ordered yet another advance.

Now the crowd behind the soldiers began to behave quite badly. A youth jumped onto a soldier's pack like a monkey. The soldier sat down hard and struggled most comically, trying to rise again. Soldier after soldier was brought down in this way. If one got back to his feet, he was pulled down again. And the soldiers began to crawl toward each other for mutual protection. They refused to shoot. They formed a defensive heap, instead, a paralyzed porcupine.

Colonel Redfield was not among them. He was nowhere to be seen.

. . .

No one was ever found who would admit to ordering the sharpshooters and the guards to open fire from the windows of the factory, but the firing began.

Fourteen people were killed outright by bullets—one of them a soldier. Twenty-three were seriously wounded.

Alexander would say when an old man that the shooting sounded no more serious than "puh-puh-popcorn," and that he thought a freakish wind had blown across the plaza below, since the people seemed to be blowing away like "luh-luh-leaves."

When it was all over, there was general satisfaction that honor had been served and that justice had been done. Law and order had been restored.

Old Daniel McCone would say to his sons as he looked out over the battlefield, vacant now except for bodies, "Like it or not, boys, that's the sort of business you're in."

Colonel Redfield would be found in a side street, naked and out of his head, but otherwise unharmed.

Young Alexander did not try to speak afterward until he had to speak, which was at Christmas dinner that afternoon. He was asked to say grace. He discovered then that he had become a bubbling booby, that his stammer was so bad now that he could not speak at all.

He would never go to the factory again. He would become Cleveland's leading art collector and the chief donor to the Cleveland Museum of Fine Arts, demonstrating that the McCone family was interested in more than money and power for money's and power's sakes.

•   •   •

His stammer was so bad for the rest of his life that he seldom ventured outside his mansion on Euclid Avenue. He had married a Rockefeller one month before his stammer became so bad. Otherwise, as he would later say, he would probably never have married at all.

He had one daughter, who was embarrassed by him, as was his wife. He would make only one friendship after the Massacre. It would be with a child. It would be with the son of his cook and his chauffeur.

The multimillionaire wanted someone who would play chess with him many hours a day. So he seduced the boy, so to speak, with simpler games first—hearts and old maid, checkers and dominoes. But he also taught him chess. Soon they were playing only chess. Their conversations were limited to conventional chess taunts and teasings, which had not changed in a thousand years.

Samples: "Have you played this game before?" "Really?" "Spot me a queen." "Is this a trap?"

The boy was Walter F. Starbuck. He was willing to spend his childhood and youth so unnaturally for this reason: Alexander Hamilton McCone promised to send him to Harvard someday.

—K.V.

# 1

LIFE GOES ON, yes—and a fool and his self-respect are soon parted, perhaps never to be reunited even on Judgment Day.

Pay attention, please, for years as well as people are characters in this book, which is the story of my life so far. Nineteen-hundred and Thirteen gave me the gift of life. Nineteen-hundred and Twenty-nine wrecked the American economy. Nineteen-hundred and Thirty-one sent me to Harvard. Nineteen-hundred and Thirty-eight got me my first job in the federal government. Nineteen-hundred and Forty-six gave me a wife. Nineteen-hundred and Forty-six gave me an ungrateful son. Nineteen-hundred and Fifty-three fired me from the federal government.

Thus do I capitalize years as though they were proper names.

Nineteen-hundred and Seventy gave me a job in the Nixon White House. Nineteen-hundred and Seventy-five sent me to prison for my own preposterous contributions to the American political scandals known collectively as "Watergate."

Three years ago, as I write, Nineteen-hundred and Seventy-seven was about to turn me loose again. I felt like a piece of garbage. I was wearing olive-drab coveralls, the prison uniform. I sat alone in a dormitory—on a cot that I had stripped of its bedding. A blanket, two sheets, and a pillowcase, which were to be returned to my government along with my uniform, were folded neatly on my lap. My speckled old hands were clasped atop these. I stared straight ahead at a wall on the second floor of a barracks at the Federal Minimum Security Adult Correctional Facility on the edge of Finletter Air Force Base—thirty-five miles from Atlanta, Georgia. I was waiting for a guard to conduct me to the Administration Building, where I would be given my release papers and my civilian clothes. There would be no one to greet me at the gate. Nowhere in the world was there anyone who had a forgiving hug for me—or a free meal or a bed for a night or two.

If anyone had been watching me, he would have seen me do something quite mysterious every five minutes or so. Without changing my blank expression, I would lift my hands from the bedding and I would clap three times. I will explain why by and by.

It was nine in the morning on April twenty-first. The guard was one hour late. A fighter plane leaped up from the tip of a nearby runway, destroyed enough energy to heat one hundred homes for a thousand years, tore the sky to shreds. I did not bat an eyelash. The event was merely tedious to old prisoners and guards at Finletter. It happened all the time.

Most of the other prisoners, all of them convicted of non-violent, white-collar crimes, had been trundled away in purple schoolbuses to work details around the base. Only a small housekeeping crew had been left behind—to wash windows, to mop floors. There were a few others around, writing or reading or napping—too sick, with heart trouble or back trouble, usually, to do manual work of any kind. I myself would have been feeding a mangle in the laundry at the base hospital if it had been a day like any other day. My health was excellent, as they say.

Was I shown no special respect in prison as a Harvard man? It was no distinction, actually. I had met or heard of at least seven others. And no sooner would I leave than my cot would be taken by Virgil Greathouse, former secretary of health, education, and welfare, who was also a Harvard man. I was quite low on the educational ladder at Finletter, with nothing but a poor bachelor's degree. I was not even a Phi Beta Kappa. We must have had twenty or more Phi Beta Kappas, a dozen or more medical doctors, an equal number of dentists, a veterinarian, a Doctor of Divinity, a Doctor of Economics, a Doctor of Philosophy in chemistry, and simply shoals of disbarred lawyers. Lawyers were so common that we had a joke for newcomers that went like this: "If you find yourself talking to somebody who hasn't been to law school, watch your step. He's either the warden or a guard."

My own poor degree was in the liberal arts, with some emphasis on history and economics. It was my plan when I entered Harvard to become a public servant, an employee rather than an elected official. I believed that there could be no higher calling in a democracy than to a lifetime in government. Since I did not know what branch of government might take me on, whether the State Department or the Bureau of Indian Affairs or whatever, I would make my wisdom as widely applicable as possible. For this reason did I take a liberal arts degree.

And I speak now of *my* plans and *my* beliefs—but, being so new to the planet in those days, I had been glad to adopt as my own the plans and beliefs of a much older man. He was a Cleveland multimillionaire named Alexander Hamilton McCone, a member of the Harvard class of Eighteen-hundred and Ninety-four. He was the reclusive, stammering son of Daniel McCone. Daniel McCone was a brilliant and brutal Scottish engineer and metallurgist, who founded the Cuyahoga Bridge and Iron Company, the largest single employer in Cleveland when I was born. Imagine being born as long ago as Nineteen-hundred and Thirteen! Will young people of today doubt me if I aver with a straight face that the Ohio skies back then were often darkened by flocks of hooting pterodactyls, and that forty-ton brontosaurs basked and crooned in the Cuyahoga River's ooze? No.

Alexander Hamilton McCone was forty-one years old when I was born into his mansion on Euclid Avenue. He was married to the former Alice Rockefeller, who was even richer than he was, and who spent most of her time in Europe with their one child, a daughter named Clara. Mother and daughter, no doubt embarrassed by Mr. McCone's terrible speech impediment, and even more dismayed, perhaps, by his wanting to do nothing with his life but read books all day long, were seldom home. Divorce was unthinkable back then.

Clara—are you still alive? She hated me. Some people did and do.

That's life.

And what was I to Mr. McCone, that I should have been born into the unhappy stillness of his mansion? My mother, born Anna Kairys in Russian Lithuania, was his cook. My father, born Stanislaus Stankiewicz in Russian Poland, was his bodyguard and chauffeur. They genuinely loved him.

Mr. McCone built a handsome apartment for them, and for me, too, on the second floor of his carriage house. And, as I grew older, I became his playmate, always indoors. He taught me hearts and old maid, checkers and dominoes—and chess. Soon we were playing only chess. He did not play well. I won almost all of the games, and it is possible that he was secretly drunk. He never tried hard to win, I thought. In any event, and very early on, he began to tell me and my parents that I was a genius, which I surely was not, and that he would send me to Harvard. He must have said to my father and mother a thousand times over the years, "You are going to find yourselves the proud parents of a perfect Harvard gentleman someday."

To that end, and when I was about ten years old, he had us change our family name from Stankiewicz to Starbuck. I would be better received at Harvard, he said, if I had an Anglo-Saxon name. Thus did Walter F. Starbuck become my name.

He himself had done badly at Harvard, had scarcely squeaked through. He had also been scorned socially, not only for his stammer but for his being the obscenely rich son of an immigrant. There was every reason for him to hate Harvard—but I watched him over the years so sentimentalize and romanticize, and finally so worship the place that, by the time I was in high school, he believed that Harvard professors were the wisest men in the history of the world. America could be paradise, if only all high posts in government were filled by Harvard men.

And, as things turned out: When I went to work for the government as a bright young man in Franklin Delano Roosevelt's Department of Agriculture, more and more posts were being filled by Harvard men. That seemed only right to me back then. It seems mildly comical to me now. Not even in prison, as I say, is there anything special about Harvard men.

While I was a student, I sometimes caught the whiff of a promise that, after I graduated, I would be better than average at explaining important matters to people who were slow at catching on. Things did not work out that way.

So there I sat in prison in Nineteen-hundred and Seventy-seven, waiting for the guard to come. I wasn't annoyed at his being an hour late so far. I was in no hurry to go anyplace, had no place in particular to go. The guard's name was Clyde Carter. He was one of the few friends I had made in prison. Our chief bond was that we had taken the same correspondence course in bartending from a diploma mill in Chicago, The Illinois Institute of Instruction, a division of The RAMJAC Corporation. On the same day and in the same mail each of us had received his Doctor of Mixology degree. Clyde had then surpassed me by taking the school's course in air conditioning, as well. Clyde was a third cousin to the President of the United States, Jimmy Carter. He was about five years younger than the President, but was otherwise his perfect spit and image. He had the same nice manners, the same bright smile.

A degree in bartending was enough for me. That was all I intended to do with the rest of my life: tend a quiet bar somewhere, ideally in a club for gentlemen.

And I lifted my old hands from the folded bedding and I clapped three times.

Another fighter plane leaped up from the tip of a nearby runway, tore the sky to shreds. I thought this: "At least I don't smoke anymore." It was true. I, who used to smoke four packages of unfiltered Pall Malls a day, was no longer a slave to King Nicotine. I would soon be reminded of how much I used to smoke, for the gray, pinstripe, three-piece Brooks Brothers suit awaiting me over in the supply room would be riddled with cigarette burns. There was a hole the size of a dime in the crotch, I remembered. A newspaper photograph was taken of me as I sat in the back of the federal marshal's green sedan, right after I was sentenced to prison. It was widely interpreted as showing how ashamed I was, haggard, horrified, unable to look anyone in the eye. It was in fact a photograph of a man who had just set his pants on fire.

I thought now about Sacco and Vanzetti. When I was young, I believed that the story of their martyrdom would cause an irresistible mania for justice to the common people to spread throughout the world. Does anybody know or care who they were anymore?

No.

I thought about the Cuyahoga Massacre, which was the bloodiest single encounter between strikers and an employer in the history of American labor. It happened in Cleveland, in front of the main gate of Cuyahoga Bridge and Iron, on Christmas morning in Eighteen-hundred and Ninety-four. That was long before I was born. My parents were still children in the Russian Empire when it happened. But the man who sent me to Harvard, Alexander Hamilton McCone, watched it from the factory clock tower in the company of his father and his older brother John. That was when he ceased to be a slight stammerer and became, when the least bit anxious about anything, a bubbling booby of totally blocked language instead.

Cuyahoga Bridge and Iron, incidentally, lost its identity, save in labor history, long ago. It was absorbed by Youngstown Steel shortly after the Second World War, and Youngstown Steel itself has now become a mere division of The RAMJAC Corporation.

Peace.

Yes, and I lifted my old hands from the folded bedding, and I clapped three times. Here was what that was all about, as silly as it was: Those three claps completed a rowdy song I had never liked, and which I had not thought about for thirty years or more. I was making my mind as blank as possible, you see, since the past was so embarrassing and the future so terrifying. I had made so many enemies over the years that I doubted that I could even get a job as a bartender somewhere. I would simply get dirtier and raggedier, I thought, since I would have no money coming in from anywhere. I would wind up on Skid Row and learn to keep the cold out by drinking wine, I thought, although I had never liked alcohol.

The worst thing, I thought, was that I would be asleep in an alley in the Bowery, say, and juvenile delinquents who loathed dirty old men would come along with a can of gasoline. They would soak me in it, and they would touch me off. And the worst thing about that, I thought, would be having my eyeballs lapped by flames.

No wonder I craved an empty mind!

But I could achieve mental vacancy only intermittently. Most of the time, as I sat there on the cot, I settled for an only slightly less perfect peace, which was filled with thoughts that need not scare me—about Sacco and Vanzetti, as I say, and about the Cuyahoga Massacre, about playing chess with old Alexander Hamilton McCone, and on and on.

Perfect blankness, when I achieved it, lasted only ten seconds or so—and then it would be wrecked by the song, sung loudly and clearly in my head by an alien voice, which required for its completion that I clap three times. The words were highly offensive to me when I first heard them, which was at a drunken stag party at Harvard during my freshman year. It was a song to be kept secret from women. It may be that no woman has ever heard it, even at this late date. The intent of the lyricist, obviously, was to so coarsen the feelings of males who sang the song that the singers could never believe again what most of us believed with all our hearts back then: that women were more spiritual, more sacred than men.

I still believe that about women. Is that, too, comical? I have loved only four women in my life—my mother, my late wife, a woman to whom I was once affianced, and one other. I will describe them all by and by. Let it be said now, though, that all four seemed more virtuous, braver about life, and closer to the secrets of the universe than I could ever be.

Be that as it may, I will now set down the words to the frightful song. And even though I have been technically responsible, because of my high position in a corporate structure in recent years, for the publication of some of the most scurrilous books about women ever written, I still find myself shrinking from setting on paper, where they have perhaps never been before, the words to the song. The tune to which they were sung, incidentally, was an old one, a tune that I call "Ruben, Ruben." It no doubt has many other names.

Readers of the words should realize, too, that I heard them sung not by middle-aged roughnecks, but by college boys, by children, really, who, with a Great Depression going on and with a Second World War coming, and with most of them mocked by their own virginity, had reason to be petrified of all the things that women of that time would expect of them. Women would expect them to earn good money after they graduated, and they did not see how they could do that, with all the businesses shutting down. Women would expect them to be brave soldiers, and there seemed every chance that they would go to pieces when the shrapnel and bullets flew. Who could be absolutely responsible for his own reactions when the shrapnel and bullets flew? There would be flame throwers and poison gas. There would be terrific bangs. The man standing beside you could have his head blown off—and his throat would be a fountain.

And women, when they became their wives, would expect them to be perfect lovers even on the wedding night—subtle, tender, raffish, respectful, titillatingly debauched, and knowing as much about the reproductive organs of both sexes as Harvard Medical School.

I recall a discussion of a daring magazine article that appeared at that time. It told of the frequency of sexual intercourse by American males in various professions and trades. Firemen were the most ardent, making love ten times a week. College professors were the least ardent, making love once a month. And a classmate of mine, who, as it happened, would actually be killed in the Second World War, shook his head mournfully and said, "Gee—I'd give anything to be a college professor."

The shocking song, then, may really have been a way of honoring the powers of women, of dealing with the fears they inspired. It might properly be compared with a song making fun of lions, sung by lion hunters on a night before a hunt.

The words were these:

> *Sally in the garden,*
> *Sifting cinders,*
> *Lifted up her leg*
> *And farted like a man.*
> *The bursting of her bloomers*
> *Broke sixteen winders.*
> *The cheeks of her ass went—*

Here the singers, in order to complete the stanza, were required to clap three times.

# 2

M Y OFFICIAL TITLE in the Nixon White House, the job I was holding when I was arrested for embezzlement, perjury, and obstruction of justice, was this: the President's special advisor on youth affairs. I was paid thirty-six thousand dollars a year. I had an office, but no secretary, in the subbasement of the Executive Office Building, directly underneath, as it happened, the office where burglaries and other crimes on behalf of President Nixon were planned. I could hear people walking overhead and raising their voices sometimes. On my own level in the subbasement my only companions were heating and air-conditioning equipment and a Coca-Cola machine that only I knew about, I think. I was the only person to patronize that machine.

Yes, and I read college and high-school newspapers and magazines, and *Rolling Stone* and *Crawdaddy*, and anything else that claimed to speak for youth. I catalogued political statements in the words of popular songs. My chief qualification for the job, I thought, was that I myself had been a radical at Harvard, starting in my junior year. Nor had I been a dabbler, a mere parlor pink. I had been cochairman of the Harvard chapter of the Young Communist League. I had been cochairman of a radical weekly paper, *The Bay State Progressive*. I was in fact, openly and proudly, a card-carrying communist until Hitler and Stalin signed a nonaggression pact in Nineteen-hundred and Thirty-nine. Hell and heaven, as I saw it, were making common cause against weakly defended peoples everywhere. After that I became a cautious believer in capitalistic democracy again.

It was once so acceptable in this country to be a communist that my being one did not prevent my winning a Rhodes Scholarship to Oxford after Harvard, and then landing a job in Roosevelt's Department of Agriculture after that. What could be so repulsive after all, during the Great Depression, especially, and with yet another war for natural wealth and markets coming, in a young man's belief that each person could work as well as he or she was able, and should be rewarded, sick or well, young or old, brave or frightened, talented or imbecilic, according to his or her simple needs? How could anyone treat me as a person with a diseased mind if I thought that war need never come again—if only common people everywhere would take control of the planet's wealth, disband their national armies, and forget their national boundaries; if only they would think of themselves ever after as brothers and sisters, yes, and as mothers and fathers, too, and children of all other common people—everywhere. The only person who would be excluded from such friendly and merciful society would be one who took more wealth than he or she needed at any time.

And even now, at the rueful age of sixty-six, I find my knees still turn to water when I encounter anyone who still considers it a possibility that there will one day be one big happy and peaceful family on Earth—the Family of Man. If I were this very day to meet myself as I was in Nineteen-hundred and Thirty-three, I would swoon with pity and respectfulness.

So my idealism did not die even in the Nixon White House, did not die even in prison, did not die even when I became, my most recent employment, a vice-president of the Down Home Records Division of The RAMJAC Corporation.

I still believe that peace and plenty and happiness can be worked out some way. I am a fool.

When I was Richard M. Nixon's special advisor on youth affairs, from Nineteen-hundred and Seventy until my arrest in Nineteen-hundred and Seventy-five, smoking four packs of unfiltered Pall Malls a day, nobody ever asked me for facts or opinions or anything. I need not even have come to work, and I might have spent my time better in helping my poor wife with the little interior-decorating business she ran out of our right little, tight little brick bungalow out in Chevy Chase, Maryland. The only visitors I ever had to my subterranean office, its walls golden-brown with cigarette tars, were the President's special burglars, whose office was above mine. They suddenly realized one day, when I had a coughing fit, that somebody was right below them, and that I might be able to hear their conversations. They performed experiments, with one of them yelling and stamping upstairs, and another one listening in my office. They satisfied themselves at last that I had heard nothing, and was a harmless old poop, in any event. The yeller and stamper was a former Central Intelligence Agency operative, a writer of spy thrillers, and a graduate of Brown University. The listener below was a former agent of the Federal Bureau of Investigation, a former district attorney, and a graduate of Fordham University. I myself, as I may have said already, was a Harvard man.

And this Harvard man, knowing full well that everything he wrote would be shredded and baled with all the rest of the White House wastepaper, unread, still turned out some two hundred or more weekly reports on the sayings and doings of youth, with footnotes, bibliographies, and appendices and all. But the conclusions implied by my materials changed so little over the years that I might as well have simply sent the same telegram each week to limbo. It would have said this:

> YOUNG PEOPLE STILL REFUSE TO SEE THE OBVIOUS IMPOSSIBILITY OF WORLD DISARMAMENT AND ECONOMIC EQUALITY. COULD BE FAULT OF NEW TESTAMENT (QUOD VIDE).
> WALTER F. STARBUCK
> PRESIDENT'S SPECIAL ADVISOR
> ON YOUTH AFFAIRS

At the end of every futile day in the subbasement I would go home to the only wife I have ever had, who was Ruth—waiting for me in our little brick bungalow in Chevy Chase, Maryland. She was Jewish, which I am not. So our only child, a son who is now a book reviewer for *The New York Times*, is half-Jewish. He has further confused racial and religious matters by marrying a black nightclub singer, who has two children by a former husband. The former husband was a nightclub comedian of Puerto Rican extraction named Jerry Cha-cha Rivera, who was shot as an innocent bystander during the robbery of a RAMJAC carwash in Hollywood. My son has adopted the children, so that they are now legally my grandchildren, my only grandchildren.

Life goes on.

My late wife Ruth, the grandmother of these children, was born in Vienna. Her family owned a rare-book store there—before the Nazis took it away from them. She was six years younger than I. Her father and mother and two siblings were killed in concentration camps. She herself was hidden by a Christian family, but was discovered and arrested, along with the head of that family, in Nineteen-hundred and Forty-two. So she herself was in a concentration camp near Munich, finally liberated by American troops, for the last two years of the war. She herself would die in her sleep in Nineteen-hundred and Seventy-four—of congestive heart failure, two weeks before my own arrest. Whither I went, and no matter how clumsily, there did my Ruth go—as long as she could. If I marveled at this out loud, she would say, "Where else could I be? What else could I do?"

She might have been a great translator, for one thing. Languages came so easily to her, as they did not to me. I spent four years in Germany after the Second World War, but never mastered German. But there was no European language that Ruth could not speak at least a little bit. She passed the time in the concentration camp, waiting for death, by getting other prisoners to teach her languages she did not know. Thus did she become fluent in Romany, the tongue of the Gypsies, and even learned the words to some songs in Basque. She might have become a portrait artist. That was another thing she had done in prison: With a finger dipped in lampblack, she had drawn on the walls likenesses of those passing through. She might have been a famous photographer. When she was only sixteen, three years before Germany annexed Austria, she photographed one hundred beggars in Vienna, all of whom were terribly wounded veterans of World War One. These were sold in portfolios, one of which I have found recently, and to my heartbroken amazement, in the collection of New York's Museum of Modern Art. She could also play the piano, whereas I am tone-deaf. I cannot even sing "Sally in the Garden" on key.

I was Ruth's inferior, you might say.

When things started to go really badly for me in the fifties and sixties, when I was unable to get a decent job anywhere, despite all the high posts I had held in government, despite all the important people I knew, it was Ruth who rescued our unpopular little family out in Chevy Chase. She began with two failures, which depressed her at first, but which would later make her laugh so hard that tears streamed from her eyes. Her first failure was as a piano player in a cocktail lounge. The proprietor, when he fired her, told her that she was too good, that his particular clientele ". . . didn't appreciate the finer things in life." Her second failure was as a wedding photographer. There was always an air of prewar doom about her photographs, which no retoucher could eradicate. It was as though the entire wedding party would wind up in the trenches or the gas chambers by and by.

But then she became an interior decorator, beguiling prospective clients with watercolors of rooms she would like to do for them. And I was her clumsy assistant, hanging draperies, holding wallpaper samples against a wall, taking telephone messages from clients, running errands, picking up swatches of this and that—and on and on. I set fire to eleven hundred dollars' worth of blue velvet draperies one time. No wonder my son never respected me.

When did he ever have a chance to?

My God—there his mother was, trying to support the family, and scrimping and saving to get by. And there his unemployed father was, always in the way and helpless, and finally setting fire to a fortune in draperies with a cigarette!

Hooray for a Harvard education! Oh, to be the proud son of a Harvard man!

Ruth was a tiny woman, incidentally—with coppery skin and straight black hair and high cheekbones and deep-set eyes. The first time I laid eyes on her, which was in Nuremberg, Germany, in late August of Nineteen-hundred and Forty-five, she was wearing voluminous army fatigues, and I mistook her for a Gypsy boy. I was a civilian employee of the Defense Department, thirty-two years old. I had never married. I had been a civilian all through the war, often exercising more real power than generals or admirals. Now I was in Nuremberg, ogling the wreckage of war for the first time. I had been sent over to oversee the feeding and housing of the American, British, French, and Russian delegations to the War Crimes Trials. I had previously set up recuperation centers for American soldiers in various resort areas in the United States, so I knew a little something about the hotel trade.

I was to be a dictator to the Germans as far as food and drink and beds were considered. My official vehicle was a white Mercedes touring car, a four-door convertible with a windshield for the backseat as well as the front. It had a siren. It had little sockets on its front fenders for flags. I of course flew American flags. This dreamboat, as young people might call it, had been an anniversary present from Heinrich Himmler, the creator of concentration camps, to his wife in the good old days. Wherever I went, I had an armed chauffeur. My father, remember, had been a millionaire's armed chauffeur.

And I was being driven down the main street, the König-strasse, one August afternoon. The War Crimes Tribunal was meeting in Berlin but was going to move to Nuremberg as soon as I could get things ready there. The street was still blocked by rubble here and there. It was being cleared away by German prisoners of war, who labored, as it happened, under the smoldering gazes of black American military policemen. The American Army was still segregated in those days. Every unit was all black or all white, except for the officers, who were usually white in any case. I do not recall having felt that there was anything odd in this scheme. I knew nothing about black people. There had been no black people on the household staff of the McCone mansion in Cleveland, no black people in my schools. Not even when I was a communist had I had a black person for a friend.

Near Saint Martha's Church on the Königstrasse, which had had its roof burned off by a firebomb, my Mercedes was halted at a security checkpoint. It was manned by white American Military Police. They were looking for people who were not where they were supposed to be, now that civilization was being started up again. They were seeking deserters from every imag-inable army, including the American one, and war criminals not yet apprehended, and lunatics and common criminals, who had simply sauntered from the approaching front lines, and citizens of the Soviet Union, who had defected to the Germans or been captured by them, who would be imprisoned or killed, if they went back home. Russians were supposed, no matter what, to go back to Russia; Poles were supposed to go back to Poland; Hungarians to Hungary; Estonians to Estonia; and on and on. Everybody, no matter what, was supposed to go home.

I was curious as to what sort of interpreters the M.P.'s were using, since I was having trouble finding good ones for my own operations. I particularly needed people who were tri-lingual, who were fluent in both German and English, and in either

French or Russian as well. They also had to be trustworthy, polite, and presentable. So I got out of my car to have a closer look at the interrogations. I discovered that they were being conducted, surprisingly, by a seeming Gypsy boy. It was my Ruth, of course. Her hair had all been cut off at a de-lousing station. She was wearing Army fatigues without any badges of unit or rank. She was beautiful to watch as she tried to elicit a glimmer of understanding from a ragbag of a man, whom the M.P.'s held before her. She must have tried seven or eight languages on him, slipping from one to another as easily as a musician changing tempos and keys. Not only that, but she altered her gestures, too, so that her hands were always doing appropriate dances to each language.

Suddenly, the man's hands were dancing as hers were, and the sounds coming from his mouth were like those she was making. As Ruth would tell me later, he was a Macedonian peasant from southern Yugoslavia. The language they had found in common was Bulgarian. He had been taken prisoner by the Germans, even though he had never been a soldier, and had been sent as a slave laborer to strengthen the forts of the Siegfried Line. He had never learned German. Now he wanted to go to America, he told Ruth, to become a very rich man. He was shipped back to Macedonia, I presume.

Ruth was then twenty-six years old—but she had eaten so badly for seven years, mostly potatoes and turnips, that she was an asexual stick. She herself, it turned out, had come to the roadblock only an hour before I had, and had been pressed into service by the M.P.'s, because of all the languages she knew. I asked an M.P. sergeant how old he thought she was, and he guessed, "Fifteen." He thought she was a boy whose voice had yet to change.

I coaxed her into the backseat of my Mercedes and I questioned her there. I learned that she had been freed from a concentration camp in springtime, about four months before—and had since eluded every agency that might have liked to help her. She should by now have been in a hospital for displaced persons. She was uninterested in ever trusting anybody with her destiny anymore. Her plan was to roam alone and out-of-doors forever, from nowhere to nowhere in a demented sort of religious ecstasy. "No one ever touches me," she said, "and I never touch anyone. I am like a bird in flight. It is so beautiful. There is only God—and me."

I thought this of her: that she resembled gentle Ophelia in *Hamlet*, who became fey and lyrical when life was too cruel to bear. I have a copy of *Hamlet* at hand, and refresh my memory as to the nonsense Ophelia sang when she would no longer respond intelligently to those who asked how she was.

This was the song:

> *How should I your true love know*
> *From another one?*
> *By his cockle hat and staff,*
> *And his sandal shoon.*
> *He is dead and gone, lady,*
> *He is dead and gone;*
> *At his head a grass-green turf,*
> *At his heels a stone —*

And on and on.

Ruth, one of millions of Europe's Ophelias after the Second World War, fainted in my motorcar.

I took her to a twenty-bed hospital in the *Kaiserburg*, the imperial castle, which wasn't even officially operating yet. It was being set up exclusively for persons associated with the War Crimes Trials. The head of it was a Harvard classmate of mine, Dr. Ben Shapiro, who had also been a communist in student days. He was now a lieutenant colonel in the Army Medical Corps. Jews were not numerous at Harvard in my day. There was a strict quota, and a low one, as to how many Jews were let in each year.

"What have we here, Walter?" he said to me in Nuremberg. I was carrying the unconscious Ruth in my arms. She weighed no more than a handkerchief. "It's a girl," I said. "She's breathing. She speaks many languages. She fainted. That's all I know."

He had an idle staff of nurses, cooks, technicians, and so on, and the finest food and medicines that the Army could give him, since he was likely to have high-ranking persons for patients by and by. So Ruth received, and for nothing, the finest care available on the planet. Why? Mostly because, I think, Shapiro and I were both Harvard men.

One year later, more or less, on October fifteenth of Nineteen-hundred and Forty-six, Ruth would become my wife. The War Crimes Trials were over. On the day we were married, and probably conceived our only child as well, *Reichsmarschall* Hermann Göring cheated the hangman by swallowing cyanide.

It was vitamins and minerals and protein and, of course, tender, loving care, that made all the difference to Ruth. After only three weeks in the hospital she was a sane and witty Viennese intellectual. I hired her as my personal interpreter and took her everywhere with me. Through another Harvard acquaintance, a shady colonel in the Quartermaster Corps in Wiesbaden—a black marketeer, I'm sure—I was able to get her a suitable wardrobe, for which, mysteriously, I was never asked to pay anyone. The woolens were from Scotland, the cottons from Egypt—the silks from China, I suppose. The shoes were French—and prewar. One pair, I remember, was alligator, and came with a bag to match. The goods were priceless, since no store in Europe, or in North America, for that matter, had offered anything like them for years. The sizes, moreover, were exactly right for Ruth. These black-market treasures were delivered to my office in cartons claiming to contain mimeograph paper belonging to the Royal Canadian Air Force. Two taciturn young male civilians delivered them in what had once been a *Wehrmacht* ambulance. Ruth guessed that one was Belgian and the other, like my mother, Lithuanian.

My accepting those goods was surely my most corrupt act as a public servant, and my *only* corrupt act—until Watergate. I did it for love.

I began to speak to Ruth of love almost as soon as she got out of the hospital and went to work for me. Her replies were kind and funny and perceptive—but above all pessimistic. She believed, and was entitled to believe, I must say, that all human beings were evil by nature, whether tormentors or victims, or idle standers-by. They could only create meaningless tragedies, she said, since they weren't nearly intelligent enough to accomplish all the good they meant to do. We were a disease, she said, which had evolved on one tiny cinder in the universe, but could spread and spread.

"How can you speak of love to a woman," she asked me early in our courtship, "who feels that it would be just as well if nobody had babies anymore, if the human race did not go on?"

"Because I know you don't really believe that," I replied. "Ruth—look at how full of *life* you are!" It was true. There was no movement or sound she made that was not at least accidentally flirtatious—and what is flirtatiousness but an argument that life must go on and on and on?

What a charmer she was! Oh, I got the credit for how smoothly things ran. My own country gave me a Distinguished Service Medal, and France made me a *chevalier* in the Légion d'honneur, and Great Britain and the Soviet Union sent me letters of commendation and thanks. But it was Ruth who worked all the miracles, who kept each guest in a state of delighted forgivingness, no matter what went wrong.

"How can you dislike life and still be so lively?" I asked her.

"I couldn't have a child, even if I wanted to," she said. "That's how lively I am."

She was wrong about that, of course. She was only guessing. She *would* give birth to a son by and by, a very unpleasant person, who, as I have already said, is now a book reviewer for *The New York Times*.

That conversation with Ruth in Nuremberg went on. We were in Saint Martha's Church, close to where fate had first brought us together. It was not yet operating as a church again. The roof had been put back on—but there was a canvas flap where the rose window used to be. The window and the altar, an old custodian told us, had been demolished by a single cannon shell from a British fighter plane. To him, judging from his solemnity, this was yet another religious miracle. And I must say that I seldom met a male German who was saddened by all the destruction in his own country. It was always the ballistics of whatever had done the wrecking that he wished to talk about.

"There is more to life than having babies, Ruth," I said.

"If I had one, it would be a monster," she said. And it came to pass.

"Never mind babies," I said. "Think of the new era that is being born. The world has learned its lesson at last, at last. The closing chapter to ten thousand years of madness and greed is being written right here and now—in Nuremberg. Books will be written about it. Movies will be made about it. It's the most important turning point in history." I believed it.

"Walter," she said, "sometimes I think you are only eight years old."

"It's the only age to be," I said, "when a new era is being born."

Clocks struck six all over town. A new voice joined the chorus of public chimes and bells. It was in fact an old voice in Nuremberg, but Ruth and I had never heard it before. It was the deep *bonging* of the *Männleinlaufen*, the bizarre clock of the distant *Frauenkirche*. That clock was built more than four hundred years ago. My ancestors, both Lithuanian and Polish, would have been fighting Ivan the Terrible back then.

The visible part of the clock consisted of seven robots, which represented seven fourteenth-century electors. They were designed to circle an eighth robot, which represented the Holy Roman Emperor Charles the Fourth, and to celebrate his exclusion, in Thirteen-hundred and Fifty-six, of the Papacy from the selection of German rulers. The clock had been knocked out by bombing. American soldiers who were clever with machinery had begun on their own time to tinker with it as soon as they occupied the city. Most Germans I had talked to were so demoralized that they did not care if the *Männleinlaufen* never ran again. But it was running again, anyway. Thanks to American ingenuity, the electors were circling Charles the Fourth again.

"Well," said Ruth, when the sounds of the bells had died away, "when you eight-year-olds kill Evil here in Nuremberg, be sure to bury it at a crossroads and drive a stake through its heart—or you just might see it again at the next full mooooooooooooooooooooooooooon."

## 3

**B**UT MY UNFLAGGING OPTIMISM prevailed. Ruth consented at last to marry me, to let me try to make her the happiest of women, despite all the ghastly things that had happened to her so far. She was a virgin, and so very nearly was I, although I was thirty-three—although, roughly speaking, half my life was over.

Oh, to be sure, I had, while in Washington, "made love," as they say, to this woman or that one from time to time. There was a WAC. There was a Navy nurse. There was a stenographer in the Department of Commerce typing pool. But I was fundamentally a fanatical monk in the service of war, war, war. There were many like me. Nothing else in life is nearly so obsessive as war, war, war.

My wedding gift to Ruth was a wood carving commissioned by me. It depicted hands of an old person pressed together in prayer. It was a three-dimensional rendering of a drawing by Albrecht Dürer, a sixteenth-century artist, whose house Ruth and I had visited many times in Nuremberg, during our courting days. That was my invention, so far as I know, having those famous hands on paper rendered in the round. Such hands have since been manufactured by the millions and are staples of dim-witted piety in gift shops everywhere.

Soon after our marriage I was transferred to Wiesbaden, Germany, outside of Frankfurt am Main, where I was placed in charge of a team of civilian engineers, which was winnowing mountains of captured German technical documents for inventions and manufacturing methods and trade secrets American industry might use. It did not matter that I knew no math or chemistry or physics—any more than it had mattered when I went to work for the Department of Agriculture that I had never been near a farm, that I had not even tended a pot of African violets on a windowsill. There was nothing that a humanist could not supervise—or so it was widely believed at the time.

Our son was born by cesarean section in Wiesbaden. Ben Shapiro, who had been my best man, and who had also been transferred to Wiesbaden, delivered the child. He had just been promoted to full colonel. In a few years Senator Joseph R. McCarthy would find that promotion to have been sinister, since it was well known that Shapiro had been a communist before the war. "Who promoted Shapiro to Wiesbaden?" he would want to know.

We named our son Walter F. Starbuck, Jr. Little did we dream that the name would become as onerous as Judas Iscariot, Jr., to the boy. He would seek legal remedy when he turned twenty-one, would have his name changed to Walter F. Stankiewicz, the name that appears over his columns in *The New York Times*. Stankiewicz, of course, was our discarded family name. And I must laugh now, remembering something my father once told me about his arrival at Ellis Island as an immigrant. He was advised that Stankiewicz had unpleasant connotations to American ears, that people would think he smelled bad, even if he sat in a bathtub all day long.

I returned to the United States with my little human family, to Washington, D.C., again, in the autumn of Nineteen-hundred and Forty-nine. My optimism became bricks and mortar and wood and nails. We bought the only house we would ever own, which was the little bungalow in Chevy Chase, Maryland. Ruth put on the mantelpiece the woodcarving of the praying hands by Albrecht Dürer. There were two things that had made her want to buy that house and no other, she said. One was that it had a perfect resting place for the hands. The other was a gnarled old tree that shaded the walk to our doorstep. It was a flowering crab apple tree.

Was she religious? No. She was from a family that was skeptical about all formal forms of worship, which was classified as Jewish by the Nazis. Its members would not have so classified themselves. I asked her once if she had ever sought the consolations of religion in the concentration camp.

"No," she said. "I knew God would never come near such a place. So did the Nazis. That was what made them so hilarious and unafraid. That was the strength of the Nazis," she said. "They understood God better than anyone. They knew how to make Him stay away."

I still ponder a toast Ruth gave one Christmas Eve, in Nineteen-hundred and Seventy-four or so. I was the only person to hear it—the only other person in the bungalow. Our son had not sent us so much as a Christmas card. The toast was this, and I suppose she might just as logically have given it on the day I met her in Nuremberg: "Here's to God Almighty, the laziest man in town."

Strong stuff.

Yes—and my speckled old hands were like the Albrecht Dürer hands atop my folded bedding, as I sat on my prison cot in Georgia, waiting for freedom to begin again.

I was a pauper.

I had emptied my savings account and cashed in my life-insurance policies and sold my Volkswagen and my brick bungalow in Chevy Chase, Maryland, in order to pay for my futile defense.

My lawyers said that I still owed them one hundred and twenty-six thousand dollars. Maybe so. Anything was possible.

Nor did I have glamor to sell. I was the oldest and least celebrated of all the Watergate coconspirators. What made me so uninteresting, I suppose, was that I had had so little power and wealth to lose. Other coconspirators had taken belly-whoppers from the tops of church steeples, so to speak. When I was arrested, I was a man sitting on a three-legged stool in the bottom of a well. All they could do to me was to saw off the legs of my little stool.

Not even I cared. My wife had died two weeks before they took me away, and my son no longer spoke to me. Still—they had to put handcuffs on me. It was the custom.

"Your name?" the police sergeant who booked me had asked.

I was impudent with him. Why not? "Harry Houdini," I replied.

A fighter plane leaped up from the tip of a nearby runway, tore the sky to shreds. It happened all the time.

"At least I don't smoke anymore," I thought.

President Nixon himself commented one time on how much I smoked. It was soon after I came to work for him—in the spring of Nineteen-hundred and Seventy. I was summoned to an emergency meeting about the shooting to death of four antiwar protesters at Kent State University by members of the Ohio National Guard. There were about forty other people at the meeting. President Nixon was at the head of the huge oval table, and I was at the foot. This was the first time I had seen him in person since he was a mere congressman—twenty years before. Until now he had no wish to see his special advisor on youth affairs. As things turned out, he would never want to see me again.

Virgil Greathouse, the secretary of health, education, and welfare, and reputedly one of the President's closest friends, was there. He would begin serving his prison term on the same day I completed mine. Vice-President Spiro T. Agnew was there. He would eventually plead *nolo contendere* to charges of accepting bribes and evading income taxes. Emil Larkin, the President's most vindictive advisor and dreaded hatchet man, was there. He would eventually discover Jesus Christ as his personal Savior as the prosecutors were about to get him for obstruction of justice and perjury. Henry Kissinger was there. He had yet to recommend the carpet-bombing of Hanoi on Christmas Day. Richard M. Helms, head of the C.I.A., was there. He would later be reprimanded for lying under oath to Congress. H.R. Haldeman and John D. Ehrlichman and Charles W. Colson and John N. Mitchell, the attorney general, were there. They, too, would be jailbirds by and by.

I had been up all the previous night, drafting and redrafting my suggestions as to what the President might say about the Kent State tragedy. The guardsmen, I thought, should be pardoned at once, and then reprimanded, and then discharged for the good of the service. The President should then order an investigation of National Guard units everywhere, to discover if such civilians in soldiers' costumes were in fact to be trusted with live ammunition when controlling unarmed crowds. The President should call the tragedy a tragedy, should reveal himself as having had his heart broken. He should declare a day or perhaps a week of national mourning, with flags flown at half-mast everywhere. And the mourning should not be just for those who died at Kent State, but for all Americans who had been killed or crippled in any way, directly or indirectly, by the Vietnam War. He would be more deeply resolved than ever, of course, to press the war to an honorable conclusion.

But I was never asked to speak, nor afterward could I interest anyone in the papers in my hand.

My presence was acknowledged only once, and then only as the butt of a joke by the President. I was so nervous as the meeting wore on that I soon had three cigarettes going all at once, and was in the process of lighting a fourth.

The President himself at last noticed the column of smoke rising from my place, and he stopped all business to stare at me. He had to ask Emil Larkin who I was.

He then gave that unhappy little smile that invariably signaled that he was about to engage in levity. That smile has always looked to me like a rosebud that had just been smashed by a hammer. The joke he made was the only genuinely witty comment I ever heard attributed to him. Perhaps that is my proper place in history—as the butt of the one good joke by Nixon.

"We will pause in our business," he said, "while our special advisor on youth affairs gives us a demonstration of how to put out a campfire."

There was laughter all around.

# 4

A DOOR in the prison dormitory below me opened and banged shut, and I supposed that Clyde Carter had come for me at last. But then the person began to sing "Swing Low, Sweet Chariot" as he clumped up the stairway, and I knew he was Emil Larkin, once President Nixon's hatchet man. This was a big man, goggle-eyed and liver-lipped, who had been a middle linebacker for Michigan State at one time. He was a disbarred lawyer now, and he prayed all day long to what he believed to be Jesus Christ. Larkin had not been sent out on a work detail or assigned any housekeeping task, incidentally, because of what all his praying on hard prison floors had done to him. He was crippled in both legs with housemaid's knee.

He paused at the top of the stairs, and there were tears in his eyes. "Oh, Brother Starbuck," he said, "it hurt so bad and it hurt so good to climb those stairs."

"I'm not surprised," I said.

"Jesus said to me," he went on, "'You have one last chance to ask Brother Starbuck to pray with you, and you've got to forget the pain it will cost you to climb those stairs, because you know what? This time Brother Starbuck is going to bend those proud Harvard knees, and he's going to pray with you.'"

"I'd hate to disappoint Him," I said.

"Have you ever done anything else?" he said. "That's all *I* used to do: disappoint Jesus every day."

I do not mean to sketch this blubbering leviathan as a religious hypocrite, nor am I entitled to. He had so opened himself to the consolations of religion that he had become an imbecile. In my time at the White House I had feared him as much as my ancestors must have feared Ivan the Terrible, but now I could be as impudent as I liked with him. He was no more sensitive to slights and jokes at his expense than a village idiot.

May I say, further, that on this very day Emil Larkin puts his money where his mouth is. A wholly-owned subsidiary of my division here at RAMJAC, Heartland House, a publisher of religious books in Cincinnati, Ohio, published Larkin's autobiography, *Brother, Won't You Pray with Me?*, six weeks ago. All of Larkin's royalties, which could well come to half a million dollars or more, excluding motion-picture and paperback rights, are to go to the Salvation Army.

"Who told you where I was?" I asked him. I was sorry he had found me. I had hoped to get out of prison without his asking me to pray with him one last time.

"Clyde Carter," he said.

This was the guard I had been waiting for, the third cousin to the President of the United States. "Where the heck is he?" I said.

Larkin said that the whole administration of the prison was in an uproar, because Virgil Greathouse, the former secretary of health, education, and welfare and one of the richest men in the country, had suddenly decided to begin serving his sentence immediately, without any further appeals, without any further delay. He was very probably the highest-ranking person any federal prison had ever been asked to contain.

I knew Greathouse mainly by sight—and of course by reputation. He was a famous tough guy, the founder and still majority stockholder in the public relations firm of Greathouse and Smiley, which specialized in putting the most favorable interpretations on the activities of Caribbean and Latin American dictatorships, of Bahamian gambling casinos, of Liberian and Panamanian tanker fleets, of several Central Intelligence Agency fronts around the world, of gangster-dominated unions such as the International Brotherhood of Abrasives and Adhesives Workers and the Amalgamated Fuel Handlers, of international conglomerates such as RAMJAC and Texas Fruit, and on and on.

He was bald. He was jowly. His forehead was wrinkled like a washboard. He had a cold pipe clamped in his teeth, even when he sat on a witness stand. I got close enough to him one time to discover that he made music on that pipe. It was like the twittering of birds. He entered Harvard six years after I graduated, so we never met there. We made eye-contact only once at the White House—at the meeting where I made a fool of myself by lighting so many cigarettes. I was just a little mouse from the White House pantry, as far as he was concerned. He spoke to me only once, and that was after we were both arrested. We came together accidentally in a courthouse corridor, where we were facing separate arraignments. He found out who I was and evidently thought I might have something on him, which I did not. So he put his face close to mine, his eyes twinkling, his pipe in his teeth, and he made me this unforgettable promise: "You say anything about me, Buster, and when you get out of jail you'll be lucky to get a job cleaning toilets in a whorehouse in Port Said."

It was after he said that, that I heard the birdcalls from his pipe.

Greathouse was a Quaker, by the way—and so was Richard M. Nixon, of course. This was surely a special bond between them, one of the things that made them best of friends for a while.

Emil Larkin was a Presbyterian.

I myself was nothing. My father had been secretly baptized a Roman Catholic in Poland, a religion that was suppressed at the time. He grew up to be an agnostic. My mother was baptized a Greek Orthodox in Lithuania, but became a Roman Catholic in Cleveland. Father would never go to church with her. I myself was baptized a Roman Catholic, but aspired to my father's indifference, and quit going to church when I was twelve. When I applied for admission to Harvard, old Mr. McCone, a Baptist, told me to classify myself as a Congregationalist, which I did.

My son is an active Unitarian, I hear. His wife told me that she was a Methodist, but that she sang in an Episcopal Church every Sunday for pay. Why not?

And on and on.

Emil Larkin, the Presbyterian, and Virgil Greathouse, the Quaker, had been thick as thieves back in the good old days. They had not only dominated the burglaries and the illegal wiretaps and the harassment of enemies by the Internal Revenue Service and so on, but the prayer breakfasts, as well. So I asked Larkin now how he felt about the reunion in prospect.

"Virgil Greathouse is no more and no less my brother than you or any other man," he said. "I will try to save him from hell, just as I am now trying to save you from hell." He then quoted the harrowing thing that Jesus, according to Saint Matthew, had promised to say in the Person of God to sinners on Judgment Day.

This is it: "Depart from me, you cursed, into the eternal fire prepared for the devil and his angels."

These words appalled me then, and they appall me now. They are surely the inspiration for the notorious cruelty of Christians.

"Jesus may have said that," I told Larkin, "but it is so unlike most of what else He said that I have to conclude that He was slightly crazy that day."

Larkin stepped back and he cocked his head in mock admiration. "I have seen some rough-tough babies in my time," he said, "but you really take the prize. You've turned every friend you ever had against you, with all your flip-flops through the years, and now you insult the last Person who still might be willing to help you, who is Jesus Christ."

I said nothing. I wished he would go away.

"Name me one friend you've got left," he said.

I thought to myself that Dr. Ben Shapiro, my best man, would have remained my friend, no matter what—might have come for me there at prison in his car and taken me to his home. But that was sentimental speculation on my part. He had gone to Israel long ago and gotten himself killed in the Six Day War. I had heard that there was a primary school named in his honor in Tel Aviv.

"Name one," Emil Larkin persisted.

"Bob Fender," I said. This was the only lifer in the prison, the only American to have been convicted of treason during the Korean War. He was *Doctor* Fender, since he held a degree in veterinary science. He was the chief clerk in the supply room where I would soon be given my civilian clothes. There was always music in the supply room, for Fender was allowed to play records of the French *chanteuse*, Edith Piaf, all day long. He was a science-fiction writer of some note, publishing many stories a year under various pseudonyms, including "Frank X. Barlow" and "Kilgore Trout."

"Bob Fender is everybody's friend and nobody's friend," said Larkin.

"Clyde Carter is my friend," I said.

"I am talking about people on the outside," said Larkin. "Who's waiting outside to help you? Nobody. Not even your own son."

"We'll see," I said.

"You're going to New York?" he said.

"Yes," I said.

"Why New York?" he said.

"It's famous for its hospitality to friendless, penniless immigrants who wish to become millionaires," I said.

"You're going to ask your son for help, even though he's never even written you the whole time you've been here?" he said. He was the mail clerk for my building, so he knew all about my mail.

"If he ever finds out I'm in the same city with him, it will be purely by accident," I said. The last words Walter had ever said to me were at his mother's burial in a small Jewish cemetery in Chevy Chase. That she should be buried in such a place and in such company was entirely my idea—the idea of an old man suddenly all alone. Ruth would have said, correctly, that it was a crazy thing to do.

She was buried in a plain pine box that cost one hundred and fifty-six dollars. Atop that box I placed a bough, broken not cut, from our flowering crab apple tree.

A rabbi prayed over her in Hebrew, a language she had never learned, although she must have had endless opportunities to learn it in the concentration camp.

Our son said this to me, before showing his back to me and the open pit and hastening to a waiting taxicab: "I pity you, but I can never love you. As far as I am concerned, you killed this poor woman. I can't think of you anymore as a father or as any sort of relative. I never want to see or hear of you again."

Strong stuff.

My prison daydream of New York City did suppose, however, that there were still old acquaintances, although I could not name them, who might help me to get a job. It is a hard daydream to let go of—that one has friends. Those who would have remained my friends, if life had gone a little bit better for me, would have been mainly in New York. I imagined that, if I were to prowl midtown Manhattan day after day, from the theater district on the west to the United Nations on the east, and from the Public Library on the south to the Plaza Hotel on the north, and past all the foundations and publishing houses and bookstores and clothiers for gentlemen and clubs for gentlemen and expensive hotels and restaurants in between, I would surely meet somebody who knew me, who remembered what a good man I used to be, who did not especially despise me—who would use his influence to get me a job tending bar somewhere.

I would plead with him shamelessly, and rub his nose in my Doctor of Mixology degree.

If I saw my son coming, so went the daydream, I would show him my back until he was safely by.

"Well," said Larkin, "Jesus tells me not to give up on anybody, but I'm close to giving up on you. You're just going to sit there, staring straight ahead, no matter what I say."

"Afraid so," I said.

"I never saw anybody more determined to be a geek than you are," he said.

A geek, of course, is a man who lies in a cage on a bed of filthy straw in a carnival freak-show and bites the heads off live chickens and makes subhuman noises, and is billed as having been raised by wild animals in the jungles of Borneo. He has sunk as low as a human being can sink in the American social order, except for his final resting place in a potter's field.

Now Larkin, frustrated, let some of his old maliciousness show. "That's what Chuck Colson called you in the White House: 'The Geek,'" he said.

"I'm sure," I said.

"Nixon never respected you," he said. "He just felt sorry for you. That's why he gave you the job."

"I know," I said.

"You didn't even have to come to work," he said.

"I know," I said.

"That's why we gave you the office without any windows and without anybody else around—so you'd catch on that you didn't even have to come to work."

"I tried to be of use anyway," I said. "I hope your Jesus can forgive me for that."

"If you're just going to make fun of Jesus, maybe you better not talk about Him at all," he said.

"Fine," I said. "You brought Him up."

"Do you know when you started to be a geek?" he said.

I knew exactly when the downward dive of my life began, when my wings were broken forever, when I realized that I would never soar again. That event was the most painful subject imaginable to me. I could not bear to think about it yet again, so I said to Larkin, looking him in the eye at last, "In the name of mercy, please leave this poor old man alone."

He was elated. "By golly—I finally got through the thick Harvard hide of Walter F. Starbuck," he said. "I touched a nerve, didn't I?"

"You touched a nerve," I said.

"Now we're getting somewhere," he said.

"I hope not," I said, and I stared at the wall again.

"I was just a little boy in kneepants in Petoskey, Michigan, when I first heard your voice," he said.

"I'm sure," I said.

"It was on the radio. My father made me and my little sister sit by the radio and listen hard. 'You listen hard,' he said. 'You're hearing history made.'"

The year would have been Nineteen-hundred and Forty-nine. I had just returned to Washington with my little human family. We had just moved into our brick bungalow in Chevy Chase, Maryland, with its flowering crab apple tree. It was autumn. There were tart little apples on the tree. My wife Ruth was about to make jelly out of them, as she would do every year. Where was my voice coming from, that it should have been heard by little Emil Larkin in Petoskey? From a committee room in the House of Representatives. With a brutal bouquet of radio microphones before me I was being questioned, principally by a young congressman from California named Richard M. Nixon, about my previous associations with communists, and about my present loyalty to the United States.

Nineteen-hundred and Forty-nine: Will young people of today doubt me if I aver with a straight face that congressional committees convened in treetops then, since saber-toothed tigers still dominated the ground? No. Winston Churchill was still alive. Joseph Stalin was still alive. Think of that. Harry S Truman was President. And the Defense Department had told me, a former communist, to form and head a task force of scientists and military men. Its mission was to propose tactics for ground forces when, as seemed inevitable, small nuclear weapons became available on the battlefield.

The committee wished to know, and especially Mr. Nixon, if a man with my political past was to be trusted with such a sensitive job. Might I hand over our tactical schemes to the Soviet Union? Might I rig the schemes to make them impractical, so that in any battle with the Soviet Union the Soviet Union would surely win?

"You know what I heard on that radio?" said Emil Larkin.

"No," I said—ever so emptily.

"I heard a man do the one thing nobody can ever forgive him for—and I don't care what their politics are. I heard him do the one thing he can't ever forgive himself for, and that was to betray his best friend."

I could not smile then at his description of what he thought he had heard, and I cannot smile at it now—but it was ludicrous all the same. It was an impossibly chowder-headed abridgement of congressional hearings and civil suits and finally a criminal trial, which were spread out over two years. As a little boy listening to the radio, he could only have heard a lot of tedious talk, not much more interesting than static. It was only as a grownup, with a set of ethics based on cowboy movies, that Larkin could have decided that he had heard with utmost clarity the betrayal of a man by his best friend.

"Leland Clewes was never my best friend," I said. This was the name of the man who was ruined by my testimony, and for a while there our last names would be paired in conversations: "Starbuck and Clewes"—like "Gilbert and Sullivan"; like "Sacco and Vanzetti"; like "Laurel and Hardy"; like "Leopold and Loeb."

I don't hear much about us anymore.

Clewes was a Yale man—my age. We first met at Oxford, where I was the coxswain and he was the bowman of a winning crew at Henley. I was short. He was tall. I am still short. He is still tall. We went to work for the Department of Agriculture at the same time and were assigned adjacent cubicles. We played tennis every Sunday morning, when the weather was clement. Those were our salad days, when we were green in judgment.

For a while there we were joint owners of a second-hand Ford Phaeton and often went out together with our girls. Phaeton was the son of Helios, the sun. He borrowed his father's flaming chariot one day and drove it so irresponsibly that parts of northern Africa were turned into deserts. In order to keep the whole planet from being desolated, Zeus had to kill him with a thunderbolt. "Good for Zeus," I say. What choice did he have?

But my friendship with Clewes was never deep and it ended when he took a girl away from me and married her. She was a member of a fine old New England family, which owned the Wyatt Clock Company in Brockton, Massachusetts, among other things. Her brother was my roommate at Harvard in my freshman year, which was how I got to know her. She was one of the four women I have ever truly loved. Sarah Wyatt was her maiden name.

When I accidently ruined him, Leland Clewes and I had not exchanged any sort of greeting for ten years or more. He and his Sarah had a child, a daughter, three years older than mine. He had become the brightest meteor in the State Department, and it was widely conceded that he would be secretary of state some day, and maybe even president. No one in Washington was better-looking and more charming than Leland Clewes.

I ruined him in this way: Under oath, and in reply to a question by Congressman Nixon, I named a number of men who were known to have been communists during the Great Depression, but who had proved themselves to be outstanding patriots during World War Two. On that roll of honor I included the name of Leland Clewes. No particular comment was made about this at the time. It was only when I got home late that afternoon that I learned from my wife, who had been listening to me and then to every news program she could find on the radio, that Leland Clewes had never been connected with communism in any way before.

By the time Ruth put on supper—and we had to eat off a packing case since the bungalow wasn't fully furnished yet—the radio was able to give us Leland Clewes's reply. He wished to appear before Congress at the earliest opportunity, in order to swear under oath that he had never been a communist, had never sympathized with any communist cause. His boss, the secretary of state, another Yale man, was quoted as saying that Leland Clewes was the most patriotic American he had ever known, and that he had proved his loyalty beyond question in negotiations with representatives of the Soviet Union. According to him, Leland Clewes had bested the communists again and again. He suggested that I might still be a communist, and that I might have been given the job of ruining Leland Clewes by my masters.

Two horrible years later Leland Clewes was convicted on six counts of perjury. He became one of the first prisoners to serve his sentence in the then new Federal Minimum Security Adult Correctional Facility on the edge of Finletter Air Force Base— thirty-five miles from Atlanta, Georgia.

Small world.

# 5

ALMOST TWENTY YEARS LATER Richard M. Nixon, having become President of the United States, would suddenly wonder what had become of me. He would almost certainly never have become President, of course, if he had not become a national figure as the discoverer and hounder of the mendacious Leland Clewes. His emissaries would find me, as I say, helping my wife with her decorating business, which she ran out of our little brick bungalow in Chevy Chase, Maryland.

Through them, he would offer me a job.

How did I feel about it? Proud and useful. Richard M. Nixon wasn't merely Richard M. Nixon, after all. He was also the President of the United States of America, a nation I ached to serve again. Should I have refused—on the grounds that America wasn't really my kind of America just then?

Should I have persisted, as a point of honor, in being to all practical purposes a basket case in Chevy Chase instead?

No.

And now Clyde Carter, the prison guard I had been waiting for so long on my cot, came to get me at last. Emil Larkin had by then given up on me and limped away.

"I'm sure sorry, Walter," said Clyde.

"Perfectly all right," I told him. "I'm in no hurry to go anywhere, and there are buses every thirty minutes." Since no one was coming to meet me, I would have to ride an Air Force bus to Atlanta. I would have to stand all the way, I thought, since the buses were always jammed long before they reached the prison stop.

Clyde knew about my son's indifference to my sufferings. Everybody in the prison knew. They also knew he was a book reviewer. Half the inmates, it seemed, were writing memoirs or spy novels or romans à clef, or what have you, so there was a lot of talk about book reviewing, and especially in *The New York Times*.

And Clyde said to me, "Maybe I ain't supposed to say this, but that son of yours ought to be shot for not coming down after his daddy."

"It's all right," I said.

"That's what you say about everything," Clyde complained. "No matter what it is, you say, 'It's all right.'"

"It usually is," I said.

"Them was the last words of Caryl Chessman," he said. "I guess they'll be your last words, too."

Caryl Chessman was a convicted kidnapper and rapist, but not a murderer, who spent twelve years on death row in California. He made all his own appeals for stays of execution, and he learned four languages and wrote two best-selling books before he was put into an airtight tank with windows in it, and made to breathe cyanide gas.

And his last words were indeed, as Clyde said, "It's all right."

"Well now, listen," said Clyde. "When you get yourself a bartending job up there in New York, I just know you're going to wind up owning that bar inside of two years' time." This was kindness on his part, and not genuine optimism. Clyde was trying to help me be brave. "And after you've got the most popular bar in New York," he went on, "I just hope you'll remember Clyde and maybe send for him. I can not only tend bar—I can also fix your air conditioning. By that time I'll be able to fix your locks, too."

I knew he had been considering enrolling in The Illinois Institute of Instruction course in locksmithing. Now, apparently, he had taken the plunge. "So you took the plunge," I said.

"I took the plunge," he said. "Got my first lesson today."

The prison was a hollow square of conventional, two-story military barracks. Clyde and I were crossing the vast parade ground at its center, I with my bedding in my arms. This was where young infantrymen, the glory of their nation, had performed at one time, demonstrating their eagerness to do or die. Now I, too, I thought, had served my country in uniform, had at every moment for two years done precisely what my country asked me to do. It had asked me to suffer. It had not asked me to die.

There were faces at some of the windows—feeble old felons with bad hearts, bad lungs, bad livers, what have you. But there was only one other figure on the parade ground itself. He was dragging a large canvas trash bag after himself as he picked up papers with a spike at the end of a long stick. He was small and old, like me. When he saw us coming, he positioned himself between us and the Administration Building, and he pointed his spike at me, indicating that he had something very important to say to me. He was Dr. Carlo di Sanza, who held a Doctorate in law from the University of Naples. He was a naturalized American citizen and was serving his second term for using the mails to promote a Ponzi scheme. He was ferociously patriotic.

"You are going home?" he said.

"Yes," I said.

"Don't ever forget one thing," he said. "No matter what this country does to you, it is still the greatest country in the world. Can you remember that?"

"Yes, sir—I think I can," I said.

"You were a fool to have been a communist," he said.

"That was a long time ago," I said.

"There are no opportunities in a communist country," he said. "Why would you want to live in a country with no opportunities?"

"It was a youthful mistake, sir," I said.

"In America I have been a millionaire two times," he said, "and I will be a millionaire again."

"I'm sure of it," I said, and I was. He would simply start up his third Ponzi scheme—consisting, as before, of offering fools enormous rates of interest for the use of their money. As before, he would use most of the money to buy himself mansions and Rolls-Royces and speedboats and so on, but returning part of it as the high interest he had promised. More and more people would come to him, having heard of him from gloatingly satisfied recipients of his interest checks, and he would use their money to write more interest checks—and on and on.

I am now convinced that Dr. di Sanza's greatest strength was his utter stupidity. He was such a successful swindler because he himself could not, even after two convictions, understand what was inevitably catastrophic about a Ponzi scheme.

"I have made many people happy and rich," he said. "Have you done that?"

"No, sir—not yet," I said. "But it's never too late to try."

I am now moved to suppose, with my primitive understanding of economics, that every successful government is of necessity a Ponzi scheme. It accepts enormous loans that can never be repaid. How else am I to explain to my polyglot grandchildren what the United States was like in the nineteen-thirties, when its owners and politicians could not find ways for so many of its people to earn even the most basic necessities, like food and clothes and fuel. It was pure hell to get shoes!

And then, suddenly, there were formerly poor people in officers' clubs, beautifully costumed and ordering filets mignon and champagne. There were formerly poor people in enlisted men's clubs, serviceably costumed and clad and ordering hamburgers and beer. A man who two years before had patched the holes in his shoes with cardboard suddenly had a Jeep or a truck or an airplane or a boat, and unlimited supplies of fuel and ammunition. He was given glasses and bridgework, if he needed them, and he was immunized against every imaginable disease. No matter where he was on the planet, a way was found to get hot turkey and cranberry sauce to him on Thanksgiving and Christmas.

What had happened?

What could have happened but a Ponzi scheme?

When Dr. Carlo di Sanza stepped aside and let Clyde and me go on, Clyde began to curse himself for his own lack of large-scale vision. "Bartender, air-conditioner repairman, locksmith—prison guard," he said. "What's the matter with me that I think so small?"

He spoke of his long association with white-collar criminals, and he told me one conclusion he had drawn: "Successful folks in this country never think about little things."

"Successful?" I said incredulously. "You're talking about convicted felons, for heaven's sake!"

"Oh, sure," he said, "but most of them have plenty of money still stashed away somewheres. Even if they don't, they know how to get plenty more. Everbody does just fine when they get out of here."

"Remember me as a striking exception," I said. "My wife had to support me for most of my married life."

"You had a million dollars one time," he said. "I'll never see a million dollars, if I live a million years." He was speaking of the *corpus delecti* of my Watergate crime, which was an old-fashioned steamer trunk containing one million dollars in unmarked and circulated twenty-dollar bills. It was an illegal campaign contribution. It became necessary to hide it when the contents of all White House safes were to be examined by the Federal Bureau of Investigation and men from the Office of the Special Prosecutor. My obscure office in the subbasement was selected as the most promising hiding place. I acquiesced.

Somewhere in there my wife died.

And then the trunk was found. The police came for me. I knew the people who brought the trunk to my office, and under whose orders they were operating. They were all high-ranking people, some of them laboring like common stevedores. I would not tell the court or my own lawyers or anyone who they were. Thus did I go to prison for a while.

I had learned this much from my mutual disaster with Leland Clewes: It was sickening to send another poor fool to prison. There was nothing quite like sworn testimony to make life look trivial and mean ever after.

Also: My wife had just died. I could not care what happened next. I was a zombie.

Even now I will not name the malefactors with the trunk. It does not matter.

I cannot, however, withhold from American history what one of the malefactors said after the trunk was set down in my office. This was it: "Whose dumb fucking idea was it to bring this shit to the White House?"

"People like you," said Clyde Carter, "find yourselves around millions of dollars all the time. If I'd of went to Harvard, maybe I would, too."

We were hearing music now. We were nearing the supply room, and it was coming from a phonograph in there. Edith Piaf was singing *"Non, Je ne Regrette Rien."* This means, of course, "No, I am not sorry about anything."

The song ended just as Clyde and I entered the supply room, so that Dr. Robert Fender, the supply clerk and lifer, could tell us passionately how much he agreed with the song. *"Non!"* he said, his teeth gnashing, his eyes blazing, *"je ne regrette rien! Rien!"*

This was, as I have already said, a veterinarian and the only American to have been convicted of treason during the Korean War. He could have been shot for what he did, since he was then a first lieutenant in the United States Army, serving in Japan and inspecting meat on its way to the troops in Korea. As a gesture of mercy, his court-martial sentenced him to life imprisonment with no chance of parole.

This American traitor bore a strong resemblance to a great American hero, Charles Augustus Lindbergh. He was tall and big-boned. He had Scandinavian blood. He was a farm boy. He was fairly fluent in a weepy sort of French from having listened to Edith Piaf for so long. He had actually been almost nowhere outside of prison but Ames, Iowa, and Osaka, Japan. He was so shy with women, he told me one time, that he was still a virgin when he reached Osaka. And then he fell crashingly in love with a female nightclub singer who passed herself off as Japanese and sang word-for-word imitations of Edith Piaf records. She was also a spy for North Korea.

"My dear friend, my dear Walter Starbuck," he said, "and how has this day gone for you so far?"

So I told him about sitting on the cot and having the same song run through my head again and again, about Sally in the garden, sifting cinders.

He laughed. He has since put me and the incident into a science fiction story of his, which I am proud to say is appearing this very month in *Playboy*, a RAMJAC magazine. The author is ostensibly Frank X. Barlow. The story is about a former judge on the planet Vicuna, two and a half galaxies away from Earth, who has had to leave his body behind and whose soul goes flying through space, looking for a habitable planet and a new body to occupy. He finds that the universe is virtually lifeless, but he comes at last to Earth and makes his first landing in the enlisted men's parking lot of Finletter Air Force Base—thirty-five miles from Atlanta, Georgia. He can enter any body he likes through its ear, and ride around inside. He wants a body so he can have some sort of social life. A soul without a body, according to the story, can't have any social life—because nobody can see it, and it can't touch anybody or make any noise.

The judge thinks he can leave a body again, any time he finds it or its destiny uncongenial. Little does he dream that the chemistries of Earthlings and Vicunians are such that, once he enters a body, he is going to be stuck inside forever. The story includes a little essay on glues previously known on Earth, and says that the strongest of these was the one that sticks mature barnacles to boulders or boats or pilings, or whatever.

"When they are very young," Dr. Fender writes in the persona of Frank X. Barlow, "barnacles can drift or creep whence-so-ever they hanker, anywhere in the seven seas and the brackish estuaries thereof. Their upper bodies are encased in cone-shaped armor. Their little tootsies dangle from the cones like clappers from dinnerbells.

"But there comes a time for every barnacle, at childhood's end, when the rim of its cone secretes a glue that will stick forever to whatever it happens to touch next. So it is no casual thing on Earth to say to a pubescent barnacle or to a homeless soul from Vicuna, 'Sit thee doon, sit thee doon.'"

The judge from Vicuna in the story tells us the way the people on his native planet said "hello" and "good-bye," and "please" and "thank you," too. It was this: "ting-a-ling." He says that back on Vicuna the people could don and doff their bodies as easily as Earthlings could change their clothing. When they were outside their bodies, they were weightless, transparent, silent awarenesses and sensibilities. They had no musical instruments on Vicuna, he said, since the people themselves were music when they floated around without their bodies. Clarinets and harps and pianos and so on would have been redundant, would have been machinery for making clumsy counterfeits of airborne souls.

But they ran out of time on Vicuna, he says. The tragedy of the planet was that its scientists found ways to extract time from topsoil and the oceans and the atmosphere—to heat their homes and power their speedboats and fertilize their crops with it; to eat it; to make clothes out of it; and so on. They served time at every meal, fed it to household pets, just to demonstrate how rich and clever they were. They allowed great gobbets of it to putrefy to oblivion in their overflowing garbage cans.

"On Vicuna," says the judge, "we lived as though there were no tomorrow."

The patriotic bonfires of time were the worst, he says. When he was an infant, his parents held him up to coo and gurgle with delight as a million years of future were put to the torch in honor of the birthday of the queen. But by the time he was fifty, only a few weeks of future remained. Great rips in reality were appearing everywhere. People could walk through walls. His own speedboat became nothing more than a steering wheel. Holes appeared in vacant lots where children were playing, and the children fell in.

So all the Vicunians had to get out of their bodies and sail out into space without further ado. "Ting-a-ling," they said to Vicuna.

"Chronological anomalies and gravitational thunderstorms and magnetic whirlpools tore the Vicunian families apart in space," the story goes on, "scattered them far and wide." The judge manages to stay with his formerly beautiful daughter for a while. She isn't beautiful anymore, of course, because she no longer has a body. She finally loses heart, because every planet or moon they come to is so lifeless. Her father, having no way to restrain her, watches helplessly as she enters a crack in a rock and becomes its soul. Ironically, she does this on the moon of Earth, with that most teeming of all planets only two hundred and thirty-nine thousand miles away!

Before he actually lands at the Air Force base, though, he falls in with a flock of turkey buzzards. He wheels and soars with them and almost enters the ear of one. For all he knows about the social situation on Earth, these carrion eaters may be members of the ruling class.

He decides that lives led at the center of the Air Force base are too busy, too unreflective for him, so he goes up in the air again and spots a much more quiet cluster of buildings, which he thinks may be a meditation center for philosophers. He has no way of recognizing the place as a minimum security prison for white-collar criminals, since there were no such institutions back on Vicuna.

Back on Vicuna, he says, convicted white-collar criminals, defilers of trustingness, had their ears plugged up, so their souls couldn't get out. Then their bodies were put into artificial ponds filled with excrement—up to their necks. Then deputy sheriffs drove high-powered speedboats at their heads.

The judge says he himself sentenced hundreds of people to this particular punishment and that the felons invariably argued that they had not broken the law, but merely violated its spirit, perhaps, just the least little bit. Before he condemned them, he would put a sort of chamberpot over his head, to make his words more resonant and awesome, and he would pronounce this formula: "Boys, you didn't just get the spirit of the law. You got its body and soul this time."

And, according to the judge, you could hear the deputies warming up their speedboats on the pond outside the court-house: *"vrooom-ah, vrooom-a, va-va-va-roooooooooooooooooooooooo-oooooooooooom!"*

# 6

THE JUDGE in Dr. Bob Fender's story tries to guess which of the philosophers in the meditation center is the wisest and most contented. He decides that it is a little old man sitting on a cot in a second-story dormitory. Every so often that little old man is so delighted with his thoughts, evidently, that he claps three times.

So the judge flies into the ear of that little old man and immediately sticks to him forever, sticks to him, according to the story ". . . as tightly as Formica to an epoxy-coated countertop." And what does he hear in that little old man's head but this:

> *Sally in the garden,*
> *Sifting cinders,*
> *Lifted up her leg*
> *And farted like a man . . .*

And so on.

It is quite an interesting story. There is a rescue of the daughter who has become the soul of a moon rock, and so on. But the true story of how its author came to commit treason in Osaka is a match for it, in my opinion, any day. Bob Fender fell in love with the North Korean agent, the Edith Piaf imitator, from a distance of about twenty feet, in a nightclub frequented by American officers. He never dared close the distance or to send her flowers or a note, but night after night he mooned at her from the same table. He was always alone and usually the biggest man by far in the club, so the singer, whose stage name was simply "Izumi," asked some of the other Americans who and what Fender was.

He was a virgin meat inspector, but his fellow officers had fun telling Izumi that he was so solitary and gloomy all the time because his work was so secret and important. They said he was in command of an elite unit that guarded atomic bombs. If she asked him about it, they said, he would claim to be a meat inspector.

So Izumi went to work on him. She sat down at his table without being asked. She reached inside his shirt and tickled his nipples and all that. She told him that she liked big, silent men, and that all other Americans talked too much. She begged him to take her home with him after the club closed at two o'clock that morning. She wanted to find out where the atomic bombs were, of course. Actually, there weren't any atomic bombs in Japan. They were on aircraft carriers and on Okinawa, and so on. For the rest of the evening she sang all her songs directly to him and to nobody else. He nearly fainted from joy and embarrassment. He had a Jeep outside.

When she got into his Jeep at two o'clock in the morning, she said she not only wanted to see where her big American lived, but where he worked. He told her that would be easy, since he lived and worked at the same place. He took her down to a new United States Army Quartermaster Corps dock in Osaka, which had a big shed running down the middle of it. At one end were some offices. At the other end was a two-room apartment for whoever the resident veterinarian happened to be. In between were great, refrigerated meat lockers, filled with carcasses Fender had inspected or would inspect. There was a fence on the land side and a guard at the gate; but as came out at the court-martial, discipline was lax. All the guard thought he had to watch out for was people trying to sneak out with sides of beef.

So the guard, who would later be acquitted by a court-martial, simply waved Dr. Fender's Jeep inside. He did not notice that there was an unauthorized woman lying on the floor.

Izumi asked to look inside some of the meat lockers, which Bob was more than glad to show her. By the time they reached his apartment, which was at the outer end of the dock, she realized that he really was nothing but a meat inspector.

"But she was so nice," Fender told me one time, "and I was so nice, if I may say so, that she stayed for the night, anyway. I was scared to death, naturally, since I had never made love before. But then I said to myself, 'Just wait a minute. Just calm down. You have always been good with every kind of animal, practically from the minute you were born. Just keep one thing in mind: You've got another nice little animal here.'"

As came out at Fender's court-martial: He and other members of the Army Veterinary Corps looked like soldiers, but they had not been trained to think like soldiers. It seemed unnecessary, since all they did anymore was inspect meat. The last veterinarian to be involved in any sort of fighting, it turned out, died at the Little Bighorn, at Custer's Last Stand. Also: There was a tendency on the part of the Army to coddle veterinarians, since they were so hard to recruit. They could make fortunes on the outside—especially in cities, looking after people's pets. This was why they gave Fender such a pleasant, private apartment on the end of a dock. He inspected meat. As long as he did that, nobody was going to think of inspecting *him*.

"If they had inspected my apartment," he told me, "they would not have found a speck of dust anywhere." They would also have found, according to him, "one of the best private collections of Japanese pottery and fabrics in Osaka." He had gone berserk for the subtlety and delicacy of all things Japanese. This art mania was surely an apology, among other things, for his own huge and—to him—ugly and useless hands and feet and all.

"Izumi kept looking back and forth between me and the beautiful things on my shelves and walls—in my cupboards, in my drawers," he told me one time. "If you could have seen her expressions change when she did that," he said, "you would have to agree with me when I say, even though it's a very conceited thing for me to say: She fell in love with me."

He made breakfast the next morning, all with Japanese utensils, although it was an American breakfast—bacon and eggs. She stayed curled up in bed while he cooked. She reminded him of the young deer, a doe he had raised when a boy. It was not a new thought. He had been taking care of that doe all night. He turned on his radio, which was tuned to the Armed Forces Network. He hoped for music. He got news instead. The biggest news was that a North Korean spy ring had been rounded up in Osaka in the wee hours of the morning. Their radio transmitter had been found. Only one member of the ring was still being hunted, and that was the woman who called herself "Izumi."

Fender, by his own account, had ". . . entered an alternate universe by then." He felt so much more at home in the new one than in the old one, simply because he was paired now with a woman, that he wasn't going to return to the old one ever again.

What Izumi told him about her loyalty to the communist cause did not sound like enemy talk to him. "It was just common sense on the part of a good person from an alternate universe," he said.

So he hid her and fed her for eleven days, being careful not to neglect his duties. On the twelfth day he was so disoriented and innocent as to ask a sailor from a ship from New Zealand, which was unloading beef, if for a thousand dollars he would take a young woman on board and away from Japan. The sailor reported this to his captain, who passed it on to American authorities. Fender and Izumi were promptly arrested, separated, and would never see each other again.

Fender was never able to find out what became of her. She vanished. The most believable rumor was that she had been turned over illegally to South Korean agents, who took her to Seoul—where she was shot without trial.

Fender regretted nothing he had done.

Now he was holding up the pants of my civilian suit, a gray, pinstripe Brooks Brothers suit, for me to see. He asked me if I remembered the large cigarette hole there had been in the crotch.

"Yes," I said.

"Find it," he said.

I could not. Nor could I find any other holes in the suit. At his own expense he had sent the suit to an invisible mender in Atlanta. "That, dear Walter," he said, "is my going-away present to you."

Almost everybody, I knew, got a going-away present from Fender. He had little else to do with all the money he made from his science-fiction tales. But the mending of my suit was by far the most personal and thoughtful one I had ever heard of. I choked up. I could have cried. I told him so.

Before he could make a reply, there were shouts and the thunder of scampering feet in offices in the front of the building—offices whose windows faced the four-lane divided highway outside. It was believed that Virgil Greathouse, the former secretary of health, education, and welfare, had arrived out front. It was a false alarm.

Clyde Carter and Dr. Fender ran out into the reception area, so that they could see, too. There were no locked doors

anywhere in the prison. Fender could have kept right on running outside, if he wanted to. Clyde didn't have a gun, and neither did any of the other guards. If Fender had made a break for
it, maybe somebody would have tried to tackle him; but I doubt
it. It would have been the first attempted escape from the prison
in its twenty-six-year history, and nobody would have had any
clear idea as to what to do.

I was incurious about the arrival of Virgil Greathouse. His
arrival, like the arrival of any new prisoner, would be a public
execution of sorts. I did not want to watch him or anybody
become less than a man. So I was all alone in the supply room.
I was grateful for the accident of privacy. I took advantage of
it. I performed what was perhaps the most obscenely intimate
physical act of my life. I gave birth to a broken, querulous little
old man by doing this: by putting on my civilian clothes.

There were white broadcloth underpants and calf-length,
ribbed black socks from the Tally-ho Gentleman's Shop in
Chevy Chase. There was a white Arrow shirt from Garfinck-
el's Department Store in Washington. There was the Brooks
Brothers suit from New York City, and a regimental-stripe tie
and black shoes from there, too. The laces on both shoes were
broken and mended with square knots. Fender obviously had
not taken a close look at them, or there would have been new
laces in those shoes.

The necktie was the most antique item. I had actually worn it
during the Second World War. Imagine that. An Englishman
I was working with on medical supply schemes for the D-Day
landings told me that the tie identified me as an officer in the
Royal Welsh Fusiliers.

"You were wiped out in the Second Battle of the Somme in
the First World War," he said, "and now, in this show, you've
been wiped out again at El Alamein. You might say, 'Not the
luckiest regiment in the world.'"

The stripe scheme is this: A broad band of pale blue is
bordered by a narrow band of forest-green above and orange
below. I am wearing that tie on this very day, as I sit here in my
office in the Down Home Records Division of The RAMJAC
Corporation.

When Clyde Carter and Dr. Fender returned to the supply
room, I was a civilian again. I felt as dazed and shy and

tremble-legged as any other newborn creature. I did not yet know what I looked like. There was one full-length mirror in the supply room, but its face was turned to the wall. Fender always turned it to the wall when a new arrival was expected. This was another example of Fender's delicacy. The new arrival, if he did not wish to, did not have to see at once how he had been transformed by a prison uniform.

Clyde's and Fender's faces, however, were mirrors enough to tell me that I was something less than a gay *boulevardier* on the order of, say, the late Maurice Chevalier. They were quick to cover their pity with horseplay; but not quick enough.

Fender pretended to be my valet in an embassy somewhere. "Good morning, Mr. Ambassador. Another crisp and bright day," he said. "The queen is expecting you for lunch at one."

Clyde said that it sure was easy to spot a Harvard man, that they all had that certain something. But neither friend made a move to turn the mirror around, so I did it myself.

Here is who I saw reflected: a scrawny old janitor of Slavic extraction. He was unused to wearing a suit and a tie. His shirt collar was much too large for him, and so was his suit, which fit him like a circus tent. He looked unhappy—on his way to a relative's funeral, perhaps. At no point was there any harmony between himself and the suit. He may have found his clothes in a rich man's ash can.

Peace.

I SAT NOW on an unsheltered park bench by the highway in front of the prison. I was waiting for the bus. I had beside me a tan canvas-and-leather suitcase designed for Army officers. It had been my constant companion in Europe during my glory days. Draped over it was an old trenchcoat, also from my glory days. I was all alone. The bus was late. Every so often I would pat the pockets of my suitcoat, making sure that I had my release papers, my government voucher for a one-way, tourist-class flight from Atlanta to New York City, my money, and my Doctor of Mixology degree. The sun beat down on me.

I had three hundred and twelve dollars and eleven cents. Two hundred and fifty of that was in the form of a government check, which could not easily be stolen from me. It was all my own money. After all the meticulous adding and subtracting that had gone on relative to my assets since my arrest, that much, to the penny, was incontrovertibly mine: three hundred and twelve dollars and eleven cents.

So here I was going out into the Free Enterprise System again. Here I was cut loose from the protection and nurture of the federal government again.

The last time this had happened to me was in Nineteen-hundred and Fifty-three, two years after Leland Clewes went to prison for perjury. Dozens of other witnesses had been found to testify against him by then—and more damagingly, too. All I had ever accused him of was membership in the Communist Party before the war, which I would have thought was about as damning for a member of the Depression generation as having stood in a breadline. But others were willing to swear that Clewes had continued to be a communist throughout the war, and had passed secret information to agents of the Soviet Union. I was flabbergasted.

That was certainly news to me, and may not even have been true. The most I had wanted from Clewes was an admission that I had told the truth about something that really didn't matter much. God knows I did not want to see him ruined and sent to jail. And the most I expected for myself was that I would be sorry for the rest of my life, would never feel quite right about myself ever again, because of what I had accidentally done to him. Otherwise, I thought, life could be expected to go on much as before.

True: I had been transferred to a less-sensitive job in the Defense Department, tabulating the likes and dislikes of soldiers of various major American races and religions, and from various educational and economic backgrounds, for various sorts of field rations, some of them new and experimental. Work of that sort, now done brainlessly and eyelessly and handlessly and at the speed of light by computers, was still being done largely by hand in those days. I and my staff now seem as archaic to me as Christian monks illuminating manuscripts with paintbrushes and gold leaf and quills.

And true: People who dealt with me at work, both inferiors and superiors, became more formal, more coldly correct, when dealing with me. They had no time anymore, seemingly, for jokes, for stories about the war. Every conversation was *schnip-schnap!* Then it was time to get back to work. I ascribed this at the time, and even told my poor wife that I admired it, to the spirit of the new, lean, keen, highly mobile and thoroughly professional Armed Forces we were shaping. They were to be a thunderbolt with which we could vaporize any new, would-be Hitler, anywhere in the world. No sooner had the people of a country lost their freedom, than the United States of America would arrive to give it back again.

And true: Ruth's and my social life was somewhat less vivid than the one I had promised her in Nuremberg. I had projected for her a telephone in our home that would never stop ringing, with old comrades of mine on the other end. They would want to eat and drink and talk all night. They would be in the primes of their lives in government service, in their late thirties or early forties, like me—so able and experienced and diplomatic and clever, and at bottom as hard as nails, that they would be the real heads and the guts of their organizations, no matter where in the hierarchy they were supposed to be. I promised Ruth that they would be blowing in from big jobs in Moscow, in Tokyo, in her home town in Vienna, in Jakarta and Timbuktu, and God knows where. What tales they would have to tell us about the world, about what was *really* going on! We would laugh and have another drink, and so on. And local people, of course, would importune us for our colorful, cosmopolitan company and for our inside information as well.

Ruth said that it was perfectly all right that our telephone did not ring—that, if it weren't for the fact that my job required me to be available at all hours of the night or day, she would rather not have a telephone in the house. As for conversations with supposedly well-informed people long into the night, she said she hated to stay up past ten o'clock, and that in the concentration camp she had heard enough supposedly inside information to last her for the rest of her days, and then some. "I am not one of those people, Walter," she said, "who finds it necessary to always know, supposedly, what is really going on."

It may be that Ruth protected herself from dread of the gathering storm, or, more accurately, from dread of the gathering silence, by reverting during the daytime, when I was at work, to the Ophelia-like elation she had felt after her liberation—when she had thought of herself as a bird all alone with God. She did not neglect the boy, who was five when Leland Clewes went to prison. He was always clean and well-fed. She did not take to secret drinking. She did, however, start to eat a lot.

And this brings me to the subject of body sizes again, something I am very reluctant to discuss—because I don't want to give them more importance than they deserve. Body sizes can be remarkable for their variations from accepted norms, but still explain almost nothing about the lives led inside those bodies. I am small enough to have been a coxswain, as I have already confessed. That explains nothing. And, by the time Leland Clewes came to trial for perjury, my wife, although only five feet tall, weighed one hundred and sixty pounds or so.

So be it.

Except for this: Our son very early on concluded that his notorious little father and his fat, foreign mother were such social handicaps to him that he actually told several playmates in the neighborhood that he was an adopted child. A neighbor woman invited my wife over for coffee during the daytime exactly once, and with this purpose: to discover if we knew who the boy's real parents were.

Peace.

So a decent interval went by after Leland Clewes was sent to prison, two years, as I say—and then I was called into the office of Assistant Secretary of the Army Shelton Walker. We had never met. He had never been in government service before. He was my age. He had been in the war and had risen to the rank of major in the Field Artillery and had made the landings in North Africa and then, on D-Day, in France. But he was essentially an Oklahoma businessman. Someone would tell me later that he owned the largest tire distributorship in the state. More startlingly to me: He was a Republican, for General of the Armies Dwight David Eisenhower had now become President—the first Republican to hold that office in twenty years.

Mr. Walker wished to express, he said, the gratitude that the whole country should feel for my years of faithful service in both war and peace. He said that I had executive skills that would surely have been more lavishly rewarded if I had employed them in private industry. An economy drive was underway, he said, and the post I held was to be terminated. Many other posts were being terminated, so that he was unable to move me somewhere else, as much as he might have liked to do so. I was fired, in short. I am unable to say even now whether he was being unkind or not when he said to me, rising and extending his hand, "You can now sell your considerable skills, Mr. Starbuck, for their true value in the open marketplace of the Free Enterprise System. Happy hunting! Good luck!"

What did I know about Free Enterprise? I know a great deal about it now, but I knew nothing about it then. I knew so little about it then that I was able to imagine for several months that private industry really would pay a lot for an all-purpose executive like me. I told my poor wife during those first months of unemployment that, yes, that was certainly an option we held, in case all else failed: that I could at any time raise my arms like a man crucified, so to speak, and fall backward into General Motors or General Electric or some such thing. A measure of the kindness of this woman to me: She never asked me why I didn't do that immediately if it was so easy—never asked me to explain why, exactly, I felt that there was something silly and not quite gentlemanly about private industry.

"We may have to be rich, even though we don't want to be," I remember telling her somewhere in there. My son was six by then, and listening—and old enough, surely, to ponder such a paradox. Could it have made any sense to him? No.

Meanwhile, I visited and telephoned acquaintances in other departments, making light of being "temporarily at liberty," as out-of-work actors say. I might have been a man with a comical injury, like a black eye or a broken big toe. Also: All my old acquaintances were Democrats like myself, allowing me to present myself as a victim of Republican stupidity and vengefulness.

But, alas, whereas life for me had been so long a sort of Virginia reel, as friends handed me on from job to job, no one could now think of a vacant post anywhere. Vacancies had suddenly become as extinct as dodo birds.

Too bad.

But the old comrades behaved so naturally and politely toward me that I could not say even now that I was being punished for what I had done to Leland Clewes—if I had not at last appealed for help to an arrogant old man outside of government, who, to my shock, was perfectly willing to show the disgust he felt for me, and to explain it in detail. He was Timothy Beame. He had been an assistant secretary of agriculture under Roosevelt before the war. He had offered me my first job in government. He, too, was a Harvard man and former Rhodes Scholar. Now he was seventy-four years old and the active head of Beame, Mearns, Weld and Weld, the most prestigious law firm in Washington.

I asked him on the telephone if he would have lunch with me. He declined. Most people declined to have lunch with me. He said he could see me for half an hour late that afternoon, but that he could not imagine what we might have to talk about.

"Frankly, sir," I said, "I'm looking for work—possibly with a foundation or a museum. Something like that."

"Ohhhhhhhhhhhhhh—looking for work, are we?" he said. "Yes—that we should talk about. Come in, by all means. How many years is it now since we've had a good talk?"

"Thirteen years, sir," I said.

"A lot of water goes over the old dam in thirteen years."

"Yes, sir," I said.

"Ta-ta," he said.

I was fool enough to keep the appointment.

His reception of me was elaborately hearty and false from the first. He introduced me to his young male secretary, told him what a promising young man I had been, clapping me on the back all the time. This was a man who may never have clapped anyone on the back in his life before.

When we got into his paneled office, Timothy Beame directed me to a leather club chair, saying, "Sit thee doon, sit thee doon." I have recently come across that same supposedly humorous expression, of course, in Dr. Bob Fender's science-fiction story about the judge from Vicuna, who got stuck forever to me and my destiny. Again: I doubt if Timothy Beame had ever addressed such an inane locution to anyone ever before. This was a bunchy, shaggy old man, incidentally—accidentally majestic as I was accidentally small. His great hands suggested that he had swung a mighty broadsword long ago, and that they were fumbling for truth and justice now. His white brows were an unbroken thicket from one side to the other, and after he had seated himself at his desk, he dipped his head forward so as to peer at me and speak to me through that hedge.

"I needn't ask what you've been up to lately," he said.

"No, sir—I guess not," I said.

"You and young Clewes have managed to make yourselves as famous as Mutt and Jeff," he said.

"To our sorrow," I said.

"I would hope so. I would certainly hope that there was much sorrow there," he said.

This was a man who, as it turned out, had only about two more months to live. He had had no hint of that, so far as I know. It was said, after he died, that he would surely have been named to the Supreme Court, if only he had managed to live until the election of another Democrat to the presidency.

"If you are truly sorrowful," he went on, "I hope you know what it is you are mourning, exactly."

"Sir—?" I said.

"You thought only you and Clewes were involved?" he said.

"Yes, sir," I said. "And our wives, of course." I meant it.

He gave a mighty groan. "That is the one thing you should not have said to me," he said.

"Sir—?" I said.

"You ninny, you Harvard abortion, you incomparably third-rate little horse's ass," he said, and he arose from his chair. "You and Clewes have destroyed the good reputation of the most unselfish and intelligent generation of public servants this country has ever known! My God—who can care about you now, or about Clewes? Too bad he's in jail! Too bad we can't find another job for you!"

I, too, got up. "Sir," I said, "I broke no law."

"The most important thing they teach at Harvard," he said, "is that a man can obey every law and still be the worst criminal of his time."

Where or when this was taught at Harvard, he did not say. It was news to me.

"Mr. Starbuck," he said, "in case you haven't noticed: We have recently come through a global conflict between good and evil, during which we grew quite accustomed to beaches and fields littered with the bodies of our own brave and blameless dead. Now I am expected to feel pity for one unemployed bureaucrat, who, for all the damage he has done to this country, should be hanged and drawn and quartered, as far as I am concerned."

"I only told the truth," I bleated. I was nauseated with terror and shame.

"You told a fragmentary truth," he said, "which has now been allowed to represent the whole! 'Educated and compassionate public servants are almost certainly Russian spies.' That's all you are going to hear now from the semiliterate old-time crooks and spellbinders who want the government back, who think it's rightly theirs. Without the symbiotic idiocies of you and Leland Clewes they could never have made the connection between treason and pity and brains. Now get out of my sight!"

"Sir," I said. I would have fled if I could, but I was paralyzed.

"You are yet another nincompoop, who, by being at the wrong place at the wrong time," he said, "was able to set humanitarianism back a full century! Begone!"

Strong stuff.

So THERE I SAT on the bench outside the prison, waiting for the bus, while the Georgia sun beat down on me. A great Cadillac limousine, with pale blue curtains drawn across its back windows, simmered by slowly on the other side of the median divider, on the lanes that would take it to the headquarters of the Air Force base. I could see only the chauffeur, a black man, who was looking quizzically at the prison. The place was not clearly a prison. A quite modest sign at the foot of the flagpole said only this: "F.M.S.A.C.F., Authorized Personnel Only."

The limousine continued on, until it found a crossover about a quarter of a mile up. Then it came back down and stopped with its glossy front fender inches from my nose. There, reflected in that perfect fender, I saw that old Slavic janitor again. This was the same limousine, it turned out, that had set off the false alarm about the arrival of Virgil Greathouse somewhat earlier. It had been cruising in search of the prison for quite some time.

The chauffeur got out, and he asked me if this was indeed the prison.

Thus was I required to make my first sound as a free man. "Yes," I said.

The chauffeur, who was a big, serenely paternal, middle-aged man in a tan whipcord uniform and black leather put-tees, opened the back door, spoke into the twilit interior. "Gentlemen," he said, with precisely the appropriate mixture of sorrow and respect, "we have reached our destination." Letters embroidered in red silk thread on his breast pocket identified his employer. "RAMJAC," they said.

As I would learn later: Old pals of Greathouse had provided him and his lawyers with swift and secret transportation from his home to prison, so that there would be almost no witnesses to his humiliation. A limousine from Pepsi-Cola had picked him up before dawn at the service entrance to the Waldorf Towers in Manhattan, which was his home. It had taken him to the Marine Air Terminal next to La Guardia, and directly out onto a runway. A corporate jet belonging to Resorts International was waiting for him there. It flew him to Atlanta, where he was met, again right out on the runway, by a curtained limousine supplied by the Southeastern District Office of The RAMJAC Corporation.

Out clambered Virgil Greathouse—dressed almost exactly as I was, in a gray, pinstripe suit and a white shirt and a regimental-stripe tie. Our regiments were different. He was a Coldstream Guard. As always, he was sucking on his pipe. He gave me the briefest of glances.

And then two sleek lawyers got out—one young, one old.

While the chauffeur went to the limousine's trunk to get the convict's luggage, Greathouse and the two lawyers looked over the prison as though it were a piece of real estate they were thinking of buying, if the price was right. There was a twinkle in the eyes of Greathouse, and he was imitating birdcalls with his pipe. He may have been thinking how tough he was. He had been taking lessons in boxing and *jujitsu* and *karate*, I would learn later from his lawyers, ever since it had become clear to him that he was really going to go to jail.

"Well," I thought to myself when I heard that, "there won't be anybody in that particular prison who will want to fight him, but he will get his back broken anyway. Everybody gets his back broken when he goes to prison for the first time. It mends after a while, but never quite the way it was before. As tough as Virgil Greathouse may be, he will never walk or feel quite the same again."

Virgil Greathouse had failed to recognize me. Sitting there on the bench, I might as well have been a corpse in the mud on a battlefield, and he might have been a general who had come forward during a lull to see how things were going, by and large.

I was unsurprised. I did think, though, that he might recognize the voice from inside the prison, which we could all hear so clearly now. It was the voice of his closest Watergate coconspirator, Emil Larkin, singing at the top of his lungs the Negro spiritual "Sometimes I Feel Like a Motherless Child."

Greathouse had no time to show his reaction to the voice, for a fighter plane leaped up from the tip of a nearby runway, tore the sky to shreds. This was a gut-ripping sound to anyone who had not heard it and heard it and heard it before. There was never a warning build-up. It was always an end-of-the-world explosion overhead.

Greathouse and the lawyers and the chauffeur flung themselves to the ground. Then they got up again, cursing and laughing and dusting themselves off. Greathouse, supposing correctly that he was being watched and sized up by people he could not see, made some boxing feints and looked up into the sky as though to say, clowningly, "Send me another one. I'm ready this time." The party did not advance on the prison, however. It waited by the limousine, expecting some sort of welcoming party. Greathouse wanted, I imagine, one last acknowledgment of his rank in society on neutral ground, a sort of surrender at Appomattox, with the warden as Ulysses S. Grant and himself as Robert E. Lee.

But the warden wasn't even in Georgia. He would have been there if he had had any advance notice that Greathouse was going to surrender on this particular day. But he was in Atlantic City, addressing a convention of the American Association of Parole Officers up there. So it was finally Clyde Carter, the spit and image of President Carter, who came out of the front door a few steps and motioned to them.

Clyde smiled. "You all come on in," he said.

So in they went, with the chauffeur bringing up the rear, carrying two valises made of buttery leather and a matching case for toiletries. Clyde relieved him of the bags at the threshold, told him politely to return to the limousine.

"You won't be needed in there," said Clyde.

So the chauffeur got back into the limousine. His name was Cleveland Lawes, a garbling of the name of the man I had ruined, Leland Clewes. He had only a grammar-school education, but he read five books a week while waiting for people, mostly RAMJAC executives and customers and suppliers. Because he had been captured by the Chinese during the Korean War, and had actually gone to China for a while and worked as a deckhand on a coastwise steamer in the Yellow Sea, he was reasonably fluent in Chinese.

Cleveland Lawes was reading *The Gulag Archipelago* now, an account of the prison system in the Soviet Union by another former prisoner, Aleksandr Solzhenitsyn.

So there I was all alone on a bench in the middle of nowhere again. I entered a period of catatonia again—staring straight ahead at nothing, and every so often clapping my old hands three times.

If it had not been for that clapping, Cleveland Lawes tells me now, he would never have become curious about me.

But I became his business by clapping my hands. He had to find out why I did it.

Did I tell him the truth about the clapping? No. It was too complicated and silly. I told him that I had been daydreaming about the past, and that whenever I remembered an especially happy moment, I would lift my hands from my lap, and I would clap three times.

He offered me a ride into Atlanta.

And there I was now, after only half an hour of freedom, sitting in the front seat of a parked limousine. So far so good.

And if Cleveland Lawes had not offered me a ride into Atlanta, he would never have become what he is today, personnel director of the Transico Division of The RAMJAC Corporation. Transico has limousine services and taxicab fleets and car-rental agencies and parking lots and garages all over the Free World. You can even rent furniture from Transico. Many people do.

I asked him if he thought his passengers would mind my coming along to Atlanta.

He said that he had never seen them before, and that he never expected to see them again—that they did not work for RAMJAC. He added the piquant detail that he had not known that his chief passenger had been Virgil Greathouse until the arrival at the prison. Until that moment Greathouse had been disguised by a false beard.

I craned my neck for a look into the backseat, and there the beard was, with one of its wire earloops hooked over a door handle.

Cleveland Lawes said as a joke that he wasn't sure Greathouse's lawyers would come back out again. "When they were looking over the prison," he said, "seemed to me they were trying it on for size."

He asked me if I had ever ridden in a limousine before. For simplicity's sake I told him, "No." As a child, of course, I had often ridden beside my father in the front seat of Alexander

Hamilton McCone's various limousines. In my youth, as I was
preparing for Harvard, I had often ridden in the backseat with
Mr. McCone, with a glass partition between myself and my
father. The partition had not seemed strange or even suggestive
to me at the time.

And when in Nuremberg I had been master of that grotesque
Fafner of a Mercedes touring car. But it had been an open car,
freakish even without the bullet holes in the trunk lid and the
rear windshield. The status it gave me among the Bavarians was
that of a pirate—in temporary possession of stolen goods that
would certainly be restolen, again and again. But, sitting there
outside the prison, I realized that I had not sat in a real limousine for perhaps forty-five years! As high as I had risen in public
service, I had never been entitled to a limousine, had never been
within three promotions of having one of my own or even the
occasional use of one. Nor had I ever so beguiled a superior who
had one that he had said to me, "Young man—I want to talk to
you more about this. You come in my car with me."

Leland Clewes, on the other hand, though not entitled to
one of his own, was forever riding around in limousines with
adoring old men.

No matter.

Calm down.

Cleveland Lawes commented that I sounded like an educated
man to him.

I admitted to having gone to Harvard.

This allowed him to tell me about his having been a prisoner
of the Chinese communists in North Korea, for the Chinese
major in charge of his prison had been a Harvard man. The
major would have been about my age, and possibly even a classmate, but I had never befriended any Chinese. According to
Lawes, he had studied physics and mathematics, so I would not
have known him in any case.

"His daddy was a big landlord," said Lawes. "When the communists came, they made his daddy kneel down in front of all
his tenants in the village, and then they chopped off his head
with a sword."

"But the son could still be a communist—after that?" I said.

"He said his daddy really had been a very bad landlord," he
said.

"Well," I said, "that's Harvard for you, I guess."

This Harvard Chinese befriended Cleveland Lawes and persuaded him to come to China instead of going back home to Georgia when the war was over. When he was a boy, a cousin of Lawes had been burned alive by a mob, and his father had been dragged out of his house one night and horsewhipped by the Ku Klux Klan, and he himself had been beat up twice for trying to register to vote, right before the Army got him. So he was easy prey for a smooth-talking communist. And he worked for two years, as I say, as a deckhand on the Yellow Sea. He said that he fell in love several times, but that nobody would fall in love with him.

"So that was what brought you back?" I asked.

He said it was the church music more than anything else. "There wasn't anybody to sing with over there," he said. "And the food," he said.

"The food wasn't any good?" I said.

"Oh, it was good," he said. "It just wasn't the kind of food I like to talk about."

"Um," I said.

"You can't just eat food," he said. "You've got to talk about it, too. And you've got to talk about it to somebody who understands that kind of food."

I congratulated him on having learned Chinese, and he replied that he could never do such a thing now. "I know too much now," he said. "I was too ignorant then to know how hard it was to learn Chinese. I thought it was like imitating birds. You know: You hear a bird make a sound, then you try to make a sound just like that, and see if you can't fool the bird."

The Chinese were nice about it when he decided that he wanted to go home. They liked him, and they went to some trouble for him, asking through circuitous diplomatic channels what would be done to him if he went home. America had no representatives in China then, and neither did any of its allies. The messages went through Moscow, which was still friendly with China then.

Yes, and this black, former private first class, whose military specialty had been to carry the base-plate of a heavy mortar, turned out to be worth negotiations at the highest diplomatic levels. The Americans wanted him back in order to punish him. The Chinese said that the punishment had to be brief and almost entirely symbolic, and that he had to be returned nearly at once to ordinary civilian life — or they would not let him go. The Americans said that Lawes would of course be expected to make some sort of public explanation of why he had come home. After that, he would be court-martialed, given a prison sentence of under three years and a dishonorable discharge, with forfeiture of all pay and benefits. The Chinese replied that Lawes had given his promise that he would never speak against the People's Republic of China, which had treated him well. If he was to be forced to break that promise, they would not let him go. They also insisted that he serve no prison time whatso-ever, and that he be paid for the time he spent as a prisoner of war. The Americans replied that he would have to be jailed at some point, since no army could allow the crime of desertion to go unpunished. They would like to jail him prior to his trial. They would sentence him to a term equal to the time he had spent as a prisoner of war, and deduct the time he had spent as a prisoner of war, and send him home. Back pay was out of the question.

And that was the deal.

"They wanted me back, you know," he told me, "because they were so embarrassed. They couldn't stand it that even one American, even a black one, would think for even a minute that maybe America wasn't the best country in the world."

I asked him if he had ever heard of Dr. Robert Fender, who was convicted of treason during the Korean War, and was right inside the prison there, measuring Virgil Greathouse for a uniform.

"No," he said. "I never kept track of other people in that kind of trouble. I never felt like it was a club or something."

I asked him if he had ever seen the legendary Mrs. Jack Graham, Jr., the majority stockholder in The RAMJAC Corporation.

"That's like asking me if I've seen God," he said.

The widow Graham had not been seen in public, at that point, for about five years. Her most recent appearance was in a courtroom in New York City, where RAMJAC was being sued by a group of its stockholders for proofs that she was still alive. The accounts in the papers amused my wife so, I remember.

"This is the America I love," she said. "Why can't it be like this all the time?"

Mrs. Graham came into the courtroom without a lawyer, but with eight uniformed bodyguards from Pinkerton, Inc., a RAMJAC subsidiary. One of them was carrying an amplifier with a loudspeaker and a microphone. Mrs. Graham was wearing a voluminous black caftan with its hood up, and with the hood pinned shut with diaper pins, so that she could peek out, but nobody could see what was inside. Only her hands were visible. Another Pinkerton was carrying an inkpad, some paper, and a copy of her fingerprints from the files of the Federal Bureau of Investigation. Her prints had been forwarded to the F.B.I. after she was convicted of drunken driving in Frankfort, Kentucky, in Nineteen-hundred and Fifty-two, soon after her husband died. She had been put on probation at that time. I myself had just been fired from government service at that time.

The amplifier was turned on, and the microphone was slipped inside her caftan, so people could hear what she was saying in there. She proved she was who she said she was by fingerprinting herself on the spot and having the prints compared with those possessed by the F.B.I. She said under oath that she was in excellent health, both physically and mentally—and in control of the company's top officers, but never face-to-face. When she instructed them on the telephone, she used a password to identify herself. This password was changed at irregular intervals. At the judge's request, I remember, she gave a sample password, and it seemed so full of magic that it still sticks in my mind. This was it: "shoemaker." Every order she gave on the phone was subsequently confirmed by mail, by a letter written entirely by her own hand. At the bottom of each letter was not only her signature, but a full set of prints from her eight little fingers and two little thumbs. She called them that: ". . . my eight little fingers and my two little thumbs."

That was that. Mrs. Jack Graham was unquestionably alive, and now she was free to disappear again.

"I've seen Mr. Leen many times," said Cleveland Lawes. He was speaking of Arpad Leen, the very public and communicative president and chairman of the board of directors of The RAMJAC Corporation. He would become my boss of bosses, and Cleveland Lawes's boss of bosses, too, when we both became corporate officers of RAMJAC. I say now that Arpad Leen is the most able and informed and brilliant and responsive executive under whom it has ever been my privilege to serve. He is a genius at acquiring companies and keeping them from dying afterward.

He used to say, "If you can't get along with me, you can't get along with anybody."

It was true, it was true.

Lawes said that Arpad Leen had come to Atlanta and been Lawes's passenger only two months before. A cluster of new stores and luxury hotels in Atlanta had gone bankrupt, and Leen had tried to snap it all up for RAMJAC. He had been outbid, however, by a South Korean religious cult.

Lawes asked me if I had any children. I said I had a son who worked for *The New York Times*. Lawes laughed and said that he and my son had the same boss now: Arpad Leen. I had missed the news that morning, so he had to explain to me that RAMJAC had just acquired control of *The New York Times* and all of its subsidiaries, which included the second-largest catfood company in the world.

"When he was down here," said Lawes, "Mr. Leen told me this was going to happen. It was the catfood company he wanted—not *The New York Times*."

The two lawyers got into the backseat of the limousine. They weren't subdued at all. They were laughing about the guard who looked like the President of the United States. "I felt like saying to him," said one, "'Mr. President, why don't you just pardon him right here and now? He's suffered enough, and he could get in some good golf this afternoon.'"

One of them tried on the false beard, and the other one said he looked like Karl Marx. And so on. They were incurious about me. Cleveland Lawes told them that I had been visiting my son. They asked me what my son was in for and I said, "Mail fraud." That was the end of the conversation.

So off we went to Atlanta. There was a curious object stuck by means of a suction cup to the glove compartment in front of me, I remember. Coming out of the cup and aimed at my breastbone was what looked like about a foot of green garden hose. At the end of the shaft was a white plastic wheel the size of a dinner plate. Once we got going, the wheel began to hypnotize me, bobbing up and down when we went over bumps, swaying this way and then that way as we went around curves.

So I asked about it. It was a toy steering wheel, it turned out. Lawes had a seven-year-old son he sometimes took with him on trips. The little boy could pretend to be steering the limousine with the plastic wheel. There had been no such toy when my own son was little. Then again, he wouldn't have enjoyed it much. Even at seven, young Walter hated to go anywhere with his mother and me.

I said it was a clever toy.

Lawes said it could be an exciting one, too, especially if the person with the real steering wheel was drunk and having close shaves with oncoming trucks and sideswiping parked cars and so on. He said that the President of the United States ought to be given a wheel like that at his inauguration, to remind him and everybody else that all he could do was pretend to steer.

He let me off at the airport.

The planes to New York City were all overbooked, it turned out. I did not get out of Atlanta until five o'clock that afternoon. That was all right with me. I skipped lunch, having no appetite. I found a paperback book in a toilet stall, so I read that for a while. It was about a man who, through ruthlessness, became the head of a big international conglomerate. Women were crazy about him. He treated them like dirt, but they just came back for more. His son was a drug addict and his daughter was a nymphomaniac.

My reading was interrupted once by a Frenchman who spoke to me in French and pointed to my left lapel. I thought at first that I had set myself on fire again, even though I didn't smoke anymore. Then I realized that I was still wearing the narrow red ribbon that identified me as a *chevalier* in the French Légion d'honneur. Pathetically enough, I had worn it all through my trial, and all the way to prison, too.

I told him in English that it had come with the suit, which I had bought secondhand, and that I had no idea what it was supposed to represent.

He became very icy. "*Permettez-moi, monsieur*," he said, and he deftly plucked the ribbon from my lapel as though it had been an insect there.

"*Merci*," I said, and I returned to my book.

When there was at last an airplane seat for me, my name was broadcast over the public-address system several times: "Mr. Walter F. Starbuck, Mr. Walter F. Starbuck . . ." It had been such a notorious name at one time; but I could not now catch sight of anyone who seemed to recognize it, who raised his or her eyebrows in lewd surmise.

Two and a half hours later I was on the island of Manhattan, wearing my trenchcoat to keep out the evening chill. The sun was down. I was staring at an animated display in the window of a store that sold nothing but toy trains.

It was not as though I had no place to go. I was close to where I was going. I had written ahead. I had reserved a room without bath or television for a week, paying in advance—in the once-fashionable Hotel Arapahoe, now a catch-as-catch-can lazaret and bagnio one minute from Times Square.

# 9

I HAD BEEN to the Arapahoe once before—in the autumn of Nineteen-hundred and Thirty-one. Fire had yet to be domesticated. Albert Einstein had predicted the invention of the wheel, but was unable to describe its probable shape and uses in the language of ordinary women and men. Herbert Hoover, a mining engineer, was President. The sale of alcoholic beverages was against the law, and I was a Harvard freshman.

I was operating under instructions from my mentor, Alexander Hamilton McCone. He told me in a letter that I was to duplicate a folly he himself had committed when a freshman, which was to take a pretty girl to the Harvard–Columbia football game in New York, and then to spend a month's allowance on a lobster dinner for two, with oysters and caviar and all that, in the famous dining room of the Hotel Arapahoe. We were to go dancing afterward. "You must wear your tuxedo," he said. "You must tip like a drunken sailor." Diamond Jim Brady, he told me, had once eaten four dozen oysters, four lobsters, four chickens, four squabs, four T-bone steaks, four pork chops, and four lamb chops there—on a bet. Lillian Russell had looked on.

Mr. McCone may have been drunk when he wrote that letter. "All work and no play," he wrote, "makes Jack a dull boy."

And the girl I took there, the twin sister of my roommate, would become one of the four women I would ever truly love. The first was my mother. The last was my wife.

Sarah Wyatt was the girl's name. She was all of eighteen, and so was I. She was attending a very easy two-year college for rich girls in Wellesley, Massachusetts, which was Pine Manor. Her family lived in Prides Crossing, north of Boston—toward Gloucester. While we were in New York City together, she would be staying with her maternal grandmother, a stockbroker's widow, in a queerly irrelevant enclave of dead-end streets and vest-pocket parks and Elizabethan apartment-hotels called "Tudor City"—near the East River, and actually bridging Forty-second Street. As luck will have it, my son now lives in Tudor City. So do Mr. and Mrs. Leland Clewes.

Small world.

Tudor City was quite new, but already bankrupt and nearly empty when I arrived by taxicab—to take my Sarah to the Hotel Arapahoe in Nineteen-hundred and Thirty-one. I was wearing a tuxedo made to my measure by the finest tailor in Cleveland. I had a silver cigarette lighter and a silver cigarette case, both gifts from Mr. McCone. I had forty dollars in my billfold. I could have bought the whole state of Arkansas for forty dollars cash in Nineteen-hundred and Thirty-one.

We come to the matter of physical size again: Sarah Wyatt was three inches taller than me. She did not mind. She was so far from minding that, when I fetched her in Tudor City, she was wearing high heels with her evening dress.

A stronger proof that she was indifferent to our disparity in size: In seven years Sarah Wyatt would agree to marry me.

She wasn't quite ready when I arrived, so I had to talk to her grandmother, Mrs. Sutton, for a while. Sarah had warned me at the football game that afternoon that I must not mention suicide to Mrs. Sutton—because Mr. Sutton had jumped out of his office window in Wall Street after the stock market crashed in Nineteen-hundred and Twenty-nine.

"It is a nice place you have here, Mrs. Sutton," I said.

"You're the only person who thinks so," she said. "It's crowded. Everything that goes on in the kitchen you can smell out here."

It was only a two-bedroom apartment. She had certainly come down in the world. Sarah said she used to have a horse farm in Connecticut and a house on Fifth Avenue, and on and on.

The walls of the little entrance hall were covered with blue ribbons from horse shows before the Crash. "I see you have won a lot of blue ribbons," I said.

"No," she said, "it was the horses that won those."

We were seated on folding chairs at a card table in the middle of the living room. There were no easy chairs, no couch. But the room was so jammed with breakfronts and escritoires and armoires and highboys and lowboys and Welsh dressers and wardrobes and grandfather clocks and so on, that I could not guess where the windows were. It turned out that she also stockpiled servants, all very old. A uniformed maid had let me in, and then exited sideways into a narrow fissure between two imposing examples of cabinetwork.

Now a uniformed chauffeur emerged from the same fissure to ask Mrs. Sutton if she would be going anywhere in "the electric" that night. Many people, especially old ladies, seemingly, had electric cars in those days. They looked like telephone booths on wheels. Under the floor were terribly heavy storage batteries. They had a top speed of about eleven miles an hour and needed to be recharged every thirty miles or so. They had tillers, like sailboats, instead of steering wheels.

Mrs. Sutton said she would not be going anywhere in the electric, so the old chauffeur said that he would be going to the hotel, then. There were two other servants besides, whom I never saw. They were all going to spend the night at a hotel so that Sarah could have the second bedroom, where they ordinarily slept.

"I suppose this all looks very temporary to you," Mrs. Sutton said to me.

"No, ma'am," I said.

"It's quite permanent," she said. "I am utterly helpless to improve my condition without a man. It was the way I was brought up. It was the way I was educated."

"Yes, ma'am," I said.

"Men in tuxedos as beautifully made as yours is should never call anyone but the Queen of England 'ma'am,'" she said.

"I'll try to remember that," I said.

"You are only a child, of course," she said.

"Yes, ma'am," I said.

"Tell me again how you are related to the McCones," she said.

I had never told anyone that I was related to the McCones. There was another lie I had told frequently, however—a lie, like everything else about me, devised by Mr. McCone. He said it would be perfectly acceptable, even fashionable, to admit that my father was penniless. But it would not do to have a household servant for a father.

The lie went like this, and I told it to Mrs. Sutton: "My father works for Mr. McCone as curator of his art collection. He also advises Mr. McCone on what to buy."

"A cultivated man," she said.

"He studied art in Europe," I said. "He is no businessman."

"A dreamer," she said.

"Yes," I said. "If it weren't for Mr. McCone, I could not afford to go to Harvard."

"'Starbuck—'" she mused. "I believe that's an old Nantucket name."

I was ready for that one, too. "Yes," I said, "but my great-grandfather left Nantucket for the Gold Rush and never returned. I must go to Nantucket sometime and look at the old records, to see where we fit in."

"A California family," she said.

"Nomads, really," I said. "California, yes—but Oregon, too, and Wyoming, and Canada, and Europe. But they were always bookish people—teachers and so on."

I was pure phlogiston, an imaginary element of long ago.

"Descended from whaling captains," she said.

"I imagine," I said. I was not at all uncomfortable with the lies.

"And from Vikings before that," she said.

I shrugged.

She had decided to like me a lot—and would continue to do so until the end. As Sarah would tell me, Mrs. Sutton often referred to me as her little Viking. She would not live long enough to see Sarah agree to marry me and then to jilt me. She died in Nineteen-hundred and Thirty-seven or so—penniless in an apartment furnished with little more than a card table, two folding chairs, and her bed. She had sold off all her treasures in order to support herself and her old servants, who would have had no place to go and nothing to eat without her. She survived them all. The maid, who was Tillie, was the last of them to die. Two weeks after Tillie died, so did Mrs. Sutton depart from this world.

Back there in Nineteen-hundred and Thirty-one, while I was waiting for Sarah to complete her toilette, Mrs. Sutton told me that Mr. McCone's father, the founder of Cuyahoga Bridge and Iron, built the biggest house where she spent her girlhood summers—in Bar Harbor, Maine. When it was finished, he gave a grand ball with four orchestras, and nobody came.

"It seemed very beautiful and noble to snub him like that," she said. "I remember how happy I was the next day. I can't help wondering now if we weren't just a little insane. I don't mean that we were insane to miss a wonderful party or to hurt the feelings of Daniel McCone. Daniel McCone was a perfectly ghastly man. What was insane was the way we all imagined that God was watching, and simply adoring us, guaranteeing us all seats at His right hand for having snubbed Daniel McCone."

I asked her what had become of the McCone mansion in Bar Harbor. My mentor had never mentioned it to me.

"Mr. and Mrs. McCone vanished from Bar Harbor the next day," she said, "with their two young sons, I believe."

"Yes," I said. One son became my mentor. The other son became chairman of the board and president of Cuyahoga Bridge and Iron.

"A month later," she said, "around Labor Day, although there was no Labor Day then—when summer was about to end—a special train arrived. There were perhaps eight freight cars and three cars of workmen, who had come all the way from Cleveland. They must have been from Mr. McCone's factory. How pale they looked! They were almost all foreigners, I remember—Germans, Poles, Italians, Hungarians. Who could tell? There had never been such people in Bar Harbor before. They slept on the train. They ate on the train. They allowed themselves to be herded like docile cattle between the mansion and the train. They removed only the finest art treasures from the mansion—only paintings and statues and tapestries and rugs that belonged in museums." Mrs. Sutton rolled her eyes. "Oh, Lord—what they didn't leave behind! And then the workmen took every pane of glass from the windows and doors and skylights. They stripped the slate from the roof. One workman was killed, I remember, by a falling slate. They bored holes in the naked roof. They loaded all the slate and glass on the train, too, so it would not be easy for anyone to make repairs. Then they went away again. No one had spoken to them, and they had not spoken to anyone.

"It was a very special departure, and nobody who saw it ever forgot it," said Mrs. Sutton. "Trains were great fun in those days, making such hullabaloos at the station with their whistles and bells. But that special train from Cleveland left as quietly as a ghost. I am sure the engineer was under orders from Daniel McCone himself not to blow the whistle or ring the bell."

Thus was the finest mansion in Bar Harbor and most of its furnishings, with sheets and blankets and quilts still on all the beds, according to Mrs. Sutton, with china and crystal still in the cupboards, with thousands of bottles of wine still in the cellar, left to die and die.

Mrs. Sutton closed her eyes, remembering the decay of the mansion year by year. "Served nobody right, Mr. Starbuck," she said.

Young Sarah now came out from between the furniture, ready at last. She wore two orchids, which I had sent to her. They, too, had been the brainstorm of Alexander Hamilton McCone.

"You are so beautiful!" I said, rising raptly from my folding chair. It was true, surely, for she was tall and slender and golden-haired—and blue-eyed. Her skin was like satin. Her teeth were like pearls. But she radiated about as much sexuality as her grandmother's card table.

This would continue to be the case for the next seven years. Sarah Wyatt believed that sex was a sort of pratfall that was easily avoided. To avoid it, she had only to remind a would-be lover of the ridiculousness of what he proposed to do to her. The first time I kissed her, which was in Wellesley the week before, I suddenly found myself being played like a tuba, so to speak. Sarah was convulsed by laughter, with her lips still pressed to mine. She tickled me. She pulled out my shirttails, leaving me in humiliating disarray. It was terrible. Nor was her laughter about sexuality girlish and nervous, something a man might be expected to modulate with tenderness and anatomical skill. It was the unbridled hee-hawing of somebody at a Marx Brothers film.

A phrase keeps asking to be used at this point: "nobody home."

It was in fact a phrase used by a Harvard classmate who also took Sarah out, but only twice, as I recall. I asked him what he thought of her, and he replied with some bitterness: "nobody home!" He was Kyle Denny, a football player from Philadelphia. Somebody told me recently that Kyle died in a fall in his bathtub on the day the Japanese bombed Pearl Harbor. He cracked his head open on a faucet.

So I can fix the date of Kyle Denny's death with pinpoint accuracy: December the seventh, Nineteen-hundred and Forty-one.

"You do look nice, my dear," said Mrs. Sutton to Sarah. She was pitifully ancient—about five years younger than I am now. I thought she might cry about Sarah's beauty, and how that beauty was sure to fade in just a few years, and on and on. She was very wise.

"I feel so silly," said Sarah.

"You don't believe you're beautiful?" said her grandmother.

"I know I'm beautiful," said Sarah. "I look in a mirror, and I think, 'I'm beautiful.'"

"What's wrong, then?" said her grandmother.

"Beautiful is such a funny thing to be," said Sarah. "Somebody else is ugly, but I'm beautiful. Walter says I'm beautiful. You say I'm beautiful. I say I'm beautiful. Everybody says, 'Beautiful, beautiful, beautiful,' and you start wondering what it is, and what's so wonderful about it."

"You make people *happy* with your beauty," said her grandmother.

"You certainly make *me* happy with it," I said.

Sarah laughed. "It's so silly," she said. "It's so dumb," she said.

"Perhaps you shouldn't think about it so much," said her grandmother.

"That's like telling a midget to stop thinking about being a midget," said Sarah, and she laughed again.

"You should stop saying everything is silly and dumb," said her grandmother.

"Everything *is* silly and dumb," said Sarah.

"You will learn differently as you grow older," her grandmother promised.

"I think everybody older just pretends to know what's going on, that it's all so serious and wonderful," said Sarah. "Older people haven't really found out anything new that I don't know. Maybe if people didn't get so serious when they got older, we wouldn't have a depression now."

"There's nothing constructive in laughing all the time," said her grandmother.

"I can cry, too," said Sarah. "You want me to cry?"

"No," said her grandmother. "I don't want to hear any more about it. You just go out with this nice young man and have a lovely time."

"I can't laugh about those poor women who painted the clocks," said Sarah. "That's one thing I can't laugh about."

"Nobody wants you to," said her grandmother. "You run along now."

Sarah was referring to an industrial tragedy that was notorious at the time. Sarah's family was in the middle of it, and sick about it. Sarah had already told me that she was sick about it, and so had her brother, my roommate, and so had their father and mother. The tragedy was a slow one that could not be stopped once it had begun, and it began in the family's clock company, the Wyatt Clock Company, one of the oldest companies in the United States, in Brockton, Massachusetts. It was an avoidable tragedy. The Wyatts never tried to justify it, and would not hire lawyers to justify it. It could not be justified.

It went like this: In the nineteen twenties the United States Navy awarded Wyatt Clock a contract to produce several thousand standardized ships' clocks that could be easily read in the dark. The dials were to be black. The hands and the numerals were to be hand-painted with white paint containing the radioactive element radium. About half a hundred Brockton women, most of them relatives of regular Wyatt Clock Company employees, were hired to paint the hands and numerals. It was a way to make pin money. Several of the women who had young children to look after were allowed to do the work at home.

Now all those women had died or were about to die most horribly with their bones crumbling, with their heads rotting off. The cause was radium poisoning. Every one of them had been told by a foreman, it had since come out in court, that she should keep a fine point on her brush by moistening it and shaping it with her lips from time to time.

And, as luck would have it, the daughter of one of those unfortunate women would become one of the four women I have ever loved in this Vale of Tears—along with my mother, my wife, and Sarah Wyatt. Mary Kathleen O'Looney was her name.

# 10

I SPEAK ONLY of Ruth as "my wife." It would not surprise me, though, if on Judgment Day Sarah Wyatt and Mary Kathleen O'Looney were also certified as having been wives of mine. I surely paired off with both of them—with Mary Kathleen for about eleven months, and with Sarah, off and on, to be sure, for about seven years.

I can hear Saint Peter saying to me: "It would appear, Mr. Starbuck, that you were something of a Don Juan."

So there I was in Nineteen-hundred and Thirty-one, sashaying into the wedding-cake lobby of the Hotel Arapahoe with beautiful Sarah Wyatt, the Yankee clock heiress, on my arm. Her family was nearly as broke as mine by then. What little they had salvaged from the crashing stock market and the failing banks would soon be dispersed among the survivors of the women who painted all those clocks for the Navy. This dispersal would be compelled in about a year by a landmark decision of the United States Supreme Court as to the personal responsibility of employers for deaths in their places of work caused by criminal negligence.

Eighteen-year-old Sarah now said of the Arapahoe lobby, "It's so dirty—and there's nobody here." She laughed. "I *love* it," she said.

At that point in time, in the filthy lobby of the Arapahoe, Sarah Wyatt did not know that I was acting with all possible humorlessness on orders from Alexander Hamilton McCone. She would tell me later that she thought I was being witty when I said we should get all dressed up. She thought we were costumed like millionaires in the spirit of Halloween. We would laugh and laugh, she hoped. We would be people in a movie.

Not at all: I was a robot programmed to behave like a genuine aristocrat.

Oh, to be young again!

The dirt in the Arapahoe lobby might not have been so obvious, if somebody had not started to do something about it and then stopped. There was a tall stepladder set against one wall.

There was a bucket at the base of it, filled with dirty water and with a brush floating on top. Someone had clearly scaled the ladder with the bucket. He had scrubbed as much of the wall as he could reach from the top. He had created a circle of cleanliness, dribbling filth at its bottom, to be sure, but as bright as a harvest moon.

I do not know who made the harvest moon. There was no one to ask. There had been no doorman to invite us in. There were no bellboys and no guests inside. There wasn't a soul behind the reception desk in the distance. The newsstand and the theater-ticket kiosk were shuttered. The doors of the unmanned elevators were propped open by chairs.

"I don't think they're in business anymore," said Sarah.

"Somebody accepted my reservation on the telephone," I said. "He called me '*monsieur*.'"

"Anybody can call anybody '*monsieur*' on the telephone," said Sarah.

But then we heard a Gypsy violin crying somewhere—sobbing as though its heart would break. And when I hear that violin's lamenting in my memory now, I am able to add this information: Hitler, not yet in power, would soon cause to be killed every Gypsy his soldiers and policemen could catch.

The music was coming from behind a folding screen in the lobby. Sarah and I dared to move the screen from the wall. We were confronted by a pair of French doors, which were held shut with a padlock and hasp. The panes in the doors were mirrors, showing us yet again how childish and rich we were. But Sarah discovered one pane that had a flaw in its silvering. She peeped through the flaw, then invited me to take a turn. I was flabbergasted. I might have been peering into the twinkling prisms of a time machine. On the other side of the French doors was the famous dining room of the Hotel Arapahoe in pristine condition, complete with a Gypsy fiddler—almost atom for atom as it must have been in the time of Diamond Jim Brady. A thousand candles in the chandeliers and on the tables became billions of tiny stars because of all the silver and crystal and china and mirrors in there.

The story was this: The hotel and the restaurant, while sharing the same building, one minute from Times Square, were under separate ownerships. The hotel had given up—was no longer taking guests. The restaurant, on the other hand, had just been completely refurbished, its owner believing that the collapse of the economy would be brief, and was caused by nothing more substantial than a temporary loss of nerve by businessmen.

Sarah and I had come in through the wrong door. I told Sarah as much, and she replied, "That is the story of my life. I always go in the wrong door first."

So Sarah and I went out into the night again and then in through the door to the place where food and drink awaited us. Mr. McCone had told me to order the meal in advance. That I had done. The owner himself received us. He was French. On the lapel of his tuxedo was a decoration that meant nothing to me, but which was familiar to Sarah, since her father had one, too. It meant, she would explain to me, that he was a *chevalier* in the Légion d'honneur.

Sarah had spent many summers in Europe. I had never been there. She was fluent in French, and she and the owner performed a madrigal in that most melodious of all languages. How would I ever have got through life without women to act as my interpreters? Of the four women I ever loved, only Mary Kathleen O'Looney spoke no language but English. But even Mary Kathleen was my interpreter when I was a Harvard communist, trying to communicate with members of the American working class.

The restaurant owner told Sarah in French, and then she told me, about the Great Depression's being nothing but a loss of nerve. He said that alcoholic beverages would be legal again as soon as a Democrat was elected President, and that life would become fun again.

He led us to our table. The room could seat at least one hundred, I would guess, but there were only a dozen other patrons there. Somehow, they still had cash. And when I try to remember them now, and to guess what they were, I keep seeing the pictures by George Grosz of corrupt plutocrats amidst the misery of Germany after World War One. I had not seen those pictures in Nineteen-hundred and Thirty-one. I had not seen anything.

There was a puffy old woman, I remember, eating alone and wearing a diamond necklace. She had a Pekingese dog in her lap. The dog had a diamond necklace, too.

There was a withered old man, I remember, hunched over his food, hiding it with his arms. Sarah whispered that he ate as though his meal were a royal flush. We would later learn that he was eating caviar.

"This must be a very expensive place," said Sarah.

"Don't worry about it," I said.

"Money is so strange," she said. "Does it make any sense to you?"

"No," I said.

"The people who've got it, and the people who don't—" she mused. "I don't think anybody understands what's really going on."

"Some people must," I said. I no longer believe that.

I will say further, as an officer of an enormous international conglomerate, that nobody who is doing well in this economy ever even wonders what is really going on.

We are chimpanzees. We are orangutans.

"Does Mr. McCone know how much longer the Depression will last?" she said.

"He doesn't know anything about business," I said.

"How can he still be so rich, if he doesn't know anything about business?" she said.

"His brother runs everything," I said.

"I wish my father had somebody to run everything for him," she said.

I knew that things were going so badly for her father that her brother, my roommate, had decided to drop out of school at the end of the semester. He would never go back to school, either. He would take a job as an orderly in a tuberculosis sanitarium, and himself contract tuberculosis. That would keep him out of the armed forces in the Second World War. He would work as a welder in a Boston shipyard, instead. I would lose touch with him. Sarah, whom I see regularly again, told me that he died of a heart attack in Nineteen-hundred and Sixty-five—in a cluttered little welding shop he ran single-handed in the village of Sandwich, on Cape Cod.

His name was Radford Alden Wyatt. He never married. According to Sarah, he had not bathed in years.

"Shirtsleeves to shirtsleeves in three generations," as the saying goes.

In the case of the Wyatts, actually, it was more like shirtsleeves to shirtsleeves in ten generations. They had been richer than most of their neighbors for at least that long. Sarah's father was now selling off at rock-bottom prices all the treasures his ancestors had accumulated—English pewter, silver by Paul Revere, paintings of Wyatts as sea captains and merchants and preachers and lawyers, treasures from the China Trade.

"It's so awful to see my father so low all the time," said Sarah. "Is your father low, too?"

She was speaking of my fictitious father, the curator of Mr. McCone's art collection. I could see him quite clearly then. I can't see him at all now. "No," I said.

"You're so lucky," she said.

"I guess so," I said. My real father was in fact in easy circumstances. My mother and he had been able to bank almost every penny they made, and the bank they put their money in had not failed.

"If only people wouldn't care so much about money," she said. "I keep telling father that I don't care about it. I don't care about not going to Europe anymore. I hate school. I don't want to go there anymore. I'm not learning anything. I'm glad we sold our boats. I was bored with them, anyway. I don't need any clothes. I have enough clothes to last me a hundred years. He just won't believe me. 'I've let you down. I've let everybody down,' he says."

Her father, incidentally, was an inactive partner in the Wyatt Clock Company. This did not limit his liability in the radium-poisoning case, but his principal activity in the good old days had been as the largest yacht broker in Massachusetts. That business was utterly shot in Nineteen-hundred and Thirty-one, of course. And it, too, in the process of dying, left him with what he once described to me as ". . . a pile of worthless accounts-receivable as high as Mount Washington, and a pile of bills as high as Pike's Peak."

He, too, was a Harvard man—the captain of the undefeated swimming team of Nineteen-hundred and Eleven. After he lost everything, he would never work again. He would be supported by his wife, who would operate a catering service out of their home. They would die penniless.

So I am not the first Harvard man who had to be supported by his wife.

Peace.

Sarah said to me at the Arapahoe that she was sorry to be so depressing, that she knew we were supposed to have fun. She said she would really try to have fun.

It was then that the waiter, shepherded by the owner, delivered the first course, specified by Mr. McCone in Cleveland, so far away. It was a half-dozen Cotuit oysters for each of us. I had never eaten an oyster before.

"*Bon appetit!*" said the owner. I was thrilled. I had never had anybody say that to me before. I was so pleased to understand something in French without the help of an interpreter. I had studied French for four years in a Cleveland public high school, by the way, but I never found anyone who spoke the dialect I learned out there. It may have been French as it was spoken by Iroquois mercenaries in the French and Indian War.

Now the Gypsy violinist came to our table. He played with all possible hypocrisy and brilliance, in the frenzied expectation of a tip. I remembered that Mr. McCone had told me to tip lavishly. I had not so far tipped anyone. So I got out my billfold surreptitiously while the music was still going on, and I took from it what I thought was a one-dollar bill. A common laborer in those days would have worked ten hours for a dollar. I was about to make a lavish tip. Fifty cents would have put me quite high up in the spendthrift class. I wadded up the bill in my right hand, so as to tip with the quick grace of a magician when the music stopped.

The trouble was this: It wasn't a one-dollar bill. It was a twenty-dollar bill.

I blame Sarah somewhat for this sensational mistake. While I was taking the money from the billfold, she was satirizing sexual love again, pretending that the music was filling her with lust. She undid my necktie, which I would be unable to retie. It had been tied by the mother of a friend with whom I was staying. Sarah kissed the tips of two of her fingers passionately, and then pressed those fingers to my white collar, leaving a smear of lipstick there.

Now the music stopped. I smiled my thanks. Diamond Jim Brady, reincarnated as the demented son of a Cleveland chauffeur, handed the Gypsy a twenty-dollar bill.

The Gypsy was quite suave at first, imagining that he had received a dollar.

Sarah, believing it to be a dollar, too, thought I had tipped much too much. "Good God," she said.

But then, perhaps to taunt Sarah with the bill that she would have liked me to take back, but which was now his, all his, the Gypsy unfolded the wad, so that its astronomical denomination became apparent to all of us for the first time. He was as aghast as we were.

And then, being a Gypsy, and hence one microsecond more cunning about money than we were, he darted out of the restaurant and into the night. I wonder to this day if he ever came back for his fiddlecase.

But imagine the effect on Sarah!

She thought I had done it on purpose, that I was stupid enough to imagine that this would be a highly erotic event for her. Never have I been loathed so much.

"You inconceivable twerp," she said. Most of the speeches in this book are necessarily fuzzy reconstructions—but when I assert that Sarah Wyatt called me an "inconceivable twerp," that is exactly what she said.

To give an extra dimension to the scolding she gave me: The word "twerp" was freshly coined in those days, and had a specific definition—it was a person, if I may be forgiven, who bit the bubbles of his own farts in a bathtub.

"You unbelievable jerk," she said. A "jerk" was a person who masturbated too much. She knew that. She knew all those things.

"Who do you think you are?" she said. "Or, more to the point, who do you think *I* am? I may be a dumb toot," she said, "but how dare you think I am such a dumb toot that I would think what you just did was glamorous?"

This was the lowest point in my life, possibly. I felt worse then than I did when I was put in prison—worse, even, than when I was turned loose again. I may have felt worse then, even, than when I set fire to the drapes my wife was about to deliver to a client in Chevy Chase.

"Kindly take me home," Sarah Wyatt said to me. We left without eating, but not without paying. I could not help myself: I cried all the way home.

I told her brokenly in the taxicab that nothing about the evening had been my own idea, that I was a robot invented and controlled by Alexander Hamilton McCone. I confessed to being half-Polish and half-Lithuanian and nothing but a chauffeur's son who had been ordered to put on the clothing and airs of a gentleman. I said I wasn't going back to Harvard, and that I wasn't even sure I wanted to live anymore.

I was so pitiful, and Sarah was so contrite and interested, that we became the closest of friends, as I say, off and on for seven years.

She would drop out of Pine Manor. She would become a nurse. While in nurse's training she would become so upset by the sickening and dying of the poor that she would join the Communist Party. She would make me join, too.

So I might never have become a communist, if Alexander Hamilton McCone had not insisted that I take a pretty girl to the Arapahoe. And now, forty-five years later, here I was entering the lobby of the Arapahoe again. Why had I chosen to spend my first nights of freedom there? For the irony of it. No American is so old and poor and friendless that he cannot make a collection of some of the most exquisite little ironies in town.

Here I was again, back where a restaurateur had first said to me, *"Bon appetit!"*

A great chunk of the original lobby was now a travel agency. What remained for overnight guests was a narrow corridor with a reception desk at the far end. It wasn't wide enough to accommodate a couch or chair. The mirrored French doors through which Sarah and I had peered into the famous dining room were gone. The archway that had framed them was still there, but it was clogged now with masonry as brutal and unadorned as the wall that kept communists from becoming capitalists in Berlin, Germany. There was a pay telephone bolted to the barrier. Its coinbox had been pried open. Its handset was gone.

And yet the man at the reception desk in the distance appeared to be wearing a tuxedo, and even a *boutonniere*!

As I advanced on him, it became apparent that my eyes had been tricked on purpose. He was in fact wearing a cotton

T-shirt on which were printed a *trompe l'oeil* tuxedo jacket and shirt, with a *boutonniere*, bow tie, shirtstuds, handkerchief in the pocket, and all. I had never seen such a shirt before. I did not find it comical. I was confused. It was not a joke somehow.

The night clerk had a beard that was real, and an even more aggressively genuine bellybutton, exposed above his low-slung trousers. He no longer dresses that way, may I say, now that he is vice-president in charge of purchasing for Hospitality Associates, Ltd., a division of The RAMJAC Corporation. He is thirty years old now. His name is Israel Edel. Like my son, he is married to a black woman. He holds a Doctor's degree in history from Long Island University, *summa cum laude*, and is a Phi Beta Kappa. When we first met, in fact, Israel had to look up at me from the pages of *The American Scholar*, the Phi Beta Kappa learned monthly. Working as night clerk at the Arapahoe was the best job he could find.

"I have a reservation," I said.

"You have a what?" he said. He was not being impudent. His surprise was genuine. No one ever made a reservation at the Arapahoe anymore. The only way to arrive there was unexpectedly, in response to some misfortune. As Israel said to me only the other day, when we happened to meet in an elevator, "Making a reservation at the Arapahoe is like making a reservation in a burn ward." He now oversees the purchasing at the Arapahoe, incidentally, which, along with about four hundred other hostelries all over the world, including one in Katmandu, is a Hospitality Associates, Ltd., hotel.

He found my letter of reservation in an otherwise vacant bank of pigeonholes behind him. "A week?" he said incredulously.

"Yes," I said.

My name meant nothing to him. His area of historical expertise was heresies in thirteenth-century Normandy. But he did glean that I was an ex-jailbird—from the slightly queer return address on my envelope: a box number in the middle of nowhere in Georgia, and some numbers after my name.

"The least we can do," he said, "is to give you the Bridal Suite."

There was in fact no Bridal Suite. Every suite had long ago been partitioned into cells. But there was one cell, and only one, which had been freshly painted and papered—as a result, I would later learn, of a particularly gruesome murder of a teen-age male prostitute in there. Israel Edel was not himself being gruesome now. He was being kind. The room really was quite cheerful.

He gave me the key, which I later discovered would open practically every door in the hotel. I thanked him, and I made a small mistake we irony collectors often make: I tried to share an irony with a stranger. It can't be done. I told him that I had been in the Arapahoe before—in Nineteen-hundred and Thirty-one. He was not interested. I do not blame him.

"I was painting the town red with a girl," I said.

"Um," he said.

I persisted, though. I told him how we had peeked through the French doors into the famous restaurant. I asked him what was on the other side of that wall now.

His reply, which he himself considered a bland statement of fact, fell so harshly on my ears that he might as well have slapped me hard in the face. He said this:

"Fist-fucking films."

I had never heard of such things. I gropingly asked what they were.

It woke him up a little, that I should be so surprised and appalled. He was sorry, as he would tell me later, to have brought a sweet little old man such ghastly news about what was going on right next door. He might have been my father, and I his little child. He even said to me, "Never mind."

"Tell me," I said.

So he explained slowly and patiently, and most reluctantly, that there was a motion-picture theater where the restaurant used to be. It specialized in films of male homosexual acts of love, and that their climaxes commonly consisted of one actor's thrusting his fist up the fundament of another actor.

I was speechless. Never had I dreamed that the First Amendment of the Constitution of the United States of America and the enchanting technology of a motion-picture camera would be combined to form such an atrocity.

"Sorry," he said.

"I doubt very much if you're to blame," I said. "Good night." I went in search of my room.

I passed the brutal wall where the French doors had been—on my way to the elevator. I paused there for a moment. My lips mouthed something that I myself did not understand for a moment. And then I realized what my lips must have said, what they had to say.

It was this, of course: "*Bon appetit.*"

# *11*

WHAT would the next day hold for me?
   I would, among other things, meet Leland Clewes, the man I had betrayed in Nineteen-hundred and Forty-nine.

But first I would unpack my few possessions, put them away nicely, read a little while, and then get my beauty sleep. I would be tidy. "At least I don't smoke anymore," I thought. The room was so clean to begin with.

Two top drawers in the dresser easily accepted all I owned, but I looked into all the other drawers anyway. Thus I discovered that the bottom drawer contained seven incomplete clarinets — without cases, mouthpieces, or bells.

Life is like that sometimes.

What I should have done, especially since I was an ex-convict, was to march back down to the front desk immediately and to say that I was the involuntary custodian of a drawerful of clarinet parts and that perhaps the police should be called. They were of course stolen. As I would learn the next day, they had been taken from a truck hijacked on the Ohio Turnpike — a robbery in which the driver had been killed. Thus, anyone associated with the incomplete instruments, should they turn up, might also be an accessory to murder. There were notices in every music store in the country, it turned out, saying that the police should be called immediately if a customer started talking about buying or selling sizeable quantities of clarinet parts. What I had in my drawer, I would guess, was about a thousandth of the stolen truckload.

But I simply closed the drawer again. I didn't want to go right back downstairs again. There was no telephone in my room. I would say something in the morning.

I was exhausted, I found. It was not yet curtain time in all the theaters down below, but I could hardly keep my eyes open. So I pulled my windowshade down, and I put myself to bed. Off I went, as my son used to say when he was little, "to seepy-bye," which is to say, "to sleep."

I dreamed that I was in an easy chair at the Harvard Club of New York, only four blocks away. I was not young again. I was not a jailbird, however, but a very successful man—the head of a medium-size foundation, perhaps, or assistant secretary of the interior, or executive director of the National Endowment for the Humanities, or some such thing. I really would have been some such thing in my sunset years, I honestly believe, if I had not testified against Leland Clewes in Nineteen-hundred and Forty-nine.

It was a compensatory dream. How I loved it. My clothes were in perfect repair. My wife was still alive. I was sipping brandy and coffee after a fine supper with several other members of the Class of Nineteen-hundred and Thirty-five. One detail from real life carried over into the dream: I was proud that I did not smoke anymore.

But then I absent-mindedly accepted a cigarette. It was simply one more civilized satisfaction to go with the good talk and my warm belly and all. "Yes, yes—" I said, recalling some youthful shenanigans. I chuckled, eyes twinkling. I put the cigarette to my lips. A friend held a match to it. I inhaled the smoke right down to the soles of my feet.

In the dream I collapsed to the floor in convulsions. In real life I fell out of my bed at the Hotel Arapahoe. In the dream my damp, innocent pink lungs shriveled into two black raisins. Bitter brown tar seeped from my ears and nostrils.

But worst of all was the *shame*.

Even as I was beginning to perceive that I was not in the Harvard Club, and that old classmates were not sitting forward in their leather chairs and looking down at me, and even after I found I could still gulp down air and it would nourish me—even then I was still strangling on shame.

I had just squandered the very last thing I had to be proud of in life: the fact that I did not smoke anymore.

And as I came awake, I examined my hands in the light that billowed up from Times Square and then bounced down on me from my freshly painted ceiling. I spread my fingers and turned my hands this way and that, as a magician might have done. I was showing an imaginary audience that the cigarette I had held only a moment before had now vanished into thin air.

But I, as magician, was as mystified as the audience as to what had become of the cigarette. I got up off the floor, woozy with disgrace, and I looked around everywhere for a cigarette's tell-tale red eye.

But there was no red eye.

I sat down on the edge of my bed, wide awake at last, and drenched in sweat. I took an inventory of my condition. Yes, I had gotten out of prison only that morning. Yes, I had sat in the smoking section of the airplane, but had felt no wish to smoke. Yes, I was now on the top floor of the Hotel Arapahoe.

No, there was no cigarette anywhere.

As for the pursuit of happiness on this planet: I was as happy as any human being in history.

"Thank God," I thought, "that cigarette was only a dream."

A T SIX O'CLOCK on the following morning, which was the prison's time for rising, I walked out into a city stunned by its own innocence. Nobody was doing anything bad to anybody anywhere. It was even hard to *imagine* badness. Why would anybody be bad?

It seemed doubtful that any great number of people lived here anymore. The few of us around might have been tourists in Angkor Wat, wondering sweetly about the religion and commerce that had caused people to erect such a city. And what had made all those people, obviously so excited for a while, decide to go away again?

Commerce would have to be reinvented. I offered a news dealer two dimes, bits of silverfoil as weightless as lint, for a copy of *The New York Times*. If he had refused, I would have understood perfectly. But he gave me a *Times*, and then he watched me closely, clearly wondering what I proposed to do with all that paper spattered with ink.

Eight thousand years before, I might have been a Phoenician sailor who had beached his boat on sand in Normandy, and who was now offering a man painted blue two bronze spearheads for the fur hat he wore. He was thinking: "Who is this crazy man?" And I was thinking: "Who is this crazy man?"

I had a whimsical idea: I thought of calling the secretary of the treasury, Kermit Winkler, a man who had graduated from Harvard two years after me, and saying this to him: "I just tried out two of your dimes on Times Square, and they worked like a dream. It looks like another great day for the coinage!"

I encountered a baby-faced policeman. He was as uncertain about his role in the city as I was. He looked at me sheepishly, as though there were every chance that I was the policeman and he was the old bum. Who could be sure of anything that early in the day?

I looked at my reflection in the black marble façade of a shuttered record store. Little did I dream that I would soon be a mogul of the recording industry, with gold and platinum recordings of moronic cacophony on my office wall.

There was something odd about the position of my arms in my reflection. I pondered it. I appeared to be cradling a baby. And then I understood that this was harmonious with my mood, that I was actually carrying what little future I thought I had as though it were a baby. I showed the baby the tops of the Empire State Building and the Chrysler Building, the lions in front of the Public Library. I carried it into an entrance to Grand Central Station, where, if we tired of the city, we could buy a ticket to simply anywhere.

Little did I dream that I would soon be scuttling through the catacombs beneath the station, and that I would learn the secret purpose of The RAMJAC Corporation down there.

The baby and I headed back west again. If we had kept going east, we would have soon delivered ourselves to Tudor City, where my son lived. We did not want to see him. Yes, and we paused before the window of a store that offered wicker picnic hampers—fitted out with Thermos bottles and tin boxes for sandwiches and so on. There was also a bicycle. I assumed that I could still ride a bicycle. I told the baby in my mind that we might buy a hamper and a bicycle and ride out on an abandoned dock some nice day and eat chicken sandwiches and wash them down with lemonade, while seagulls soared and keened over-head. I was beginning to feel hungry. Back in prison I would have been full of coffee and oatmeal by then.

I passed the Century Association on West Forty-third Street, a gentleman's club where, shortly after the Second World War, I had once been the luncheon guest of Peter Gibney, the com-poser, a Harvard classmate of mine. I was never invited back. I would have given anything now to be a bartender in there, but Gibney was still alive and probably still a member. We had had a falling out, you might say, after I testified against Leland Clewes. Gibney sent me a picture postcard, so that my wife and the postman could read the message, too.

"Dear shithead," it said, "why don't you crawl back under a damp rock somewhere?" The picture was of the Mona Lisa, with that strange smile of hers.

Down the block was the Coffee Shop of the Hotel Royalton, and I made for that. The Royalton, incidentally, like the Arapa-hoe, was a Hospitality Associates, Ltd., hotel; which is to say, a RAMJAC hotel. By the time I reached the coffee-shop door, however, my self-confidence had collapsed. Panic had taken its place. I believed that I was the ugliest, dirtiest little old bum in Manhattan. If I went into the coffee shop, everybody would be nauseated. They would throw me out and tell me to go to the Bowery, where I belonged.

But I somehow found the courage to go in anyway—and imagine my surprise! It was as though I had died and gone to heaven! A waitress said to me, "Honeybunch, you sit right down, and I'll bring you your coffee right away." I hadn't said anything to her.

So I did sit down, and everywhere I looked I saw customers of every description being received with love. To the waitresses everybody was "honeybunch" and "darling" and "dear." It was like an emergency ward after a great catastrophe. It did not matter what race or class the victims belonged to. They were all given the same miracle drug, which was coffee. The catastrophe in this case, of course, was that the sun had come up again.

I thought to myself, "My goodness—these waitresses and cooks are as unjudgmental as the birds and lizards on the Galapagos Islands, off Ecuador." I was able to make the comparison because I had read about those peaceful islands in prison, in a *National Geographic* loaned to me by the former lieutenant governor of Wyoming. The creatures there had had no enemies, natural or unnatural, for thousands of years. The idea of anybody's wanting to hurt them was inconceivable to them.

So a person coming ashore there could walk right up to an animal and unscrew its head, if he wanted to. The animal would have no plan for such an occasion. And all the other animals would simply stand around and watch, unable to draw any lessons for themselves from what was going on. A person could unscrew the head of every animal on an island, if that was his idea of business or fun.

I had the feeling that if Frankenstein's monster crashed into the coffee shop through a brick wall, all anybody would say to him was, "You sit down here, Lambchop, and I'll bring you your coffee right away."

The profit motive was not operating. The transactions were on the order of sixty-eight cents, a dollar ten, two dollars and sixty-three . . . I would find out later that the man who ran the cash register was the owner, but he would not stay at his post to rake the money in. He wanted to cook and wait on people, too, so that the waitresses and cooks kept having to say to him, "That's my customer, Frank. Get back to the cash register," or "I'm the cook here, Frank. What's this mess you've started here? Get back to the cash register," and so on.

His full name was Frank Ubriaco. He is now executive vice-president of the McDonald's Hamburgers Division of The RAMJAC Corporation.

I could not help noticing that he had a withered right hand. It looked as though it had been mummified, although he could still use his fingers some. I asked my waitress about it. She said he had literally French-fried that hand about a year ago. He accidentally dropped his wristwatch into a vat of boiling cooking oil. Before he realized what he was doing, he had plunged his hand into the oil, trying to rescue the watch, which was a very expensive Bulova Accutron.

So out into the city I went again, feeling much improved.

I sat down to read my newspaper in Bryant Park, behind the Public Library at Forty-second Street. My belly was full and as warm as a stove. It was no novelty for me to read *The New York Times*. About half the inmates back at the prison had mail subscriptions to the *Times*, and to *The Wall Street Journal*, too, and *Time* and *Newsweek* and *Sports Illustrated*, too, and on and on. And *People*. I subscribed to nothing, since the prison trash baskets were forever stuffed with periodicals of every kind.

There was a sign over every trash basket in prison, incidentally, which said, "Please!" Underneath that word was an arrow that pointed straight down.

In leafing through the *Times*, I saw that my son, Walter Stankiewicz, *né* Starbuck, was reviewing the autobiography of a Swedish motion-picture star. Walter seemed to like it a lot. I gathered that she had had her ups and downs.

What I particularly wanted to read, though, was the *Times*'s account of its having been taken over by The RAMJAC Corporation. The event might as well have been an epidemic of cholera in Bangladesh. It was given three inches of space on the bottom corner of an inside page. The chairman of the board of RAMJAC, Arpad Leen, said in the story that RAMJAC contemplated no changes in personnel or editorial policy. He pointed out that all publications taken over by RAMJAC in the past, including those of Time, Incorporated, had been allowed to go on as they wished, without any interference from RAMJAC.

"Nothing has changed but the ownership," he said. And I must say, as a former RAMJAC executive myself, that we didn't change companies we take over very much. If one of them started to die, of course—then our curiosity was aroused.

The story said that the publisher of the *Times* had received a handwritten note from Mrs. Jack Graham ". . . welcoming him to the RAMJAC family." It said she hoped he would stay on in his present capacity. Beneath the signature were the prints of all her fingers and thumbs. There could be no question about the letter's being genuine.

I looked about myself in Bryant Park. Lilies of the valley had raised their little bells above the winter-killed ivy and glassine envelopes that bordered the walks. My wife Ruth and I had lilies of the valley and ivy growing under the flowering crab apple tree in the front yard of our little brick bungalow in Chevy Chase, Maryland.

I spoke to the lilies of the valley. "Good morning," I said.

Yes, and I must have gone into a defensive trance again. Three hours passed without my budging from the bench.

I was aroused at last by a portable radio that was turned up loud. The young man carrying it sat down on a bench facing mine. He appeared to be Hispanic. I did not learn his name. If he had done me some kindness, he might now be an executive in The RAMJAC Corporation. The radio was tuned to the news. The newscaster said that the air quality that day was unacceptable.

Imagine that: unacceptable air.

The young man did not appear to be listening to his own radio. He may not even have understood English. The newscaster spoke with a barking sort of hilarity, as though life were a comical steeplechase, with unconventional steeds and hazards and vehicles involved. He made me feel that even I was a contestant—in a bathtub drawn by three aardvarks, perhaps. I had as good a chance as anybody to win.

He told about another man in the steeplechase, who had been sentenced to die in an electric chair in Texas. The doomed man had instructed his lawyers to fight anybody, including the governor and the President of the United States, who might want to grant him a stay of execution. The thing he wanted more than anything in life, evidently, was death in the electric chair.

Two joggers came down the path between me and the radio. They were a man and a woman in identical orange-and-gold sweatsuits and matching shoes. I already knew about the jogging craze. We had had many joggers in prison. I found them smug.

About the young man and his radio. I decided that he had bought the thing as a prosthetic device, as an artificial enthusiasm for the planet. He paid as little attention to it as I paid to my false front tooth. I have since seen several young men like that in groups—with their radios tuned to different stations, with their radios engaged in a spirited conversation. The young men themselves, perhaps having been told nothing but "shut up" all their lives, had nothing to say.

But now the young man's radio said something so horrifying that I got off my bench, left the park, and joined the throng of Free Enterprisers charging along Forty-second Street toward Fifth Avenue.

The story was this: An imbecilic young female drug addict from my home state of Ohio, about nineteen years old, had had a baby whose father was unknown. Social workers put her and the baby into a hotel not unlike the Arapahoe. She bought a full-grown German shepherd police dog for protection, but she forgot to feed it. Then she went out one night on some unspecified errand, and she left the dog to guard the baby. When she got back, she found that the dog had killed the baby and eaten part of it.

What a time to be alive!

So there I was marching as purposefully as anybody toward Fifth Avenue. According to plan, I began to study the faces coming at me, looking for a familiar one that might be of some use to me. I was prepared to be patient. It would be like panning for gold, I thought, like looking for a glint of the precious in a dish of sand.

When I had got no farther than the curb at Fifth Avenue, though, my warning systems went off earsplittingly: "*Beep, beep, beep! Honk, honk, honk! Rowrr, rowrr, rowrr!*"

Positive identification had been made!

Coming right at me was the husk of the man who had stolen Sarah Wyatt from me, the man I had ruined back in Nineteen-hundred and Forty-nine. He had not seen *me* yet. He was Leland Clewes!

He had lost all his hair, and his feet were capsizing in broken shoes, and the cuffs of his trousers were frayed, and his right arm appeared to have died. Dangling at the end of it was a battered sample case. Clewes had become an unsuccessful salesman, as I would find out later, of advertising matchbooks and calendars.

He is nowadays, incidentally, a vice-president in the Diamond Match Division of The RAMJAC Corporation.

In spite of all that had happened to him, though, his face, as he came toward me, was illuminated as always with an adolescent, goofy good will. He had worn that expression even in a photograph of his entering prison in Georgia, with the warden looking up at him as the secretary of state used to do. When Clewes was young, older men were always looking up at him as though to say, "That's my boy."

Now he saw me!

The eye-contact nearly electrocuted me. I might as well have stuck my nose into a lamp socket!

I went right past him and in the opposite direction. I had nothing to say to him, and no wish to stand and listen to all the terrible things he was entitled to say to me.

When I gained the curb, though, and the lights changed, and we were separated by moving cars, I dared to look back at him.

Clewes was facing me. Plainly, he had not yet come up with a name for me. He pointed at me with his free hand, indicating that he knew I had figured in his life in some way. And then he made that finger twitch like a metronome, ticking off possible names for me. This was fun for him. His feet were apart, his knees were bent, and his expression said that he remembered this much, anyway: We had been involved years ago in some sort of wildness, in a boyish prank of some kind.

I was hypnotized.

As luck would have it, there were religious fanatics behind him, barefoot and chanting and dancing in saffron robes. Thus did he appear to be a leading man in a musical comedy.

Nor was I without my own supporting cast. Willy-nilly, I had placed myself between a man wearing sandwich boards and a top hat, and a little old woman who had no home, who carried all her possessions in shopping bags. She wore enormous purple-and-black basketball shoes. They were so out of scale with the rest of her that she looked like a kangaroo.

My companions were both speaking to passers-by. The man in the sandwich boards was saying such things as "Put women back in the kitchen," and "God never meant women to be the equals of men," and so on. The shopping-bag lady seemed to be scolding strangers for their obesity, calling them, as I understood her, "stuck-up fats," and "rich fats," and "snooty fats," and "fats" of a hundred other varieties.

The thing was: I had been away from Cambridge, Massachusetts, so long that I could no longer detect that she was calling people "farts" in the accent of the Cambridge working class.

And in the toe of one of her capacious basketball shoes, among other things, were hypocritical love letters from me. Small world!

Good God! What a reaper and binder life can be sometimes!

When Leland Clewes, on the other side of Fifth Avenue, realized who I was, he formed his mouth into a perfect "O." I could not hear his saying "Oh," but I could see his saying "Oh." He was making fun of our encounter after all these years, overacting his surprise and dismay like an actor in a silent movie.

Plainly, he was going to come back across the street as soon as the lights changed. Meanwhile, all those fake Hindu imbeciles in saffron robes continued to chant and dance behind him.

There was still time for me to flee. What made me hold my ground, I think, was this: the need to prove myself a gentleman. During the bad old days, when I had testified against him, people who wrote about us, speculating as to who was telling the truth and who was not, concluded for the most part that he was a real gentleman, descended from a long line of gentlemen, and that I was a person of Slavic background only pretending to be a gentleman. Honor and bravery and truthfulness, then, would mean everything to him and very little to me.

Other contrasts were pointed out, certainly. With every new edition of the papers and news magazines, seemingly, I became shorter and he became taller. My poor wife became more gross and foreign, and his wife became more of an American golden girl. His friends became more numerous and respectable, and mine couldn't even be found under damp rocks anymore. But what troubled me most in my very bones was the idea that he was honorable and I was not. Thus, twenty-six years later, did this little Slavic jailbird hold his ground.

Across the avenue he came, the former Anglo-Saxon champion, a happy, ramshackle scarecrow now.

I was bewildered by his happiness. "What," I asked myself, "can this wreck have to be so happy about?"

So there we were reunited, with the shopping-bag lady looking on and listening. He put down his sample case and he extended his right hand. He made a joke, echoing the meeting of Henry Morton Stanley and David Livingstone in Darkest Africa: "Walter F. Starbuck, I presume."

And we might as well have been in Darkest Africa, for all anybody knew or cared about us anymore. Most people, if they remembered us at all, believed us dead, I suppose. And we had never been as significant in American history as we had sometimes thought we were. We were, if I may be forgiven, farts in a windstorm—or, as the shopping-bag lady would have called us, "fats in a windstorm."

Did I harbor any bitterness against him for having stolen my girl so long ago? No. Sarah and I had loved each other, but we would never have been happy as man and wife. We could never have gotten a sex life going. I had never persuaded her to take sex seriously. Leland Clewes had succeeded where I had failed—much to her grateful amazement, I am sure.

What tender memories did I have of Sarah? Much talk about human suffering and what could be done about it—and then infantile silliness for relief. We collected jokes for each other, to use when it was time for relief. We became addicted to talking to each other on the telephone for hours. Those talks were the most agreeable narcotic I have ever known. We became disembodied—like free-floating souls on the planet Vicuna. If there was a long silence, one or the other of us would end it with the start of a joke.

"What is the difference between an enzyme and a hormone?" she might ask me.

"I don't know," I would say.

"You can't hear an enzyme," she would say, and the silly jokes would go on and on—even though she had probably seen something horrible at the hospital that day.

## 13

I WAS ABOUT TO SAY to him gravely, watchfully but sincerely, "How are you, Leland? It is good to see you again."

But I never got to say it. The shopping-bag lady, whose voice was loud and piercing, cried out, "Oh, my God! Walter F. Starbuck! Is that really you?" I do not intend to reproduce her accent on the printed page.

I thought she was crazy. I thought that she would have parroted any name Clewes chose to hang on me. If he had called me "Bumptious Q. Bangwhistle," I thought, she would have cried, "Oh, my God! Bumptious Q. Bangwhistle! Is that really you?"

Now she began to lean her shopping bags against my legs, as though I were a convenient fireplug. There were six of them, which I would later study at leisure. They were from the most expensive stores in town—Henri Bendel, Tiffany's, Sloane's, Bergdorf Goodman, Bloomingdale's, Abercrombie and Fitch. All but Abercrombie and Fitch, incidentally, which would soon go bankrupt, were subsidiaries of The RAMJAC Corporation. Her bags contained mostly rags, pickings from garbage cans. Her most valuable possessions were in her basketball shoes.

I tried to ignore her. Even as she entrapped me with her bags, I kept my gaze on the face of Leland Clewes. "You're looking well," I said.

"I'm feeling well," he said. "And so is Sarah, you'll be happy to know."

"I'm glad to hear it," I said. "She's a very good girl." Sarah was no girl anymore, of course.

Clewes told me now that she was still doing a little nursing, as a part-time thing.

"I'm glad," I said.

To my horror, I felt as though a sick bat had dropped from the eaves of a building and landed on my wrist. The shopping-bag lady had taken hold of me with her filthy little hand.

"This is your wife?" he said.

"My what?" I said. He thought I had sunk so low that this awful woman and I were a pair! "I never saw her before in my life!" I said.

"Oh, Walter, Walter, Walter," she keened, "how can you say such a thing?"

I pried her hand off me; but the instant I returned my attention to Clewes, she snapped it onto my wrist again.

"Pretend she isn't here," I said. "This is crazy. She has nothing to do with me. I will not let her spoil this moment, which means a great deal to me."

"Oh, Walter, Walter, Walter," she said, "what has become of you? You're not the Walter F. Starbuck I knew."

"That's right," I said, "because you never knew any Walter F. Starbuck, but this man did." And I said to Clewes, "I suppose you know that I myself have spent time in prison now."

"Yes," he said. "Sarah and I were very sorry."

"I was let out only yesterday morning," I said.

"You have some trying days ahead," he said. "Is there somebody to look after you?"

"I'll look after you, Walter," said the shopping-bag lady. She leaned closer to me to say that so fervently, and I was nearly suffocated by her body odor and her awful breath. Her breath was laden not only with the smell of bad teeth but, as I would later realize, with finely-divided droplets of peanut oil. She had been eating nothing but peanut butter for years.

"You can't take care of anybody!" I said to her.

"Oh—you'd be surprised what all I could do for you," she said.

"Leland," I said, "all I want to say to you is that I know what jail is now, and, God damn it, the thing I'm sorriest about in my whole life is that I had anything to do with sending you to jail."

"Well," he said, "Sarah and I have often talked about what we would like to say most to you."

"I'm sure," I said.

"And it's this:" he said, "'Thank you very much, Walter. My going to prison was the best thing that ever happened to Sarah and me.' I'm not joking. Word of honor: It's true."

I was amazed. "How can that be?" I said.

"Because life is supposed to be a test," he said. "If my life had kept going the way it was going, I would have arrived in heaven never having faced any problem that wasn't as easy as pie to solve. Saint Peter would have had to say to me, 'You never lived, my boy. Who can say what you are?'"

"I see," I said.

"Sarah and I not only have love," he said, "but we have love that has stood up to the hardest tests."

"It sounds very beautiful," I said.

"We would be proud to have you see it," he said. "Could you come to supper sometime?"

"Yes—I suppose," I said.

"Where are you staying?" he said.

"The Hotel Arapahoe," I said.

"I thought they'd torn that down years ago," he said.

"No," I said.

"You'll hear from us," he said.

"I look forward to it," I said.

"As you'll see," he said, "we have nothing in the way of material wealth; but we need nothing in the way of material wealth."

"That's intelligent," I said.

"I'll say this though:" he said, "The food is good. As you may remember, Sarah is a wonderful cook."

"I remember," I said.

And now the shopping-bag lady offered the first proof that she really did know a lot about me. "You're talking about that Sarah Wyatt, aren't you?" she said.

There was a silence among us, although the uproar of the metropolis went on and on. Neither Clewes nor I had mentioned Sarah's maiden name.

I finally managed to ask her, woozy with shapeless misgivings, "How do you know that name?"

She became foxy and coquettish. "You think I don't know you were two-timing me with her the whole time?" she said.

Given that much information, I no longer needed to guess who she was. I had slept with her during my senior year at Harvard, while still squiring the virginal Sarah Wyatt to parties and concerts and athletic events.

She was one of the four women I had ever loved. She was the first woman with whom I had had anything like a mature sexual experience.

She was the remains of Mary Kathleen O'Looney!

I WAS HIS CIRCULATION MANAGER," said Mary Kathleen to Leland Clewes very loudly. "Wasn't I a good circulation manager, Walter?"

"Yes—you certainly were," I said. That was how we met: She presented herself at the tiny office of *The Bay State Progressive* in Cambridge at the start of my senior year, saying that she would do absolutely anything I told her to do, as long as it would improve the condition of the working class. I made her circulation manager, put her in charge of handing out the paper at factory gates and along breadlines and so on. She had been a scrawny little thing back then, but tough and cheerful and highly visible because of her bright red hair. She was such a hater of capitalism, because her mother was one of the women who died of radium poisoning after working for the Wyatt Clock Company. Her father had gone blind after drinking wood alcohol while a night watchman in a shoe-polish factory.

Now what was left of Mary Kathleen bowed her head, responded modestly to my having agreed that she had been a good circulation manager, and presented her pate to Leland Clewes and me. She had a bald spot about the size of a silver dollar. The tonsure that fringed it was sparse and white.

Leland Clewes would tell me later that he almost fainted. He had never seen a woman's bald spot before.

It was too much for him. He closed his blue eyes and he turned away. When he manfully faced us again, he avoided looking directly at Mary Kathleen—just as the mythological Perseus had avoided looking at the Gorgon's head.

"We must get together soon," he said.

"Yes," I said.

"You'll be hearing from me soon," he said.

"I hope so," I said.

"Must rush," he said.

"I understand," I said.

"Take care," he said.

"I will," I said.

He was gone.

Mary Kathleen's shopping bags were still banked around my legs. I was as immobilized and eye-catching as Saint Joan of Arc at the stake. Mary Kathleen still grasped my wrist, and she would not lower her voice.

"Now that I've found you, Walter," she cried, "I'll never let you go again!"

Nowhere in the world was this sort of theater being done anymore. For what it may be worth to modern impresarios: I can testify from personal experience that great crowds can still be gathered by melodrama, provided that the female in the piece speaks loudly and clearly.

"You used to tell me all the time how much you loved me, Walter," she cried. "But then you went away, and I never heard from you again. Were you just lying to me?"

I may have made some responsive sound. "Bluh," perhaps, or "fluh."

"Look at me in the eye, Walter," she said.

Sociologically, of course, this melodrama was as gripping as *Uncle Tom's Cabin* before the Civil War. Mary Kathleen O'Looney wasn't the only shopping-bag lady in the United States of America. There were tens of thousands of them in major cities throughout the country. Ragged regiments of them had been produced accidentally, and to no imaginable purpose, by the great engine of the economy. Another part of the machine was spitting out unrepentent murderers ten years old, and dope fiends and child batterers and many other bad things. People claimed to be investigating. Unspecified repairs were to be made at some future time.

Good-hearted people were meanwhile as sick about all these tragic by-products of the economy as they would have been about human slavery a little more than a hundred years before. Mary Kathleen and I were a miracle that our audience must have prayed for again and again: the rescue of at least one shopping-bag lady by a man who knew her well.

Some people were crying. I myself was about to cry.

"Hug her," said a woman in the crowd.

I did so.

I found myself embracing a bundle of dry twigs that was wrapped in rags. That was when I myself began to cry. I was crying for the first time since I had found my wife dead in bed one morning—in my little brick bungalow in Chevy Chase, Maryland.

## 15

M Y NOSE, thank God, had conked out by then. Noses are merciful that way. They will report that something smells awful. If the owner of a nose stays around anyway, the nose concludes that the smell isn't so bad after all. It shuts itself off, deferring to superior wisdom. Thus is it possible to eat Limburger cheese—or to hug the stinking wreckage of an old sweetheart at the corner of Fifth Avenue and Forty-second Street.

It felt for a moment as though Mary Kathleen had died in my arms. To be perfectly frank, that would have been all right with me. Where, after all, could I take her from there? What could be better than her receiving a hug from a man who had known her when she was young and beautiful, and then going to heaven right away?

It would have been wonderful. Then again, I would never have become executive vice-president of the Down Home Records Division of The RAMJAC Corporation. I might at this very moment be sleeping off a wine binge in the Bowery, while a juvenile monster soaked me in gasoline and touched me off with his Cricket lighter.

Mary Kathleen now spoke very softly. "God must have sent you," she said.

"There, there," I said. I went on hugging her.

"There's nobody I can trust anymore," she said.

"Now, now," I said.

"Everybody's after me," she said. "They want to cut off my hands."

"There, there," I said.

"I thought you were dead," she said.

"No, no," I said.

"I thought everybody was dead but me," she said.

"There, there," I said.

"I still believe in the revolution, Walter," she said.

"I'm glad," I said.

"Everybody else lost heart," she said. "I never lost heart."

"Good for you," I said.

"I've been working for the revolution every day," she said.

"I'm sure," I said.

"You'd be surprised," she said.

"Get her a hot bath," said somebody in the crowd.

"Get some food in her," said somebody else.

"The revolution is coming, Walter—sooner than you know," said Mary Kathleen.

"I have a hotel room where you can rest awhile," I said. "I have a little money. Not much, but some."

"Money," she said, and she laughed. Her scornful laughter about money had not changed. It was exactly as it had been forty years before.

"Shall we go?" I said. "My room isn't far from here."

"I know a better place," she said.

"Get her some One-a-Day vitamins," said somebody in the crowd.

"Follow me, Walter," said Mary Kathleen. She was growing strong again. It was Mary Kathleen who now separated herself from me, and not the other way around. She became raucous again. I picked up three of her bags, and she picked up the other three. Our ultimate destination, it would turn out, was the very top of the Chrysler Building, the quiet showroom of The American Harp Company up there. But first we had to get the crowd to part for us, and she began to call people in our way "capitalist fats" and "bloated plutocrats" and "bloodsuckers" and all that again.

Her means of locomotion in her gargantuan basketball shoes was this: She barely lifted the shoes from the ground, shoving one forward and then the other, like cross-country skis, while her upper body and shopping bags swiveled wildly from side to side. But that oscillating old woman could go like the wind! I panted to keep up with her, once we got clear of the crowd. We were surely the cynosure of all eyes. Nobody had ever seen a shopping-bag lady with an assistant before.

When we got to Grand Central Station, Mary Kathleen said that we had to make sure we weren't being followed. She led me up and down escalators, ramps, and stairways, looking over her shoulders for pursuers all the time. We scampered through the Oyster Bar three times. She brought us at last to an iron door at the end of a dimly lit corridor. We surely were all alone. Our hearts were beating hard.

When we had recovered our breaths, she said to me, "I am going to show you something you mustn't tell anybody about."

"I promise," I said.

"This is our secret," she said.

"Yes," I said.

I had assumed that we were as deep in the station as anyone could go. How wrong I was! Mary Kathleen opened the iron door on an iron staircase going down, down, down. There was a secret world as vast as Carlsbad Caverns below. It was used for nothing anymore. It might have been a sanctuary for dinosaurs. It had in fact been a repair shop for another family of extinct monsters—locomotives driven by steam.

Down the steps we went.

My God—what majestic machinery there must have been down there at one time! What admirable craftsmen must have worked there! In conformance with fire laws, I suppose, there were lightbulbs burning here and there. And there were little dishes of rat poison set around. But there were no other signs that anyone had been down there for years.

"This is my home, Walter," she said.

"Your what?" I said.

"You wouldn't want me sleeping outdoors, would you?" she said.

"No," I said.

"Be glad, then," she said, "that I have such a nice and private home."

"I am," I said.

"You not only talked to me—you hugged me," she said. "That's how I knew I could trust you."

"Um," I said.

"You're not after my hands," she said.

"No," I said.

"You know there are millions of poor souls out on the street, looking for a toilet somebody will let them use?" she said.

"I suppose that's true," I said.

"Look at this," she said. She led me into a chamber that contained row on row of toilets.

"It's good to know they're here," I said.

"You won't tell anybody?" she said.

"No," I said.

"I'm putting my life in your hands, telling you my secrets like this," she said.

"I'm honored," I said.

And then out of the catacombs we climbed. She led me through a tunnel under Lexington Avenue, and up a staircase into the lobby of the Chrysler Building. She skied across the floor to a waiting elevator, with me trotting behind. A guard shouted at us, but we got into the elevator before he could stop us. The doors shut in his angry face as Mary Kathleen punched the button for the topmost floor.

We had the car all to ourselves, and upward we flew. Within a trice the doors slithered open on a place of unearthly beauty and peace within the building's stainless-steel crown. I had often wondered what was up there. Now I knew. The crown came to a point seventy feet above us. Between us and the point, as I looked upward in awe, there was nothing but a lattice of girders and air, air, air.

"What a glorious waste of space!" I thought. But then I saw that there were tenants after all. Myriads of bright yellow little birds were perched on the girders, or flitting through the prisms of light admitted by the bizarre windows, by the great triangles of glass that pierced the crown.

The vast floor at whose edge we stood was carpeted in grassy green. There was a fountain splashing at its center. There were garden benches and statues everywhere, and here and there a harp.

As I have already said, this was the showroom of The American Harp Company, which had recently become a subsidiary of The RAMJAC Corporation. The company had occupied this space since the building opened in Nineteen-hundred and Thirty-one. All the birds I saw, which were prothonotary warblers, were descended from a single pair released back then.

There was a Victorian gazebo near the elevator, which contained the desks of the salesman and his secretary. A woman was sobbing in there. What a morning it was for tears! What a book this is for tears!

The oldest man I had ever seen came tottering out of the gazebo. He wore a swallowtail coat and striped trousers and spats. He was the sole salesman, and had been since

Nineteen-hundred and Thirty-one. He was the man who had released from the hot cage of his hands and into this enchanted space the first two prothonotary warblers. He was ninety-two years old! He looked like John D. Rockefeller at the end of his life, or like a mummy. The only moisture left in him, seemingly, was faint dew on the surface of his eyes. He was not entirely defenseless, however. He was president of a pistol club that shot at targets shaped like men on weekends, and he had a loaded Luger the size of a Doberman pinscher in his desk. He had been looking forward to a robbery for quite some time.

"Oh—it's you," he said to Mary Kathleen, and she said that, yes, it was.

She was accustomed to coming here almost every day and sitting for several hours. The understanding was that she was to get out of sight with her shopping bags, in case a customer came in. There was a further understanding, which Mary Kathleen had now violated.

"I thought I told you," he said to her, "that you were never to bring anybody else with you, or even to tell anybody else how nice it was up here."

Since I was carrying three shopping bags, he concluded that I was another derelict, a shopping-bag man.

"He isn't a bum," said Mary Kathleen. "He's a Harvard man."

He did not believe this for a minute. "I see," he said, and he looked me up and down. He himself had never even graduated from grammar school, incidentally. There had been no laws against child labor when he was a boy, and he had gone to work in the Chicago factory of The American Harp Company at the age of ten. "I've heard that you can always tell a Harvard man," he said, "but you can't tell him much."

"I never thought there was anything special about Harvard men," I said.

"That makes two of us," he said. He was being most unpleasant, and clearly wanted me out of there. "This is not the Salvation Army," he said. This was a man born during the presidency of Grover Cleveland. Imagine that! He said to Mary Kathleen, "Really—I'm most disappointed in you, bringing somebody else along. Should we expect three tomorrow, and twenty the day after that? Christianity does have its limits, you know."

I now made a blunder that would land me back in *el calabozo* before noon on what was to have been my first full day of freedom. "As a matter of fact," I said, "I'm here on business."

"You wish to buy a harp?" he said. "They're seven thousand dollars and up, you know. How about a kazoo instead?"

"I was hoping you could advise me," I said, "as to where I could buy clarinet parts—not whole clarinets, but just clarinet parts." I was not serious about this. I was extrapolating a business fantasy from the contents of my bottom drawer at the Arapahoe.

The old man was secretly electrified. Thumbtacked to the bulletin board in the gazebo was a circular that advised him to call the police in case anyone expressed interest in buying or selling clarinet parts. As he would tell me later, he had stuck it up there months before—"like a lottery ticket bought in a moment of folly." He had never expected to win. His name was Delmar Peale.

Delmar was nice enough later on to make me a present of the circular, which I hung on my office wall at RAMJAC. I became his superior in the RAMJAC family, since American Harp was a subsidiary of my division.

I was certainly no superior of his the first time we met, though. He played cat-and-mouse with me. "Many clarinet parts, or a few?" he asked cunningly.

"Quite a few, actually," I said. "I realize that you yourself don't handle clarinets—"

"You've come to the right place all the same," he hastened to assure me. "I know everyone in the business. If you and Madam X would like to make yourselves comfortable, I would be glad to make some telephone calls."

"You're too kind," I said.

"Not at all," he said.

"Madam X," incidentally, was the only name he had for Mary Kathleen. That was what she had told him her name was. She had simply barged in one day, trying to escape from people she thought were after her. He had worried a lot about shopping-bag ladies, and he was a practicing Christian, so he had let her stay.

Meanwhile, the sobbing in the gazebo was abating some.

Delmar conducted us to a bench far from the gazebo, so we could not hear him call the police. He had us sit down. "Comfy?" he said.

"Yes, thank you," I said.

He rubbed his hands. "How about some coffee?" he said.

"It makes me too nervous," said Mary Kathleen.

"With sugar and cream, if it's not too much trouble," I said.

"No trouble at all," he said.

"What's the trouble with Doris?" said Mary Kathleen. That was the name of the secretary who was crying in the gazebo. Her full name was Doris Kramm. She herself was eighty-seven years old.

At my suggestion, *People* magazine recently did a story on Delmar and Doris as being almost certainly the oldest boss-and-secretary team in the world, and perhaps in all history. It was a cute story. One picture showed Delmar with his Luger, and quoted him to the effect that anybody who tried to rob The American Harp Company ". . . would be one unhappy robber pretty quick."

He told Mary Kathleen now that Doris wept because she had had two hard blows in rapid succession. She had been notified on the previous afternoon that she was going to have to retire immediately, now that RAMJAC had taken over. The retirement age for all RAMJAC employees everywhere, except for supervisory personnel, was sixty-five. And then that morning, while she was cleaning out her desk, she got a telegram saying that her great-grandniece had been killed in a head-on collision after a high-school senior prom in Sarasota, Florida. Doris had no descendents of her own, he explained, so her collateral relatives meant a lot to her.

Delmar and Doris, incidentally, did almost no business up there, and continue to do almost no business up there. I was proud, when I became a RAMJAC executive, that American Harp Company harps were the finest harps in the world. You would have thought that the best harps would come from Italy or Japan or West Germany by now, with American craftsmanship having become virtually extinct. But no—musicians even in those countries and even in the Soviet Union agreed: Only an American Harp Company harp can cut the mustard. But the harp business is not and can never be a volume business, except in heaven, perhaps. So the profit picture, the bottom line, was ridiculous. It is so ridiculous that I recently undertook an investigation of why RAMJAC had ever acquired American Harp. I learned that it was in order to capture the incredible lease on the top of the Chrysler Building. The lease ran until the year Two-thousand and Thirty-one, at a rent of two hundred dollars a month! Arpad Leen wanted to turn the place into a restaurant.

That the company also owned a factory in Chicago with sixty-five employees was a mere detail. If it could not be made to show a substantial profit within a year or two, RAMJAC would close it down.

Peace.

# 16

MARY KATHLEEN O'LOONEY was, of course, the legendary Mrs. Jack Graham, the majority stockholder in The RAMJAC Corporation. She had her inkpad and pens and writing paper in her basketball shoes. Those shoes were her bank vaults. Nobody could take them off of her without waking her up.

She would claim later that she had told me who she really was on the elevator.

I could only reply, "If I had heard you say that, Mary Kathleen, I surely would have remembered it."

If I had known who she really was, all her talk about people who wanted to cut off her hands would have made a lot more sense. Whoever got her hands could pickle them and throw away the rest of her, and control The RAMJAC Corporation with just her fingertips. No wonder she was on the run. No wonder she dared not reveal her true identity anywhere.

No wonder she dared not trust anybody. On this particular planet, where money mattered more than anything, the nicest person imaginable might suddenly get the idea of wringing her neck so that their loved ones might live in comfort. It would be the work of the moment—and easily forgotten as the years went by. Time flies.

She was so tiny and weak. Killing her and cutting off her hands would have been little more horrifying than what went on ten thousand times a day at a mechanized chicken farm. RAMJAC owns Colonel Sanders Kentucky Fried Chicken, of course. I have seen that operation as it looks backstage.

About my not having heard her say she was Mrs. Jack Graham on the elevator:

I do remember that I had trouble with my ears toward the top of the elevator ride, because of the sudden change in altitude. We shot up about a thousand feet, with no stops on the way. Also: Temporarily deaf or not, I had my conversational automatic pilot on. I was not thinking about what she was saying, or what I was saying, either. I thought that we were both so far outside the mainstream of human affairs that all we could do was comfort each other with animal sounds. I remember her saying at one point that she owned the Waldorf-Astoria Hotel, and I thought I had not heard her right.

"I'm glad," I said.

So, as I sat beside her on the bench in the harp showroom, she thought I had a piece of key information about her, which I did not have. And Delmar Peale had meanwhile called the police and had also sent Doris Kramm out, supposedly for coffee, but really to find a policeman out on the street somewhere.

As it happened, there was a small riot going on in the park adjacent to the United Nations, only three blocks away. Every available policeman was over there. Out-of-work white youths armed with baseball bats were braining men they thought were homosexuals. They threw one of them into the East River, who turned out to be the finance minister of Sri Lanka.

I would meet some of those youths later at the police station, and they would assume that I, too, was a homosexual. One of them exposed his private parts to me and said, "Hey, Pops—you want some of this? Come and get it. Yum, yum, yum," and so on.

But my point is that the police could not come and get me for nearly an hour. So Mary Kathleen and I had a nice long talk. She felt safe in this place. She felt safe with me. She dared to be sane.

It was most touching. Only her body was decrepit. Her voice and the soul it implied might well have belonged still to what she used to be, an angrily optimistic eighteen-year-old.

"Everything is going to be all right now," she said to me in the showroom of The American Harp Company. "Something always told me that it would turn out this way. All's well that ends well," she said.

What a fine mind she had! What fine minds all of the four women I've loved have had! During the months I more or less lived with Mary Kathleen, she read all the books I had read or pretended to have read as a Harvard student. Those volumes had been chores to me, but they were a cannibal feast to Mary Kathleen. She read my books the way a young cannibal might eat the hearts of brave old enemies. Their magic would become hers. She said of my little library one time: "the greatest books in the world, taught by the wisest men in the world at the greatest university in the world to the smartest students in the world."

Peace.

And contrast Mary Kathleen, if you will, with my wife Ruth, the Ophelia of the death camps, who believed that even the most intelligent human beings were so stupid that they could only make things worse by speaking their minds. It was thinkers, after all, who had set up the death camps. Setting up a death camp, with its railroad sidings and its around-the-clock crematoria, was not something a moron could do. Neither could a moron explain why a death camp was ultimately humane.

Again: peace.

So there Mary Kathleen and I were—among all those harps. They are very strange-looking instruments, now that I think about them, and not very far from poor Ruth's idea of civilization even in peacetime—impossible marriages between Greek columns and Leonardo da Vinci's flying machines.

Harps are self-destructive, incidentally. When I found myself in the harp business at RAMJAC, I had hoped that American Harp had among its assets some wonderful old harps that would turn out to be as valuable as Stradivari's and the Amatis' violins. There was zero chance for this dream's coming true. The tensions in a harp are so tremendous and unrelenting that it becomes unplayable after fifty years and belongs on a dump or in a museum.

I discovered something fascinating about prothonotary warblers, too. They are the only birds that are housebroken in captivity. You would think that the harps would have to be protected from bird droppings by canopies—but not at all! The warblers deposit their droppings in teacups that are set around. In a state of nature, evidently, they deposit their droppings in other birds' nests. That is what they think the teacups are.

Live and learn!

But back to Mary Kathleen and me among all those harps—with the prothonotary warblers overhead and the police on their way:

"After my husband died, Walter," she said, "I became so unhappy and lost that I turned to alcohol." That husband would have been Jack Graham, the reclusive engineer who had founded The RAMJAC Corporation. He had not built the company from scratch. He had been born a multimillionaire. So far as I knew, of course, she might have been talking about a plumber or a truck driver or a college professor or anyone.

She told about going to a private sanitarium in Louisville, Kentucky, where she was given shock treatments. These blasted all her memories from Nineteen-hundred and Thirty-five until Nineteen-hundred and Fifty-five. That would explain why she thought she could still trust me now. Her memories of how callously I had left her, and of my later betrayal of Leland Clewes and all that, had been burned away. She was able to believe that I was still the fiery idealist I had been in Nineteen-hundred and Thirty-five. She had missed my part in Watergate. Everybody had missed my part in Watergate.

"I had to make up a lot of memories," she went on, "just to fill up all the empty spaces. There had been a war, I knew, and I remembered how much you hated fascism. I saw you on a beach somewhere—on your back, in a uniform, with a rifle, and with the water washing gently around you. Your eyes were wide open, Walter, because you were dead. You were staring straight up at the sun."

We were silent for a moment. A yellow bird far above us warbled as though its heart would break. The song of a prothonotary warbler is notoriously monotonous, as I am the first to admit. I am not about to risk the credibility of my entire tale by claiming that prothonotary warblers rival the Boston Pops Orchestra with their songs. Still—they are capable of expressing heartbreak—within strict limits, of course.

"I've had the same dream of myself," I said. "Many's the time, Mary Kathleen, that I've wished it were true."

"No! No! No!" she protested. "Thank God you're still alive! Thank God there's somebody still alive who cares what happens to this country. I thought maybe I was the last one. I've wandered this city for years now, Walter, saying to myself, 'They've all died off, the ones who cared.' And then there you were."

"Mary Kathleen," I said, "you should know that I just got out of prison."

"Of course you did!" she said. "All the good people go to prison all the time. Oh, thank God you're still alive! We will remake this country and then the world. I couldn't do it by myself, Walter."

"No—I wouldn't think so," I said.

"I've just been hanging on for dear life," she said. "I haven't been able to do anything but survive. That's how alone I've been. I don't need much help, but I do need some."

"I know the problem," I said.

"I can still see enough to write, if I write big," she said, "but I can't read the stories in newspapers anymore. My eyes—" She said she sneaked into bars and department stores and motel lobbies to listen to the news on television, but that the sets were almost never tuned to the news. Sometimes she would hear a snatch of news on somebody's portable radio, but the person owning it usually switched to music as soon as the news began.

Remembering the news I had heard that morning, about the police dog that ate a baby, I told her that she wasn't really missing much.

"How can I make sensible plans," she said, "if I don't know what's going on?"

"You can't," I said.

"How can you base a revolution on *Lawrence Welk* and *Sesame Street* and *All in the Family*?" she said. All these shows were sponsored by RAMJAC.

"You can't," I said.

"I need solid information," she said.

"Of course you do," I said. "We all do."

"It's all such crap," she said. "I find this magazine called *People* in garbage cans," she said, "but it isn't about people. It's about crap."

This all seemed so pathetic to me: that a shopping-bag lady hoped to plan her scuttlings about the city and her snoozes among ash cans on the basis of what publications and radio and television could tell her about what was really going on.

It seemed pathetic to her, too. "Jackie Onassis and Frank Sinatra and the Cookie Monster and Archie Bunker make their moves," she said, "and then I study what they have done, and then I decide what Mary Kathleen O'Looney had better do.

"But now I have you," she said. "You can be my eyes—and my brains!"

"Your eyes, maybe," I said. "I haven't distinguished myself in the brains department recently."

"Oh—if only Kenneth Whistler were alive, too," she said.

She might as well have said, "If only Donald Duck were alive, too." Kenneth Whistler was a labor organizer who had been my idol in the old days—but I felt nothing about him now, had not thought about him for years.

"What a trio we would make," she went on. "You and me and Kenneth Whistler!"

Whistler would have been a bum, too, by now, I supposed—if he hadn't died in a Kentucky mine disaster in Nineteen-hundred and Forty-one. He had insisted on being a worker as well as a labor organizer, and would have found modern union officials with their soft, pink palms intolerable. I had shaken hands with him. His palm had felt like the back of a crocodile. The lines in his face had had so much coal dust worked into them that they looked like black tattoos. Strangely enough, this was a Harvard man—the class of Nineteen-hundred and Twenty-one.

"Well," said Mary Kathleen, "at least there's still us—and now we can start to make our move."

"I'm always open to suggestions," I said.

"Or maybe it isn't worth it," she said.

She was talking about rescuing the people of the United States from their economy, but I thought she was talking about life in general. So I said of life in general that it probably was worth it, but that it did seem to go on a little too long. My life would have been a masterpiece, for example, if I had died on a beach with a fascist bullet between my eyes.

"Maybe people are just no good anymore," she said. "They all look so mean to me. They aren't like they were during the Depression. I don't see anybody being kind to anybody anymore. Nobody will even speak to me."

She asked me if I had seen any acts of kindness anywhere. I reflected on this and I realized that I had encountered almost nothing but kindness since leaving prison. I told her so.

"Then it's the way I look," she said. This was surely so. There was a limit to how much reproachful ugliness most people could bear to look at, and Mary Kathleen and all her shopping-bag sisters had exceeded that limit.

She was eager to know about individual acts of kindness toward me, to have it confirmed that Americans could still be good-hearted. So I was glad to tell her about my first twenty-four hours as a free man, starting with the kindnesses shown to me by Clyde Carter, the guard, and then by Dr. Robert Fender, the supply clerk and science-fiction writer. After that, of course, I was given a ride in a limousine by Cleveland Lawes.

Mary Kathleen exclaimed over these people, repeated their names to make sure she had them right. "They're saints!" she said. "So there are still saints around!"

Thus encouraged, I embroidered on the hospitality offered to me by Dr. Israel Edel, the night clerk at the Arapahoe, and then by the employees at the Coffee Shop of the Hotel Royalton on the following morning. I was not able to give her the name of the owner of the shop, but only the physical detail that set him apart from the populace. "He had a French-fried hand," I said.

"The saint with the French-fried hand," she said wonderingly.

"Yes," I said, "and you yourself saw a man I thought was the worst enemy I had in the world. He was the tall, blue-eyed man with the sample case. You heard him say that he forgave me for everything I had done, and that I should have supper with him soon."

"Tell me his name again," she said.

"Leland Clewes," I said.

"Saint Leland Clewes," she said reverently. "See how much you've helped me already? I never could have found out about all these good people for myself." Then she performed a minor mnemonic miracle, repeating all the names in chronological order. "Clyde Carter, Dr. Robert Fender, Cleveland Lawes, Israel Edel, the man with the French-fried hand, and Leland Clewes."

Mary Kathleen took off one of her basketball shoes. It wasn't the one containing the inkpad and her pens and paper and her will and all that. The shoe she took off was crammed with memorabilia. There were hypocritical love letters from me, as I've said. But she was particularly eager for me to see a snapshot of what she called ". . . my two favorite men."

It was a picture of my one-time idol, Kenneth Whistler, the Harvard-educated labor organizer, shaking hands with a small and goofy-looking college boy. The boy was myself. I had ears like a loving cup.

That was when the police finally came clumping in to get me.

"I'll rescue you, Walter," said Mary Kathleen. "Then we'll rescue the world together."

I was relieved to be getting away from her, frankly. I tried to seem regretful about our parting. "Take care of yourself, Mary Kathleen," I said. "It looks like this is good-bye."

# 17

I HUNG THAT SNAPSHOT of Kenneth Whistler and myself, taken in the autumn of Nineteen-hundred and Thirty-five, dead center in the Great Depression, on my office wall at RAMJAC—next to the circular about stolen clarinet parts. It was taken by Mary Kathleen, with my bellows camera, on the morning after we first heard Whistler speak. He had come all the way to Cambridge from Harlan County, Kentucky, where he was a miner and a union organizer, to address a rally whose purpose was to raise money and sympathy for the local chapter of the International Brotherhood of Abrasives and Adhesives Workers.

The union was run by communists then. It is run by gangsters now. As a matter of fact, the start of my prison sentence overlapped with the end of one being served at Finletter by the lifetime president of the I.B.A.A.W. His twenty-three-year-old daughter was running the union from her villa in the Bahamas while he was away. He was on the telephone to her all the time. He told me that the membership was almost entirely black and Hispanic now. It was lily-white back in the thirties—Scandinavians mostly. I don't think a black or Hispanic would have been allowed to join back in the good old days.

Times change.

Whistler spoke at night. On the afternoon before he spoke, I made love to Mary Kathleen O'Looney for the first time. It was mixed up in our young minds, somehow, with the prospect of hearing and perhaps even touching a genuine saint. How better to present ourselves to him or to any holy person, I suppose, than as Adam and Eve—smelling strongly of apple juice?

Mary Kathleen and I made love in the apartment of an associate professor of anthropology named Arthur von Strelitz. His specialty was the headhunters of the Solomon Islands. He spoke their language and respected their taboos. They trusted him. He was unmarried. His bed was unmade. His apartment was on the third floor of a frame house on Brattle Street.

A footnote to history: Not only that house, but that very apartment would be used later as a set in a very popular motion

picture called *Love Story*. It was released during my early days
with the Nixon administration. My wife and I went to see it
when it came to Chevy Chase. It was a made-up story about
a wealthy Anglo-Saxon student who married a poor Italian
student, much against his father's wishes. She died of cancer.
The aristocratic father was played brilliantly by Ray Milland.
He was the best thing in the movie. Ruth cried all through the
movie. We sat in the back row of the theater for two reasons:
so I could smoke and so there wouldn't be anybody behind her
to marvel at how fat she was. But I could not really concentrate
on the story, because I knew the apartment where so much of
it was happening so well. I kept waiting for Arthur von Strelitz
or Mary Kathleen O'Looney or even me to appear.

Small world.

Mary Kathleen and I had the place for a weekend. Von Strelitz had given me the key. He had then gone to visit some other
German émigré friends on Cape Ann. He must have been about
thirty then. He seemed old to me. He was born into an aristocratic family in Prussia. He was lecturing at Harvard when
Hitler became dictator of Germany in the spring of Nineteen-
hundred and Thirty-three. He declined to go home. He applied
for American citizenship instead. His father, who never communicated with him in any way again, would command a corps
of S.S. and die of pneumonia during the Siege of Leningrad. I
know how his father died, since there was testimony about his
father at the War Crimes Trials in Nuremberg, where I was in
charge of housekeeping.

Again: small world.

His father, acting on written orders from Martin Bormann,
who was tried *in absentia* in Nuremberg, caused to be executed
all persons, civilian and military, taken prisoner during the siege.
The intent was to demoralize the defenders of Leningrad. Leningrad, incidentally, was younger than New York City. Imagine
that! Imagine a famous European city, full of imperial treasures
and worth besieging, and yet much younger than New York.

Arthur von Strelitz would never learn how his father died. He
himself would be rowed ashore from an American submarine in
the Solomon Islands, as a spy, while they were still occupied by
the Japanese. He would never be heard of again.

Peace.

He thought it was urgent, I remember, that mankind and womankind be defined. Otherwise, he was sure, they were doomed forever to be defined by the needs of institutions. He had mainly factories and armies in mind.

He was the only man I ever knew who wore a monocle.

Now Mary Kathleen O'Looney, age eighteen, lay in his bed. We had just made love. It would be very pretty to paint her as naked now—a pink little body. But I never saw her naked. She was modest. Never could I induce her to take off all her clothes.

I myself stood stark naked at a window, with my private parts just below the sill. I felt like the great god Thor.

"Do you love me, Walter?" Mary Kathleen asked my bare backside.

What could I reply but this: "Of course I do."

There was a knock on the door. I had told my coeditor at *The Bay State Progressive* where I could be found in case of emergency. "Who is it?" I said.

There was a sound like a little gasoline engine on the other side of the door. It was Alexander Hamilton McCone, my mentor, who had decided to come to Cambridge unannounced—to see what sort of life I was leading on his money. He sounded like a motor because of the Cuyahoga Massacre in Eighteen-hundred and Ninety-four. He was trying to say his own name.

# 18

I HAD SOMEHOW NEGLECTED to tell him that I had become a communist.

Now he had found out about that. He had come first to my room in Adams House, where he was told that I was most likely at *The Progressive*. He had gone to *The Progressive* and had ascertained what sort of publication it was and that I was its coeditor. Now he was outside the door with a copy folded under his arm.

I remained calm. Such was the magic of having emptied my seminal vesicles so recently.

Mary Kathleen, obeying my silent arm signals, hid herself in the bathroom. I slipped on a robe belonging to von Strelitz. He had brought it home from the Solomon Islands. It appeared to be made of shingles, with wreaths of feathers at its collar and cuffs.

Thus was I clad when I opened the door and said to old Mr. McCone, who was in his early sixties then, "Come in, come in."

He was so angry with me that he could only continue to make those motor sounds: "bup-bup-bup-bup-bup . . ." But he meanwhile did a grotesque pantomime of how repulsed he was by the paper, whose front-page cartoon showed a bloated capitalist who looked just like him; by my costume; by the unmade bed; by the picture of Karl Marx on von Strelitz's wall.

Out he went again, slamming the door behind him. He was through with me!

Thus did my childhood end at last. I had become a man.

And it was as a man that I went that night, with Mary Kathleen on my arm, to hear Kenneth Whistler speak at the rally for my comrades in the International Brotherhood of Abrasives and Adhesives Workers.

How could I be so serene, so confident? My tuition for the year had already been paid, so I would graduate. I was about to get a full scholarship to Oxford. I had a superb wardrobe in good repair. I had been saving most of my allowance, so that I had a small fortune in the bank.

If I had to, I could always borrow money from Mother, God rest her soul.

What a daring young man I was!

What a treacherous young man I was! I already knew that I would abandon Mary Kathleen at the end of the academic year. I would write her a few love letters and then fall silent after that. She was too low class.

Whistler had a big bandage over one temple and his right arm was in a plaster cast that night. This was a Harvard graduate, mind you, and from a good family in Cincinnati. He was a Buckeye, like me. Mary Kathleen and I supposed that he had been beat up by the forces of evil yet again—by the police or the National Guard, or by goons or organizers of yellow-dog unions.

I held Mary Kathleen's hand.

Nobody had ever told her he loved her before.

I was wearing a suit and a necktie, and so were most of the men there. We wanted to show that we were as decent and sober citizens as anyone. Kenneth Whistler might have been a businessman. He had even found time to shine his shoes.

Those used to be important symbols of self-respect: shined shoes.

Whistler began his speech by making fun of his bandages. "The Spirit of Seventy-six," he said.

Everybody laughed and laughed, although the occasion was surely not a happy one. All the members of the union had been fired about a month before—for joining a union. They were makers of grinding wheels, and there was only one company in the area that could use their skills. That was the Johannsen Grinder Company, and that was the company that had fired them. They were specialized potters, essentially, shaping soft materials and then firing them in kilns. The fathers or grandfathers of most of them had actually been potters in Scandinavia, who were brought to this country to learn this new specialty.

The rally took place in a vacant store in Cambridge. Appropriately enough, the folding chairs had been contributed by a funeral home. Mary Kathleen and I were in the first row.

Whistler, it turned out, had been injured in a routine mining accident. He said he had been working as "a robber," taking out supporting pillars of coal from a tunnel where the seam had otherwise been exhausted. Something had fallen on him.

And he went seamlessly from talk of such dangerous work in such a dark place to a recollection of a tea dance at the Ritz fifteen years before, where a Harvard classmate named Nils Johannsen had been caught using loaded dice in a crap game in the men's room. This was the same person who was now the president of Johannsen Grinder, who had fired all these workers. Johannsen's grandfather had started the company. He said that Johannsen had had his head stuck in a toilet bowl at the Ritz, and that the hope was that he would never use loaded dice again.

"But here he is," said Whistler, "using loaded dice again."

He said that Harvard could be held responsible for many atrocities, including the executions of Sacco and Vanzetti, but that it was innocent of having produced Nils Johannsen. "He never attended a lecture, never wrote a paper, never read a book while he was there," he said. "He was asked to leave at the end of his sophomore year.

"Oh, I pity him," he said. "I even understand him. How else could he ever amount to anything if he did not use loaded dice? How has he used loaded dice with you? The laws that say he can fire anybody who stands up for the basic rights of workers—those are loaded dice. The policemen who will protect his property rights but not your human rights—those are loaded dice."

Whistler asked the fired workers how much Johannsen actually knew or cared about grinding wheels. How shrewd this was! The way to befriend working people in those days, and to get them to criticize their society as brilliantly as any philosopher, was to get them to talk about the one subject on which they were almost arrogantly well-informed: their work.

It was something to hear. Worker after worker testified that Johannsen's father and grandfather had been mean bastards, too, but that they at least knew how to run a factory. Raw materials of the highest quality arrived on time in their day—machinery was properly maintained, the heating plant and the toilets worked, bad workmanship was punished and good workmanship was rewarded, no defective grinding wheel ever reached a customer, and on and on.

Whistler asked them if one of their own number could run the factory better than Nils Johannsen did. One man spoke for them all on that subject: "God, yes," he said, "anyone here."

Whistler asked him if he thought it was right that a person could inherit a factory.

The man's considered answer was this: "Not if he's afraid of the factory and everybody in it—no. No, siree."

This piece of groping wisdom impresses me still. A sensible prayer people could offer up from time to time, it seems to me, might go something like this: "Dear Lord—never put me in the charge of a frightened human being."

Kenneth Whistler promised us that the time was at hand for workers to take over their factories and to run them for the benefit of mankind. Profits that now went to drones and corrupt politicians would go to those who worked, and to the old and the sick and the orphaned. All people who could work would work. There would be only one social class—the working class. Everyone would take turns doing the most unpleasant work, so that a doctor, for example, might be expected to spend a week out of each year as a garbage man. The production of luxury goods would stop until the basic needs of every citizen were met. Health care would be free. Food would be cheap and nourishing and plentiful. Mansions and hotels and office buildings would be turned into small apartments, until everyone was decently housed. Dwellings would be assigned by means of a lottery. There would be no more wars and eventually no more national boundaries, since everyone in the world would belong to the same class with identical interests—the interests of the working class.

And on and on.

What a spellbinder he was!

Mary Kathleen whispered in my ear, "You're going to be just like him, Walter."

"I'll try," I said. I had no intention of trying.

The most embarrassing thing to me about this autobiography, surely, is its unbroken chain of proofs that I was never a serious man. I have been in a lot of trouble over the years, but that was all accidental. Never have I risked my life, or even my comfort, in the service of mankind. Shame on me.

People who had heard Kenneth Whistler speak before begged him to tell again about leading the pickets outside Charlestown Prison when Sacco and Vanzetti were executed. And it seems strange to me now that I have to explain who Sacco and Vanzetti were. I recently asked young Israel Edel at RAMJAC, the former night clerk at the Arapahoe, what he knew about Sacco and Vanzetti, and he told me confidently that they were rich, brilliant thrill-killers from Chicago. He had them confused with Leopold and Loeb.

Why should I find this unsettling? When I was a young man, I expected the story of Sacco and Vanzetti to be retold as often and as movingly, to be as irresistible, as the story of Jesus Christ some day. Weren't modern people, if they were to marvel creatively at their own lifetimes, I thought, entitled to a Passion like Sacco and Vanzetti's, which ended in an electric chair?

As for the last days of Sacco and Vanzetti as a modern Passion: As on Golgotha, three lower-class men were executed at the same time by a state. This time, though, not just one of the three was innocent. This time two of the three were innocent.

The guilty man was a notorious thief and killer named Celestino Madeiros, convicted of a separate crime. As the end drew near, he confessed to the murders for which Sacco and Vanzetti had been convicted, too.

Why?

"I seen Sacco's wife come here with the kids, and I felt sorry for the kids," he said.

Imagine those lines spoken by a good actor in a modern Passion Play.

Madeiros died first. The lights of the prison dimmed three times.

Sacco died next. Of the three, he was the only family man. The actor portraying him would have to project a highly intelligent man who, since English was his second language and since he was not clever with languages, could not trust himself to say anything complicated to the witnesses as he was strapped into the electric chair.

"Long live anarchy," he said. "Farewell, my wife, and child, and all my friends," he said. "Good evening, gentlemen," he said. "Farewell, Mother," he said. This was a shoemaker. The lights of the prison dimmed three times.

Vanzetti was the last. He sat down in the chair in which Madeiros and Sacco had died before anyone could indicate that this was what he was expected to do. He began to speak to the witnesses before anyone could tell him that he was free to do this. English was his second language, too, but he could make it do whatever he pleased.

Listen to this:

"I wish to tell you," he said, "that I am an innocent man. I never committed any crime, but sometimes some sin. I am innocent of all crime—not only this one, but all crime. I am an innocent man." He had been a fish peddler at the time of his arrest.

"I wish to forgive *some* people for what they are now doing to me," he said. The lights of the prison dimmed three times.

The story yet again:

Sacco and Vanzetti never killed anybody. They arrived in America from Italy, not knowing each other, in Nineteen-hundred and Eight. It was the same year in which my parents arrived.

Father was nineteen. Mother was twenty-one.

Sacco was seventeen. Vanzetti was twenty. American employers at that time wanted the country to be flooded with labor that was cheap and easily cowed, so that they could keep wages down.

Vanzetti would say later, "In the immigration station, I had my first surprise. I saw the steerage passengers handled by the officials like so many animals. Not a word of kindness, of encouragement, to lighten the burden of tears that rest heavily upon the newly arrived on American shores."

Father and Mother used to tell me much the same thing. They, too, were made to feel like fools who had somehow gone to great pains to deliver themselves to a slaughterhouse.

My parents were recruited at once by an agent of the Cuyahoga Bridge and Iron Company in Cleveland. He was instructed to hire only blond Slavs, Mr. McCone once told me, on his father's theory that blonds would have the mechanical ingenuity and robustness of Germans, but tempered with the passivity of Slavs. The agent was to pick up factory workers, and a few presentable domestic servants for the various McCone households, as well. Thus did my parents enter the servant class.

Sacco and Vanzetti were not so lucky. There was no broker in human machinery who had a requisition for shapes like theirs. "Where was I to go? What was I to do?" wrote Vanzetti. "Here was the promised land. The elevated rattled by and did not answer. The automobiles and the trolleys sped by heedless of me." So he and Sacco, still separately and in order not to starve to death, had to begin at once to beg in broken English for any sort of work at any wage—going from door to door.

Time passed.

Sacco, who had been a shoemaker in Italy, found himself welcome in a shoe factory in Milford, Massachusetts, a town where, as chance would have it, Mary Kathleen O'Looney's mother was born. Sacco got himself a wife and a house with a garden. They had a son named Dante and a daughter named Inez. Sacco worked six days a week, ten hours each day. He also found time to speak out and give money and take part in demonstrations for workers on strike for better wages and more humane treatment at work and so on. He was arrested for such activities in Nineteen-hundred and sixteen.

Vanzetti had no trade and so went from job to job—in restaurants, in a quarry, in a steel mill, in a rope factory. He was an ardent reader. He studied Marx and Darwin and Hugo and Gorki and Tolstoi and Zola and Dante. That much he had in common with Harvard men. In Nineteen-hundred and Sixteen he led a strike against the rope factory, which was The Plymouth Cordage Company in Plymouth, Massachusetts, now a subsidiary of RAMJAC. He was blacklisted by places of work far and wide after that, and became a self-employed peddler of fish to survive.

And it was in Nineteen-hundred and Sixteen that Sacco and Vanzetti came to know each other well. It became evident to both of them, thinking independently, but thinking always of the brutality of business practices, that the battlefields of World War One were simply additional places of hideously dangerous work, where a few men could supervise the wasting of millions of lives in the hopes of making money. It was clear to them, too, that America would soon become involved. They did not wish to be compelled to work in such factories in Europe, so they both joined the same small group of Italian-American anarchists that went to Mexico until the war was over.

Anarchists are persons who believe with all their hearts that governments are enemies of their own people.

I find myself thinking even now that the story of Sacco and Vanzetti may yet enter the bones of future generations. Perhaps it needs to be told only a few more times. If so, then the flight into Mexico will be seen by one and all as yet another expression of a very holy sort of common sense.

Be that as it may: Sacco and Vanzetti returned to Massachusetts after the war, fast friends. Their sort of common sense, holy or not, and based on books Harvard men read routinely and without ill effects, had always seemed contemptible to most of their neighbors. Those same neighbors, and those who liked to guide their destinies without much opposition, now decided to be terrified by that common sense, especially when it was possessed by the foreign-born.

The Department of Justice drew up secret lists of foreigners who made no secret whatsoever about how unjust and self-deceiving and ignorant and greedy they thought so many of the leaders were in the so-called "Promised Land." Sacco and Vanzetti were on the list. They were shadowed by government spies.

A printer named Andrea Salsedo, who was a friend of Vanzetti's, was also on the list. He was arrested in New York City by federal agents on unspecified charges, and held incommunicado for eight weeks. On May third of Nineteen-hundred and Twenty, Salsedo fell or jumped or was pushed out of the fourteenth-story window of an office maintained by the Department of Justice.

Sacco and Vanzetti organized a meeting that was to demand an investigation of the arrest and death of Salsedo. It was scheduled for May ninth in Brockton, Massachusetts, Mary Kathleen O'Looney's home town. Mary Kathleen was then six years old. I was seven.

Sacco and Vanzetti were arrested for dangerous radical activities before the meeting could take place. Their crime was the possession of leaflets calling for the meeting. The penalties could be stiff fines and up to a year in jail.

But then they were suddenly charged with two unsolved murders, too. Two payroll guards had been shot dead during a robbery in South Braintree, Massachusetts, about a month before.

The penalties for that, of course, would be somewhat stiffer, would be two painless deaths in the same electric chair.

# 19

Vanzetti, for good measure, was also charged with an attempted payroll robbery in Bridgewater, Massachusetts. He was tried and convicted. Thus was he transmogrified from a fish peddler into a known criminal before he and Sacco were tried for murder.

Was Vanzetti guilty of this lesser crime? Possibly so, but it did not matter much. Who said it did not matter much? The judge who tried the case said it did not matter much. He was Webster Thayer, a graduate of Dartmouth College and a descendent of many fine New England families. He told the jury, "This man, although he may not have actually committed the crime attributed to him, is nevertheless morally culpable, because he is the enemy of our existing institutions."

Word of honor: This was said by a judge in an American court of law. I take the quotation from a book at hand: *Labor's Untold Story*, by Richard O. Boyer and Herbert M. Morais. (United Front: San Francisco, 1955.)

And then this same Judge Thayer got to try Sacco and the known criminal Vanzetti for murder. They were found guilty about one year after their arrest—in July of Nineteen-hundred and Twenty-one, when I was eight years old.

They were finally electrocuted when I was fifteen. If I heard anybody in Cleveland say anything about it, I have forgotten now.

I talked to a messenger boy in an elevator in the RAMJAC Building the other morning. He was about my age. I asked him if he remembered anything about the execution when he was a boy. He said that, yes, he had heard his father say he was sick and tired of people talking about Sacco and Vanzetti all the time, and that he was glad it was finally over with.

I asked him what line of work his father had been in.

"He was a bank president in Montpelier, Vermont," he said. This was an old man in a war-surplus United States Army overcoat.

Al Capone, the famous Chicago gangster, thought Sacco and Vanzetti should have been executed. He, too, believed that they were enemies of the American way of thinking about America. He was offended by how ungrateful to America these fellow Italian immigrants were.

According to *Labor's Untold Story*, Capone said, "Bolshevism is knocking at our gates. . . . We must keep the worker away from red literature and red ruses."

Which reminds me of a story written by Dr. Robert Fender, my friend back in prison. The story was about a planet where the worst crime was ingratitude. People were executed all the time for being ungrateful. They were executed the way people used to be executed in Czechoslovakia. They were defenestrated. They were thrown out of altitudinous windows.

The hero in Fender's story was finally thrown out of a window for ingratitude. His last words, as he went sailing out of a window thirty floors up, were these: "Thanks a miiiiiiiiiiiiiiiiiiiilllionnnnnnnnnn!"

Before Sacco and Vanzetti could be executed for ingratitude in the Massachusetts style, however, huge crowds turned out in protest all over the world. The fish peddler and the shoemaker had become planetary celebrities.

"Never in our full life," said Vanzetti, "could we hope to do such work for tolerance, for justice, for man's understanding of man, as now we do by accident."

If this were done as a modern Passion Play, the actors playing the authorities, the Pontius Pilates, would still have to express scorn for the opinions of the mob. But they would be in favor rather than against the death penalty this time.

And they would never wash their hands.

They were in fact so proud of what they were about to do that they asked a committee composed of three of the wisest, most respected, most fair-minded and impartial men within the boundaries of the state to say to the world whether or not justice was about to be done.

It was only this part of the Sacco and Vanzetti story that Kenneth Whistler chose to tell—that night so long ago, when Mary Kathleen and I held hands while he spoke.

He dwelt most scornfully on the resonant credentials of the three wise men.

One was Robert Grant, a retired probate judge, who knew what the laws were and how they were meant to work. The chairman was the president of Harvard, and he would still be president when I became a freshman. Imagine that. He was A. Lawrence Lowell. The other, who according to Whistler ". . . knew a lot about electricity, if nothing else," was Samuel W. Stratton, the president of the Massachusetts Institute of Technology.

During their deliberations, they received thousands of telegrams, some in favor of the executions, but most opposed. Among the telegraphers were Romain Rolland, George Bernard Shaw, Albert Einstein, John Galsworthy, Sinclair Lewis, and H.G. Wells.

The triumvirate declared at last that it was clear to them that, if Sacco and Vanzetti were electrocuted, justice would be done.

So much for the wisdom of even the wisest human beings.

And I am now compelled to wonder if wisdom has ever existed or can ever exist. Might wisdom be as impossible in this particular universe as a perpetual-motion machine?

Who was the wisest man in the Bible, supposedly—wiser even, we can suppose, than the president of Harvard? He was King Solomon, of course. Two women claiming the same baby appeared before Solomon, asking him to apply his legendary wisdom to their case. He suggested cutting the baby in two.

And the wisest men in Massachusetts said that Sacco and Vanzetti should die.

When their decision was rendered, my hero Kenneth Whistler was in charge of pickets before the Massachusetts State House in Boston, by his own account. It was raining.

"Nature sympathized," he said, looking straight at Mary Kathleen and me in the front row. He laughed.

Mary Kathleen and I did not laugh with him. Neither did anybody else in the audience. His laugh was a chilling laugh about how little Nature ever cares about what human beings think is going on.

And Whistler kept his pickets before the State House for ten more days, until the night of the execution. Then he led them through the winding streets and across the bridge to Charlestown, where the prison was. Among his pickets were Edna St. Vincent Millay and John Dos Passos and Heywood Broun.

National Guardsmen and police were waiting for them. There were machine gunners on the walls, with their guns aimed out at the general populace, the people who wanted Pontius Pilate to be merciful.

And Kenneth Whistler had with him a heavy parcel. It was an enormous banner, long and narrow and rolled up tight. He had had it made that morning.

The prison lights began their dimming.

When they had dimmed nine times, Whistler and a friend hurried to the funeral parlor where the bodies of Sacco and Vanzetti were to be displayed. The state had no further use for the bodies. They had become the property of relatives and friends again.

Whistler told us that two pairs of sawhorses had been set up in the front room of the funeral parlor, awaiting the coffins. Now Whistler and his friend unfurled their banner, and they nailed it to the wall over the sawhorses.

On the banner were painted the words that the man who had sentenced Sacco and Vanzetti to death, Webster Thayer, had spoken to a friend soon after he passed the sentence:

> DID YOU SEE WHAT I DID TO THOSE
> ANARCHIST BASTARDS THE OTHER DAY?

# 20

Sacco and Vanzetti never lost their dignity—never cracked up. Walter F. Starbuck finally did.

I seemed to hold up quite well when I was arrested in the showroom of The American Harp Company. When old Delmar Peale showed the two policemen the circular about the stolen clarinet parts, when he explained what I was to be arrested for, I even smiled. I had the perfect alibi, after all: I had been in prison for the past two years.

When I told them that, though, it did not relax them as much as I had hoped. They decided that I was perhaps more of a desperado than they had at first supposed.

The police station was in an uproar when we arrived. Television crews and newspaper reporters were trying to get at the young men who had rioted in the gardens of the United Nations, who had thrown the finance minister of Sri Lanka into the East River. The Sri Lankan had not been found yet, so it was assumed that the rioters would be charged with murder.

Actually, the Sri Lankan would be rescued by a police launch about two hours later. He would be found clinging to a bell buoy off Governor's Island. The papers the next morning would describe him as "incoherent." I can believe it.

There was no one to question me at once. I was going to have to be locked up for a while. The police station was so busy that there wasn't even an ordinary cell for me. I was given a chair in the corridor outside the cells. It was there that the rioters insulted me from behind bars, imagining that I would enjoy nothing so much as making love to them.

I was eventually taken to a padded cell in the basement. It was designed to hold a maniac until an ambulance could come for her or him. There wasn't a toilet in there, because a maniac might try to bash his or her brains out on a toilet's rim. There was no cot, no chair. I would have to sit or lie on the padded floor. Oddly enough, the only piece of furniture was a large bowling trophy, which somebody had stored in there. I got to know it well.

So there I was back in a quiet basement again.

And, as had happened to me when I was the President's special advisor on youth affairs, I was forgotten again.

I was accidentally left there from noon until eight o'clock that night, without food or water or a toilet or the slightest sound from the outside—on what was to have been my first full day of freedom. Thus began a test of my character that I failed.

I thought about Mary Kathleen and all she had been through. I still did not know that she was Mrs. Jack Graham, but she had told me something else very interesting about herself: After I left Harvard, after I stopped answering her letters or even thinking much about her anymore, she hitchhiked to Kentucky, where Kenneth Whistler was still working as a miner and an organizer. She arrived at sundown at the shack where he was living alone. The place was unlocked, having nothing inside worth stealing. Whistler was still at work. Mary Kathleen had brought food with her. When Whistler came home, there was smoke coming out of his chimney. There was a hot meal waiting for him inside.

That was how she got down into the coalfields. And that was how she happened, when Kenneth Whistler became violent late at night because of alcohol, to run out into the moonlit street of a shanty town and into the arms of a young mining engineer. He was, of course, Jack Graham.

And then I regaled myself with a story by my prison friend Dr. Robert Fender, which he had published under the name of "Kilgore Trout." It was called "Asleep at the Switch." It was about a huge reception center outside the Pearly Gates of heaven—filled with computers and staffed by people who had been certified public accountants or investment counselors or business managers back on Earth.

You could not get into heaven until you had submitted to a full review of how well you had handled the business opportunities God, through His angels, had offered to you on Earth.

All day long and in every cubicle you could hear the experts saying with utmost weariness to people who had missed this opportunity and then that one: "And there you were, asleep at the switch again."

How much time had I spent in solitary by then? I will make a guess: five minutes.

"Asleep at the Switch" was quite a sacrilegious story. The hero was the ghost of Albert Einstein. He himself was so little interested in wealth that he scarcely heard what his auditor had to say to him. It was some sort of balderdash about how he could have become a billionaire, if only he had gotten a second mortgage on his house in Bern, Switzerland, in Nineteen-hundred and Five, and invested the money in known uranium deposits before telling the world that $E = Mc^2$.

"But there you were—asleep at the switch again," said the auditor.

"Yes," said Einstein politely, "it does seem rather typical."

"So you see," said the auditor, "life really was quite fair. You did have a remarkable number of opportunities, whether you took them or not."

"Yes, I see that now," said Einstein.

"Would you mind saying that in so many words?" said the auditor.

"Saying what?" said Einstein.

"That life was fair."

"Life was fair," said Einstein.

"If you don't really mean it," said the auditor, "I have many more examples to show you. For instance, just forgetting atomic energy: If you had simply taken the money you put into a savings bank when you were at the Institute for Advanced Studies at Princeton, and you had put it, starting in Nineteen-hundred and Fifty, say, into IBM and Polaroid and Xerox—even though you had only five more years to live—" The auditor raised his eyes suggestively, inviting Einstein to show how smart he could be.

"I would have been rich?" said Einstein.

"'Comfortable,' shall we say?" said the auditor smugly. "But there you were again—" And again his eyebrows went up.

"Asleep at the switch?" asked Einstein hopefully.

The auditor stood and extended his hand, which Einstein accepted unenthusiastically. "So you see, Doctor Einstein," he said, "we can't blame God for everything, now can we?" He handed Einstein his pass through the Pearly Gates. "Good to have you aboard," he said.

So into heaven Einstein went, carrying his beloved fiddle. He thought no more about the audit. He was a veteran of countless border crossings by then. There had always been senseless questions to answer, empty promises to make, meaningless documents to sign.

But once inside heaven Einstein encountered ghost after ghost who was sick about what his or her audit had shown. One husband and wife team, which had committed suicide after losing everything in a chicken farm in New Hampshire, had been told that they had been living the whole time over the largest deposit of nickel in the world.

A fourteen-year-old Harlem child who had been killed in a gang fight was told about a two-carat diamond ring that lay for weeks at the bottom of a catch basin he passed every day. It was flawless and had not been reported as stolen. If he had sold it for only a tenth of its value, four hundred dollars, say, according to his auditor, and speculated in commodities futures, especially in cocoa at that time, he could have moved his mother and sisters and himself into a Park Avenue condominium and sent himself to Andover and then to Harvard after that.

There was Harvard again.

All the auditing stories that Einstein heard were told by Americans. He had chosen to settle in the American part of heaven. Understandably, he had mixed feelings about Europeans, since he was a Jew. But it wasn't only Americans who were being audited. Pakistanis and pygmies from the Philippines and even communists had to go through the very same thing.

It was in character for Einstein to be offended first by the mathematics of the system the auditors wanted everybody to be so grateful for. He calculated that if every person on Earth took full advantage of every opportunity, became a millionaire and then a billionaire and so on, the paper wealth on that one little planet would exceed the worth of all the minerals in the universe in a matter of three months or so. Also: There would be nobody left to do any useful work.

So he sent God a note. It assumed that God had no idea what sorts of rubbish His auditors were talking. It accused the auditors rather than God of cruelly deceiving new arrivals about the opportunities they had had on Earth. He tried to guess the auditors' motives. He wondered if they might not be sadists.

The story ended abruptly. Einstein did not get to see God. But God sent out an archangel who was boiling mad. He told Einstein that if he continued to destroy ghosts' respect for the audits, he was going to take Einstein's fiddle away from him for all eternity. So Einstein never discussed the audits with anybody ever again. His fiddle meant more to him than anything.

The story was certainly a slam at God, suggesting that He was capable of using a cheap subterfuge like the audits to get out of being blamed for how hard economic life was down here.

I made my mind a blank.

But then it started singing about Sally in the garden again.

Mary Kathleen O'Looney, exercising her cosmic powers as Mrs. Jack Graham, had meanwhile telephoned Arpad Leen, the top man at RAMJAC. She ordered him to find out what the police had done with me, and to send the toughest lawyer in New York City to rescue me, no matter what the cost.

He was to make me a RAMJAC vice-president after that. While she was at it, she said, she had a list of other good people who were to be rounded up and also made vice-presidents. These were the people I had told her about, of course—the strangers who had been so nice to me.

She also ordered him to tell Doris Kramm, the old secretary at The American Harp Company, that she didn't have to retire, no matter how old she was.

Yes, and there in my padded cell I told myself a joke I had read in *The Harvard Lampoon* when a freshman. It had amazed me back then because it seemed so dirty. When I became the President's special advisor on youth affairs, and had to read college humor again, I discovered that the joke was still being published many times a year—unchanged. This was it:

*SHE: How dare you kiss me like that?*
*HE: I was just trying to find out who ate all the macaroons.*

So I had a good laugh about that there in solitary. But then I began to crack. I could not stop saying to myself, "Macaroons, macaroons, macaroons . . ."

Things got much worse after that. I sobbed. I bounced myself off the walls. I took a crap in a corner. I dropped the bowling trophy on top of the crap.

I screamed a poem I had learned in grammar school:

*Don't care if I do die,*
*Do die, do die!*
*Like to make the juice fly,*
*Juice fly, juice fly!*

I may even have masturbated. Why not? We old folks have much richer sex lives than most young people imagine.

I eventually collapsed.

At seven o'clock that night the toughest attorney in New York entered the police station upstairs. He had traced me that far. He was a famous man, known to be extremely ferocious and humorless in prosecuting or defending almost anyone. The police were thunderstruck when such a dreaded celebrity appeared. He demanded to know what had become of me.

Nobody knew. There was no record anywhere of my having been released or transferred elsewhere. My lawyer knew I hadn't gone home, because he had already asked after me there. Mary Kathleen had told Arpad Leen and Leen had told the lawyer that I lived at the Arapahoe.

They could not even find out what I had been arrested for.

So all the cells were checked. I wasn't in any of them, of course. The people who had brought me in and the man who had locked me up had all gone off-duty. None of them could be reached at home.

But then the detective who was trying to placate my lawyer remembered the cell downstairs and decided to have a look inside it, just in case.

When the key turned in the lock, I was lying on my stomach like a dog in a kennel, facing the door. My stocking feet extended in the direction of the bowling trophy and the crap. I had removed my shoes for some reason.

When the detective opened the door, he was appalled to see me, realizing how long I must have been in there. The City of New York had accidentally committed a very serious crime against me.

"Mr. Starbuck—?" he asked anxiously.

I said nothing. I did sit up. I no longer cared where I was or what might happen next. I was like a hooked fish that had done all the fighting it could. Whatever was on the other end of the line was welcome to reel me in.

When the detective said, "Your lawyer is here," I did not protest even inwardly that nobody knew I was in jail, that I had no lawyer, no friends, no anything. So be it: My lawyer was there.

Now the lawyer showed himself. It would not have surprised me if he had been a unicorn. He was, in fact, almost that fantastic—a man who, when only twenty-six years old, had been chief counsel of the Senate Permanent Investigating Committee, whose chairman was Senator Joseph R. McCarthy, the most spectacular hunter of disloyal Americans since World War Two.

He was in his late forties now—but still unsmiling and nervously shrewd. During the McCarthy Era, which came after Leland Clewes and I had made such fools of ourselves, I had hated and feared this man. He was on my side now.

"Mr. Starbuck," he said, "I am here to represent you, if you want me to. I have been retained on your behalf by The RAMJAC Corporation. Roy M. Cohn is my name."

What a miracle-worker he was!

I was out of the police station and into a waiting limousine before you could say, "*Habeas corpus!*"

Cohn, having delivered me to the limousine, did not himself get in. He wished me well without shaking my hand, and was gone. He never touched me, never gave any indication that he knew that I, too, had played a very public part in American history in olden times.

So there I was in a limousine again. Why not? Anything was possible in a dream. Hadn't Roy M. Cohn just gotten me out of jail, and hadn't I left my shoes behind? So why shouldn't the dream go on—and have Leland Clewes and Israel Edel, the night clerk at the Arapahoe, already sitting in the back of the limousine, with a space between them for me? This it did.

They nodded to me uneasily. They, too, felt that life wasn't making good sense just now.

What was going on, of course, was that the limousine was cruising around Manhattan like a schoolbus, picking up people Mary Kathleen O'Looney had told Arpad Leen to hire as RAMJAC vice-presidents. This was Leen's personal limousine. It was what I have since learned is called a "stretch" limousine. The American Harp Company could have used the backseat for a showroom.

Clewes and Edel and the next person we were going to pick up had all been telephoned personally by Leen—after some of his assistants had found out more about who they were and where they were. Leland Clewes had been found in the phonebook. Edel had been found behind the desk at the Arapahoe. One of the assistants had gone to the Coffee Shop of the Royalton to ask for the name of a person who worked there and had a French-fried hand.

Other calls had gone to Georgia—one to the RAMJAC regional office, asking if they had a chauffeur named Cleveland Lawes working for them, and another one to the Federal Minimum Security Adult Correctional Facility at Finletter Air Force Base, asking if they had a guard named Clyde Carter and a prisoner named Dr. Robert Fender there.

Clewes asked me if I understood what was going on.

"No," I said. "This is just the dream of a jailbird. It's not supposed to make sense."

Clewes asked me what had happened to my shoes.

"I left them in the padded cell," I said.

"You were in a padded cell?" he said.

"It's very nice," I said. "You can't possibly hurt yourself."

A man in the front seat next to the chauffeur now turned his face to us. I knew him, too. He had been one of the lawyers who had escorted Virgil Greathouse into prison on the morning before. He was Arpad Leen's lawyer, too. He was worried about my having lost my shoes. He said we would go back to the police station and get them.

"Not on your life!" I said. "They've found out by now that I threw the bowling trophy down in the shit, and they'll just arrest me again."

Edel and Clewes now drew away from me some.

"This has to be a dream," said Clewes.

"Be my guest," I said. "The more the merrier."

"Gentlemen, gentlemen—" said the lawyer genially. "Please, you mustn't worry so. You are about to be offered the opportunity of your lives."

"When the hell did she see me?" said Edel. "What was the wonderful thing she saw me do?"

"We may never know," said the lawyer. "She seldom explains herself, and she's a mistress of disguise. She could be anybody."

"Maybe she was that big black pimp that came in after you last night," Edel said to me. "I was nice to him. He was eight feet tall."

"I missed him," I said.

"You're lucky," said Edel.

"You two know each other?" said Clewes.

"Since childhood!" I said. I was going to blow this dream wide open by absolutely refusing to take it seriously. I was damn well going to get back to my bed at the Arapahoe or my cot in prison. I didn't care which.

Maybe I could even wake up in the bedroom of my little brick bungalow in Chevy Chase, Maryland, and my wife would still be alive.

"I can promise you she wasn't the tall pimp," said the lawyer. "That much we can be sure of: Whatever she looks like, she is not tall."

"Who isn't tall?" I said.

"Mrs. Jack Graham," said the lawyer.

"Sorry I asked," I said.

"You must have done her some sort of favor, too," the lawyer said to me, "or done something she saw and admired."

"It's my Boy Scout training," I said.

So we came to a stop in front of a rundown apartment building on the Upper West Side. Out came Frank Ubriaco, the owner of the Coffee Shop. He was dressed for the dream in a pale-blue velvet suit and green-and-white cowboy boots with high, high heels. His French-fried hand was elegantly sheathed in a white kid glove. Clewes pulled down a jumpseat for him.

I said hello to him.

"Who are you?" he said.

"You served me breakfast this morning," I said.

"I served everybody breakfast this morning," he said.

"You know him, too?" said Clewes.

"This is my town," I said. I addressed the lawyer, more convinced than ever that this was a dream, and I told him, "All right—let's pick up my mother next."

He echoed me uncertainly. "Your mother?"

"Sure. Why not? Everybody else is here," I said.

He wanted to be cooperative. "Mr. Leen didn't say anything specific about your not bringing anybody else along. You'd like to bring your mother?"

"Very much," I said.

"Where is she?" he said.

"In a cemetery in Cleveland," I said, "but that shouldn't slow *you* down."

He thereafter avoided direct conversations with me.

When we got underway again, Ubriaco asked those of us in the backseat who we were.

Clewes and Edel introduced themselves. I declined to do so.

"They're all people who caught the eye of Mrs. Graham, just as you did," said the lawyer.

"You guys know her?" Ubriaco asked Clewes and Edel and me.

We all shrugged.

"Jesus Christ," said Ubriaco. "This better be a pretty good job you got to offer. I like what I do."

"You'll see," said the lawyer.

"I broke a date for you monkeys," said Ubriaco.

"Yes—and Mr. Leen broke a date for you," said the lawyer. "His daughter is having her debut at the Waldorf tonight, and he won't be there. He'll be talking to you gentlemen instead."

"Fucking crazy," said Ubriaco. Nobody else had anything to say. As we crossed Central Park to the East Side, Ubriaco spoke again. "Fucking debut," he said.

Clewes said to me, "You're the only one who knows everybody else here. You're in the middle of this thing somehow."

"Why wouldn't I be?" I said. "It's my dream."

And we were delivered without further conversation to the penthouse dwelling of Arpad Leen. We were told by the lawyer to leave our shoes in the foyer. It was the custom of the house. I, of course, was already in my stocking feet.

Ubriaco asked if Leen was a Japanese, since the Japanese commonly took off their shoes indoors.

The lawyer assured him that Leen was a Caucasian, but that he had grown up in Fiji, where his parents ran a general store. As I would find out later, Leen's father was a Hungarian Jew, and his mother was a Greek Cypriot. His parents met when they were working on a Swedish cruise ship in the late twenties. They jumped ship in Fiji, and started the store.

Leen himself looked like an idealized Plains Indian to me. He could have been a movie star. And he came out into the foyer in a striped silk dressing gown and black socks and garters. He still hoped to make it to his daughter's debut.

Before he introduced himself to us, he had to tell the lawyer an incredible piece of news. "You know what the son of a bitch is in prison for?" he said. "Treason! And we're supposed to get him out and give him a job. Treason! How do you get somebody out of jail who's committed treason? How do we give him even a lousy job without every patriot in the country raising hell?"

The lawyer didn't know.

"Well," said Leen, "what the hell. Get me Roy Cohn again. I wish I were back in Nashville."

This last remark alluded to Leen's having been the leading publisher of country music in Nashville, Tennessee, before his little empire was swallowed up by RAMJAC. His old company, in fact, was the nucleus of the Down Home Records Division of RAMJAC.

Now he looked us over and he shook his head in wonderment. We were a freakish crew. "Gentlemen," he said, "you have all been noticed by Mrs. Jack Graham. She didn't tell me where or when. She said you were honest and kind."

"Not me," said Ubriaco.

"You're free to question her judgment, if you want," said Leen. "I'm not. I have to offer you good jobs. I don't mind doing that, though, and I'll tell you why: She never told me to do anything that didn't turn out to be in the best interests of the company. I used to say that I never wanted to work for anybody, but working for Mrs. Jack Graham has been the greatest privilege of my life." He meant it.

He did not mind making us all vice-presidents. The company had seven hundred vice-presidents of this and that on the top level, the corporate level, alone. When you got out into the subsidiaries, of course, the whole business of presidents and vice-presidents started all over again.

"*You* know what she looks like?" Ubriaco wanted to know.

"I haven't seen her recently," said Leen. This was an urbane lie. He had never seen her, which was a matter of public record.

He would confess to me later that he did not even know how he had come to Mrs. Graham's attention. He thought she might have seen an article on him in the Diners Club magazine, which had featured him in their "Man on the Move" department.

In any event, he was abjectly loyal to her. He loved and feared his idea of Mrs. Graham the way Emil Larkin loved and feared his idea of Jesus Christ. He was luckier than Larkin in his worship, of course, since the invisible superior being over him called him up and wrote him letters and told him what to do.

He actually said one time, "Working for Mrs. Graham has been a religious experience for me. I was adrift, no matter how much money I was making. My life had no purpose until I became president of RAMJAC and placed myself at her beck and call."

All happiness is religious, I have to think sometimes.

Leen said he would talk to us one by one in his library. "Mrs. Graham didn't tell me about your backgrounds, what your special interests might be — so you're just going to have to tell me about yourselves." He said for Ubriaco to come into the library first, and asked the rest of us to wait in the living room. "Is there anything my butler can bring you to drink?" he said.

Clewes didn't want anything. Edel asked for a beer. I, still hoping to blow the dream wide open, ordered a *pousse-café*, a rainbow-colored drink that I had never seen, but which I had studied while earning my Doctor of Mixology degree. A heavy liqueur was put into the bottom of a glass, then a lighter one of a different color was carefully spooned in on top of that, and then a lighter one still on top of that, and on and on, with each bright layer undisturbed by the one above or below.

Leen was impressed with my order. He repeated it, to make sure he had heard it right.

"If it's not too much trouble," I said. It was no more trouble, surely, than building a full-rigged ship model in a bottle, say.

"No problem!" said Leen. This, I would learn, was a favorite expression of his. He told the butler to give me a *pousse-café* without further ado.

He and Ubriaco went into the library, and the rest of us entered the living room, which had a swimming pool. I had never seen a living room with a swimming pool before. I had heard of such a thing, of course, but hearing of and actually seeing that much water in a living room are two very different things.

I knelt by the pool and swirled my hand in the water, curious about the temperature, which was soupy. When I withdrew my hand and considered its wetness, I had to admit to myself that the wet was undreamlike. My hand was really wet and would remain so for some time, unless I did something about it.

All this was really going on. As I stood, the butler arrived with my *pousse-café*.

Outrageous behavior was not the answer. I was going to have to start paying attention again. "Thank you," I said to the butler.

"You're welcome, sir," he replied.

Clewes and Edel were seated at one end of a couch about half a block long. I joined them, wanting their appreciation for how sedate I had become.

They were continuing to speculate as to when Mrs. Graham might have caught them behaving so virtuously.

Clewes mourned that he had not had many opportunities to be virtuous, selling advertising matchbooks and calendars from door to door. "About the best I can do is let a building custodian tell me his war stories," he said. He remembered a custodian in the Flatiron Building who claimed to have been the first American to cross the bridge over the Rhine at Remagan, Germany, during World War Two. The capture of this bridge had been an immense event, allowing the Allied Armies to pour at high speed right into the heart of Germany. Clewes doubted that the custodian could have been Mrs. Jack Graham, though.

Israel Edel supposed that Mrs. Graham could be disguised as a man, though. "I sometimes think that about half our customers at the Arapahoe are transvestites," he said.

The possibility of Mrs. Graham's being a transvestite would be brought up again soon, and most startlingly, by Arpad Leen.

Meanwhile, though, Clewes got back on the subject of World War Two. He got personal about it. He said that he and I, when we were wartime bureaucrats, had only imagined that we had something to do with defeats and victories. "The war was won by fighters, Walter. All the rest was dreams."

It was his opinion that all the memoirs written about that war by civilians were swindles, pretenses that the war had been won

by talkers and writers and socialites, when it could only have
been won by fighters.

A telephone rang in the foyer. The butler came in to say that
the call was for Clewes, who could take it on the telephone on
the coffee table in front of us. The telephone was black-and-
white plastic and shaped like "Snoopy," the famous dog in the
comic strip called "Peanuts." Peanuts was owned by what was
about to become my division of RAMJAC. To converse on
that telephone, as I would soon discover, you had to put your
mouth over the dog's stomach and stick his nose in your ear.
Why not?

It was Clewes's wife Sarah, my old girlfriend, calling from
their apartment. She had just come home from a private nursing
case, had found his note, which said where he was and what he
was doing there and how he could be reached by telephone.

He told her that I was there, too, and she could not believe it.
She asked to talk to me. So Clewes handed me the plastic dog.

"Hi," I said.

"This is crazy," she said. "What are you doing there?"

"Drinking a *pousse-café* by the swimming pool," I said.

"I can't imagine you drinking a *pousse-café*," she said.

"Well, I am," I said.

She asked how Clewes and I had met. I told her. "Such a small
world, Walter," she said, and so on. She asked me if Clewes
had told me that I had done them a big favor when I testified
against him.

"I would have to say that that opinion is moot," I told her.

"Is what?" she said.

"Moot," I said. It was a word she had somehow never heard
before. I explained it to her.

"I'm so dumb," she said. "There's so much I don't know,
Walter." She sounded just like the same old Sarah on the telephone. It could have been Nineteen-hundred and Thirty-five
again, which made what she said next especially poignant: "Oh,
my God, Walter! We're both over sixty years old! How is that
possible?"

"You'd be surprised, Sarah," I said.

She asked me to come home with Clewes for supper, and I
said I would if I could, that I didn't know what was going to
happen next. I asked her where she lived.

It turned out that she and Clewes lived in the basement of the same building where her grandmother used to live—in Tudor City. She asked me if I remembered her grandmother's apartment, all the old servants and furniture jammed into only four rooms.

I said I did, and we laughed.

I did not tell her that my son also lived somewhere in Tudor City. I would find out later that there was nothing vague about his proximity to her, with his musical wife and his adopted children. Stankiewicz of *The New York Times* was in the same building, and notoriously so, because of the wildness of the children—and only three floors above Leland and Sarah Clewes.

She said that it was good that we could still laugh, despite all we had been through. "At least we still have our sense of humor," she said. That was something Julie Nixon had said about her father after he got bounced out of the White House: "He still has his sense of humor."

"Yes—at least that," I agreed.

"Waiter," she said, "what's this fly doing in my soup?"

"What?" I said.

"What's this fly doing in my soup?" she persisted.

And then it came back to me: This was the opening line in a daisychain of jokes we used to tell each other on the telephone. I closed my eyes. I gave the answering line, and the telephone became a time machine for me. It allowed me to escape from Nineteen-hundred and Seventy-seven and into the fourth dimension.

"I believe that's the backstroke, madam," I said.

"Waiter," she said, "there's also a needle in my soup."

"I'm sorry, madam," I said, "that's a typographical error. That should have been a noodle."

"Why do you charge so much for cream?" she said.

"It's because the cows hate to squat on those little bottles," I said.

"I keep thinking it's Tuesday," she said.

"It *is* Tuesday," I said.

"That's what I keep thinking," she said. "Tell me, do you serve flannelcakes?"

"Not on the menu today," I said.

"Last night I dreamed I was eating flannelcakes," she said.

"That must have been very nice," I said.

"It was terrible," she said. "When I woke up, the blanket was gone."

She, too, had reason to escape into the fourth dimension. As I would find out later, her patient had died that night. Sarah had liked her a lot. The patient was only thirty-six, but she had a congenitally defective heart—huge and fatty and weak.

And imagine, if you will, the effect this conversation was having on Leland Clewes, who was sitting right next to me. My eyes were closed, as I say, and I was in such an ecstasy of time-lessness and placelessness that I might as well have been having sexual intercourse with his wife before his eyes. He forgave me, of course. He forgives everybody for everything. But he still had to be impressed by how lazily in love Sarah and I could still be on the telephone.

What is more protean than adultery? Nothing in this world.

"I am thinking of going on a diet," said Sarah.

"I know how you can lose twenty pounds of ugly fat right away," I said.

"How?" she said.

"Have your head cut off," I said.

Clewes could hear only my half of the conversation, of course, so he could only hear the premise or the snapper of a joke, but never both. Some of the lines were highly suggestive.

I asked Sarah, I remember, if she smoked after intercourse.

Clewes never heard her reply, which was this: "I don't know. I never looked." And then she went on: "What did you do before you were a waiter?"

"I used to clean birdshit out of cuckoo clocks," I said.

"I have often wondered what the white stuff in birdshit was," she said.

"That's birdshit, too," I told her. "What kind of work do *you* do?"

"I work in the bloomer factory," she said.

"Is it a good job in the bloomer factory?" I inquired archly.

# 21

"OH," SHE SAID, "I can't complain. I pull down about ten thousand a year." Sarah coughed, and that, too, was a cue, which I nearly missed.

"That's quite a cough you have there," I said in the nick of time.

"It won't stop," she said.

"Take two of these pills," I said. "They're just the thing."

So she made swallowing sounds: "gluck, gluck, gluck." And then she asked what was in the pills.

"The most powerful laxative known to medical science," I said.

"Laxative!" she said.

"Yes," I said, "now you don't dare cough."

We did the joke, too, about a sick horse I supposedly had. I have never really owned a horse. The veterinarian gave me half a pound of purple powder that I was to give the horse, supposedly. The veterinarian told me to make a tube out of paper, and to put the powder inside the tube, and then to slip the tube into the horse's mouth, and to blow it down its throat.

"How is the horse?" said Sarah.

"Oh, the horse is fine," I said.

"You don't look so good," she said.

"No," I said, "that is because the horse blew first."

"Can you still imitate your mother's laugh?" she said.

This was not the premise of yet another joke. Sarah genuinely wanted to hear me imitate my mother's laugh, something I used to do a lot for Sarah on the telephone. I had not tried the trick in years. I not only had to make my voice high: I also had to make it beautiful.

The thing was this: Mother never laughed out loud. She had been trained to stifle her laughter when a servant girl in Lithuania. The idea was that a master or guest, hearing a servant laughing somewhere in the house, might suspect that the servant was laughing about him.

344

So when my mother could not help laughing, she made tiny, pure sounds like a music box—or perhaps like bells far away. It was accidental that they were so beautiful.

So—forgetful of where I was, I now filled my lungs and tightened my throat, and to please my old girlfriend, I reincarnated the laughing part of my mother.

It was at that point that Arpad Leen and Frank Ubriaco came back into the living room. They heard the end of my song.

I told Sarah that I had to hang up now, and I did hang up.

Arpad Leen stared at me hard. I had heard women speak of men's undressing them mentally. Now I was finding out what that felt like. As things turned out, that was exactly what Leen was doing to me: imagining what I would look like with no clothes on.

He was beginning to suspect that I was Mrs. Jack Graham, checking up on him while disguised as a man.

# 22

I COULD NOT KNOW THAT, of course—that he thought I might be Mrs. Graham. So his subsequent courting of me was as inexplicable as anything that had happened to me all day.

I tried to believe that he was being so attentive in order to soften the bad news he had to give me by and by: that I was simply not RAMJAC material, and that his limousine was waiting down below to take me back, still jobless, to the Arapahoe. But the messages in his eyes were more passionate than that. He was ravenous for my approval of everything he did.

He told me, and not Leland Clewes or Israel Edel, that he had just made Frank Ubriaco a vice-president of the McDonald's Hamburgers Division of RAMJAC.

I nodded that I thought that was nice.

The nod was not enough for Leen. "I think it's a wonderful example of putting the right man in the right job," he said. "Don't you? That's what RAMJAC is all about, don't you think—putting good people where they can use their talents to the fullest?"

The question was for me and nobody else, so I finally said, "Yes."

I had to go through the same thing after he had interviewed and hired Clewes and Edel. Clewes was made a vice-president of the Diamond Match Division, presumably because he had been selling advertising matchbooks for so long. Edel was made a vice-president of the Hilton Department of the Hospitality Associates, Ltd., Division, presumably because of his three weeks of experience as a night clerk at the Arapahoe.

It was then my turn to go into the library with him. "Last but not least," he said coyly. After he closed the door on the rest of the house, his flirtatiousness became even more outrageous. "Come into my parlor," he murmured, "said the spider to the fly." He winked at me broadly.

I hated this. I wondered what had happened to the others in here.

There was a Mussolini-style desk with a swivel chair behind it. "Perhaps *you* should sit there," he said. He made his eyebrows go up and down. "Doesn't that look like your kind of chair? Eh? Eh? Your kind of chair?"

This could only be mockery, I thought. I responded to it humbly. I had had no self-respect for years and years. "Sir," I said, "I don't know what's going on."

"Ah," he said, holding up a finger, "that *does* happen sometimes."

"I don't know how you found me, or even if I'm who you think I am," I said.

"I haven't told you yet who I think you are," he said.

"Walter F. Starbuck," I said bleakly.

"If you say so," he said.

"Well," I said, "whoever I am, I'm not much anymore. If you're really offering jobs, all I want is a little one."

"I'm under orders to make you a vice-president," he said, "orders from a person I respect very much. I intend to obey."

"I want to be a bartender," I said.

"Ah!" he said. "And mix *pousse-cafés*!"

"I can, if I have to," I said. "I have a Doctor of Mixology degree."

"You also have a lovely high voice when you want to," he said.

"I think I had better go home now," I said. "I can walk. It isn't far from here." It was only about forty blocks. I had no shoes; but who needed shoes? I would get home somehow without them.

"When it's time to go home," he said, "you shall have my limousine."

"It's time to go home now," I said. "I don't care how I get there. It has been a very tiring day for me. I don't feel very clever. I just want to sleep. If you know anybody who needs a bartender, even part-time, I can be found at the Arapahoe."

"What an actor you are!" he said.

I hung my head. I didn't even want to look at him or at anybody anymore. "Not at all," I said. "Never was."

"I will tell you something very strange," he said.

"I won't understand it," I said.

"Everyone here tonight remembers having seen you, but they've never seen each other before," he said. "How would you explain that?"

"I have no job," I said. "I just got out of prison. I've been walking around town with nothing to do."

"Such a complicated story," he said. "You were in *prison*, you say?"

"It happens," I said.

"I won't ask what you were in prison for," he said. What he meant, of course, was that I, as Mrs. Graham disguised as a man, did not have to go on telling taller and taller lies, unless it entertained me to do so.

"Watergate," I said.

"Watergate!" he exclaimed. "I thought I knew the names of almost all the Watergate people." As I would find out later, he not only knew their names: He knew many of them well enough to have bribed them with illegal campaign contributions, and to have chipped in for their defenses afterward. "Why is it that I have never heard the name Starbuck associated with Watergate before?"

"I don't know," I said, my head still down. "It was like being in a wonderful musical comedy where the critics mentioned everybody but me. If you can find an old program, I'll show you my name."

"The prison was in Georgia, I take it," he said.

"Yes," I said. I supposed that he knew that because Roy M. Cohn had looked up my record when he had to get me out of jail.

"That explains Georgia," he said.

I couldn't imagine why anybody would want Georgia explained.

"So that's how you know Clyde Carter and Cleveland Lawes and Dr. Robert Fender," he said.

"Yes," I said. Now I started to be afraid. Why would this man, one of the most powerful corporate executives on the planet, bother to find out so much about a pathetic little jailbird like me? Was there a suspicion somewhere that I knew some spectacular secret that could still be revealed about Watergate? Might he be playing cat-and-mouse with me before having me killed some way?

"And Doris Kramm," he said, "I'm sure you know her, too."

I was so relieved not to know her! I was innocent after all! His whole case against me would collapse now. He had the wrong man, and I could prove it! I did not know Doris Kramm! "No, no, no," I said. "I don't know Doris Kramm."

"The lady you asked me not to retire from The American Harp Company," he said.

"I never asked you anything," I said.

"A slip of the tongue," he said.

And then horror grew in me as I realized that I really did know Doris Kramm. She was the old secretary who had been sobbing and cleaning out her desk at the harp showroom. I wasn't about to tell him that I knew her, though.

But he knew I knew her, anyway! He knew everything! "You will be happy to learn that I telephoned her personally and assured her that she did not have to retire, after all. She can stay on as long as she likes. Isn't that lovely?"

"No," I said. It was as good an answer as any. But now I was remembering the harp showroom. I felt as though I had been there a thousand years ago, perhaps, in some other life, before I was born. Mary Kathleen O'Looney had been there. Arpad Leen, in his omniscience, would surely mention her next.

And then the nightmare of the past hour suddenly revealed itself as having been logical all along. I knew something that Leen himself did not know, that probably nobody in the world but me knew. It was impossible, but it had to be true: Mary Kathleen O'Looney and Mrs. Jack Graham were the same.

It was then that Arpad Leen raised my hand to his lips and kissed it. "Forgive me for penetrating your disguise, madam," he said, "but I assume you made it so easy to penetrate on purpose. Your secret is safe with me. I am honored at last to meet you face to face."

He kissed my hand again, the same hand Mary Kathleen's dirty little claw had grasped that morning. "High time, madam," he said. "We have worked together so well so long. High time."

My revulsion at being kissed by a man was so fully automatic that I became a veritable Queen Victoria! My rage was imperial, although my language came straight from the playgrounds of my Cleveland adolescence. "What the hell do you think you're doing?" I demanded to know. "I'm no God damn woman!" I said.

I have spoken of losing my self-respect over the years. Arpad Leen had now lost his in a matter of seconds, with this preposterous misapprehension of his.

He was speechless and white.

When he tried to recover, he did not recover much. He was beyond apologizing, too shattered to exhibit charm or cleverness of any kind. He could only grope for where the truth might lie.

"But you know her," he said at last. There was resignation in his voice, for he was acknowledging what was becoming clear to me, too: that I was more powerful than he was, if I wanted to be.

I confirmed this for him. "I know her well," I said. "She will do whatever I tell her, I'm sure." This last was gratuitous. It was vengeful.

He was still a very sick man. I had come between his God and him. It was his turn to hang his head. "Well," he said, and there was a long pause, "speak well of me, if you can."

More than anything now, I wanted to rescue Mary Kathleen O'Looney from the ghastly life the dragons in her mind had forced her to lead. I knew where I could find her.

"I wonder if you could tell me," I said to the broken Leen, "where I could find a pair of shoes to fit me at this time of night."

His voice came to me as though from the place where I was going next, the great cavern under Grand Central Station. "No problem," he said.

# 23

THE NEXT THING I KNEW, I, all alone, having made certain that no one was following me, was descending the iron staircase into the cavern. Every few steps I called ahead, crooningly, comfortingly, "It's Walter, Mary Kathleen. It's Walter here."

How was I shod? I was wearing black patent leather evening slippers with little bows at the insteps. They had been given to me by the ten-year-old son of Arpad Leen, little Dexter. They were just my size. Dexter had been required to buy them for dancing school. He did not need them anymore. He had delivered his first successful ultimatum to his parents: He had told them that he would commit suicide if they insisted that he keep on going to dancing school. He hated dancing school that much.

What a dear boy he was—in his pajamas and bathrobe after a swim in the living room. He was so sympathetic and concerned for me, for a little old man who had no shoes for his little feet. I might have been a kindly elf in a fairy tale, and he might have been a princeling, making a gift to the elf of a pair of magic dancing shoes.

What a beautiful boy he was. He had big brown eyes. His hair was a crown of black ringlets. I would have given a lot for a son like that. Then again, my own son, I imagine, would have given a lot for a father like Arpad Leen.

Fair is fair.

"It's Walter, Mary Kathleen," I called again. "It's Walter here." At the bottom of the steps, I came across the first clue that all might not be well. It was a shopping bag from Bloomingdale's—lying on its side, vomiting rags and a doll's head and a copy of *Vogue*, a RAMJAC publication.

I straightened it up and stuffed things back into its mouth, pretending that that was all that needed to be done to put things right again. That is when I saw a spot of blood on the floor. That was something I couldn't put back where it belonged. There were many more farther on.

And I don't mean to draw out the suspense here to no purpose, to give readers a *frisson*, to let them suppose that I would find Mary Kathleen with her hands cut off, waving her bloody stumps at me. She had in fact been sideswiped by a Checker cab on Vanderbilt Avenue, and had refused medical attention, saying that she was fine, just fine.

But she was far from fine.

There was a possible irony here, one I am, however, unable to confirm. There was a very good chance that Mary Kathleen had been creamed by one of her own taxicabs.

Her nose was broken, which was where the blood had come from. There were worse things wrong with her. I cannot name them. No inventory was ever taken of everything that was broken in Mary Kathleen.

She had hidden herself in a toilet stall. The drops of blood showed me where to look. There could be no doubt as to who was in there. Her basketball shoes were visible beneath the door.

At least there was not a corpse in there. When I crooned my name and my harmlessness again, she unlatched the door and pulled it open. She was not using the toilet, but simply sitting on it. She might as well have been using it, her humiliation by life was now so complete. Her nosebleed had stopped, but it had left her with an Adolf Hitler mustache.

"Oh! You poor woman!" I cried.

She was unimpressed by her condition. "I guess that's what I am," she said. "That's what my mother was." Her mother, of course, had died of radium poisoning.

"What happened to you?" I said.

She told me about being hit by a taxi. She had just mailed a letter to Arpad Leen, confirming all the orders she had given to him on the telephone.

"I'll get an ambulance," I said.

"No, no," she said. "Stay here, stay here."

"But you need help!" I said.

"I'm past that," she said.

"You don't even know what's wrong with you," I said.

"I'm dying, Walter," she said. "That's enough to know."

"Where there's life there's hope," I said, and I prepared to run upstairs.

"Don't you dare leave me alone again!" she said.

"I'm going to save your life!" I said.

"You've got to hear what I have to say first!" she said. "I've been sitting here thinking, 'My God—after all I've gone through, after all I've worked for, there isn't going to be anybody to hear the last things I have to say.' You get an ambulance, and there won't be anybody who understands English on that thing."

"Can I make you more comfortable?" I said.

"I am comfortable," she said. There was something to that claim. Her layers and layers of clothing were keeping her warm. Her little head was supported in a corner of the stall and cushioned against the metal by a pillow of rags.

There was meanwhile an occasional grumbling in the living rock around us. Something else was dying upstairs, which was the railroad system of the United States. Half-broken locomotives were dragging completely broken passenger cars in and out of the station.

"I know your secret," I said.

"Which one?" she said. "There are so many now."

I expected it to be a moment of high drama when I told her that I knew she was the majority stockholder in RAMJAC. It was a fizzle, of course. She had told me that already, and I had failed to hear.

"Are you going deaf, Walter?" she said.

"I hear you all right, now," I said.

"On top of everything else," she said, "am I going to have to yell my last words?"

"No," I said. "But I don't want to listen to any more talk about last words. You're so rich, Mary Kathleen! You can take over a whole hospital, if you want to—and make them make you well again!"

"I hate this life," she said. "I've done everything I can to make it better for everybody, but there probably isn't that much that anybody can do. I've had enough of trying. I want to go to sleep now."

"But you don't have to live this way!" I said. "That's what I came here to tell you. I'll protect you, Mary Kathleen. We'll hire people we can trust absolutely. Howard Hughes hired Mormons—because they have such high moral standards. We'll hire Mormons, too."

"Oh Lord, Walter," she said, "you think I haven't tried Mormons?"

"You have?" I said.

"I was up to my ears in Mormons one time," she said, and she told me as gruesome a tale as I ever expect to hear.

It happened when she was still living expensively, still trying to find ways to enjoy her great wealth at least a little bit. She was a freak that many people would have liked to photograph or capture or torment in some way—or kill. People would have liked to kill her for her hands or her money, but also for revenge. RAMJAC had stolen or ruined many other businesses and had even had a hand in the toppling of governments in countries that were small and weak.

So she dared not reveal her true identity to anyone but her faithful Mormons, and she had to keep moving all the time. And so it came to pass that she was staying on the top floor of a RAMJAC hotel in Managua, Nicaragua. There were twenty luxury suites on the floor, and she hired them all. The two stairways from the floor below were blocked with brutal masonry, like the archway in the lobby of the Arapahoe. The controls on the elevators were set so that only one could reach the top, and that one was manned by a Mormon.

Not even the manager of the hotel, supposedly, knew who she really was. But everyone in Managua, surely, must have suspected who she really was.

Be that as it may: She rashly resolved to go out into the city alone one day, to taste however briefly what she had not tasted for years—what it was like to be just another human being in the world. So out she went in a wig and dark glasses.

She befriended a middle-aged American woman whom she found weeping on a bench in a park. The woman was from St. Louis. Her husband was a brewmaster in the Anheuser-Busch Division of RAMJAC. They had come to Nicaragua for a second honeymoon on the advice of a travel agent. The husband had died that morning of amoebic dysentery.

So Mary Kathleen took her back to the hotel and put her into one of the many unused suites she had, and told some of her Mormons to arrange to have the body and the widow flown to St. Louis on a RAMJAC plane.

When Mary Kathleen went to tell her about the arrangements, she found the woman strangled with a cord from the draperies. This was the really horrible part, though: Whoever had done it had obviously believed the woman was Mary Kathleen. Her hands were cut off. They were never found.

Mary Kathleen went to New York City soon after that. She began to watch shopping-bag ladies through field glasses from her suite in the Waldorf Towers. General of the Armies Douglas MacArthur lived on the floor above her, incidentally.

She never went out, never had visitors, never called anyone. No hotel people were allowed in. The Mormons brought the food from downstairs, and made the beds, and did all the cleaning. But one day she received a threatening note, anyway. It was in a pink, scented envelope atop her most intimate lingerie. It said that the author knew who she was and held her responsible for the overthrow of the legitimate government of Guatemala. He was going to blow up the hotel.

Mary Kathleen could take it no more. She walked out on her Mormons, who were surely loyal, but unable to protect her. She began to protect herself with layers and layers of clothing she found in garbage cans.

"If your money made you so unhappy," I said, "why didn't you give it away?"

"I am!" she said. "After I die, you look in my left shoe, Walter. You will find my will in there. I leave The RAMJAC Corporation to its rightful owners, the American people." She smiled. It was harrowing to see such cosmic happiness expressed by gums and a rotten tooth or two.

I thought she had died. She had not.

"Mary Kathleen—?" I said.

"I'm not dead yet," she said.

"I really am going to get help now," I said.

"If you do, I'll die," she said. "I can promise that now. I can die when I want to now. I can pick the time."

"Nobody can do that," I said.

"Shopping-bag ladies can," she said. "It's our special dispensation. We can't say when we will start dying. But once we do start, Walter, we can pick the exact time. Would you like me to die right now, at the count of ten?"

"Not now, not ever," I said.

"Then stay here," she said.

So I did. What else could I do?

"I want to thank you for hugging me," she said.

"Any time," I said.

"Once a day is enough," she said. "I've had my hug today."

"You were the first woman I ever really made love to," I said. "Do you remember that?"

"I remember the hugs," she said. "I remember you said you loved me. No man had ever said that to me before. My mother used to say it to me a lot—before she died."

I was starting to cry again.

"I know you never meant it," she said.

"I did, I did," I protested. "Oh, my God—I did."

"It's all right," she said. "You couldn't help it that you were born without a heart. At least you tried to believe what the people with hearts believed—so you were a good man just the same."

She stopped breathing. She stopping blinking. She was dead.

# Epilogue

THERE WAS MORE. There is always more.

It was nine o'clock in the evening of my first full day of freedom. I still had three hours to go. I went upstairs and told a policeman that there was a dead shopping-bag lady in the basement.

His duties had made him cynical. He said to me, "So what else is new?"

So I stood by the body of my old friend in the basement until the ambulance attendants came, just as any other faithful animal would have done. It took a while, since it was known that she was dead. She was stiffening up when they got there. They commented on that. I had to ask them what they had just said, since they did not speak in English. It turned out that their first language was Urdu. They were both from Pakistan. Their English was primitive. If Mary Kathleen had died in their presence instead of mine, they would have said, I am sure, that she spoke gibberish at the end.

I inquired of them, in order to calm the sobs that were welling up inside me, to tell me a little about Urdu. They said it had a literature as great as any in the world, but that it had begun as a spare and ugly artificial language invented in the court of Ghenghis Khan. Its purpose in the beginning was military. It allowed his captains to give orders that were understood in every part of the Mongol Empire. Poets would later make it beautiful.

Live and learn.

I gave the police Mary Kathleen's maiden name. I gave them my true name as well. I was not about to be cute with the police. Neither was I ready to have anyone learn yet that Mrs. Jack Graham was dead. The consequences of that announcement would surely be an avalanche of some kind.

I was the only person on the planet who could set it off. I was not ready to set it off yet. This was not cunning on my part, as some people have said. It was my natural awe of an avalanche.

I walked home, a harmless little elf in his magic dancing shoes, to the Hotel Arapahoe. Much straw had been spun into gold that day, and much gold had been spun into straw. And the spinning had just begun.

There was a new night clerk, naturally, since Israel Edel had been summoned to Arpad Leen's. This new man had been sent over to fill in on short notice. His regular post was behind the desk at the Carlyle, also a RAMJAC hotel. He was exquisitely dressed and groomed. He was mortified, having to deal with whores and people fresh out of jails and lunatic asylums and so on.

He had to tell me that: that he really belonged to the Carlyle, and that he was only filling in. This was not the real him.

When I told him my name, he said that there was a package for me, and a message, too.

The police had returned my shoes and had picked up the clarinet parts from my bureau. The message was from Arpad Leen. It was a holograph, like Mary Kathleen's will, which I had in the inner pocket of my suitcoat—along with my Doctor of Mixology degree. The pockets of my raincoat were stuffed with other materials from Mary Kathleen's shoes. They bulged like saddlebags.

Leen wrote that the letter was for my eyes only. He said that in the midst of the confusion at his penthouse he had never gotten around to offering a specific job to me. He suggested that I would be happy in his old division, which was Down Home Records. It now included *The New York Times* and Universal Pictures and Ringling Bros. and Barnum & Bailey and Dell Publishing, among other things. There was also a catfood company, he said, which I needn't worry about. It was about to be transferred to the General Foods Division. It had belonged to the *Times*.

"If this is not your cup of tea," he wrote, "we'll find something that is. I am absolutely thrilled to know that we will have an observer for Mrs. Graham among us. Please give her my warmest regards."

There was a postscript. He said that he had taken the liberty of making an appointment for me at eleven the next morning with someone named Morty Sills. There was an address. I assumed that Sills was a RAMJAC personnel director or something. It turned out that he was a tailor.

Once again a multimillionaire was sending Walter F. Starbuck to his own tailor, to be made into a convincing counterfeit of a perfect gentleman.

• • •

On the following morning I was still numbed by my dread of the avalanche. I was four thousand dollars richer and technically a thief. Mary Kathleen had had four one-thousand-dollar bills as insoles for her basketball shoes.

There was nothing in the papers about the death of Mary Kathleen. Why would there have been? Who cared? There was an obituary for the patient Sarah Clewes had lost—the woman with the bad heart. She left three children behind. Her husband had died in an automobile accident a month before, so the children were orphans now.

As I was being measured for a suit by Morty Sills, I found it unbearable to think of Mary Kathleen's not being claimed by anyone. Clyde Carter was there, too, fresh off the plane from Atlanta. He, too, was getting a brand-new wardrobe, even before Arpad Leen had seen him.

He was scared.

I told him not to be.

So I went to the morgue after lunch, and I claimed her. It was easily done. Who else would want that tiny body? It had no relatives. I was its only friend.

I had one last look at it. It was nothing. There was nobody in there anymore. "Nobody home."

I found a mortician only one block away. I had him pick up the body and embalm it and put it into a serviceable casket. There was no funeral. I did not even accompany it to the grave, which was a crypt in a great concrete honeycomb in Morristown, New Jersey. The cemetery had advertised in the *Times* that morning. Each crypt had a tasteful little bronze door on which the tenant's name was engraved.

Little did I dream that the man who did the engraving of the doors would be arrested for drunken driving about two years later, and would comment on what an unusual name the arresting officer had. He had come across it only once before—at his lugubrious place of work. The name of the officer, a Morris County deputy sheriff, actually, was Francis X. O'Looney.

O'Looney would become curious as to how the woman in the crypt was related to him.

O'Looney, using the sparse documents at the cemetery, would trace Mary Kathleen back to the morgue in New York City. There he would get a set of her fingerprints. On the outside chance that she had been arrested or had spent time in a mental institution, he would send the prints to the F.B.I.

Thus would RAMJAC be brought tumbling down.

•  •  •

There was a bizarre sidelight to the case. O'Looney, before he finally found out who Mary Kathleen really was, fell in love with his dream of her when she was young. He had it all wrong, incidentally. He dreamed that she was tall and buxom and black-haired, whereas she had been short and scrawny and red-haired. He dreamed that she was an immigrant who had gone to work for an eccentric millionaire in a spooky mansion, and that she had been both attracted and repelled by this man, and that he had abused her to the point of death.

All this came out in divorce proceedings brought against O'Looney by his wife of thirty-two years. It was front-page stuff in the tabloids for a week or more. O'Looney was already famous by then. The papers called him "The man who blew the whistle on RAMJAC," or variations on that theme. Now his wife was claiming that his affections had been alienated by a ghost. He wouldn't sleep with her anymore. He stopped brushing his teeth. He was chronically late to work. He became a grandfather, and he didn't care. He wouldn't even look at the baby.

What was particularly sick about his behavior was that, even after he found out what Mary Kathleen had really been like, he stayed in love with the original dream.

"Nobody can ever take that away from me," he said. "It's the most precious thing I own."

He has been relieved of his duties, I hear. His wife is suing him again—this time for her share in the small fortune he got for the movie rights to his dream. The film is to be shot in a spooky old mansion in Morristown. If you can believe the gossip columns, there is to be a talent search for an actress to play the Irish immigrant girl. Al Pacino has already agreed to play Sheriff O'Looney, and Kevin McCarthy to play the eccentric millionaire.

• • •

So I dallied too long, and now I must go to prison again, they say. My high jinks with Mary Kathleen's remains were not crimes in and of themselves, since corpses have no more rights than do orts from last night's midnight snack. My actions were accessory, however, to the commission of a class E felony, which according to Section 190.30 of the Penal Law of New York State consists of unlawfully concealing a will.

I had entombed the will itself in a safe-deposit box of Manufacturers Hanover Trust Company, a division of RAMJAC.

I have tried to explain to my little dog that her master must go away for a while—because he violated Section 190.30. I have told her that laws are written to be obeyed. She understands nothing. She loves my voice. All news from me is good news. She wags her tail.

• • •

I lived very high. I bought a duplex with a low-interest company loan. I cashed stock options for clothes and furniture. I became a fixture at the Metropolitan Opera and the New York City Ballet, coming and going by limousine.

I gave intimate parties at my home for RAMJAC authors and recording artists and movie actors and circus performers—Isaac Bashevis Singer, Mick Jagger, Jane Fonda, Gunther Gebel-Williams, and the like. It was fun. After RAMJAC acquired the Marlborough Gallery and Associated American Artists, I had painters and sculptors to my parties, too.

How well did I do at RAMJAC? During my incumbency, my division, including subsidiaries under its control, both covert and overt, won eleven platinum records, forty-two gold records, twenty-two Oscars, eleven National Book Awards, two American League pennants, two National League pennants, two World Series, and fifty-three Grammies—and we never failed to show a return on capital of less than 23 percent. I even engaged in corporate in-fighting, preventing the transfer of the catfood company from my division to General Foods. It was exciting. I got really mad.

We just missed getting another Nobel prize in literature several times. But then we already had two: Saul Bellow and Mr. Singer.

I myself have made *Who's Who* for the first time in my life. This is a slightly tarnished triumph, admittedly, since my own division controls Gulf & Western, which controls *Who's Who*. I put it all in there, except for the prison term and the name of my son: where I was born, where I went to college, various jobs I've held, my wife's maiden name.

* * *

Did I invite my own son to my parties—to chat with so many heroes and heroines of his? No. Did he quit the *Times* when I became his superior there? No. Did he write or telephone greetings of any sort? No. Did I try to get in touch with him? Only once. I was in the basement apartment of Leland and Sarah Clewes. I had been drinking, something I don't enjoy and rarely do. And I was physically so close to my son. His apartment was only thirty feet above my head.

It was Sarah who had made me telephone him.

So I dialed my son's number. It was about eight o'clock at night. One of my little grandchildren answered, and I asked him his name.

"Juan," he said.

"And your last name?" I said.

"Stankiewicz," he said. In accordance with my wife's will, incidentally, Juan and his brother, Geraldo, were receiving reparations from West Germany for the confiscation of my wife's father's bookstore in Vienna by the Nazis after the *Anschluss*, Germany's annexation of Austria in Nineteen-hundred and Thirty-eight. My wife's will was an old one, written when Walter was a little boy. The lawyer had advised her to leave the money to her grandchildren so as to avoid one generation of taxes. She was trying to be smart about money. I was out of work at the time.

"Is your daddy home?" I said.

"He's at the movies," he said.

I was so relieved. I did not leave my name. I said I would call back later.

. . .

As for what Arpad Leen suspected about me: Like anyone else, he was free to suspect as much or as little as he pleased. There were no more fingerprinted messages from Mrs. Graham. The last one confirmed in writing that Clewes and I and Ubriaco and Edel and Lawes and Carter and Fender were to be made vice-presidents.

There was a deathly silence after that—but there had been deathly silences before. One lasted two years. Leen meanwhile operated under the mandate of a letter Mary Kathleen had sent him in Nineteen-hundred and Seventy-one, which said only this: "acquire, acquire, acquire."

She had certainly picked the right man for the job. Arpad Leen was born to acquire and acquire and acquire.

What was the biggest lie I told him? That I saw Mrs. Graham once a week, and that she was happy and well and quite satisfied with the way things were going.

As I testified before a grand jury: He gave every evidence of believing me, no matter what I said about Mrs. Graham.

I was in an extraordinary position theologically with respect to that man. I knew the answers to so many of the ultimate questions he might want to ask about that life of his.

Why did he have to go on acquiring and acquiring and acquiring? Because his deity wanted to give the wealth of the United States to the people of the United States. Where was his deity? In Morristown, New Jersey. Was she pleased with how he was doing his job? She was neither pleased nor displeased, since she was as dead as a doornail. What should he do next? Find another deity to serve.

I was in an extraordinary position theologically with respect to his millions of employees, too, of course, since he was a deity to them, and supposedly knew exactly what he wanted and why.

. . .

Well—it is all being sold off now by the federal government, which has hired twenty thousand new bureaucrats, half of them lawyers, to oversee the job. Many people assumed that RAMJAC owned everything in the country. It was something of an anticlimax, then, to discover that it owned only 19 percent of it—not even one-fifth. Still—RAMJAC was enormous when compared with other conglomerates. The second largest conglomerate in the Free World was only half its size. The next five after that, if combined, would have been only about two-thirds the size of RAMJAC.

There are plenty of dollars, it turns out, to buy all the goodies the federal government has to sell. The President of the United States himself was astonished by how many dollars had been scattered over the world through the years. It was as though he had told everybody on the planet, "Please rake your yard and send the leaves to me."

There was a photograph on an inside page of the *Daily News* yesterday of a dock in Brooklyn. There was about an acre of bales that looked like cotton on the dock. These were actually bales of American currency from Saudi Arabia, cash on the barrelhead, so to speak, for the McDonald's Hamburgers Division of RAMJAC.

The headline said this: "HOME AT LAST!"

Who is the lucky owner of all those bales? The people of the United States, according to the will of Mary Kathleen O'Looney.

•   •   •

What, in my opinion, was wrong with Mary Kathleen's scheme for a peaceful economic revolution? For one thing, the federal government was wholly unprepared to operate all the businesses of RAMJAC on behalf of the people. For another thing: Most of those businesses, rigged only to make profits, were as indifferent to the needs of the people as, say, thunderstorms. Mary Kathleen might as well have left one-fifth of the weather to the people. The businesses of RAMJAC, by their very nature, were as unaffected by the joys and tragedies of human beings as the rain that fell on the night that Madeiros and Sacco and Vanzetti died in an electric chair. It would have rained anyway.

The economy is a thoughtless weather system—and nothing more.

Some joke on the people, to give them such a thing.

•  •  •

There was a supper party given in my honor last week—a "going away party," you might say. It celebrated the completion of my last full day at the office. The host and hostess were Leland Clewes and his lovely wife Sarah. They have not moved out of their basement apartment in Tudor City, nor has Sarah given up private nursing, although Leland is now pulling down about one hundred thousand dollars a year at RAMJAC. Much of their money goes to the Foster Parents Program, a scheme that allows them to support individual children in unfortunate circumstances in many parts of the world. They are supporting fifty children, I think they said. They have letters and photographs from several of them, which they passed around.

I am something of a hero to certain people, which is a novelty. I single-handedly extended the life of RAMJAC by two years and a little more. If I had not concealed the will of Mary Kathleen, those at the party would never have become vice-presidents of RAMJAC. I myself would have been thrown out on my ear—to become what I expect to be anyway, if I survive my new prison term, which is a shopping-bag man.

Am I broke again? Yes. My defense has been expensive. Also: My Watergate lawyers have caught up with me. I still owe them a lot for all they did for me.

Clyde Carter, my former guard in Georgia and now a vice-president of the Chrysler Air Temp Division of RAMJAC, was there with his lovely wife Claudia. He did a side-splitting imitation of his cousin the President, saying, "I will never lie to you," and promising to rebuild the South Bronx and so on.

Frank Ubriaco was there with his lovely new wife Marilyn, who is only seventeen. Frank is fifty-three. They met at a discotheque. They seem very happy. She said that what attracted her to him at first was that he wore a white glove on only one hand. She had to find out why. He told her at first that the hand had been burned by a Chinese communist flame thrower during the Korean War, but later admitted that he had done it to himself with a Fry-o-lator. They have started a collection of tropical fish. They have a coffee table that contains tropical fish.

Frank invented a new sort of cash register for the McDonald's Hamburgers Division. It was getting harder all the time to find employees who understood numbers well, so Frank took the numbers off the keys of the cash register and substituted pictures of hamburgers and milkshakes and French fries and Coca-Colas and so on. The person totting up a bill would simply punch the pictures of the various things a customer had ordered, and the cash register would add it up for him.

Frank got a big bonus for that.

My guess is that the Saudis will keep him on.

There was a telegram to me from Dr. Robert Fender, still in prison in Georgia. Mary Kathleen had wanted RAMJAC to make him a vice-president, too, but there was no way to get him out of prison. Treason was just too serious a crime. Clyde Carter had written to him that I was going back to prison myself, and that there was going to be a party for me, and that he should send a telegram.

This was all it said: "Ting-a-ling."

That was from his science-fiction story about the judge from the planet Vicuna, of course, who had to find a new body to occupy, and who flew into my ear down there in Georgia, and found himself stuck to my feelings and destiny until I died.

According to the judge in the story, that was how they said both hello and good-bye on Vicuna: "Ting-a-ling."

"Ting-a-ling" was like the Hawaiian "aloha," which also means both hello and good-bye.

"Hello and good-bye." What else is there to say? Our language is much larger than it needs to be.

I asked Clyde if he knew what Fender was working on now.

"A science-fiction novel about economics," said Clyde.

"Did he say what pseudonym he's going to use?" I said.

"'Kilgore Trout,'" said Clyde.

· · ·

My devoted secretary, Leora Borders, and her husband, Lance, were there. Lance was just getting over a radical mastectomy. He told me that one mastectomy in two hundred was performed on a man. Live and learn!

There were several other RAMJAC friends who should have been there, but dared not come. They feared that their reputations, and hence their futures as executives, might be tainted if it were known that they were friendly with me.

There were telegrams from other people I had had to my famous little parties—John Kenneth Galbraith and Salvador Dalí and Erica Jong and Liv Ullmann and the Flying Farfans and on and on.

Robert Redford's telegram, I remember, said this: "Hang tough."

The telegrams were something less than spontaneous. As Sarah Clewes would admit under questioning, she had been soliciting them all week long.

Arpad Leen sent a spoken message through Sarah, which was meant for my ears alone: "Good show." That could be taken a million different ways.

He was no longer presiding over the dismemberment of RAMJAC, incidentally. He had been hired away by American Telephone and Telegraph Company, which had just been bought by a new company in Monaco named BIBEC. Nobody has been able to find out who or what BIBEC is, so far. Some people think it's the Russians.

At least I will have some real friends outside of prison this time.

There was a bowl of yellow tulips on the table for a centerpiece. It was April again.

It was raining outside. Nature sympathized.

• • •

I was seated at the place of honor—to the right of my hostess, of Sarah Clewes, the nurse. Of the four women I ever loved, she was always the easiest one to talk to. That may be because I had never promised her anything, and so had never let her down. Oh, Lord—the things I used to promise my mother and my poor wife and poor Mary Kathleen!

Young Israel Edel and his not-so-lovely wife Norma were there. I say that she was not-so-lovely for the simple reason that she has always hated me. I don't know why. I have never insulted her, and she is certainly as pleased as Punch with the upturn her husband's career has taken. He would still be a night clerk, if it weren't for me. The Edels are renovating a brownstone in Brooklyn Heights with all the money he makes. Still—every time she looks at me, I feel like something the cat dragged in. It is just one of those things. I think she may be slightly crazy. She miscarried twins about a year ago. That might have something to do with it. She may have some sort of chemical imbalance as a result of that. Who knows?

She wasn't seated next to me anyway, thank God. Another black woman was. That was Eucharist Lawes, the lovely wife of Cleveland Lawes, the former RAMJAC chauffeur. He is a vice-president of the Transico Division now. That is really his wife's name: Eucharist. It means *happy gratitude*, and I don't know why more people don't name their daughters that. Everybody calls her "Ukey."

Ukey was homesick for the South. She said the people were friendlier and more relaxed and more natural down there. She was after Cleveland to retire in or near Atlanta, especially now that the Transico Division had been bought by Playgrounds International, which everybody knows is a front for the Mafia. It just can't be proved.

My own division was being snapped up by I.G. Farben, a West German concern.

"It won't be the same old RAMJAC," I said to Ukey. "That's for sure."

There were presents—some silly, some not. Israel Edel gave me a rubber ice-cream cone with a squeaker in it—a plaything for my little dog, who is a female Lhasa apso, a golden dustmop without a handle. I could never have a dog when I was young, because Alexander Hamilton McCone hated dogs. So this is the only dog I have ever known at all well—and she sleeps with me. She snores. So did my wife.

I have never bred her, but now, according to the veterinarian, Dr. Howard Padwee, she is experiencing a false pregnancy and believes the rubber ice-cream cone to be a puppy. She hides it in closets. She carries it up and down the stairs of my duplex. She is even secreting milk for it. She is getting shots to make her stop doing that.

I observe how profoundly serious Nature has made her about a rubber ice-cream cone—brown rubber cone, pink rubber ice cream. I have to wonder what equally ridiculous commitments to bits of trash I myself have made. Not that it matters at all. We are here for no purpose, unless we can invent one. Of that I am sure. The human condition in an exploding universe would not have been altered one iota if, rather than live as I have, I had done nothing but carry a rubber ice-cream cone from closet to closet for sixty years.

Clyde Carter and Leland Clewes chipped in on a far more expensive present, which is a chess-playing computer. It is about the size of a cigar box, but most of the space is taken up by a compartment for the playing pieces. The computer itself is not much bigger than a package of cigarettes. It is called "Boris." Boris has a long, narrow little window in which he announces his moves. He can even joke about the moves I make. "Really?" he will say; or, "Have you played this game before?" or, "Is this a trap?" or, "Spot me a queen."

Those are standard chess jokes. Alexander Hamilton McCone and I exchanged those same tired jokes endlessly when, for the sake of a Harvard education in my future, I agreed to be his chess-playing machine. If Boris had existed in those days, I probably would have gone to Western Reserve, and then become a tax assessor or an office manager in a lumberyard, or an insurance salesman, or some such thing. Instead, I am the most disreputable Harvard graduate since Putzi Hänfstaengl, who was Hitler's favorite pianist.

At least I gave ten thousand dollars to Harvard before the lawyers came and took away all my money again.

•   •   •

It was time for me now at the party to respond to all the toasts that had been offered to me. I stood. I had not had a drop of alcohol.

"I am a recidivist," I said. I defined the word as describing a person who habitually relapsed into crime or antisocial behavior.

"A good word to know," said Leland Clewes.

There was laughter all around.

"Our lovely hostess has promised two more surprises before the evening is over," I said. These would turn out to be the trooping in of my son and his little human family from upstairs, and the playing of a phonograph recording of part of my testimony before Congressman Richard M. Nixon of California and others so long ago. It had to be played at seventy-eight revolutions per minute. Imagine that. "As though I hadn't had surprises enough!" I said.

"Not enough nice ones, old man," said Cleveland Lawes.

"Say it in Chinese," I said. He had, of course, been a prisoner of war of the Chinese for a while.

Lawes said something that certainly sounded like Chinese.

"How do we know he wasn't ordering sweet-and-sour pork?" said Sarah.

"You don't," said Lawes.

We had begun our feast with oysters, so I announced that oysters were not the aphrodisiacs many people imagined them to be.

There were boos, and then Sarah Clewes beat me to the punch line of that particular joke. "Walter ate twelve of them the other night," she said, "and only four of them worked!"

She had lost another patient the day before.

There was more laughter all around.

And I was suddenly offended and depressed by how silly we were. The news, after all, could hardly have been worse. Foreigners and criminals and other endlessly greedy conglomerates were gobbling up RAMJAC. Mary Kathleen's legacy to the people was being converted to mountains of rapidly deteriorating currency, which were being squandered in turn on a huge new bureaucracy and on legal fees and consultants' fees, and on and on. What was left, it was said by the politicians, would help to pay the interest on the people's national debt, and would buy them more of the highways and public buildings and advanced weaponry they so richly deserved.

Also: I was about to go to jail again.

So I elected to complain about our levity. "You know what is finally going to kill this planet?" I said.

"Cholesterol!" said Frank Ubriaco.

"A total lack of seriousness," I said. "Nobody gives a damn anymore about what's really going on, what's going to happen next, or how we ever got into such a mess in the first place."

Israel Edel, with his doctor's degree in history, took this to be a suggestion that we become even sillier, if possible. So he began to make booping and beeping sounds. Others chimed in with their own *beeps* and *boops*. They were all imitating supposedly intelligent signals from outer space, which had been received by radio telescopes only the week before. They were the latest news sensation, and had in fact driven the RAMJAC story off the front pages. People were beeping and booping and laughing, not just at my party, but everywhere.

Nobody was prepared to guess what the signals meant. Scientists did say, though, that if the signals were coming from whence they appeared to come, they had to be a million years old or more. If Earth were to make a reply, it would be the start of a very slow conversation, indeed.

• • •

So I gave up on saying anything serious. I told another joke, and I sat down.

The party ended, as I say, with the arrival of my son and daughter-in-law and their two children, and with the playing of a phonograph recording of the closing minutes of my testimony before a congressional committee in Nineteen-hundred and Forty-nine.

My daughter-in-law and my grandchildren found it natural and easy, seemingly, to accord me the honors due a grandfather who, when all was said and done, was a clean and dapper and kindly old man. The model for what the children found to love in me, I suppose, was Santa Claus.

My son was a shock. He was such a homely and unhealthy and unhappy-looking young man. He was short like me, and nearly as fat as his poor mother had become toward the end. I still had most of my hair, but he was bald. The baldness must have been inherited from the Jewish side of his family.

He was a chain-smoker of unfiltered cigarettes. He coughed a lot. His suit was riddled with cigarette holes. I glanced at him while the record was playing, and I saw that he was so nervous that he had three cigarettes all going at one time.

He had shaken my hand with the correct wretchedness of a German general surrendering at Stalingrad, say. I was still a monster to him. He had been cajoled into coming against his better judgment—by his wife and Sarah Clewes.

Too bad.

The record changed nothing. The children, kept up long after their bedtime, squirmed and dozed.

The record was meant to honor me, to let people who might not know about it hear for themselves what an idealistic young man I had been. The part in which I accidentally betrayed Leland Clewes as a former communist was on another record, I presume. It was not played.

Only my very last sentences were of much interest to me. I had forgotten them.

Congressman Nixon had asked me why, as the son of immigrants who had been treated so well by Americans, as a man who had been treated like a son and been sent to Harvard by an American capitalist, I had been so ungrateful to the American economic system.

The answer I gave him was not original. Nothing about me has ever been original. I repeated what my one-time hero, Kenneth Whistler, had said in reply to the same general sort of question long, long ago. Whistler had been a witness at a trial of strikers accused of violence. The judge had become curious about him, had asked him why such a well-educated man from such a good family would so immerse himself in the working class.

My stolen answer to Nixon was this: "Why? The Sermon on the Mount, sir."

There was polite applause when the people at the party realized that the phonograph record had ended.

Good-bye.

—W.F.S.

# *Index*

# DEADEYE DICK

*For Jill*

Who is Celia? What is she?
That all her swains commend her?

—OTTO WALTZ
(1892–1960)

# Preface

"DEADEYE DICK," like "Barnacle Bill," is a nickname for a sailor. A deadeye is a rounded wooden block, usually bound with rope or iron, and pierced with holes. The holes receive a multiplicity of lines, usually shrouds or stays, on an old-fashioned sailing ship. But in the American Middle West of my youth, "Deadeye Dick" was an honorific often accorded to a person who was a virtuoso with firearms.

So it is a sort of lungfish of a nickname. It was born in the ocean, but it adapted to life ashore.

• • •

There are several recipes in this book, which are intended as musical interludes for the salivary glands. They have been inspired by *James Beard's American Cookery*, Marcella Hazan's *The Classic Italian Cook Book*, and Bea Sandler's *The African Cookbook*. I have tinkered with the originals, however—so no one should use this novel for a cookbook.

Any serious cook should have the reliable originals in his or her library anyway.

• • •

There is a real hotel in this book, the Grand Hotel Oloffson in Port au Prince, Haiti. I love it, and so would almost anybody else. My dear wife Jill Krementz and I have stayed there in the so-called "James Jones Cottage," which was built as an operating room when the hotel was headquarters for a brigade of United States Marines, who occupied Haiti, in order to protect American financial interests there, from 1915 until 1934.

The exterior of that austere wooden box has subsequently been decorated with fanciful, jigsaw gingerbread, like the rest of the hotel.

The currency of Haiti, by the way, is based on the American dollar. Whatever an American dollar is worth, that is what a Haitian dollar is worth, and actual American dollars are in general circulation. There seems to be no scheme in Haiti, however,

381

for retiring worn-out dollar bills, and replacing them with new ones. So it is ordinary there to treat with utmost seriousness a dollar which is as insubstantial as a cigarette paper, and which has shrunk to the size of an airmail stamp.

I found one such bill in my wallet when I got home from Haiti a couple of years ago, and I mailed it back to Al and Sue Seitz, the owners and host and hostess of the Oloffson, asking them to release it into its natural environment. It could never have survived a day in New York City.

•  •  •

James Jones (1921–1977), the American novelist, was actually married to his wife Gloria in the James Jones Cottage, before it was called that. So it is a literary honor to stay there.

There is supposedly a ghost—not of James Jones, but of somebody else. We never saw it. Those who have seen it describe a young white man in a white jacket, possibly a medical orderly of some kind. There are only two doors, a back door opening into the main hotel, and a front door opening onto a porch. This ghost is said to follow the same route every time it appears. It comes in through the back door, searches for something in a piece of furniture which isn't there anymore, and then goes out the front door. It vanishes when it passes through the front door. It has never been seen in the main hotel or on the porch.

It may have an uneasy conscience about something it did or saw done when the cottage was an operating room.

•  •  •

There are four real painters in this book, one living and three dead. The living one is my friend in Athens, Ohio, Cliff McCarthy. The dead ones are John Rettig, Frank Duveneck, and Adolf Hitler.

Cliff McCarthy is about my age and from my part of America, more or less. When he went to art school, it was drummed into him that the worst sort of painter was eclectic, borrowing from here and there. But now he has had a show of thirty years of his work, at Ohio University, and he says, "I notice that I have been eclectic." It's strong and lovely stuff he does. My own favorite is "The Artist's Mother as a Bride in 1917." His mother is all dressed up, and it's a warm time of year, and somebody has persuaded her to pose in the bow of a rowboat. The rowboat is in a perfectly still, narrow patch of water, a little river, probably, with the opposite bank, all leafy, only fifty yards away. She is laughing.

There really was a John Rettig, and his painting in the Cincinnati Art Museum, "Crucifixion in Rome," is as I have described it.

There really was a Frank Duveneck, and I in fact own a painting by him, "Head of a Young Boy." It is a treasure left to me by my father. I used to think it was a portrait of my brother Bernard, it looks so much like him.

And there really was an Adolf Hitler, who studied art in Vienna before the First World War, and whose finest picture may in fact have been "The Minorite Church of Vienna."

• • •

I will explain the main symbols in this book.

There is an unappreciated, empty arts center in the shape of a sphere. This is my head as my sixtieth birthday beckons to me.

There is a neutron bomb explosion in a populated area. This is the disappearance of so many people I cared about in Indianapolis when I was starting out to be a writer. Indianapolis is there, but the people are gone.

Haiti is New York City, where I live now.

The neutered pharmacist who tells the tale is my declining sexuality. The crime he committed in childhood is all the bad things I have done.

• • •

This is fiction, not history, so it should not be used as a reference book. I say, for example, that the United States Ambassador to Austria-Hungary at the outbreak of the First World War was Henry Clowes, of Ohio. The actual ambassador at that time was Frederic Courtland Penfield of Connecticut.

I also say that a neutron bomb is a sort of magic wand, which kills people instantly, but which leaves their property unharmed. This is a fantasy borrowed from enthusiasts for a Third World War. A real neutron bomb, detonated in a populated area, would cause a lot more suffering and destruction than I have described.

I have also misrepresented Creole, just as the viewpoint character, Rudy Waltz, learning that French dialect, might do. I say that it has only one tense—the present. Creole only seems to have that one tense to a beginner, especially if those speaking it to him know that the present is the easiest tense for him.

Peace.

—K.V.

# 1

To the as-yet-unborn, to all innocent wisps of undifferentiated nothingness: Watch out for life.

I have caught life. I have come down with life. I was a wisp of undifferentiated nothingness, and then a little peephole opened quite suddenly. Light and sound poured in. Voices began to describe me and my surroundings. Nothing they said could be appealed. They said I was a boy named Rudolph Waltz, and that was that. They said the year was 1932, and that was that. They said I was in Midland City, Ohio, and that was that.

They never shut up. Year after year they piled detail upon detail. They do it still. You know what they say now? They say the year is 1982, and that I am fifty years old.

Blah blah blah.

• • •

My father was Otto Waltz, whose peephole opened in 1892, and he was told, among other things, that he was the heir to a fortune earned principally by a quack medicine known as "Saint Elmo's Remedy." It was grain alcohol dyed purple, flavored with cloves and sarsaparilla root, and laced with opium and cocaine. As the joke goes: It was absolutely harmless unless discontinued.

He, too, was a Midland City native. He was an only child, and his mother, on the basis of almost no evidence whatsoever, concluded that he could be another Leonardo da Vinci. She had a studio built for him on a loft of the carriage house behind the family mansion when he was only ten years old, and she hired a rapscallion German cabinetmaker, who had studied art in Berlin in his youth, to give Father drawing and painting lessons on weekends and after school.

It was a sweet racket for both teacher and pupil. The teacher's name was August Gunther, and his peephole must have opened in Germany around 1850. Teaching paid as well as cabinetmaking, and, unlike cabinetmaking, allowed him to be as drunk as he pleased.

After Father's voice changed, moreover, Gunther could take him on overnight visits by rail to Indianapolis and Cincinnati and Louisville and Cleveland and so on, ostensibly to visit galleries and painters' studios. The two of them also managed to get drunk, and to become darlings of the fanciest whorehouses in the Middle West.

Was either one of them about to acknowledge that Father couldn't paint or draw for sour apples?

●    ●    ●

Who else was there to detect the fraud? Nobody. There wasn't anybody else in Midland City who cared enough about art to notice if Father was gifted or not. He might as well have been a scholar of Sanskrit, as far as the rest of the town was concerned.

Midland City wasn't a Vienna or a Paris. It wasn't even a St. Louis or a Detroit. It was a Bucyrus. It was a Kokomo.

●    ●    ●

Gunther's treachery was discovered, but too late. He and Father were arrested in Chicago after doing considerable property damage in a whorehouse there, and Father was found to have gonorrhea, and so on. But Father was by then a fully committed, eighteen-year-old good-time Charley.

Gunther was denounced and fired and blacklisted. Grandfather and Grandmother Waltz were tremendously influential citizens, thanks to Saint Elmo's Remedy. They spread the word that nobody of quality in Midland City was ever to hire Gunther for cabinetwork or any other sort of work—ever again.

Father was sent to relatives in Vienna, to have his gonorrhea treated and to enroll in the world-famous Academy of Fine Arts. While he was on the high seas, in a first-class cabin aboard the *Lusitania*, his parents' mansion burned down. It was widely suspected that the showplace was torched by August Gunther, but no proof was found.

Father's parents, rather than rebuild, took up residence in their thousand-acre farm out near Shepherdstown—leaving behind the carriage house and a cellar hole.

This was in 1910—four years before the outbreak of the First World War.

• • •

So Father presented himself at the Academy of Fine Arts with a portfolio of pictures he had created in Midland City. I myself have examined some of the artwork of his youth, which Mother used to moon over after he died. He was good at cross-hatching and shading a drapery, and August Gunther must have been capable in those areas, too. But with few exceptions, everything Father depicted wound up looking as though it were made of cement—a cement woman in a cement dress, walking a cement dog, a herd of cement cattle, a cement bowl of cement fruit, set before a window with cement curtains, and so on.

He was no good at catching likenesses, either. He showed the Academy several portraits of his mother, and I have no idea what she looked like. Her peephole closed long before mine opened. But I do know that no two of Father's portraits of her resemble each other in the least.

Father was told to come back to the Academy in two weeks, at which time they would tell him whether they would take him in or not.

He was in rags at the time, with a piece of rope for a belt, and with patched trousers and so on—although he was receiving an enormous allowance from home. Vienna was then the capital of a great empire, and there were so many elaborate uniforms and exotic costumes, and so much wine and music that it seemed to Father to be a fancy dress ball. So he decided to come to the party as a starving artist. What fun!

And he must have been very good-looking then, for he was, in my opinion, the best-looking man in Midland City when I got to know him a quarter of a century later. He was slender and erect to the end. He was six feet tall. His eyes were blue. He had curly golden hair, and he had lost almost none of it when his peephole closed, when he was allowed to stop being Otto Waltz, when he became just another wisp of undifferentiated nothingness again.

• • •

So he came back in two weeks, and a professor handed him back his portfolio, saying that his work was ludicrous. And there was another young man in rags there, and he, too, had his portfolio returned with scorn.

His name was Adolf Hitler. He was a native Austrian. He had come from Linz.

And Father was so mad at the professor that he got his revenge right then and there. He asked to see some of Hitler's work, with the professor looking on. He picked a picture at random, and he said it was a brilliant piece of work, and he bought it from Hitler for more cash on the spot than the professor, probably, could earn in a month or more.

Only an hour before, Hitler had sold his overcoat so that he could get a little something to eat, even though winter was coming on. So there is a chance that, if it weren't for my father, Hitler might have died of pneumonia or malnutrition in 1910.

Father and Hitler paired off for a while, as people will—comforting and amusing each other, jeering at the art establishment which had rejected them, and so on. I know they took several long walking trips, just the two of them. I learned of their good times together from Mother. When I was old enough to be curious about Father's past, World War Two was about to break out, and Father had developed lockjaw as far as his friendship with Hitler was concerned.

Think of that: My father could have strangled the worst monster of the century, or simply let him starve or freeze to death. But he became his bosom buddy instead.

That is my principal objection to life, I think: It is too easy, when alive, to make perfectly horrible mistakes.

• • •

The painting Father bought from Hitler was a watercolor which is now generally acknowledged as having been the best thing the monster ever did as a painter, and it hung for many years over my parents' bed in Midland City, Ohio. Its title was: "The Minorite Church of Vienna."

# 2

FATHER WAS so well received in Vienna, known to one and all as an American millionaire disguised as a ragged genius, that he roistered there for nearly four years. When the First World War broke out in August of 1914, he imagined that the fancy dress ball was to become a fancy dress picnic, that the party was to be moved out into the countryside. He was so happy, so naive, so self-enchanted, that he asked influential friends if they couldn't get him a commission in the Hungarian Life Guard, whose officers' uniforms included a panther skin.

He adored that panther skin.

He was summoned by the American ambassador to the Austro-Hungarian Empire, Henry Clowes, who was a Cleveland man and an acquaintance of Father's parents. Father was then twenty-two years old. Clowes told Father that he would lose his American citizenship if he joined a foreign army, and that he had made inquiries about Father, and had learned that Father was not the painter he pretended to be, and that Father had been spending money like a drunken sailor, and that he had written to Father's parents, telling them that their son had lost all touch with reality, and that it was time Father was summoned home and given some honest work to do.

"What if I refuse?" said Father.

"Your parents have agreed to stop your allowance," said Clowes.

So Father went home.

• • •

I do not believe he would have stayed in Midland City, if it weren't for what remained of his childhood home, which was its fanciful carriage house. It was hexagonal. It was stone. It had a conical slate roof. It had a naked skeleton inside of noble oak beams. It was a little piece of Europe in southwestern Ohio. It was a present from my great-grandfather Waltz to his homesick wife from Hamburg. It was a stone-by-stone replica of a structure in an illustration in her favorite book of German fairy tales.

It still stands.

I once showed it to an art historian from Ohio University, which is in Athens, Ohio. He said that the original might have been a medieval granary built on the ruins of a Roman watchtower from the time of Julius Caesar. Caesar was murdered two thousand years ago.

Think of that.

•   •   •

I do not think my father was entirely ungifted as an artist. Like his friend Hitler, he had a flair for romantic architecture. And he set about transforming the carriage house into a painter's studio fit for the reincarnated Leonardo da Vinci his doting mother still believed him to be.

Father's mother was as crazy as a bedbug, my own mother said.

•   •   •

I sometimes think that I would have had a very different sort of soul, if I had grown up in an ordinary little American house—if our home had not been vast.

Father got rid of all the horse-drawn vehicles in the carriage house—a sleigh, a buckboard, a surrey, a phaeton, a brougham, and who-knows-what-all? Then he had ten horse stalls and a tack room ripped out. This gave him for his private enjoyment more uninterrupted floor-space beneath a far higher ceiling than was afforded by any house of worship or public building in the Midland City of that time.

Was it big enough for a basketball game? A basketball court is ninety-four feet long and fifty feet wide. My childhood home was only eighty feet in diameter. So, no—it lacked fourteen feet of being big enough for a basketball game.

•   •   •

There were two pairs of enormous doors in the carriage house, wide enough to admit a carriage and a team of horses. One pair faced north, one pair faced south. Father had his workmen take down the northern pair, which his old mentor, August

Gunther, made into two tables, a dining table and a table on which Father's paints and brushes and palette knives and charcoal sticks and so on were to be displayed.

The doorway was then filled with what remains the largest window in the city, admitting copious quantities of that balm for all great painters, northern light.

It was before this window that Father's easel stood.

·   ·   ·

Yes, he had been reunited with the disreputable August Gunther, who must have been in his middle sixties then. Old Gunther had only one child, a daughter named Grace, so Father was like a son to him. A more suitable son for Gunther would be hard to imagine.

Mother was just a little girl then, and living in a mansion next door. She was terrified of old Gunther. She told me one time that all nice little girls were supposed to run away from him. Right up until the time Mother died, she cringed if August Gunther was mentioned. He was a hobgoblin to her. He was the bogeyman.

As for the pair of great doors facing south: Father had them bolted shut and padlocked, and the workmen caulked the cracks between and around them, to keep out the wind. And then August Gunther cut a front door into one of them. That was the entrance to Father's studio, what would later be my childhood home.

A hexagonal loft encircled and overhung the great chamber. This was partitioned off into bedrooms and bathrooms and a small library.

Above that was an attic under the conical slate roof. Father had no immediate use for the attic, so it was left in its primitive condition.

It was all so impractical—which I guess was the whole idea.

Father was so elated by the vastness of the ground floor, which was paved with cobblestones laid in sand, that he considered putting the kitchen up on a loft. But that would have put the servants and all their hustle and bustle and cooking smells up among the bedrooms. There was no basement to put them in.

So he reluctantly put the kitchen on the ground floor, tucked under a loft and partitioned off with old boards. It was cramped and stuffy. I would love it. I would feel so safe and cozy in there.

•  •  •

Many people found our house spooky, and the attic in fact was full of evil when I was born. It housed a collection of more than three hundred antique and modern firearms. Father had bought them during his and Mother's six-month honeymoon in Europe in 1922. Father thought them beautiful, but they might as well have been copperheads and rattlesnakes.

They were murder.

# 3

MY MOTHER'S PEEPHOLE opened in Midland City in 1901. She was nine years younger than Father. She, like him, was an only child—the daughter of Richard Wetzel, the founder and principal stockholder of the Midland County National Bank. Her name was Emma.

She was born into a mansion teeming with servants, right next door to my father's childhood home, but she would die penniless in 1978, four years ago now, in a little shitbox she and I shared in the suburb of Midland City called Avondale.

• • •

She remembered seeing Father's childhood home burn down when she was nine years old, when Father was on his way to Vienna. But Father made a far greater impression on her than the fire when he came home from Vienna and looked over the carriage house with the idea of turning it into a studio.

She had her first glimpse of him through the privet hedge between the two properties. This was a bird-legged, buck-toothed, skinny thirteen-year-old, who had never seen men dressed in anything but overalls or business suits. Her parents had spoken glowingly of Father, since he was rich and came from an excellent family. They had suggested playfully that she could do worse than marry him someday.

So now she peeked at him through the hedge, her heart beating madly, and, great God! He was all scarlet and silver, except for a panther skin over one shoulder—and a sable busby with a purple plume on his head.

He was wearing one of the many souvenirs he had brought home from Vienna, which was the dress uniform of a major in the Hungarian Life Guard, the regiment he had hoped to join.

• • •

A real Hungarian Life Guard back in the Austro-Hungarian Empire might have been putting on a field gray uniform about then.

Father's friend Hitler, who was an Austrian, had managed to join the German rather than the Austrian army—because he admired all things German so much. He was wearing field gray.

•   •   •

Father was living with his parents out near Shepherdstown at the time, but all his souvenirs were stored in the carriage house. And, on the day that Mother saw him in the uniform, he had begun opening trunks and packing cases, with his old mentor, August Gunther, looking on. He had put on the uniform to make Gunther laugh.

They came outside, lugging a table between them. They were going to have lunch in the shade of an ancient walnut tree. They had brought beer and bread and sausage and cheese and roast chicken, all of which had been produced locally. The cheese, incidentally, was Liederkranz, which most people assume is a European cheese. Liederkranz was invented in Midland City, Ohio, in about 1865.

•   •   •

So Father, setting down for a lusty lunch with old Gunther, was aware that a little girl was watching everything through the hedge, and he made jokes about her which she could hear. He said to Gunther that he had been away so long that he could no longer remember the names of American birds. There was a bird in the hedge there, he said, and he described Mother as though she were a bird, and he asked old Gunther what to call the bird.

And Father approached the supposed little bird with a piece of bread in his hand, asking if little birds like her ate bread, and Mother fled into her parents' house.

She told me this. Father told me this.

•   •   •

But she came out again, and she found a better place to spy from—where she could see without being seen. There were puzzling new arrivals at the picnic. They were two short, dark youths, who had evidently been wading. They were barefoot, and their trousers were wet above the knees. Mother had never seen anything quite like them for this reason: The two, who were brothers, were Italians, and there had never been Italians in Midland City before.

They were Gino Maritimo, eighteen, and Marco Maritimo, twenty. They were in one hell of a lot of trouble. They weren't expected at the picnic. They weren't even supposed to be in the United States. Thirty-six hours before, they had been stokers aboard an Italian freighter which was taking on cargo in Newport News, Virginia. They had jumped ship in order to escape military conscription at home, and because the streets of America were paved with gold. They spoke no English.

Other Italians in Newport News boosted them and their cardboard suitcases into an empty boxcar in a train that was bound for God-knows-where. The train began to move immediately. The sun went down. There were no stars, no moon that night. America was blackness and *clackety-clack*.

How do I know what the night was like? Gino and Marco Maritimo, as old men, both told me so.

•   •   •

Somewhere in the seamless darkness, which may have been West Virginia, Gino and Marco were joined by four American hoboes, who at knife-point took their suitcases, their coats, their hats, and their shoes.

They were lucky they didn't have their throats slit for fun. Who would have cared?

•   •   •

How they wished that their peepholes would close! But the nightmare went on and on. And then it became a daymare. The train stopped several times, but in the midst of such ugliness that Gino and Marco could not bring themselves to step out into it, to somehow start living there. But then two railroad detectives with long clubs made them get out anyway, and, like it or lump it, they were on the outskirts of Midland City, Ohio, on the other side of Sugar Creek from the center of town.

They were terribly hungry and thirsty. They could either await death, or they could invent something to do. They invented. They saw a conical slate roof on the other side of the river, and they walked toward that. In order to keep putting one foot in

front of the other, they pretended that it was of utmost importance that they reach that structure and no other.

They waded across Sugar Creek, rather than draw attention
to themselves on the bridge. They would have swum the creek,
if it had been that deep.

And now here they were, as astonished as my mother had
been to see a young man all dressed in scarlet and silver, with a
sable busby on his head.

When Father looked askance at the two of them from his
seat under the oak, Gino, the younger of the brothers, but their
leader, said in Italian that they were hungry and would do any
sort of work for food.

Father replied in Italian. He was good with languages. He
was fluent in French and German and Spanish, too. He told the
brothers that they should by all means sit down and eat, if they
were as hungry as they appeared to be. He said that nobody
should ever be hungry.

He was like a god to them. It was so easy for him to be like
a god to them.

After they had eaten, he took them up into the attic above the
loft, the future gun room. There were two old cots up there.
Light and air came from windows in a cupola at the peak of the
roof. A ladder, its bottom bolted to the center of the attic floor,
led up into the cupola. Father told the brothers that they could
make the attic their home, until they found something better.

He said he had some old shoes and sweaters and so on, if they
wanted them, in his trunks below.

He put them to work the next day, ripping out the stalls and
tack room.

And no matter how rich and powerful the Maritimo brothers
subsequently became, and no matter how disreputable and poor
Father became, Father remained a god to them.

# 4

AND SOMEWHERE in there, before America entered the First World War against the German Empire and the Austro-Hungarian Empire and the Ottoman Empire, Father's parents had their peepholes closed by carbon monoxide from a faulty heating system in their farmhouse out near Shepherdstown.

So Father became a major stockholder in the family business, the Waltz Brothers Drug Company, to which he had contributed nothing but ridicule and scorn.

And he attended stockholders' meetings in a beret and a paint-stained smock and sandals, and he brought old August Gunther along, claiming Gunther was his lawyer, and he protested that he found his two uncles and their several sons, who actually ran the business, intolerably humorless and provincial and obsessed by profits, and so on.

He would ask them when they were going to stop poisoning their fellow citizens, and so on. At that time, the uncles and cousins were starting the first chain of drugstores in the history of the country, and they were especially proud of the soda fountains in those stores, and had spent a lot of money to guarantee that the ice cream served at those fountains was the equal of any ice cream in the world. So Father wanted to know why ice cream at a Waltz Brothers Drugstore always tasted like library paste, and so on.

He was an artist, you see, interested in enterprises far loftier than mere pharmacy.

And now is perhaps the time for me to name my own profession. Guess what? I, Rudy Waltz, the son of that great artist Otto Waltz, am a registered pharmacist.

• • •

Somewhere in there, one end of a noble oak timber was dropped on Father's left foot. Alcohol was involved in the accident. During a wild party at the studio, with tools and building materials lying all around, Father got a structural idea which had to be carried out at once. Nothing would do but that the drunken guests become common laborers under Father's command, and a young dairy farmer named John Fortune lost his grip on a timber. It fell on Father's foot, smashing the bones of his instep. Two of his toes died, and had to be cut away.

Thus was Father rendered unfit for military service when America got into World War One.

•   •   •

Father once said to me when he was an old man, after he had spent two years in prison, after he and Mother had lost all their money and art treasures in a lawsuit, that his greatest disappointment in life was that he had never been a soldier. That was almost the last illusion he had, and there might have been some substance to it—that he had been born to serve bravely and resourcefully on a battlefield.

He certainly envied John Fortune to the end. The man who crushed his foot went on to become a hero in the trenches in the First World War, and Father would have liked to have fought beside him—and, like Fortune, come home with medals on his chest. The only remotely military honor Father would ever receive was a citation from the governor of Ohio for Father's leadership of scrap drives in Midland County during World War Two. There was no ceremony. The certificate simply arrived in the mail one day.

Father was in prison over at Shepherdstown when it came. Mother and I brought it to him on visitors' day. I was thirteen then. It would have been kinder of us to burn it up and scatter its ashes over Sugar Creek. That certificate was the crowning irony, as far as Father was concerned.

"At last I have joined the company of the immortals," he said. "There are only two more honors for me to covet now." One was to be a licensed dog. The other was to be a notary public.

And Father made us hand over the certificate so that he could wipe his behind with it at the earliest opportunity, which he surely did.

Instead of saying good-bye that day, he said this, a finger in the air: "Nature calls."

•   •   •

And somewhere in there, in the autumn of 1916, to be exact, the old rascal August Gunther died under most mysterious circumstances. He got up two hours before dawn one day, and prepared and ate a hearty breakfast while his wife and daughter slept. And he set out on foot, armed with a double-barreled ten-gauge shotgun which my father had given to him, meaning to join Father and John Fortune and some other young bucks in gun pits on the edge of a meadow on John Fortune's father's dairy farm. They were going to shoot geese which had spent the night on the backwaters of Sugar Creek and on Crystal Lake. The meadow had been baited with cracked corn.

He never reached the gun pits, or so the story went.

So he must have died somewhere in the intervening five miles, which included the Sugar Creek Bridge. One month later, his headless body was found at the mouth of Sugar Creek just west of Cincinnati, about to start its voyage to the Mississippi and the Gulf of Mexico and beyond.

What a vacation from Midland City!

And when I was little, the decapitation of August Gunther so long ago, sixteen years before my birth, was the most legendary of all the unsolved crimes committed in my hometown. And I had a ghoulish ambition. I imagined that I would be famous and admired, if only I could find August Gunther's missing head. And after that the murderer would have to confess, for some reason, and he would be taken off to be punished, and so on—and the mayor would pin a medal on me.

Little did I suspect back then that I myself, Rudy Waltz, would become a notorious murderer known as "Deadeye Dick."

• • •

My parents were married in 1922, four years after the end of the First World War. Father was thirty and Mother was twenty-one. Mother was a college graduate, having taken a liberal arts degree at Oberlin College in Oberlin, Ohio. Father, who certainly encouraged people to believe that he had spent time at some great and ancient European university, was in fact only a high school graduate. He could certainly lecture on history or race or biology or art or politics for hours, although he had read very little.

Almost all his opinions and information were cannibalized from the educations and miseducations of his roistering companions in Vienna before the First World War.

And one of these pals was Hitler, of course.

•    •    •

The wedding and the reception took place in the Wetzel mansion, next door to the studio. The Wetzels and the Waltzes were
proudly agnostic, so the ceremony was performed by a judge.
Father's best man was John Fortune, the war hero and dairy
farmer. Mother's attendants were friends from Oberlin.

Father's immediate relatives, the uncles and cousins who
earned his living for him, came with their mates to the wedding, but they stayed for only a few minutes of the reception,
behaving correctly but coldly, and then they departed en masse.
Father had given them every reason to loathe him.

Father laughed. According to Mother, he announced to the
rest of the guests that he was sorry, but that his relatives had to
go back to the countinghouse.

He was quite the bohemian!

•    •    •

So then he and Mother went on a six-month honeymoon in
Europe. While they were away, the Waltz Brothers Drug Company was moved to Chicago, where it already had a cosmetics
factory and three drugstores.

When Mother and Father came home, they were the only
Waltzes in town.

•    •    •

It was during the honeymoon that Father acquired his
famous gun collection, or most of it—at a single whack. He
and Mother visited what was left of the family of a friend from
the good old days in Vienna, Rudolf von Furstenberg, outside
of Salzburg, Austria. Rudolf had been killed in the war, and
so had his father and two brothers, and I am named after him.
His mother and his youngest brother survived, but they were
bankrupt. Everything on the estate was for sale.

So Father bought the collection of more than three hundred
guns, which encompassed almost the entire history of firearms
up until 1914 or so. Several of the weapons were American,
including a Colt .45 revolver and a .30-06 Springfield rifle. As
powerful as those two guns were, Father taught me how to fire

them and handle their violent kicks, and to clean them, and to take them apart and put them back together again while blindfolded, when I was only ten years old.

God bless him.

•    •    •

And Mother and Father bought a lot of the von Furstenbergs' furniture and linens and crystal, and some battle-axes and swords, chain maces, and helmets and shields.

My brother and I were both conceived in a von Furstenberg bed, with a coat of arms on the headboard, and with "The Minorite Church of Vienna," by Adolf Hitler, on the wall over that.

•    •    •

Mother and Father went looking for Hitler, too, on their honeymoon. But he was in jail.

He had risen to the rank of corporal in the war, and had won an Iron Cross for delivering messages under fire. So Father had close friends who had been heroes on both sides of the war.

•    •    •

Father and Mother also bought the enormous weather vane from the gatehouse of the von Furstenberg estate, and put it atop their cupola back home, making the studio taller than anything in the county, except for the dome of the county courthouse, a few silos, the Fortunes' dairy barn, and the Midland County National Bank.

That weather vane was instantly the most famous work of art in Midland City. Its only competition was a statue of a Union soldier on foot in Fairchild Park. Its arrow alone was twelve feet long, and one hollow copper horseman chased another one down that awesome shaft. The one in back was an Austrian with a lance. The one in front, fleeing for his life, was a Turk with a scimitar.

This engine, swinging now toward Detroit, now toward Louisville, and so on, commemorated the lifting of the Turkish siege of Vienna in 1683.

When I was little, I asked my brother Felix, who is seven years older than I am, and who used to lie to me every chance he got, to explain to me and a playmate the significance of the weather vane. He was in high school then. He already had the beautiful, deep purple voice which would prove to be his fortune in the communications industry.

"If the Austrians hadn't won," he said in a solemn rumble, "Mother would be in a harem now. Father would be passing out towels in a steam bath, and you and I and your friend here would probably have our balls cut off."

I believed him at the time.

# 5

ADOLF HITLER became chancellor of Germany in 1933, when I was one year old. Father, who had not seen him since 1914, sent his heartiest congratulations and a gift, Hitler's watercolor, "The Minorite Church of Vienna."

Hitler was charmed. He had fond memories of Father, he said, and he invited him to come to Germany as his personal guest, to see the new social order he was building, which he expected to last a thousand years or more.

Mother and Father and Felix, who was then nine, went to Germany for six months in 1934, leaving me behind and in the care of servants, all black people. Why should I have gone? I was only two. It was surely then that I formed the opinion that the servants were my closest relatives. I aspired to do what they did so well—to cook and bake and wash dishes, and to make the beds and wash and iron and spade the garden, and so on.

It still makes me as happy as I can be to prepare a good meal in a house which, because of me, is sparkling clean.

• • •

I have no conscious memory of what my real relatives looked like when they came home from Germany. Perhaps a hypnotist could help me come up with one. But I have since seen photographs of them—in a scrapbook Mother kept of those exciting days, and also in old copies of the *Midland City Bugle-Observer*. Mother is wearing a dirndl. Father is wearing lederhosen and knee socks. Felix, although technically not entitled to do so, since he never joined the organization, was wearing the khaki uniform and Sam Browne belt, and the armband with swastika and ornamental dagger of the Hitler Youth. Even if Felix had been a German boy, he would have been too young to wear an outfit like that, but Father had a tailor in Berlin make it up for him anyway.

Why not?

• • •

And as soon as those relatives of mine got home, according to the paper, Father flew his favorite gift from Hitler from the horizontal shaft of the weather vane. It was a Nazi flag as big as a bedsheet.

Again: This was only 1934, and World War Two was still a long way off. It was a long way off, that is, if five years can be considered a long way off. So flying a Nazi flag in Midland City was no more offensive than flying a Greek or Irish or Confederate flag, or whatever. It was a playful, exuberant thing to do, and, according to Mother, the community was proud and envious of Father and her and Felix. Nobody else in Midland City was friendly with a head of state.

I myself am in one picture in the paper. It is of our entire family in the street in front of the studio, looking up at the Nazi flag. I am in the arms of Mary Hoobler, our cook. She would teach me everything she knew about cooking and baking, by and by.

•  •  •

Mary Hoobler's corn bread: Mix together in a bowl half a cup of flour, one and a half cups of yellow cornmeal, a teaspoon of salt, a teaspoon of sugar, and three teaspoons of baking powder. Add three beaten eggs, a cup of milk, a half cup of cream, and a half cup of melted butter.

Pour it into a well-buttered pan and bake it at four hundred degrees for fifteen minutes.

Cut it into squares while it is still hot. Bring the squares to the table while they are still hot, and folded in a napkin.

•  •  •

When we all posed in the street for our picture in the paper, Father was forty-two. According to Mother, he had undergone a profound spiritual change in Germany. He had a new sense of purpose in life. It was no longer enough to be an artist. He would become a teacher and political activist. He would become a spokesman in America for the new social order which was being born in Germany, but which in time would be the salvation of the world.

This was quite a mistake.

• • •

How to make Mary Hoobler's barbecue sauce: Sauté a cup of chopped onions and three chopped garlic cloves in a quarter of a pound of butter until tender. Add a half cup of catsup, a quarter cup of brown sugar, a teaspoon of salt, two teaspoons of freshly ground pepper, a dash of Tabasco, a tablespoon of lemon juice, a teaspoon of basil, and a tablespoon of chili powder.

Bring to a boil and simmer for five minutes.

• • •

So for two years and a little bit more, Father lectured and showed films and lantern slides of the new Germany all over the Middle West. He told heartwarming stories about his friend Hitler, and explained Hitler's theories about the variously superior and inferior human races as being simple chemistry. A pure Jew was this. A pure German was that. Cross a Pole with a Negro, you were certain to get an amusing laborer.

It must have been terrible.

I remember the Nazi flag hanging on the wall of our living room—or I think I do. I certainly heard about it. It used to be the first thing that visitors saw when they came in. It was so colorful. Everything else was so dull by comparison—the timbers and stone walls, the great tables made of carriage-house doors; Father's rustic easel, which looked like a guillotine, silhouetted against the north window; the medieval weapons and armor rusting here and there.

• • •

I close my eyes and I try to see the flag in my memory. I can't. I shiver, though—because our house, except for the kitchen, was always so cold in the wintertime.

• • •

That house was a perfect son of a bitch to heat. Father wanted to see the bare stones of the walls, and the bare boards that supported the slate roof over the gun room.

Even at the end of his life, when my brother Felix was paying the heating bill, Father would not hear of insulation.

"After I am dead," he said.

•    •    •

Mother and Father and Felix never used to complain about the cold. They wore lots of clothes in the house, and said everybody else's house in America was too warm, and that all that heat slowed the blood and made people lazy and stupid and so on.

That, too, must have been part of the Nazi thing.

They would make me come out of the little kitchen and into the vast draftiness of the rest of the ground floor, so that I would grow up hardy and vigorous, I suppose. But I was soon back in the kitchen again, where it was so hot and fragrant. It was comical in there, too, since it was the only room in the house where any meaningful work was going on, and yet it was as cramped as a ship's galley. The people who did nothing, who were merely waited on, had all the space.

And on cold days, and even on days that weren't all that cold, the rest of the servants, the yardman and the upstairs maid and so on, all black, would crowd into the kitchen with the cook and me. They liked being crowded together. When they were little, they told me, they slept in beds with a whole lot of brothers and sisters. That sounded like a lot of fun to me. It still sounds like a lot of fun to me.

There in the crowded kitchen, everybody would talk and talk and talk so easily, just blather and blather and laugh and laugh. I was included in the conversation. I was a nice little boy. Everybody liked me.

"What you got to say about that, Mister Rudy?" a servant would ask me, and I would say something, anything, and everybody would pretend I had said something wise or intentionally funny.

If I had died in childhood, I would have thought life was that little kitchen. I would have done anything to get back into that kitchen again—on the coldest day in the wintertime.

Carry me back to old Virginny.

•    •    •

Somewhere in there the Nazi flag came down. Father stopped traveling. According to my brother Felix, who was an eighth-grader at the time, Father wouldn't even leave the house or talk on the telephone, or look at his mail for three months or more. He went into such a deep depression that it was feared that he might commit suicide, so that Mother took the gun-room key from his key ring. He never missed it. He had no inclination to visit his beloved firearms.

Felix says that Father might have crashed like that, no matter what was really going on in the outside world. But the mail and telephone calls he was receiving were getting meaner all the time, and G-men had visited him, and suggested that he register as an agent for a foreign power, in order to comply with the law of the land. The man who had been his best man at his wedding, John Fortune, had stopped speaking to him, and had been going around town, to Father's certain knowledge, declaring Father to be a dangerous nincompoop.

Which Father surely was.

Fortune himself was of totally Germanic extraction. His last name was simply an Anglicization of the German word for luck, which is *Glück*.

Fortune would never give Father an opportunity to mend the rupture between them, for, in 1938, he suddenly took off for the Himalayas, in search of far higher happiness and wisdom than was available, evidently, in Midland City, Ohio. His wife had died of cancer. He was childless. There had been some defect in his or his wife's reproductive apparatus. The family dairy farm went bankrupt, and was taken over by the Midland County National Bank.

And John Fortune is buried now in bib overalls—in the capital city of Nepal, which is Katmandu.

# 6

MIDLAND CITY has now been depopulated by a neutron bomb explosion. It was a big news story for about ten days or so. It might have been a bigger story, a signal for the start of World War Three, if the Government hadn't acknowledged at once that the bomb was made in America. One newscast I heard down here in Haiti called it "a friendly bomb."

The official story is that an American truck was transporting this American bomb on the Interstate, and the bomb went off. There was this flash. It was an accident, supposedly. The truck, if there really was a truck, seems to have been right opposite the new Holiday Inn and Dwayne Hoover's Exit 11 Pontiac Village when the bomb went off.

Everybody in the county was killed, including five people awaiting execution on death row in the Adult Correctional Institution at Shepherdstown. I certainly lost a lot of acquaintances all at once.

But most of the structures are still left standing and furnished. I am told that every one of the television sets in the new Holiday Inn is still fully operable. So are all the telephones. So is the ice-cube maker behind the bar. All those sensitive devices were only a few hundred yards from the source of the flash.

So nobody lives in Midland City, Ohio, anymore. About one hundred thousand people died. That was roughly the population of Athens during the Golden Age of Pericles. That is two-thirds of the population of Katmandu.

And I do not see how I can get out of asking this question: Does it matter to anyone or anything that all those peepholes were closed so suddenly? Since all the property is undamaged, has the world lost anything it loved?

• • •

Midland City isn't radioactive. New people could move right in. There is talk now of turning it over to Haitian refugees.

Good luck to them.

• • •

There is an arts center there. If the neutrons were going to knock over anything, you might think, it would have been the Mildred Barry Center for the Arts, since it looks so frail and exposed—a white sphere on four slender stilts in the middle of Sugar Creek.

It has never been used. The walls of its galleries are bare. What a delightful opportunity it would represent to Haitians, who are the most prolific painters and sculptors in the history of the world.

The most gifted Haitian could refurbish my father's studio. It is time a real artist lived there—with all that north light flooding in.

•  •  •

Haitians speak Creole, a French dialect which has only a present tense. I have lived in Haiti with my brother for the past six months, so I can speak it some. Felix and I are innkeepers now. We have bought the Grand Hotel Oloffson, a gingerbread palace at the base of a cliff in Port au Prince.

Imagine a language with only a present tense. Our headwaiter, Hippolyte Paul De Mille, who claims to be eighty and have fifty-nine descendants, asked me about my father.

"He is dead?" he said in Creole.

"He is dead," I agreed. There could be no argument about that.

"What does he do?" he said.

"He paints," I said.

"I like him," he said.

•  •  •

Haitian fresh fish in coconut cream: Put two cups of grated coconut in cheesecloth over a bowl. Pour a cup of hot milk over it, and squeeze it dry. Repeat this with two more cups of hot milk. The stuff in the bowl is the sauce.

Mix a pound of sliced onions, a teaspoon of salt, a half teaspoon of black pepper, and a teaspoon of crushed pepper. Sauté the mixture in butter until soft but not brown. Add four pounds of fresh fish chunks, and cook them for about a minute on each side.

Pour the sauce over the fish, cover the pan, and simmer for ten minutes. Uncover the pan and baste the fish until it is done—and the sauce has become creamy.

Serves eight vaguely disgruntled guests at the Grand Hotel Oloffson.

•   •   •

Imagine a language with only a present tense. Or imagine my father, who was wholly a creature of the past. To all practical purposes, he spent most of his adult life, except for the last fifteen years, at a table in a Viennese café before the First World War. He was forever twenty years old or so. He would paint wonderful pictures by and by. He would be a devil-may-care soldier by and by. He was already a lover and a philosopher and a nobleman.

I don't think he even noticed Midland City before I became a murderer. It was as though he were in a space suit, with the atmosphere of prewar Vienna inside. He used to speak so inappropriately to my playmates, and to Felix's friends, whenever we were foolish enough to bring them home.

At least I didn't go through what Felix went through when he was in junior high school. Back then, Father used to say "Heil Hitler" to Felix's guests, and they were expected to say "Heil Hitler" back, and it was all supposed to be such lusty fun.

"My God," Felix said only the other afternoon, "—it was bad enough that we were the richest kids in town, and everybody else was having such a hard time, and there was all this rusty medieval shit hanging on the walls, as though it were a torture chamber. Couldn't we at least have had a father who didn't say 'Heil Hitler,' to everyone, including Izzy Finkelstein?"

•   •   •

About how much money we had, even though the Great Depression was going on: Father sold off all his Waltz Brothers Drug Company stock in the 1920s, so when the chain fell apart during the Depression, it meant nothing to him. He bought Coca-Cola stock, which acted the way he did, as though it didn't even know a depression was going on. And Mother still had all the bank stock she had inherited from her father. Because of all the prime farmland it had acquired through foreclosures, it was as good as gold.

This was dumb luck.

•   •   •

It was soda fountains as much as the Depression that wrecked the Waltz Brothers chain. Pharmacists have no business being in the food business, too. Leave the food business to those who know and love it.

One of Father's favorite jokes, I remember, was about the boy who flunked out of pharmacy school. He didn't know how to make a club sandwich.

•   •   •

There is still one Waltz Brothers Drugstore left, I have heard, in Cairo, Illinois. It certainly has nothing to do with me, or with any of my relatives, wherever they may be. I gather that it is part of a cute, old-fashioned urban renewal scheme in downtown Cairo. The streets are cobblestoned, like the floor of my childhood home. The streetlights are gas.

And there is an old-fashioned pool hall and an old-fashioned saloon and an old-fashioned firehouse and an old-fashioned drugstore with a soda fountain. Somebody found an old sign from a Waltz Brothers drugstore, and they hung it up again.

It was so quaint.

I hear they have a poster inside, too, which sings the praises of Saint Elmo's Remedy.

They wouldn't dare really stock Saint Elmo's Remedy today, of course, it was so bad for people. The poster is just a joke. But they have a modern prescription counter, where you can get barbiturates and amphetamines and methaqualones and so on.

Science marches on.

•   •   •

By the time I was old enough to bring guests home, Father had stopped mentioning Hitler to anyone. That much about the present had got through to him, anyway: The subject of Hitler and the new order in Germany seemed to make people angrier with each passing day, so he had better find something else to talk about.

And I do not mean to mock him. He had been just another wisp of undifferentiated nothingness, like the rest of us, and then all the light and sound poured in.

But he assumed that my playmates were thoroughly familiar with Greek mythology and legends of King Arthur's Round Table and the plays of Shakespeare and Cervantes' *Don Quixote*, Goethe's *Faust* and Wagnerian opera and on and on—all of which were no doubt lively subjects in Viennese cafés before the First World War.

So he might say to the eight-year-old son of a tool-checker over at Green Diamond Plow, "You look at me as though I were Mephistopheles. Is that who you think I am? Eh? Eh?"

My guest was expected to answer.

Or he might say to a daughter of a janitor over at the YMCA, offering her a chair, "Do sit down in the Siege Perilous, my dear. Or do you dare?"

Almost all my playmates were children of uneducated parents in humble jobs, since the neighborhood had gone downhill fast after all the rich people but Father and Mother moved away.

Father might say to another one, "I am Daedalus! Would you like me to give you wings so you can fly with me? We can join the geese and fly south with them! But we mustn't fly too close to the sun, must we. Why mustn't we fly too close to the sun, eh? Eh?"

And the child was expected to answer.

On his deathbed at the County Hospital, when Father was listing all his virtues and vices, he said that at least he had been wonderful with children, that they had all found him a lot of fun. "I understand them," he said.

• • •

He gave his most dumbfoundingly inappropriate greeting, however, not to a child but to a young woman named Celia Hildreth. She was a high school senior, as was my brother—and Felix had invited her to the senior prom. This would have been in the springtime of 1943, almost exactly a year before I became a murderer—a double murderer, actually. World War Two was going on.

Felix was the president of his class—because of that deep voice of his. God spoke through him—about where the senior prom should be held, and whether people should have their nicknames under their pictures in the yearbook, and on and on. And he was in the midst of an erotic catastrophe, to which he had made me privy, although I was only eleven years old. Irreconcilable differences had arisen between him and his sweetheart for the past semester and a half, Sally Freeman, and Sally had turned to Steve Adams, the captain of the basketball team, for consolation.

This left the president of the class without a date for the prom, and at a time when every girl of any social importance had been spoken for.

Felix executed a sociological master stroke. He invited a girl who was at the bottom of the social order, whose parents were illiterate and unemployed, who had two brothers in prison, who got very poor grades and engaged in no extracurricular activities, but who, nonetheless, was one of the prettiest young women anybody had ever seen.

Her family was white, but they were so poor that they lived in the black part of town. Also: The few young men who had tried to trifle with her, despite her social class, had spread the word that, no matter what she looked like, she was as cold as ice.

This was Celia Hildreth.

So she could have had scant expectation of being invited to the senior prom. But miracles do happen. A new Cinderella is born every minute. One of the richest, cutest boys in town, and the president of the senior class, no less, invited her to the senior prom.

•   •   •

So, a few weeks in advance of the prom, Felix talked a lot about how beautiful Celia Hildreth was, and what an impression he was going to make when he appeared with a movie star on his arm. Everybody else there was supposed to feel like a fool for having ignored Celia for so long.

And Father heard all this, and nothing would do but that Felix bring Celia by the studio, on the way to the prom, so that Father, an artist after all, could see for himself if Celia was as beautiful as Felix said. Felix and I had by then given up bringing home friends for any reason whatsoever. But in this instance Father had a means for compelling Felix to introduce him to Celia. If Felix wouldn't do that, then Felix couldn't use the car that night. He and Celia would have to ride a bus to the senior prom.

•  •  •

Haitian banana soup: Stew two pounds of goat or chicken with a half cup of chopped onions, a teaspoon of salt, half a teaspoon of black pepper, and a pinch of crushed red pepper. Use two quarts of water. Stew for an hour.

Add three peeled yams and three peeled bananas, cut into chunks. Simmer until the meat is tender. Take out the meat.

What is left is eight servings of Haitian banana soup.

*Bon appétit!*

•  •  •

So Father, without enough to do, as usual, was as excited by the approach of prom night as the most bubble-headed senior. He would say over and over:

> "Who is Celia? What is she?
> That all her swains commend her?"

Or he would protest in the middle of a silence at supper, "She can't be that beautiful! No girl could be that beautiful."

It was to no avail for Felix to tell him that Celia was no world's champion of feminine pulchritude. Felix said many times, "She's just the prettiest girl in the senior class, Dad," but Father imagined a grander adversary. He, the highest judge of beauty in the city, and Celia, one of the most beautiful women ever to live, supposedly, were about to meet eye-to-eye.

Oh, he was leading scrap drives in those days, and he was an air-raid warden, too. And he had helped the War Department to draw up a personality profile of Hitler, who he now said was a brilliant homicidal maniac. But he still felt drab and superannuated and so on, with so many battle reports in the paper and on the radio, and with so many uniforms around. His spirits needed a boost in the very worst way.

And he had a secret. If Felix had guessed it, Felix wouldn't have brought Celia within a mile of home. He would have taken her to the prom on a bus.

This was it: When Celia was introduced to Father, he would be wearing the scarlet-and-silver uniform of a major in the Hungarian Life Guard, complete with sable busby and panther skin.

# 7

L ISTEN: When Felix was ready to fetch Celia, Father wasn't even in his painter's costume. He was wearing a sweater and slacks, and he promised Felix yet again that he simply wanted to catch a glimpse of this girl, and that he wasn't going to put on any kind of a show for her. It was all going to be very ordinary and brief, and even boring.

About the automobile: It was a Keedsler touring car, manufactured right in Midland City in 1932, when a Keedsler was in every respect the equal or the superior of a German Mercedes or a British Rolls-Royce. It was a bizarre and glorious antique even in 1943. Felix had put the top down. There was a separate windshield for the back seat. The engine had sixteen cylinders, and the two spare tires were mounted in shallow wells in the front fenders. The tires looked like the necks of plunging horses.

So Felix burbled off toward the black part of town in that flabbergasting apparatus. He was wearing a rented tuxedo, with a gardenia in his lapel. There was a corsage of two orchids for Celia on the seat beside him.

Father stripped down to his underwear, and Mother brought him the uniform. She was in on this double-cross of Felix. She thought everything Father did was wonderful. And while Father was getting dressed again, she went around turning off electric lights and lighting candles. She and Father, without anybody's much noticing it, had earlier in the day put candles everywhere. There must have been a hundred of them.

Mother got them all lit, just about the time Father topped off his scarlet-and-silver uniform with the busby.

And I myself, standing on the balcony outside my bedroom on the loft, was as enchanted as Mother and Father expected Celia Hildreth to be. I was inside a great beehive filled with fireflies. And below me was the beautiful King of the Early Evening.

My mind had been trained by heirloom books of fairy tales, and by the myths and legends which animated my father's conversation, to think that way. It was second nature for me, and for Felix, too, and for no other children in Midland City, I am sure, to see candle flames as fireflies—and to invent a King of the Early Evening.

And now the King of the Early Evening, with a purple plume in his busby, gave this order: "Ope, ope the portals!"

• • •

What portals were there to open? There were only two, I thought. There was the front door on the south, and there was the kitchen door on the northeast. But Father seemed to be calling for something far more majestic than opening both of those.

And then he advanced on the two huge carriage-house doors, in one of which our front door was set. I had never thought of them as doors. They were a wall of my home which was made of wood rather than stone. Now Father took hold of the mighty bolt which had held them shut for thirty years. It resisted him for only a moment, and then slid back, as it had been born to do.

Until that moment, I had seen that bolt as just another dead piece of medieval iron on the wall. In the proper hands, perhaps it could have killed an enemy.

I had felt the same way about the ornate hinges. But they weren't more junk from Europe. They were real Midland City, Ohio, hinges, ready to work at any time.

I had stolen downstairs now, awe in every step I took.

The King of the Early Evening put his shoulder to one carriage-house door and then the other. A wall of my home vanished. There were stars and a rising moon where it had been.

# 8

A ND MOTHER AND FATHER AND I all hid as Felix arrived with Celia Hildreth in the Keedsler touring car. Felix, too, was dazed by the lovely transformation of our home. When he switched off the Keedsler's idling engine, it was as though it went on idling anyway. In a voice just like the engine's, he was reassuring Celia that she needn't be afraid, even though she had never seen anything like this house before.

I heard her say this: "I'm sorry. I can't help being scared. I want to get out of here." I was just inside the great new doorway.

That should have been enough for Felix. He should have gotten her out of there. As she would say in a few minutes, she hadn't even wanted to go to the prom, but her parents had told her she had to, and she hated her dress and was ashamed to have anybody see her in it, and she didn't understand rich people, and didn't want to, and she was happiest when she was all alone and nobody could stare at her, and nobody could say things to her that she was supposed to reply to in some fancy, ladylike way—and so on.

Felix used to say that he didn't get her out of there because he wanted to show Father that he could keep a promise, even if Father couldn't. He admits now, though, that he forgot her entirely. He got out of the car, but he didn't go to Celia's side, to open her door for her and offer his arm.

All alone, he walked to the center of the great new doorway, and he stopped there, and he put his hands on his hips, and he looked all around at the galaxy of tiny conflagrations.

He should have been angry, and he would get angry later. He would be like a dog with rabies later on. But, at that moment, he could only acknowledge that his father, after years of embarrassing enthusiasms and ornate irrelevancies, had produced an artistic masterpiece.

Never before had there been such beauty in Midland City.

• • •

And then Father stepped out from behind a vertical timber, the very one which had mashed his left foot so long ago. He was only a yard or two from Felix, and he held an apple in his hand. Celia could see him through the windshield of the Keedsler. He called out, with our house as an echo chamber, "Let Helen of Troy come forward—to claim this apple, if she dare!"

Celia stayed right where she was. She was petrified.

And Felix, having allowed things to go this far, was fool enough to think that maybe she could get out of the car and accept the apple, even though there was no way she could have any idea what was going on.

What did she know of Helen of Troy and apples? For that matter, what did Father know? He had the legend all garbled, as I now realize. Nobody ever gave Helen of Troy an apple—not as a prize, anyway.

It was the goddess Aphrodite who was given a golden apple in the legend—as a prize for being the most beautiful of all the goddesses. A young prince, named Paris, a mortal, chose her over the other two finalists in the contest—Athena and Hera.

So, as though it would have made the least bit of difference on that spring night in 1943, Father should have said, "Let Aphrodite come forward—to claim this apple, if she dare!"

It would have been better still, of course, if he had had himself bound and gagged in the gun room on the night of the senior prom.

As for Helen of Troy, and how she fitted into the legend, not that Celia Hildreth had ever heard of her: She was the most beautiful mortal woman on earth, and Aphrodite donated her to Paris in exchange for the apple.

There was just one trouble with Helen. She was already married to the king of Sparta, so that Paris, a Trojan, had to kidnap her.

Thus began the Trojan War.

• • •

So Celia got out of the car, all right, but she never went to get the apple. As Felix approached her, she tore off her corsage and she kicked off her high-heeled golden dancing shoes, bought, no doubt, like her white dress and maybe her underwear, at prodigious financial sacrifice. And fear and anger and stocking feet, and that magnificent face, made her as astonishing as anyone I have ever encountered in a legend from any culture.

Midland City had a goddess of discord all its own.

This was a goddess who could not dance, would not dance, and hated everybody at the high school. She would like to claw away her face, she told us, so that people would stop seeing things in it that had nothing to do with what she was like inside. She was ready to die at any time, she said, because what men and boys thought about her and tried to do to her made her so ashamed. One of the first things she was going to do when she got to heaven, she said, was to ask somebody what was written on her face and why had it been put there.

•   •   •

I reconstruct all the things that Celia said that night as Felix and I sit side by side here in Haiti, next to our swimming pool.

She said, we both remember, that black people were kinder and knew more about life than white people did. She hated the rich. She said that rich people ought to be shot for living the way we did, with a war going on.

And then, leaving her shoes and corsage behind her, she struck out on foot for home.

•   •   •

She only had about fourteen blocks to go. Felix went after her in the Keedsler, creeping along beside her, begging her to get in. But she ditched him by cutting through a block where the Keedsler couldn't go. And he never found out what happened to her after that. They didn't meet again until 1970, twenty-seven years later. She was then married to Dwayne Hoover, the Pontiac dealer, and Felix had just been fired as president of the National Broadcasting Company.

He had come home to find his roots.

# 9

M Y DOUBLE MURDER went like this:
In the spring of 1944, Felix was ordered to active duty in the United States Army. He had just finished up his second semester in the liberal arts at Ohio State. Because of his voice, he had become a very important man on the student radio station, and was also elected vice-president of the freshman class.

He was sworn in at Columbus, but was allowed to spend one more night at home, and part of the next morning, which was Mother's Day, the second Sunday in May.

There were no tears, nor should there have been any, since the Army was going to use him as a radio announcer. But we could not have known that, so we did not cry because Father said that our ancestors had always been proud and happy to serve their country in time of war.

Marco Maritimo, I remember, who by then, in partnership with his brother Gino, had become the biggest building contractor in town, had a son who was drafted at the very same time. And Marco and his wife brought their son over to our house on the night before Mother's Day, and the whole family cried like babies. They didn't care who saw them do it.

They were right to cry, too, as things turned out. Their son Julio would be killed in Germany.

• • •

At dawn on Mother's Day, while Mother was still asleep, Father and Felix and I went out to the rifle range of the Midland County Rod and Gun Club, as we had done at least a hundred times before. It was a Sunday-morning ritual, this discharging of firearms. Although I was only twelve, I had fired rifles and pistols and shotguns of every kind. And there were plenty of other fathers and sons, blazing away and blazing away.

Police Chief Francis X. Morissey was there, I remember, with Bucky, his son. Morissey was one of the bunch who had been goose-hunting with Father and John Fortune back in 1916, when old August Gunther disappeared. Only recently have I learned that it was Morissey who killed old Gunther. He accidentally discharged a ten-gauge shotgun about a foot from Gunther's head.

There was no head left.

So Father and the rest, in order to keep Morissey's life from being ruined by an accident that could have happened to anyone, launched Gunther's body for a voyage down Sugar Creek.

•  •  •

On the morning of Mother's Day, Father and Felix and I didn't have any exotic weapons along. Since Felix was headed for battle, seemingly, we brought only the Springfield .30-06. The Springfield was no longer the standard American infantry weapon. It had been replaced by the Garand, by the M-1. But it was still used by snipers, because of its superb accuracy.

We all shot well that morning, but I shot better than anybody, which was much commented upon. But only after I had shot a pregnant housewife that afternoon would anybody think to award me my unshakable nickname, Deadeye Dick.

•  •  •

I got one trophy out on the range that morning, though. When we were through firing, Father said to Felix, "Give your brother Rudy the key."

Felix was puzzled. "What key is that?" he said.

And Father named the Holy of Holies, as far as I was concerned. Felix himself hadn't come into possession of it until he was fifteen years old, and I had never even touched it. "Give him," said Father, "the key to the gun-room door."

•  •  •

I was certainly very young to receive the key to the gun room. At fifteen, Felix had probably been too young, and I was only twelve. And after I shot the pregnant housewife, it turned out that Father had only the vaguest idea how old I was. When the police came, I heard him say that I was sixteen or so.

There was this: I was tall for my age. I was tall for any age, since the general population is well under six feet tall, and I was six feet tall. I suppose my pituitary gland was out of kilter for a little while, and then it straightened itself out. I did not become a freakish adult, except for my record as a double murderer, as other people my age more or less caught up with me.

But I was abnormally tall and weak for a time there. I may have been trying to evolve into a superman, and then gave it up in the face of community disapproval.

•   •   •

So after we got home from the Rod and Gun Club, and I could feel the key to the gun room burning a hole in my pocket, there was yet another proof that I had to be a man now, because Felix was leaving. I had to chop the heads off two chickens for supper that night. This was another privilege which had been accorded Felix, who used to make me watch him.

The place of execution was the stump of the walnut tree, under which Father and old August Gunther had been lunching when the Maritimo brothers arrived in Midland City so long ago. There was a marble bust on a pedestal, which also had to watch. It was another piece of loot from the von Furstenberg estate in Austria. It was a bust of Voltaire.

And Felix used to play God to the chickens, saying in that voice of his, "If you have any last words to say, now is the time to say them," or "Take your last look at the world," and so on. We didn't raise chickens. A farmer brought in two chickens every Sunday morning, and they had their peepholes closed by a machete in Felix's right hand almost immediately.

Now, with Felix watching, and about to catch a train for Columbus and then a bus for Fort Benning, Georgia, it was up to me to do.

So I grabbed a chicken by its legs, and I flopped it down on the stump, and I said in a voice like a penny whistle, "Take your last look at the world."

Off came its head.

•   •   •

Felix kissed Mother, and he shook Father's hand, and he boarded the train at the train station. And then Mother and Father and I had to hurry on home, because we were expecting a very important guest for lunch. She was none other than Eleanor Roosevelt, the wife of the President of the United States. She was visiting war plants in the boondocks to raise morale.

Whenever a famous visitor came to Midland City, he or she was usually brought to Father's studio at one point or another, since there was so little else to see. Usually, they were in Midland City to lecture or sing or play some instrument, or whatever, at the YMCA. That was how I got to meet Nicholas Murray Butler, the president of Columbia University, when I was a boy—and Alexander Woollcott, the wit and writer and broadcaster, and Cornelia Otis Skinner, the monologist, and Gregor Piatigorsky, the cellist, and on and on.

They all said what Mrs. Roosevelt was about to say: "It's hard to believe I'm in Midland City, Ohio."

Father used to sprinkle a few drops of turpentine and linseed oil on the hot-air registers, so the place would smell like an active studio. When a guest walked in, there was always some classical record on the phonograph, but never German music after Father decided that being a Nazi wasn't such a good idea after all. There was always imported wine, even during the war. There was always Liederkranz cheese, and Father would tell the story of its invention.

And the food was excellent, even when war came and there was strict rationing of meat, since Mary Hoobler was so resourceful with catfish and crayfish from Sugar Creek, and with unrationed parts of animals which other people didn't consider edible.

●   ●   ●

Mary Hoobler's chitlins: Take the small intestine of a pig, cut it up into two-inch sections, and wash and wash them, changing the water often, until no fatty particles remain.

Boil them for three or four hours with onions, herbs, and garlic. Serve with greens and grits.

●   ●   ●

That is what we served Eleanor Roosevelt for lunch on Mother's Day in 1944—Mary Hoobler's chitlins. She was most appreciative, and she was very democratic, too. She went out into the kitchen and talked to Mary and the other servants there. She had Secret Service agents along, of course, and one of them said to Father, I remember, "I hear you have quite a collection of guns."

So the Secret Service had checked us out. They surely knew, too, that Father had been an admirer of Hitler, but was now reformed, supposedly.

The same man asked what music was playing on the phonograph.

"Chopin," said Father. And then, when the agent appeared to have another question, Father guessed it and answered it: "A Pole," he said. "A Pole, a Pole, a Pole."

And Felix and I, comparing notes here in Haiti, now realize that all our distinguished visitors from out of town had been tipped off that Father was a phony as a painter. Not one of them ever asked to see examples of Father's work.

•   •   •

If somebody had been ignorant enough or rude enough to ask, he would have shown them, I suppose, a small canvas clamped into the rugged framework of his easel. His easel was capable of holding a canvas eight feet high and twelve feet wide, I would guess. As I have already said, and particularly in view of the room's other decorations, it was easily mistaken for a guillotine.

The small canvas, whose back was turned toward visitors, was where a guillotine's fallen blade might be. It was the only picture I ever saw on the easel, as long as Father and I were on the same planet together, and some of our guests must have gone to the trouble of looking at its face. I think Mrs. Roosevelt did. I am sure the Secret Service agents did. They wanted to see everything.

And what they saw on that canvas were brushstrokes laid down exuberantly and confidently, and promisingly, too, in prewar Vienna, when Father was only twenty years old. It was only a sketch so far—of a nude model in the studio he rented after he moved out of the home of our relatives over there. There was a skylight. There was wine and cheese and bread on a checkered tablecloth.

Was Mother jealous of that naked model? No. How could she be? When that picture was begun, Mother was only eleven years old.

•   •   •

That rough sketch was the only respectable piece of artwork by my father that I ever saw. After he died in 1960, and Mother and I moved into our little two bedroom shitbox out in Avondale, we hung it over our fireplace. That was the same fireplace that would eventually kill Mother, since its mantelpiece had been made with radioactive cement left over from the Manhattan Project, from the atomic bomb project in World War Two.

It is still somewhere in the shitbox, I presume, since Midland City is now being protected against looters by the National Guard. And its special meaning for me is this: It is proof that sometime back when my father was a young, young man, he must have had a moment or two when he felt that he might have reason to take himself and his life seriously.

I can hear him saying to himself in astonishment, after he had roughed in that promising painting: "My God! I'm a painter after all!"

Which he wasn't.

•  •  •

So, during a lunch of chitlins, topped off with coffee and crackers and Liederkranz, Mrs. Roosevelt told us how proud and unselfish and energetic the men and women were over the tank-assembly line at Green Diamond Plow. They were working night and day over there. And even at lunchtime of Mother's Day, the studio trembled as tanks rumbled by outside. The tanks were on the way to the proving ground which used to be John Fortune's dairy farm, and which would later become the Maritimo Brothers' jumble of little shitboxes known as Avondale.

Mrs. Roosevelt knew that Felix had just left for the Army, and she prayed that he would be safe. She said that the hardest part of her husband's job was that there was no way to win a battle without many persons being injured or killed.

Like Father, she assumed, because I was so tall, that I must be about sixteen. Anyway, she guessed it was touch-and-go whether I myself would be drafted by and by. She certainly hoped not.

For my own part, I hoped that my voice changed before then.

She said that there would be a wonderful new world when the war was won. Everybody who needed food or medicine would get it, and people could say anything they wanted, and could choose any religion that appealed to them. Leaders wouldn't dare to be unjust anymore, since all the other countries would gang up on them. For this reason, there could never be another Hitler. He would be squashed like a bug before he got very far.

And then Father asked me if I had cleaned the Springfield rifle yet. That was something I got along with the key to the gun room: the duty to clean the guns.

Felix says now that Father made such an honor and fetish out of the key to the gun room because he was too lazy to ever clean a gun.

•  •  •

Mrs. Roosevelt, I remember, made some polite inquiry about my familiarity with firearms. And it was news to Mother, too, that I had the key to the gun room now.

So Father told them both that Felix and I knew more about small arms than most professional soldiers, and he said most of the things the National Rifle Association still says about how natural and beautiful it is for Americans to have love affairs with guns. He said that he had taught Felix and me about guns when we were so young in order to make our safety habits second nature. "My boys will never have a shooting accident," he said, "because their respect for weapons has become a part of their nervous systems."

I wasn't about to say so, but I had some doubts at that point about the gun safety habits of Felix, and of his friend Bucky Morissey, too—the son of the chief of police. For the past couple of years, anyway, Felix and Bucky, without Father's knowledge, had been helping themselves to various weapons in the gun room, and had picked off crows perched on headstones in Calvary Cemetery, and had cut off telephone service to several farms by shooting insulators along the Shepherdstown Turnpike, and had blasted God-only-knows how many mailboxes all over the county, and had actually loosed a couple of rounds at a herd of sheep out near Sacred Miracle Cave.

Also: After a big Thanksgiving Day football game between Midland City and Shepherdstown, a bunch of Shepherdstown tough guys had caught Felix and Bucky walking home from the football field. They were going to beat up Felix and Bucky, but

Felix dispersed them by pulling from the belt under his jacket a fully loaded Colt .45 automatic.

He wasn't kidding around.

•   •   •

But Father knew nothing of this, obviously, as he blathered on about safety habits. And, after Mrs. Roosevelt made her departure, he sent me up to the gun room, to clean the Springfield without further delay.

So this was Mother's Day to most people, but to me it was the day during which, ready or not, I had been initiated into manhood. I had killed the chickens. Now I had been made master of all these guns and all this ammunition. It was something to savor. It was something to think about and I had the Springfield in my arms. It loved to be held. It was born to be held.

I liked it so much, and it liked me so much, since I had fired it so well that morning, that I took it with me when I climbed the ladder up into the cupola. I wanted to sit up there for a while, and look out over the roofs of the town, supposing that my brother might be going to his death, and hearing and feeling the tanks in the street below. Ah, sweet mystery of life.

I had a clip of ammunition in my breast pocket. It had been there since morning. It felt good. So I pushed it down into the rifle's magazine, since I knew the rifle enjoyed that so. It just ate up those cartridges.

I slid forward the bolt, which caught the topmost cartridge and delivered it into the chamber. I locked the bolt. Now the rifle was cocked, with a live cartridge snugly home.

For a person as familiar with firearms as I was, this represented no commitment whatsoever. I could let down the hammer gently, without firing the cartridge. And then I could withdraw the bolt, which would extract the live cartridge and throw it away.

But I squeezed the trigger instead.

# 10

Eleanor Roosevelt, with her dreams of a better world than this one, was well on her way to some other small city by then—to raise morale. So she never got to hear me shoot.

Mother and Father heard me shoot. So did some of the neighbors. But nobody could be sure of what he or she had heard, with the tanks making such an uproar on their way to the proving ground. Their new engines backfired plenty the first time they tasted petroleum.

Father came upstairs to find out if I was all right. I was better than that. I was at one with the universe. I heard him coming, but I was unconcerned—even though I was still at an open window in the cupola with the Springfield in my arms.

He asked me if I had heard a bang. I said I had.

He asked me if I knew what the bang had been. I said, "No."

I took my own sweet time about descending from the cupola. Firing the Springfield over the city was now part of my treasure-house of memories.

I hadn't aimed at anything. If I thought of the bullet's hitting anything, I don't remember now. I was the great marksman, anyway. If I aimed at nothing, then nothing is what I would hit.

The bullet was a symbol, and nobody was ever hurt by a symbol. It was a farewell to my childhood and a confirmation of my manhood.

Why didn't I use a blank cartridge? What kind of a symbol would that have been?

• • •

I put the spent cartridge in a wastebasket for spent cartridges, which would be given to a scrap drive. It became a member of that great wartime fraternity, Cartridge Cases Anonymous.

I took the Springfield apart and cleaned it. I put it back together again, which I could have done when blindfolded, and I restored it to its rack.

What a friend it had been to me.

I rejoined polite society downstairs, locking the gun room behind me. All those guns weren't for just anybody to handle. Some people were fools where guns were concerned.

•   •   •

So I helped Mary Hoobler clean up after Mrs. Roosevelt. My participation in housework had become invisible. My parents had always had servants, after all, sort of ghostly people. Mother and Father were incurious as to who it was, exactly, who brought something or took something away.

I certainly wasn't effeminate. I had no interest in dressing like a girl, and I was a good shot, and I played a little football and baseball and so on. What if I liked cooking? The greatest cooks in the world were men.

Out in the kitchen, where Mary Hoobler washed and I dried, Mary said that the most important thing in her life had now happened. She had met Mrs. Roosevelt, and she would tell her grandchildren about it, and everything for her was downhill now. Nothing that important could ever happen to her again.

The front doorbell rang. The great carriage-house doors had of course been closed and bolted after the fiasco with poor Celia Hildreth the year before. We had an ordinary front door again.

So I answered the door. Mother and Father never answered the door. It was police chief Morissey out there. He looked very unhappy and secretive. He told me that he didn't want to come in, and he particularly didn't want to disturb my mother—so I was to tell Father to come out for a talk with him. He said I should be in on it, too.

I give my word of honor: I had not the slightest inkling of what the trouble might be.

So I got Father. He and Chief Morissey and I were going to do some more man business, business that women might be better off not hearing about. They might not understand. I was drying my hands on a tea towel.

And Morissey himself, as I know now but didn't know then, had accidentally killed August Gunther with a firearm when he was young.

And he said quietly to Father and me that Eloise Metzger, the pregnant wife of the city editor of the *Bugle-Observer*, George Metzger, had just been shot dead while running a vacuum cleaner in the guest room on the second floor of her home over on Harrison Avenue, about eight blocks away. There was a bullet hole in the window.

Her family downstairs had become worried when the vacuum cleaner went on running and running without being dragged around at all.

Chief Morissey said that Mrs. Metzger couldn't have felt any pain, since the bullet got her right between the eyes. She never knew what hit her.

The bullet had been recovered from the guest-room floor, and it was virtually undamaged, thanks to its copper jacket, in spite of all it had been through.

"Now I am asking you two as an old friend of the family," said Morissey, "and before any official investigation has begun, and I am just another human being and family man standing here before you: Does either one of you have any idea where a .30-caliber copper-jacketed rifle bullet could have come from about an hour ago?"

I died.

But I didn't die.

•  •  •

Father knew exactly where it had come from. He had heard the bang. He had seen me at the top of the ladder in the cupola, with the Springfield in my arms.

He made a wet hiss, sucking in air through his clenched teeth. It is the sound stoics make when they have been hurt a good deal. He said, "Oh, Jesus."

"Yes," said Morissey. And everything about his manner said that no possible good could come from our being made to suffer for this unfortunate accident, which could have happened to anyone. He, for one, would do all in his power to make whatever we had done somehow understandable and acceptable to the community. Perhaps, even, we could convince the community that the bullet had come from somewhere else.

We certainly didn't have the only .30-caliber rifle in town.

I myself began to feel a little better. Here was this wise and powerful adult, the chief of police, no less, and he clearly believed that I had done no bad thing. I was unlucky. I would never be that unlucky again. That was for sure.

I took a deep breath. That was for sure.

# *11*

So everything was going to be okay.

And Father's life and Mother's life and my life would have been okay, I firmly believe, if it weren't for what Father did next.

He felt that, given who he was, he had no option other than to behave nobly. "The boy did it," he said, "but it is I who am to blame."

"Now, just a minute, Otto—" Morissey cautioned him.

But Father was off and running, into the house, shouting to Mother and Mary Hoobler and anybody else who could hear him, "I am to blame! I am to blame!"

And more police came, not meaning to arrest me or Father, or to even question us, but simply to report to Morissey. They certainly weren't going to do anything mean, unless Morissey told them to.

So they heard Father's confession, too: "I am to blame!"

• • •

What, incidentally, was a pregnant mother of two doing, operating a vacuum cleaner on Mother's Day? She was practically asking for a bullet between the eyes, wasn't she?

• • •

Felix missed all the fun, of course, since he was on a troop bus bound for Georgia. He had been put in charge of his particular bus, because of his commanding vocal cords—but that was pretty small stuff compared to what Father and I were doing.

And Felix has made surprisingly few comments over the years on that fateful Mother's Day. Just now, though, here in Haiti, he said to me, "You know why the old man confessed?"

"No," I said.

"It was the first truly consequential adventure life had ever offered him. He was going to make the most of it. At last something was happening to him! He would keep it going as long as he could!"

• • •

Father really did make quite a show of it. Not only did he make an unnecessary confession, but then he took a hammer and a prybar and a chisel, and the machete I had used on the chickens, and he went clumping upstairs to the gun-room door. He himself had a key, but he didn't use it. He hacked and smashed the lock away.

Everybody was too awed to stop him.

And never, may I say, would the moment come when he would give the tiniest crumb of guilt to me. The guilt was all his, and would remain entirely, exclusively his for the rest of his life. So I was just another bleak and innocent onlooker, along with Mother and Mary Hoobler and Chief Morissey, and maybe eight small-city cops.

He broke all his guns, just whaled away at them in their racks with the hammer. He at least bent or dented all of them. A few old-timers shattered. What would those guns be worth today, if Felix and I had inherited them? I will guess a hundred thousand dollars or more.

Father ascended the ladder into the cupola, where I had been so recently. He there accomplished what Marco Maritimo later said should have been impossible for one man with such small and inappropriate tools. He cut away the base of the cupola, and he capsized it. It twisted free from its last few feeble moorings, and it went bounding down the slate roof, and it went crashing, weather vane and all, onto Chief Morissey's police car in the driveway below.

There was silence after that.

I and the rest of Father's audience were at the foot of the gun-room ladder, looking up. What a hair-raising melodrama Father had given to Midland City, Ohio. And it was over now. There the leading character was above us, crimson faced and panting, but somehow most satisfied, too, exposed to wind and sky.

# *12*

I THINK FATHER was surprised when he and I were taken away to jail after that. He never said anything to confirm this, but I think, and Felix agrees, that he was sufficiently adrift to imagine that wrecking the guns and decapitating the house would somehow settle everything. He intended to pay for his crime, the trusting of a child with firearms and live ammunition, before the bill could even be presented. What class!

That was surely one of the messages his pose at the top of the ladder, against the sky, had conveyed to me, and I had been glad to believe it: "Paid in full, by God—paid in full!"

But they took us down to the hoosegow.

Mother went to bed, and didn't get out of it for a week.

Marco and Gino Maritimo, who had dozens of workmen at their command, came over to put a tar-paper cap on the big hole in the roof personally, before the sun went down. Nobody had called them. Everybody in town had heard about the kinds of trouble we were in by then. Most of the sympathy, naturally enough, was going to the husband and two children of the woman I had shot.

And Eloise Metzger had been pregnant—which, as I have already said, made me a double murderer.

You know what it says in the Bible? "Thou shalt not kill."

• • •

Chief Morissey gave up on rescuing Father and me, since Father seemed to find it so rewarding to damn and doom himself. Throwing up his hands and departing, he left us in the hands of a mild old lieutenant and a stenographer. Father told me to describe exactly how I had fired the rifle, and I answered simply and truthfully. The stenographer wrote it down.

And then Father had this to say, for his own part, which was also duly recorded: "This is only a boy here. His mother and I are morally and legally responsible for his actions, except when it comes to the handling of firearms. I alone am responsible for whatever he does with guns, and I alone am responsible for the terrible accident which happened this afternoon. He has been a good boy up to now, and will be a sturdy and decent man in due time. I have no words of reproach to utter to him now. I gave him a gun and ammunition when he was much too young to have them without any supervision." He had by then found out I was only twelve, and not sixteen or so. "Leave him out of this. Leave my poor wife out of this. I, Otto Waltz, being of sound mind, do now declare under oath and in fear for my soul, that I alone am to blame."

• • •

And I think he was surprised, again, when we weren't allowed to go home after that. What more could anybody want after a confession that orotund?

But he was led off to cells in the basement of police headquarters, and I was taken to a much smaller cellblock on the top floor, the third floor, which was reserved for women and for children under the age of sixteen. There was only one other prisoner up there, a black woman from out of town, who had been taken off a Greyhound bus after beating up the white driver. She was from the Deep South, and she was the one who introduced me to the idea of birth's being an opening peephole, and of death's being when that peephole closes again.

The idea must have been ordinary, back wherever it was she came from. She said she was sorry she had beat up the bus driver, who had spoken to her insultingly because of her race. "I didn't ask my peephole to open. It just open one day, and I hear the people saying, 'That's a black one there. Unlucky to be black.' And that poor driver they took off to the hospital, his peephole done open, and he hear the people saying, 'That's a white one there. Lucky to be white.'"

A while later she said, "My peephole open, I see this woman, I say, 'Who you?' She say, 'I's you mama.' I say, 'How we doing, Mama?' She say, 'Ain't doing good. Ain't got no money, ain't got no work, ain't got no house, your daddy on the chain gang, and I already got seven other children whose peepholes opened up on them.' And I said, 'Mama, if you know how to close up my peephole again, you just go ahead and do it.' And she say, 'Don't you tempt me like that, child. That's the devil talking through you.'"

She asked me what a white boy in nice clothes was doing in jail. So I told her that I had had an accident while cleaning a rifle. It had gone off somehow, and killed a woman far away. I was beginning to work up a defense, even if Father didn't believe in making one.

"Oh, my Lord," she said, "—you done closed a peephole. That can't feel good. That can't feel good."

•   •   •

It felt to me then as though my peephole had just opened, and I wasn't even used to all the sights and sounds yet, but my father had already chopped the top off our house, and everybody was saying I was a killer. This was a planet where everything happened much too fast.

I could hardly catch my breath.

But police headquarters seemed quiet enough. Not much could happen on a Sunday night.

How common was it to have a known killer in a cell in Midland City? I had no way of knowing then, but I have since looked up the crime statistics for 1944. A killer was quite a novelty. There were only eight detected homicides of any sort. Three were drunken driving accidents. One was a sober driving accident. One was a fight in a black nightclub. One was a fight in a white bar. One was the shooting of a brother-in-law mistaken for a burglar. And there was Eloise Metzger and me.

Because of my age, I could not be prosecuted. Only Father could be prosecuted. Chief Morissey had explained that to me very early in the game—at a time when he thought there was all sorts of hope for both Father and me. So I felt safe, although embarrassed.

Little did I know that Morissey had meanwhile concluded that Father and I were dangerous imbeciles, since we seemed determined to confess to far more than was necessary, to inflame the community by seeming almost proud of my having shot Mrs. Metzger. Mrs. Metzger and her survivors were nothing. Father and I, on the other hand, confessing so boisterously, appeared to think we were movie stars.

We were no longer protected by Morissey, and a tentative, moody, slow-motion and incomplete lynching was about to begin. First, as I lay facedown on my cot, trying to blot out what my life had come to be, a bucket of ice-cold water was thrown all over me.

Two policemen hoisted me to my feet and shackled my hands behind my back. They put leg-irons on my ankles, and they dragged me into an office on the same floor, in order to fingerprint me, they said.

I was tall, but I was weak, and I weighed about as much as a box of kitchen matches. The one manly feat of strength of which I was capable was the mastery of a bucking gun. Instructed by my father and my brother on the range at the Rod and Gun Club, I had learned to knit together whatever strength and weight I had so as to absorb any shock a man-sized rifle or shotgun or pistol might wish to deal to me—to absorb it with amusement and satisfaction, and to get ready to fire again and again.

I was not only fingerprinted. I was faceprinted, too. The police pushed my hand and then my face into a shallow pan of gummy black ink.

I was straightened up, and one of the policemen commented that I was a proper-looking nigger now. Until that moment, I had been willing to believe that policemen were my best friends and everybody's best friends.

•   •   •

I was about to be put on display to concerned members of the community—in a holding pen for suspected criminals awaiting trial, in the basement of the old County Courthouse across the street. It was ten at night. It was still Mother's Day. The courthouse was empty. The upper floors would remain dark. Only the basement lights would be on.

It was the feeling of the police that I should not look good, and that I bear some marks of their displeasure with what I had done. But they couldn't beat me up, as they might have beaten up an adult offender, since that might evoke sympathy. So they had rolled my face in goo.

All this was in clear violation of the Bill of Rights of the Constitution of the United States.

•   •   •

So I was put in this large cage in the basement of the court-house. It was rectangular, and made of heavy-duty mesh fencing and vertical iron pipes. It was open to observers on all four sides. It contained wooden benches for about thirty people, I would say. There were plenty of cuspidors, but no toilet. Any caged person having to go to the toilet had to say so, and then to be escorted to a nearby lavatory.

I was unshackled.

The audience had yet to arrive, but the policemen who had brought me there, and who were now separated from me by wire, showed me what I was going to see a lot of—fingers hooked through the mesh. Person after person, bellying up to the wire for a good look at me, would, almost automatically, hook his or her fingers through the mesh.

Look at the monkey.

•   •   •

Who were the people who came to look at the monkey? Many were simply friends or relatives of policemen, responding to oral invitations along these lines, no doubt: "If you want to see the kid who shot that pregnant woman this afternoon, we've got him in the courthouse basement. I can get you in. Keep it under your hat, though. Don't tell anyone else. We don't want a mob to form."

But the honored visitors were substantial citizens, grave community leaders with a presumed need to know everything. There was something the policeman on the telephone thought it important for them to see—so they had better see it. Duty called. Some brought members of their families. I even remember a babe in arms.

So far as I know, only two people told the inviters that displaying a boy in a cage was a terrible thing to do, and stunk of the Middle Ages and so on. They were, of course, Gino and Marco Maritimo, virtually our family's only steadfast friends. And I know of this only because the brothers themselves told me about it. They had received the obscene invitation, offered as though nothing could be more civilized, soon after capping the hole in our roof where the cupola had been.

•   •   •

I have mentioned Alexander Woollcott, the writer and wit and broadcaster and so on, who was a guest at our house one time. He coined that wonderful epithet for writers, "ink-stained wretches."

He should have seen me in my cage.

•   •   •

I sat on the same bench for two hours. I said nothing, no matter what was said to me. Sometimes I sat bolt upright. Sometimes I bent over, with my head down and my inky hands over my inky ears or eyes. Toward the end, my bladder was full to bursting. I peed in my pants rather than speak. Why not? I was a geek. I was a wild man from Borneo.

•   •   •

I have since determined, from talking to old, old people, that I was the only Midland City criminal to have been put on public display since the days of public hangings on the courthouse lawn. My punishment was more than cruel and unusual. It was unique. But it made sense to just about everybody—with the exception of the Maritimo brothers, as I have said, and, surprisingly, George Metzger, the city editor of the *Bugle-Observer*, the husband of the woman I had killed that afternoon.

Before George Metzger arrived, though, members of my audience behaved as though they were quite accustomed to taunting bad people. They may have done a lot of it in their dreams. They clearly felt entitled to respectful attention from me.

So I heard a lot of things like "Hey you—it's you I'm talking to. Yes you!" and "God damn it, you look me in the eye, you son of a bitch," and so on.

I was told about friends or relatives who had been hurt or killed in the war. Some of the casualties were victims of industrial accidents right there at home. The moral arithmetic was simple. Here all those soldiers and sailors and workers in war plants were risking their all to add more goodness to the world, whereas I had just subtracted some.

What was my own opinion of myself? I thought I was a defective human being, and that I shouldn't even be on this planet anymore. Anybody who would fire a Springfield .30-06 over the rooftops of a city had to have a screw loose.

If I had begun to reply to the people, I think that's what I would have babbled over and over again: "I have a screw loose somewhere, I have a screw loose somewhere, I have a screw loose somewhere."

•  •  •

Celia Hildreth came by the cage. I hadn't seen her for a year, since the awful night of the senior prom, but I had no trouble recognizing her. She was still the most beautiful woman in town. I can't imagine that the police had seen fit to invite her. It was her escort, surely, who had been invited. She was on the arm of Dwayne Hoover, who was then some sort of civilian inspector for the Army Air Corps, I think.

Something had kept him out of uniform. I knew who he was because he was good with automobiles, and Father had hired him from time to time to do some work on the Keedsler. Dwayne would eventually marry Celia and become the most successful automobile dealer in the area.

Celia would commit suicide by eating Drāno, a drain-clearing compound of lye and zinc chips, in 1970, twelve years ago now. She killed herself in the most horrible way I can think of—a few months before the dedication of the Mildred Barry Memorial Center for the Arts.

Celia knew the arts center was going to open, and the newspaper and the radio station and the politicians and so on all said what a difference it was going to make in the quality of life in Midland City. But there was the can of Drāno, with all its dire warnings, and she just couldn't wait around anymore.

I have seen unhappiness in my time.

N OW THAT I have known Haiti, with its voodooism, with its curses and charms and zombies and good and bad spirits which can inhabit anybody or anything, and so on, I wonder if it mattered much that it was I who was in the cage in the basement of the old courthouse so long ago. A curiously carved bone or stick, or a dried mud doll with straw hair would have served as well as I did, there on the bench, as long as the community believed, as Midland City believed of me, that it was a package of evil magic.

Everybody could feel safe for a while. Bad luck was caged. There was bad luck, cringing on the bench in there.

See for yourself.

• • •

At midnight, all the civilians were shooed out of the basement. "That's it, folks," said the police, and "Show's over, folks," and so on. They were frank to call me a show. I was regional theater.

But I wasn't let out of the cage. It would have been nice to take a bath, and to go to bed between clean sheets, and to sleep until I died.

There was more to come. Six policemen were still in the basement with me—three in uniform and three in plain clothes, and all with pistols. I could name the manufacturers of the pistols, and their calibers. There wasn't a pistol there that I couldn't have taken apart and cleaned properly, and put together again. I knew where the drops of oil should go. If they had put their pistols in my hands, I could have made them this guarantee: The pistols would never jam.

It can be a very frustrating thing if a pistol jams.

The six remaining policemen were the producers of the Rudy Waltz Show, and their poses in the basement indicated that we had reached an intermission, that there was more to come. They ignored me for the moment, as though a curtain had descended.

They were electrified by a call from upstairs. "He's here!" was the call, as a door upstairs opened and shut. They echoed that. "He's here, he's here." They wouldn't say who it was, but it was somebody somehow marvelous. Now I heard his footsteps on the stairs.

I thought it might be an executioner. I thought it might be Police Chief Francis X. Morissey, that old family friend, who had yet to show himself. I thought it might be my father.

It was George Metzger, the thirty-five-year-old widower of the woman I had shot. He was fifteen years younger than I am now, a mere spring chicken—but, as children will, I saw him as an old man. He was bald on top. He was skinny, and his posture was bad, and he was dressed like almost no other man in Midland City—in gray flannel trousers and a tweed sport coat, what I would recognize much later at Ohio State as the uniform of an English professor. All he did was write and edit at the *Bugle-Observer* all day long.

I did not know who he was. He had never been to our house. He had been in town only a year. He was a newspaper gypsy. He had been hired away from the *Indianapolis Times*. It would come out at legal proceedings later on that he was born to poor parents in Kenosha, Wisconsin, and had put himself through Harvard, and that he had twice worked his way to Europe on cattle boats. The adverse information about him, which was brought out by our lawyer, was that he had once belonged to the Communist party, and had attempted to enlist in the Abraham Lincoln Brigade during the Spanish Civil War.

He wore horn-rimmed spectacles, and his eyes were red from crying, or maybe from too much cigarette smoke. He was smoking when he came down the stairs, followed by the detective who had gone to get him. He behaved as though he himself were a criminal, puffing on the same cigarette he would be smoking when he was propped against the basement wall in front of a firing squad.

I wouldn't have been surprised if the police had shot this unhappy stranger while I watched. I was beyond surprise. I am still beyond surprise. The consequences of my having shot a pregnant woman were bound to be complicated beyond belief.

How can I bear to remember that first confrontation with George Metzger? I have this trick for dealing with all my worst

memories. I insist that they are plays. The characters are actors.
Their speeches and movements are stylized, arch. I am in the
presence of art.
 So:

*The curtain rises on a basement at midnight. Six* POLICEMEN
*stand around the walls.* RUDY, *a boy, covered with ink, is in a cage
in the middle of the room. Down the stairs, smoking a cigarette, comes*
GEORGE METZGER, *whose wife has just been shot by the boy. He is
followed by a* DETECTIVE, *who has the air of a master of ceremonies.
The* POLICE *are fascinated by what is about to happen. It is bound
to be interesting.*

 METZGER (*appalled by* RUDY's *appearance*): Oh, my God.
   What is it?
 DETECTIVE: That's what shot your wife, Mr. Metzger.
 METZGER: What have you done to him?
 DETECTIVE: Don't worry about him. He's fine. You want
   him to sing and dance? We can make him sing and dance.
 METZGER: I'm sure. (*Pause*) All right. I've looked at him.
   Will you take me back home to my children now?
 DETECTIVE: We were hoping you'd have a few words to say
   to him.
 METZGER: Is that required?
 DETECTIVE: No, sir. But the boys and me here—we figured
   you should have this golden opportunity.
 METZGER: It sounded so official—that I was to come with
   you. (*Catching on, troubled*) This is not an official assembly.
   This is—(*Pause*) informal.
 DETECTIVE: Nobody's even here. I'm home in bed, you're
   home in bed. All the other boys are home in bed. Ain't
   that right, boys?

 (POLICEMEN *assent variously, making snoring sounds and
 so on.*)

 METZGER (*morbidly curious*): What would it please you
   gentlemen to have me do?
 DETECTIVE: If you was to grab a gun away from one of
   us, and it was to go off, and if the bullet was to hit young

Mr. Rich Nazi Shitface there, I wouldn't blame you. But it would be hard for us to clean up the mess afterwards. A mess like that can go on and on.

METZGER: So I should limit my assault to words, you think?

DETECTIVE: Some people talk with their hands and feet.

METZGER: I should beat him up.

DETECTIVE: Heavens to Betsy, no. How could you think such a thing?

(POLICEMEN *display mock horror at the thought of a beating.*)

METZGER: Just asking.

DETECTIVE: Get him out here, boys.

(*Two* POLICEMEN *hasten to unlock the cage and drag* RUDY *out of it.* RUDY *struggles in terror.*)

RUDY: It was an accident! I'm sorry! I didn't know! (*and so on*)

(*The two* POLICEMEN *hold* RUDY *in front of* METZGER, *so that* METZGER *can hit and kick him as much as he likes.*)

DETECTIVE (*to both* RUDY *and* METZGER): A lot of people fall down stairs. We have to take them to the hospital afterwards. It's a very common accident. Up to now, it's happened with mean drunks and to niggers who don't seem to understand their place. We never had a smart-ass kid murderer on our hands before.

METZGER (*uninterested in doing anything, giving up on life*): What a day this has been.

DETECTIVE: Don't want to hit him where it shows? Pull his pants down, boys, so this man can whap his ass. (POLICE-MEN *pull down* RUDY's *pants, turn him around, and bend him over*) Somebody get this man something to whap an ass with.

(*Unoccupied* POLICEMEN *search for a suitable whip.* POLICE-MAN ONE *finds a piece of cable on the floor about two feet long, proudly brings it to* METZGER, *who accepts it listlessly.*)

METZGER: Many thanks.
POLICEMAN ONE: Any time.
RUDY: I'm sorry! It was an accident!

(*All wait in silence for the first blow.* METZGER *does not move, but speaks to a higher power instead.*)

METZGER: God—there should not be animals like us. There should be no lives like ours.

(METZGER *drops the whip, turns, walks to the stairs, clumps up them. Nobody moves. A door upstairs opens and closes.* RUDY *is still bent over. Twenty seconds pass.*)

POLICEMAN ONE (*in a dream*): Jesus—how's he gonna get home?
DETECTIVE (*in a dream*): Walk. It's nice out.
POLICEMAN ONE: How far away does he live?
DETECTIVE: Six blocks from here.

(*Curtain.*)

• • •

It wasn't exactly like that, of course. I don't have total recall. It was a lot like that.

I was allowed to straighten up and pull up my pants. I had such a little pecker then. They still wouldn't let me wash, but Mr. Metzger had succeeded in warning these fundamentally innocent, hayseed policemen of how crazy they had become.

So I wasn't bopped around much anymore, and pretty soon I would be taken home to my mother.

Since it was Mr. Metzger's wife I had shot, he had the power not only to make the police take it easy with me, but to persuade the whole town to more or less forgive me. This he did—in a very short statement which appeared on the front page of the *Bugle-Observer*, bordered in black, a day and a half after my moment of fatal carelessness:

"My wife has been killed by a machine which should never have come into the hands of any human being. It is called a firearm. It makes the blackest of all human wishes come true at once, at a distance: that something die.

"There is evil for you.

"We cannot get rid of mankind's fleetingly wicked wishes. We can get rid of the machines that make them come true.

"I give you a holy word: DISARM."

# 14

WHILE I WAS in the cage, another bunch of policemen had been beating up Father in the police station across the street. He should never have refused the easy way out which Police Chief Morissey had offered him. But it was too late now.

The police actually threw him down a flight of stairs. They didn't just pretend that was what had happened to him. There was a lot of confused racist talk, evidently. Father would later remember lying at the bottom of the stairs, with somebody standing over him and asking him, "Hey, Nazi—how does it feel to be a nigger now?"

They brought me to see him after my confrontation with George Metzger. He was in a room in the basement, all bunged up, and entirely broken in spirit.

"Look at your rotten father," he said. "What a worthless man I am." If he was curious about my condition, he gave no sign of it. He was so theatrically absorbed by his own helplessness and worthlessness that I don't think he even noticed that his own son was all covered with ink. Nor did he ever ask me what I had just been through.

Nor did he consider the propriety of my hearing what he was determined to confess next, which was how his character had been corrupted at an early age by liquor and whores. I would never have known of the wild times he and old August Gunther used to have, when they were supposedly visiting museums and studios. Felix would never have known of them, if I hadn't told him. Mother never did know, I'm sure. I certainly never told her.

And that might have been bearable information for a twelve-year-old, since it had all happened so long ago. But then Father went on to say that he *still* patronized prostitutes regularly, although he had the most wonderful wife in the world.

He was all in pieces.

•  •  •

The police had become subdued by then. Some of them may have been wondering what on earth they thought they had been doing.

Word may have come down from Chief Morissey that enough was enough. Father and I had no lawyer to secure our rights for us. Father refused to call a lawyer. But the district attorney or somebody must have said that I should be sent home without any further monkey business.

Anyway—after being shown my father, I was told to sit on a hard bench in a corridor and wait. I was left all alone, still covered with ink. I could have walked out of there. Policemen would come by, and hardly give me a glance.

And then a young one in uniform stopped in front of me, acting like somebody who had been told to carry the garbage out, and he said, "On your feet, killer. I've got orders to take you home."

There was a clock on the wall. It was one o'clock in the morning. The law was through with me, except as a witness. Under the law, I was only a witness to my father's crime of criminal negligence. There would be a coroner's inquest. I would have to testify.

•   •   •

So this ordinary patrolman drove me home. He kept his eye on the road, but his thoughts were all of me. He said that I would have to think about Mrs. Metzger, lying cold in the ground, for the rest of my life, and that, if he were me, he would probably commit suicide. He said that he expected some relative of Mrs. Metzger would get me sooner or later, when I least expected it—maybe the very next day, or maybe when I was a man, full of hopes and good prospects, and with a family of my own. Whoever did it, he said, would probably want me to suffer some.

I would have been too addled, too close to death, to get his name, if he hadn't insisted that I learn it. It was Anthony Squires, and he said it was important that I commit it to memory, since I would undoubtedly want to make a complaint about him, since policemen were expected to speak politely at all times, and that, before he got me home, he was going to call me a little Nazi

cocksucker and a dab of catshit and he hadn't decided what all
yet.

He explained, too, why he wasn't in the armed forces, even
though he was only twenty-four years old. Both his eardrums
were broken, he said, because his father and mother used to beat
him up all the time. "They held my hand over the fire of a gas
range once," he said. "You ever had that done to you?"

"No," I said.

"High time," he said. "Or too late, maybe. That's locking the
barn after the horse is stolen."

And I of course reconstruct this conversation from a leaky
old memory. It went something like that. I can give my word of
honor that one thing was said, however: "You know what I'm
going to call you from now on," he said, "and what I'm going
to tell everybody else to call you?"

"No," I said.

And he said, "Deadeye Dick."

• • •

He did not accompany me to the door of our home, which
was dark inside. There was no moon. His headlights picked
out a strange broken form in the driveway. It hadn't been there
on the previous morning. It was of course the wreckage of the
cupola and the famous weather vane. It had been pulled off the
top of the police chief's car and left there in the driveway.

The front door was locked, which wasn't unusual. It was
always locked at night, since the neighborhood had deteriorated
so, and since we had so many supposed art treasures inside. I
had a key in my pocket, but it wasn't the right key.

It was the key to the gun-room door.

• • •

Patrolman Anthony Squires, incidentally, would many years
later become chief of detectives, and then suffer a nervous
breakdown. He is dead now. He was working as a part-time
bartender at the new Holiday Inn when he had his peephole
closed by ye olde neutron bomb.

• • •

Mrs. Gino Maritimo's *spuma di cioccolata*: Break up six ounces of semisweet chocolate in a saucepan. Melt it in a 250-degree oven.

Add two teaspoons of sugar to four egg yolks, and beat the mixture until it is pale yellow. Then mix in the melted chocolate, a quarter cup of strong coffee, and two tablespoons of rum.

Whip two-thirds of a cup of cold, heavy whipping cream until it is stiff. Fold it into the mixture.

Whip four egg whites until they form stiff peaks, then fold them into the mixture. Stir the mixture ever so gently, then spoon it into cups, each cup a serving. Refrigerate for twelve hours.

Serves six.

• • •

So Mother's Day of 1944 was over. I was locked out of my own home as the wee hours of a new day began. I shuffled through the darkness to our back door, the only other door. That, too, was locked.

No one had been told to expect me, and we had no servants who lived with us. So there was only my mother to awaken inside. I did not want to see her.

I had not cried yet about what I had done, and about all that had been done to me. Now I cried, standing outside the back door.

I grieved so noisily that dogs barked at me.

Someone inside the fortress manipulated the brass jewelry of the back door's lock. The door opened for me. There stood my mother, Emma, who was herself a child. Outside of school, she had never had any responsibilities, any work to do. Her servants had raised her children. She was purely ornamental.

Nothing bad was supposed to happen to her—ever. But here she was in a thin bathrobe now, without her husband or servants, or her basso profundo elder son. And there I was, her gangling, flute-voiced younger son, a murderer.

She wasn't about to hug me, or cover my inky head with kisses. She was not what I would call demonstrative. When Felix went off to war, she shook his hand by way of encouragement—and then blew a kiss to him when his train was a half a mile away.

And, oh, Lord, I don't mean to make a villain of this woman, with whom I spent so many years. After Father died, I would be paired off with her, like a husband with a wife. We had each other, and that was about all we had. She wasn't wicked. She simply wasn't useful.

"What is that all over you?" she said. She meant the ink. She was protecting herself. She didn't want to get it on her, too.

She was so far from imagining what I might want that she did not even get out of the doorway so I could come inside. I wanted to get into my bed and pull the covers over my head. That was my plan. That is still pretty much my plan.

So, keeping me outside, and not even sure whether she wanted to let me in or not, seemingly, she asked me when Father was coming home, and whether everything was going to be all right now, and so on.

She needed good news, so I gave it to her. I said that I was fine, and that Father was fine. Father would be home soon, I said. He just had to explain some things. She let me in, and I went to bed as planned.

Misinformation of that sort would continue to pacify her, day after day, year after year, until nearly the end of her life. At the end of her life, she would become combative and caustically witty, a sort of hick-town Voltaire, cynical and skeptical and so on. An autopsy would reveal several small tumors in her head, which doctors felt almost certainly accounted for this change in personality.

•  •  •

Father was sent to prison for two years, and he and Mother were sued successfully by George Metzger for everything they had—except for a few essential pieces of furniture and the crudely patched roof over their heads. All Mother's wealth, it turned out, was in Father's name.

Father did nothing effective to defend himself. Against all advice, he was his own lawyer. He pled guilty right after he was arrested, and he pled guilty again at the coroner's inquest, where he made no comment on what was evident to everyone—that he had very recently been beaten black and blue. Nor, as his own lawyer and mine, did he put on the record that any number of laws had been violated when I, only twelve years old, had been smeared with ink and exposed to public scorn.

The community was to be ashamed of nothing. Father was to be ashamed of everything. My father, the master of so many grand gestures and attitudes, turned out to be as collapsible as a paper cup. He had always known, evidently, that he wasn't worth a good God damn. He had only kept going, I think, because all that money, which could buy almost anything, kept coming in and coming in.

The shock to me wasn't that my father was so collapsible.

The shock to me was that Mother and I were so unsurprised.

Nothing had changed.

•   •   •

After we got home from the inquest, incidentally, which happened the day before Mrs. Metzger's funeral, we got a telephone call from my brother Felix at Fort Benning. Even before basic training had begun, he said, an officer had recommended that he be made an acting corporal, and that he go to Officers' Candidate School in thirteen weeks. This was because he had exhibited such leadership on the troop bus.

And I didn't talk, but I listened in on an extension.

Felix asked how everything was going with us, and neither Mother nor Father would tell him the truth.

Mother said to him, "You know us. We're just like Old Man River. We just keep rollin' along."

# 15

FATHER WAS DEFENDED by a lawyer in the lawsuit, but he was a jailbird by then. As things turned out, he would have been better off simply to hand over everything to George Metzger without a trial. At least he wouldn't have had to listen to proofs that he had admired Hitler, and that he had never done an honest day's work, and that he only pretended to be a painter, and that he had no education beyond high school, and that he had been arrested several times during his youth in other cities, and that he had regularly insulted his working relatives, and on and on.

There were enough ironies, certainly, to sink a battleship. The young lawyer who represented George Metzger had offered his services first to Father. He was Bernard Ketchum, and the Maritimo brothers had brought him to the coroner's inquest, urging Father to hire him and start using him then and there. He wasn't in the armed forces because he was blind in one eye. When he was little, a playmate had shot him in the eye with a beebee gun.

Ketchum was ruthless on Metzger's behalf, just as he would have been ruthless with Metzger, if Father had hired him. He certainly never let the jury forget that Mrs. Metzger had been pregnant. He made the embryo a leading personality in town. It was always "she," since it was known to have been a female. And, although Ketchum himself had never seen her, he spoke familiarly of her perfectly formed little fingers and toes.

Years later, Felix and I would have reason to hire Ketchum, to sue the Nuclear Regulatory Commission and the Maritimo Brothers Construction Company and the Ohio Valley Ornamental Concrete Company for killing our mother with a radioactive mantelpiece.

That is how Felix and I got the money to buy this hotel, and old Ketchum is also a partner.

My instructions to Ketchum were these: "Don't forget to tell the jury about Mother's perfectly formed little fingers and toes."

• • •

After Father lost the lawsuit, we had to let all the servants go. There was no way to pay them, and Mary Hoobler and all the rest of them left in tears. Father was still in prison, so at least he was spared those wrenching farewells. Nor did he experience that spooky morning after, when Mother and I awoke in our separate rooms, and came out onto the balcony overhanging the main floor, and listened and sniffed.

Nothing was being cooked.

No one was straightening up the room below, and waiting for the time when she could make our beds.

This was new.

I of course got breakfast. It was easy and natural for me to do. And thus did I begin a life as a domestic servant to my mother and then to both my parents. As long as they lived, they never had to prepare a meal or wash a dish or make a bed or do the laundry or dust or vacuum or sweep, or shop for food. I did all that, and maintained a B average in school, as well.

What a good boy was I!

•   •   •

Eggs à la Rudy Waltz (age thirteen): Chop, cook, and drain two cups of spinach. Blend with two tablespoons of butter, a teaspoon of salt, and a pinch of nutmeg. Heat and put into three oven-proof bowls or cups.

Put a poached egg on top of each one, and sprinkle with grated cheese. Bake for five minutes at 375 degrees.

Serves three: the papa bear, the mama bear, and the baby bear who cooked it—and who will clean up afterwards.

•   •   •

As soon as the suit was settled, George Metzger took off for Florida with his two children. So far as I know, not one of them was ever seen in Midland City again. They had lived there a very short time, after all. Before they could put down roots, a bullet had come from nowhere for no reason, and drilled Mrs. Metzger between the eyes. And they hadn't made any friends to whom they would write year after year.

The two children, Eugene and Jane, in fact, found themselves as much outcasts as I was when we all returned to school. And we, in turn, were no worse off, socially, than the few children whose fathers or brothers had been killed in the war. We were all lepers, willy-nilly, for having shaken hands with Death.

We might as well have rung bells wherever we went, as lepers were often required to do in the Dark Ages.

Curious.

•   •   •

Eugene and Jane were named, I found out only recently, for Eugene V. Debs, the labor hero from Terre Haute, Indiana, and Jane Addams, the Nobel prize–winning social reformer from Cedarville, Illinois. They were much younger than me, so we were in different schools. It was only recently, too, that I learned that they had found themselves as leprous as I was, and what had become of them in Florida, and on and on.

The source of all this information about the Metzgers has been, of course, their lawyer, who is now our lawyer, Bernard Ketchum.

Only at the age of fifty, thirty-eight years after I destroyed Mrs. Metzger's life, my life, and my parents' life with a bullet, have I asked anyone how the Metzgers were. It was right here by the swimming pool at two in the morning. All the hotel guests were asleep, not that they are ever all that numerous. Felix and his new wife, his fifth wife, were there. Ketchum and his first and only wife were there. And I was there. Where was my mate? Who knows? I think I am a homosexual, but I can't be sure. I have never made love to anyone.

Nor have I tasted alcohol, except for homeopathic doses of it in certain recipes—but the others had been drinking champagne. Not since I was twelve, for that matter, have I swallowed coffee or tea, or taken a medicine, not even an aspirin or a laxative or an antacid or an antibiotic of any sort. This is an especially odd record for a person who is, as I am, a registered pharmacist, and who was the solitary employee on the night shift of Midland City's only all-night drugstore for years and years.

So be it.

I had just served the others and myself, as a surprise, *spuma di cioccolata*, which I had made the day before. There was one serving left over.

And we certainly all had plenty of things to think about, both privately and publicly, since our hometown had so recently been depopulated by the neutron bomb. We might so easily have had our peepholes closed, too, if we hadn't come down to take over the hotel.

When we heard about that fatal flash back home, in fact, I had quoted the words of William Cowper, which a sympathetic English teacher had given me to keep from killing myself when I was young:

> God moves in a mysterious way
> His wonders to perform;
> He plants his footsteps in the sea,
> And rides upon the storm.

So I said to Ketchum, after we had finished our chocolate seafoams, our *spume di cioccolata*, "Tell us about the Metzgers."

And Felix dropped his spoon. Curiosity about the Metzgers had been the most durable of all our family taboos. The taboo had surely existed in large measure for my own protection. Now I had broken it as casually as I had served dessert.

Old Ketchum was impressed, too. He shook his head wonderingly, and he said, "I never expected to hear a member of the Waltz family ask how any of the Metzgers were."

"I wondered out loud only once," said Felix, "—after I came home from the war. That was enough for me. I'd had a good time in the war, and I'd made a lot of contacts I could use afterwards, and I was pretty sure I was going to make a lot of money and become a big shot fast."

And he did become a big shot, of course. He eventually became president of NBC, with a penthouse and a limousine and all.

He also "tapped out early," as they say. After he was canned by NBC twelve years ago, when he was only forty-four, he couldn't find suitable work anywhere.

This hotel has been a godsend to Felix.

"So I was a citizen of the world when I came home," Felix went on. "Any city in any country, including my own hometown, was to me just another place where I might live or might not live. Who gave a damn? Anyplace you could put a microphone was home enough for me. So I treated my own mother and father and brother as natives of some poor, war-ravaged town I was passing through. They told me their troubles, as natives will, and I gave them my absentminded sympathy. I cared some. I really did.

"I tried to look at the lighter side, as passers-through will, and I speculated as to what the formerly penniless Metzgers might be doing with their million dollars or so.

"And Mother, one of the most colorless women I would ever know, until she developed all those brain tumors toward the end," Felix went on, "—she slapped me. I was in uniform, but I hadn't been wounded or anything. I had just been a radio announcer.

"And then Father shouted at me, 'What the Metzgers do with their money is none of our business! It's theirs, do you hear me? I never want it mentioned again! We are poor people! Why should we break our hearts and addle our brains with rumors about the lives of millionaires?'"

·   ·   ·

According to Ketchum, George Metzger took his family to Florida because of a weekly newspaper which was for sale in Cedar Key, and because it was always warm down there, and because it was so far from Midland City. He bought the paper for a modest amount, and he invested the rest of the money in two thousand acres of open land near Orlando.

"A fool and his money can be a winning combination," said Ketchum of that investment made back in 1945. "That unprepossessing savannah, friends and neighbors, which George put in the name of his two children, and which they still own, became the magic carpet on which has been constructed the most successful family entertainment complex in human history, which is Walt Disney World."

There was water music throughout this conversation. We were far from the ocean, but a concrete dolphin expectorated lukewarm water into the swimming pool. The dolphin had come with the hotel, like the voodooist headwaiter, Hippolyte Paul De Mille. God only knows what the dolphin is connected to. God only knows what Hippolyte Paul De Mille is connected to.

He claims he can make a long-dead corpse stand up and walk around, if he wants it to.

I am skeptical.

"I surprise you," he says in Creole. "I show you someday."

•   •   •

George Metzger, according to Ketchum, is still alive, and a man of very modest means by choice—and still running a weekly paper in Cedar Key. He had kept enough money for himself, anyway, that he did not have to care whether anybody liked his paper or not. And very early on, in fact, he had lost most of his advertisers and subscribers to a new weekly, which did not share his exotic views on war and firearms and the brotherhood of man and so on.

So only his children were rich.

"Does anybody read his paper?" said Felix.

"No," said Ketchum.

"Did he ever remarry?" I said.

"No," said Ketchum.

Felix's fifth wife, Barbara, and the first loving wife he had ever had, in my opinion, found the solitude of old George Metzger in Cedar Key intolerable. She was a native of Midland City like the rest of us, and a product of its public schools. She was an X-ray technician. That was how Felix had met her. She had X-rayed his shoulder. She was only twenty-three. She was pregnant by Felix now, and so happy to be pregnant. She was such a true believer in how life could be enriched by children.

She was carrying Felix's first legitimate child. He had one illegitimate child, fathered in Paris during the war, and now in parts unknown. All his wives, though, had been very sophisticated about birth control.

And this lovely Barbara Waltz said of old George Metzger, "But he has those children, and they must adore him, and know what a hero he is."

"They haven't spoken to him for years," said Ketchum, with ill-concealed satisfaction. He plainly liked it when life went badly. That was comical to him.

Barbara was stricken. "Why?" she said.

Ketchum's own two children, for that matter, no longer spoke to him, and had fled Midland City—and so had escaped the neutron bomb. They were sons. One had deserted to Sweden during the Vietnam War, and was working with alcoholics there. The other was a welder in Alaska who had flunked out of Harvard Law School, his father's alma mater.

"Your baby will be asking you that wonderful question soon enough," said Ketchum, as amused by his own bad luck as by anybody else's "—'Why, why, why?'"

Eugene Debs Metzger, it turned out, lived in Athens, Greece, and owned several tankers, which flew the flag of Liberia.

His sister, Jane Addams Metzger, who found her mother dead and vacuum cleaner still running so long ago, a big, homely girl, as I recall, and big and homely still, according to Ketchum, was living with a refugee Czech playwright on Molokai, in the Hawaiian Islands, where she owned a ranch and was raising Arabian horses.

"She sent me a play by her lover," said Ketchum. "She thought maybe I could find a producer for it, since, of course, there in Midland City, Ohio, I was falling over producers every time I turned around."

And my brother Felix parodied the line about there being a broken heart for every light on Broadway in New York City. He substituted the name of Midland City's main drag. "There's a broken heart for every light on old Harrison Avenue," he said. And he got up, and went for more champagne.

His way up the stairs to the hotel proper was blocked by a Haitian painter, who had fallen asleep while waiting for a tourist, any tourist, to come back from a night on the town. He had garish pictures of Adam and Eve and the serpent, and of Haitian village life, with all the people with their hands in their pockets, since the artist couldn't draw hands very well, and so on, lining the staircase on either side.

Felix did not disturb him. He stepped over him very respectfully. If Felix had seemed to kick him intentionally, Felix would have been in very serious trouble. This is no ordinary colonial situation down here. Haiti as a nation was born out of the only successful slave revolt in all of human history. Imagine that. In no other instance have slaves overwhelmed their masters, begun to govern themselves and to deal on their own with other nations, and repelled foreigners who felt that natural law required them to be slaves again.

So, as we had been warned when we bought the hotel here, any white or lightly colored person who struck or even menaced

a Haitian in a manner suggesting a master-and-slave relationship would find himself in prison.

This was understandable.

•    •    •

While Felix was away, I asked Ketchum if the Czech refugee's
play was any good. He said that he was in no position to judge,
and that neither was Jane Metzger, since it was written in Czech.
"It is a comedy, I'm told," he said. "It could be very funny."

"Funnier than my play, certainly," I said. And here is an
eerie business: Twenty-three years ago, back in 1959, I entered
a playwriting contest sponsored by the Caldwell Foundation,
and I won, and my prize was a professional production of my
play at the Theatre de Lys in Greenwich Village. It was called
*Katmandu*. It was about John Fortune, Father's dairy farmer
friend and then enemy, who is buried in Katmandu.

I stayed with my brother and his third wife, Genevieve. They
lived in the Village, and I slept on their couch. Felix was only
thirty-four, but he was already general manager of radio station
WOR, and was about to head up the television department of
Batten, Barton, Durstine & Osborn, the advertising agency. He
was already having his clothes made in London.

And *Katmandu* opened and closed in a single night. This was
my one fling away from Midland City, my one experience, until
now, with inhabiting a place where I was not Deadeye Dick.

# 16

THE NEW YORK CITY CRITICS found it hilarious that the author of *Katmandu* held a degree in pharmacy from Ohio State University. They found it obvious, too, that I had never seen India or Nepal, where half my play took place. How delicious they would have found it, if only they had known, that I had begun to write the play when I was only a junior in high school. How pathetic they would have found it, if only they had known, that I had been told that I should become a writer, that I had the divine spark, by a high school English teacher who had never been anywhere, either, who had never seen anything important, either, who had no sex life, either. And what a perfect name she had for a role like that: Naomi Shoup.

She took pity on me, and on herself, too, I'm sure. What awful lives we had! She was old and alone, and considered to be ridiculous for finding joy on a printed page. I was a social leper. I would have had no time for friends anyway. I went food shopping right after school, and started supper as soon as I got home. I did the laundry in the broken-down Maytag wringer-washer in the furnace room. I served supper to Mother and Father, and sometimes guests, and cleaned up afterwards. There would be dirty dishes from breakfast and lunch as well.

I did my homework until I couldn't keep my eyes open any longer, and then I collapsed into bed. I often slept in my clothing. And then I got up at six in the morning and did the ironing and vacuuming. And then I served breakfast to Mother and Father, and put a hot lunch for them in the oven. And then I made all the beds and I went to school.

"And what are your parents up to while you're doing all that housework?" Miss Shoup asked me. She had summoned me from a study hall, where I had been fast asleep, to a conference in her tiny office. There was a photograph of Edna St. Vincent Millay on her wall. She had to tell me who she was.

I was too embarrassed to tell old Miss Shoup the truth about what Mother and Father did with their time. They were zombies. They were in bathrobes and bedroom slippers all day long—unless company was expected. They stared into the distance a lot. Sometimes they would hug each other very lightly and sigh. They were the walking dead.

The next time Hippolyte Paul De Mille offers to raise a corpse for my amusement, I will say to him, "It is nothing I do not see yesterday."

• • •

So I told Miss Shoup that Father did carpentry around the house, and of course painted and drew a lot, and ran a little antique business. The last time Father had touched any tools, in fact, was when he decapitated the house and smashed up his guns. I had never seen him paint or draw. His antique business consisted of trying to sell off what little was left of all the loot he had brought back from Europe in his glory days.

That was one way we went on eating—and heating. Another source of cash was a small legacy Mother received from a relative in Germany. She inherited it after the lawsuit was settled. Otherwise, the Metzgers would have got that, too. But most of our money came from Felix, who was extraordinarily generous without our ever asking him for anything.

And I told Miss Shoup that Mother gardened and helped me a lot with the housework, and helped Father with his antique business, and wrote letters to friends, and read a lot, and so on.

What Miss Shoup wanted to see me about, though, was an essay on this assigned subject: "The Midland City Person I Most Admire." My hero was John Fortune, who died in Katmandu when I was only six years old. She turned my ears crimson by saying that it was the finest piece of writing by a student that she had seen in forty years of teaching. She began to weep.

"You really must become a writer," she said. "And you must get out of this deadly town, too—as soon as you can.

"You must find what I should have had the courage to look for," she said, "what we should all have the courage to look for."

"What is that?" I said.

Her answer was this: "Your own Katmandu."

• • •

She had been watching me recently, she confessed. "You seem to be talking to yourself."

"Who else is there to talk to?" I said. "It's not talking anyway."

"Oh?" she said. "What is it?"

"Nothing," I said. I had never told anybody what it was, nor did I tell her. "It's just a nervous habit," I said. She would have liked it if I had told her all my secrets, but I never gave her that satisfaction.

It seemed safest and wisest to be as cold as ice to her, and to everyone.

But the answer to her question was this: I was singing to myself. It was scat singing, an invention of the black people. They had found it a good way to shoo the blues away, and so had I. "Booby dooby wop wop," I would sing to myself, and, "Skaddy wee, skeedy wah," and so on. "Beedy op! Beedy op!"

And the miles went by, and the years went by. "Foodly yah, foodly yah. Zang reepa dop. Faaaaaaaaaaaaaaaaaa!"

•   •   •

Linzer torte (from the *Bugle-Observer*): Mix half a cup of sugar with a cup of butter until fluffy. Beat in two egg yolks and half a teaspoon of grated lemon rind.

Sift a cup of flour together with a quarter teaspoon of salt, a teaspoon of cinnamon, and a quarter teaspoon of cloves. Add this to the sugar-and-butter mixture. Add one cup of unblanched almonds and one cup of toasted filberts, both chopped fine.

Roll out two-thirds of the dough until a quarter of an inch thick. Line the bottom and sides of an eight-inch pan with dough. Slather in a cup and a half of raspberry jam. Roll out the rest of the dough, make it into eight thin pencil shapes about ten inches long. Twist them a little, and lay them across the top in a decorative manner. Crimp the edges.

Bake in a preheated 350-degree oven for about an hour, and then cool at room temperature.

A great favorite in Vienna, Austria, before the First World War!

•   •   •

So I said nothing to my parents about wanting to become a writer until I had served a surprise dessert which I had gotten out of the paper, which was Linzer torte.

Father roused himself from living death sufficiently to say that the dessert took him back forty years. And, before he could sink out of sight again, I told him what Naomi Shoup had said to me.

"Half woman and half bird," he said.

"Sir?" I said.

"Miss Shoup," he said.

"I don't understand," I said.

"She is obviously a siren," he said. "A siren is half woman, half bird."

"I know what a siren is," I said.

"Then you know they lure sailors with their sweet songs to shipwrecks on rocks," he said.

"Yes, sir," I said. Since shooting Mrs. Metzger, I had taken to calling all grown men "sir." Like the secret scat singing, it somehow made my hard life just a trifle easier. I was a make-believe soldier of the lowest rank.

"What did Odysseus do in order to sail by the sirens safely?" he asked me.

"I forget," I said.

"He did what you must do now, whenever anybody tells you that you have an artistic gift of any kind," he said. "I only wish my father had told me what I tell you now."

"Sir?" I said.

"Plug your ears with wax, my boy—and lash yourself to the mast," he said.

•  •  •

"I wrote a thing about John Fortune, and she said it was good," I persisted. I did very little of that, I must say—persisting. During my time in the cage, all covered with ink, I concluded that the best thing for me and for those around me was to want nothing, to be enthusiastic about nothing, to be as unmotivated as possible, in fact, so that I would never again hurt anyone.

To put it another way: I wasn't to touch anything on this planet, man, woman, child, artifact, animal, vegetable, or mineral—since it was very likely to be connected to a push-pull detonator and an explosive charge.

And the fact that I had been working for the past month, late at night, on a major essay on a subject that excited me, was news to my parents. They never asked me what I might be doing at school.

School.

"John Fortune?" said Father. "What did you find to say about him?"

"I'll show you my essay," I said. Miss Shoup had given it back to me.

"No, no," said Father. "Just tell me." Now that I think about it, he may have been dyslectic. "I'd be interested to hear what you have to say about him, because I knew him well."

"I know," I said.

"Why didn't you ask me about him?" he said.

"I didn't want to bother you," I said. "You have so much to think about." I didn't say so, but I also knew that the loss of John Fortune as a friend, over Father's admiration of Hitler, was a painful subject for Father. I had caused him enough pain. I had caused everybody enough pain.

"He was a fool," said Father. "There is no wisdom to be found in Asia. It was that damn fool book that killed him."

"*Lost Horizon* — by James Hilton," I said. This was a very popular novel published in 1933, one year after my peephole opened. It told of a tiny, isolated country, a secret from the rest of the world, where no one ever tried to hurt anybody else, and where everybody was happy and nobody grew old. Hilton located this imaginary Garden of Eden somewhere in the Himalayas, and he called it "Shangri-La."

It was this book which inspired John Fortune to take off for the Himalayas after his wife died. It was possible back then for even an educated person, which Fortune wasn't, to suspect that contentment might be hidden somewhere on the map, like the treasure of Captain Kidd. Katmandu had certainly been visited by travelers often enough, but they all had to get there the way John Fortune got there, which was on a footpath from the Indian border — through mountains and jungle. A road wasn't put through until 1952, the year I graduated from pharmacy school.

And, my God, they've got a big airport there now. It can handle jets. My dentist, Herb Stacks, has been there three times so far, and his waiting room is chock-a-block with Nepalese art. That was how he and his family escaped the neutron bomb. They were in Katmandu at the time.

• • •

Father behaved as though I had pulled off a miracle of extra-sensory perception, knowing about John Fortune and *Lost Horizon*. "How could you possibly know that?" he said.

"I went through old newspapers at the public library," I said.

"Oh," he said. I don't think he had ever used the public library. "They keep old newspapers there?" he said with some surprise.

"Yes, sir," I said.

"Goodness—there must be a lot of them," he said. "Day after day, week after week." He asked me if people were in the library all the time, ". . . dredging up the past like that?" It may have seemed wrong to him that his own past in the newspaper hadn't been carted off to the dump. And I had come across a little of that, some of his letters to the editor in praise of Hitler.

"Well," he said, "—I certainly hope you never read that book."

"*Lost Horizon*?" I said. "I already have."

"You mustn't take it seriously," he said. "It's all bunk. This is as much Shangri-La as anywhere."

Now, at the age of fifty, I believe this to be true.

And, here in Haiti, I have begun to verbalize that sentiment, so intolerable to me when I was a teen-ager. We are going to have to go back to Midland City soon, at the pleasure of our government, to collect whatever personal property we want, and to file our claims against our government. It now seems certain: The entire county is to become a refugee center, possibly fenced.

A dark thought: Perhaps the neutron bomb explosion wasn't so accidental after all.

In any event, and in anticipation of our brief return to our hometown, I have in conversation given Midland City this code name, which the Ketchums and my brother and his wife accept without protest: "Shangri-La."

THE NIGHT I told Father I wanted to be a writer, the night of the Linzer tortes, he ordered me to become a pharmacist instead, which I did. As Felix has pointed out, Father and Mother were understandably edgy about losing their last servant, among other things.

And Father made a ritual of lighting a cigar, and then he shook out the match and dropped it in what was left of the Linzer torte, and then he said again, "Be a pharmacist! Go with the grain of your heritage! There is no artistic talent in this family, nor will there ever be! You can imagine how much it hurts me to say so. We are business people, and that's all we can ever hope to be."

"Felix is gifted," I said.

"And so is every circus freak," said Father. "Yes—he has the deepest voice in the world, but have you ever listened to what he actually says when he's using his own mind, when some genuinely gifted person hasn't written something for him to say?"

I made no reply and he went on: "You and I and your mother and your brother are descended from solid, stolid, thick-skulled, unimaginative, unmusical, ungraceful German stock whose sole virtue is that it can never leave off working. You see in me a man who was flattered and lied to and coddled out of his proper destiny, which was a life in business, in rendering some sort of plodding but useful service to his community. Don't throw away your destiny the way I did. Be what you were born to be. Be a pharmacist!"

• • •

So I became a pharmacist. But I never gave up on being a writer, too, although I stopped talking about it. I cut poor old Naomi Shoup dead the next time she dared mention my divine spark to me. I told her that I had no wish to be distracted from my first love, which was pharmacy. Thus was I without a single friend in this world again.

I was permitted a certain number of electives when I enrolled as a pharmacy major at Ohio State. And, with nobody watching, so to speak, I took a course in playwriting in my sophomore year. I had by then heard of James Thurber, who had grown up right there in Columbus, and then gone on to New York City to write comically about the same sorts of people I had known in Midland City. And his biggest hit had been a play, *The Male Animal*.

"Scooby dooby do-wop! Deedly-ah! Deedly ah!" Maybe I could be like him.

So I turned my essay on John Fortune into a play.

•  •  •

Who was doing the housework back home meanwhile? I was still doing most of it. I wasn't your typical college boy, any more than I had been your typical high school boy. I still lived at home, but made the hundred-mile round-trip to Columbus three or four times a week, depending on what my schedule was.

I cut down on fancy cooking, I must say. I served an awful lot of canned stew in those days, and sometimes I didn't get around to serving it until midnight, either. Mother and Father groused a little bit, but not all that much.

Who was paying my tuition? My brother was.

•  •  •

I agree now that *Katmandu* was a ridiculous play. What made me keep working on it so long, even after I graduated and went to work as the night man at Schramm's Drugstore, were the lines at the very end. They so much deserved to be spoken in a theater. They weren't even my lines. They were the last words of John Fortune himself, which I found in an old *Bugle-Observer*.

The thing was this: He simply disappeared somewhere in Asia in 1938. He had sent postcards back from San Francisco, and then Honolulu, and then Fiji, and then Manila, and Madras, and so on. But then the cards stopped. The very last one came from Agra, India, the site of the Taj Mahal.

One letter I found in the paper, published in 1939, long before anybody in Midland City found out what finally happened to Fortune, said this: "At least he saw the Taj Mahal."

But then, right at the end of World War Two, the *Bugle-Observer* got a letter from a British doctor who had been a prisoner of the Japanese for years and years. His name was David Brokenshire. It is easy for me to remember that, since he became a character in my play.

This Dr. Brokenshire had walked all alone on the footpath to Katmandu. He was studying folk medicine. So he had been in Nepal for about a year, when some natives brought to him a white man on a stretcher. The man had collapsed in front of the palace. He had just arrived, and he had double pneumonia. It was John Fortune, of course, and his costume was so strange to both the Englishman and the Nepalese that he was asked to say what it was. The answer was this: "Plain old, honest Ohio bib overalls."

So John Fortune's peephole closed and he was buried there in Katmandu, but not before he scrawled a message which Broken-shire promised to deliver sooner or later to the *Bugle-Observer* back in Midland City. But the doctor was in no hurry to get to the nearest mailbox. He went wandering into Tibet instead, and then northern Burma, and then China, where the Japanese captured him. They thought he was a spy. He didn't even know there was a war going on.

He wrote a book about it later. I read it. It is hard to find, but worth looking for. It is quite interesting.

But the point is that he didn't get to send John Fortune's last words, along with a map of where in Katmandu Fortune was buried, to Midland City until six years after Fortune's death. The words were these:

"To all my friends and enemies in the buckeye state. Come on over. There's room for everybody in Shangri-La."

# 18

KATMANDU, my contribution to Western civilization, has been performed three times before paying audiences— once at the Theatre de Lys in New York City in 1960, in the same month that Father died, and then twice on the stage of Fairchild High School in Midland City three years later. The female lead of the Midland City production was, incidentally, none other than Celia Hildreth Hoover, to whom Father had tried to present an apple so long ago.

In the first act of the play, which was set in Midland City, Celia, who in real life would eventually swallow Drāno, played the ghost of John Fortune's wife. In the second act, she was a mysterious Oriental woman he meets at the Taj Mahal. She offers to show him the way to Shangri-La, and leads the way over mountains and through jungle on the path to Katmandu. And then, after Fortune speaks his message for the people back in Midland City and dies, she doesn't say anything, but she reveals herself as the ghost of his wife again.

It isn't an easy part, and Celia had never done any acting at all before. She was only the wife of a Pontiac dealer, but I think she was actually at least as good as the professional actress who did it in New York City. She was certainly more beautiful. She hadn't yet been made all raddled and addled and snaggletoothed and haggard by amphetamine.

I forget the name of the actress in New York City now. I think maybe she dropped out of acting after *Katmandu*.

•  •  •

Speaking of amphetamine: Father's old friend Hitler was evidently one of the first people to experience its benefits. I read recently that his personal doctor kept him bright eyed and bushy tailed right up to the end with bigger and bigger doses of vitamins and amphetamine.

•  •  •

I went straight from pharmacy school to a job as all-night man at Schramm's Drugstore, six days a week from midnight to dawn. I still lived with my parents, but now I was able to make a substantial contribution to their support and my own. It was a dangerous job, since Schramm's, the only business establishment of any sort that was open all night, was a sort of lighthouse for lunatics and outlaws. My predecessor, old Malcolm Hyatt, who went to high school with my father, was killed by a robber from out of town. The robber swung off the Shepherdstown Turnpike, and closed old Hyatt's peephole with a sawed-off shotgun, and then swung back onto the Interstate again.

He was apprehended at the Indiana border, and tried and convicted, and sentenced to die over at Shepherdstown. They closed his peephole with electricity. In one microsecond he was hearing and seeing all sorts of things. In the next microsecond he was a wisp of undifferentiated nothingness again.

Served him right.

· · ·

The drugstore was owned by a man named Horton in Cincinnati, incidentally. There weren't any Schramms left in town. There used to be dozens of Schramms in town.

There used to be dozens of Waltzes in town, too. But when I went to work at Schramm's, there were only four of us— Mother, Father, and me, and my brother's first wife Donna. She was half of a set of what used to be identical twins. She and Felix were divorced, but she still called herself Donna Waltz. So she wasn't a real Waltz, a blood Waltz.

And she would never have been a Waltz of any sort, if Felix hadn't accidentally put her through a windshield the day after he was discharged from the Army. He hardly knew her, since her family had moved to Midland City from Kokomo, Indiana, while he was at war. He couldn't even tell her from her twin, Dina.

They were out joyriding in her father's car. Thank God it wasn't our car, anyway. We didn't have a car anymore. We didn't have shit anymore, and Father was still in prison. But Felix was driving. He was at the wheel. And the brakes locked. It was a prewar Hudson. There weren't any postwar cars yet.

So Donna went through the windshield, and she didn't look anything like her sister anymore. And Felix married her after she got out of the hospital. She was only eighteen years old, but she had a full set of false teeth, uppers and lowers.

Felix now refers to his first marriage as a "shotgun wedding." Her relatives and friends felt it was his duty to marry her, whether he loved her or not—and Felix says that he felt that way, too. Usually, when people talk about shotgun weddings, they have pregnancy in mind. A man has impregnated a woman, so he has to marry her.

Felix didn't get his first wife pregnant before he married her, but he put her through a windshield. "I might as well have got her pregnant," he said the other night. "Putting her through a windshield came to very much the same sort of thing."

• • •

Very early on at Schramm's, long before I ran off to New York City to see my play produced, a drunk came in at about two A.M., maybe, and he squinted at the sign on the prescription counter which said, RUDOLPH WALTZ, R.PH.

He evidently knew something of our family's distinguished history, although I don't think we had ever met before. And he was drunk enough to say to me, "Are you the one who shot the woman, or are you the one who put the woman through the windshield?"

He wanted a chocolate malted milkshake, I remember. Schramm's hadn't had a soda fountain for at least five years. He wanted one anyway. "You just give me a little milk and ice cream and chocolate syrup, and I'll make it myself," he said. And then he fell down.

• • •

He didn't call me "Deadeye Dick." Very rarely did anybody do that to my face. But my nickname was said often enough behind my back in all sorts of crowds—in stores, at movies, in eating places. Or maybe somebody would shout it at me from a passing car. It was a thing for drunks or young people to do. No mature and respectable person ever called me "Deadeye Dick."

But one unsettling aspect of the all-night job at Schramm's, one I hadn't anticipated, was the telephone there. Hardly a night passed that some young person, feeling wonderfully daring and

witty, no doubt, would telephone to ask me if I was Deadeye
Dick.

I always was. I always will be.

•   •   •

There was plenty of time for reading on the job, and there
were any number of magazines on the racks. And most of the
business I did at night wasn't at all complicated, didn't have
anything to do with pharmacy. Mainly, I sold cigarettes and,
surprisingly, watches and the most expensive perfumes. The
watches and perfumes were presents, of course, for birthdays
and anniversaries which were remembered only after every
other store in town had closed.

So I was reading *Writer's Digest* one night, and I came across
an announcement of the Caldwell Foundation's contest for play-
wrights. The next thing I knew, I was back in the stock room,
pecking away on the rattletrap Corona portable typewriter we
used for making labels. I was writing a new draft of *Katmandu*.

And I won first prize.

•   •   •

Sauerbraten à la Rudolph Waltz, R.Ph.: Mix in a saucepan a
cup of wine vinegar, half a cup of white wine, half a cup of cider
vinegar, two sliced onions, two sliced carrots, a rib of celery,
chopped, two bay leaves, six whole allspice, crushed, two cloves,
two tablespoons of crushed peppercorns, and a tablespoon of
salt. Bring just to a boil.

Pour it hot over a four-pound rump roast, rolled and tied, in
a deep bowl. Turn the meat around and around in the mixture.
Cover the bowl and refrigerate for three days. Turn the meat in
the mixture several times a day.

Take the meat out of the marinade and dry it. Sear it on all
sides in eight tablespoons of beef drippings in a braising pan.
When it is nicely browned, take it out of the pan and pour out
the drippings. Put the meat back in the pan, heat up the marinade, and pour it over the meat. Simmer for about three hours.
Pour off the liquid, strain, and remove the excess fat. Keep the
meat hot in the braising pan.

Melt three tablespoons of butter in a saucepan, and blend in
three tablespoons of flour and a tablespoon of sugar. Gradually

pour in the marinade, and stir until you have a uniform sauce. Add one cup of crushed ginger-snaps, and simmer the sauce for about six minutes.

That's it!

•   •   •

For three days I did not tell Mother and Father that I had won the contest. It takes that long to make sauerbraten. The sauerbraten was a complete surprise, since Mother and Father never went into the kitchen. They simply waited at the table like good little children, to see what was going to come out of there.

When they had eaten all the sauerbraten they wanted, and said again and again how good it was, I spoke as follows to them: "I am now twenty-seven years old. I have been cooking for you for twelve years now, and I have enjoyed every minute of it. But now I have won a playwriting contest, and my play is going to be produced professionally in New York City three months from now. I will of course have to be there for six weeks of rehearsals.

"Felix says I can stay with him and Genevieve," I went on. "I will sleep on their couch. Their apartment is only three blocks from the theater." Genevieve, incidentally, is the wife Felix now refers to as "Anyface." She had almost no eyebrows, and very thin lips, so that, if she wanted anything memorable in the way of features, she had to paint them on.

I told Mother and Father that I had hired Cynthia Hoobler, the daughter-in-law of our old cook Mary Hoobler, to come in and care for them while I was gone. I would pay her from money I had saved.

I expected no trouble, since the servant problem was all taken care of, and got none. These people, after all, were like characters at the end of a novel or a play, who have been wrong about all sorts of things throughout the action, and finally something has settled their hash.

Mother spoke first. "Goodness," she said. "Good luck."

"Yes," said Father. "Good luck."

Little did I dream that Father had only a few more months to live then.

# 19

TIME FLEW. In a twinkling I was on Christopher Street in Greenwich Village at high noon, gazing up at a theater marquee as snowflakes kissed my face. It was February 14, 1960. My father was still in good health, as far as I knew. The words on the marquee were these:

KATMANDU
A NEW DRAMA
BY RUDY WALTZ

Rehearsals were over. We would open that night.

Father had had his studio, with its dusty skylight and nude model in Vienna, where he had found out he couldn't paint. Now I had my name up on a theater marquee in New York City, where I had found out I couldn't write. The play was a catastrophe. The more the poor actors rehearsed it, the more stupid and depressing it became.

The actors and the director, and the representatives of the Caldwell Foundation, which would never sponsor another play contest, had stopped speaking to me. I was barred from the theater. It wasn't that I had made impossible demands. My offense was that I seemed to know less about the play than anybody. I simply was not worth talking to.

If I was asked about this line or that one, it was as though I had never heard it before. I was likely to say something like "My goodness—I wonder what I meant by that."

Nor did I seem at all interested in rediscovering why I had said this or that.

The thing was this: I was startled not to be Deadeye Dick anymore. Suddenly nobody knew that I was remarkable for having shot and killed a pregnant woman. I felt like a gas which had been confined in a labeled bottle for years, and which had now been released into the atmosphere.

I no longer cooked. It was Deadeye Dick who was always trying to nourish back to health those he had injured so horribly.

I no longer cared about the play. It was Deadeye Dick, tormented by guilt in Midland City, who had found old John

476

Fortune's quite pointless death in Katmandu, as far away from his hometown as possible, somehow magnificent. He himself yearned for distance and death.

So, there in Greenwich Village, looking up at my name on the marquee, I was nobody. My braincase might as well have been filled with stale ginger ale.

Thus, when the actors were still talking to me, could I have had a conversation like this with poor Sheldon Woodcock, the actor who was playing John Fortune:

"You've got to help me get a handle on this part," he said.

"You're doing fine," I said.

"I don't feel like I'm doing fine," he said. "The guy is so inarticulate."

"He's a simple farmer," I said.

"That's just it—he's too simple," he said. "I keep thinking he has to be an idiot, but he isn't an idiot, right?"

"Anything but," I said.

"He never says why he wants to get to Katmandu," he said. "All these people either try to help him get to Katmandu or keep him from getting to Katmandu, and I keep thinking, 'Why the hell should anybody care whether he gets to Katmandu or not?' Why not Tierra del Fuego? Why not Dubuque? He's such a lunk, does it make any difference where he is?"

"He's looking for Shangri-La," I said. "He says that many times—that he wants to find Shangri-La."

"Thirty-four times," he said.

"I beg your pardon?" I said.

"He says that thirty-four times: 'I am looking for Shangri-La.'"

"You counted?" I said.

"I thought somebody better," he said. "That's a lot of times to say anything in just two hours—especially if the person who says it says practically nothing else."

"Cut some of them, if you want," I said.

"Which ones?" he said.

"Whichever ones seem excessive to you," I said.

"And what do I say instead?" he said.

"What would you like to say?" I said.

So he swore under his breath, but then he pulled himself together. I would be barred from the theater soon after this.

"Maybe you don't realize this," he said with bitter patience, "but actors don't make up what they say on the stage. They look like they've made it up, if they're any good, but actually a person called a 'playwright' has first written down every word."

"Then just say what I've written," I said. The secret message in this advice was that I was so light-headed, being away from home for the first time in my life, that I didn't care what happened next. The play was going to be a big flop, but nobody in New York knew what I looked like anyway. I wasn't going to be arrested. I wasn't going to be displayed in a cage, all covered with ink.

I wasn't going home again, either. I would get a job as a pharmacist somewhere in New York. Pharmacists can always find work. And I would do what my brother Felix did—send money home. And then, step by step, I would experiment with having a home of my own and a life of my own, maybe try pairing off with this kind of person or that one, to see how that went.

"Tell me again about my great death scene in the arms of Dr. Brokenshire in Katmandu, with the sitar music," said Woodcock.

"Okay," I said.

"I think I'm in Shangri-La," he said.

"That's right," I said.

"And I know I'm dying," he said. "I don't just think I'm sick, and I'm going to get better again."

"The doctor makes it clear you're dying," I said.

"Then how can I believe I'm in Shangri-La?" he said.

"Pardon me?" I said.

"Another thing I say all through the play," he said, "is that nobody dies in Shangri-La. But here I'm dying, so how can I be in Shangri-La?"

"I'll have to think about it," I said.

"You mean this is the first time you've thought about it?" he said.

And on and on like that.

"Seventeen times," he said.

"Pardon me?" I said.

"Seventeen times I say that nobody dies in Shangri-La."

• • •

So, with opening night only a few hours away, I dawdled from the theater to my brother's duplex apartment, three blocks away. The snowflakes were few, and they melted when they landed. I had given up reading or listening to news since I had come to New York, and so did not know that the Ice Age was reclaiming southwestern Ohio with the most terrible blizzard in history there.

At just about the time the curtain went up on *Katmandu*, that blizzard would come busting in the back door of the old carriage house back home, and then it would fling open the great front portals from the inside, just as Father had done for Celia Hildreth so long ago.

People talk a lot about all the homosexuals there are to see in Greenwich Village, but it was all the neuters that caught my eye that day. These were my people—as used as I was to wanting love from nowhere, as certain as I was that almost anything desirable was likely to be booby-trapped.

I had a fairly funny idea. Someday all we neuters would come out of our closets and form a parade. I even decided what banner our front rank should carry, as wide as Fifth Avenue. A single word would be printed on it in letters four feet high:

EGREGIOUS.

Most people think that word means terrible or unheard of or unforgivable. It has a much more interesting story than that to tell. It means "outside the herd."

Imagine that—thousands of people, outside the herd.

•  •  •

I let myself into Felix's duplex. The place was faintly reminiscent of our childhood home, since the master bedroom was upstairs, and opened onto a balcony that overhung the living-dining room. Felix and I had already rearranged some of the furniture—to better accommodate the party we would be giving after the show. Caterers would bring the food. As I say, I didn't give a damn about food anymore.

And nobody in his right mind was going to come to the party anyway.

It wasn't my party anyway, any more than it was my stupid play. I had regressed to being the boy I used to be—before I shot Mrs. Metzger. I was barely twelve years old.

I supposed that I would have the place to myself all afternoon. Felix and his wife Genevieve, "Anyface," were at radio station WOR, I thought. She still had her job as a receptionist there, and Felix was cleaning out his desk there, preparing to move on to bigger things at Batten, Barton, Durstine & Osborn.

They, in turn, had every reason to assume that I would be at the theater, making last-minute changes in the play. I had not told them that I had been barred from there.

So I wandered up on the balcony, and I sat on a hard-backed chair there. It must have been something I used to do in the carriage house when I was genuinely innocent and twelve years old—to sit very still on the balcony, and to appreciate every sound that floated up to me. It wasn't eavesdropping. It was music appreciation.

And thus it was that I overheard the final dissolution of my brother's second marriage, and some unkind character sketches of Felix and myself and our parents and Genevieve, and some others I did not know. Genevieve came bursting into the apartment first, so angry that she was spitting like a cat, and then, half a minute later, Felix entered. She had come in one cab, and he had chased her in another. And down below me, and out of my line of sight, an acrimonious, atonal duet for viola and string bass was improvised. They both had such noble voices. She was the viola, and he was the bass.

Or maybe it was a comedy. Maybe it is amusing when physically attractive, well-to-do great apes in an urban setting hate each other so much:

## DUPLEX
### A NEW COMEDY
### BY RUDY WALTZ.

*The curtain rises on a Greenwich Village duplex, severely modern, expensive, white. There are fresh flowers. There is fresh fruit. There is impressive electronic apparatus for reproducing music.* GENEVIEVE WALTZ, *a beautiful young woman whose features must be painted on like those of a China doll, enters through the front door, terminally furious. Her young and successful husband,* FELIX, *wearing clothes made in London, follows almost at once. He is just as mad. On the balcony sits* RUDY WALTZ, *a neutered pharmacist from Ohio,* FELIX's *kid brother. He is large and good-looking, but is so sexless and shy that he might as well be made out of canned tuna fish. Incredibly, he has written a play which is going to open in a few hours. He knows it is no good. He considers himself a big mistake. He considers life a big mistake. It probably shouldn't be going on. It is all he can do to give life the benefit of the doubt. There is a frightful secret in his past, which he and his brother have withheld from* GENEVIEVE, *that he is a murderer. All three are products of public school systems in the Middle West, although* GENEVIEVE *now sounds vaguely British, and* FELIX *sounds like a Harvard-educated secretary of state. Only* RUDY *is still a twanging hick.*

GENEVIEVE: Leave me alone. Go back to work.

FELIX: I'll help you pack.

GENEVIEVE: I can pack all right.

FELIX: Can you kick your own butt as you go out the door?

GENEVIEVE: You're sick. You're from a very sick family. Thank God we never had a child.

FELIX: There was a young man from Dundee,

Who buggered an ape in a tree.

The results were most horrid,

All ass and no forehead,

Three balls and a purple goatee.

GENEVIEVE: I didn't know your father was from Dundee. (*She opens a closet*) Look at all the pretty suitcases in here.

FELIX: Fill 'em up. I want every trace of you out of here.

GENEVIEVE: Some of my perfume may have gotten into the draperies. You should probably burn them in the fireplace.

FELIX: Just pack, baby. Just pack.

GENEVIEVE: It's my house as much as it's your house. That's just a theory, of course.

FELIX: I'll pay you off. I'll buy you out.

GENEVIEVE: And I'll give your brother my clothes. He can have all my stuff here. I don't even have to pack. I'll just walk out of here, and start out new.

FELIX: What is that supposed to mean?

GENEVIEVE: Starting out new? Well, you go to Bendel's or Saks or Bloomingdale's, naked except for a credit card—

FELIX: My brother and your clothes.

GENEVIEVE: I think he would enjoy being a woman. I think that's what he was meant to be. That would be nice for you, too, since then you could marry him. I want you to be happy, as hard as that may be for you to believe.

FELIX: That is the end.

GENEVIEVE: We passed that long ago.

FELIX: That is the *very* end.

GENEVIEVE: And the very, very end is coming up. Just get out of here and let me pack.

FELIX: I am to have no feelings of loyalty toward members of my own family?

GENEVIEVE: I was part of your family. Don't you remember that ceremony we went through at City Hall? You probably thought it was an opera, where you were supposed to sing, "I do." If you're from such a close-knit family, why weren't any of its members there?

FELIX: You were in such a hurry to get married.

GENEVIEVE: Was I? I guess I was. I was glad to get married. There was going to be so much happiness. And there was happiness, too, wasn't there?

FELIX: Some. Sure.

GENEVIEVE: Until your brother came along.

FELIX: It's not his fault.

GENEVIEVE: It's your fault.

FELIX: Tell me how.

GENEVIEVE: The very, very end is coming up now. Are you sure you want to hear it?

FELIX: How is it my fault?

GENEVIEVE: You are so ashamed of him. You must be ashamed of your parents, too. Otherwise, why have I never met them?

FELIX: They're too sick to leave home.

GENEVIEVE: And we, with an income of over one hundred thousand dollars a year, have been too poor to visit them. Are they dead?

FELIX: No.

GENEVIEVE: Are they in a crazy house?

FELIX: No.

GENEVIEVE: I'm very good at visiting people in crazy houses. My own mother was in a crazy house when I was in high school, and I visited her. She was wonderful. I was wonderful. I told you my mother was in the crazy house for a while.

FELIX: Yes.

GENEVIEVE: I thought you should know—in case we wanted a baby. It isn't anything to be ashamed of, anyway. Or is it?

FELIX: Nothing to be ashamed of.

GENEVIEVE: So tell me the worst about your parents.

FELIX: Nothing.

GENEVIEVE: Then I'll tell you what's wrong with them. They're not good enough for you. You deserve something far more classy. What a snob you are.

FELIX: It's more complicated.

GENEVIEVE: I doubt it. I can't remember anything about you that was the least bit complicated. Making a good impression at all costs—that accounted for everything.

FELIX: There's a little more to me than that, thank you.

GENEVIEVE: No. There was nothing to you but urbane perfection, until your brother arrived—and turned out to be a circus freak.

FELIX: Don't you call him that.

GENEVIEVE: I'm telling you what you think of him. And what was my duty as a wife? To protect your perfection as much as possible: To pretend that there was absolutely nothing wrong with him. At least I never cringed. You did all the cringing.

FELIX: Cringing?

GENEVIEVE: With your head in your hands, whenever he's around. You could die of shame. You think he hasn't noticed that? You think he hasn't noticed that we're all set up for entertaining, but we somehow never have people in?

FELIX: I've been protecting him.

GENEVIEVE: Protecting you, you mean. This lovely fight we've had—it wasn't about anything I said to him. I've been very nice to him. It was what I said to you that you couldn't stand.

FELIX: With a million people listening.

GENEVIEVE: Five other people in the reception room. And not one heard what I said—because I whispered it to you. But people as far as Chicago must have heard what you yelled back at me. I was actually happily married this morning—for a few seconds—before you yelled at me. I was feeling very pretty and cherished as I sat at the reception desk. We had made love this morning, as you may remember. You had better burn the bottom sheet—along with the draperies. There were five strangers in the reception room, imagining, I think, what sort of life and lover I must have to be so impish and gay—so early in the morning. Into the reception room comes a young broadcasting executive, flawlessly groomed, urbane and sexy. What marvelous New York bullshit! He is the lover! He stops and kisses her, and then she whispers in his ear. It was almost as though New York City were true. A couple of spunky kids from the Middle West, making it big in Gotham.

FELIX: You shouldn't have whispered what you did.

GENEVIEVE: I'll say it again: "Tell your brother to take a bath."

FELIX: What a time to say a thing like that.

GENEVIEVE: His play is opening tonight, and he stinks to high heaven. He hasn't taken a bath since he's been here.

FELIX: You call a remark like that romantic?

GENEVIEVE: I call it family life. I call it intimacy. That's all over now. (*She hauls a suitcase from the closet, opens it, flops it gaping on the couch*) Look how hungry that suitcase is.

FELIX: I'm sorry I said what I said.

GENEVIEVE: You yelled. You yelled, "Shut the fuck up!" You yelled, "If you don't like my relatives, get the hell out of my life!"

FELIX: It was over in a minute.

GENEVIEVE: You bet your English boots it was. And I walked out of that office, never to return. I'm gone, old friend. What a bore and a boor you were to follow me. What a hick.

(*The closet contains mostly sporting goods, ski parkas, wetsuits, warm-up jackets, and so on.* GENEVIEVE *sorts through these,*

*throwing what she wants on the couch, near the open suitcase.*
FELIX's *manly bumptiousness decays as he watches. He is a*
*person of weak character, an actor who can't bear to be ignored.*
*He elects to recapture* GENEVIEVE's *attention by becoming*
*pitiful and harrowingly frank.*)

FELIX (*loudly abject*): It's true, it's true, it's true.
GENEVIEVE (*uninterested*): We never did go scuba diving.
FELIX: I *am* ashamed of my family! You're right! You got me!

(RUDY *doesn't do anything through all this. He just sits.*)

GENEVIEVE: Scuba was next.
FELIX: Father served a prison term, if you want to know.
GENEVIEVE (*unexpectedly fascinated*): Really?
FELIX: Now you know.
GENEVIEVE: What for?

(*Pause.*)

FELIX: Murder.
GENEVIEVE (*moved*): Oh, my God. How awful.
FELIX: Now you know. There's a nice piece of gossip for the
    broadcast industry.
GENEVIEVE: Never mind the gossip. What it must have
    done to your brother—what it must have done to you.
FELIX: I'm all right.
GENEVIEVE: There's no reason why you should be. And
    your poor brother—no wonder he is the way he is. I
    thought he had been born defective, that the umbilical
    cord had strangled him or something. I thought he was
    an idiot savant.
FELIX: What's an idiot savant?
GENEVIEVE: Somebody who's stupid in every possible way
    but one—like playing the piano.
FELIX: He can't play the piano.
GENEVIEVE: But he wrote a play—and it's going to be
    produced. He may not take baths. He may not have any
    friends. He may be so shy he's afraid to talk to anybody. But
    he wrote a play, and he has an extraordinary vocabulary.

He has a bigger vocabulary than both of us put together, and sometimes he says something that is really very funny or wise.

FELIX: He has a degree in pharmacy.

GENEVIEVE: I thought he was an idiot savant in that way, too—theater and pharmacy. But he's the son of a murderer. No wonder he's the way he is. No wonder he wants to be invisible. I saw him walking down Christopher Street last Sunday, and he was as big and handsome as Gary Cooper, but nobody else could see him. He went into a coffee shop, and sat down at the counter, but he couldn't get waited on—because he wasn't there. No wonder.

FELIX: Don't ask for details of the murder.

(*Pause.*)

GENEVIEVE: That's a request I'm bound to honor. Is he in prison now?

FELIX: No—but he might as well be. He might as well be dead.

GENEVIEVE: Everything stops—as I suddenly understand.

FELIX: Please stay, Gen. I don't want to be one of those jerks who gets married and divorced, married and divorced, married and divorced again. Something's very wrong with them.

GENEVIEVE: I can't ever go back to the radio station again—not after that scene. It was so embarrassing.

FELIX: I don't want you to work anymore anyway.

GENEVIEVE: I enjoy work. I enjoy having money of my own. What would I do—sit around the house all day?

FELIX: Have a baby.

GENEVIEVE: Oh, my goodness.

FELIX: Why not?

GENEVIEVE: Do you really think I would make a good mother?

FELIX: The best.

GENEVIEVE: What would you want—a boy or a girl?

FELIX: Either one. Whatever it was, I'd love it.

GENEVIEVE: Oh, my, oh, my. I think I'm going to cry now.

FELIX: Just don't walk out on me. I love you so.

GENEVIEVE: I won't.

FELIX: Do you believe I love you?

GENEVIEVE: I'd better, I guess.

FELIX: I'm going back to the office. I'll clean out my desk. I'll apologize to everybody for the scene I made. It was all my fault. My brother does stink. He should take a bath, and I thank you for saying so. Promise me you'll be here when I get back.

GENEVIEVE: Promise.

(FELIX *exits through the front door.* GENEVIEVE *starts putting things back in the closet.*)

RUDY: Ahem.

GENEVIEVE: Hello?

RUDY: Ahem.

GENEVIEVE: (*scared*): Who's up there, please?

RUDY (*standing, showing himself*): It's me.

GENEVIEVE: Oh, my.

RUDY: I didn't want to scare you.

GENEVIEVE: You heard all that.

RUDY: I didn't want to interrupt.

GENEVIEVE: We don't believe half of what we said.

RUDY: It's all right. I was going to take a bath anyway.

GENEVIEVE: You don't even have to.

RUDY: The house back home is so cold in the winter. You get out of the habit of taking baths. We all get used to the way we smell.

GENEVIEVE: I'm so sorry you heard.

RUDY: It's okay. I don't have any more feelings than a rubber ball. You said how nobody sees me, how I never can get waited on . . . ?

GENEVIEVE: You heard that, too.

RUDY: That's because I'm a neuter. I'm no sex. I'm out of the sex game entirely. Nobody knows how many neuters there are, because they're invisible to most people. I'll tell you something, though: There are millions in this town. They should have a parade sometime, with big signs saying,

TRIED SEX ONCE, THOUGHT IT WAS STUPID, NO SEX
FOR TEN YEARS, FEEL WONDERFUL, FOR ONCE IN YOUR
LIFE, THINK ABOUT SOMETHING BESIDES SEX.

GENEVIEVE: You really can be funny sometimes.

RUDY: Idiot savant. No good at life, but very funny sometimes with the commentary.

GENEVIEVE: I'm sorry about your father.

RUDY: He never murdered anybody.

GENEVIEVE: He didn't?

RUDY: He wouldn't hurt a fly. But he was still a very bad
father to have. Felix and I stopped bringing friends home,
because he was so embarrassing. He wasn't anything and he
never did anything, but he still thought he was so important. He was very spoiled as a child, I guess. We used to get
him to help us with our homework, and then we'd get to
school and find out that everything he said was wrong. You
know what happens if you give a raccoon a lump of sugar?

GENEVIEVE: No.

RUDY: Raccoons always wash their food before they eat it.

GENEVIEVE: I've heard that. Back in Wisconsin, we had
raccoons.

RUDY: A raccoon will take a lump of sugar down to the
water, and wash it and wash it and wash it.

(*Pause.*)

GENEVIEVE: Aha! Until the sugar's gone.

RUDY: And that's what growing up was like for Felix and me.
We had no father when we got through. Mother still thinks
he's the greatest man in the world.

GENEVIEVE: But you still love your parents anyway.

RUDY: Neuters don't love anybody. They don't hate anybody
either.

GENEVIEVE: But you've been keeping house for your parents for years and years, haven't you? Or isn't that true?

RUDY: Neuters make very good servants. They're not your
great seekers of respect, and they usually cook pretty well.

GENEVIEVE (*feeling creepy*): You're a very strange person,
Rudy Waltz.

RUDY: That's because *I'm* the murderer.

GENEVIEVE: What?
RUDY: There's a murderer in the family, all right — but it isn't
    Father. It's me.

(*Pause.*)

(*Curtain.*)

· · ·

Thus did I prevent my brother's fathering a child back then.
Genevieve cleared out of the duplex, not wishing to be there
alone with a murderer, and she and Felix never got together
again. The child they had talked about having would be twenty-
two years old now. The child Eloise Metzger was carrying when
I shot her would be thirty-eight! Think of that.

Who knows what those people would be doing now, instead
of drifting around nowhere, mere wisps of undifferentiated
nothingness. They could be so busy now.

· · ·

To this day, I have never told Felix about how I overheard his
conversation with Genevieve from the balcony, and about how
I scared her out of the duplex, never to return. I wrecked the
marriage. It was an accident-prone time in my life, just as it was
an accident-prone time in my life when I shot Mrs. Metzger.

That's all I can say.

· · ·

I had to let my sister-in-law know that I was somebody to be
reckoned with — that I was a murderer. That was my claim to
fame.

# 20

THE MORNING AFTER *Katmandu* opened and closed, Felix and I were flying over a landscape as white and blank as our lives. Felix had lost his second wife. I was the laughingstock of New York. We were in a six-passenger private plane, traversing a southwestern Ohio which appeared to be as lifeless as a polar ice cap. Somewhere down there was Midland City. The power was off. The phone lines were out.

How could anyone still be alive down there?

The sky was clear, anyway, and the air was still. The blizzard which had done this was now raging somewhere off Labrador.

• • •

Felix and I were in a plane which belonged to Barrytron, Ltd., a manufacturer of sophisticated weapons systems, the largest single employer in Midland City. With us were Fred T. Barry, the founder and sole owner of Barrytron, and his mother, Mildred, and their pilot.

Mr. Barry was a bachelor and his mother was a widow, and they were tireless globe-trotters. Felix and I learned from their conversation that they had been to cultural events all over the planet—arm-in-arm at film festivals and premieres of new ballets and operas, at openings of museum shows, and on and on. And I would be the last to mock them for being such frivolous gadabouts, since it was my play which had brought them and their airplane to New York City. They did not know me or Felix, nor had they more than a nodding acquaintance with our parents. But they had found it imperative that they be at the opening of the only full-length play by a citizen of Midland City which had ever been produced commercially.

How could I not like them for that?

What is more: This mother-and-son team had stayed to the very end of *Katmandu*. Only twenty people did that, including Felix and me. I know. I counted the house. And the Barrys clapped and whistled and stamped as the curtain came down. They were so uninhibited. And Mrs. Barry could certainly whistle. She had been born in England, and in her youth she had been an imitator in music halls of various birds of the British Empire.

•  •  •

Mr. Barry thought a lot more of his mother than I thought of mine. After his mother died, he would try to immortalize her by having the Maritimo Brothers Construction Company build an arts center on stilts in Sugar Creek, and naming it in her honor.

My own mother effectively wrecked that scheme, persuading the community that the arts center and its contents were monstrosities. After that came the neutron bomb. There is nobody left in Midland City anymore to know or care who Mildred Barry might have been.

The scheme for turning the empty husks of my town into housing for refugees moves forward apace, incidentally. The President himself has called it "a golden opportunity."

Bernard Ketchum, our resident shyster here at the Grand Hotel Oloffson, says that Haitian refugees should follow the precedent set by white people, and simply discover Florida or Virginia or Massachusetts or whatever. They could come ashore, and start converting people to voodooism.

"It's a widely accepted principle," he says, "that you can claim a piece of land which has been inhabited for tens of thousands of years, if only you will repeat this mantra endlessly: 'We discovered it, we discovered it, we discovered it. . . .'"

•  •  •

Fred Barry's mother Mildred had an English accent which she had done nothing to modify, although she had lived in Midland City for a quarter of a century or more.

Her black servants, I know, were very fond of her. She knew exactly what kind of a fool she was, and she loved to keep her servants laughing at her all the time.

There in that little plane, she imitated the bulbul of Malaysia and the morepork owl of New Zealand, and so on. I identified a basic mistake my parents had made about life: They thought that it would be very wrong if anybody ever laughed at them.

•  •  •

I keep wanting to say that Fred T. Barry was the grandest neuter I ever saw. He certainly had no sex life. He didn't even have friends. It was all right with him if life ended at any time, obviously, since this was a suicidal flight we were on. He didn't care much if I died, either, or Felix or his mother—or the pilot, who had gone to high school with my brother, and who was scared stiff. If we had an engine failure before we reached Cincinnati, the nearest open runway, where could we land?

But the satisfaction Mr. Barry found in the company of his mother and in their harum-scarum visits to athletic and cultural events all over the world was anything but proof of neutrality. If he liked any part of life that much, he couldn't march in the great parade of neuters in the sweet by-and-by.

Or his mother, either.

• • •

Fred and his mother really had liked *Katmandu*, and they had stayed up late afterwards, so they could get early editions of the morning newspapers and read the reviews. One of the things that made them really mad was that none of the critics had stayed long enough to find out whether John Fortune had found Shangri-La or not.

Mr. Barry said that he would like to see the play performed sometime with an all-Ohio cast. He said that he didn't think New York actors could fully appreciate why it might be important for a simple farmer to die on a quest for wisdom in Asia, even if there wasn't all that much wisdom to find over there.

And that would actually come to pass in three years, as I've said: The Midland County Mask and Wig Club would revive *Katmandu* on the high school stage, and they would give the female lead to poor Celia Hoover.

Oh, my.

• • •

I keep calling Fred T. Barry "Mr. Barry," as though he were older than God. My goodness, he was only about fifty back then—which is my age now. His mother was maybe seventy-five, with eight more years to go until she tried to rescue a bat she found clinging upside down to her living room draperies.

Mr. Barry was a self-educated inventor and super-salesman. He had entered the armaments business more or less by accident. The timer on an automatic washing machine which he had been manufacturing in the old Keedsler Automobile Works turned out to have military applications. It was ideal for timing the release of bombs from airplanes—so as to create a desired pattern of explosions on the ground. When the war was over, orders for much more sophisticated weapons systems started coming in, and Mr. Barry brought in more and more brilliant scientists and engineers and technicians to keep up with the game.

A lot of them were Japanese. My father played host to the first Italians to settle in Midland City. Mr. Barry brought in the first Japanese.

I'll never forget the first Japanese to come into Schramm's Drugstore when I was on all-night duty there. I have mentioned that the store was a lighthouse for lunatics—and that Japanese was a lunatic of a sort, almost literally a lunatic, since the word "lunatic" has to do with craziness and the moon. This Japanese didn't want to buy anything. He wanted me to come outside and see something wonderful in the moonlight.

Guess what it was. It was the conical slate roof of my childhood home, only a few blocks away. The peak of the cone, where the cupola used to be, was capped with very light gray tar roofing, with bits of sand stuck to it. In the light of a full moon, it was glittering white—like snow.

The Japanese smiled and pointed up at the roof. He had no idea that the building meant anything to me. Here was the thought he wanted to share with me, the only other person awake at the time: "Fujiyama," he said, "—the sacred volcano of Japan."

•  •  •

Mr. Barry, like a lot of self-educated people, was full of obscure facts which he had found for himself, and which nobody else seemed to know. He asked me, for instance, if I knew Sir Galahad had been a Jew.

I said politely that I hadn't. It was his airplane. I expected to be annoyed by an anti-Semitic joke of some kind. I was mistaken.

"Not even the Jews know Sir Galahad was a Jew," he went on. "Jesus, yes—Galahad no. Every Jew I meet, I ask him, 'How come you people don't boast more about Sir Galahad?' And I even tell them where they can check it out, if they want to. 'Start with the Holy Grail,' I say."

According to Fred T. Barry, a Jew named Joseph of Arimathea took Christ's goblet when the Last Supper was over. He believed Christ to be divine.

Joseph brought the goblet to the Crucifixion, and some of Christ's blood fell into it. Joseph was arrested for his Christian sympathies. He was thrown into prison without food or water, but he survived for several years. He had the goblet with him, and every day it filled up with food and drink.

So the Romans let him go. They couldn't have known about the goblet, or they surely would have taken it from him. And Joseph went to England to spread the word about Christ. The goblet fed him on the way. And this wandering Jew founded the first Christian church in England—at Glastonbury. He stuck his staff into the ground there, and it became a tree which bloomed every Christmas Eve.

Imagine that.

Joseph had children, who inherited the goblet, which came to be known as the "Holy Grail."

But sometime during the next five hundred years, the Holy Grail was lost. King Arthur and his knights would become obsessed with finding it again—the most sacred relic in England. Knight after knight failed. Supernatural messages indicated that their hearts weren't pure enough for them to find the Grail.

But then Sir Galahad presented himself at Camelot, and it was evident to everyone that his heart was perfectly pure. And he did find the Grail. He was not only spiritually entitled to it. He was legally entitled to it as well, since he was the last living descendant of that wandering Jew, Joseph of Arimathea.

• • •

Mr. Barry told me what the "stock" part of a "laughingstock" was. It was a tree stump used as a target by archers. I had told him that I guessed I was the laughingstock of New York.

Fred's mother said to me, speaking of herself, "Shake hands with the laughingstock of Midland City, and the laughingstock of Venice, Italy, and the laughingstock of Madrid, Spain, and the laughingstock of Vancouver, British Columbia, and the laughingstock of Cairo, Egypt, and of just about every important city you can name."

• • •

Felix got to talking to the pilot, Tiger Adams, about Celia Hildreth, who had become Celia Hoover. Tiger, who had been a year ahead of Felix in high school, had taken her out once, which was par for the course. He guessed that she was lucky to have married an automobile dealer who didn't care what was under her hood.

"A cream puff," he said. At that time, this was a common description for an automobile which was flashy and loaded with accessories—and never mind whether it ran or not.

He had one interesting piece of information, which I had also heard: that the place to see Celia was at the YMCA at night, where she was enrolled in several self-improvement programs— calligraphy and modern dance and business law, and things like that. This had been going on for a couple of years or more.

Felix, hunching forward, asked Adams how Dwayne Hoover took it, having his wife go off night after night. And Adams replied that Dwayne had probably given up interesting her in sex. It was a futile undertaking. Dwayne was consoling himself, no doubt, in somebody else's arms.

"And that's probably a chore for him," Adams went on, "like having his teeth cleaned." He laughed. "It's something everybody should do at least twice a year," he said.

"Some sexy town," said Felix.

"Some towns had better pay attention to business," said Adams. "It would be a terrible thing for the country if they were all like Hollywood and New York."

• • •

And after we set down on the one runway that was open at Cincinnati, it was evident to me that the runway had been cleared at great expense and just for us. That was how important

Fred T. Barry was. It turned out that he was on an emergency mission, although he and his mother had said nothing about that to us. The Air Force was deeply concerned about sensitive work that Barrytron was doing for them. They had a helicopter waiting to take him straight to Midland City, so that he could evaluate and remedy any damage the blizzard might have done to the plant.

In order that we might come along with him, Mr. Barry said that Felix and I were two of his top executives. So up we went again, this time in a clattering contraption invented by Leonardo da Vinci. Leonardo had obviously modeled it on some mythological creature—half eagle, half cow.

That was Fred T. Barry's image: "Half eagle, half cow."

He made me a present of another image, too, as the shadow of our heavier-than-air machine skittered over the unbroken snowfield where Route 53, the highway from Cincinnati to Midland City, used to be.

I was in a permanent cringe in my seat, going over in my mind all the terrible things about the blizzard which I had heard and read in New York. Thousands were obviously dying or dead below us. It would take a long time to find all the bodies, and there would be so much rebuilding to do. Midland City and Shepherdstown, when the snow melted, would look like French towns on the front in the First World War.

But Fred T. Barry, as cheerful as ever, said to me, "It's nothing but a big pillow fight."

"Sir—?" I said.

"Human beings always treat blizzards as though they were the end of the world," he said. "They're like birds when the sun goes down. Birds think the sun is never going to come up again. Sometime, just listen to the birds when the sun goes down."

"Sir—?" I said.

"This will all melt in a few days or a few weeks," he said, "and it will turn out that everybody is all right, and nothing much got hurt. You'll hear on the news that so-and-so many people were killed by the blizzard, but they would have died anyway. Somebody dies of cancer he's had for eleven years, and the radio says the blizzard got him."

So I relaxed some. I sat up straighter.

"Blizzard is nothing but a great big pillow fight," he said.

His mother laughed. Mother and son were so unvain and unafraid. They had such nice times.

●    ●    ●

But Fred T. Barry must have been temporarily regretful that he'd said that—when we got a good look from the air at the carriage house. We had circled over the city, so we approached the conical roof from the north. Wind had piled snow halfway up the big north window. The drift hid the back door, the kitchen door, entirely. Seeing it from a distance, I imagined that the drift would actually make the place cozier, would shield it from the wind.

But we were horrified when we saw the south side. The great doors, which had last been thrown open for Celia Hildreth in 1943, were agape again. The back door had blown open, we would find out later, and the gale it admitted had flung open the great doors from the inside. The enormous open doorway appeared to have tried to vomit the snow which had piled up inside. How deep was the snow inside? Six feet or more.

# 21

FRED T. BARRY and his mother were left off by the helicopter on a rooftop at Barrytron. Mr. Barry maintained the hoax that Felix and I were his employees, and he instructed the pilot sternly that he was to take us wherever we wanted to go, and to stand by until we were through with him. We had all been such great pals, and gone through so much together, and the mood was that we should really see a lot more of each other, and that most people in Midland City weren't as amusing and worldly as we were, and so on.

But I would not see or hear from Mr. Barry for ten more years, and I would never lay eyes on his mother again. Out of sight, out of mind. That's how it was with the Barrys.

So Felix and I used that Air Force helicopter like a taxicab. We went back to the carriage house. There were no footprints there. We had jackets and hats and gloves, but no boots. We were wearing ordinary street shoes, and these filled with snow as we wallowed and tumbled and writhed our way inside. Maybe Mother and Father were under all that snow. If so, they were dead.

We got to the staircase, whose bottom half was buried. Knowing our parents, we supposed that they had gone to bed when the blizzard hit. They wouldn't have got out of bed, we surmised, even after all hell cut loose downstairs. So Felix and I entered their bedroom. The bed was empty. Not only that, but it was stripped of its blankets and sheets. So, maybe Mother and Father had wrapped themselves in bedding, and gone downstairs after all.

I went up one more flight to what used to be the gun room, while Felix checked the other rooms on the loft.

We were expecting to find bodies as hard and stiff as andirons. It was so cold inside. These words popped into my head: "Dead storage."

I heard Felix call from the balcony: "Anybody home?" And then, as I came down from the gun room, he looked up at me, and he said, haggardly, "Nice to be home again."

• • •

We found Mother and Father at the County Hospital. Father was dying of double pneumonia, coupled with kidney failure. Mother had frostbitten fingers and feet. Father was very sick before the blizzard ever hit, and had been about to go to the hospital anyway.

Before the streets became completely impassable, Mother had walked out into the storm in a bathrobe and bedroom slippers and a nightgown, with the Hungarian Life Guard tunic over her shoulders and the sable busby on her head. She was out there long enough to suffer frostbite, but she managed to flag down a snowplow. And the snowplow took her and Father, all bundled up in bedclothes, to the hospital, which had its own diesel-powered electric plant.

When Felix and I came into the lobby of the hospital, not knowing if our parents were there or not, we were appalled by the mess. Hundreds of healthy people had sought shelter there, although nobody was supposed to go there unless seriously ill. The sanitary facilities were swamped, and the refugees had begun to infest the entire hospital, in search of food and water and places to lie down.

These were my people. They had become pioneers again. They were starting a new settlement.

They were ten deep at the information counter, which Felix and I were trying to approach, too. You would have thought it was a bar on the Klondike. So I told Felix that I would keep trying to get up to the counter, while he went looking for familiar faces which might have news of our parents.

I had a feeling, while I inched forward in the crowd, that invisible insects were buzzing around my head. The hospital lobby was surely hot and humid enough for real insects, but the ones that nagged and niggled around me were a condition of my spirit. There had been no such swarms in New York City, but here they were again in my own hometown. They were little bits of information I had about this person, or that person, or which this or that person had about me.

I was a Midland City celebrity, of course, so every so often I heard or thought I heard these words: "Deadeye Dick."

I gave no sign that I heard them. What would have been the point of my looking this or that person in the eye, accusing him or her of having called me "Deadeye Dick"? I deserved the name.

When I got to within a rank of the information counter, I learned that the other people were there principally to gain some measure of respect. No truly urgent questions were being put to the three frazzled women behind the counter.

Typical questions:

"What's the latest news, miss?"

"If we want blankets, where do we go?"

"Do you know that they're out of toilet paper in the ladies' room?"

"How sick do you have to be to get a room?"

"Could I have some dimes for when the telephones start working again?"

"Is that clock right?"

"Can we use just one burner in the kitchen for about fifteen minutes?"

"Dr. Mitchell is my doctor. I'm not sick, but would you please tell him I'm here anyway?"

"Is there a list of everybody who's here? Do you want my name?"

"Is there some office where they'll cash a personal check for me?"

"Can I help some way?"

"My mother's got this pain in her left leg that won't go away. What should I do?"

"What is the Power and Light Company doing?"

"Should I tell somebody that I've got a legful of shrapnel from the First World War?"

I came to admire the three women behind the counter. They were patient and polite, for the most part. One of them blew up ever so briefly at the man with the legful of shrapnel. Her initial reply had somehow left him unsatisfied, and he told her that she had no business in the medical profession, if she wouldn't listen to what people were trying to tell her about themselves. I had a vague idea who he was, and I had my doubts about his ever having been in any war. I was pretty sure he was one of the Gatch brothers, who used to work for the Maritimo Brothers

Construction Company, until they were caught stealing tools and building materials.

If he was who I was pretty sure he was, he had a daughter who was two years ahead of me in school, Mary or Martha or Marie, maybe, who was a shoplifter. She was always trying to turn people into friends by making them presents of things she stole.

And the woman behind the counter told him bitterly that she was just an ordinary housewife, who had volunteered to help at the hospital, and that she hadn't been to sleep for twenty-four hours. It was late afternoon by then.

I realized that I knew who she was, too—not approximately, but exactly. Twenty-four hours of sleeplessness had made her, in my eyes, anyway, an idealized representative of compassionate, long-suffering women of all ages everywhere. She denied that she was a nurse, but she was a nurse anyway, without vanity or guile.

I have a tendency, anyway, to swoon secretly in the presence of nurturing women, since my own mother was such a cold and aggressively helpless old bat.

Who was this profoundly beautiful and unselfish woman behind the counter? What a surprise! This was Celia Hoover, née Hildreth, the wife of the Pontiac dealer—once believed to be the dumbest girl in high school. I wanted Felix to get a look at her, but I could not spot him anywhere. The last time he had seen her, she had been cutting through a vacant lot in the nighttime, way back in 1943.

•   •   •

She was a robot in back of the counter. Her memory was blasted by weariness. I asked her if Mr. and Mrs. Otto Waltz were in the hospital, and she looked in a card file. She told me mechanically that Otto Waltz was in intensive care, in critical condition, and could not have visitors, and that Emma Wetzel Waltz was not in serious condition, and had been given a bed in a makeshift ward which had been set up in the basement.

So there was a member of our distinguished family down in a basement again.

I had never been in the basement of the hospital before. But I had known this much about it even when I was a little boy: That was where they had the city morgue.

That had been the first stop for Eloise Metzger, after I shot her between the eyes.

•  •  •

I found Felix standing in a corner of the lobby, agog at the crowd. He hadn't done anything to try and find Mother and Father. He was useless. "Help me, Rudy," he said, "—I'm seventeen years old again." It was true.

"Somebody just called me the 'Velvet Fog,'" he marveled. This was the sobriquet of a famous singer of popular music named Mel Tormé. Felix had also been nicknamed that in high school.

"Whoever called me that," he said, "said it sneeringly, as though I should be ashamed of myself. It was a real fat guy, with cold blue eyes. A grown man in a business suit. Nobody's spoken to me like that since the Army took me away from here."

It was easy for me to guess who he was talking about. It had to be Jerry Mitchell, who had been Felix's worst enemy in high school. "Jerry Mitchell," I said.

"That was Jerry?" said Felix. "He's so heavy. He's lost so much hair!"

"Not only that," I said, "but he's a doctor now."

"I pity his patients," said Felix. "He used to torture cats and dogs, and say he was performing scientific experiments."

And there was prophecy in that. Dr. Mitchell was building a big practice on the principle that nobody in modern times should ever be the least uncomfortable or dissatisfied, since there were now pills for everything. And he would buy himself a great big house out in Fairchild Heights, right next door to Dwayne and Celia Hoover, and he would encourage Celia and his own wife, and God only knows who all else, to destroy their minds and spirits with amphetamine.

About that insect swarm around my head, all those bits of information I had on this person and that one: Dr. Jerome Mitchell was married to the former Barbara Squires, the younger sister of Anthony Squires. Anthony Squires was the policeman who had given me the nickname Deadeye Dick.

•  •  •

Father's deathbed scene went like this: Mother and Felix and I were there, right by his bed. Gino and Marco Maritimo, faithful to the end, had driven to the hospital atop their own bulldozer. It would later turn out that these two endearing old poops had done hundreds of thousands of dollars' worth of damage on the way, tearing up hidden automobiles and fences and fire hydrants and mailboxes, and so on. They had to stay out in the corridor, since they weren't blood relatives.

Father was under an oxygen tent. He was all shot up with antibiotics, but his body couldn't fight off the pneumonia. Too much else was wrong. The hospital had shaved off his thick, youthful hair and mustache, so that an accidental spark couldn't make them burn like gunpowder in the presence of all that oxygen. He seemed to be asleep, but having nightmares, fighting with his eyes closed, when Felix and I came in.

Mother had already been there for hours. Her frostbitten hands and feet were enclosed in plastic bags filled with a yellow salve, so that she couldn't touch any of us. This turned out to be an experimental treatment for frostbite, invented right there in Midland City that very morning, by a Doctor Miles Pendleton. We assumed that all frostbite victims had their damaged parts encased in plastic and salve. Mother, in fact, was probably the only person in history to be treated that way.

She was a human guinea pig, and we didn't even know it.

No harm done, luckily.

• • •

Father's peephole closed forever at sunset on the day after the opening and closing of my play. He was sixty-eight. The only word Felix and I heard from him was his very last one, which was this: "Mama." It was Mother who told us about his earlier deathbed assertions—that he had at least been good with children, that he had always tried to behave honorably, and that he hoped he had at least brought some appreciation of beauty to Midland City, even if he himself hadn't been an artist.

• • •

He mentioned guns, according to Mother, but he didn't editorialize about them. All he said was, "Guns."

The wrecked guns, including the fatal Springfield, had been donated to a scrap drive during the war—along with the weather vane. They might have killed a lot more people when they were melted up and made into shells or bombs or hand grenades or whatever.

Waste not, want not.

· · ·

As far as I know, he had only one big secret which he might have told on his deathbed: Who killed August Gunther, and what became of Gunther's head. But he didn't tell it. Who would have cared? Would there have been any social benefit in prosecuting old Francis X. Morissey, who had become chief of police and was about to retire, for accidentally blowing Gunther's head off with a ten-gauge shotgun forty-four years ago?

Let sleeping dogs lie.

· · ·

When Felix and I got to Father, he was a baby again. He thought his mother was somewhere around. He died believing that he had once owned one of the ten greatest paintings in the world. This wasn't "The Minorite Church of Vienna" by Adolf Hitler. Father had nothing to say about Hitler as he died. He had learned his lesson about Hitler. One of the ten greatest paintings in the world, as far as he was concerned, was "Crucifixion in Rome," by John Rettig, which he had bought for a song in Holland, during his student days. It now hangs in the Cincinnati Art Museum.

"Crucifixion in Rome," in fact, was one of the few successes in the art marketplace, or in any sort of marketplace, which Father experienced in his threescore years and eight. When he and Mother had to put up all their treasures for sale, in order to pay off the Metzgers, they had imagined that their paintings alone were worth hundreds of thousands of dollars. They advertised in an art magazine, I remember, that an important art collection was to be liquidated, and that serious collectors and museum curators could see it by appointment in our house.

About five people did come all the way to Midland City for a look, I remember, and found the collection ludicrous. One man, I remember, wanted a hundred pictures for a motel he was furnishing in Biloxi, Mississippi. The rest really seemed to know and care about art.

But the only painting anybody wanted was "Crucifixion in Rome." The Cincinnati Art Museum bought it for not much money, and the museum wanted it not because its greatness was so evident, I'm sure, but because it had been painted by a native of Cincinnati. It was a tiny thing, about the size of a shirt cardboard—about the size of Father's work in progress, the nude in his Vienna studio.

John Rettig, in fact, died in the year I was born, which was 1932. Unlike me, he got out of his hometown and stayed out. He took off for the Near East and then Europe, and he finally settled in Volendam, Holland. That became his home, and that was where Father discovered him before the First World War.

Volendam was John Rettig's Katmandu. When Father met him, this man from Cincinnati was wearing wooden shoes.

•  •  •

"Crucifixion in Rome" is signed "John Rettig," and it is dated 1888. So it was painted four years before Father was born. Father must have bought it in 1913 or so. Felix thinks there is a possibility that Hitler was with Father on that skylarking trip to Holland. Maybe so.

"Crucifixion in Rome" is indeed set in Rome, which I have never seen. I know enough, though, to recognize that it is chock-a-block with architectural anachronisms. The Colosseum, for example, is in perfect repair, but there is also the spire of a Christian church, and some architectural details and monuments which appear to be more recent, even, than the Renaissance, maybe even nineteenth century. There are sixty-eight tiny but distinct human figures taking part in some sort of celebration amid all this architecture and sculpture. Felix and I counted them one time, when we were young. Hundreds more are implied by impressionistic smears and dots. Banners fly. Walls are festooned with ropes of leaves. What fun.

Only if you look closely at the painting will you realize that two of the sixty-eight figures are not having such a good time. They are in the lower left-hand corner, and are harmonious with the rest of the composition, but they have in fact just been hung from crosses.

The picture is a comment, I suppose, but certainly a bland one, on man's festive inhumanity to men—even into what to John Rettig were modern times.

It has the same general theme, I guess, of Picasso's "Guernica," which I have seen. I went to see "Guernica" at the Museum of Modern Art in New York City, during a lull in the rehearsals of *Katmandu*.

Some picture!

# 22

I WENT FOR A WALK through hospital corridors all alone after Father died. A few people may or may not have murmured "Deadeye Dick" behind my back. It was a busy place.

I came upon strange beauty unexpectedly in a fourth-floor cul-de-sac. It was in a dazzlingly sunny patients' lounge. The unexpected beauty was in the form of Celia Hoover, née Hildreth, again. She had fallen asleep on a couch, and her eleven-year-old son was watching over her. She had evidently brought him with her to the hospital, rather than leave him alone at home in the blizzard.

He was seated stiffly on the edge of the couch. Even in sleep, she was keeping him captive. She was holding his hand. I had the feeling that, if he had tried to get up, she would have awakened enough to make him sit back down again.

That seemed all right with him.

. . .

Yes—well—and ten years later, in 1970, that same boy would be a notorious homosexual, living away from home in the old Fairchild Hotel. His father, Dwayne Hoover, had disowned him. His mother had become a recluse. He eked out a living as a piano player at night in the Tally-ho Room of the new Holiday Inn.

I was again what I had been before the fiasco of my play in New York, the all-night man at Schramm's Drugstore. Father was buried in Calvary Cemetery, not all that far from Eloise Metzger. We buried him in a painter's smock, and with his left thumb hooked through a palette. Why not?

The city had taken the old carriage house for fifteen years of back taxes. The first floor now sheltered the carcasses of trucks and buses which were being cannibalized for parts. The upper floors were dead storage for documents relating to transactions by the city before the First World War.

Mother and I inhabited a little two-bedroom shitbox out in the Maritimo Brothers development known as "Avondale." Mother and I moved into it about three months after Father died. It was virtually a gift from Gino and Marco Maritimo. We didn't even have a down payment. Mother and I were both dead broke, and Felix hadn't started to make really big money yet, and he was about to pay alimony to two ex-wives instead of one. Old Gino and Marco told us to move in anyway, and not to worry. The price they were asking, it turned out, was so far below the actual value of the house that we had no trouble getting a mortgage. It had been a model house, too, which meant it was already landscaped, and there were Venetian blinds already on all the windows, and a flagstone walk running up to the front door, and a post lantern out front, and all sorts of expensive options which most Avondale buyers passed up, like a full basement and genuine tile in the bathroom, and a cedar closet in Mother's bedroom, and a dishwasher and a garbage disposal unit and a wall oven and a built-in breakfast nook in the kitchen, and a fireplace with an ornate mantelpiece in the living room, and an outdoor barbecue, and an eight-foot cedar fence around the backyard, and on and on.

• • •

So, in 1970, at the age of thirty-eight, I was still cooking for my mother, and making her bed every day, and doing her laundry, and so on. My brother, forty-four then, was president of the National Broadcasting Company, and living in a penthouse overlooking Central Park, and one of the ten best-dressed men in the country, supposedly, and breaking up with his fourth wife. According to a gossip column Mother and I read, he and his fourth wife had divided the penthouse in half with a line of chairs. Neither one was supposed to go in the other one's territory.

Felix was also due to be fired any day, according to the same column, because the ratings of NBC prime time television shows were falling so far behind those of the other networks.

Felix denied this.

• • •

Yes—and Fred T. Barry had lost his mother, and the Maritimo Brothers Construction Company was building the Mildred Barry Memorial Center for the Arts on stilts in the middle of Sugar Creek. I hadn't seen Mr. Barry for ten years.

But Tiger Adams, his pilot, came into Schramm's Drugstore one morning, at about two A.M. I asked him how Mr. Barry was, and he said that he had almost no interest in anything anymore, except for the arts center.

"He says he wants to give southwestern Ohio its own Taj Mahal," he told me. "He's sick with loneliness, of course. If it weren't for the arts center, I think maybe he would have killed himself."

So I looked up the Taj Mahal at the downtown public library the next afternoon. The library was about to be torn down, since the neighborhood had deteriorated so much. Nice people didn't like to go there anymore in the winter, since there were always so many bums inside, just keeping warm.

I had of course heard of the Taj Mahal before. Who hasn't? And it had figured in my play. Old John Fortune saw the Taj Mahal before he died. That was the last place he sent a postcard from. But I had never known why and when and how it had been built, exactly.

It turned out that it was completed in 1643, three hundred and one years before I shot Eloise Metzger. It took twenty thousand workmen twenty-two years to build it.

It was a memorial to something Fred T. Barry never had, and which I have never had, which is a wife. Her name was Arjumand Banu Begum. She died in childbirth. Her husband, who ordered the Taj Mahal to be built at any cost, was the Mogul emperor Shah Jahan.

●  ●  ●

Tiger Adams gave me news of somebody else I hadn't seen for quite a while. He said that, two nights before, he had been coming in for a night landing at Will Fairchild Memorial Airport, and he had had to pull up at the last second because there was somebody out on the runway.

Whoever it was fell down in a heap right in the middle of the runway, and then just stayed there. There were only two people inside the airport at that hour—one in the tower, and the other waxing floors down below. So the floor waxer, who was one of the Gatch brothers, drove out on the runway in his own car.

He had to half-drag the mystery person into his car. It turned out to be Celia Hoover. She was barefoot, and wearing her husband's trenchcoat over a nightgown, and about five miles from home. She had evidently gone for a long walk, even though she was barefoot—and she had got on the runway in the dark, thinking it was a road. And then the landing lights had come on all of a sudden, and the Barrytron Learjet had put a part in her hair.

Nobody notified the police or anybody. Gatch just took her home.

Gatch later told Tiger then there hadn't been anybody at her house to wonder where she had been, to be relieved that she was all right, and so on. She just went inside all alone, and presumably went to bed all alone. After she went inside, one light upstairs went on for about three minutes, and then went off again. It looked like a bathroom light.

According to Tiger, Gatch said this to the blacked-out house: "Sleep tight, honeybunch."

•    •    •

That isn't quite right. There had been a dog to welcome her home, but she hadn't paid any attention to the dog. She had put no value, as far as Gatch could see, on the dog's delight. She didn't pet it or thank it, or anything—or tell it to come on upstairs with her.

The dog was Dwayne Hoover's Labrador retriever, Sparky, but Dwayne was hardly ever home anymore. Sparky would have been glad to see just about anybody. Sparky was glad to see Gatch.

•    •    •

So, while I try not to become too concerned about anybody, while my feeling ever since I shot Eloise Metzger has been that I don't really belong on this particular planet, I had loved Celia at least a little bit. She had been in my play, after all, and had taken the play very seriously—which made her a sort of child or sister of mine.

To have been a perfectly uninvolved person, a perfect neuter, I should never have written a play.

To have been a perfect neuter, I shouldn't have bought a new Mercedes, either. That's correct: Ten years after Father died, I had saved so much money, working night after night, and living so modestly out in Avondale, that I bought a white, four-door Mercedes 280, and still had plenty of money left over.

It felt like a very funny accident. There Deadeye Dick was all of a sudden, driving this big white dreamboat around town, evidently talking to himself a mile a minute. What I was really doing, of course, was chasing the blues with scat singing. "Feedily watt a boo boo," I'd sing in my Mercedes, and "Rang-a-dang wee," and so on. "Foodily at! Foodily at!"

•  •  •

The most troubling news Tiger Adams had about Celia was this: During the seven years since she had been in my play, she had become as ugly as the Wicked Witch of the West in *The Wizard of Oz*.

Those were Tiger's exact words to me: "My God, Rudy, you wouldn't believe it—that poor woman has become as ugly as the Wicked Witch of the West in *The Wizard of Oz*."

•  •  •

A week later, she paid me a call at the drugstore—at about midnight, the witching hour.

# 23

I HAD JUST COME to work. I was standing at the back door, gazing at my new Mercedes, and listening to the seeming muted roar of waves breaking on a beach not far away. The seeming surf was in fact the sound of gigantic trucks with eighteen wheels, moving at high speed on the Interstate. The night was balmy. All I needed was a ukulele. I was so content.

My back was to the stock room, with its cures for every ailment known to man. A little bell dinged in the stock room, telling me that someone had just entered the front of the store. It could be a killer, of course. There was always a chance that it was a killer, or at least a robber. In the ten years since Father had died, I had been robbed in the store six times.

What a hero I was.

So I went to wait on the customer, or whatever it was. I left the back door unlocked. If it was a robber, I would try to get out the back door and hide among the weeds and garbage cans. He or she would have to help himself or herself. I would not be there to obey his or her orders to cooperate.

The customer, or whatever it was, was inspecting dark glasses on a carousel. Who needed dark glasses at midnight?

It was small for a human being. But it was certainly big enough to carry a sawed-off shotgun under its voluminous trenchcoat, the hem of which scarcely cleared the floor.

"Can I help you?" I said cheerily. Perhaps it had a headache or hemorrhoids.

It faced me, and it showed me the raddled, snaggletoothed ruins of the face of Celia Hoover, once the most beautiful girl in town.

Again—my memory writes a playlet.

*The curtain rises on the interior of a seedy drugstore in the poorest part of a small Middle-Western city, shortly after midnight.* RUDY WALTZ, *a fat, neutered pharmacist, is shocked to recognize a demented speed freak, a hag, as* CELIA HOOVER, *once the most beautiful girl in town.*

RUDY: Mrs. Hoover!

CELIA: My hero!

RUDY: Not me.

CELIA: Yes! Yes! You! My hero of theatrical literature!

RUDY (*pained*): Oh, please—

CELIA: That play of yours—it changed my life.

RUDY: You were certainly good in it.

CELIA: All those wonderful words that came out of me—
those were your words. I could never have thought up
words that beautiful to say in a million years. I almost lived
and died without ever saying anything worth listening to.

RUDY: You made my words sound a lot better than they
really were.

CELIA: I was on that stage, and there were all these people
out there, all bug-eyed, hearing all those wonderful words
coming out of dumb old Celia Hoover. They couldn't
believe it.

RUDY: It was a magic time in my life, too.

CELIA (*imitating the audience*): "Author! Author!"

RUDY: We were the toast of the town at curtain call. Now,
then—what can I get you here?

CELIA: A new play.

RUDY: I've written my first and last play, Celia.

CELIA: Wrong! I have come to inspire you—with this new
face of mine. Look at my new face! Make up the words that
should come out of a face like this. Write a crazy-old-lady
play!

RUDY (*looking out at the street*): Where did you park your car?

CELIA: I always wanted a face like this. I wish I could have
been born with a face like this. It would have saved a lot of
trouble. Everybody could have said, "Just leave that crazy
old lady alone."

RUDY: Is your husband home?

CELIA: You're my husband. That's what I came to tell you.

RUDY: Celia—you are not well. What's your doctor's name?

CELIA: You are my doctor. You are the only person in this
town who ever made me glad to be alive—with the medicine of your magic words! Give me more words!

RUDY: You've lost your shoes.

CELIA: I threw my shoes away! In your honor! I threw all my shoes away. They're all in the garbage can.

RUDY: How did you get here?

CELIA: I walked here—and I'll walk home again.

RUDY: There's broken glass everywhere in this neighborhood.

CELIA: I would gladly walk over glowing coals for you. I love you. I need you so.

(RUDY *considers this declaration, comes to a cynical conclusion, which makes him tired.*)

RUDY (*emptily*): Pills.

CELIA: What a team we'd make—the crazy old lady and Deadeye Dick.

RUDY: You want pills from me—without a prescription.

CELIA: I love you.

RUDY: Sure. But it's pills, not love, that make people walk over broken glass at midnight. What'll it be, Celia—amphetamine?

CELIA: As a matter of fact—

RUDY: As a matter of fact—?

CELIA (*as though it were a perfectly routine order, certain to be filled*): Pennwalt Biphetamine, please.

RUDY: "Black beauties."

CELIA: I've never heard them called that.

RUDY: You know how black and glistening they are.

CELIA: You heard what I call them.

RUDY: You can't get them here.

CELIA (*indignantly*): They've been prescribed for me for years!

RUDY: I'll bet they have! But you've never been here before—with or without a prescription.

CELIA: I came here to ask you to write another play.

RUDY: You came here because you've been shut off everyplace else. And I wouldn't give you any more of that poison, if you had a prescription signed by God Almighty. Now you're going to tell me you don't love me after all.

CELIA: I can't believe you're so mean.

RUDY: And who was it who was so nice to you for so long? Dr. Mitchell, I'll bet—hand in hand with the Fairchild

Heights Pharmacy. Too late, they got scared to death of what they'd done to you.

CELIA: What makes you so afraid of love?

*(Telephone behind prescription counter rings.* RUDY *goes to answer.)*

RUDY: Excuse me. *(Into telephone)* Schramm's. *(He listens to a brief question blankly)* So they say. *(He hangs up)* Somebody wanted to know if I was Deadeye Dick. Now, then, Mrs. Hoover—my understanding of the effects of long-term use of amphetamine leads me to expect that you will very soon become abusive. I can take that if I have to, but I'd rather get you home some way.

CELIA: You think you know so much.

RUDY: Is there someplace I can reach your husband? Is he home?

CELIA: Detroit.

RUDY: Your son's just a few blocks away.

CELIA: I hate his guts, and he hates mine.

RUDY: We seem to be living the crazy-old-lady play. I'll call Dr. Mitchell.

CELIA: He's not my doctor anymore. Dwayne beat him up last week—for giving me all those pills so long.

RUDY: Good for Dwayne.

CELIA: Isn't that nice? And as soon as Dwayne gets back from Detroit, he's going to put me in the crazy house.

RUDY: You do need help. You need a lot of help.

CELIA: Then put your arms around me! (RUDY *freezes*) And no Pennwalt Biphetamine, either. No anything here. *(She gravely sweeps a display of cosmetics from a counter to the floor.)*

RUDY: Please don't do any more of that.

CELIA: Oh—I'll pay for all damages, any damages I decide to do. Money is not a problem. *(She brings forth a handful of gold coins from her trench-coat pocket)* See?

RUDY: Gold pieces!

CELIA: Sure! I don't fool around. My husband's a coin collector, you know.

RUDY: There's got to be several thousand dollars there.

CELIA: Yours, all yours, honeybunch. (*She scatters the coins at his feet*) Now give me a hug, or give me some Pennwalt Biphetamine.

(RUDY *goes to the telephone, dials.*)

RUDY (*singing softly to himself, waiting for an answer on the phone*): Skeedee-wah, skeedee-woo. (*Etc.*)
CELIA: Who are you calling?
RUDY: The police.
CELIA: You big tub of lard! (*She topples a carousel of dark glasses.*) You fat Nazi bastard!
RUDY (*into telephone*): This is Rudy Waltz—over at Schramm's. Who's this? Oh—Bob! I didn't recognize your voice. I need a little help here.
CELIA: You need a lot of help here! (*She sets about wrecking everything she can get her hands on*) Killer! Mama's boy!
RUDY (*into telephone*): Not a criminal matter. It's a mental case.

(*Curtain.*)

•  •  •

But she got out of there before the police could come. When they arrived, they could see all the damage she had done, but she herself was roaming shoeless out in the night again. That is the second story I have told about Celia which ends with her fleeing barefoot.

History repeats itself.

The police went looking for her—to protect her. She could get robbed or raped. She could be attacked by dogs. She could be hit by a car.

Meanwhile, I set about cleaning up the mess she had made. The store wasn't mine, so I was in no position to forgive and forget. Celia's husband was going to have to find out what she had done, and then he would be asked to cough up a thousand dollars or more. Celia had gone after the most expensive perfumes. Celia had gone after the watches, too, but they were still okay. It is virtually impossible to harm a Timex watch. For some reason, the less you pay for a watch, the surer you can be that it will never stop.

My conscience was active as I worked. Should I have hugged her or given her amphetamine? My feeling was that chemicals had wrecked her brains, and that she wasn't Celia Hoover anymore. She was a monster. If I did write a play for her new face, I thought, she wouldn't be able to learn her lines. Somebody else would have to play her—in a fright wig, and with several teeth blacked out.

What wonderful things could a writer put into the mouth of a crazy old lady like her anyway? My mind got this far with the problem, anyway: She could certainly shake up an audience if she let it think she was about a hundred years old for a while, and then told her true age. Celia was only forty-four when she took the drugstore apart.

I tinkered, too, with the idea of having the voice of God coming from the back of the theater. Whoever played God would have to have a voice like my brother's.

The actress playing Celia could ask why God had ever put her on earth.

And then the voice from the back of the theater could rumble: "To reproduce. Nothing else really interests Me. All the rest is frippery."

• • •

She had reproduced, of course, which was certainly more than I had done. And I got it into my head to stop cleaning up for a minute and call up her son, Bunny. He would probably be in his room at the Fairchild Hotel, fresh home from work at the new Holiday Inn.

He was wide awake. Somebody had told me that Bunny was heavily into cocaine. That could merely be a rumor.

I told him who I was, and I said his mother had just been in the store, and that, in my opinion, she really needed help. "I just thought you should know," I said.

Out of the corner of my eye, I saw that a mouse was listening to me. It was going to have to guess what was going on, since it could hear only my half of the conversation.

So this disinherited young homosexual at the other end of the line laughed and laughed. Bunny wouldn't make any specific comments on his mother's poor health. His laughter was a terrible thing to hear. He sure hated her.

But then he settled down some, and he told me that maybe I should spend more time worrying about my own relatives.

"What do you mean by that?" I said. The little ears of the mouse were fine-tuning themselves to my voice, not wishing to miss a syllable.

"Your brother's just been canned by NBC," he said.

I said that that was just gossip.

He said it wasn't gossip anymore. He had just heard it over the radio. "It's official," he said. "They finally caught up with him."

"What is that supposed to mean?" I asked him.

"He's just another big fake from Midland City," he said. "Everybody here is fake."

"That's a nice thing to say about your own hometown," I said.

"Your father was a fake. He couldn't paint good pictures. I'm a fake. I can't really play the piano. You're a fake. You can't write decent plays. It's perfectly all right, as long as we all stay home. That's where your brother made his mistake. He went away from home. They catch fakes out in the real world, you know. They catch 'em all the time."

He laughed some more, and I hung up on him.

But then the phone rang right away, and it was my brother calling from his penthouse in Manhattan. It was absolutely true, he said. It was official: He had been canned. "It's the best thing that ever happened to me," he said.

"If that's the case, I'm glad for you," I said. I was standing there, with broken eyeglasses and gold pieces crunching under my feet. The police had come and gone so quickly that I hadn't had a chance to tell them about the gold.

Gold! Gold! Gold!

"For the first time in my life," said Felix, "I have the opportunity to find out who I really am. From now on, women can see me as a real human being, instead of a high-ranking corporate executive who can make them big shots, too."

I told him that I could see how that might be a relief. His wife at that time was named Charlotte, so I asked him how Charlotte was taking things.

"She is what I am talking about," he said. "She didn't marry Felix Waltz. She married the president of the National Broadcasting Company."

I had never met Charlotte. She had sounded nice enough, the few times I had talked to her on the phone—maybe just a touch insincere. She was trying to treat me like family, I guess. She thought she had to be warm, no matter what I really was. I don't know whether she ever found out I was a murderer.

But now Felix was saying that she was insane.

"That's putting it a little strong, I expect," I said.

It turned out that Charlotte was so mad at him that she had cut all the buttons off his clothes—every coat, every suit, every shirt, every pair of pajamas. Then she had thrown all the buttons down the incinerator.

People can sure get mad at each other. They are liable to do anything.

"What's Mom's reaction?" he said.

"She hasn't heard yet," I said. "I guess it'll be in the paper in the morning."

"Tell her I've never been happier," he said.

"Okay," I said.

"She's going to take it pretty hard, I guess," he said.

"Not as hard as she might have a few months ago," I said. "She's got some exciting problems of her own, for a change."

"She's sick?" he said.

"No, no, no," I said. Of course, she was sick, but I had no way of knowing that. "She's been appointed to the board of directors of the new arts center—"

"You told me," he said. "That was certainly very nice of Fred T. Barry to appoint her."

"Well—now she's fighting him tooth and nail about modern art," I said. "She's raising hell about the first two works of art he's bought, even though he paid for them with his own money."

"That doesn't sound like Mother," said Felix.

"One of them's a statue by Henry Moore—" I said.

"The English sculptor?" said Felix.

"Right. And the other one is a painting by somebody named Rabo Karabekian," I said. "The statue is already in the sculpture garden, and Mother says it's nothing but a figure eight on its side. The picture is supposed to go up just inside the front door, so it's the first thing you see when you come in. It's green. It's about the size of a barn door. It has one vertical orange stripe, and it's called 'The Temptation of Saint Anthony.' Mother wrote a letter to the paper, saying the picture was an insult to the memory of Father, and to the memory of every serious artist who ever lived."

The telephone went dead. I will never know why. It was nothing I did on my end. It could have been caused by something the mouse on my end did. The mouse had gone away. It could have been fooling with the telephone wires in the wall. Or maybe, in the basement of my brother's building in New York City, somebody was putting a tap on his line. Maybe a private detective, working for his wife, wanted to get the goods on him—to be used in a divorce action later on. Anything is possible.

Then the telephone came alive again. Felix was talking about coming home to Midland City to rediscover his roots. He said the exact opposite of what Bunny Hoover had said to me. He said that everybody in New York City was phony, and that it was the people of Midland City who were real. He named a lot of friends from high school. He was going to drink beer with them and go hunting with them.

He mentioned some girls, too. It wasn't quite clear what he could do with them, since they were all married, and had children, or had left town. But he didn't mention Celia Hoover, and I didn't remind him of her—didn't tell him that she had become a crazy old bat, and that she had just taken the drugstore apart.

It's interesting that he didn't mention Celia for this reason: He would later declare, under the influence of drugs a doctor had prescribed for him, that she was the only woman he had ever loved, and that he should have married her.

Celia was dead by then.

# 24

I WOULD BE GLAD to attempt a detailed analysis of Celia Hoover's character, if I thought her character had much of anything to do with her suicide by Drāno. As a pharmacist, though, I see no reason not to give full credit to amphetamine.

Here is the warning which the law requires as a companion now for each shipment of amphetamine as it leaves the factory:

"Amphetamine has been extensively abused. Tolerance, extreme psychological dependence, and severe social disability have occurred. There are reports of patients who have increased dosages to many times that recommended. Abrupt cessation following prolonged high dosage results in extreme fatigue and mental depression; changes are also noted in the sleep EEG.

"Manifestations of chronic intoxication with amphetamine include severe dermatoses, marked insomnia, irritability, hyperactivity, and personality changes. The most severe manifestation of chronic intoxication is psychosis, often indistinguishable from schizophrenia."

Want some?

•  •  •

The late twentieth century will go down in history, I'm sure, as an era of pharmaceutical buffoonery. My own brother came home from New York City—bombed on Darvon and Ritalin and methaqualone and Valium, and God only knows what all. He had prescriptions for every bit of it. He said he was home to discover his roots, but, after I heard about all the pills he was taking, I thought he would be lucky to find his own behind with both hands. I thought it was a miracle that he had even found the right exit off the Interstate.

As it was, he had an accident on his way home—in a brand new white Rolls-Royce convertible. The car itself was drug-inspired madness. The day after he was fired and his fourth wife walked out on him, he bought a seventy-thousand-dollar motorcar.

He loaded it up like a truck with his buttonless wardrobe, and took off for Midland City. And when he first got home, his conversation, if you could call it that, was repetitious, obsessed. There were only two things he wanted to do: One was to find his roots, and the other was to find some woman who would sew all his buttons back on. The only buttons he had were on the clothes on his back. He had been particularly vulnerable to an attack on his buttons, too, since his suits and coats were made in London, with buttons instead of zippers on their flies, and with buttons at the wrists which actually buttoned and unbuttoned. He put on one of his buttonless coats for Mother and me, and those floppy cuffs made him look like a pirate in *Peter Pan*.

•  •  •

There was a big dent in the left front fender of that brand new Rolls-Royce, and a crease and a sort of chalky blue stripe that ran back from the dent and across the left-hand door. Felix had sideswiped something blue, and he was as curious about what it might have been as we were.

It remains a mystery to the present day, although Felix, I am happy to say, is now drug free, except for alcohol and caffeine, which he uses in moderation. He remembers proposing marriage to a girl he picked up at a tollbooth on the Ohio Turnpike. "She bailed out in downtown Mansfield," he said the other night. He had swung off the turnpike and into Mansfield, to buy her a color television set or a stereo or anything she wanted, as proof of how much he liked her.

"That could have been where I got the dent," he said.

He was able to identify the drug which had made him so brainlessly ardent, too. "Methaqualone," he said.

•  •  •

I think now about all the little shitbox houses I have driven by in my life, and that all Americans have driven by in their lives—shitbox houses with very expensive cars in the driveway, and maybe even a yacht on a trailer, too. And suddenly there was Mother's and my little shitbox, with a new Mercedes under the carport, and a new Rolls-Royce convertible on the front lawn. That was where Felix first parked his car when he got home—on the lawn. We were lucky he didn't take down the post lantern, and half the shrubbery, too.

So in he came, saying, "The prodigal son is home! Kill the fatted calf!" and so on. Mother and I had known he was coming, but we hadn't known exactly when. We were all dressed up, and about to go out, and were going to leave the side door unlocked for him.

I was wearing my best suit, which was as tight as the skin of a knackwurst. I had put on a lot of weight recently. It was the fault of my own good cooking. I had been trying out a lot of new recipes, with considerable success. And Mother, who hadn't put on an ounce in fifty years, was wearing the black dress Felix had bought her for Father's funeral.

"Where do you two think you're going?" said Felix.

So Mother told him. "We're going to Celia Hoover's funeral," she said.

That was the first Felix had heard that his date for the senior prom was no longer among the living. The last he had seen of her, she had been running away from him barefoot, and into a vacant lot—at night.

If he was going to catch her now, he would have to go wherever it was that the dead people went.

•  •  •

That would make a good scene in a movie: Felix in heaven, wearing a tuxedo for the senior prom carrying Celia's golden slippers, and calling out over and over again, "Celia! Celia! Where are you? I have your dancing shoes."

•  •  •

So nothing would do but that Felix come to the funeral with us. Methaqualone had persuaded him that he and Celia had been high school sweethearts, and that he should have married her. "She was what I was looking for all the time, and I never even realized it," he said.

I think now that Mother and I should have driven him to the County Hospital for detoxification. But we got into his car with him, and told him where the funeral was. The top was down, which was no way to go to a funeral, and Felix himself was a mess. His necktie was askew, and his shirt was filthy, and he had a two-day growth of beard. He had found time to buy a Rolls-Royce, but it hadn't occurred to him that he might have bought some new shirts with buttons, too. He wasn't going to have another shirt with buttons until he could find some woman who would sew all his buttons on.

• • •

Off we went to the First Methodist Church, with Felix at the wheel and Mother in the back seat. As luck would have it, Felix almost closed the peephole of his first wife, Donna, as she was getting out of her Thunderbird in front of her twin sister's house on Arsenal Avenue. It would have been her fault, if she had died, since she didn't look to see what was coming before she disembarked on the driver's side. But it would have made for an ugly case in court, since Felix had already put her through a windshield once, and he was still paying her a lot of alimony, and the business about all the pills he was taking would have come out, and so on. Worst of all, as far as a jury was concerned, I'm sure, would have been the fact that he was a bloated plutocrat in a Rolls-Royce.

Felix didn't even recognize her, and I don't think she recognized him, either. When I told him who it was he had almost hit, he spoke of her most unkindly. He recalled that her scalp was crisscrossed with scars, because of her trip through the windshield. When he used to run his fingers through her hair, he would encounter those scars, and he would get this crazy idea that he was a quarterback. "I would look downfield for an end who was open for a forward pass," he said.

• • •

It was at the church, though, that Felix and his good friend methaqualone became embarrassing. We got there late, so we had to sit toward the back, where those least concerned with the deceased should have been sitting anyway. If we were going to make any disturbance, people would have to swivel around in their pews to see who we were.

The service started quietly enough. I heard only one person crying, and she was way up front, and I think it was Lottie Davis, the Hoovers' black maid. She and Dwayne were the only people there to do a whole lot of crying, since practically nobody else had seen Celia for seven years—since she had starred in *Katmandu*.

Her son wasn't there.

Her doctor wasn't there.

Both her parents were dead, and all her brothers and sisters had drifted off to God-knows-where. One brother, I know, was killed in the Korean War. And somebody swore, I remember, that he had seen her sister Shirley as an extra in the remake of the movie *King Kong*. Maybe so.

There were maybe two hundred mourners there. Most of them were employees and friends and customers and suppliers of Dwayne's. The word was all over town of how in need of support he was, of how vocally ashamed he was to have been such a bad husband that his wife had committed suicide. He had been quoted to me as having made a public announcement in the Tally-ho Room of the new Holiday Inn, the day after Celia killed herself: "I take half the blame, but the other half goes to that son-of-bitching Doctor Jerry Mitchell. Watch out for the pills your doctor tells your wife to take. That's all I've got to say."

● ● ●

It must have been a startling scene. From five until six thirty or so every weekday night, the Tally-ho Room, the cocktail lounge, was a plenary session of the oligarchy of Midland City. A few powerful people, most notably Fred T. Barry, were involved in planetary games, so that the deliberations at the Tally-ho Room were beneath their notice. But anyone doing big business or hoping to do big business strictly within the county was foolish not to show his face there at least once a week, if only to drink a glass of ginger ale. The Tally-ho Room did a very big trade in ginger ale.

Dwayne owned a piece of the new Holiday Inn, incidentally. His automobile dealership was right next door, on the same continuous sheet of blacktop. And the Tally-ho Room was where his disinherited son, Bunny, played the piano. The story was that Bunny applied for the job there, and the manager of the Inn asked Dwayne how he felt about it, and Dwayne said he had never heard of Bunny, so he did not care if the Inn hired him or not, as long as he could play the piano.

And then Dwayne added, supposedly, that he himself hated piano music, since it interfered with conversation. All he asked was that there be no piano playing until eight o'clock at night. That way, although he did not say so, Dwayne Hoover would never have to lay eyes on his disgraceful son.

•   •   •

I daydreamed at Celia's funeral. There was no reason to expect that anything truly exciting or consoling would be said. Not even the minister, the Reverend Charles Harrell, believed in heaven or hell. Not even the minister thought that every life had a meaning, and that every death could startle us into learning something important, and so on. The corpse was a mediocrity who had broken down after a while. The mourners were mediocrities who would break down after a while.

The city itself was breaking down. Its center was already dead. Everybody shopped at the outlying malls. Heavy industry had gone bust. People were moving away.

The planet itself was breaking down. It was going to blow itself up sooner or later anyway, if it didn't poison itself first. In a manner of speaking, it was already eating Drāno.

There in the back of the church, I daydreamed a theory of what life was all about. I told myself that Mother and Felix and the Reverend Harrell and Dwayne Hoover and so on were cells in what was supposed to be one great big animal. There was no reason to take us seriously as individuals. Celia in her casket there, all shot through with Drāno and amphetamine, might have been a dead cell sloughed off by a pancreas the size of the Milky Way.

How comical that I, a single cell, should take my life so seriously!

I found myself smiling at a funeral.

I stopped smiling. I glanced around to see if anyone had noticed. One person had. He was at the other end of our pew, and he did not look away when I caught him gazing at me. He went right on gazing, and it was I who faced forward again. I had not recognized him. He was wearing large sunglasses with mirrored lenses. He could have been anyone.

•   •   •

But then I became the center of attention for the full congregation, for Reverend Harrell had mentioned my name. He was talking about Rudy Waltz. I was Rudy Waltz. To whoever might be watching our insignificant lives under an electron microscope: We cells have names, and, if we know little else, we know our names.

Reverend Harrell told the congregation of the six weeks when he and the late Celia Hoover, née Hildreth, and the playwright Rudy Waltz had known blissful unselfishness which could serve as a good example for the rest of the world. He was talking about the local production of *Katmandu*. He had played the part of John Fortune, the Ohio pilgrim to nowhere, and Celia had played the ghost of his wife. He was a gifted actor. He resembled a lion.

For all I know, Celia may have fallen in love with him. For all I know, Celia may have fallen in love with me. In any case, the Reverend and I were clearly unavailable.

As only a gifted actor could, the Reverend made the Mask and Wig Club's production of *Katmandu*, and especially Celia's performance, sound as though it had enriched lives all over town. My own calculation is that people were as moved by the play as they might have been by a good game of basketball. The auditorium was a nice enough place to be that night.

• • •

Reverend Harrell said it was sad that Celia had not lived to see the completion of the Mildred Barry Memorial Center for the Arts in Sugar Creek, but that her performance in *Katmandu* was proof that the arts were important in Midland City before the center was built.

He declared that the most important arts centers a city could have were human beings, not buildings. He called attention to me again. "There in the back sits an arts center named 'Rudy Waltz,'" he said.

It was then that Felix and his friend methaqualone began wailing. Felix was as loud as a fire engine, and he could not stop.

# 25

THERE WAS JUST a prayer and some music after that, thank God, and then the recessional, with the pallbearers wheeling the casket out to the hearse. Otherwise, Felix's sobbing could have wrecked the funeral. Mother and I gave up on going to the burial. We had no thought but to get Felix out of the church and into the County Hospital. It was all we could do not to get out ahead of the casket.

We had come late, so we were parked fairly far out on the parking lot, and there were a number of neighborhood children paying their respects to the Rolls-Royce. They had never seen one before, I'm sure, but they knew what it was. They were so reverent, that they might have been attending an open-casket funeral right there in the parking lot.

Celia Hoover's casket, by the way, was closed. That must have been because of the Drāno.

We got Felix into the back seat without any trouble. He sat there with the top down, sobbing away. I think we could have sent him up a tree, and he would have been up among the branches and birds' nests, sobbing away.

But he wouldn't give us the keys. The keys were too materialistic a concern for him to consider at such a time. So I had to go through his pockets, while Mother told me to hurry up, hurry up. I happened to glance in the direction of the church, and I saw that Dwayne Hoover, maybe having told everybody to stay behind, that he had some private business with Felix to conduct, was coming in our direction.

He might have been expected to remain close to the hearse, and to duck curious and possibly accusing eyes by getting into the undertaker's Cadillac limousine behind it. But, no—he was going to trudge fifty yards out into the parking lot instead, and we were the only people out there, since we had fled the church so quickly. So it was like a scene in a cowboy movie, with the townspeople all huddled together, and with a half-broken, tragic, great big man going to meet destiny all alone.

The hearse could wait.

He had business to settle first.

· · ·

If this confrontation scene were done as a playlet, the set could be very simple. A curb along the back of the stage might indicate the edge of a parking lot. A Rolls-Royce with its top down, which is the expensive part, could be parked next to that, aimed left. Flats behind the curb could be painted with trees and shrubbery. A tasteful wooden sign might make the location more specific, saying:

FIRST METHODIST CHURCH
VISITORS' PARKING
ALL PERSONS WELCOME.

Felix would be sobbing in the back seat of the Rolls-Royce. Mother, whose name was Emma, and I, whose name is Rudy, would be between the convertible and the audience. Emma would have the heebie-jeebies, wanting to get out of there, and Rudy would be frisking Felix for the keys.

FELIX: Who cares about the keys?
EMMA: Hurry up—oh, please hurry up.
RUDY: How many pockets can they put in a London suit? God damn it, Felix.
FELIX: You're making me sorry I came home.
EMMA: I could die.
FELIX: I loved her so much.
RUDY: Did you ever!

(RUDY *happens to look in the direction of the church, off right, and is appalled to see* DWAYNE *approaching.*)

RUDY: Oh, my God.
FELIX: Pray for her. That's what I'm going to do.
RUDY: *Felix*—get out of the car.
EMMA: Let him stay there. Get him to hunker down.
RUDY: Mother—look behind you. Here comes Dwayne.
(EMMA *looks, hates what she sees.*)

EMMA: Oh. You'd think he'd stay with the body.

RUDY: Felix—get out of the car, because I think somebody just might want to beat the shit out of you.

FELIX: I just got home.

RUDY: I'm not kidding. Here comes Dwayne. He beat the shit out of Doctor Mitchell a week ago. This could be your turn.

FELIX: I've got to fight him?

RUDY: Get out of the car and run!

(FELIX *gets out of the car, muttering and complaining. His tears have abated some. The danger is so unreal to him that he doesn't even look to see where the danger may be coming from. He is distracted by the dent and scratch on the side of the car as* DWAYNE *enters right and stops.*)

FELIX: Oh, look at that. What a shame.

DWAYNE: It really is—a beautiful machine like that.

(FELIX *straightens up and turns to look at him.*)

FELIX: Hello. You're the husband.

DWAYNE: Where do you fit in?

FELIX: What?

DWAYNE: I'm the husband, and I never felt worse in my life—but I couldn't cry the way you cried. I never heard anybody cry like you did, male or female. Where do you fit in?

FELIX: We were sweethearts in high school.

(*As* DWAYNE *thinks this over,* FELIX *takes a bottle of pills from a pocket and starts to open it.*)

EMMA: No more pills!

RUDY: My brother isn't well.

EMMA: He's insane—and I used to be so proud of him.

DWAYNE: I'd be sorry to believe he was crazy. I'm hoping he was crying because he was sane.

EMMA: He can't fight. He never could.

RUDY: We're on our way to the hospital.

FELIX: Just a damn minute here. I was crying because I'm sane. I'm the sanest person in this whole shit-storm! What the hell's going on?

EMMA: Go ahead and get your brains beat out.

FELIX: You must be the worst mother a person ever had.

EMMA: I never disgraced myself and my family in public, I'll tell you that.

FELIX: You never sewed on a button, either. You never hugged or kissed me.

EMMA: Who could blame me?

FELIX: You never did anything a mother's supposed to do.

DWAYNE: Just tell me more about why you cried!

FELIX: We were raised by servants—do you know that? This lady here ought to get switches and coal every Mother's Day! My brother and I know so much about black people and so little about white people, we should be in a minstrel show.

DWAYNE: He really is crazy, isn't he?

FELIX: Amos 'n' Andy.

EMMA: I have never been so humiliated in my life, and as a younger woman I have traveled all over this world.

DWAYNE: At least you never had a wife commit suicide. Or a husband.

EMMA: I know you've been through so much, and then all this on top of it.

DWAYNE: I don't know what part of the world you could have visited, where having the person you were married to commit suicide wasn't the most humiliating thing that could happen.

EMMA: You go back to your friends. And again, I'm so ashamed of my son, I wish he were dead. Go back to your friends.

DWAYNE: Those people back there? You know something? I think maybe I would have come walking out here alone, even if you hadn't been out here. If you hadn't given me a logical place to stop, I might have kept walking until I was in Katmandu. I'm the only person in town who hasn't been to Katmandu. My dentist's been to Katmandu.

EMMA: You go to Herb Stacks, too?

DWAYNE: Sure. Celia, too—or used to.

EMMA: I wonder why we never met there?

FELIX: Because he uses Gleem toothpaste with Fluoristan.

EMMA: I can't be responsible for what he says. I can't imagine how he got control of an entire major television network.

DWAYNE: Celia never told me that you and she were sweethearts. That was her big complaint right up to the end, you know—that nobody had ever loved her, so why should she even go to the dentist anymore?

EMMA: Radio, too. He was also in charge of radio.

FELIX: You're interrupting an important conversation—as usual. Mr. Hoover—yes, Celia and I were not only sweethearts in high school, but I realized there in church that she was the only woman I had ever loved, and maybe the only woman I will ever love. I hope I have not offended you.

DWAYNE: I'm glad. I may not look glad, but I am glad. They're going to honk the horn of the hearse any minute— to tell me to hurry up, that the cemetery's about to close. She was like this Rolls-Royce here, you know?

FELIX: The most beautiful woman I ever knew. No offense, no offense.

DWAYNE: No offense. Anybody who wants to can say she was the most beautiful woman he ever saw. You should have married her, not me.

FELIX: I wasn't worthy of her. Look at the dent I put in the Rolls-Royce.

DWAYNE: You scraped up against something blue.

FELIX: Listen. She lasted a lot longer with you than she would have lasted with me. I'm one of the worst husbands there ever was.

DWAYNE: Not as bad as me. I just ran away from her, she was so unhappy, and I didn't know what to do about it—and there wasn't anybody else to take her off my hands. I'm good for selling cars. I can really sell cars. I can fix cars. I can really fix cars. But I sure couldn't fix that woman. Never even knew where to get the tools. I put her up on blocks and forgot her. I only wish you'd come along in time to rescue the both of us. But you did me a big favor today.

At least I don't have to think my poor wife went all the way through life without finding out what love was.

FELIX: Where am I? What have I said? What have I done?

DWAYNE: You come on along to the cemetery. I don't care if you're crazy or not. You'll make this automobile dealer feel a little bit better, if you'll just cry some more—while we put my poor wife in the ground.

(*Curtain.*)

# 26

W E ALL SEE our lives as stories, it seems to me, and I am convinced that psychologists and sociologists and historians and so on would find it useful to acknowledge that. If a person survives an ordinary span of sixty years or more, there is every chance that his or her life as a shapely story has ended, and all that remains to be experienced is epilogue. Life is not over, but the story is.

Some people, of course, find inhabiting an epilogue so uncongenial that they commit suicide. Ernest Hemingway comes to mind. Celia Hoover, née Hildreth, comes to mind.

My own father's story ended, it seems to me, and it must have seemed to him, when he took all the blame for my having shot Eloise Metzger—and then the police threw him down the iron staircase. He could not be an artist, and he could not be a soldier—but he could at least be heroically honorable and truthful, should an opportunity to be so present itself.

That was the story of his life which he carried in his head.

The opportunity presented itself. He was heroically honorable and truthful. He was thrown down the staircase—like so much garbage.

It was then that these words should have appeared somewhere:

THE END.

But they didn't. But his life as a story was over anyway. The remaining years were epilogue—a sort of junk shop of events which were nothing more than random curiosities, boxes and bins of whatchamacallits.

This could be true of nations, too. Nations might think of themselves as stories, and the stories end, but life goes on. Maybe my own country's life as a story ended after the Second World War, when it was the richest and most powerful nation on earth, when it was going to ensure peace and justice everywhere, since it alone had the atom bomb.

THE END.

534

Felix likes this theory a lot. He says that his own life as a story ended when he was made president of the National Broadcasting Company, and was celebrated as one of the ten best-dressed men in the country.

### THE END.

He says, though, that his epilogue rather than his story has been the best part of his life. This must often be the case.

Bernard Ketchum told us about one of Plato's dialogues, in which an old man is asked how it felt not to be excited by sex anymore. The old man replies that it was like being allowed to dismount from a wild horse.

Felix says that that was certainly how he felt when he was canned by NBC.

•   •   •

It may be a bad thing that so many people try to make good stories out of their lives. A story, after all, is as artificial as a mechanical bucking bronco in a drinking establishment.

And it may be even worse for nations to try to be characters in stories.

Perhaps these words should be carved over doorways of the United Nations and all sorts of parliaments, big and small: LEAVE YOUR STORY OUTSIDE.

•   •   •

I got off the wild horse of my own life story at Celia Hoover's funeral, I think—when Reverend Harrell forgave me in public for having shot Eloise Metzger so long ago. If it wasn't then, it was only a couple of years after that, when Mother was finally killed by the radioactive mantelpiece.

I had paid her back as best I could for ruining her life and Father's. She was no longer in need of personal services. The case was closed.

•   •   •

We probably never would have found out that it was the mantelpiece that killed her, if it weren't for an art historian from Ohio University over at Athens. His name was Cliff McCarthy. He was a painter, too. And Cliff McCarthy never would have got involved in our lives, if it hadn't been for all the publicity Mother received for objecting to the kind of art Fred T. Barry was buying for the arts center. He read about her in *People* magazine. Then again, Mother almost certainly wouldn't have become so passionate about taking Fred T. Barry on in the first place, if it hadn't been for little tumors in her brain, which had been caused by the radioactive mantelpiece.

Wheels within wheels!

*People* magazine described Mother as the widow of an Ohio painter. Cliff McCarthy had been working for years, financed by a Cleveland philanthropist, on a book which was to include every serious Ohio painter, but he had never heard of Father. So he visited our little shitbox, and he photographed Father's unfinished painting over the fireplace. That was all there was to photograph, so he took several exposures of that with a big camera on a tripod. He was being polite, I guess.

But the camera used flat packs of four-by-five film, and he had exposed some of it elsewhere, so he got several packs out of his camera bag.

He accidentally left one behind—on the mantelpiece. One week later he swung off the Interstate, on his way to someplace else, and he picked up the pack.

Three days after that, he called me on the telephone to say that the film in the pack had all turned black, and that a friend of his who taught physics had offered the opinion that the film had been close to something which was highly radioactive.

●   ●   ●

He gave me another piece of news on the telephone, too. He had been looking at a diary kept by the great Ohio painter Frank Duveneck at the end of his life. He died in 1919, at the age of seventy-one. Duveneck spent his most productive years in Europe, but he returned to his native Cincinnati after his wife died in Florence, Italy.

"Your father is in the diary!" said McCarthy. "Duveneck heard about this wonderful studio a young painter was building in Midland City, and on March 16, 1915, he went and had a look at it."

"What did he say?" I asked.

"He said it was certainly a beautiful studio, such as any artist in the world would have given his eyeteeth to have."

"I mean, what did he say about Father?" I said.

"He liked him, I think," said McCarthy.

"Look," I said, "—I'm aware that my father was a fraud, and Father knew it, too. Duveneck was probably the only really important painter who ever saw Father's masquerade. No matter how cutting it is, please tell me what Duveneck said."

"Well—I'll read it to you," said McCarthy, and he did: "'Otto Waltz should be shot. He should be shot for seeming to prove the last thing that needs to be proved in this part of the world: that an artist is a person of no consequence.'"

• • •

I asked around about who was in charge of civil defense. I hoped that whoever it was would have a Geiger counter, or some other method of measuring radioactivity. It turned out that the director of civil defense for the county was Lowell Ulm, who owned the car wash on the Shepherdstown Turnpike by the airport. He was who you were supposed to call in case of World War Three. He did have a Geiger counter.

So he came over after work. He had to go home for the Geiger counter first. That innocent-looking mantelpiece, before which Mother had spent so many hours, either gazing into the flames or up at Father's unfinished painting, was a killer. Lowell Ulm said this: "Jesus Christ! This thing is hotter than a Hiroshima baby carriage!"

• • •

Mother and I were moved into the new Holiday Inn, while workmen dressed like astronauts on the moon performed radical surgery on our little Avondale shitbox. The irony was, of course, that, if Mother had been a typical mother, out in the kitchen or down in the basement or out shopping most of the time, and if I had been a typical son, waiting to be fed, and lounging around the living room, I would have been the one to get the fatal dose of radiation.

At least Gino and Marco Maritimo were both dead by then, presumably feeling nothing. They would have been heartsick to learn that the house which they had practically given to us was so dangerous. Marco had his peephole closed by natural causes about a month before Celia Hoover's funeral, and then Gino was killed in a freak accident at the arts center a few months after that. He was trying to get the center's drawbridge to work right, with the dedication ceremonies only a week away, and he was electrocuted. Two people died during the construction of the Mildred Barry Memorial Center for the Arts.

I have no idea how many people were killed during the construction of the Taj Mahal. Hundreds upon hundreds, probably. Beauty seldom comes cheap.

•   •   •

But Gino and Marco's sons certainly took the mantelpiece seriously. They were as embarrassed as their fathers would have been, and they told us a lot more than they should have, since Felix and I would eventually decide to sue their corporation and a lot of other people by and by. The mantelpiece, they told us, came from a scrap heap in weeds back of an ornamental concrete company outside of Cincinnati. Old Gino had found it there, and couldn't see anything wrong with it, and had bought it cheap for the model house, which became our house, at Avondale.

With a lot of luck, and the help of a few honest people, we were able to trace the cement that went into the mantelpiece all the way back to Oak Ridge, Tennessee, where pure uranium 235 was produced for the bomb they dropped on Hiroshima in 1945. The government somehow allowed that cement to be sold off as war surplus, even though many people had known how hot it was.

In this case, the government was about as careless as a half-wit boy up in a cupola with a loaded Springfield rifle—on Mother's Day.

•   •   •

When Mother and I moved back into our little shitbox, we didn't have a fireplace anymore. We had been away for only twenty-four hours, but a Sheetrock wall had replaced the fireplace, and the whole living room had been repainted. The Maritimo Brothers Construction Company had done all that at their own expense. It wasn't even possible to tell that we had once had a fireplace.

Felix wasn't around to see the transformation. He had taken a job under an assumed name, although his employers knew who he really was, or who he really had been, as an announcer on a radio station in South Bend, Indiana. This wasn't a humiliation. It was what he wanted to do, what he said he had been born to do. He was drug free. We were so proud of him.

•   •   •

Mother said a significant thing when she saw we didn't have a fireplace anymore. "Oh, dear—I don't know if I want to go on living without a fireplace."

"What part of her life," you might ask, "was story, and what part was epilogue?" I think her case was similar to Father's, in that, by the time my brother and I came along, there was nothing left but epilogue. The circumstances of her early life virtually decreed that she live only a pipsqueak story, which was over only a few moments after it had begun. She had nothing to atone for, for example, since she was never tempted to do anything bad in the first place. And she wasn't going to go seeking any kind of Holy Grail, since that was clearly a man's job, and she already had a cup that overflowed and overflowed with good things to eat and drink anyway.

I suppose that's really what so many American women are complaining about these days: They find their lives short on story and overburdened with epilogue.

Mother's story ended when she married the handsomest rich man in town.

M OTHER SAID that thing about not knowing if she wanted to go on living, if she couldn't have a fireplace—and then the telephone rang. Mother answered. I used to be the one to answer the telephone, but now she always beat me to it. Almost every call was thrillingly for her, since she had become the local Saint Joan of Arc in a holy war against nonrepresentational art.

A year had passed since the dedication of the Mildred Barry Memorial Center for the Arts, with speeches and performances by noted creative persons from all over the country. Now it was virtually as empty and unvisited as the old Sears, Roebuck downtown, or the railroad station, where the Monon and New York Central railroads used to intersect, but which didn't even have tracks anymore.

Mother had been bounced off the board of directors of the center, for her disruptive behavior at meetings, and for her unfriendly comments on the center in the press and before church groups and garden clubs and so on. She was much in demand as a sparkling, prickly public speaker. Fred T. Barry, for his part, had become as silent as the center itself. I saw his Lincoln limousine a couple of times, but the back windows were opaque, so I have no idea whether he was in there or not. I would see his company jet parked out at the airport sometimes, but never him. I expected to hear news of Mr. Barry from time to time, as in the past, from employees of his who happened into the drugstore. But then it became evident that Mr. Barry's employees were boycotting Schramm's Drugstore, both night and day, because my mother's younger son was an employee there.

So it was a surprise that Mother now found herself talking on the telephone to none other than Fred T. Barry. He hoped, with all possible courtliness, that Mother would be home during the next hour, and willing to receive him. He had never been in our little shitbox before. I doubt, in fact, that he had ever before been in Avondale.

Mother told him to come ahead. Those were her exact words, delivered in the flat tones of someone who had never lost a fight: "Come ahead, if you want to."

•    •    •

Mother and I had not yet begun to speculate seriously about what the radioactive mantelpiece might have done to our health, nor had we been encouraged to do so. Nor would we ever be encouraged to do so. Ulm, the director of civil defense and car-wash tycoon, had been getting advice on our case over the telephone from somebody at the Nuclear Regulatory Commission in Washington, D.C., to the effect that the most important thing was that nobody panic. In order to prevent panic, the workmen who had torn out our fireplace, wearing protective clothing provided by Ulm, had been sworn to secrecy—in the name of patriotism, of national security.

The cover story, provided by Washington, D.C., and spread throughout Avondale while Mother and I were staying at the new Holiday Inn, was that our house had been riddled by termites, and that the protective clothing was necessary, since the workmen had killed the insects with cyanide.

Insects.

So we did not panic. Good citizens don't. We waited calmly for Fred T. Barry. I was at the picture window, peering out at the street between slats of the Venetian blinds. Mother was reclining in the Barcalounger my brother Felix had given her three Christmases ago. She was vibrating almost imperceptibly, and a reassuring drone came from underneath her. She had the massage motor turned on low.

Mother said that she didn't feel any different, now that she knew she had been exposed to radioactivity. "Do you feel any different?" she asked.

"No," I said. This sort of conversation is going to become increasingly common, I think, as radioactive materials get spread around the world.

"If we were in such great danger," she said, "you'd think we would have noticed something. There would have been dead bugs on the mantelpiece, don't you think—or the plants would have gotten funny spots or something?"

Meanwhile, little tumors were blooming in her head.

"I'm so sorry they told the neighbors we had termites," she said. "I wish they could have thought of something else. It's like telling everybody we had leprosy."

It turned out that she had had a traumatic experience with termites in childhood, which she had never mentioned to me. She had suppressed the memory all those years, but now she told me, full of horror, of walking into the music room of her father's mansion, which she had believed to be so indestructible when she was a little girl, and seeing what looked like foam, boiling out the floor and a baseboard near the grand piano, and out of the legs and the keyboard of the piano itself.

"There were billions and billions of bugs with shiny wings, acting for all the world like a liquid," she said. "I ran and got Father. He couldn't believe his eyes, either. Nobody had played the piano for years. If somebody had played it, maybe it would have driven the bugs out of there. Father gave a piano leg a little kick, and it crumpled like it was made out of cardboard. The piano fell down."

•   •   •

This was clearly one of the most memorable events of her whole life, and I had never heard of it before.

If she had died in childhood, she would have remembered life as the place you went, in case you wanted to see bugs eat a grand piano.

•   •   •

So Fred T. Barry arrived in his limousine. He was so old now, and Mother was so old now, and they had had this long fight about whether modern art was any good or not. I let him in, and Mother received him while lying on the Barcalounger.

"I have come to surrender, Mrs. Waltz," he said. "You should be very proud of yourself. I have lost all interest in the arts center. It can be turned into a chicken coop, for all I care. I am leaving Midland City forever."

"I am sure you had the best intentions, Mr. Barry," she said. "I never doubted that. But the next time you try to give somebody a wonderful present, make sure they want it first. Don't try to stuff it down their throats."

He sold his company to the RAMJAC Corporation for a gazoolian bucks. A firm that acquires American farmland for Arabs bought his farm. As far as I know, no Arab has ever come to take a look at it. He himself moved to Hilton Head, South Carolina, and I have heard nothing about him since. He was so bitter that he left no endowment behind to maintain the arts center, and the city was so broke that it could only let the place go to rack and ruin.

And then, one day, there was this flash.

•  •  •

Mother died a year after Fred T. Barry surrendered to her. When she was in the hospital for the last time, she thought she was in a spaceship. She thought I was Father, and that we were headed for Mars, where we were going to have a second honeymoon.

She was as alive as anybody, and utterly mistaken about everything. She wouldn't let go of my hand.

"That picture," she said, and she would smile and give my hand a squeeze. I was supposed to know which of all the pictures in the world she meant. I thought for a while that it was Father's unfinished masterpiece from his misspent youth in Vienna. But in a moment of clarity, she made it clear that it was a scrapbook photograph of her in a rowboat on a small river somewhere, maybe in Europe. Then again, it could have been Sugar Creek. The boat is tied to shore. There aren't any oars in place. She isn't going anywhere. She wears a summer dress and a garden hat. Somebody has persuaded her to pose in the boat, with water around her and dappled with shade. She is laughing. She has just been married, or is about to be married.

She will never be happier. She will never be more beautiful.

Who could have guessed that that young woman would take a rocket-ship trip to Mars someday?

•  •  •

She was seventy-seven when she died, so that all sorts of things, including plain old life, could have closed her peephole. But the autopsy revealed that she had been healthy as a young horse, except for tumors in her head. Tumors of that sort, moreover, could only have been caused by radiation, so Felix and I hired Bernard Ketchum to sue everybody who had bought or sold in any form the radioactive cement from Oak Ridge.

It took a while to win, and I meanwhile kept going to work six nights a week at Schramm's Drugstore, and keeping house in the little shitbox out in Avondale. There isn't all that much difference between keeping house for two and keeping house for one.

My Mercedes continued to give me an indecent amount of pleasure.

At one point there, through a misunderstanding, I was suspected of abducting and murdering a little girl. So the state police scientists impounded the Mercedes, and they went over it inch by inch with fingerprint powder and a vacuum cleaner and so on. When they gave it back to me, along with a clean bill of health, they said they had never seen anything like it. The car was seven years old then, and had over a hundred thousand miles on it, but every hair in it and every fingerprint on it belonged to just one person, the owner.

"You aren't what we would call real sociable," one trooper said. "How come you got a car with four doors?"

•  •  •

Polka-dot brownies: Melt half a cup of butter and a pound of light-brown sugar in a two-quart saucepan. Stir over a low fire until just bubbly. Cool to room temperature. Beat in two eggs and a teaspoon of vanilla. Stir in a cup of sifted flour, a half teaspoon of salt, a cup of chopped filberts, and a cup of semisweet chocolate in small chunks.

Spread into a well-greased nine-by-eleven baking pan. Bake at two hundred and thirty-five degrees for about thirty-five minutes.

Cool to room temperature, and cut into squares with a well-greased knife.

•  •  •

I think I was about as happy as anybody else in Midland City, and maybe in the country, as I waited for all the lawsuits to come to a head. But there you have a problem in relativity again. I continued to be comforted by music of my own making, the scat singing, the brainless inward fusillades of "skeedee wahs"

and "bodey oh dohs," and so on. I had a Blaupunkt FM-AM ste-
reophonic radio in my Mercedes, but I hardly ever turned it on.

As for scat singing: I came across what I consider a most
amusing graffito, written in ball-point pen on tile in the men's
room at Will Fairchild Memorial Airport one morning. It was
dawn, and I was seized by an attack of diarrhea on my way home
from work, just as I was passing the airport. It was caused, I'm
sure, by my having eaten so many polka-dot brownies before
going to work the night before.

So I swung into the airport, and jumped out of my four-door
Mercedes. I didn't expect to get into the building. I just wanted
to get out of sight. But there was another car in the parking lot
at that unlikely hour. So I tried a side door, and it was unlocked.

In I flew, and up to the men's room, noting in flight that
somebody was running a floor-waxing machine. I relieved
myself, and became as calm and respectable as any other citizen
again, or even more so. For a few moments there, I was happier than happy, healthier than healthy, and I saw these words
scrawled on the tiles over a wash basin:

> "To be is to do" — Socrates
> "To do is to be" — Jean-Paul Sartre.
> "Do be do be do" — Frank Sinatra.

# *Epilogue*

I HAVE NOW SEEN with my own eyes what a neutron bomb can do to a small city. I am back at the Hotel Oloffson after three days in my old hometown. Midland City was exactly as I remembered it, except that there were no people living there. The security is excellent. The perimeter of the flash area is marked by a high fence topped with barbed wire, with a watchtower every three hundred yards or so. There is a minefield in front of that, and then a low barbed wire entanglement beyond that, which wouldn't stop a truly determined person, but which is meant as a friendly warning about the mines.

It is possible for a civilian to visit inside the fence only in daylight. After nightfall, the flash area becomes a free-fire zone. Soldiers are under orders to shoot anything that moves, and their weapons are equipped with infrared sights. They can see in the dark.

And in the daytime, the only permissible form of transportation for a civilian inside is a bright purple school bus, driven by a soldier, and with other soldiers aboard as stern and watchful guides. Nobody gets to bring his own car inside or to walk where he likes, even if he has lost his business and all his relatives and everything. It is all government property now. It belongs to all the people, instead of just some of them.

We were a party of four—Felix and myself and Bernard Ketchum, our lawyer, and Hippolyte Paul De Mille, the headwaiter from the Oloffson. Ketchum's wife and Felix's wife had declined to come along. They were afraid of radioactivity, and Felix's wife was especially afraid of it, since she was with child. We were unable to persuade those superstitious souls that the whole beauty of a neutron bomb explosion was that there was no lingering radiation afterwards.

Felix and I had run into the same sort of ignorance when it was time to bury Mother next to Father in Calvary Cemetery. People refused to believe that she herself wasn't radioactive. They were sure that she would make all the other bodies glow in the dark, and that she would seep into the water supply and so on.

For Mother to be personally radioactive, she would have had to bite a piece out of the mantelpiece, and then fail to excrete it. If she had done that, it's true, she would have been a holy terror for twenty thousand years or more.

But she didn't.

·   ·   ·

We brought old Hippolyte Paul De Mille along, who had never been outside Haiti before, on the pretext that he was the brother of a Haitian cook for Dr. Alan Maritimo, the veterinarian, and his wife. Alan was a maverick in the Maritimo family, who had declined to go into the building business. His entire household was killed by the flash. Ketchum had put together fake affidavits which entitled Hippolyte Paul to pass through the gate in a purple school bus with the rest of us.

We went to this trouble for Hippolyte Paul because he was our most valuable employee. Without him and his goodwill, the Grand Hotel Oloffson would have been a worthless husk. It was worth our while to keep him happy.

But Hippolyte Paul, in his excitement about the trip, had volunteered to make us a highly specific gift, which we intended to refuse politely at the proper time. He said that if there was any ghost we thought should haunt Midland City for the next few hundred years, he would raise it from its grave and turn it loose, to wander where it would.

We tried very hard not to believe that he could do that.

But he could, he could.

Amazing.

·   ·   ·

There was no odor. We expected a lot of odor, but there was none. Army engineers had buried all the dead under the block-square municipal parking lot across the street from police headquarters, where the old courthouse had stood. They had then repaved the lot, and put the dwarf arboretum of parking meters back in place. The whole process had been filmed, we were told—from parking lot to mass grave, and then back to parking lot again.

My brother Felix, in that rumbling voice of his, speculated that a flying saucer might someday land on the mass grave, and conclude that the whole planet was asphalt, and that parking meters were the only living things. We were sitting in a school bus. We weren't allowed to get out at that point.

"Maybe it will look like the Garden of Eden to some bug-eyed monsters," Felix went on. "They will love it. They will crack open the parking meters with the butts of their zap-pistols, and they will feast on all the slugs and beer-can tops and coins."

• • •

We caught sight of several movie crews, and they were given as the reason we weren't to touch anything, even though it might unquestionably have been our own property. It was as though we were in a national park, full of endangered species. We weren't even to pick a little flower to sniff. It might be the very last such flower anywhere.

When our school bus took us to Mother's and my little shit-box out in Avondale, for example, I wandered to the Meekers' house next door. Young Jimmy Meeker's tricycle, with white sidewall tires, was sitting in the driveway, waiting patiently for its master. I put my hand on the seat, meaning to roll it back and forth just a few inches, and to wonder what life in Midland City had been all about.

And such a yell I heard!

Captain Julian Pefko, who was in charge of our party, yelled at me, "Hands in your pockets!" That was one of the rules: Whenever men were outside the school bus, they were to keep their hands in their pockets. Women, if they had pockets, were to do the same. If they didn't have pockets, they were to keep their arms folded across their bosoms. Pefko reminded me that we were under martial law as long as we were inside the fence. "One more dumb trick like that, mister," he told me, "and you're on your way to the stockade. How would you like twenty years on the rockpile?" he said.

"I wouldn't, sir," I said. "I wouldn't like that at all."

And there wasn't any more trouble after that. We certainly all behaved ourselves. You can learn all kinds of habits quickly under martial law.

The reason everything had to be left exactly where it was, of course, was so that camera crews could document, without the least bit of fakery, the fundamental harmlessness of a neutron bomb.

Skeptics would be put to flight, once and for all.

•   •   •

The empty city did not give me the creeps, and Hippolyte Paul actually enjoyed it. He didn't miss the people, since he had no people to miss. Limited to the present tense, he kept exclaiming in Creole, "How rich they are! How rich they are!"

But Felix finally found my serenity something to complain about. "Jesus Christ!" he exploded as our second afternoon in the flash area was ending. "Would you show just a trace of emotion, please?"

So I told him, "This isn't anything I haven't seen on practically every day of my adult life. The sun is setting instead of rising—but otherwise this is what Midland

City always looked like and felt like to me when I locked up Schramm's Drugstore at dawn:

"Everybody has left town but me."

•   •   •

We were allowed into Midland City in order to photograph and make lists of all the items of personal property which were certainly ours, or which might be ours, or which we thought we might inherit, once all the legal technicalities were unscrambled. As I say, we weren't allowed to actually touch anything. The penalty for trying to smuggle anything out of the flash area, no matter how worthless, was twenty years in prison for civilians. For soldiers, the penalty was death.

As I say, the security was quite wonderful, and we heard many visitors who had certainly been more horribly bereaved than we were praise the military for its smart appearance and efficiency. It was almost as though Midland City were at last being run the way it should have been run all along.

But, as we were to discover on the morning of our third and final day, where the minefield outside the fence ended, highly treasonous opinion of the Federal Government began. The farmers on the fringe of the flash area, in the past as politically inert as mastodons, had been turned into bughouse social commentators by the flash.

They had lost their shopping centers, of course.

So Felix and I and Ketchum and Hippolyte Paul were having breakfast at the Quality Motor Court out by Sacred Miracle Cave, where we were staying, and where our purple school bus would pick us up, and two farmers in bib overalls, just like old John Fortune in Katmandu, were passing out leaflets in the coffee shop. The Quality Motor Court was not then under martial law. I understand that all motels within fifty miles of Midland City have now been placed under martial law.

These two said the same thing over and over again as they offered their leaflets: "Read the truth and then write your congressman." About half the customers refused to even look at the leaflets, but we each took one.

The organization which wanted us to write our congressmen, it turned out, was "Farmers of Southwestern Ohio for Nuclear Sanity." They said that it was all well and good that the Federal Government should be making idealistic plans for Midland City, as a haven for refugees from less fortunate countries or whatever. But they also felt that there should be some public discussion, that "the veil of silence should be lifted" from the mystery of how all the previous inhabitants had wound up under the municipal parking lot.

They confessed that they were fighting a losing battle in trying to make anybody outside of southwestern Ohio care what had happened to someplace called "Midland City." As far as the farmers knew, Midland City had never even been mentioned on a major network television show until after the flash. They were wrong about that, incidentally. It was certainly network news during the Blizzard of 1960, but I can't remember any other time. Power went off during the blizzard, so the farmers had no way of knowing that Midland City had finally made the TV.

They missed it!

But that didn't weaken the argument of their leaflet, to wit: that the United States of America was now ruled, evidently, by a small clique of power brokers who believed that most Americans were so boring and ungifted and small time that they could be slain by the tens of thousands without inspiring any long-term regrets on the part of anyone. "They have now proved this with Midland City," said the leaflet, "and who is to say that Terre Haute or Schenectady will not be next?"

That was certainly the most inflammatory of their beliefs— that Midland City had been neutron-bombed on purpose, and not from a truck, but from a missile site or a high-flying airplane. They had hired a mathematician from, they said, "a great university," to make calculations independent of the Government's, as to where the flash had originated. The mathematician could not be named, they said, for fear that retaliatory action would be taken against him, but it was his opinion, based largely on the pattern of livestock deaths on the outer perimeter of the flash, that the center of the flash was near Exit 11 on the Interstate, all right, but at least sixty feet above the pavement. That certainly suggested a package which had arrived by air.

Either that, or a truck had been hauling a neutron bomb in an enormous pop-up toaster.

• • •

Bernard Ketchum asked the farmer who had given us our leaflets to name the clique which had supposedly neutron-bombed Midland City. This was the answer he got: "They don't want us to know their name, so they don't have a name. You can't fight back against something that don't have a name."

"The military-industrial complex?" said Ketchum archly. "The Rockefellers? The international conglomerates? The CIA? The Mafia?"

And the farmer said to him, "You like any of them names? Just help yourself. Maybe that's who it is, maybe it ain't. How's a farmer supposed to find out? It's whoever it was shot President Kennedy and his brother—and Martin Luther King."

So there we had it—the ever-growing ball of American paranoia, the ball of string a hundred miles in diameter, with the unsolved assassination of John F. Kennedy at its core.

"You mention the Rockefellers," said the farmer. "If you ask me, they don't know any more'n I do about who's really running things, what's really going on."

• • •

Ketchum asked him why these nameless, invisible forces would want to depopulate Midland City—and then maybe Terre Haute and Schenectady after that.

"Slavery!" was the farmer's prompt reply.

"I beg your pardon?" said Ketchum.

"They aim to bring slavery back," said the farmer. He wouldn't tell us his name, for fear of reprisals, but I had a hunch he was an Osterman. There were several Ostermans with farms out around Sacred Miracle Cave.

"They never gave up on it," he said. "The Civil War wasn't going to make any difference in the long run, as far as they were concerned. Sooner or later, they knew in their hearts, we'd get back to owning slaves."

Ketchum said jocularly that he could understand the desirability of a slave economy, especially in view of all the trouble so many American industries were having with foreign competition. "But I fail to see the connection between slaves and empty cities," he said.

"What we figure," said the farmer: "These slaves aren't going to be Americans. They're going to come by the boatload from Haiti and Jamaica and places like that, where there's such terrible poverty and overpopulation. They're going to need housing. What's cheaper—to use what we've already got, or to build new?"

He let us think that over for a moment, and then he added, "And guess what? You've seen that fence with the watchtowers. Do you honestly believe that fence is ever coming down?"

• • •

Ketchum said he certainly wished he knew who these sinister forces were.

"I'll make a wild guess," said the farmer, "and you're going to laugh at it, because the people I'll name want to be laughed at until it's too late. They don't want anybody worrying about whether they're taking over the country from top to bottom—until it's too late."

This was his wild guess: "The Ku Klux Klan."

• • •

My own guess is that the American Government had to find out for certain whether the neutron bomb was as harmless as it was supposed to be. So it set one off in a small city which nobody cared about, where people weren't doing all that much with their lives anyhow, where businesses were going under or moving away. The Government couldn't test a bomb on a foreign city, after all, without running the risk of starting World War Three.

There is even a chance that Fred T. Barry, with all his contacts high in the military, could have named Midland City as the ideal place to test a neutron bomb.

•   •   •

At the end of our third day in Midland City, Felix became tearful and risked the displeasure of Captain Julian Pefko by asking him if we could please, on the way to the main gate, have our purple school bus make a slight detour past Calvary Cemetery, so we could visit our parents' grave.

For all his rough and ready manners, Pefko, like so many professional soldiers, turned out to have an almond macaroon for a heart. He agreed.

•   •   •

Almond macaroons: Preheat an oven to three hundred degrees, and work one cup of confectioners' sugar into a cup of almond paste with your fingertips. Add three egg whites, a dash of salt, and a half teaspoon of vanilla.

Fit unglazed paper onto a cookie sheet. Sprinkle with granulated sugar. Force the almond paste mixture through a round pastry tube, so that uniform gobs, nicely spaced, drop onto the glazed paper. Sprinkle with granulated sugar.

Bake about twenty minutes. Tip: Put the sheet of macaroons on a damp cloth, paper side down. This will make it easier to loosen the cookies from the paper.

Cool.

•   •   •

Calvary Cemetery has never been any comfort to me, so I almost stayed in the purple school bus. But then, after all the others had got out, I got out, too—to stretch my legs. I strolled into the old part of the cemetery, which had been all filled up, by and large, before I was born. I stationed myself at the foot of the most imposing monument in the bone orchard, a sixty-two-foot gray marble obelisk with a stone football on top. It celebrated George Hickman Bannister, a seventeen-year-old whose peephole was closed while he was playing high school football on the morning of Thanksgiving in 1924. He was from a poor family, but thousands of people had seen him die, our parents not among them—and many of them had chipped in to buy him the obelisk.

Our parents had no interest in sports.

Maybe twenty feet away from the obelisk was the most fanciful marker in the cemetery, a radial, air-cooled airplane engine reproduced in pink marble, and fitted with a bronze propeller. This was the headstone of Will Fairchild, the World War One ace in the Lafayette Escadrille, after whom the airport was named. He hadn't died in the war. He had crashed and burned, again with thousands watching, in 1922, while stunt flying at the Midland County Fair.

He was the last of the Fairchilds, a pioneering family after which so much in the city was named. He had failed to reproduce before his peephole closed.

Inscribed in the bronze propeller were his name and dates, and the euphemism fliers in the Lafayette Escadrille used for death in an airplane in wartime: "Gone West."

"West," to an American in Europe, of course, meant "home."

Here he was home.

Somewhere near me, I knew, was the headless body of old August Gunther, who had taken Father when a youth to the fanciest whorehouse in the Corn Belt. Shame on him.

I raised my eyes to the horizon, and there, on the other side of shining Sugar Creek, was the white-capped slate roof of my childhood home. In the level rays of the setting sun, it did indeed resemble a postcard picture of Fujiyama, the sacred volcano of Japan.

Felix and Ketchum were at a distance, visiting more contemporary graves. Felix would tell me later that he had managed to maintain his aplomb while visiting Mother and Father, but that he had gone all to pieces when, turning away from their markers, he discovered that he had been standing on Celia Hoover's grave.

Eloise Metzger, the woman I had shot, was also over there somewhere. I had never paid her a call.

I heard my brother go to pieces over Celia Hoover's grave, and I looked in his direction. I saw that Hippolyte Paul De Mille was attempting to cheer him up.

I was not alone, by the way. A soldier with a loaded M-16 was with me, making certain that I kept my hands in my pockets. We weren't even to touch tombstones. And Felix and Hippolyte Paul and Bernard Ketchum also kept their hands in their pockets, no matter how much they might have wanted to gesticulate among the tombstones.

And then Hippolyte Paul De Mille said something to Felix in Creole which was so astonishing, so offensive, that Felix's grief dropped away like an iron mask. Hippolyte Paul had offered to raise the ghost of Celia Hoover from the grave, if Felix would really like to see her again.

There was a clash between two cultures, or I have never seen one.

To Hippolyte Paul, raising a spirit from a grave was the most ordinary sort of favor for a gifted metaphysician to offer a friend. He wasn't proposing to exhume a zombie, a walking corpse with dirt and rags clinging to it, and so on, a clearly malicious thing to do. He simply wanted to give Felix a misty but recognizable ghost to look at, and to talk to, although the ghost would not be able to reply to him, if that might somehow comfort him.

To Felix, it seemed that our Haitian headwaiter was offering to make him insane, for only a lunatic would gladly meet a ghost.

So these two very different sorts of human beings, their hands thrust deep into their pockets, talked past each other in a mixture of English and Creole, while Ketchum and Captain Pefko and a couple of other soldiers looked on.

Hippolyte Paul was at last so deeply hurt that he turned his back on Felix and walked away. He was coming in my direction, and I signaled with my head that he should keep coming, that

I would explain the misunderstanding, that I understood his point of view as well as my brother's, and so on.

If he stayed mad at Felix, there went the Grand Hotel Oloffson.

"She doesn't feel anything. She doesn't know anything," he said to me in Creole. He meant that Celia's ghost wouldn't have caused any embarrassment or inconvenience or discomfort of any sort to Celia herself, who could feel nothing. The ghost would be nothing more than an illusion, based harmlessly on whatever Celia used to be.

"I know. I understand," I said. I explained that Felix had been upset about a lot of things lately, and that Hippolyte Paul would be mistaken to take anything Felix said too much to heart.

Hippolyte Paul nodded uncertainly, but then he brightened. He said that there was surely somebody in the cemetery that I would like to see again.

The soldier guarding us understood none of this, of course.

"You are nice," I said in Creole. "You are too generous, but I am happy as I am."

The old headwaiter was determined to work his miracle, whether we wanted it or not. He argued that we owed it both to the past and to the future to raise some sort of representative ghost which would haunt the city, no matter who lived there, for generations to come.

So, for the sake of the hotel, I told him to go ahead and raise one, but from the part of the cemetery where we stood, where I didn't know anyone.

So he raised the ghost of Will Fairchild. The old barnstormer was wearing goggles and a white silk scarf and a black leather helmet and all, but no parachute.

I remembered what Father had told me about him one time: "Will Fairchild would be alive today, if only he had worn a parachute."

So there was Hippolyte Paul De Mille's gift to whoever was going to inhabit Midland City next: the restless ghost of Will Fairchild.

And I, Rudy Waltz, the William Shakespeare of Midland City, the only serious dramatist ever to live and work there, will now make my own gift to the future, which is a legend.

I have invented an explanation of why Will Fairchild's ghost is likely to be seen roaming almost anywhere in town—in the empty arts center, in the lobby of the bank, out among the little shitboxes of Avondale, out among the luxurious homes of Fairchild Heights, in the vacant lot where the public library stood for so many years. . . .

Will Fairchild is looking for his parachute.

• • •

You want to know something? We are still in the Dark Ages. The Dark Ages—they haven't ended yet.

# GALÁPAGOS

In memory of Hillis L. Howie
(1903–1982), amateur naturalist—
A good man who
took me and my best friend Ben Hitz
and some other boys
out to the American Wild West
from Indianapolis, Indiana,
in the summer of 1938.

Mr. Howie introduced us to real Indians
and had us sleep out of doors every night
and bury our dung,
and he taught us how to ride horses,
and he told us the names of many plants
    and animals,
and what they needed to do
in order to stay alive
and reproduce themselves.

One night Mr. Howie scared us half to death
on purpose,
screaming like a wildcat near our camp.
A real wildcat screamed back.

In spite of everything, I still believe
people are really good at heart.
—*Anne Frank (1929–1944)*

# BOOK ONE

## The Thing Was

# 1

T HE THING WAS:
      One million years ago, back in 1986 A.D., Guayaquil
was the chief seaport of the little South American democracy of Ecuador, whose capital was Quito, high in the Andes
Mountains. Guayaquil was two degrees south of the equator,
the imaginary bellyband of the planet after which the country
itself was named. It was always very hot there, and humid, too,
for the city was built in the doldrums—on a springy marsh
through which the mingled waters of several rivers draining
the mountains flowed.

This seaport was several kilometers from the open sea. Rafts
of vegetable matter often clogged the soupy waters, engulfing
pilings and anchor lines.

. . .

Human beings had much bigger brains back then than they
do today, and so they could be beguiled by mysteries. One such
mystery in 1986 was how so many creatures which could not
swim great distances had reached the Galápagos Islands, an
archipelago of volcanic peaks due west of Guayaquil—separated
from the mainland by one thousand kilometers of very deep
water, very cold water fresh from the Antarctic. When human
beings discovered those islands, there were already geckos and
iguanas and rice rats and lava lizards and spiders and ants and
beetles and grasshoppers and mites and ticks in residence, not
to mention enormous land tortoises.

What form of transportation had they used?

Many people were able to satisfy their big brains with this
answer: They came on natural rafts.

. . .

Other people argued that such rafts became waterlogged and
rotted to pieces so quickly that nobody had ever seen one out of
sight of land, and that the current between the islands and the
mainland would carry any such rustic vessel northward rather
than westward.

Or they asserted that all those landlubberly creatures had walked dry-shod across a natural bridge or had swum short distances between stepping-stones, and that one such formation or another had since disappeared beneath the waves. But scientists using their big brains and cunning instruments had by 1986 made maps of the ocean floor. There wasn't a trace, they said, of an intervening land mass of any kind.

•   •   •

Other people back in that era of big brains and fancy thinking asserted that the islands had once been part of the mainland, and had been split off by some stupendous catastrophe.

But the islands didn't look as though they had been split off from anything. They were clearly young volcanoes, which had been vomited up right where they were. Many of them were such newborns out there that they could be expected to blow again at any time. Back in 1986, they hadn't even sprouted much coral yet, and so were without blue lagoons and white beaches, amenities many human beings used to regard as foretastes of an ideal afterlife.

A million years later, they do possess white beaches and blue lagoons. But when this story begins, they were still ugly humps and domes and cones and spires of lava, brittle and abrasive, whose cracks and pits and bowls and valleys brimmed over not with rich topsoil or sweet water, but with the finest, driest volcanic ash.

•   •   •

Another theory back then was that God Almighty had created all those creatures where the explorers found them, so they had had no need for transportation.

•   •   •

Another theory was that they had been shooed ashore there two by two—down the gangplank of Noah's ark.

If there really was a Noah's ark, and there may have been—I might entitle my story "A Second Noah's Ark."

# 2

THERE WAS NO MYSTERY a million years ago as to how a thirty-five-year-old American male named James Wait, who could not swim a stroke, intended to get from the South American continent to the Galápagos Islands. He certainly wasn't going to squat on a natural raft of vegetable matter and hope for the best. He had just bought a ticket at his hotel in downtown Guayaquil for a two-week cruise on what was to be the maiden voyage of a new passenger ship called the *Bahía de Darwin*, Spanish for "Darwin Bay." The first Galápagos trip for the ship, which flew the Ecuadorian flag, had been publicized and advertised all over the world during the past year as "the Nature Cruise of the Century."

Wait was traveling alone. He was prematurely bald and he was pudgy, and his color was bad, like the crust on a pie in a cheap cafeteria, and he was bespectacled, so that he might plausibly claim to be in his fifties, in case he saw some advantage in making such a claim. He wished to seem harmless and shy.

He was the only customer now in the cocktail lounge of the Hotel El Dorado, on the broad Calle Diez de Agosto, where he had taken a room. And the bartender, a twenty-year-old descendent of proud Inca noblemen, named Jesús Ortiz, got the feeling that this drab and friendless man, who claimed to be a Canadian, had had his spirit broken by some terrible injustice or tragedy. Wait wanted everybody who saw him to feel that way.

Jesús Ortiz, who is one of the nicest people in this story of mine, pitied rather than scorned this lonesome tourist. He found it sad, as Wait had hoped he would, that Wait had just spent a lot of money in the hotel boutique—on a straw hat and rope sandals and yellow shorts and a blue-and-white-and-purple cotton shirt, which he was wearing now. Wait had had considerable dignity, Ortiz thought, when he had arrived from the airport in a business suit. But now, at great expense, he had turned himself into a clown, a caricature of a North American tourist in the tropics.

The price tag was still stapled to the hem of Wait's crackling new shirt, and Ortiz, very politely and in good English, told him so.

"Oh?" said Wait. He knew the tag was there, and he wanted it to remain there. But he went through a charade of self-mocking embarrassment, and seemed about to pluck off the tag. But then, as though overwhelmed by some sorrow he was trying to flee from, he appeared to forget all about it.

• • •

Wait was a fisherman, and the price tag was his bait, a way of encouraging strangers to speak to him, to say in one way or another what Ortiz had said: "Excuse me, Señor, but I can't help noticing—"

Wait was registered at the hotel under the name on his bogus Canadian passport, which was Willard Flemming. He was a supremely successful swindler.

Ortiz himself was in no danger from him, but an unescorted woman who looked as though she had a little money, and who was without a husband and past childbearing, surely would have been. Wait had so far courted and married seventeen such persons—and then cleaned out their jewelry boxes and safe-deposit boxes and bank accounts, and disappeared.

He was so successful at what he did that he had become a millionaire, with interest-bearing savings accounts under various aliases in banks all over North America, and he had never been arrested for anything. For all he knew, nobody was even trying to catch him. As far as the police were concerned, he reasoned, he was one of seventeen faithless husbands, each with a different name, instead of a single habitual criminal whose real name was James Wait.

• • •

It is hard to believe nowadays that people could ever have been as brilliantly duplicitous as James Wait—until I remind myself that just about every adult human being back then had a brain weighing about three kilograms! There was no end to the evil schemes that a thought machine that oversized couldn't imagine and execute.

So I raise this question, although there is nobody around to answer it: Can it be doubted that three-kilogram brains were once nearly fatal defects in the evolution of the human race?

A second query: What source was there back then, save for our overelaborate nervous circuitry, for the evils we were seeing or hearing about simply everywhere?

My answer: There was no other source. This was a very innocent planet, except for those great big brains.

# 3

The Hotel El Dorado was a brand-new, five-story tourist accommodation—built of unadorned cement block. It had the proportions and mood of a glass-front bookcase, high and wide and shallow. Each bedroom had a floor-to-ceiling wall of glass looking westward—toward the waterfront for deep-draft vessels dredged in the delta three kilometers away.

In the past, that waterfront had teemed with commerce, and ships from all over the planet had delivered meat and grain and vegetables and fruit and vehicles and clothing and machinery and household appliances, and so on, and carried away, in fair exchange, Ecuadorian coffee and cocoa and sugar and petroleum and gold, and Indian arts and crafts, including "Panama" hats, which had always come from Ecuador and not from Panama.

But there were only two ships out there now, as James Wait sat in the bar, nursing a rum and Coca-Cola. He was not a drinker, actually, since he lived by his wits, and could not afford to have the delicate switches of the big computer in his skull short-circuited by alcohol. His drink was a theatrical prop—like the price tag on his ridiculous shirt.

He was in no position to judge whether the state of affairs at the waterfront was normal or not. Until two days before, he had never even heard of Guayaquil, and this was the first time in his life he had ever been below the equator. As far as he was concerned, the El Dorado was no different from all the other characterless hostelries he had used as hideouts in the past—in Moose Jaw, Saskatchewan, in San Ignacio, Mexico, in Watervliet, New York, and on and on.

He had picked the name of the city where he was now from an arrivals-and-departures board at Kennedy International Airport in New York City. He had just pauperized and deserted his seventeenth wife—a seventy-year-old widow in Skokie, Illinois, right outside Chicago. Guayaquil sounded to him like the last place she would ever think of looking for him.

This woman was so ugly and stupid, she probably never should have been born. And yet Wait was the second person to have married her.

And he wasn't going to stay at the El Dorado very long, either, since he had bought a ticket for "the Nature Cruise of the Century" from the travel agent who had a desk in the lobby. It was late in the afternoon now, and hotter than the hinges of hell outside. There was no breeze outside, but he did not care, since he was inside, and the hotel was air conditioned, and he would soon be away from there anyway. His ship, the *Bahía de Darwin*, was scheduled to sail at high noon on the very next day, which was Friday, November 28, 1986—a million years ago.

•   •   •

The bay for which Wait's means of transportation was named fanned south from the Galápagos Island of Genovesa. Wait had never heard of the Galápagos Islands before. He expected them to be like Hawaii, where he had once honeymooned, or Guam, where he had once hidden out—with broad white beaches and blue lagoons and swaying palms and nut-brown native girls.

The travel agent had given him a brochure which described the cruise, but Wait hadn't looked inside it yet. It was supine on the bar in front of him. The brochure was truthful about how forbidding most of the islands were, and warned prospective passengers, as the hotel travel agent had not warned Wait, that they had better be in reasonably good physical condition and have sturdy boots and rough clothing, since they would often have to wade ashore and scramble up rock faces like amphibious infantry.

•   •   •

Darwin Bay was named in honor of the great English scientist Charles Darwin, who had visited Genovesa and several of its neighbors for five weeks back in 1835—when he was a mere stripling of twenty-six, nine years younger than Wait. Darwin was then the unpaid naturalist aboard Her Majesty's Ship *Beagle*, on a mapping expedition that would take him completely around the world and would last five years.

In the cruise brochure, which was intended to delight nature-lovers rather than pleasure-seekers, Darwin's own description of a typical Galápagos island was reproduced, and was taken from his first book, *The Voyage of the Beagle*:

"Nothing could be less inviting than the first appearance. A broken field of black basaltic lava, thrown into the most rugged waves, and crossed by great fissures, is everywhere covered by stunted, sun-burnt brushwood, which shows little signs of life. The dry and parched surface, being heated by the noon-day sun, gave to the air a close and sultry feeling, like that from a stove: we fancied even that the bushes smelt unpleasantly."

Darwin continued: "The entire surface . . . seems to have been permeated, like a sieve, by the subterranean vapours: here and there the lava, whilst soft, had been blown into great bubbles; and in other parts, the tops of caverns similarly formed have fallen in, leaving circular parts with steep sides." He was vividly reminded, he wrote, ". . . of those parts of Staffordshire, where the great iron foundries are most numerous."

•  •  •

There was a portrait of Darwin behind the bar at the El Dorado, framed in shelves and bottles—an enlarged reproduction of a steel engraving, depicting him not as a youth in the islands, but as a portly family man back home in England, with a beard as lush as a Christmas wreath. That same portrait was on the bosom of T-shirts for sale in the boutique, and Wait had bought two of those. That was what Darwin looked like when he was finally persuaded by friends and relatives to set down on paper his notions of how life forms everywhere, including himself and his friends and relatives, and even his Queen, had come to be as they were in the nineteenth century. He thereupon penned the most broadly influential scientific volume produced during the entire era of great big brains. It did more to stabilize people's volatile opinions of how to identify success or failure than any other tome. Imagine that! And the name of his book summed up its pitiless contents: *On the Origin of Species by Means of Natural Selection, or the Preservation of Favoured Races in the Struggle for Life.*

•  •  •

Wait had never read that book, nor did the name Darwin mean anything to him, although he had successfully passed himself off as an educated man from time to time. He was considering claiming, during "the Nature Cruise of the Century," to be a mechanical engineer from Moose Jaw, Saskatchewan, whose wife had recently died of cancer.

Actually, his formal education had stopped after two years of instruction in automobile repair and maintenance at the vocational high school in his native city of Midland City, Ohio. He was then living in the fifth of a series of foster homes, essentially an orphan, since he was the product of an incestuous relationship between a father and a daughter who had run away from town, forever and together, soon after he was born.

When he himself was old enough to run away, he hitchhiked to the island of Manhattan. A pimp there befriended him and taught him how to be a successful homosexual prostitute, to leave price tags on his clothes, to really enjoy lovers whenever possible, and so on. Wait was once quite beautiful.

When his beauty began to fade, he became an instructor in ballroom dancing at a dance studio. He was a natural dancer, and he had been told back in Midland City that his parents had been very good dancers, too. His sense of rhythm was probably inherited. And it was at the dance studio that he met and courted and married the first of his seventeen wives so far.

•   •   •

All through his childhood, Wait was severely punished by foster parents for nothing and everything. It was expected by them that, because of his inbred parentage, he would become a moral monster.

So here that monster was now—in the Hotel El Dorado, happy and rich and well, as far as he knew, and keen for the next test of his survival skills.

•   •   •

Like James Wait, incidentally, I, too, was once a teenage runaway.

# 4

THE ANGLO-SAXON Charles Darwin, underspoken and gentlemanly, impersonal and asexual and blankly observant in his writings, was a hero in teeming, passionate, polyglot Guayaquil because he was the inspiration for a tourist boom. If it weren't for Darwin, there would not have been a Hotel El Dorado or a *Bahía de Darwin* to accommodate James Wait. There would have been no boutique to clothe him so comically.

If Charles Darwin had not declared the Galápagos Islands marvelously instructive, Guayaquil would have been just one more hot and filthy seaport, and the islands would have been worth no more to Ecuador than the slag heaps of Staffordshire.

Darwin did not change the islands, but only people's opinion of them. That was how important mere opinions used to be back in the era of great big brains.

Mere opinions, in fact, were as likely to govern people's actions as hard evidence, and were subject to sudden reversals as hard evidence could never be. So the Galápagos Islands could be hell in one moment and heaven in the next, and Julius Caesar could be a statesman in one moment and a butcher in the next, and Ecuadorian paper money could be traded for food, shelter, and clothing in one moment and line the bottom of a birdcage in the next, and the universe could be created by God Almighty in one moment and by a big explosion in the next—and on and on.

Thanks to their decreased brainpower, people aren't diverted from the main business of life by the hobgoblins of opinions anymore.

•  •  •

White people discovered the Galápagos Islands in 1535 when a Spanish ship came upon them after being blown off course by a storm. Nobody was living there, nor were remains of any human settlement ever found there.

This unlucky ship wished nothing more than to carry the Bishop of Panama to Peru, never losing sight of the South American coast. There was this storm, which rudely hustled it westward, ever westward, where prevailing human opinion insisted there was only sea and more sea.

But when the storm lifted, the Spaniards found that they had delivered their bishop into a sailor's nightmare where the bits of land were mockeries, without safe anchorages or shade or sweet water or dangling fruit, or human beings of any kind. They were becalmed, and running out of water and food. The ocean was like a mirror. They put a longboat over the side, and towed their vessel and their spiritual leader out of there.

They did not claim the islands for Spain, any more than they would have claimed hell for Spain. And for three full centuries after revised human opinion allowed the archipelago to appear on maps, no other nation wished to own it. But then in 1832, one of the smallest and poorest countries on the planet, which was Ecuador, asked the peoples of the world to share this opinion with them: that the islands were part of Ecuador.

No one objected. At the time, it seemed a harmless and even comical opinion. It was as though Ecuador, in a spasm of imperialistic dementia, had annexed to its territory a passing cloud of asteroids.

But then young Charles Darwin, only three years later, began to persuade others that the often freakish plants and animals which had found ways to survive on the islands made them extremely valuable, if only people would look at them as he did—from a scientific point of view.

Only one English word adequately describes his transformation of the islands from worthless to priceless: *magical*.

•  •  •

Yes, and by the time of James Wait's arrival in Guayaquil, so many persons with an interest in natural history had come there, on their way to the islands to see what Darwin had seen, to feel what Darwin had felt, that three cruise ships had their home port there, the newest of which was the *Bahía de Darwin*. There were several modern tourist hotels, the newest of which was the El Dorado, and there were souvenir shops and boutiques and restaurants for tourists all up and down the Calle Diez de Agosto.

The thing was, though: When James Wait got there, a world-wide financial crisis, a sudden revision of human opinions as to the value of money and stocks and bonds and mortgages and so on, bits of paper, had ruined the tourist business not only in Ecuador but practically everywhere. So that the El Dorado was the only hotel still open in Guayaquil, and the *Bahía de Darwin* was the only cruise ship still prepared to sail.

The El Dorado was staying open only as an assembly point for persons with tickets for "the Nature Cruise of the Century," since it was owned by the same Ecuadorian company which owned the ship. But now, less than twenty-four hours before the cruise was to begin, there were only six guests, including James Wait, in the two-hundred-bed hotel. And the other five guests were:

*Zenji Hiroguchi, twenty-nine, a Japanese computer genius;

Hisako Hiroguchi, twenty-six, his very pregnant wife, who was a teacher of ikebana, the Japanese art of flower arranging;

*Andrew MacIntosh, fifty-five, an American financier and adventurer of great inherited wealth, a widower;

Selena MacIntosh, eighteen, his congenitally blind daughter;

And Mary Hepburn, fifty-one, an American widow from Ilium, New York, whom practically nobody in the hotel had seen because she had stayed in her room on the fifth floor, and had taken all her meals up there, since arriving all alone the night before.

The two with stars by their names would be dead before the sun went down. This convention of starring certain names will continue throughout my story, incidentally, alerting readers to the fact that some characters will shortly face the ultimate Darwinian test of strength and wiliness.

•  •  •

I was there, too, but perfectly invisible.

# 5

THE *BAHÍA DE DARWIN* was also doomed, but not yet ready for a star by her name. It would be five more sundowns before her engines quit forever, and ten more years before she sank to the ocean floor. She was not only the newest and largest and fastest and most luxurious cruise ship based in Guayaquil. She was the only one designed specifically for the Galápagos tourist trade, whose destiny, from the moment her keel was laid, was understood to be a steady churning out to the islands and back again, out to the islands and back again.

She was built in Malmö, Sweden, where I myself worked on her. It was said by the skeleton crew of Swedes and Ecuadorians who delivered her from Malmö to Guayaquil that a storm she passed through in the North Atlantic would be the last rough water or cold weather she would ever know.

She was a floating restaurant and lecture hall and nightclub and hotel for one hundred paying guests. She had radar and sonar, and an electronic navigator which gave continuously her position on the face of the earth, to the nearest hundred meters. She was so thoroughly automated that a person all alone on the bridge, with no one in the engine room or on deck, could start her up, hoist her anchor, put her in gear, and drive her off like a family automobile. She had eighty-five flush toilets and twelve bidets, and telephones in the staterooms and on the bridge which, via satellite, could reach other telephones anywhere.

She had television, so people could keep up with the news of the day.

Her owners, a pair of old German brothers in Quito, boasted that their ship would never be out of touch with the rest of the world for an instant. Little did they know.

• • •

She was seventy meters long.

The ship on which Charles Darwin was the unpaid naturalist, the *Beagle*, was only twenty-eight meters long.

When the *Bahía de Darwin* was launched in Malmö, eleven hundred metric tons of saltwater had to find someplace else to go. I was dead by then.

When the *Beagle* was launched in Falmouth, England, only two hundred and fifteen metric tons of saltwater had to find someplace else to go.

The *Bahía de Darwin* was a metal motor ship.

The *Beagle* was a sailboat made out of trees, and carried ten cannons for repelling pirates and savages.

•   •   •

The two older cruise ships with which the *Bahía de Darwin* was meant to compete had gone out of business before the struggle could begin. Both had been booked to capacity for many months to come, but then, because of the financial crisis, they had been swamped with cancellations. They were anchored in backwaters of the marshland now, out of sight of the city, and far from any road or habitation. Their owners had stripped them of their electronic gear and other valuables—in anticipation of a prolonged period of lawlessness.

Ecuador, after all, like the Galápagos Islands, was mostly lava and ash, and so could not begin to feed its nine million people. It was bankrupt, and so could no longer buy food from countries with plenty of topsoil, so the seaport of Guayaquil was idle, and the people were beginning to starve to death.

Business was business.

•   •   •

Neighboring Peru and Colombia were bankrupt, too. The only ship at the Guayaquil waterfront other than the *Bahía de Darwin* was a rusty Colombian freighter, the *San Mateo*, stranded there for want of the means to buy food or fuel. She was anchored offshore, and had been there so long that an enormous raft of vegetable matter had built up around her anchor line. A baby elephant might have reached the Galápagos Islands on a raft that size.

Mexico and Chile and Brazil and Argentina were likewise bankrupt—and Indonesia and the Philippines and Pakistan and India and Thailand and Italy and Ireland and Belgium and Turkey. Whole nations were suddenly in the same situation as the *San Mateo*, unable to buy with their paper money and coins, or their written promises to pay later, even the barest essentials. Persons with anything life sustaining to sell, fellow citizens as well as foreigners, were refusing to exchange their goods for money. They were suddenly saying to people with nothing but paper representations of wealth, "Wake up, you idiots! Whatever made you think paper was so valuable?"

• • •

There was still plenty of food and fuel and so on for all the human beings on the planet, as numerous as they had become, but millions upon millions of them were starting to starve to death now. The healthiest of them could go without food for only about forty days, and then death would come.

And this famine was as purely a product of oversize brains as Beethoven's Ninth Symphony.

It was all in people's heads. People had simply changed their opinions of paper wealth, but, for all practical purposes, the planet might as well have been knocked out of orbit by a meteor the size of Luxembourg.

# 6

THIS FINANCIAL CRISIS, which could never happen today, was simply the latest in a series of murderous twentieth century catastrophes which had originated entirely in human brains. From the violence people were doing to themselves and each other, and to all other living things, for that matter, a visitor from another planet might have assumed that the environment had gone haywire, and that the people were in such a frenzy because Nature was about to kill them all.

But the planet a million years ago was as moist and nourishing as it is today—and unique, in that respect, in the entire Milky Way. All that had changed was people's opinion of the place.

To the credit of humanity as it used to be: More and more people were saying that their brains were irresponsible, unreliable, hideously dangerous, wholly unrealistic—were simply no damn good.

In the microcosm of the Hotel El Dorado, for example, the widow Mary Hepburn, who had been taking all her meals in her room, was cursing her own brain sotto voce for the advice it was giving her, which was to commit suicide.

"You are my enemy," she whispered. "Why would I want to carry such a terrible enemy inside of me?" She had been a biology teacher in the public high school in Ilium, New York, now defunct, for a quarter of a century, and so was familiar with the very odd tale of the evolution of a then-extinct creature named by human beings the "Irish elk." "Given a choice between a brain like you and the antlers of an Irish elk," she told her own central nervous system, "I'd take the antlers of the Irish elk."

These animals used to have antlers the size of ballroom chandeliers. They were fascinating examples, she used to tell her students, of how tolerant nature could be of clearly ridiculous mistakes in evolution. Irish elk survived for two and a half million years, in spite of the fact that their antlers were too unwieldy for fighting or self-defense, and kept them from seeking food in thick forests and heavy brush.

• • •

Mary had also taught that the human brain was the most admirable survival device yet produced by evolution. But now her own big brain was urging her to take the polyethylene garment bag from around a red evening dress in her closet there in Guayaquil, and to wrap it around her head, thus depriving her cells of oxygen.

• • •

Before that, her wonderful brain had entrusted a thief at the airport with a suitcase containing all her toilet articles and clothes which would have been suitable for the hotel. That had been her carry-on luggage on a flight from Quito to Guayaquil. At least she still had the contents of the suitcase she had checked through rather than carried, which included the evening dress in the closet, which was for parties on the *Bahía de Darwin*. She was also still in possession of a wet suit and flippers and mask for diving, two bathing suits, a pair of rugged hiking boots, and a set of war surplus United States Marine Corps combat fatigues for trips ashore, which she was wearing now. As for the pants suit she had worn on the flight from Quito: Her big brain had persuaded her to send it to the hotel laundry, to believe the sad-eyed hotel manager when he said she could surely have it back by morning, in time for breakfast. But, much to the embarrassment of the manager, that, too, had disappeared.

But the worst thing her brain had done to her, other than recommending suicide, was to insist that she come to Guayaquil despite all the news about the planetary financial crisis, despite the near certainty that "the Nature Cruise of the Century," booked to capacity only a month before, would be called off for want of passengers.

Her colossal thinking machine could be so petty, too. It would not let her go downstairs in her combat fatigues on the grounds that everybody, even though there was practically nobody in the hotel, would find her comical in such a costume. Her brain told her: "They'll laugh at you behind your back, and think you're crazy and pitiful, and your life is over anyway. You've lost your husband and your teaching job, and you don't have any children or anything else to live for, so just put yourself out of your misery with the garment bag. What could be easier? What could be more painless? What could make more sense?"

•  •  •

To give her brain its due: It wasn't entirely its fault that 1986 really had been a perfectly awful year so far. The year had started out so promisingly, too, with Mary's husband, Roy, in seemingly perfect health and secure in his job as a millwright at GEFFCo, the principal industry in Ilium, and with the Kiwanis giving her a banquet and a plaque celebrating her twenty-five years of distinguished teaching, and the students naming her the most popular teacher for the twelfth year in a row.

At the start of 1986, she said, "Oh, Roy—we have so much to be thankful for: we're so lucky compared to most people. I could cry for happiness."

And he said, putting his arms around her, "Well now, you just go ahead and cry." She was fifty-one and he was fifty-nine, and they were great lovers of the out-of-doors, hiking and skiing and mountain-climbing and canoeing and running and bicycling and swimming, so they both had lean and youthful bodies. They did not smoke or drink, and they ate mostly fresh fruits and vegetables, with a little fish from time to time.

They had also handled their money well, giving their savings, in financial terms, the same sort of sensible nourishment and exercise that they gave themselves.

The tale of fiscal wisdom which Mary could tell about herself and Roy, of course, would be a thrill to James Wait.

•  •  •

And, yes, Wait, that eviscerator of widows, was speculating about Mary Hepburn as he sat in the bar of the El Dorado, although he had not met her yet, nor learned for certain how well fixed she was. He had seen her name on the hotel register, and had asked the young manager about her.

Wait liked what little the manager was able to tell him. This shy and lonesome schoolteacher upstairs, although younger than any of the wives he had ruined so far, sounded to him like his natural prey. He would stalk her at leisure during "the Nature Cruise of the Century."

•   •   •

If I may insert a personal note at this point: When I was alive,
I often received advice from my own big brain which, in terms
of my own survival, or the survival of the human race, for that
matter, can be charitably described as questionable. Example: It
had me join the United States Marines and go fight in Vietnam.

Thanks a lot, big brain.

THE NATIONAL CURRENCIES of all six guests at the El Dorado, the four Americans, one claiming to be a Canadian, and the two Japanese, were still as good as gold everywhere on the planet. Again: The value of their money was imaginary. Like the nature of the universe itself, the desirability of their American dollars and yen was all in people's heads.

And if Wait, who did not even know that there was a financial crisis going on, had carried out his masquerade as a Canadian to the extent of bringing Canadian dollars into Ecuador, he would not have been as well received as he was. Although Canada had not gone bankrupt, people's imaginations in more and more places, including Canada itself, were making them unhappy about trading anything really useful for Canadian dollars anymore.

A similar decay in imagined value was happening to the British pound and the French and Swiss francs and the West German mark. The Ecuadorian sucre, meanwhile, named in honor of Antonio José de Sucre (1795–1830), a national hero, had come to be worth less than a banana peel.

• • •

Up in her room, Mary Hepburn was wondering if she had a brain tumor, and that was why her brain was giving her the worst possible advice all the time. It was a natural thing for her to suspect, since it was a brain tumor which had killed her husband Roy only three months before. It hadn't been enough for the tumor to kill him, either. It had to addle his memory and destroy his judgment first.

She had to wonder, too, when his tumor had begun to do that to him—whether it wasn't the tumor which had made him sign them up for "the Nature Cruise of the Century" in the promising January of that ultimately horrible year.

• • •

Here was how she found out he had signed them up for the cruise: She came home from work one afternoon, expecting

Roy still to be at GEFFCo. He got off work an hour later than she did. But there Roy was, already home, and it turned out that he had quit at noon. This was a man who adored the work he did with machinery, and who had never taken off so much as an hour from his job during his twenty-nine years with GEFFCo—not for sickness, since he was never sick, not for anything.

She asked him if he was sick, and he said that he had never felt better in his life. He was proud of himself in what seemed to Mary the manner of an adolescent who was tired of being thought a good boy all the time. This was a man whose words were few and well-chosen, never silly or immature. But now he said incredibly, and with an inane expression to match, as though she were his disapproving mother: "I played hookey."

It had to have been the tumor that said that, Mary now thought in Guayaquil. And the tumor couldn't have picked a worse day for carefree truancy, for there had been an ice storm the night before, and then wind-driven sleet all day. But Roy had gone up and down Clinton Street, the main street of Ilium, stopping in store after store and telling the salespeople that he was playing hookey.

So Mary tried to be happy about that, to say and mean that it was time he loosened up and had some fun—although they had always had a lot of fun on weekends and during vacations, and at work, as far as that went. But a miasma overlay this unexpected escapade. And Roy himself, during their early supper, seemed puzzled by the afternoon. So that was that. He didn't think he would do it again, and they could forget the incident, except maybe to laugh about it now and then.

But then, right before bedtime, while they were staring at the glowing embers in the fieldstone fireplace which Roy had built with his own two horny hands, Roy said, "There's more."

"There's more of what?" said Mary.

"About this afternoon," he said. "One of the places I went was the travel agency." There was only one such establishment in Ilium, and not doing well.

"So?" she said.

"I signed us up for something," he said. It was as though he were remembering a dream. "It's all paid for. It's all taken care of. It's done. In November, you and I are flying to Ecuador, and we are going to take 'the Nature Cruise of the Century.'"

•   •   •

Roy and Mary Hepburn were the very first persons to respond to the advertising and publicity program for the maiden voyage of the *Bahía de Darwin*, which ship was nothing but a keel and a pile of blueprints in Malmö, Sweden, at the time. The Ilium travel agent had just received a poster announcing the cruise. He was just Scotch-taping it to his wall when Roy Hepburn walked in.

•   •   •

If I may interject a personal note: I myself had been working as a welder in Malmö for about a year, but the *Bahía de Darwin* had not yet materialized sufficiently so as to require my services. I would literally lose my head to that steel maiden only when springtime came. Question: Who hasn't lost his or her head in the springtime?

•   •   •

But to continue:

The travel poster in Ilium depicted a very strange bird standing on the edge of a volcanic island, looking out at a beautiful white motor ship churning by. This bird was black and appeared to be the size of a large duck, but it had a neck as long and supple as a snake. The queerest thing about it, though, was that it seemed to have no wings, which was almost the truth. This sort of bird was endemic to the Galápagos Islands, meaning that it was found there and nowhere else on the planet. Its wings were tiny and folded flat against its body, in order that it might swim as fast and deep as a fish could. This was a much better way to catch fish than, as so many fish-eating birds were required to do, to wait for fish to come to the surface and then crash down on them with beaks agape. This very successful bird was called by human beings a "flightless cormorant." It could go where the fish were. It didn't have to wait for fish to make a fatal error.

Somewhere along the line of evolution, the ancestors of such a bird must have begun to doubt the value of their wings, just as, in 1986, human beings were beginning to question seriously the desirability of big brains.

If Darwin was right about the Law of Natural Selection, cormorants with small wings, just shoving off from shore like fishing boats, must have caught more fish than the greatest of their aviators. So they mated with each other, and those children of theirs who had the smallest wings became even better fisherpeople, and so on.

•   •   •

Now the very same sort of thing has happened to people, but not with respect to their wings, of course, since they never had wings—but with respect to their hands and brains instead. And people don't have to wait any more for fish to nibble on baited hooks or blunder into nets or whatever. A person who wants a fish nowadays just goes after one like a shark in the deep blue sea.

It's so easy now.

# 8

EVEN BACK IN JANUARY, there were any number of reasons Roy Hepburn should not have signed up for that cruise. It wasn't evident then that a world economic crisis was coming, and that the people of Ecuador would be starving when the ship was supposed to sail. But there was the matter of Mary's job. She did not yet know that she was about to be laid off, to be forced into early retirement, so she could not see how she, in good conscience, could take off three weeks in late November and early December, right in the middle of a semester.

Also, although she had never been there, she had grown very bored with the Galápagos Archipelago. There was such a wealth of films and slides and books and articles about the islands, which she had used over and over in her courses, that she could not imagine any surprise that might await her there. Little did she know.

She and Roy hadn't been out of the United States during their entire marriage. If they were going to kick up their heels and take a really glamorous trip, she thought, she would much rather go to Africa, where the wildlife was so much more thrilling, and the survival schemes were so much more dangerous. When all was said and done, the creatures of the Galápagos Islands were a pretty listless bunch, when compared with rhinos and hippos and lions and elephants and giraffes and so on.

The prospect of the voyage, in fact, made her confess to a close friend, "All of a sudden I have this feeling that I never want to see another blue-footed booby as long as I live!"

Little did she know.

• • •

Mary muted her misgivings about the trip, though, when talking to Roy, confident that he would perceive on his own that he had suffered a mild brain malfunction. But by March, Roy was out of his job, and Mary knew she was going to be let go in June. The timing of the cruise, anyway, became practical. And the cruise loomed huge in Roy's increasingly erratic imagination as ". . . the only good thing we've got to look forward to."

•  •  •

Here was what had happened to their jobs: GEFFCo had furloughed almost its entire work force, blue-collar and white-collar alike, in order to modernize the Ilium operation. A Japanese company, Matsumoto, was doing the job. Matsumoto was also automating the *Bahía de Darwin*. This was the same company which employed *Zenji Hiroguchi, the young computer genius who would be staying with his wife at the Hotel El Dorado the same time that Mary was there.

When the Matsumoto Corporation got through installing computers and robots, only twelve human beings would be able to run everything. So people young enough to have children, or at least ambitious dreams for the future, left town in droves. It was, as Mary Hepburn would say on her eighty-first birthday, two weeks before a great white shark ate her, ". . . as though the Pied Piper had passed through town." Suddenly, there were almost no children to educate, and the city was bankrupt for want of taxpayers. So Ilium High School would graduate its last class in June.

•  •  •

In April Roy was diagnosed as having an inoperable brain tumor. "The Nature Cruise of the Century" thereupon became what he was staying alive for. "I can hang on that long at least, Mary. November—that's not far away, is it?"

"No," she said.

"I can hang on that long."

"You could have years, Roy," she said.

"Just let me take that cruise," he said. "Let me see penguins on the equator," he said. "That'll be good enough for me."

•  •  •

While Roy was mistaken about more and more things, he was right about there being penguins on the Galápagos Islands. They were skinny things underneath their headwaiters' costumes. They had to be. If they had been swaddled in fat like their relatives on the ice floes to the south, half a world away, they would have roasted to death when they came ashore on the lava to lay their eggs and tend their young.

Like those of the flightless cormorants, their ancestors, too, had abandoned the glamor of aviation—electing to catch more fish instead.

•   •   •

About that mystifying enthusiasm a million years ago for turning over as many human activities as possible to machinery: What could that have been but yet another acknowledgment by people that their brains were no damn good?

# 9

WHILE ROY HEPBURN was dying, and while the whole city of Ilium was dying, for that matter, and while both the man and the city were being killed by growths inimical to a healthy and happy humanity, Roy's big brain persuaded him that he had been a sailor at the United States atomic bomb tests at Bikini Atoll, equatorial like Guayaquil, in 1946. He was going to sue his own government for millions, he said, because the radiation he had absorbed there had first prevented his and Mary's having children, and now it had caused his brain cancer.

Roy had served a hitch in the Navy, but otherwise his case against the United States of America was a weak one, since he was born in 1932, and his country's lawyers would have no trouble proving that. That would make him fourteen years old at the time of his supposed exposure.

That anachronism did not prevent his having vivid memories of the terrible things his government had made him do to so-called lower animals. As he told it, he worked virtually unassisted, first driving stakes into the ground all over the atoll, and then tying different sorts of animals to the stakes. "I guess they chose me," he said, "because animals have always trusted me."

This much was true: Animals all trusted Roy. While he had no formal education past high school, except for the apprentice program at GEFFCo, and while Mary had a master's degree in zoology from Indiana University, Roy was much better at actually relating to animals than Mary was. He could talk to birds in their own languages, for example, something she could never have done, since her ancestors were notoriously tone deaf on both sides of her family. There was no dog or farm animal, not even a guard dog at GEFFCo or a sow with piglets, so vicious that Roy couldn't, within five minutes or less, turn it into a friend of his.

So Roy's tears were understandable when he remembered tying animals to all those stakes. Such a cruel experiment had been performed on animals, of course, on sheep and pigs and cattle and horses and monkeys and ducks and chickens and geese, but surely not on a zoo such as Roy described. To hear him tell it, he had tethered peacocks and snow leopards and gorillas and crocodiles and albatrosses to the stakes. In his big brain, Bikini became the exact reverse of Noah's ark. Two of every sort of animal had been brought there in order to be atom-bombed.

•  •  •

The craziest detail in his story, which did not seem at all crazy to him, of course, was this one: "Donald was there." Donald was a golden retriever male who was roaming the neighborhood there in Ilium at that very moment, probably, maybe right outside the Hepburns' house, and was only four years old.

"It was all very hard," Roy would say, "but the hardest part was tying Donald to one of those stakes. I kept putting it off until I couldn't put it off any longer. Tying Donald to a stake was the last thing I had to do. He let me do it, and after I did it he licked my hand and wagged that tail of his. And I said to him, and I'm not ashamed to say I cried: "So long, old pal. You're going to a different world now. It's sure to be a better one, since no other world could be as bad as this one is."

•  •  •

While Roy began putting on such performances, Mary was still teaching every weekday, still assuring the few students she had left that they should thank God for their great big brains. "Would you rather have the neck of a giraffe or the camouflage of a chameleon or the hide of a rhinoceros or the antlers of an Irish elk?" she would ask, and so on.

She was still spouting the same old malarkey.

Yes, and then she would go home to Roy, and his demonstrations of how misleading a brain could be. He was never hospitalized, except briefly for tests. And he was docile. He wasn't to drive a car anymore, but he understood that, and did not seem to resent it when Mary hid the keys to his Jeep station wagon. He even said that maybe they should sell it, since it didn't look like they were going to do much camping anymore. So Mary didn't have to hire a nurse to watch over Roy while she worked. Retired people in the neighborhood were glad to pick up a few dollars, keeping him company and making sure he didn't hurt himself in some way.

He was certainly no trouble to them. He watched a lot of television and enjoyed playing for hours, never leaving the yard, with Donald, the golden retriever who had died, supposedly, on Bikini Atoll.

•   •   •

As Mary delivered what was to be her last lecture about the Galápagos Islands, though, she would be stopped in midsentence for five seconds by a doubt which, if expressed in words, might have come out something like this: "Maybe I'm just a crazy lady who has wandered off the street and into this classroom and started explaining the mysteries of life to these young people. And they believe me, although I am utterly mistaken about simply everything."

She had to wonder, too, about all the supposedly great teachers of the past, who, although their brains were healthy, had turned out to be as wrong as Roy about what was really going on.

# *10*

Ow MANY GALÁPAGOS ISLANDS were there a million years ago? There were thirteen big ones, seventeen small ones, and three hundred and eighteen tiny ones, some nothing more than rocks rising only a meter or two above the surface of the ocean.

There are now fourteen big ones, seven small ones, and three hundred and twenty-six tiny ones. Quite a lot of volcanic activity still goes on. I make a joke: The gods are still angry.

And the northernmost of the islands, so all alone, so far from the rest, is still Santa Rosalia.

• • •

Yes, and a million years ago, on August 3, 1986, a man named *Roy Hepburn was on his deathbed in his right little, tight little home in Ilium, New York. There at the very end, what he lamented most was that he and his wife Mary had never had children. He could not urge his wife to try to have children by someone else after he was gone, since she had ceased to ovulate.

"We Hepburns are extinct as the dodoes now," he said, and he rambled on with the names of many other creatures which had become fruitless, leafless twigs on the tree of evolution. "The Irish elk," he said. "The ivory-billed woodpecker," he said. "*Tyrannosaurus rex*," he said, and on and on. Right up to the end, though, his dry sense of humor would pop up unexpectedly. He made two jocular additions to the lugubrious roll call, both of which were indeed without progeny. "Smallpox," he said, and then, "George Washington."

• • •

Right to the end, he believed with all his heart that his own government had done him in with radiation. He said to Mary, and to the doctor and the nurse who were there because the end could surely come at any moment now: "If only it had been just God Almighty who was mad at me!"

Mary took that to be his curtain line. He certainly looked dead after that.

But then, after ten seconds, his blue lips moved again. Mary leaned close to hear his words. She would be glad for the rest of her life that she had not missed them.

"I'll tell you what the human soul is, Mary," he whispered, his eyes closed. "Animals don't have one. It's the part of you that knows when your brain isn't working right. I always knew, Mary. There wasn't anything I could do about it, but I always knew."

And then he scared the wits out of Mary and everybody in the room by sitting up straight, his eyes open wide and fiery. "Get the Bible!" he commanded, in a voice which could be heard throughout the house.

This was the only time anything to do with formal religion was mentioned during the whole of his illness. He and Mary were no churchgoers; or prayers in even dire circumstances, but they did have a Bible somewhere. Mary wasn't quite sure where.

"Get the Bible!" he said again. "Woman, get the Bible!" He had never called her "woman" before.

So Mary went to look for it. She found it in the spare bedroom, along with Darwin's *The Voyage of the Beagle* and *A Tale of Two Cities*, by Charles Dickens.

*Roy sat up, and he called Mary "woman" again. "Woman—" he commanded, "put your hand on the Bible and repeat after me: 'I, Mary Hepburn, hereby make two solemn promises to my beloved husband on his deathbed.'"

So she said that. She expected, and in fact hoped, that the two promises would be so bizarre, perhaps having to do with suing the government, that there would be no possibility of her keeping either one. But she was not to be so lucky.

The first promise was that she do her best to get married again as soon as possible, and not waste time in moping and feeling sorry for herself.

The second was that she go to Guayaquil in November and take "the Nature Cruise of the Century" for both of them.

"My spirit will be with you every inch of the way," he said. And he died.

•   •   •

So here she was in Guayaquil, suspecting that she had a brain tumor herself. Her brain had her in the closet now, removing the garment bag from the red evening dress, which she called her "Jackie dress." She had given it that nickname because one of her fellow passengers was supposed to be Jacqueline Kennedy Onassis, and Mary wanted to look nice for her.

But there in the closet, Mary knew that the widow Onassis surely wasn't going to be crazy enough to come to Guayaquil—not with soldiers patrolling the streets and on rooftops, and digging foxholes and machine-gun pits in the parks.

While slipping the bag off the dress, she dislodged the dress from its hanger, and it fell to the floor. It made a red puddle there.

She did not pick it up, since she believed that she had no more use for earthly things. But she was not yet ready for a star before her name. She would in fact live for thirty more years. She would, moreover, employ certain vital materials on the planet in such a way as to make her, without question, the most important experimenter in the history of the human race.

# 11

I F MARY HEPBURN had been in a mood to eavesdrop instead of kill herself, she might have put an ear to the back of her closet and heard susurruses next door. She had no idea who her neighbors were on either side, since there hadn't been any other guests when she arrived the night before, and she hadn't been out of her room since then.

But the makers of the susurruses were *Zenji Hiroguchi, the computer genius, and his pregnant wife Hisako, the teacher of ikebana, the Japanese art of flower arranging.

Her neighbors on the other side were Selena MacIntosh, the blind, teenage daughter of *Andrew MacIntosh, and Kazakh, her seeing-eye dog, also a female. Mary had heard no barking, because Kazakh never barked.

Kazakh never barked or played with other dogs or investigated interesting smells or noises or chased animals which had been the natural prey of her ancestors because, when she was a puppy, big-brained human beings had showed her hate and withheld food whenever she did any of those things. They let her know from the first that that was the kind of planet she was on: that natural canine activities were against the law—all of them.

They removed her sex organs so that she would never be distracted by sexual urgencies. And I was about to say that the cast of my story would soon boil down to just one male and a lot of females, including a female dog. But Kazakh wasn't really a female anymore, thanks to surgery. Like Mary Hepburn, she was out of the evolutionary game. She wasn't going to leave her genes to anyone.

•  •  •

Beyond Selena and Kazakh's room, with an open connecting door, lay the quarters of Selena's lusty father, the financier and adventurer *Andrew MacIntosh. He was a widower. He and the widow Mary Hepburn might have got along quite nicely, since they were such ardent outdoors people. But they would never meet. As I have already said, *Andrew MacIntosh and *Zenji Hiroguchi would be dead before the sun went down.

James Wait, incidentally, had been given a room all alone on the second floor as far as possible from the other guests. His big brain was congratulating him on seeming harmless and ordinary, but it was wrong about that. The hotel manager had spotted Wait as a crook of some kind.

• • •

This hotel manager, whose name was *Siegfried von Kleist, was a lugubrious, middle-aged member of the old and generally prosperous German community in Ecuador. His two paternal uncles in Quito owned the hotel and the *Bahía de Darwin*, too, and they had put him in charge of the hotel for only two weeks, a period drawing to a close now, to oversee the reception of the passengers for "the Nature Cruise of the Century." He was generally an idler, having inherited considerable money, but had been shamed by his uncles into, so to speak, "pulling his own weight" in this particular family enterprise.

He was unmarried and had never reproduced, and so was insignificant from an evolutionary point of view. He might also have been considered as a marriage possibility for Mary Hepburn. But he, too, was doomed. *Siegfried von Kleist would survive the sunset, but three hours after that he would be drowned by a tidal wave.

It was now four o'clock in the afternoon. This native Ecuadorian Hun, with his watery blue eyes and drooping moustache, actually looked as though he expected to die that evening, but he could no more foretell the future than I could. Both of us felt that afternoon that the planet was wobbling on its axis, and that anything could happen next.

*Zenji Hiroguchi and *Andrew MacIntosh, incidentally, would die of gunshot wounds.

• • •

*Siegfried von Kleist is not important to my story, but his only sibling, his brother Adolf, three years his senior and also a bachelor, surely is. Adolf von Kleist, the Captain of the *Bahía de Darwin*, would in fact become the ancestor of every human being on the face of the earth today.

With the help of Mary Hepburn, he would become a latter-day Adam, so to speak. The biology teacher from Ilium, however, since she had ceased ovulating, would not, could not, become his Eve. So she had to be more like a god instead.

And this supremely important brother of the insignificant hotel manager was at that moment arriving at Guayaquil International Airport on a nearly empty transport plane from New York City, where he had been doing publicity for "the Nature Cruise of the Century."

• • •

If Mary had listened in on the Hiroguchis through her closet wall, she wouldn't have understood what was troubling them, since their susurruses were in Japanese, the only language in which they were fluent. *Zenji knew a little English and Russian. Hisako knew a little Chinese. Neither one knew any Spanish or Quechuan or German or Portuguese, the commonest languages in Ecuador.

They, too, it turned out, were bitter about what their supposedly wonderful brains had done to them. They felt especially foolish about having allowed themselves to be delivered into such a nightmare, since *Zenji was widely regarded as being one of the smartest men in the world. And it was his fault, not hers, that they had in effect become prisoners of the dynamic *Andrew MacIntosh.

Here is how that happened: *MacIntosh had visited Japan with his blind daughter and her dog about a year before, and had met *Zenji, and had seen the wonderful work he was doing as a salaried employee for Matsumoto. Technologically speaking, *Zenji, although only twenty-nine, had become a grandfather. He had earlier sired a pocket computer capable of translating many spoken languages instantaneously, and he had named it "Gokubi." And then, at the time of the MacIntoshes' visit to Japan, *Zenji had come up with a pilot model for a new generation of simultaneous voice translators, and he had named it "Mandarax."

So *Andrew MacIntosh, whose investment banking firm raised money for businesses and itself by the sale of stocks and bonds, took young *Zenji aside and told him that he was an idiot to be on salary, that *MacIntosh could help him form a corporation of his own which would make him almost instantly a billionaire in dollars or a trillionaire in yen.

So *Zenji said that he would like time to think about it.

This exploratory conversation took place in a Tokyo sushi restaurant. Sushi was raw fish wrapped around cold rice, a popular dish a million years ago. Little did anybody dream back then that everybody would be eating practically nothing but raw fish in the sweet by-and-by.

The florid, boisterous American entrepreneur and the reserved, relatively doll-like Japanese inventor communicated through Gokubi, since neither spoke the other's language at all well. There were then thousands upon thousands of Gokubis in use all over the world. The two men could not use Mandarax, since the only working model of Mandarax was under heavy guard in *Zenji's office back at Matsumoto. So *Zenji's big brain began to play with the idea of becoming as rich as the richest man in his country, who was the Emperor of Japan.

A few months later, in the following January, the same January during which Mary and Roy Hepburn thought they had so much to be grateful for, *Zenji got a letter from *MacIntosh asking him a full ten months in advance to be his guest on his estate outside of Mérida, Yucatán, in Mexico, and then on the maiden voyage of an Ecuadorian luxury ship called the *Bahía de Darwin*, in whose financing he had had a hand.

*MacIntosh had said in the letter in English, which had to be translated for *Zenji: *Let us take this opportunity to get to really know each other.*

• • •

What he meant to get from *Zenji, probably in Yucatán, or surely during "the Nature Cruise of the Century," was *Zenji's signature on an agreement to head a new corporation, whose stock *MacIntosh would merchandize.

Like James Wait, *MacIntosh was a fisherman of sorts. He hoped to catch investors, using for bait not a price tag on his shirt but a Japanese computer genius.

And now it appears to me that the tale I have to tell, spanning a million years, doesn't change all that much from beginning to end. In the beginning, as in the end, I find myself speaking of human beings, regardless of their brain size, as fisherfolk.

•  •  •

So it was November now, and the Hiroguchis were in Guayaquil. On the advice of *MacIntosh, *Zenji had lied to his employers about where he was going. He had led them to believe that he was exhausted by the creation of Mandarax, and that he and Hisako wished to have two months all by themselves, far from any reminders of work, and incommunicado. He put his piece of misinformation into their big brains: he had chartered a schooner with crew, whose name he did not wish to reveal, sailing from a Mexican port whose name he did not wish to reveal, for a cruise through the islands of the Caribbean.

And, although the passenger list for "the Nature Cruise of the Century" had been widely publicized, *Zenji's employers never learned that their most productive employee and his wife were also expected to be aboard. Like James Wait, they were traveling under false identities.

And, again like James Wait, they had evanesced!

Anybody looking for them would not be able to find them anywhere. Any big-brained search for them wouldn't even start on the correct continent.

# 12

T HERE IN THEIR HOTEL ROOM next to Mary Hepburn's, the Hiroguchis were susurruing away about *Andrew MacIntosh's being an actual maniac. This was an exaggeration. *MacIntosh was surely wild and greedy and inconsiderate, but not insane. Most of what his big brain believed to be going on was actually going on. When he flew Selena and Kazakh and the Hiroguchis from Mérida to Guayaquil in his private Learjet, with himself at the controls, he had known that the city would be under martial law, or something close to it, and that the stores would all be closed, and that there would be increasingly hungry people milling around, and that the *Bahía de Darwin* would not sail as scheduled, probably, and so on.

The communications facilities in his Yucatecan mansion had kept him absolutely up to date on what was going on in Ecuador or anyplace else he might have reason to care about. At the same time he had kept the Hiroguchis, but not his blind daughter, in the dark, so to speak, about what was likely awaiting them.

His true purpose in coming to Guayaquil, which, again, he had revealed to his daughter but not to the Hiroguchis, was to buy as many Ecuadorian assets as possible at rock-bottom prices, including, perhaps, even the El Dorado and the *Bahía de Darwin*—and gold mines and oil fields, and on and on. He was moreover going to bond *Zenji Hiroguchi to himself forever by sharing these business opportunities with him, to lend him money so that he, too, could become a major property owner in Ecuador.

• • •

*MacIntosh had told the Hiroguchis to stay in their room at the El Dorado—because he would soon be bringing wonderful news for them. He had been on the telephone all afternoon, call-ing Ecuadorian financiers and banks, and the news he expected to bring was about all the properties he and the Hiroguchis could call their own in a day or two.

And then he was going to say: "And to hell with 'the Nature Cruise of the Century'!"

•  •  •

The Hiroguchis could no longer conceive of any good news for themselves which could be delivered by *Andrew MacIntosh. They honestly believed him to be a madman, which misconception, ironically, had been impressed upon them by *Zenji's own creation, which was Mandarax. There were now ten such instruments in the world, nine back in Tokyo, and one which *Zenji had brought along for the cruise. Mandarax, unlike Gokubi, was not only a translator, but also could diagnose with respectable accuracy one thousand of the most common diseases which attacked *Homo sapiens*, including twelve varieties of nervous breakdown.

What Mandarax did in the medical field was simplicity itself, actually. Mandarax was programed to do what real doctors did, which was to ask a series of questions, each answer suggesting the next question, such as: "How is your appetite?" and then, "Do your bowels move regularly?" and, perhaps, "What did the stool look like?" and so on.

In Yucatán, the Hiroguchis had followed such a daisy chain of questions and answers, describing for Mandarax the behavior of *Andrew MacIntosh. Mandarax had at last displayed these words in Japanese on the screen, which was about the size of a playing card: *Pathological personality.*

•  •  •

Unfortunately for the Hiroguchis, but not for Mandarax, which couldn't feel anything or care about anything, the computer was not programed to explain that this was a rather mild affliction compared to most, and that those who had it were rarely hospitalized, that they were, in fact, among the happiest people on the planet—and that their behavior merely caused pain to those around them, and almost never to themselves. A real doctor might have gone on to say that millions of people walking the streets every day fell into a gray area, where it was difficult to say with any degree of certainty whether or not their personalities were pathological.

But the Hiroguchis were ignorant of medical matters, and so responded to the diagnosis as though it were a dread disease. So, one way or another, they wanted to get away from

*Andrew MacIntosh, and then all the way back to Tokyo. But they remained dependent on him, as much as they wished they weren't. They had learned from the mournful-looking hotel manager, speaking to him through Mandarax, that all commercial flights out of Guayaquil had been canceled, and that none of the companies with planes for charter seemed to be answering their phones.

So that left the petrified Hiroguchis with only two possible ways of egress from Guayaquil: either on *MacIntosh's Learjet, or aboard the *Bahía de Darwin*, if, as was becoming harder and harder to believe, it would really sail next day.

# *13*

*Z*ENJI HIROGUCHI begat Gokubi one million and five years
ago, and then, one million years ago, this young genius
begat Mandarax. Yes, and at the time of his begetting of Mandarax, his wife was about to give birth to his first human child.

There had been concern about the genes the mother, Hisako,
might have passed on to her fetus, since her own mother had
been exposed to radiation when the United States of America
dropped an atomic bomb on Hiroshima, Japan. So a sample of
Hisako's amniotic fluid was tested back in Tokyo for clues that
the child might be abnormal. That fluid, incidentally, would be
identical in salinity with that of the ocean into which the *Bahía
de Darwin* would disappear.

The tests declared the fetus normal.

They also gave away the secret of its sex. It would come into
the world as a little girl, yet another female in this tale.

• • •

The tests were incapable of detecting minor defects in the
fetus, such as that it might be as tone deaf as Mary Hepburn,
which it wasn't—or that it might be covered with a fine, silky
pelt like a fur seal's, which would actually turn out to be the case.

The only human being *Zenji Hiroguchi would ever beget
was a darling but furry daughter he would never see.

She would be born on Santa Rosalia, at the northern-most
extremity of the Galápagos Islands. Her name would be Akiko.

• • •

When Akiko became an adult on Santa Rosalia, she would be
very much like her mother on the inside, but in a different sort
of skin. The evolutionary sequence from Gokubi to Mandarax,
by contrast, was a radical improvement in the contents of a package, but with few perceptible changes in the wrapper. Akiko was
protected from sunburn, and from the chilly water when she
swam, and the abrasiveness of lava when she chose to sit or lie
down—whereas her mother's bare skin was wholly defenseless

against these ordinary hazards of island life. But Gokubi and Mandarax, as different as they were inside, inhabited nearly identical shells of high-impact black plastic, twelve centimeters high, eight wide, and two thick.

Any fool could tell Akiko from Hisako, but only an expert could tell Gokubi from Mandarax.

• • •

Gokubi and Mandarax both had pressure-sensitive buttons on their backs, set flush with their cases, by means of which a person might communicate with whatever it was that had been put inside. On the face of each was an identical screen on which images could be caused to appear, and which also functioned as a solar cell, charging tiny batteries which, again, were exactly the same in Gokubi and Mandarax.

Each had a microphone the size of a pinhead at the upper right-hand corner of its screen. It was by means of this that Gokubi or Mandarax heard spoken language, and then, in accordance with instructions from its buttons, translated it into words on its screen.

An operator of either instrument had to be as quick and graceful with his hands as a magician, if a bilingual conversation was to flow at all naturally. If I were an English-speaking person talking to a Portuguese, say, I would have to hold the instrument somewhere near the mouth of the Portuguese, but with the screen close enough to my eyes for me to read the written translation into English of what he was saying. And then I would have to flip it over quickly, so that the instrument could hear me, and so he could read from the screen what I was saying.

No person living today has hands clever enough or a brain big enough to operate a Gokubi or a Mandarax. Nobody can thread a needle, either—or play the piano, or pick his or her nose, as the case may be.

• • •

Gokubi could translate among only ten languages. Mandarax could translate among a thousand. Gokubi had to be told what language it was hearing. Mandarax could identify every one of the thousand languages after hearing only a few words, and begin to translate those words into the operator's language without being told.

Both were highly accurate clocks and perpetual calendars. The clock of *Zenji Hiroguchi's Mandarax lost only eighty-two seconds between the time he checked into the Hotel El Dorado and, thirty-one years later, when Mary Hepburn and the instrument were eaten by a great white shark.

Gokubi would have kept track of time just as accurately, but in all other respects Mandarax left its father far behind. Not only could Mandarax traffic in one hundred times more languages than its progenitor and correctly diagnose more diseases than the majority of physicians of that time. It could also name on command important events which happened in any given year. If you punched out on its back *1802*, for example, the year of Charles Darwin's birth, Mandarax would tell you that Alexandre Dumas and Victor Hugo were also born then, and that Beethoven completed his Second Symphony, and that France suppressed a Negro rebellion in Santo Domingo, and that Gottfried Treviranus coined the term *biology*, and that the Health and Morals of Apprentices Act became law in Britain, and on and on. That was also the year in which Napoleon became President of the Italian Republic.

Mandarax knew the rules, too, for two hundred games, and could recite the basic principles laid down by masters for fifty different arts and crafts. It could moreover recall on command any one of twenty thousand popular quotations from literature. So that, if you punched out on its back the word *Sunset*, for example, these lofty sentiments would appear on its screen:

> *Sunset and evening star,*
> *And one clear call for me!*
> *And may there be no moaning of the bar,*
> *When I put out to sea.*
> Alfred, Lord Tennyson
> (1809–1892)

• • •

*Zenji Hiroguchi's Mandarax was about to be marooned for thirty-one years on Santa Rosalia, along with his pregnant

wife and Mary Hepburn and the blind Selena MacIntosh and
Captain Adolf von Kleist, and six other people, all females. But
under those particular circumstances, Mandarax wasn't really
much help.

The uselessness of all its knowledge would so anger the Captain that he threatened to throw it into the ocean. On the last
day of his life, when he was eighty-six and Mary was eighty-one,
he would actually carry out that threat. As the new Adam, it
might be said, his final act was to cast the Apple of Knowledge
into the deep blue sea.

•   •   •

Under the circumstances peculiar to Santa Rosalia, the
medical advice of Mandarax was bound to sound like mockery.
When Hisako Hiroguchi entered a deep depression which was
to last until her death, to last for nearly twenty years, Mandarax recommended new hobbies, new friends, a change of scene
and perhaps profession, and lithium. When the kidneys of
Selena MacIntosh began to fail when she was only thirty-eight,
Mandarax suggested that a compatible donor for a transplant
be located as soon as possible. Hisako's furry daughter Akiko,
when Akiko was six, came down with pneumonia, apparently
caught from a fur seal who was her best friend, and Mandarax
recommended antibiotics. Hisako and the blind Selena were
then living together and raising Akiko together, almost like
husband and wife.

And when Mandarax was asked to come up with quotations
from world literature which could be used in a celebration of
some event on the slag heap of Santa Rosalia, the instrument
almost always came up with clunkers. Here were its thoughts
when Akiko gave birth, at the age of twenty-four, to her own
furry daughter and the first member of the second generation
of human beings to be born on the island:

> *If I were hanged on the highest hill,*
> *Mother o' mine, O mother o' mine!*
> *I know whose love would follow me still,*
> *Mother o' mine, O mother o' mine!*
> Rudyard Kipling (1865–1936)

and

> In the dark womb where I began
> My mother's life made me a man.
> Through all the months of human birth
> Her beauty fed my common earth.
> I cannot see, nor breathe, nor stir,
> But through the death of some of her.
>                     John Masefield (1878–1967)

and

> Lord, who ordainest for mankind
>     Benignant toils and tender cares!
> We thank Thee for the ties that bind
>     The mother to the child she bears.
>                     William Cullen Bryant
>                         (1794–1878)

and

> Honor thy father and thy mother; that thy days may be long
> upon the land which the Lord thy God giveth thee.
>                                         The Bible

The father of Akiko's daughter was the oldest of the Captain's children, Kamikaze, only thirteen years old.

## 14

THERE WOULD BE MANY BIRTHS but no formal marriages to celebrate during the first forty-one years of the colony on Santa Rosalia, from which all humanity is now descended. There were surely pairings off from the very first. Hisako and Selena paired off for the rest of their lives. The Captain and Mary Hepburn paired off for the first ten years—until she did something which he considered absolutely unforgivable, which was to make unauthorized use of his sperm. And the six other females, while living together as a family, also formed pairs within an already very intimate sisterhood.

When the first Santa Rosalia marriage was performed by Kamikaze and Akiko in the year 2027, all of the original colonists had long since vanished into the sinuous blue tunnel which leads into the Afterlife, and Mandarax was studded with barnacles on the floor of the South Pacific. If Mandarax were still around, it would have had mostly unpleasant things to say about matrimony, such as:

> *Marriage: a community consisting of a master, a mistress, and two slaves, making in all, two.*
> Ambrose Bierce (1842–?)

and

> *Marriage from love, like vinegar from wine—*
> *A sad, sour, sober beverage—by time*
> *Is sharpen'd from its high celestial flavour,*
> *Down to a very homely household savour.*
> Lord Byron (1788–1824)

and so on.

The last human marriage in the Galápagos Islands, and thus the last one on Earth, was performed on Fernandina Island in the year 23,011. Nobody today has any idea what a marriage is. I have to say that Mandarax's cynicism about the institution back in its heyday was largely justified. My own parents made each other miserable by getting married, and Mary Hepburn, when she was an old lady on Santa Rosalia, once told the furry Akiko that she and Roy had been, quite possibly, the only happily married couple in all of Ilium.

What made marriage so difficult back then was yet again that instigator of so many other sorts of heartbreak: the oversize brain. That cumbersome computer could hold so many contradictory opinions on so many different subjects all at once, and switch from one opinion or subject to another one so quickly, that a discussion between a husband and wife under stress could end up like a fight between blindfolded people wearing roller skates.

The Hiroguchis, for example, whose susurrations Mary had heard through the back of her closet, were then changing their opinions of themselves and each other, and of love and sex and work and the world and so on, with lightning speed.

In one second, Hisako would think that her husband was very stupid, and that she was going to have to rescue herself and her female fetus. But then in the next second she would think that he was as brilliant as everybody said he was, and that she could just stop worrying, that he would get them out of this mess very easily and soon.

In one second *Zenji was inwardly cursing her for her helplessness, for being such a dead weight, and in the next he was vowing in his head to die, if necessary, for this goddess and her unborn daughter.

Of what possible use was such emotional volatility, not to say craziness, in the heads of animals who were supposed to stay together long enough, at least, to raise a human child, which took about fourteen years or so?

•  •  •

*Zenji found himself saying in the midst of a silence, "Something else is bothering you." He meant that something more personal than the general mess they were in was burning her up, and had been burning her up for quite some time.

"No," she said. That was another thing about those big brains: They found it easy to do what Mandarax could never do, which was lie and lie.

"Something's been bothering you for the past week," he said. "Why don't you just spit it out? Tell me what it is."

"Nothing," she said. Who would want to spend fourteen years with a computer like that, when you could never be sure whether it was telling the truth or not?

They were conversing in Japanese, and not in the idiomatic American English of a million years ago, which I have employed throughout this story. *Zenji, incidentally, was toying nervously with Mandarax, passing it from one hand to the other, and had unintentionally set it so that it was translating anything either one of them said into Navaho.

•   •   •

"Well—if you must know—" said Hisako at last, "back in Yucatán I was playing with Mandarax one afternoon on the *Omoo*," which was *MacIntosh's one-hundred-meter yacht. "You were diving for sunken treasure." This was something *MacIntosh actually had *Zenji doing, although *Zenji could scarcely swim: scuba-diving down forty meters to a Spanish galleon, and bringing up broken dishes and cannonballs. *MacIntosh also had his blind daughter Selena diving, her right wrist attached to his right ankle by a three-meter nylon cord.

"I accidentally found out something Mandarax could do which you somehow forgot to tell me Mandarax could do," Hisako went on. "Do you want to guess what it was?"

"No, I do not," he said. It was his turn to lie.

"Mandarax," she said, "turns out to be a very good teacher of the art of flower arranging." That was what she had been so proud of being, of course. But her self-respect had been severely crippled by the discovery that a little black box could not only teach what she taught, but could do so in a thousand different tongues.

"I was going to tell you. I meant to tell you," he said. This was another lie, and her learning that Mandarax knew ikebana was as improbable as her guessing the combination to a bank vault. She had been very reluctant to learn how to work Mandarax, and would remain so until she died.

But, by golly if she hadn't fiddled with the buttons there on the *Omoo* until, suddenly, Mandarax was telling her that the most beautiful flower arrangements had one, two, or at the most three, elements. In arrangements of three elements, said Mandarax, all three might be the same, or two of the three might be the same, but all three should never be different. Mandarax told her the ideal ratios between the altitudes of the elements in arrangements of more than one element, and between the elements and the diameters and altitudes of their vases or bowls—or sometimes baskets.

Ikebana turned out to be as easily codified as the practice of modern medicine.

•   •   •

\*Zenji Hiroguchi had not himself taught Mandarax ikebana or anything else it knew. He had left that to underlings. The underling who taught Mandarax ikebana had simply taken a tape recorder to Hisako's famous ikebana class, and then boiled things down.

•   •   •

\*Zenji said to Hisako that he had had Mandarax learn ikebana as a pleasant surprise for Mrs. Onassis, to whom he intended to present the instrument on the final night of "the Nature Cruise of the Century." "I did it for her," he said, "because she is supposed to be such a lover of beauty."

This happened to be the truth, but Hisako did not believe him. That was how bad things had become back in 1986. Nobody believed anybody anymore, since there was so much lying going on.

"Oh, yes," said Hisako, "I am sure you did it for Mrs. Onassis, and to honor your wife as well. You have placed me among the immortals." She was talking about the heavy thinkers Mandarax could quote.

She turned really mean now, and wanted to diminish his accomplishments as much as he, in her opinion, had diminished her own. "I must be awfully stupid," she said, a statement Mandarax faithfully translated into written Navaho. "It has taken me an unforgivably long time to realize how much malice there is, how much contempt for others there is, in what you do."

"You, \*Doctor Hiroguchi," she went on, "think that everybody but yourself is just taking up space on this planet, and we make too much noise and waste valuable natural resources and have too many children and leave garbage around. So it would be a much nicer place if the few stupid services we are able to perform for the likes of you were taken over by machinery. That wonderful Mandarax you're scratching your ear with now: what is that but an excuse for a mean-spirited egomaniac never to pay or even thank any human being with a knowledge of languages or mathematics or history or medicine or literature or ikebana or anything?"

•   •   •

I have already given my own opinion as to the cause for the craze back then for having machines do everything that human beings did—and I mean *everything*. I just want to add that my father, who was a science-fiction writer, once wrote a novel about a man whom everybody laughed at because he was building sports robots. He created a golf robot who could make a hole in one every time, and a basketball robot who could hit the basket every time, and a tennis robot who served an ace every time, and so on.

At first, people couldn't see any use for robots like that, and the inventor's wife walked out on him, the way Father's wife, incidentally, had walked out on him—and his children tried to put him into a nuthouse. But then he let advertisers know that his robots would also endorse automobiles or beer or razors or wristwatches or perfume or whatever. He made a fortune, according to my father, because so many sports enthusiasts wanted to be exactly like those robots.

Don't ask me why.

# 15

ANDREW MACINTOSH, meanwhile, was in his blind daughter's room, waiting for the telephone to ring—to bring him the good news which he would then share with the Hiroguchis. He was fluent in Spanish, and he had been on the telephone all afternoon with his offices on the island of Manhattan and with frightened Ecuadorian financiers and officials. He was doing business in his daughter's room because he wanted her to hear what he was doing. These two were very close. Selena had never known a mother, since her mother had died while giving birth to her.

I think of Selena now, with her meaningless green eyes, as an experiment by Nature—since her blindness was inherited and she could pass it on. She was eighteen there in Guayaquil, with her best reproductive years ahead of her. She would be only twenty-eight when Mary Hepburn asked her if she would like to take part in her unauthorized experiments on Santa Rosalia with the Captain's sperm. Selena would refuse. But if she had found any advantages in blindness, she could have passed them on.

• • •

Little did young Selena know in Guayaquil, as she listened to her sociopathic father wheel and deal on the telephone, that her destiny was to pair off with Hisako Hiroguchi, two rooms away, and to raise a furry baby.

In Guayaquil she was paired off with her father, who apparently owned the planet they were on, and who could do whatever he pleased whenever he pleased, and wherever he pleased. Her big brain told her that she was going to get through life safely and amusingly inside a sort of electromagnetic bubble created by her father's indomitable personality, which would continue to protect her even after he died—even after it came to be his turn to enter the blue tunnel into the Afterlife.

• • •

Before I forget: On Santa Rosalia, Selena's blindness gave her one advantage over all the other colonists which was a great joy to her, but which, nonetheless, was not worth passing on to yet another generation:

More than anybody else on the island, Selena enjoyed the feel of little Akiko's fur.

•   •   •

*Andrew MacIntosh had told the top financial people in Ecuador that he was prepared to transfer instantly to any designated fiduciary in Ecuador fifty million American dollars, still as good as gold. Most of the supposed wealth held by American banks at that point had become so wholly imaginary, so weightless and impalpable, that any amount of it could be transferred instantly to Ecuador, or anyplace else capable of receiving a written message by wire or radio.

*MacIntosh was waiting to hear from Quito what properties Ecuadorians would be willing to put into the names of himself, his daughter, and the Hiroguchis, also instantly, in exchange for such a sum.

It wasn't even going to be his own money. He had arranged to borrow it, whatever it was, from the Chase Manhattan Bank. They found it somewhere, whatever it was, to loan to him.

Yes, and if the deal went through, Ecuador could wire or radio pieces of the mirage to fertile countries and get real food in return.

And the people would eat up all the food, gobble, gobble, yum, yum, and it would become nothing but excrement and memories. What then for little Ecuador?

•   •   •

*MacIntosh's call was supposed to come at five-thirty on the dot. He had half an hour more to wait and he ordered two rare filet mignons with all the trimmings from room service. There were still plenty of good things to eat at the El Dorado, hoarded for arriving passengers for "the Nature Cruise of the Century," and especially for Mrs. Onassis. Soldiers at that moment were stringing barbed wire at a distance of one block in every direction around the hotel—to protect the food.

The same thing was happening at the waterfront. Barbed wire was being strung around the *Bahía de Darwin*, which, as everyone in Guayaquil knew, had been provisioned to serve three gourmet meals a day, no two alike, for fourteen days—to one hundred passengers. A person looking at the beautiful ship, and capable of doing a little arithmetic, might have had this thought: "I am so hungry, and my wife and children are so hungry, and my mother and father are so hungry—and there are forty-two hundred delicious meals in there."

●   ●   ●

The man who brought the two filet mignon suppers to Selena's room had made such calculations, and carried in his big brain an inventory of the good things to eat in the hotel's larder as well. He himself wasn't hungry yet, since the hotel staff was still being fed. His family, a small one by Ecuadorian standards, consisting of a pregnant wife, her mother, his father, and an orphaned nephew he was raising, were also well enough fed so far. Like all the other employees, he had been stealing food from the hotel for his family.

This was Jesús Ortiz, the young Inca bartender who had recently been serving James Wait downstairs. He had been pressed into service as a room waiter by *Siegfried von Kleist, the manager, who himself had taken over as bartender. The hotel was suddenly short-handed. The two regular room-service waiters seemed to have disappeared. That might be all right, that they had disappeared, since no large volume of room service had been expected. They might be asleep somewhere.

So Ortiz had those two steaks for his big brain to think about in the kitchen, and then in the elevator, and then in the corridor outside Selena's room. The hotel's employees were not eating and stealing food that good. They were generally proud of that. They were still saving the best for what they spoke of as "Señora Kennedy," actually Mrs. Onassis, which was their collective term for all the famous and rich and powerful people who were still supposed to be coming.

Ortiz's brain was so big that it could show him movies in his head which starred him and his dependents as millionaires. And this man, little more than a boy, was so innocent that he believed the dream could come true, since he had no bad habits and was willing to work so hard, if only he could get some hints on succeeding in life from people who were already millionaires.

He had tried, without much satisfaction, to get some advice on living well from James Wait downstairs, who, while so laughably unprepossessing, had a wallet stuffed, as Ortiz had observed respectfully, with credit cards and American twenty-dollar bills.

He thought this about the steaks, too, as he knocked on Selena's door: The people inside there deserved them, and that he would deserve them, too, once he had become a millionaire. And this was a highly intelligent and enterprising young man. Working in Guayaquil hotels since he was ten years old, he had become fluent in six languages, which was more than half as many languages as Gokubi knew, and six times as many languages as James Wait or Mary Hepburn knew, and three times as many languages as the Hiroguchis knew, and two times as many languages as the MacIntoshes knew. He was also a good cook and baker, and had taken a course in accounting and another in business law in night school.

So his inclination was to like whatever he saw and heard as Selena let him into the room. He already knew her green eyes were blind. Otherwise, he would have been fooled. She did not act or look as though she were blind. She was so beautiful. His big brain had him fall in love with her.

●  ●  ●

*Andrew MacIntosh was standing at the floor-to-ceiling window wall, looking out over the marsh and slums at the *Bahía de Darwin*, which he expected to be his, or perhaps Selena's, or perhaps the Hiroguchis', before the sun went down. The person who was going to call him at five-thirty, the head of an emergency consortium of financiers in Quito, high in the clouds, was Gottfried von Kleist, chairman of the board of the largest bank of Ecuador, an uncle of the manager of the El Dorado and the captain of the *Bahía de Darwin*, and co-owner with his elder brother Wilhelm of the ship and the hotel.

Turning to look at Ortiz, who had just come in with the filet mignons, *MacIntosh was rehearsing in his head the first thing he was going to say to Gottfried von Kleist in Spanish: "Before you tell me the rest of the good news, dear colleague, give me your word of honor that I am gazing at my own ship in the distance, from the top floor of my own hotel."

• • •

*MacIntosh was barefoot and wearing nothing but a pair of khaki shorts whose fly was unbuttoned and under which he wore no underwear, so that his penis was no more a secret than the pendulum on a grandfather clock.

• • •

Yes, and I pause to marvel now at how little interested this man was in reproduction, in being a huge success biologically—despite his exhibitionistic sexuality and his mania for claiming as his own property as many of the planet's life-support systems as possible. The most famous amassers of survival schemes back then typically had very few children. There were exceptions, of course. Those who did reproduce a lot, though, and who might be thought to want so much property for the comfort of their descendants, commonly made psychological cripples of their own children. Their heirs were more often than not zombies, easily fleeced by men and women as greedy as the person who had left them much too much of everything a human animal could ever want or need.

*Andrew MacIntosh didn't even care if he himself lived or died—as evidenced by his enthusiasms for skydiving and the racing of high-performance motor vehicles and so on.

So I have to say that human brains back then had become such copious and irresponsible generators of suggestions as to what might be done with life, that they made acting for the benefit of future generations seem one of many arbitrary games which might be played by narrow enthusiasts—like poker or polo or the bond market, or the writing of science-fiction novels.

More and more people back then, and not just *Andrew MacIntosh, had found ensuring the survival of the human race a total bore.

It was a lot more fun, so to speak, to hit and hit a tennis ball.

• • •

The seeing-eye dog Kazakh sat by the baggage rack at the foot of Selena's king-size bed. Kazakh was a female German shepherd. She was at ease, and free to be herself, since she was not at the moment wearing her harness and handle. And her small brain, cued by the smell of meat, made her look up at Ortiz with her big brown eyes most hopefully, and to wag her tail.

Dogs back then were far superior to people when it came to distinguishing between different odors. Thanks to Darwin's Law of Natural Selection, all human beings now have senses of smell as acute as Kazakh's. And they have surpassed dogs in one respect: They can smell things underwater.

Dogs still can't even swim underwater, although they have had a million years in which to learn. They goof around as much as ever. They can't even catch fish yet. And I would have to say that the whole rest of the animal world has done strikingly little to improve its survival tactics in all that time, except for humankind.

# 16

W HAT *ANDREW MACINTOSH now said to Jesús Ortiz
was so offensive, and, in view of the hunger pangs
spreading throughout Ecuador, so dangerous, that his big
brain really must have been sick in some serious way—if giving
a damn what happened next was a sign of mental health. The
outrageous insult he was about to offer to this friendly and
good-hearted waiter, moreover, was not deliberate.

This was a boxy man of medium stature, his head a box set
atop a larger one, and with very thick arms and legs. He was
as lusty and able an outdoorsman as Mary Hepburn's husband
Roy had been, but eager to take terrifying chances, too, which
Roy had never been. *MacIntosh had teeth so big and white perfect, and he gave Ortiz such a good look, Ortiz was reminded
of keys on a grand piano.

*MacIntosh said to him in Spanish, "Uncover the steaks and
put them both on the floor for the dog, and then get out of
here."

• • •

Speaking of teeth: There have never been dentists on Santa
Rosalia or any of the other human colonies in the Galápagos
Islands. As would have been the case a million years ago, a
typical colonist can expect to be edentate by the time he or she
is thirty years old, having suffered many skull-cracking tooth-
aches on the way. And this is more than a blow to mere vanity,
surely, since teeth set in living gums are now people's only tools.

Really. Except for their teeth, people now have no tools at all.

• • •

Mary Hepburn and the Captain had good teeth when they
arrived on Santa Rosalia, although they were both well over
thirty, thanks to regular visits to dentists, who drilled out rot
and drained abscesses and so on. But they were toothless when
they died. Selena MacIntosh was so young when she died in a
suicide pact with Hisako Hiroguchi that she still had a lot of

her teeth, but by no means all of them. Hisako was completely toothless then.

And if I were criticizing human bodies as they were a million years ago, the kind of body I had, as though they were machines somebody intended to put on the market, I would have two main points to make—one of which I have surely made by now in my story: "The brain is much too big to be practical." The other would be: "Something is always going wrong with our teeth. They don't last anything like a lifetime, usually. What chain of events in evolution should we thank for our mouthfuls of rotting crockery?"

It would be nice to say that the Law of Natural Selection, which has done people so many favors in such a short time, had taken care of the tooth problem, too. In a way it has, but its solution has been draconian. It hasn't made teeth more durable. It has simply cut the average human life span down to about thirty years.

·  ·  ·

Now back to Guayaquil, and *Andrew MacIntosh's telling Jesús Ortiz to put the filet mignons on the floor:

"I beg your pardon, sir?" said Ortiz in English.

"Put them both in front of the dog," said *MacIntosh.

So Ortiz did that, his big brain in total confusion, revising entirely Ortiz's opinion of himself, humanity, the past and future, and the nature of the universe.

Before Ortiz had time to straighten up from serving the dog, *MacIntosh said yet again, "Get out of here."

·  ·  ·

It pains me even now, even a million years later, to write about such human misbehavior.

A million years later, I feel like apologizing for the human race. That's all I can say.

·  ·  ·

If Selena was Nature's experiment with blindness, then her father was Nature's experiment with heartlessness. Yes, and Jesús Ortiz was Nature's experiment with admiration for the rich, and I was Nature's experiment with insatiable voyeurism, and my father was Nature's experiment with cynicism, and my mother was Nature's experiment with optimism, and the Captain of the *Bahía de Darwin* was Nature's experiment with ill-founded self-confidence, and James Wait was Nature's experiment with purposeless greed, and Hisako Hiroguchi was Nature's experiment with depression, and Akiko was Nature's experiment with furriness, and on and on.

I am reminded of one of my father's novels, *The Era of Hopeful Monsters*. It was about a planet where the humanoids ignored their most serious survival problems until the last possible moment. And then, with all the forests being killed and all the lakes being poisoned by acid rain, and all the groundwater made unpotable by industrial wastes and so on, the humanoids found themselves the parents of children with wings or antlers or fins, with a hundred eyes, with no eyes, with huge brains, with no brains, and on and on. These were Nature's experiments with creatures which might, as a matter of luck, be better planetary citizens than the humanoids. Most died, or had to be shot, or whatever, but a few were really quite promising, and they intermarried and had young like themselves.

I will now call my own lifetime a million years ago "the Era of Hopeful Monsters," with most of the monsters novel in terms of personality rather than body type. And there are no such experiments, either with bodies or personalities, going on at the present time.

• • •

Big brains back then were not only capable of being cruel for the sake of cruelty. They could also feel all sorts of pain to which lower animals were entirely insensitive. No other sort of animal on earth could feel, as Jesús Ortiz felt as he descended in the elevator to the lobby, that he had been mangled by what *MacIntosh had said to him. He could not even be sure that there was enough of himself left to make living worthwhile.

And his brain was so complicated that he was seeing all sorts of pictures inside his skull which no lower animal could ever see, all as imaginary, as purely matters of human opinion, as the fifty million dollars *Andrew MacIntosh was prepared to transfer instantly from Manhattan to Ecuador when the right words came over the telephone. He saw a picture of Señora Kennedy,

Jacqueline Kennedy Onassis, which was indistinguishable from pictures he had seen of the Virgin Mary. Ortiz was a Roman Catholic. Everybody in Ecuador was a Roman Catholic. The von Kleists were all Roman Catholics. Even the cannibals in the Ecuadorian rain forest, the elusive Kanka-bonos, were Roman Catholics.

This Señora Kennedy was beautiful and sad and pure and kind and all powerful. In the mind of Ortiz, though, she also presided over a host of minor deities, who were also going to take part in "the Nature Cruise of the Century," which included the six guests already at the hotel. Ortiz had expected nothing but goodness from any of them, and felt, as had most Ecuadorians until hunger started to set in, that their coming to Ecuador would be a glorious moment in their nation's history, and that every conceivable luxury should be lavished on them.

But now the truth about one of these supposedly wonderful visitors, *Andrew MacIntosh, had polluted Ortiz's mental picture not only of all the other minor deities, but of Señora Kennedy herself.

So that head-and-shoulders portrait grew fangs like a vampire, and the skin dropped off the face, but the hair stayed on. It was a grinning skull now, wishing nothing but pestilence and death for little Ecuador.

•   •   •

It was a scary picture, and Ortiz could not make it go away. He thought that he might be able to ditch it in the heat outside, so he crossed the lobby, heedless of *Siegfried von Kleist's calls from the bar. *Von Kleist was asking him what was the matter, where was he going, and so on. Ortiz was the hotel's best employee, the most loyal and resourceful and uniformly cheerful one, and *von Kleist really needed him.

•   •   •

Here is why the hotel manager had no children, incidentally, although he was heterosexual and his sperm looked fine under a microscope and so on: There was a fifty-fifty chance that he was a carrier of an inherited and incurable disease of the brain, unknown in the present day, called Huntington's chorea.

Back then, Huntington's chorea was one of the thousand most common diseases which Mandarax could diagnose.

It is a matter of pure, gambling-casino luck that there are no carriers of Huntington's chorea today. It was the same dumb luck which had made *Siegfried von Kleist a possible carrier back then. His father had learned that he was a carrier only in middle life, after he had reproduced twice.

And that meant, of course, that *Siegfried's taller and older and more glamorous brother, Adolf, the captain of the *Bahía de Darwin*, might also be a carrier. So *Siegfried, who was about to die without issue, and Adolf, who would eventually become the common sire of the entire human race, had both, for admirably unselfish reasons, declined to engage in biologically significant copulation a million years ago.

• • •

*Siegfried and Adolf kept it a secret that they might have this defect in their genes. That secrecy spared them personal embarrassment, surely—but it protected all their relatives, too. If it had been generally known that the brothers might transmit Huntington's chorea to their offspring, all the von Kleists would likely have found it difficult to make good marriages, even though there was no chance that they, too, were carriers.

The thing was: The disease, if they had it, had come to the brothers through their paternal grandmother, who was the second wife of their paternal grandfather, and who had only one child—their father, the Ecuadorian sculptor and architect, Sebastian von Kleist.

How bad a defect was it? Well—it was certainly a lot worse than having a child all covered with fur.

In fact, of all the horrible diseases known to Mandarax, Huntington's chorea may have been the worst. It was surely the most treacherous, the nastiest, of all surprises. It usually lay in ambush, and undetectable by any known test, until the wretch who had inherited it was well into his or her adult years. The father of the brothers, for example, led an unclouded and productive life until he was fifty-four—at which time he began to dance involuntarily, and to see things which weren't there. And then he killed his wife, a fact which was hushed up. The murder was reported to the police, and so treated by them, as a household accident.

• • •

So these two brothers had been expecting to go crazy at any moment, to start dancing and hallucinating, for twenty-five years now. Each one had a fifty-fifty chance of doing that. If either one went crazy, that would be proof that he could pass on the defect to yet another generation. If either one became an old, old man without going crazy, that would be proof that he was not a carrier, nor would any of his descendants be carriers, either. It would turn out that he might have reproduced with impunity.

• • •

As things turned out, the flip of a coin, the Captain was not a carrier, but his brother was. At least poor *Siegfried wasn't going to suffer long. He started going crazy when he had only a few more hours to live—on the afternoon of Thursday, November 27, 1986. There he was, standing in back of the bar at the El Dorado, with James Wait seated before him and the portrait of Charles Darwin at his back. He had just seen his most trustworthy employee, Jesús Ortiz, go out the front door, terribly upset about something.

And then *Siegfried's big brain had him swoon into madness for a moment, and then back to sanity again.

• • •

At that early stage of the disease, the only stage the unlucky brother would know, it was still possible for his soul to recognize that his brain had become dangerous, and to help him maintain a semblance of mental health through sheer willpower. So he kept a straight face and tried to return to business as usual by putting a question to Wait.

"What do you do for a living, Mr. Flemming?" he inquired.

When *Siegfried spoke these words, they came back to him hellishly, as though he were shouting into an empty steel barrel at the top of his lungs. He had become extremely sensitive to noises.

And Wait's reply, although spoken softly, was also an ear splitter. "I used to be an engineer," said Wait, "but I lost interest in that and in everything, to tell the truth, after my wife died. I guess you'd call me a survivor now."

•   •   •

So Jesús Ortiz left the hotel after having been so hideously insulted by *Andrew MacIntosh. He intended to walk all over the neighborhood until he had calmed down some. But he soon discovered that barbed wire and soldiers had turned the area around the hotel into a cordon sanitaire. The necessity for such a barrier was also evident. Crowds of people of all ages on the other side of the wire looked at him as soulfully as had Kazakh, the seeing-eye dog, hoping against hope that he might have food for them.

He stayed within the fence, and walked around the hotel again and again. On each of three laps he passed the open doorway of the laundry room. Right inside was a gray steel box fixed to the wall. He knew what it contained: the junctions which married the hotel's telephones to the outside world. A good citizen of a million years ago might have thought of such a box, "What the telephone company hath joined together, let no man put asunder."

Yes, and such was the overt sentiment in the brain of Jesús Ortiz. He would never harm a box that important to so many people. But brains back then were so big that they could actually deceive their owners. His brain wanted him to disconnect all the telephones the first time he went past the laundry room, but it knew how opposed his soul was to bad citizenship. So, in order to keep him from becoming paralyzed, his brain kept reassuring him, in effect, "No, no — of course we would never do such a thing."

On the fourth lap, it got him into the laundry room, but also gave him a cover story for what he was doing in there. Good citizen that he was, he was searching for the green pants suit of a hotel guest, Mary Hepburn, which had apparently disappeared into some other universe the night before.

And then he opened the box and ripped apart the junctions. In a matter of seconds, a typical brain of a million years ago had turned the best citizen in Guayaquil into a ravening terrorist.

## 17

O N THE ISLAND OF MANHATTAN, a middle-aged American publicity man contemplated the collapse of his masterpiece, which was "the Nature Cruise of the Century." He had just moved into new offices within the hollow crown of the Chrysler Building, formerly the showroom of a harp company which found itself bankrupt—like the City of Ilium and Ecuador and the Philippines and Turkey, and on and on. His name was Bobby King.

He was in the same time zone as Guayaquil, and a line drawn due south from the deep crease in his brow to just below the equator would have found a terminal in an even deeper crease in the brow of *Andrew MacIntosh in Guayaquil. *MacIntosh was trying to shout life into a dead telephone. *MacIntosh might as well have been holding a stuffed Galápagos marine iguana alongside his boxy head as he cried out ever more imperiously: "Hello! Hello!"

Bobby King had a stuffed Galápagos marine iguana on his desk; had in fact amused more than one visitor by pretending that he had mistaken it for his telephone, holding it alongside his head and saying, "Hello! Hello!"

He was in no joking mood now, though, surely. In his own way, he had done as much as Charles Darwin to make the Galápagos Islands famous—with a ten-month campaign of publicity and advertising which had persuaded millions of people all over the planet that the maiden voyage of the *Bahía de Darwin* would indeed be "the Nature Cruise of the Century." In the process, he had made celebrities of many of the islands' creatures, the flightless cormorants, the blue-footed boobies, the larcenous frigate birds, and on and on.

His clients were the Ministry of Travel of Ecuador, Ecuatoriana Airlines, and the owners of the Hotel El Dorado and the *Bahía de Darwin*, the paternal uncles of *Siegfried and Captain Adolf von Kleist. Neither the hotel manager nor the Captain had to work for livings, incidentally. They were fabulously well to do through inheritance, but felt that they should keep busy all the same.

628

It now appeared certain to King, although he had not been told so yet, that his work had been for nothing, that "the Nature Cruise of the Century" would not take place.

As for the stuffed marine iguana on his desk: He had made that reptile the totemic animal for the cruise—had caused its image to be painted on either side of the *Bahía de Darwin*'s bow, and to appear as a logo in every ad and at the top of every publicity release.

In real life, the creature could be more than a meter long, and look as fearsome as a Chinese dragon. Actually, though, it was no more dangerous to life forms of any sort, with the exception of seaweed, than a liverwurst. Here is what its life is like in the present day, which is exactly what its life was like a million years ago:

It has no enemies, so it sits in one place, staring into the middle distance at nothing, wanting nothing, worried about nothing, until it is hungry. It then waddles down to the ocean and swims slowly and not all that ably until it is a few meters from shore. Then it dives like a submarine, and stuffs itself with seaweed, which is at that time indigestible. The seaweed is going to have to be cooked before it is digestible.

So the marine iguana pops to the surface, swims ashore, and sits on the lava in the sunshine again. It is using itself for a covered stewpot, getting hotter and hotter while the sunshine cooks the seaweed. It continues to stare into the middle distance at nothing, as before, but with this difference: It now spits up increasingly hot saltwater from time to time.

During the million years I have spent in these islands, the Law of Natural Selection has found no way to improve, or, for that matter, to worsen this particular survival scheme.

• • •

King knew that six persons had actually reached Guayaquil, and were in the Hotel El Dorado at that very moment, still expecting to take "the Nature Cruise of the Century." This was a minor shock to him. He had assumed that those who had made their own arrangements to get there would surely stay away, since the news from the area was so bad.

He had the names of all six. One was entirely unknown to him, a Canadian named Willard Flemming. That was actually

James Wait, of course. King could not imagine how this person had gotten onto the passenger list, which, with the exception of Mary Hepburn and a Japanese veterinarian and his wife, was supposed to be composed of newsmakers and trend-setters of the highest potency.

It puzzled King that Mary Hepburn was down there, but not her husband, Roy. He hadn't heard that Roy was dead. And he knew something about the Hepburns, even though they were complete nobodies on a passenger list of celebrities, because they were the very first persons to sign up for "the Nature Cruise of the Century." That was at a time when King had reason to doubt that any really famous person could be induced to make the trip.

When the Hepburns signed on, in fact, King had played with the idea of turning them into mini-celebrities somehow, with appearances on talk shows and newspaper interviews and so on. He would never meet them, but he did talk to Mary on the telephone, hoping against hope that there might be something interesting about the Hepburns, even though they held the most ordinary sorts of jobs in a drab industrial town with the highest unemployment rate in the country. One or the other might have a famous ancestor or relative, or Roy might have been a hero in some war, or they might have won a lottery, or they might have suffered a recent tragedy, or whatever.

And parts of King's conversation with Mary back in January had gone like this:

"Well—I am a distant relative of Daniel Boone," she said. "My maiden name was Boone, and I was born in Kentucky."

"That's wonderful!" said King. "You're his great-great-great-granddaughter or what?"

"I don't think it's quite that direct," she said. "It never meant much to me, so I never tried to get it straight."

"But your maiden name was Boone."

"Yes, but that's just a coincidence. My father's name was Boone, but he wasn't any relative of Daniel Boone. I'm related to Daniel Boone on my mother's side."

"If your father's name was Boone, and he was a Kentuckian, then he had to be related to Daniel Boone some way, don't you think?" said King.

"Not necessarily," she said, "because his father was a horse trainer from Hungary named Miklós Gömbös, who changed his name to Michael Boone."

On the subject of prizes or honors she or Roy might have won, Mary said that her husband certainly deserved plenty of them for all the good work he had done at GEFFCo, but that that company didn't believe in anything of that sort except for its very top executives.

"No military medals — nothing like that," he said.

"He was in the Navy," she said, "but he didn't fight."

If King had called three months later, of course, and gotten Roy on the phone, he would have received an earful about Roy's tragic exploits during the bomb tests in the Pacific.

"You have children?" said King.

"Not in the usual sense," said Mary. "But I consider every student a child of mine, and Roy is active in scouting, and he considers every member of his troop to be a son of his."

"That's a wonderful attitude," said King, "and it has been awfully nice to talk to you, and I hope you and your husband enjoy the trip."

"I'm sure we will," she said, "but I still have to get up enough nerve to tell the principal that I want three weeks off right in the middle of a semester."

"You'll have so many wonderful things to tell your students when you get back," said King, "that he'll be glad to let you go." King, incidentally, had never seen the Galápagos Islands first-hand, and never would. Like Mary Hepburn, he had certainly seen plenty of pictures of them.

"Oh —" said Mary as he was about to hang up, "you were asking about honors and prizes and medals and all that . . ."

"Yes?" said King.

"I'm just about to get a kind of prize, or what feels like a prize to me. I'm not supposed to know about it, so I probably shouldn't tell you about it."

"My lips are sealed," said King.

"I just happened to find out about it by accident," said Mary. "But this year's senior class is going to dedicate its yearbook to me. They give me a nickname in the dedication, which I just happened to see in a printshop where I was picking up some birth announcements for a friend. She had twins—a boy and a girl."

"Aha!" said King.

"Do you know the nickname those nice young people are giving me?" said Mary.

"No," said King.

"'Mother Nature Personified,'" said Mary.

•   •   •

And there are no tombs in the Galápagos Islands. The ocean gets all the bodies to use as it will. But if there were a tombstone for Mary Hepburn, no other inscription would do but this one: "Mother Nature Personified." In what way was she so like Mother Nature? In the face of utter hopelessness on Santa Rosalia, she still wanted human babies to be born there. Nothing could keep her from doing all she could to keep life going on and on and on.

# 18

WHEN BOBBY KING heard that Mary Hepburn was one of the six unfortunate enough to have reached Guayaquil, he thought about her for the first time in months. He thought that perhaps Roy was with her, since they had sounded like such an inseparable couple, and that his name had been omitted accidentally by the Hotel El Dorado's manager, whose teletyped communications were becoming more hectic by the hour.

• • •

King knew about me, by the way, although not by name.

He knew a workman had been killed during the building of the ship.

But he no more wanted to publicize this piece of information, which might imply to the superstitious that the *Bahía de Darwin* had a ghost, than the von Kleist family wished it known that one of its members was hospitalized with Huntington's chorea, and that two more of its members had a fifty-fifty chance of being carriers of that disease.

• • •

Did the Captain ever tell Mary Hepburn during their years together on Santa Rosalia that he might be a carrier of Huntington's chorea? He revealed that terrible secret only after they had been marooned ten years, and he realized that she had been playing fast and loose with his sperm.

• • •

Of the six guests at the El Dorado, King was acquainted with only two: *Andrew MacIntosh and his blind daughter Selena— and, of course, Kazakh, Selena's dog. Anybody who knew the MacIntoshes also knew the dog, although Kazakh, thanks to surgery and training, had virtually no personality. The MacIntoshes were frequenters of several restaurants which were King's clients, and *MacIntosh, but not the dog and the daughter, had been on talk shows with some of his clients. King had watched the shows with Selena and the dog on a backstage monitor. It was his impression that the daughter had little more personality than the dog when she wasn't right next to her father. And her father was all she could talk about.

*Andrew MacIntosh certainly enjoyed his exposure on talk shows. He was a welcome guest on them because he was so outrageous. He held forth about what fun life was if you had unlimited money to spend. He pitied and scorned people who weren't rich, and so on.

Thanks to the rigors of Santa Rosalia, Selena would develop a personality very distinct from her father's before she went down the blue tunnel into the Afterlife. She would also be fluent in Japanese. In the era of big brains, life stories could end up any which way.

Look at mine.

•   •   •

After Roy and Mary Hepburn, the MacIntoshes and the Hiroguchis were the next people to join the passenger list for "the Nature Cruise of the Century." That was in February. The Hiroguchis were to be *MacIntosh's guests, and they would travel under false names, so that *Zenji Hiroguchi's employers would not discover that he was negotiating a business deal with *MacIntosh.

As far as King and *Siegfried von Kleist and anybody else connected with the cruise knew, the Hiroguchis were the Kenzaburos, and *Zenji was a veterinarian.

That meant that fully half of the guests at the El Dorado weren't who they were supposed to be. As a fillip to all this big-brained deceiving going on, Mary Hepburn's war-surplus combat fatigues still bore the embroidered last name of their previous owner over the left breast pocket, which was Kaplan. And when she and James Wait finally met in the cocktail lounge, he would tell her his false name and she would tell him her true name, but he would keep calling her "Mrs. Kaplan" anyway, and extol the Jewish people and so on.

And they would later be married by the Captain on the sundeck of the *Bahía de Darwin*, and as far as she knew, she had become the wife of Willard Flemming, and as far as he knew, he had become the husband of Mary Kaplan.

This sort of confusion would be impossible in the present day, since nobody has a name anymore—or a profession, or a life story to tell. All that anybody has in the way of a reputation anymore is an odor which, from birth to death, cannot be modified. People are who they are, and that is that. The Law of Natural Selection has made human beings absolutely honest in that regard. Everybody is exactly what he or she seems to be.

•    •    •

When *Andrew MacIntosh signed up for three staterooms on the *Bahía de Darwin*'s maiden voyage, Bobby King had reason to be mystified. *MacIntosh had a private yacht, the *Omoo*, which was nearly as large as the cruise ship, and so could have gone to the Galápagos Islands on his own—without submitting to the close contacts with strangers and the disciplines which would be imposed by "the Nature Cruise of the Century." The cruise passengers, for example, would not be able to go ashore whenever they pleased, and to behave there however they pleased. They were to be escorted and supervised at all times by guides, all of them trained by scientists at the Darwin Research Station on Santa Cruz Island, and all of them holding graduate degrees in one of the natural sciences.

So when King, making his rounds of restaurants and clubs one night, saw *MacIntosh and his daughter and her dog and two other people having a late supper in a celebrity hangout called Elaine's, he stopped by their table to say how pleased he was that they were taking the cruise. He wanted very much to hear why they were taking it—so that he might use their reasons as inducements for other newsmakers to come along.

Only after greeting the MacIntoshes did King realize who the other two people at the table were. He knew them both to speak to, and he did so now. The woman was the most admired female on the planet, Mrs. Jacqueline Bouvier Kennedy Onassis, and her escort that evening was the great dancer, Rudolf Nureyev.

Nureyev, incidentally, was a former citizen of the Soviet Union, who had been granted political asylum in Great Britain. And I was still alive then, and I was a United States citizen who had been granted political asylum in Sweden.

Yes, and we both liked to dance.

•   •   •

At the risk of reminding *MacIntosh that he owned an ocean-going yacht, King asked him what he had found so attractive about the *Bahía de Darwin*. *MacIntosh, who was highly intelligent and well read, thereupon delivered a speech on the damage selfish and ignorant persons had done to the Galápagos Islands while going ashore unsupervised. This material was all lifted from an article in the *National Geographic* magazine, which he read from cover to cover every month. The magazine's point was that Ecuador would require a navy the size of the combined fleets of the world to keep persons from going ashore on the islands and doing as they pleased, so that the fragile habitats could be preserved only if individuals were educated to exercise self-restraint. "No good citizen of the planet," said the article, "should ever go ashore unless escorted by a well-trained guide."

•   •   •

When Mary Hepburn and the Captain and Hisako Hiroguchi and Selena MacIntosh and the rest of them were marooned on Santa Rosalia, they would not have a trained guide along. And, for their first few years there, they would raise perfect hell with the fragile habitat.

Just in the nick of time they realized that it was their own habitat they were wrecking—that they weren't merely visitors.

•   •   •

There in Elaine's Restaurant, *MacIntosh angered his spellbound audience with tales of boots crushing the camouflaged nests of iguanas, of greedy fingers stealing the eggs of boobies, and on and on. His most moving atrocity story by far, though, again lifted from the *National Geographic*, was of persons cradling fur seal pups in their arms as though they were human infants—for the sake of photographs. When the pup was returned to its mother, he said bitterly, she would no longer nurse it because its smell had been changed.

"So what happens to that darling pup, which has just had the great honor of being cuddled by a bighearted nature lover?"

asked *MacIntosh. "It starves to death — all for the sake of a photograph."

So his answer to Bobby King's question was that he was setting a good example he hoped others would follow by taking "the Nature Cruise of the Century."

•  •  •

It is a joke to me that this man should have presented himself as an ardent conservationist, since so many of the companies he served as a director or in which he was a major stockholder were notorious damagers of the water or the soil or the atmosphere. But it wasn't a joke to *MacIntosh, who had come into this world incapable of caring much about anything. So, in order to hide this deficiency, he had become a great actor, pretending even to himself that he cared passionately about all sorts of things.

With the same degree of conviction, he had earlier given his daughter an entirely different explanation of why they were going to the islands on the *Bahía de Darwin* instead of the *Omoo*. The Hiroguchis might feel trapped on the *Omoo*, with nobody but the MacIntoshes to talk to. They might panic under such circumstances, and *Zenji might refuse to negotiate anymore, and ask to be put ashore at the nearest port so that he and his wife could fly back home.

Like so many other pathological personalities in positions of power a million years ago, he might do almost anything on impulse, feeling nothing much. The logical explanations for his actions, invented at leisure, always came afterwards.

And let that sort of behavior back in the era of the big brains be taken as a capsule history of the war I had the honor to fight in, which was the Vietnam War.

L IKE MOST pathological personalities, *Andrew MacIntosh never cared much whether what he said was true or
not—and so he was tremendously persuasive. And he so moved
the widow Onassis and Rudolf Nureyev that they asked Bobby
King for more information about "the Nature Cruise of the
Century," which he sent to them on the following morning by
special messenger.

As luck would have it, there was going to be a documentary
about the lives of blue-footed boobies on the islands shown
on educational television that evening, so King enclosed notes
saying that they might want to watch it. These birds would later
become crucial to the survival of the little human colony on
Santa Rosalia. If those birds hadn't been so stupid, so incapable
of learning that human beings were dangerous, the first settlers
would almost certainly have starved to death.

• • •

The high point of that program, like the high point of Mary
Hepburn's lectures on the islands at Ilium High School, was
film footage of the courtship dance of the blue-footed boobies.
The dance went like this:

There were these two fairly large sea birds standing around
on the lava. They were about the size of flightless cormorants,
and had the same long, snaky necks and fish-spear beaks. But
they had not given up on aviation, and so had big, strong wings.
Their legs and webbed feet were bright, rubbery blue. They
caught fish by crashing down on them from the sky.

Fish! Fish! Fish!

They looked alike, although one was a male and the other
was a female. They seemed to be on separate errands, and not
interested in each other in the least—although there wasn't
much business for either one of them to do on the lava, since
they didn't eat bugs or seeds. They weren't looking for nesting
materials, since it was much too early in the game for that.

The male stopped doing what he was so busy doing, which
was nothing. He caught sight of the female. He looked away

from her, and then back again, standing still and making no
sound. They both had voices, but at no point in the dance
would either make a sound.

She looked this way and that, and then her gaze met his accidentally. They were then five meters apart or more.

When Mary showed the film of the dance at the high school,
she used to say at this point, as though she were speaking for the
female: "What on Earth could this strange person want with
me? Really! How bizarre!"

The male raised one bright blue foot. He spread it in air like
a paper fan.

Mary Hepburn, again in the persona of the female, used to
say, "What is that supposed to be? A Wonder of the World?
Does he think that's the only blue foot in the islands?"

The male put that foot down and raised the other one, bringing himself one pace closer to the female. Then he showed her
the first one again, and then the second one again, looking her
straight in the eye.

Mary would say for her, "I'm getting out of here." But the
female didn't get out of there. She seemed glued to the lava as
the male showed her one foot and then the other one, coming
closer all the time.

And then the female raised one of her blue feet, and Mary
used to say, "You think you've got such beautiful feet? Take a
look at this, if you want to see a beautiful foot. Yes, and I've got
another one, too."

The female put down one foot and raised the other one,
bringing herself one pace closer to the male.

Mary used to shut up then. There would be no more anthro-
pomorphic jokes. It was up to the birds now to carry the show.
Advancing toward each other in the same grave and stately
manner, neither bird speeding up or slowing down, they were
at last breast to breast and toe to toe.

At Ilium High School, the students did not expect to see the
birds copulate. The film was so famous, since Mary had shown
it in the auditorium in early May, as an educational celebration
of springtime, for years and years, that everybody knew that
they would not get to see the birds copulate.

What those birds did on camera, though, was supremely
erotic all the same. Already breast to breast and toe to toe, they

made their sinuous necks as erect as flagpoles. They tilted their heads back as far as they would go. They pressed their long throats and the undersides of their jaws together. They formed a tower, the two of them—a single structure, pointed on top and resting on four blue feet.

Thus was a marriage solemnized.

There were no witnesses, no other boobies to celebrate what a nice couple they were or how well they had danced. In the film Mary Hepburn used to show at the high school, which was the same film Bobby King thought Mrs. Onassis and Rudolf Nureyev might enjoy watching on educational television, the only witnesses were the big-brained members of the camera crew.

The name of the film was *Sky-Pointing*, the same name big-brained scientists gave to the moment when the beaks of both birds were pointed in the direction exactly opposite to the pull of gravity.

And Mrs. Onassis was so moved by this film that she had her secretary call Bobby King the next morning, to inquire if it was too late to reserve two outside staterooms on the main deck of the *Bahía de Darwin* for "the Nature Cruise of the Century."

# *20*

MARY HEPBURN used to give her students extra credit if they would write a little poem or essay about the courtship dance. Something like half of them would turn something in, and about half who did thought the dance was proof that animals worshiped God. The rest of the responses were all over the place. One student turned in a poem which Mary would remember to her dying day, and which she taught to Mandarax. The student was named Noble Claggett, and he would be killed in the war in Vietnam—but there his poem would be inside of Mandarax, along with bits by some of the greatest writers who ever lived. It went like this:

> *Of course I love you,*
> *So let's have a kid*
> *Who will say exactly*
> *What its parents did;*
> *"Of course I love you,*
> *So let's have a kid*
> *Who will say exactly*
> *What its parents did;*
> *'Of course I love you,*
> *So let's have a kid*
> *Who will say exactly*
> *What its parents did—'"*
> *Et cetera.*
>> Noble Claggett
>> (1947–1966)

Some students would ask permission to write about some other Galápagos Islands creature, and Mary, being such a good teacher, would of course answer, "Yes." And the favorite alternates were those teasers and robbers of the boobies, the great frigate birds. These James Waits of the bird world survived on fish which boobies caught, and got their nesting materials from nests which boobies built. A certain sort of student found this hilarious, and such a student was almost invariably male.

And a unique physical feature of male great frigate birds was also bound to attract the attention of immature human males concerned with erectile performances of their own sex organs. Each male great frigate bird at mating time tried to attract the attention of females by inflating a bright red balloon at the base of his throat. At mating time, a typical rookery when viewed from the air resembled an enormous party for human children, at which every child had received a red balloon. The island would in fact be paved with male great frigate birds with their heads tilted back, their qualifications as husbands inflated by their lungs to the bursting point—while, overhead, the females wheeled.

One by one the females would drop from the sky, having chosen this or that red balloon.

•   •   •

After Mary Hepburn showed her film about the great frigate birds, and the windowshades in the classroom were raised and the lights turned back on, some student, again almost invariably a male, was sure to ask, sometimes clinically, sometimes as a comedian, sometimes bitterly, hating and fearing women: "Do the females always try to pick the biggest ones?"

So Mary was ready with a reply as consistent, word by word, as any quotation known by Mandarax: "To answer that, we would have to interview female great frigate birds, and no one has done that yet, so far as I know. Some people have devoted their lives to studying them, though, and it is their opinion that the females are in fact choosing the red balloons which mark the best nesting sites. That makes sense in terms of survival, you see.

"And that brings us back to the really deep mystery of the blue-footed boobies' courtship dance, which seems to have absolutely no connection with the elements of booby survival, with nesting or fish. What does it have to do with, then? Dare we call it 'religion'? Or, if we lack that sort of courage, might we at least call it 'art'?

"Your comments, please."

•   •   •

The courtship dance of the blue-footed boobies, which Mrs. Onassis suddenly wanted to see so much in person, has not changed one iota in a million years. Neither have these birds learned to be afraid of anything. Neither have they shown the slightest inclination to give up on aviation and become submarines.

As for the meaning of the courtship dance of the blue-footed boobies: The birds are huge molecules with bright blue feet and have no choice in the matter. By their very nature, they have to dance exactly like that.

Human beings used to be molecules which could do many, many different sorts of dances, or decline to dance at all—as they pleased. My mother could do the waltz, the tango, the rumba, the Charleston, the Lindy hop, the jitterbug, the Watusi, and the twist. Father refused to do any dances, as was his privilege.

## 21

WHEN MRS. ONASSIS said she wanted to go on "the Nature Cruise of the Century," then everybody wanted to go, and Roy and Mary Hepburn were almost entirely forgotten, with their pitiful little cabin below the waterline. By the end of March, King was able to release a passenger list headed by Mrs. Onassis, and followed by names almost as glamorous as hers—Dr. Henry Kissinger, Mick Jagger, Paloma Picasso, William F. Buckley, Jr., and of course *Andrew MacIntosh, and Rudolf Nureyev and Walter Cronkite, and on and on. *Zenji Hiroguchi, traveling under the name Zenji Kenzaburo, was said in the release to be a world famous expert in animal diseases, so as to make him seem more or less in scale with all the other passengers.

Two names were left off the list as a matter of delicacy, so as not to raise the embarrassing question of who they were, exactly, since they were really nobody at all. They were Roy and Mary Hepburn, with their pitiful little cabin below the waterline.

But then this slightly bobtailed list became the official list. So when Ecuatoriana Airlines in May sent a telegram to everybody on the list, notifying them that there would be a special overnight flight for any of them who happened to be in New York City on the evening before the *Bahía de Darwin* was to sail, Mary Hepburn was not among those notified. Limousines would pick them up anywhere in the city, and take them to the airport. Each seat on the plane could be converted into a bed, and the tourist seats had been replaced with cabaret tables and a dance floor, where a company from the Ecuadorian Ballet Folklórico would perform characteristic dances of various Indian tribes, including the fire dance of the elusive Kanka-bonos. Gourmet meals would be served, along with wines worthy of the greatest restaurants in France. All this would be free of charge, but Roy and Mary Hepburn never heard about it.

Yes, and they never got a letter that everybody else got in June—from Dr. José Sepúlveda de la Madrid, the president of Ecuador, inviting them to a state breakfast in their honor at the

Hotel El Dorado, followed by a parade in which they would ride in horse-drawn carriages decked with flowers—from the hotel to the waterfront, where they would board the ship.

Nor did Mary get a telegram King sent to everybody else on the first of November, which acknowledged that storm clouds on the economic horizon were indeed worrisome. The economy of Ecuador, however, remained sound, so that there was no reason to believe that the *Bahía de Darwin* would not sail as planned. What the letter didn't say, although King knew it, was that the passenger list had been cut approximately in half by cancellations from virtually every country represented there but Japan and the United States. So that almost everybody still intent on going would be on that special flight from New York City.

And now King's secretary came into his office to tell him that she had just heard on the radio that the State Department had just advised American citizens not to travel in Ecuador at the present time.

So that was that for what King considered the finest piece of work he had ever done. Without knowing anything about naval architecture, he had made a ship more attractive by persuading its owners not to call it, as they were about to do, the *Antonio José de Sucre*, but the *Bahía de Darwin*. He had transformed what was to have been a routine, two-week trip out to the islands and back into the nature cruise of the century. How had he worked such a miracle? By never calling it anything but "the Nature Cruise of the Century."

If, as now seemed certain to King, the *Bahía de Darwin* would not set out on "the Nature Cruise of the Century" at noon the next day, certain side effects of his campaign would endure. He had taught people a lot of natural history with his publicity releases about the wonders which Mrs. Onassis and Dr. Kissinger and Mick Jagger and so on would see. He had created two new celebrities: Robert Pépin, the chef King had declared to be "the greatest chef in France" after hiring him to run the galley for the maiden voyage, and Captain Adolf von Kleist, the captain of the *Bahía de Darwin*, who, with his big nose and air of hiding some unspeakable personal tragedy from the world, had turned out to be on television talk shows a first-rate comedian.

King had in his files a transcript of the Captain's performance on *The Tonight Show,* starring Johnny Carson. On that show, as on all the others, the Captain was dazzling in the gold-and-white uniform he was entitled to wear as an admiral in the Ecuadorian Naval Reserve. The transcript went like this:

• • •

CARSON: "Von Kleist" doesn't sound like a very South American name somehow.

CAPTAIN: It's Inca—one of the commonest Inca names, in fact, like "Smith" or "Jones" in English. You read the accounts of the Spanish explorers who destroyed the Inca Empire because it was so un-Christian—

CARSON: Yes—?

CAPTAIN: I assume you've read them.

CARSON: They're on my bedside table—along with *Ecstasy and Me,* the autobiography of Hedy Lamarr.

CAPTAIN: Then you know that one out of every three Indians they burned for heresy was named von Kleist.

CARSON: How big is the Ecuadorian navy?

CAPTAIN: Four submarines. They are always underwater. They never come up.

CARSON: Never come up?

CAPTAIN: Not for years and years.

CARSON: But they keep in touch by radio?

CAPTAIN: No. They maintain radio silence. It's their own idea. We would be glad to hear from them, but they prefer to maintain radio silence.

CARSON: Why have they stayed underwater so long?

CAPTAIN: You will have to ask them about that. Ecuador is a democracy, you know. Even those of us in the Navy have very wide latitude in what we can or cannot do.

CARSON: Some people think Hitler might still be alive—and living in South America. Do you think there's any chance of that?

CAPTAIN: I know there are persons in Ecuador who would love to have him for dinner.

CARSON: Nazi sympathizers.

CAPTAIN: I don't know about that. It's possible, I suppose.

CARSON: If they would be glad to have Hitler for dinner—

CAPTAIN: Then they must be cannibals. I was thinking of the Kanka-bonos. They are glad to have almost anybody for dinner. They are—what is the English word? It's on the tip of my tongue.

CARSON: I think I'll pass on this one.

CAPTAIN: They are—they are—the Kanka-bonos are—

CARSON: Take your time.

CAPTAIN: Aha! They are "apolitical." That's the word. Apolitical is what the Kanka-bonos are.

CARSON: But they are citizens of Ecuador?

CAPTAIN: Yes. Of course. I told you it was a democracy. One cannibal, one vote.

CARSON: There is a question which several ladies have asked me to ask you, and maybe it is too personal—

CAPTAIN: Why a man of my beauty and charm should never have tasted the joys of marriage?

CARSON: I've had some experience in these matters myself—as you may or may not know.

CAPTAIN: It would not be fair to the woman.

CARSON: Now things are getting too personal. Let's talk about blue-footed boobies. Maybe now is the time to show the film you brought.

CAPTAIN: No, no. I'm perfectly willing to discuss my failure to plight a troth. It would not be fair of me to marry a woman, since at any time I might be given command of a submarine.

CARSON: And you would have to go under, and never come up again.

CAPTAIN: That is the tradition.

• • •

King sighed massively. The passenger list was on his desktop, with about half the names crossed off—Mexicans and Argentinians and Italians and Filipinos, and so on, foolish enough to have kept their fortunes in their own national currencies. The names remaining, save for the six persons already in Guayaquil, were all in the New York City area, easily reached by telephone.

"I guess we have some telephoning to do," King said to his secretary.

She offered to do the calling. He said, "No." It was not a duty he felt free to delegate. He had persuaded all these celebrities to take part in the cruise, had wooed the most potent newsmakers among them as a lover might. Now he was going to have to give them the bad news personally, as a responsible lover should. At least he wouldn't have much trouble finding most of them. There were forty-two of them, counting mates or companions who were nonentities, but they had organized themselves into a few dinner parties, duly reported in gossip columns that day, in order to pass pleasantly the hours remaining until limousines came to cushion and muffle them away to Kennedy International Airport—for Ecuatoriana's special ten o'clock flight to Guayaquil.

And at least he wouldn't have to talk about getting back their money for them. The trip wasn't to have cost them a nickel—and they had already received free matched luggage and toiletries, and Panama hats besides.

For the sad amusement of himself and his secretary, King now played his joke with the stuffed marine iguana. He picked it up and held it alongside his head as though it were a telephone, and he said, "Mrs. Onassis? I am afraid I have some disappointing news for you. You're not going to get to see the courtship dance of the blue-footed boobies after all."

• • •

King's apologetic telephoning was a gallant formality. No one still expected to board the plane at ten that night. By ten that night, incidentally, *Andrew MacIntosh, *Zenji Hiroguchi, and the Captain's brother *Siegfried would all be dead, and would all have completed their short journeys through the blue tunnel into the Afterlife.

All the people on the passenger list that King talked to had already made new plans for the coming two weeks. Many would go skiing within the safe boundaries of the United States instead. At one dinner party for six, everybody had already decided to go to a combination fat farm and tennis camp in Phoenix, Arizona.

And the last call King made before leaving his office was to a man who had become a very close friend during the past ten months, who was Dr. Teodoro Donoso, a poet and physician from Quito, who was Ecuador's ambassador to the United

Nations. He had earned his medical degree at Harvard, and several other Ecuadorians King had dealt with had been educated in the United States. The Captain of the *Bahía de Darwin*, Adolf von Kleist, was a graduate of the United States Naval Academy at Annapolis. The Captain's brother *Siegfried was a graduate of the Cornell Hotel School at Ithaca, New York.

There was a lot of noise from what sounded like a wild party going on at the embassy, which Dr. Donoso suppressed by closing a door.

"What are those people celebrating?" King asked.

"It's the Ballet Folklórico," said the Ambassador, "rehearsing the fire dance of the Kanka-bonos."

"They don't know the trip's been called off?" said King.

It turned out that they did know, and that they intended to stay in the United States in order to earn dollars for their families back home by performing in nightclubs and theaters a dance Bobby King had made so famous in his publicity—the fire dance of the Kanka-bonos.

"Are there any real Kanka-bonos in the bunch?" said King.

"My guess is that there aren't any real Kanka-bonos anywhere," said the Ambassador. He had in fact written a twenty-six line poem called "The Last Kanka-bono," about the extinction of a little tribe in the Ecuadorian rain forest. At the start of the poem, there were eleven Kanka-bonos. At the end there was just one, and he wasn't feeling well. This was an exercise in fiction, however, since the poet, like most Ecuadorians, had never seen a Kanka-bono. He had heard that the tribe was down to only fourteen members, so that their final extinction by the encroachments of civilization seemed inevitable.

Little did he know that in a matter of less than a century the blood of every human being on earth would be predominantly Kanka-bono, with a little von Kleist and Hiroguchi thrown in.

And this astonishing turn of events would be made to happen, in large part, by one of the only two absolute nobodies on the original passenger list for "the Nature Cruise of the Century." That was Mary Hepburn. The other nobody was her husband, who himself played a crucial role in shaping human destiny by booking, when facing his own extinction, that one cheap little cabin below the waterline.

# 22

Ambassador Donoso's twenty-six lines of mourning for "The Last Kanka-bono" were premature, to say the least. He should have wept on paper for "The Last Mainland South American" and "The Last Mainland North American" and "The Last Mainland European" and "The Last Mainland African" and "The Last Mainland Asian" instead.

He guessed right, at any rate, as to what was going to happen to the morale of the people of Ecuador within the next hour or so, when he said to Bobby King on the telephone: "Everybody down there is just going to fall apart when they find out that Mrs. Onassis isn't coming after all."

"Things can change so much in just thirty days," said King. "'The Nature Cruise of the Century' was supposed to be just one of many things Ecuadorians had to look forward to. Suddenly it became the only thing."

"It is as though we prepared a great crystal bowl of champagne punch," said Donoso, "and then, overnight, it turned into a rusty bucket of nitroglycerin." He said that "the Nature Cruise of the Century" had at least postponed Ecuador's facing up to its insoluble economic problems for a week or two. The governments of Colombia to the north and Peru to the south and east had already been overthrown, and were now military dictatorships. The new leaders of Peru, in fact, in order to divert the big brains of their people from all their troubles, were just about to declare war on Ecuador.

• • •

"If Mrs. Onassis were to go there now," said Donoso, "people would receive her as though she were a rescuer, a worker of miracles. She would be expected to summon ships laden with food to Guayaquil—and to have United States bombers drop cereal and milk and fresh fruit for the children by parachute!"

Nobody nowadays, I must say, expects to be rescued from anything, once he or she is more than nine months old. That's how long human childhood lasts nowadays.

* * *

I myself was rescued from folly and carelessness until I was ten years old—until Mother walked out on Father and me. I was on my own after that. Mary Hepburn didn't become independent of her parents until she received her master's degree at the age of twenty-two. Adolf von Kleist, the Captain of the *Bahía de Darwin*, was regularly bailed out by his parents from gambling debts and charges of drunken driving and assault and resisting arrest and vandalism and so on until he was twenty-six—when his father came down with Huntington's chorea and murdered his mother. Only then did he begin to assume responsibility for mistakes he made.

Back when childhoods were often so protracted, it is unsurprising that so many people got into the lifelong habit of believing, even after their parents were gone, that somebody was always watching over them—God or a saint or a guardian angel or the stars or whatever.

People have no such illusions today. They learn very early what kind of a world this really is, and it is a rare adult indeed who hasn't seen a careless sibling or parent eaten alive by a killer whale or shark.

* * *

A million years ago, there were passionate arguments about whether it was right or wrong for people to use mechanical means to keep sperm from fertilizing ova or to dislodge fertilized ova from uteri—in order to keep the number of people from exceeding the food supply.

That problem is all taken care of nowadays, without anybody's having to do anything unnatural. Killer whales and sharks keep the human population nice and manageable, and nobody starves.

* * *

Mary Hepburn used to teach not only general biology at Ilium High School, but a course in human sexuality, too. This necessitated her describing various birth-control devices which she herself had never used, since her husband was the only lover she had ever had, and she and Roy had wanted to have babies from the very first.

She, who had failed to get pregnant despite years of profound sexual intimacies with Roy, had to admonish her students about how easy it was for a human female to get pregnant from the most fleeting, insensate, seemingly inconsequential contact with a male. And after she had been teaching a few years, most of her cautionary tales involved students she had known personally—right there at Ilium High.

Scarcely a semester passed at the high school without at least one unwanted pregnancy, and during the memorable spring semester of 1981 there were six. And, true enough, about half of these babies having babies spoke of true love for those with whom they had mated. But the other half swore, in the face of contradictory evidence which could only be described as overwhelming, that they had never, to the best of their recollection, engaged in any activity which could result in the birth of a child.

And Mary would say to a female colleague at the end of the memorable spring semester of 1981, "For some people, getting pregnant is as easy as catching cold." And there certainly was an analogy there: Colds and babies were both caused by germs which loved nothing so much as a mucous membrane.

•  •  •

After ten years on Santa Rosalia Island, Mary Hepburn would discover firsthand exactly how easily a teenage virgin could be made pregnant by the seed of a male who was seeking sexual release and nothing else, who did not even like her.

# 23

So, WITHOUT ANY IDEA that he was going to become the sire of all humankind, I got into the head of Captain Adolf von Kleist as he rode in a taxicab from Guayaquil International Airport to the *Bahía de Darwin*. I did not know that humanity was about to be diminished to a tiny point, by luck, and then, again by luck, to be permitted to expand again. I believed that the chaos involving billions of big-brained people thrashing around every which way, and reproducing and reproducing, would go on and on. It did not seem likely that an individual could be significant in such an unplanned uproar.

My choosing the Captain's head for a vehicle, then, was the equivalent of putting a coin in a slot machine in an enormous gambling casino, and hitting a jackpot right away.

It was his uniform which attracted me as much as anything. He was wearing the white-and-gold uniform of a Reserve admiral. I myself had been a private, and so was curious to know what the world looked like to a person of very high military rank and social standing.

And I was mystified to find his big brain thinking about meteorites. That was often my experience back then: I would get into the head of somebody in what to me was a particularly interesting situation, and discover that the person's big brain was thinking about things which had nothing to do with the problem right at hand.

Here was the thing about the Captain and meteorites: He had paid little attention to most of his instructors at the United States Naval Academy, and had graduated at the very bottom of his class. He in fact would have been expelled for cheating in an examination on celestial navigation, if his parents hadn't interceded through diplomatic channels. But he had been impressed by one lecture on the subject of meteorites. The instructor said that showers of great boulders from outer space had been quite common over the eons, and their impacts had been so terrific, possibly, as to have caused the extinction of many life forms, including the dinosaurs. He said that human beings had every reason to expect more such planet smashers at any time, and should devise apparatus for distinguishing between enemy missiles and meteorites.

Otherwise, utterly meaningless wrath from outer space could trigger World War Three.

And this apocalyptic warning so suited the wiring of the Captain's brain, even before his father came down with Huntington's chorea, that he would ever after believe that that was indeed the most likely way in which humanity would be exterminated: by meteorites.

To the Captain, it was such a much more honorable and poetical and even beautiful way for humanity to die than World War Three would be.

•  •  •

When I got to know his big brain better, I understood that there was a certain logic to his thinking about meteorites while he was looking out at Guayaquil with its hungry crowds under martial law. Even without the glamor of a meteorite shower, the world appeared to be ending for the people of Guayaquil.

•  •  •

In a sense, too, this man had already been hit by a meteorite: by the murder of his mother by his father. And his feeling that life was a meaningless nightmare, with nobody watching or caring what was going on, was actually quite familiar to me.

That was how I felt after I shot a grandmother in Vietnam. She was as toothless and bent over as Mary Hepburn would be at the end of her life. I shot her because she had just killed my best friend and my worst enemy in my platoon with a single hand-grenade.

This episode made me sorry to be alive, made me envy stones. I would rather have been a stone at the service of the Natural Order.

•  •  •

The Captain went straight from the airport to his ship, without stopping off at the hotel to see his brother. He had been drinking champagne during the long flight from New York City, and so had a splitting headache.

And when we got aboard the *Bahía de Darwin*, it was obvious to me that his functions as captain, like his functions as a Reserve admiral, were purely ceremonial. Others would be doing the navigating and engineering and maintaining crew discipline and so on while he socialized with the distinguished passengers. He knew very little about the operation of the ship, nor did he feel he needed to know much about it. His familiarity with the Galápagos Islands was likewise sketchy. He had made ceremonial visits as an admiral to the naval base on the island of Baltra and the Darwin Research Station on Santa Cruz— again as essentially a passenger on board a ship of which he was nominally the commander. But all the rest of the islands were terra incognita to him. He would have been a more instructive guide on the ski slopes of Switzerland, say, or on the carpets of the casino at Monte Carlo, or to the stables serving at Palm Beach polo fields.

But again—what did that matter? On "the Nature Cruise of the Century," there would be guides and lecturers trained at the Darwin Research Station and holding graduate degrees in the natural sciences. The Captain intended to listen to them carefully, and learn about the islands right along with the rest of the passengers.

●   ●   ●

Riding in the Captain's skull, I had hoped to find out what it was like to be a supreme commander. I found out, instead, what it was like to be a social butterfly. We were received with all possible signs of military respect when we came up the gangplank. But, once aboard, no officers or crewmen asked us for instructions about anything as they made the final preparations for the arrival of Mrs. Onassis and the rest of them.

So far as the Captain knew, the ship was still going to sail the next day. He had not been told otherwise. Since he had been back in Ecuador for only an hour, and still had a bellyful of good New York food and a champagne headache, it had yet to dawn on him what awful trouble he and his ship were in.

●   ●   ●

There is another human defect which the Law of Natural Selection has yet to remedy: When people of today have full bellies, they are exactly like their ancestors of a million years ago: very slow to acknowledge any awful troubles they may be in. Then is when they forget to keep a sharp lookout for sharks and whales.

This was a particularly tragic flaw a million years ago, since the people who were best informed about the state of the planet, like *Andrew MacIntosh, for example, and rich and powerful enough to slow down all the waste and destruction going on, were by definition well fed.

So everything was always just fine as far as they were concerned.

For all the computers and measuring instruments and news gatherers and evaluators and memory banks and libraries and experts on this and that at their disposal, their deaf and blind bellies remained the final judges of how urgent this or that problem, such as the destruction of North America's and Europe's forests by acid rain, say, might really be.

And here was the sort of advice a full belly gave and still gives, and which the Captain's full belly gave him when the first mate of the *Bahía de Darwin*, Hernando Cruz, told him that none of the guides had shown up or been heard from, and that a third of the crewmen had deserted so far, feeling that they had better look after their families: "Be patient. Smile. Be confident. Everything will turn out for the best somehow."

MARY HEPBURN had seen and appreciated the Captain's comical performance on *The Tonight Show*, and then another one on *Good Morning America*. To that extent, she felt she already knew him some before her big brain made her come to Guayaquil.

He was on *The Tonight Show* two weeks after Roy died, and he was the first person to make her laugh out loud after that sad event. There she was in the living room of her little house, with the houses on all sides of hers empty and for sale, and heard herself laugh out loud about the ridiculous Ecuadorian submarine fleet, whose tradition was to go underwater and never come up again.

She supposed then that von Kleist was a lot like Roy in loving nature and machinery. Otherwise, why would he have been chosen to be the Captain of the *Bahía de Darwin*?

Now her big brain had her say out loud to the Captain's image on the cathode-ray tube, to the considerable embarrassment of her soul, although there was no one to hear her: "Would you by any chance like to marry me?"

• • •

It would turn out that she knew at least a little bit more about machinery than he did, just from living with Roy. After Roy died, and the lawn mower wouldn't start, for example, she was able to change the spark plug and get it going—something the Captain could never have done.

And she knew a whole lot more about the islands. It was Mary who correctly identified the island on which they would be marooned. The Captain, grasping for shreds of self-respect and authority after his big brain had made such a mess of things, declared the island to be Rábida, which it surely wasn't and which, in any case, he had never seen.

And what allowed Mary to recognize Santa Rosalia were the dominant sorts of finches there. These drab little birds, incidentally, so uninteresting to most tourists and to Mary's students, had been as exciting to young Charles Darwin as the great land tortoises or the boobies or marine iguanas, or any other creatures there. The thing was: The finches looked very much alike, but they were in fact divided into thirteen species, each species with its own peculiar diet and method for getting food.

None had close relatives on the mainland of South America or anywhere. Their ancestors might, too, have arrived on Noah's ark or a natural raft, since it was wholly out of character for a finch to set out on a flight of a thousand kilometers over open ocean.

There were no woodpeckers on the islands, but there was a finch which ate what woodpeckers would have eaten. It couldn't peck wood, and so it took a twig or a spine from a cactus in its blunt little beak, and used that to dig insects out of their hiding places.

Another sort of finch was a bloodsucker, surviving by pecking at the long neck of an unheeding booby until it had raised little beads of blood. Then it sipped that perfect diet to its heart's content. This bird was called by human beings: *Geospiza difficilis*.

The principal nesting place of these queer finches, their Garden of Eden, was the Island of Santa Rosalia. She would probably never have heard of that island, so removed from the rest of the archipelago, and so rarely visited by anyone, if it weren't for its swarms of *Geospiza difficilis*. And she surely wouldn't have lectured so much about it if the bloodsuckers hadn't been the only finches she could make her students give much of a damn about.

Great teacher that she was, she would go along with her students by describing the birds as ". . . ideal pets for Count Dracula." This entirely fictitious count, she knew, was a far more significant person to most of her students than George Washington, for instance, who was merely the founder of their country.

They were better informed about Dracula, too, so that Mary could expand her joke admitting that he might not enjoy *Geospiza difficilis* as a pet after all, since he, whom she then called "*Homo transylvaniensis*," slept all through the daytime, whereas *Geospiza difficilis* slept all through the night. "So perhaps," she would decide with mock sadness, "the best pet for Count Dracula remains a member of the family Desmodontidae—which is a scientific way of saying: 'vampire bat.'"

•  •  •

And then she would top that joke by saying, "If you should find yourself on Santa Rosalia, and you have killed a specimen of *Geospiza difficilis*, what must you do to make sure that it stays dead forever?" Her answer was this: "You must bury it at a crossroads, of course, with a little stake driven through its heart."

•  •  •

What was so thought provoking about all sorts of Galápagos finches to young Charles Darwin, though, was that they were behaving as best they could like a wide variety of much more specialized birds on the continents. He was still prepared to believe, if it turned out to make sense, that God Almighty had created all the creatures just as Darwin found them on his trip around the world. But his big brain had to wonder why the Creator in the case of the Galápagos Islands would have given every conceivable job for a small land bird to an often ill-adapted finch? What would have prevented the Creator, if he thought the islands should have a woodpecker-type bird, from creating a real woodpecker? If he thought a vampire was a good idea, why didn't he give the job to a vampire bat instead of a finch, for heaven's sakes? A vampire finch?

•  •  •

And Mary used to state the same intellectual problem to her students, concluding: "Your comments, please."

•  •  •

When she went ashore for the first time on the black peak where the *Bahía de Darwin* had been run aground, Mary stumbled. She broke her fall in such a way as to abrade the knuckles on her right hand. It wasn't a painful event. She made the most cursory examination of her injuries. There were these scratches from which beads of blood arose.

But then a finch, utterly fearless, lit on her finger. She was unsurprised, since she had heard many stories of finches landing on people's heads and hands and drinking cups or whatever.

So she resolved to enjoy this welcome to the islands, and held her hand still, and spoke sweetly to the bird. "And which of the thirteen sorts of finch are you?" she said.

As though it understood her question, the bird now showed her what sort it was by sipping up the red beads on her knuckles.

So she took another look around at the island, never imagining that she was going to spend the rest of her life there, providing thousands of meals for vampire finches. She said to the Captain, for whom she had lost all respect, "You say this is Rábida Island?"

"Yes," he said. "I'm quite sure of it."

"Well, I hate to tell you this after all you've been through, but you're wrong again," she said. "This has to be Santa Rosalia."

"How can you be so sure?" he said.

And she said, "This little bird just told me so."

# 25

O N THE ISLAND OF MANHATTAN, Bobby King turned out the light in his office atop the Chrysler Building, said good-night to his secretary, and went home. He will not appear in this tale again. Nothing more he did from that moment on until, many busy years later, he entered the blue tunnel into the Afterlife, would have the slightest bearing on the future of the human race.

In Guayaquil at the same moment that Bobby King reached home, *Zenji Hiroguchi was leaving his room at the Hotel El Dorado, angry with his pregnant wife. She had said unforgivable things about his motives in creating Gokubi and then Mandarax. He pressed the button for the elevator, and snapped his fingers and breathed very shallowly.

And then out into the corridor came the person he least wanted to see, the cause of all his troubles as far as he was concerned, who was *Andrew MacIntosh.

"Oh—there you are," said *MacIntosh. "I was just going to tell you that there is some sort of trouble with the telephones. As soon as they're fixed, I will have very good news for you."

*Zenji, whose genes live on today, was so jangled by his wife and now by *MacIntosh that he could not speak. So he punched out this message on the keys of Mandarax in Japanese, and had Mandarax display the words to *MacIntosh on its little screen: *I do not wish to talk now. I am very upset. Please leave me alone.*

Like Bobby King, incidentally, *MacIntosh would have no further influence on the future of the human race. If his daughter had agreed ten years later to be artificially inseminated on Santa Rosalia, it might have been a very different story. I think it's safe to say that he would have liked very much to participate in Mary Hepburn's experiments with the Captain's sperm. If Selena had been more venturesome, everybody today might then have been descended as he was, from the stout-hearted Scottish warriors who had repelled invading Roman legions so long ago. What a missed opportunity! As Mandarax would have it:

*For of all sad words of tongue or pen,*
*The saddest are these: "It might have been!"*
John Greenleaf Whittier (1807–1892)

"What can I do to help?" said *MacIntosh. "I'll do anything to help. Just name it."

*Zenji found that he couldn't even shake his head. The best he could do was to close his eyes tight. And then the elevator arrived, and *Zenji thought the top of his head would blow off when *MacIntosh got into it with him.

"Look—" said *MacIntosh on the way down, "I'm your friend. You can tell me anything. If I'm what's bothering you, you can tell me to take a flying fuck at a rolling doughnut, and I'll be the first to sympathize. I make mistakes. I'm human."

•  •  •

When they got down to the lobby, *Zenji's big brain gave him the impractical, almost infantile advice that he should somehow run away from *MacIntosh—that he could beat this athletic American in a footrace.

So right out the front door of the hotel he went, and onto the cordoned-off section of the Calle Diez de Agosto, with *MacIntosh right beside him.

The two of them were across the lobby and out into the sunset so quickly that the unlucky von Kleist brother, *Siegfried, behind the bar in the cocktail lounge, couldn't even shout a warning to them in time. Too late, he cried, "Please! Please! I wouldn't go out there, if I were you!" And then he ran after them.

•  •  •

Many events which would have repercussions a million years later were taking place in a small space on the planet in a very short time. While the unlucky von Kleist brother was running after *MacIntosh and *Hiroguchi, the lucky one was taking a shower in his cabin just aft of the bridge of the *Bahía de Darwin*. He wasn't doing anything particularly important to the future of humankind, other than surviving, other than staying alive, but his first mate, whose name was Hernando Cruz, was about to take a radically influential action.

Cruz was outside on the sun deck, gazing, as it happened, at the only other ship in sight, the Colombian freighter *San Mateo*, long anchored in the estuary. Cruz was a stocky, bald man about the Captain's age, who had made fifty cruises out to the islands and back on other ships. He had been part of the skeleton crew which brought the *Bahía de Darwin* from Malmö. He had supervised her outfitting in Guayaquil, while the nominal captain had made a publicity tour of the United States. This man had stocked his big brain with a perfect understanding of every part of the ship, from the mighty diesels below to the ice-maker behind the bar in the main saloon. He moreover knew the personal strengths and weaknesses of every crewman, and had earned his respect.

This was the real captain, who would really run the ship while Adolf von Kleist, potching around in the shower now and singing, would charm the passengers at mealtimes, and dance with each and every one of the ladies at night.

Cruz was least concerned with what he happened to be looking at, the *San Mateo* and the great raft of vegetable matter which had accumulated around her anchor line. That rusty little ship had become such a permanent fixture that it might as well have been a lifeless rock out there. But now he saw that a small tanker had come alongside the *San Mateo*, and was nursing it as a whale might have nursed a calf. It was excreting diesel fuel through a flexible tube. That would be mother's milk to the engine of the *San Mateo*.

What had happened was that the *San Mateo*'s owners had received a large number of United States dollars in exchange for Colombian cocaine, and smuggled those dollars into Ecuador, where they were traded not only for diesel fuel, but for the most precious commodity of all, which was food, which was fuel for human beings. So there was still a certain amount of international commerce going on.

Cruz could not divine the details of the corruption which had made the fueling and provisioning of the *San Mateo* possible, but he surely meditated on corruption in general, to wit: Anybody who had liquid wealth, whether he deserved it or not, could have anything he wanted. The captain in the shower was such a person, as Cruz was not. The painstakingly accumulated lifetime savings of Cruz, all in sucres, had turned to trash.

He envied the elation the *San Mateo*'s crewmen were feeling, now that they were going home. Since rising at dawn, Cruz himself had been thinking seriously about going home. He had a pregnant wife and eleven children in a nice house out by the airport, and they were scared. They certainly needed him, and yet, until now, abandoning a ship to which he was duty bound, no matter for what reason, had seemed to him a form of suicide, an obliteration of all that was admirable in his character and reputation.

But now he decided to walk off the *Bahía de Darwin* anyway. He patted the rail around the sun deck, and he said this softly in Spanish: "Good luck, my Swedish princess. I shall dream of you."

His case was very much like that of Jesús Ortiz, who had disconnected the El Dorado's telephones. His big brain had concealed from his soul until the last possible moment its conclusion that it was now time for him to act antisocially.

• • •

That left Adolf von Kleist completely in charge, although he did not know shit from Shinola about navigation, the Galápagos Islands, or the operation and maintenance of a ship that size.

The combination of the Captain's incompetence and the decision of Hernando Cruz to go to the aid of his own flesh and blood, although the stuff of low comedy at the time, has turned out to be of incalculable value to present-day humankind. So much for comedy. So much for supposedly serious stuff.

• • •

If "the Nature Cruise of the Century" had come off as planned, the division of duties between the Captain and his first mate would have been typical of the management of so many organizations a million years ago, with the nominal leader specializing in sociable balderdash, and with the supposed second-in-command burdened with the responsibility of understanding how things really worked, and what was really going on.

The best-run nations commonly had such symbiotic pairings at the top. And when I think about the suicidal mistakes nations used to make in olden times, I see that those polities were trying to get along with just an Adolf von Kleist at the top, without an Hernando Cruz. Too late, the surviving inhabitants of such a nation would crawl from ruins of their own creation and realize that, throughout all their self-imposed agony, there had been absolutely nobody at the top who had understood how things really worked, what it was all about, what was really going on.

# 26

THE LUCKY VON KLEIST BROTHER, the common sire of everybody alive today, was tall and thin, and had a beak like an eagle's. He had a great head of curly hair which had once been golden, which now was white. He had been put in command of the *Bahía de Darwin*, with the understanding that his first mate would do all the serious thinking, for the same reason *Siegfried had been put in charge of the hotel: His uncles in Quito had wanted a close relative to watch over their famous guests and valuable property.

The Captain and his brother had beautiful homes in the chilly mists above Quito, which they would never see again. They had also inherited considerable wealth from their murdered mother and both sets of grandparents. Almost none of it was in worthless sucres. Almost all of it was managed by the Chase Manhattan Bank in New York City, which had caused it to be represented by U.S. dollars and Japanese yen.

Dancing there in the shower stall, the Captain did not think he had much to worry about, as troubled as things seemed to be in Guayaquil. No matter what happened, Hernando Cruz would know what to do.

His big brain came up with what he thought might be a good idea to pass on to Cruz after he had dried himself off. If it looked like crewmen were about to desert, he thought, Cruz could remind them that the *Bahía de Darwin* was technically a ship of war, which meant that deserters would be subject to strict punishment under regulations of the Navy.

This was bad law, but he was right that the ship on paper was a part of the Ecuadorian Navy. The Captain himself, in his role as admiral, had welcomed her to that fighting force when she arrived from Malmö during the summer. Her decks had yet to be carpeted, and the bare steel was dotted here and there with plugged holes which could accept the mounts for machine guns and rocket launchers and racks of depth charges and so on, should war ever come.

She would then become an armored troop carrier, with, as the Captain had said on *The Tonight Show*, ". . . ten bottles of Dom Pérignon and one bidet for every hundred enlisted men."

·   ·   ·

The Captain had some other ideas in the shower, but they had all come from Hernando Cruz. For instance: If the cruise was canceled, which seemed almost a certainty, then Cruz and a few men would anchor the ship out on the marsh somewhere, away from looters. Cruz could think of no reason for the Captain to come along on a trip like that.

If all hell broke loose, and there seemed no safe place for the ship anywhere near the city, then Cruz planned to take her out to the naval base on the Galápagos island of Baltra. Again, Cruz hadn't been able to think of a reason for the Captain to come along.

Or, if the celebrities from New York City were still, incredibly, going to arrive the next morning, then it would be vital that the Captain be aboard to greet and reassure them. While waiting for them, Cruz would anchor the *Bahía de Darwin* offshore, like the Colombian freighter *San Mateo*. He would bring the ship back to the wharf only when the celebrities were right there, ready to board. He would get them out into the safety of the open ocean as quickly as possible, and then, depending on the news, he might actually take them on the promised tour of the islands.

More likely, though: He would deliver them to some safer port than Guayaquil, but surely no port in Peru or Chile or Colombia, which was to say the entire west coast of South America. The citizens in all those countries were at least as desperate as those of Ecuador.

Panama was a possibility.

If necessary, Hernando Cruz intended to take the celebrities all the way to San Diego. There was certainly more than enough food and fuel and water on the ship for a trip that long. And the celebrities could telephone their friends and relatives en route, telling them that, no matter how bad the news from the rest of the world might be, they were living high on the hog as usual.

·   ·   ·

One emergency plan the Captain didn't consider there in the shower was that he himself take full charge of the ship, with only Mary Hepburn to help him—and that he run it aground on Santa Rosalia, which would become the cradle of all humankind.

Here is a quotation well known to Mandarax:

*A little neglect may breed great mischief . . . for want of a nail the shoe was lost; for want of a shoe the horse was lost; for want of a horse the rider was lost.*

Benjamin Franklin (1706–1790)

Yes, and a little neglect can breed good news just as easily. For want of Hernando Cruz aboard the *Bahía de Darwin*, humanity was saved. Cruz would never have run the ship aground on Santa Rosalia.

And now he was driving away from the waterfront in his Cadillac El Dorado, its trunk packed solid with delicacies intended for "the Nature Cruise of the Century." He had stolen all that food for his family at dawn that day, long before the troops and the hungry mob arrived.

His vehicle, which he had bought with graft from the outfitting and provisioning of the *Bahía de Darwin*, had the same name as the hotel—the same name as the legendary city of great riches and opportunity which his Spanish ancestors had sought but never found. His ancestors used to torture Indians—to make them tell where El Dorado was.

It is hard to imagine anybody's torturing anybody nowadays. How could you even capture somebody you wanted to torture with just your flippers and your mouth? How could you even stage a manhunt, now that people can swim so fast and stay underwater for so long? The person you were after would not only look pretty much like everybody else, but could also be hiding out at any depth practically anywhere.

•   •   •

Hernando Cruz had done his bit for humanity.

The Peruvian Air Force would soon do its bit, as well, but not until six o'clock that evening, after *Andrew MacIntosh and *Zenji Hiroguchi were dead—at which time Peru would declare war on Ecuador. Peru had been bankrupt for fourteen days longer than Ecuador, so that hunger was that much more advanced there. Ground soldiers were going home, and taking their weapons with them. Only the small Peruvian Air Force was still reliable, and the military junta was keeping it that way by giving its members the best of whatever food was still around.

One thing which made the Air Force such a high morale unit was that its equipment, bought on credit and delivered before the bankruptcy, was so up to date. It had eight new French fighter-bombers and each of these planes, moreover, was equipped with an American air-to-ground missile with a Japanese brain which could home in on radar signals, or on heat from an engine, depending on instructions from the pilot. The pilot was in turn being instructed by computers on the ground and in his cockpit. The warhead of each missile carried a new Israeli explosive which was capable of creating one fifth as much devastation as the atomic bomb the United States dropped on the mother of Hisako Hiroguchi during World War Two.

This new explosive was regarded as a great boon to big-brained military scientists. As long as they killed people with conventional rather than nuclear weapons, they were praised as humanitarian statesmen. As long as they did not use nuclear weapons, it appeared, nobody was going to give the right name to all the killing that had been going on since the end of the Second World War, which was surely "World War Three."

•  •  •

The Peruvian junta gave this as its official reason for going to war: that the Galápagos Islands were rightfully Peru's, and that Peru was going to get them back again.

•  •  •

Nobody today is nearly smart enough to make the sorts of weapons even the poorest nations had a million years ago. Yes, and they were being used all the time. During my entire life-time, there wasn't a day when, somewhere on the planet, there weren't at least three wars going on.

And the Law of Natural Selection was powerless to respond to such new technologies. No female of any species, unless, maybe, she was a rhinoceros, could expect to give birth to a baby who was fireproof, bombproof, or bulletproof.

The best that the Law of Natural Selection could come up with in my time was somebody who wasn't afraid of anything, even though there was so much to fear. I knew a few people like that in Vietnam—to the extent that such people were knowable. And such a person was *Andrew MacIntosh.

*27*

S ELENA MACINTOSH would never know for certain that her father was dead until she was reunited with him at the far end of the blue tunnel into the Afterlife. All she could be sure of was that he had departed her room at the El Dorado, and exchanged some words with *Zenji Hiroguchi out in the corridor. Then the two went down together in the elevator. After that, she would never again receive news about either one of them.

Here is the story on her blindness, by the way: She had retinitis pigmentosa, caused by a defective gene inherited on the female side. She had got it from her mother, who could see perfectly well, and who had concealed from her husband the certainty that this was a gene she carried.

This was another disease with which Mandarax was familiar, since it was one of the top one thousand serious diseases of *Homo sapiens*. Mandarax, when asked about it by Mary on Santa Rosalia, would pronounce Selena's case a severe one, since she was blind at birth. It was more usual for retinitis pigmentosa, said Mandarax, son of Gokubi, to let its hosts and hostesses see the world clearly for as long as thirty years sometimes. Mandarax confirmed, too, what Selena herself had told Mary: that if she had a baby, there was a fifty-fifty chance that it would be blind. And if that baby was a female, whether it went blind or not, and that baby grew up and reproduced, there would be a fifty-fifty chance that its child would be blind.

• • •

It is amazing that two such relatively rare hereditary defects, retinitis pigmentosa and Huntington's chorea, should have been causes for worry to the first human settlers of Santa Rosalia, since the settlers numbered only ten.

As I have already said, the Captain luckily turned out not to be a carrier. Selena was surely a carrier. If she had reproduced, though, I think humankind would still be free of retinitis pigmentosa now—thanks to the Law of Natural Selection, and sharks and killer whales.

• • •

Here is how her father and *Zenji Hiroguchi died, incidentally, while she and her dog Kazakh listened to the noise of the
crowd outside: They were shot in their heads from behind, so
they never knew what hit them. And the soldier who shot them
is another person who should be credited with having done a
little something whose effects are still visible after a million
years. I am not talking about the shootings. I am talking about
his breaking into the back door of a shuttered souvenir shop
which faced the El Dorado.

If he had not burglarized that shop, there would almost certainly be no human beings on the face of the earth today. I mean
it. Everybody alive today should thank God that this soldier
was insane.

His name was Private Geraldo Delgado, and he had deserted
his unit, taking his first-aid kit and canteen and trenchknife,
automatic assault rifle and two grenades and several clips of
ammunition and so on with him. He was only eighteen years
old, and was a paranoid schizophrenic. He should never have
been issued live ammunition.

His big brain was telling him all sorts of things that were not
true—that he was the greatest dancer in the world, that he was
the son of Frank Sinatra, that people envious of his dancing
ability were attempting to destroy his brains with little radios,
and on and on.

Delgado, facing starvation like so many other people in
Guayaquil, thought his big problem was enemies with little
radios. And when he broke in through the back door of what
was plainly a defunct souvenir shop, it wasn't a souvenir shop
to him. To him it was the headquarters of the Ecuadorian Ballet
Folklórico, and he was now going to get his chance to prove that
he really was the greatest dancer in the world.

• • •

There are still plenty of hallucinators today, people who
respond passionately to all sorts of things which aren't really
going on. This could be a legacy from the Kanka-bonos. But
people like that can't get hold of weapons now, and they're easy
to swim away from. Even if they found a grenade or a machine

gun or a knife or whatever left over from olden times, how could they ever make use of it with just their flippers and their mouths?

•   •   •

When I was a child in Cohoes, my mother took me to see the circus in Albany one time, although we could not afford it and Father did not approve of circuses. And there were trained seals and sea lions there who could balance balls on their noses and blow horns and clap their flippers on cue and so on.

But they could never have loaded and cocked a machine gun, or pulled the pin on a hand grenade and thrown it any distance with any accuracy.

•   •   •

As to how a person as crazy as Delgado got into the army in the first place: He looked all right and he acted all right when he talked to the recruiting officer, just as I did when I enlisted in the United States Marines. And Delgado was taken in during the previous summer, about the time Roy Hepburn died, for short-term service specifically associated with "the Nature Cruise of the Century." His unit was to be a spit-and-polish drill team which was to strut its stuff before Mrs. Onassis and the rest of them. They were going to have assault rifles and steel helmets and all that, but surely not live ammunition.

And Delgado was a wonderful marcher and polisher of brass buttons and shiner of shoes. But then Ecuador was convulsed by this economic crisis, and live ammunition was passed out to the soldiery.

He was a harrowing example of quick evolution, but then so was any soldier. When I was through with Marine boot camp, and I was sent to Vietnam and issued live ammunition, I bore almost no resemblance to the feckless animal I had been in civilian life. And I did worse things than Delgado.

•   •   •

Now, then: The store that Delgado broke into was in a block of locked business establishments facing the El Dorado. The soldiers who had strung barbed wire around the hotel considered the stores as part of their barrier. So that when Delgado broke open the back door of one, and then unlocked its front door just a hair and peeked out, he had made a hole in the barrier, through which somebody else might pass. This breach was his contribution to the future of humankind, since very important people would pass through it in a very short while, and reach the hotel.

•   •   •

When Delgado looked out through the crack in the door, he saw two of his enemies. One of them was flourishing a little radio which could scramble his brains—or so he thought. This wasn't a radio. It was Mandarax, and the two supposed enemies were *Zenji Hiroguchi and *Andrew MacIntosh. They were walking briskly along the inside of the barricade, as they were entitled to do, since they were guests at the hotel.

*Hiroguchi was still boiling mad, and *MacIntosh was joshing him about taking life too seriously. They went right past the store where Delgado was lurking. So Delgado stepped out through the front door and shot them both in what he believed to be self-defense.

So I don't have to put stars in front of the names of Zenji Hiroguchi and Andrew MacIntosh anymore. I only did that to remind readers that they were the two of the six guests at the El Dorado who would be dead before the sun went down.

They were dead now, and the sun was going down on a world where so many people believed, a million years ago, that only the fit survived.

•   •   •

Delgado, the survivor, disappeared into the store again, and headed for the back door, where he expected to find more enemies to outsurvive.

But there were only six little brown beggar children out there—all girls. When this horrifying military freak leapt out at the little girls with all his killing equipment, they were too hungry and too resigned to death to run away. They opened their mouths instead—and rolled their brown eyes, and patted their stomachs, and pointed down their gullets to show how hungry they were.

Children all over the world were doing that back then, and not just in that one back alley in Ecuador.

So Delgado just kept going, and he was never caught and punished or hospitalized or whatever. He was just one more soldier in a city teeming with soldiers, and nobody had gotten a good look at his face, which, in the shadow of his steel helmet, wasn't all that different from anybody else's face anyway. And, like the great survivor he was, he would rape a woman the next day and become the father of one of the last ten million children or so to be born on the South American mainland.

• • •

After he was gone, the six little girls went into the shop, seeking food or anything which might be traded for food. These were orphans from the Ecuadorian rain forest across the mountains to the east—from far, far away. Their parents had all been killed by insecticides sprayed from the air, and a bush pilot had brought them to Guayaquil, where they had become children of the streets.

These children were predominantly Indian, but had Negro ancestors as well—African slaves who had escaped into the rain forest long ago.

These were Kanka-bonos. They would grow to womanhood on Santa Rosalia, where, along with Hisako Hiroguchi, they would become the mothers of all modern humankind.

• • •

Before they could get to Santa Rosalia, though, they would first have to reach the hotel. And the soldiers and the barricades would surely have stopped them from getting there, if Private Geraldo Delgado had not opened up that pathway through the store.

# 28

THESE CHILDREN would become six Eves to Captain von Kleist's Adam on Santa Rosalia, and they wouldn't have been in Guayaquil if it weren't for a young Ecuadorian bush pilot named Eduardo Ximénez. During the previous summer, on the day after Roy Hepburn was buried, in fact, Ximénez was flying his own four-passenger amphibious plane over the rain forest, near the headwaters of the Tiputini River, which flowed to the Atlantic rather than the Pacific Ocean. He had just delivered a French anthropologist and his survival equipment to a point downstream, on the border of Peru, where the Frenchman planned to begin a search for the elusive Kanka-bonos.

Ximénez was headed next for Guayaquil, five hundred kilometers away and across two high and rugged mountain barriers. In Guayaquil, he was to pick up two Argentinian millionaire sportsmen, and take them to the landing field on the Galápagos island of Baltra, where they had chartered a deep-sea fishing boat and crew. They would not be going after just any sort of fish, either. They hoped to hook great white sharks, the same creatures who, thirty-one years later, would swallow Mary Hepburn and Captain von Kleist and Mandarax.

• • •

Ximénez saw from the air these letters trampled in the mud of the riverbank: *SOS*. He landed on the water and then made his plane waddle ashore like a duck.

He was greeted by an eighty-year-old Roman Catholic priest from Ireland named Father Bernard Fitzgerald, who had lived with the Kanka-bonos for half a century. With him were the six little girls, the last of the Kanka-bonos. He and they had trampled the letters in the riverbank.

Father Fitzgerald, incidentally, had a great-grandfather in common with John F. Kennedy, the first husband of Mrs. Onassis and the thirty-fifth president of the United States. If he had mated with an Indian, which he never did, everybody now alive might claim to be an Irish blue blood—not that anybody today claims to be much of anything.

After only about nine months of life, people even forget who their mothers were.

●   ●   ●

The girls had been at choir practice with Father Fitzgerald when everybody else in the tribe got sprayed. Some of the victims were still dying, so the old priest was going to stay with them. He wanted Ximénez, though, to take the girls someplace where somebody could look after them.

So in only five hours those girls were flown from the Stone Age to the Electronics Age, from the freshwater swamps of the jungle to the brackish marshes of Guayaquil. They spoke only Kanka-bono, which only a few dying relatives in the jungle and, as things would turn out, one dirty old white man in Guayaquil could understand.

Ximénez was from Quito, and had no place of his own where he could put up the girls in Guayaquil. He himself hired a room at the Hotel El Dorado, the same room which would later be occupied by Selena MacIntosh and her dog. On the advice of police he took the girls to an orphanage next door to the cathedral downtown, where nuns gladly accepted responsibility for them. There was still plenty of food for everyone.

Ximénez then went to the hotel, and he told the story to the bartender there, who was Jesús Ortiz, the same man who would later disconnect all the telephones from the outside world.

●   ●   ●

So Ximénez was one aviator who had quite a lot to do with the future of humanity. And another one was an American named Paul W. Tibbets. It was Tibbets who had dropped an atomic bomb on Hisako Hiroguchi's mother during World War Two. People would probably be as furry as they are today, even if Tibbets hadn't dropped the bomb. But they certainly got furrier faster because of him.

●   ●   ●

The orphanage put out a call for anybody who could speak Kanka-bono, to serve as an interpreter. An old drunk and petty thief appeared, a purebred white man who, amazingly, was a grandfather of the lightest of the girls. When a youngster, he had gone prospecting for valuable minerals in the rain forest, and had lived with the Kanka-bonos for three years. He had welcomed Father Fitzgerald to the tribe when the priest first arrived from Ireland.

His name was Domingo Quezeda, and he was from excellent stock. His father had been head of the Philosophy Department of the Central University in Quito. If they were so inclined, then, people today might claim to be descended from a long line of aristocratic Spanish intellectuals.

* * *

When I was a little boy in Cohoes, and could detect nothing in the life of our little family about which I could be proud, my mother told me that I had the blood of French noblemen flowing in my veins. I would probably be living in a chateau on a vast estate over there, she said, if it hadn't been for the French Revolution. That was on her side of the family. I was also somehow related through her, she went on, to Carter Braxton, one of the signers of the Declaration of Independence. I should hold my head up high, she said, because of the blood flowing in my veins.

I thought that was pretty good. So then I disturbed my father at his typewriter, and asked him what my heritage was from his side of the family. I didn't know then what sperm was, and so wouldn't understand his answer for several years. "My boy," he said, "you are descended from a long line of determined, resourceful, microscopic tadpoles—champions every one."

* * *

Old Quezeda, stinking like a battlefield, told the girls that they could trust only him, which was easy enough for them to believe, since he was the grandfather of one and the only person who would converse with them. They had to believe everything he said. They were without the means to be skeptical, since their new environment had nothing in common with the rain forest. They had many truths they were prepared to defend stubbornly and proudly, but none of them applied to anything they had so far seen in Guayaquil, except for one, a classically fatal belief in urban areas a million years ago: Relatives would never want to hurt them. Quezeda in fact wished to expose them to terrible dangers as thieves and beggars, and, as soon as was remotely possible, as prostitutes. He would do this in order to feed his big brain's thirst for self-esteem and alcohol. He was at last going to be a man of wealth and importance.

He took the girls on walks around the city, showing them, as far as the nuns at the orphanage were aware, the parks and the cathedral and the museums and so on. He was in fact teaching them what was hateful about tourists, and where to find them and how to fool them, and where they were most likely to keep their valuables. And they played the game of spotting policemen before policemen spotted them, and memorizing good hiding places in the downtown area, should any enemy try to catch them.

•  •  •

It was "just pretend" for the girls' first week in the city. But then Grandfather Domingo Quezeda and the girls, as far as the nuns and the police were concerned, vanished entirely. That vile old ancestor of all humanity had moved the girls into an empty shed by the waterfront—a shed, as it happened, belonging to one of the two older cruise ships with which the *Bahía de Darwin* was meant to compete. The shed was empty because tourism had declined to the point where the old ship was out of business.

At least the girls had each other. And during their early years on Santa Rosalia, until Mary Hepburn made them the gift of babies, that was what they were most grateful for: At least they had each other—and their own language and their own religious beliefs and jokes and songs and so on.

And that was what they would leave to their children on Santa Rosalia when they entered, one by one, the blue tunnel into the Afterlife: the comforts of at least having each other, and the Kanka-bono language, and the Kanka-bono religion, and the Kanka-bono jokes and songs.

•  •  •

During their bad old days in Guayaquil, old Quezeda offered his stinking body for their experimentation as he taught them, as little as they were, the fundamental skills and attitudes of prostitutes.

They were certainly in need of rescue, long before the economic crisis. Yes, and one dusty window of the shed which was their gruesome schoolhouse framed the stern of the *Bahía de Darwin* right outside. Little did they know that that beautiful white ship would soon be their Noah's ark.

• • •

The girls finally ran away from the old man. They began to live in the streets, still begging and stealing. But, for reasons they could not understand, tourists became harder and harder to find, and, at last, there didn't seem to be anything to eat anywhere. They were truly hungry now, as they approached simply anyone, opening their mouths wide and rolling their eyes and pointing down their little throats to show how long it had been since they had eaten.

And late one afternoon, they were attracted by the sounds of the crowd around the El Dorado. They found that the back door of a shuttered shop was open, and out came Geraldo Delgado, who had just shot Andrew MacIntosh and Zenji Hiroguchi. So they went into the shop and out of the front door. They were inside the barrier set up by the soldiers, so there was nobody to stop them from entering the El Dorado, where they would throw themselves on the mercy of James Wait in the cocktail lounge.

# 29

MARY HEPBURN was meanwhile murdering herself up in her room, lying on her bed with the polyethylene sheath of her "Jackie dress" wrapped around her head. The sheath was now all steamed up inside, and she hallucinated that she was a great land tortoise lying on its back in the hot and humid hold of a sailing ship of long ago. She pawed the air in perfect futility, just as a land tortoise on its back would have done.

As she had often told her students, sailing ships bound out across the Pacific used to stop off in the Galápagos Islands to capture defenseless tortoises, who could live on their backs without food or water for months. They were so slow and tame and huge and plentiful. Sailors would capsize them without fear of being bitten or clawed. Then they would drag them down to waiting longboats on the shore, using the animals' own useless suits of armor for sleds.

They would store them on their backs in the dark, paying no further attention to them until it was time for them to be eaten. The beauty of the tortoises to the sailors was that they were fresh meat which did not have to be refrigerated or eaten right away.

• • •

Every school year back in Ilium, Mary could count on some student's being outraged that human beings should have treated such trusting creatures so cruelly. This gave her the opportunity to say that the natural order had dealt harshly with such tortoises long before there was such an animal as man.

There used to be millions of them, lumbering over every temperate land mass of any size, she would say.

But then some tiny animals evolved into rodents. These easily found and ate the eggs of the tortoises—all of the eggs.

So, very quickly, that was that for the tortoises everywhere, except for those on a few islands which remained rodent free.

• • •

It was prophetic that Mary should imagine herself to be a land tortoise as she suffocated, since something very much like what had happened to most of the land tortoises so long ago was then beginning to happen to most of humankind.

Some new creature, invisible to the naked eye, was eating up all the eggs in human ovaries, starting at the annual Book Fair at Frankfurt, Germany. Women at the fair were experiencing a slight fever, which came and went in a day or two, and sometimes blurry vision. After that, they would be just like Mary Hepburn: They couldn't have babies anymore. Nor would any way be discovered for stopping this disease. It would spread practically everywhere.

The near extinction of mighty land tortoises by little rodents was certainly a David-and-Goliath story. Now here was another one.

•   •   •

Yes, and Mary came close enough to death to see the blue tunnel into the Afterlife. At that point, she rebelled against her big brain, which had brought her that far. She unwrapped the garment bag from her head, and, instead of dying, she went downstairs, where she found James Wait feeding peanuts and olives and maraschino cherries and cocktail onions from behind the bar to the six Kanka-bono girls.

This tableau of clumsy charity would remain imprinted in her brain for the rest of her life. She would believe ever after that he was an unselfish, compassionate, lovable human being. He was about to suffer a fatal heart attack, so nothing would ever happen to revise her high opinion of this loathsome man.

On top of everything else, this man was a murderer.

His murder had gone like this:

He was a homosexual prostitute on the island of Manhattan, and a bloated plutocrat picked him up in a bar, asking him if he realized that the price tag was still on the hem of his lovely new blue velour shirt. This man had royal blood in his veins! This was Prince Richard of Croatia-Slavonia, a direct descendant of James the First of England and Emperor Frederick the Third of Germany and Emperor Franz Joseph of Austria and King Louis the Fifteenth of France. He ran an antique shop on upper Madison Avenue, and he wasn't homosexual. He wanted young

Wait to strangle him with a silken sash from his dressing gown, and then to loosen the sash after having brought him as close as possible to death.

Prince Richard had a wife and two children, who were on a skiing vacation in Switzerland, and his wife was young enough to be ovulating still, so young Wait may have prevented yet another carrier of those noble genes from being born.

There was this, too: If Prince Richard hadn't been murdered, he and his wife might have been invited by Bobby King to take part in "the Nature Cruise of the Century."

• • •

His widow would become a very successful designer of neckties, calling herself "Princess Charlotte," although she was a commoner, the daughter of a Staten Island roofer, and not entitled to that rank, or the use of his coat of arms. That crest nonetheless appeared on every tie she designed.

The late Andrew MacIntosh owned several Princess Charlotte ties.

• • •

Wait spread-eagled this porky, chinless blue-blood face up on a four-poster bed which the Prince said had belonged to Eleonore of Palatinate-Neuburg, the mother of King Joseph the First of Hungary. Wait tied him to the thick posts with nylon ropes already cut to length. These had been stored in a secret drawer under the flounce at the foot of the bed. This was an old drawer, and had one time concealed secrets of the sex life of Eleonore of Palatinate-Neuburg.

"Tie me nice and tight, so I can't get away," Prince Richard told young Wait, "but don't cut off the circulation. I would hate to get gangrene."

His big brain had had him doing this at least once a month for the past three years: hiring strangers to tie him up and strangle him just a little bit. What a survival scheme!

• • •

Prince Richard of Croatia-Slavonia, possibly with the ghosts of his progenitors looking on, instructed young James Wait to strangle him to the point where he lost consciousness. Then

Wait, whom he knew only as "Jimmy," was to count slowly to twenty in this manner: "One thousand and one, one thousand and two . . ." and so on.

Possibly with King James and Emperor Frederick and Emperor Franz Joseph and King Louis looking on, the Prince, one of several claimants to the throne of Yugoslavia, warned "Jimmy" not to touch any part of his body or clothing, save for the sash around his neck. He would experience orgasm, but "Jimmy" was not to attempt to enhance that event with his mouth or hands. "I am not a homosexual," he said, "and I've hired you as a sort of valet—not as a prostitute.

"This may be hard for you to believe, Jimmy," he went on, "if you lead the kind of life I think you lead, but this is a spiritual experience for me, so keep it spiritual. Otherwise: no hundred-dollar tip. Do I make myself clear? I am an unusual man."

• • •

He didn't tell Wait about it, but his big brain put on quite a movie for him while he was unconscious. It showed him one end of a writhing piece of blue tubing, about five meters in diameter, big enough to drive a truck through, and lit up inside like the funnel of a tornado. It did not roar like a tornado, however. Instead, unearthly music, as though from a glass harmonica, came from the far end, which appeared to be about fifty meters away. Depending on how the tube twisted, Prince Richard could catch glimpses of the opening in the far end, a golden dot and hints of greenery.

This, of course, was the tunnel into the Afterlife.

• • •

So Wait put a small rubber ball into the mouth of this would-be liberator of the Yugoslavs, as he had been told to do, and sealed the mouth with a precut piece of adhesive tape which had been stuck to a bedpost.

Then he strangled the Prince, cutting off the blood supply to his big brain and the air supply to his lungs. Instead of counting slowly to twenty after the Prince lost consciousness and had his orgasm and saw the writhing tube, he counted slowly to three hundred instead. That was five minutes.

It was Wait's big brain's idea. It wasn't anything he himself had particularly wanted to do.

•  •  •

If he had ever been brought to trial for the murder, or the manslaughter, or whatever the government chose to call his crime, he would probably have pleaded temporary insanity. He would have claimed that his big brain simply wasn't working right at the time. There wasn't a person alive a million years ago who didn't know what that was like.

Apologies for momentary brain failures were the staple of everybody's conversations: "Whoops," "Excuse me," "I hope you're not hurt," "I can't believe I did that," "It happened so fast I didn't have time to think," "I have insurance against this kind of a thing," and "How can I ever forgive myself?" and "I didn't know it was loaded," and on and on.

•  •  •

There were beads and dollops of human sperm on the Prince's crested satin sheets, full of royal tadpoles racing each other to nowhere, as young Wait let himself out of the triple apartment on Sutton Place. He hadn't stolen anything, and he hadn't left any fingerprints. The doorman of the building, who had seen him coming and going, was able to tell the police very little about his appearance, save that he was young and white and slender, and wore a blue velour shirt from which the price tag had not been removed.

And there was something prophetic, too, in those millions of royal tadpoles on a satin sheet, with no place meaningful to go. The whole world, as far as human sperm was concerned, with the exception of the Galápagos Islands, was about to become like that satin sheet.

Dare I add this: "In the nick of time"?

# *30*

I WILL NOW PUT A STAR in front of the name of *James Wait, indicating that, after *Siegfried von Kleist, he will be the next to die. *Siegfried would go into the blue tunnel first, in about an hour and a half, and *Wait would follow in about fourteen hours, having first married Mary Hepburn on the sun deck of the *Bahía de Darwin* when it was well at sea.

• • •

Quoth Mandarax so long ago:

> *All is well that ends well.*
> John Heywood (1497?–1580?)

This was surely the case with the life of *James Wait. He had come into this world as a child of the devil, supposedly, and beatings had begun almost immediately. But here he was so close to the end now, astonished by the joy of feeding the Kanka-bono girls. They were so grateful, and helping them was such an easy thing to do, since the bar was stocked with snacks and garnishes and condiments. The opportunity to be charitable had simply never presented itself before, but here it was now, and he was loving it. To these children, Wait was life itself.

And then the widow Hepburn appeared, as he had been hoping she would all afternoon. Nor did he have to win her trust. She liked him immediately because he was feeding the children, and she said to him, because she had seen so many hungry children on her way to the hotel from Guayaquil International Airport the previous afternoon: "Oh, good for you! Good for you!" She assumed then, and would never believe differently, that this man had seen the children outside, and had invited them in so he could feed them.

"Why can't I be like you?" Mary went on. "Here I've been upstairs, doing nothing but feeling sorry for myself, when I should have been down here like you—sharing whatever we have with all those poor children out there. You make me so

686

ashamed—but my brains just haven't been working right lately. Sometimes I could just kill my brains."

She spoke to the children in English, a language they would never understand. "Does that taste good?" she said, and "Where are your mommies and daddies?" and that sort of thing.

The little girls would never learn English, since Kanka-bono would from the first be the language of the majority on Santa Rosalia. In a century and a half, it would be the language of the majority of humankind. Forty-two years after that, Kanka-bono would be the only language of humankind.

· · ·

There was no urgency about Mary's getting the girls better things to eat. A diet of peanuts and oranges, of which there were plenty behind the bar, was ideal. The girls spit out whatever wasn't good for them—the cherries and the green olives and the little onions. They needed no help with eating.

So Mary and *Wait were free to simply watch and chat, and get to know each other.

*Wait said that he thought people were put on earth to help each other, and that was why he was feeding the children. He said that children were the future of the world, and so the planet's greatest natural resource.

"Permit me to introduce myself," he said. "I am Willard Flemming of Moose Jaw, Saskatchewan."

Mary said who and what she was, an ex-teacher and a widow.

He said how much he admired teachers, and how important they had been to him when he was young. "If it hadn't been for my teachers in high school," he said, "I never would have gone to MIT. I probably wouldn't have gone to college at all—probably would have been an automobile mechanic like my father."

"So what did you become?" she said.

"Less than nothing, since my wife died of cancer," he said.

"Oh!" she said. "I'm so sorry!"

"Well—it's not your fault, is it," he said.

"No," she said.

"Before that," he said, "I was a windmill engineer. I had this crazy idea that there was all this clean, free energy around. Does that sound crazy to you?"

"It's a beautiful idea," she said. "It was something my husband and I talked about."

"The power and light companies hated me," he said, "and the oil barons and the coal barons and the atomic energy trust."

"I should think they would!" she said.

"They can stop worrying about me now," he said. "I closed up shop after my wife died, and I've been roaming the world ever since. I don't even know what I'm looking for. I very much doubt if there's anything worth finding. I'm just sure of one thing: I can never love again."

"You have so much to give the world!" she said.

"If I ever did love again," he said, "it wouldn't be with the sort of silly, pretty little ball of fluff so many men seem to want today. I couldn't stand it."

"I wouldn't think so," she said.

"I've been spoiled," he said.

"I expect you deserved it," she said.

"And I ask myself, 'What good is money now?'" he said. "I'm sure your husband was as good a husband as my wife was a wife—"

"He really was a very good man," she said, "a perfectly wonderful man."

"So you're certainly asking the same question: 'What good is money to a person all alone?'" he said. "Suppose you have a million dollars . . ."

"Oh, Lord!" she said. "I don't have anything like that."

"All right—a hundred thousand, then . . ."

"That's a little more like it," she said.

"It's just trash now, right?" he said. "What happiness can it buy?"

"A certain amount of creature comfort, anyway," she said.

"You've got a nice house, I imagine," he said.

"Quite nice," she said.

"And a car, or maybe two or three cars, and all that," he said.

"One car," she said.

"A Mercedes, I'll bet," he said.

"A Jeep," she said.

"And you've probably got stocks and bonds, just like I do," he said.

"Roy's company had a stock bonus plan," she said.

"Oh, sure," he said. "And an insurance plan, and a retirement plan—and all the rest of the middle-class dream of security."

"We both worked," she said. "We both contributed."

"I wouldn't have a wife who didn't work," he said. "My wife worked for the phone company. After she died, the death benefits, after they were all added up, turned out to be quite a bit. But they just wanted to make me cry. They were just more reminders of how empty my life had become. And her little jewel box, with all the rings and pins and necklaces I'd given her over the years, and no children to pass it on to."

"We didn't have children, either," she said.

"It seems we have a lot in common," he said. "So who will you leave your jewelry to?"

"Oh—there isn't much," she said. "I guess the only valuable piece is a string of pearls Roy's mother left me. It has a diamond clasp. There are so few times I wear jewelry, I'd almost forgotten those pearls until this very moment."

"I certainly hope they're insured," he said.

H OW PEOPLE used to talk and talk back then! Everybody was going, "Blah-blah-blah," all day long. Some of them would even do it in their sleep. My father used to blather in his sleep a lot—especially after Mother walked out on us. I would be sleeping on the couch, and it would be in the middle of the night, and there wouldn't be anybody else in the house but us—and I would hear him going, "Blah-blah-blah," in the bedroom. He would be quiet for a little while, and then he would go, "Blah-blah-blah," again.

And sometimes when I was in the Marines, or later in Sweden, somebody would wake me up to tell me to stop talking in my sleep. I would have no recollection of what I might have said. I would have to ask what I had been talking about, and it was always news to me. What could most of that blah-blah-blahing have been, both night and day, but the spilling of useless, uncalled-for signals from our preposterously huge and active brains?

There was no shutting them down! Whether we had anything for them to do or not, they ran all the time! And were they ever loud! Oh, God, were they ever loud.

When I was still alive, there were these portable radios and tape-players some young people carried with them wherever they went in cities in the United States, playing music at a volume capable of drowning out a thunderstorm. These were called "ghetto blasters." It wasn't enough, a million years ago, that we already had ghetto blasters inside our heads!

• • •

Even at this late date, I am still full of rage at a natural order which would have permitted the evolution of something as distracting and irrelevant and disruptive as those great big brains of a million years ago. If they had told the truth, then I could see some point in everybody's having one. But these things lied all the time! Look at how *James Wait was lying to Mary Hepburn!

And now *Siegfried von Kleist returned to the cocktail lounge, having witnessed the shooting of Zenji Hiroguchi and Andrew MacIntosh. If his big brain had been a truth machine, he might have given Mary and *Wait information to which they were surely entitled, and which might have been very useful to them, in case they wished to survive: that he was in the first stages of a mental crack-up, that two hotel guests had just been shot, that the crowd outside couldn't be held back much longer, that the hotel was out of touch with the rest of the world, and so on.

But no. He maintained a placid exterior. He did not wish his remaining four guests to panic. As a result, they would never find out what became of Zenji Hiroguchi and Andrew MacIntosh. For that matter, they would never hear the news, which would be announced in about an hour, that Peru had declared war on Ecuador, and neither would the Captain. When Peruvian rockets hit targets in the Guayaquil area, they would believe the Captain when he said what his big brain honestly believed to be the truth, not that it felt any compunction to tell the truth: that they were being showered by meteorites.

And, as long as there was anybody on Santa Rosalia curious as to why his or her ancestors had come there—and that sort of curiosity would finally peter out only after about three thousand years—that was the story: They were driven off the mainland by a shower of meteorites.

Quoth Mandarax:

> *Happy is the nation without a history.*
> Cesare Bonesana, Marchese di Beccaria
> (1738–1794)

So, in a perfectly calm tone of voice, *Siegfried, the Captain's brother, asked *Wait to go upstairs, and to ask Selena MacIntosh and Hisako Hiroguchi to come down, and to help them with their luggage. "Be careful not to alarm them," he said. "Let them know that everything is perfectly all right. Just to be safe, I am going to take you all out to the airport." Guayaquil International Airport, incidentally, would be the first target to be devastated by Peruvian rocketry.

He handed Mandarax to *Wait, so that *Wait would be able to communicate with Hisako. He had recovered the instrument from beside the body of Zenji. Both bodies had been moved out of sight—into the burglarized souvenir shop. *Siegfried himself had covered them with souvenir bedspreads, which bore the same portrait of Charles Darwin which hung behind the bar.

•   •   •

So *Siegfried von Kleist shepherded Mary Hepburn and Hisako Hiroguchi and *James Wait and Selena MacIntosh and *Kazakh out to a gaily decorated bus parked in front of the hotel. This bus was to have carried musicians and dancers out to the airport—to regale the celebrities from New York. The six Kanka-bono girls came right along with them, and I have put a star in front of the dog's name because she would soon be killed and eaten by those children. It was no time to be a dog.

Selena wanted to know where her father was, and Hisako wanted to know where her husband was. *Siegfried said that they had gone ahead to the airport. His plan was to somehow get them on a plane, whether a commercial flight or a charter flight or a military flight, which would get them safely out of Ecuador. The truth about Andrew MacIntosh and Zenji Hiroguchi would be the last thing they heard from him before the plane took off—at which time they might still survive, no matter how frenzied with grief they became.

As a sop to Mary, he agreed to take the six girls along. He could make no sense of their language, even with the help of Mandarax. The best Mandarax could do was to identify one word in twenty, maybe, as being closely related to Quechuan, the lingua franca of the Inca Empire. Here and there Mandarax thought it might have heard a little Arabic, too, the lingua franca of the African slave trade so long ago.

Now, there is a big-brain idea I haven't heard much about lately: human slavery. How could you ever hold somebody in bondage with nothing but your flippers and your mouth?

# 32

J UST AS EVERYBODY got nicely settled in the bus in front of the El Dorado, the news came over several radios in the crowd that "the Nature Cruise of the Century" had been canceled. That meant to the crowd, and to the soldiers, too, who were just civilians in soldier suits, that the food in the hotel now belonged to everyone. Take it from somebody who has been around for a million years: When you get right down to it, food is practically the whole story every time.

Quoth Mandarax:

> *First comes fodder, then comes morality.*
> Bertolt Brecht (1898–1956)

So there was a rush for the hotel's entrances which momentarily engulfed the bus, although the bus and the people in it were of no interest to the food rioters. They banged on the sides of the bus, however, and yelled—agonized by the realization that others were already inside the hotel, and that there would be no food left for them.

It was certainly very frightening to be on the bus. It might be turned over. It might be set on fire. Rocks might be thrown, making shrapnel of window glass. The place for survivors to be was on the floor in the aisle. Hisako Hiroguchi performed her first intimate act with blind Selena, instructing her with her hands and murmured Japanese to kneel in the aisle with her head down. Then Hisako knelt beside her and *Kazakh, and put her arm across her back.

How tenderly Hisako and Selena would care for each other during the coming years! What a beautiful and sweet-natured child they would rear! How I admired them!

• • •

Yes, and *James Wait found himself posing yet again as a protector of children. He was sheltering with his own body the terrified Kanka-bono girls in the aisle. He had meant only to save himself, if he could, but Mary Hepburn had grabbed both

693

his hands and pulled him toward her so that they formed a living fort. If there was to be flying glass, it would bite into them and not into the little girls.

Quoth Mandarax:

*Greater love hath no man than this, that a man lay down his life for his friends.*
                                        St. John (4 B.C.?–30?)

It was while *Wait was in this position that his heart began to fibrillate—which is to say that its fibers began to twitch in an uncoordinated manner, so that the march of the blood in his circulatory system was no longer orderly. Here heredity was operating again. He had no way of knowing this, but *Wait's father and mother, who were also father and daughter, were both then dead of heart attacks which had struck when they were in their early forties.

It was a lucky thing for humanity that *Wait did not live long enough to take part in the Santa Rosalia mating games. Then again, it might not have made all that much difference if people today had inherited his time-bomb heart, since nobody would have lived long enough for the bomb to go off anyway. Anybody *Wait's age today would be a regular Methuselah.

• • •

Down at the waterfront, meanwhile, another mob, another fibrillating organ in the social system of Ecuador, was stripping the *Bahía de Darwin* not only of its food, but of its television sets and telephones and radar and sonar and radios and light bulbs and compasses and toilet paper and carpeting and soap and pots and pans and charts and mattresses and outboard motors and inflatable landing craft, and on and on. These survivors would even try to steal the winch which lowered or raised the anchors, but succeeded only in damaging it beyond repair.

At least they left the lifeboats—but bereft of their emergency food supplies.

And Captain von Kleist, in fear of his life, had been driven up into the crow's nest, clad only in his underwear.

• • •

The crowd at the El Dorado swept past the bus like a tidal wave—leaving it high and dry, so to speak. It was free to go where it pleased. There was nobody much around, except for a few people lying down here and there, injured or killed in the rush.

So *Siegfried von Kleist, heroically suppressing the spasms and ignoring the hallucinations symptomatic of Huntington's chorea, took his place in the driver's seat. He thought it best that his ten passengers stay in the aisle where they were—invisible from the outside, and calming one another with body heat.

He started the engine, and saw that he had a full tank of gasoline. He turned on the air conditioning. He announced in English, the only language he had in common with any of his passengers, that it would be very cool inside in a minute or two. This was a promise he could keep.

It was twilight outside now, so he turned on his parking lights.

• • •

It was at about that time that Peru declared war on Ecuador. Two of Peru's fighter bombers were then over Ecuadorian territories, one with its rocket tuned to the radar signals coming from Guayaquil International Airport, and the other with its rocket tuned to radar signals coming from the naval base on the Galápagos Island of Baltra, lair of a sail training ship, six Coast Guard ships, two oceangoing tugs, a patrol submarine, a dry dock, and, high and dry in the dry dock, a destroyer. The destroyer was the largest ship in the Ecuadorian Navy, save for one—the *Bahía de Darwin*.

Quoth Mandarax:

*It was the best of times, it was the worst of times, it was the age of wisdom, it was the age of foolishness, it was the epoch of belief, it was the epoch of incredulity, it was the season of Light, it was the season of Darkness, it was the spring of hope, it was the winter of despair, we had everything before us, we had nothing before us, we were all going direct to Heaven, we were all going direct the other way.*

Charles Dickens (1812–1870)

# 33

I SOMETIMES SPECULATE as to what humanity might have become if the first settlers on Santa Rosalia had been the original passenger list and crew for "the Nature Cruise of the Century"—Captain von Kleist, surely, and Hisako Hiroguchi and Selena MacIntosh and Mary Hepburn, and, instead of the Kanka-bono girls, the sailors and officers and Jacqueline Onassis and Dr. Henry Kissinger and Rudolf Nureyev and Mick Jagger and Paloma Picasso and Walter Cronkite and Bobby King and Robert Pépin, "the greatest chef in France," and, of course, Andrew MacIntosh and Zenji Hiroguchi, and on and on.

The island could have supported that many individuals—just barely. There would have been some struggles, some fights, I guess—some killings, even, if food or water ran short. And I suppose some of them would have imagined that Nature or something was very pleased if they emerged victorious. But their survival wouldn't have amounted to a hill of beans, as far as evolution was concerned, if they didn't reproduce, and most of the women on the passenger list were past child-bearing age, and so not worth fighting for.

During the first thirteen years on Santa Rosalia, before Akiko reached puberty, in fact, the only fertile women would have been Selena, who was blind, and Hisako Hiroguchi, who had already given birth to a baby all covered with fur, and three others who were normal. And probably all of them would have been impregnated by victors, even against their will. But in the long run, I don't think it would have made much difference which males did the impregnating, Mick Jagger or Dr. Henry Kissinger or the Captain or the cabin boy. Humanity would still be pretty much what it is today.

In the long run, the survivors would still have been not the most ferocious strugglers but the most efficient fisherfolk. That's how things work in the islands here.

•  •  •

There were live Maine lobsters who also came within a hair of having their survival skills tested by the Galápagos Archipelago. Before the *Bahía de Darwin* was looted, there were two hundred of them in aerated tanks of saltwater in the hold.

The waters around Santa Rosalia were surely cold enough for them, but perhaps too deep. There was this about them, at any rate: They were like human beings in that they could eat almost anything, if they had to.

And Captain von Kleist, when he was an old, old man, remembered those lobsters in their tanks. The older he became, the more vivid were his recollections of events of the long ago. And after supper one night, he amused Akiko, the furry daughter of Hisako Hiroguchi, with a science-fiction fantasy whose premise was that the Maine lobsters had made it to the islands, and that a million years had passed, as they have indeed passed now—and that lobsters had become the dominant species on the planet, and had built cities and theaters and hospitals and public transportation and so on. He had lobsters playing violins and solving murders and performing microsurgery and subscribing to book clubs and so on.

The moral of the story was that the lobsters were doing exactly what human beings had done, which was to make a mess of everything. They all wished that they could just be ordinary lobsters, particularly since there were no longer human beings around who wanted to boil them alive.

That was all they had had to complain about in the first place: being boiled alive. Now, just because they hadn't wanted to be boiled alive anymore, they had to support symphony orchestras, and on and on. The viewpoint character in the Captain's story was the underpaid second chair French horn player in the Lobsterville Symphony Orchestra who had just lost his wife to a professional ice hockey player.

•   •   •

When he made up that story, he had no idea that humanity elsewhere was on the verge of extinction, and that other life forms were facing less and less opposition, in case they had a tendency to become dominant. The Captain would never hear about that, and neither would anybody else on Santa Rosalia.

And I am speaking only of the dominance of large life forms over other large life forms. Truth be told, the planet's most victorious organisms have always been microscopic. In all the encounters between Davids and Goliaths, was there ever a time when a Goliath won?

On the level of the big creatures, then, the visible strugglers, lobsters were surely poor candidates for becoming as elaborately constructive and destructive as humankind. If the Captain had told his mordant fable about octopi instead of lobsters, though, it might not have been quite so ridiculous. Back then, as now, those squishy creatures had highly developed brains, whose basic function was to control their versatile arms. Their situation, one might think, wasn't all that different from that of human beings, with hands to control. Presumably, their brains could do other things with their arms and brains than catch fish.

But I have yet to see an octopus, or any sort of animal, for that matter, which wasn't entirely content to pass its time on earth as a food gatherer, to shun the experiments with unlimited greed and ambition performed by humankind.

•  •  •

As for human beings making a comeback, of starting to use tools and build houses and play musical instruments and so on again: They would have to do it with their beaks this time. Their arms have become flippers in which the hand bones are almost entirely imprisoned and immobilized. Each flipper is studded with five purely ornamental nubbins, attractive to members of the opposite sex at mating time. These are in fact the tips of four suppressed fingers and a thumb. Those parts of people's brains which used to control their hands, moreover, simply don't exist anymore, and human skulls are now much more streamlined on that account. The more streamlined the skull, the more successful the fisher person.

•  •  •

If people can swim as fast and far as fur seals now, what is to prevent their swimming all the way back to the mainland, whence their ancestors came? Answer: nothing.

Plenty have tried it or will try it during periods of fish shortages or overpopulation. But the bacterium which eats human
eggs is always there to greet them.

So much for exploration.

Then again, it is so peaceful here, why would anybody want
to live on the mainland? Every island has become an ideal place
to raise children, with waving coconut palms and broad white
beaches—and limpid blue lagoons.

And all the people are so innocent and relaxed now, all
because evolution took their hands away.

Quoth Mandarax:

> *In works of labour, or of skill,*
> *I would be busy, too;*
> *For Satan finds some mischief still*
> *For idle hands to do.*
> Isaac Watts (1674–1748)

# 34

THERE WAS THIS PERUVIAN PILOT a million years ago, a young lieutenant colonel who had his fighter-bomber skipping from wisp to wisp of finely divided matter at the very edge of the planet's atmosphere. His name was Guillermo Reyes, and he was able to survive at such an altitude because his suit and helmet were inflated with an artificial atmosphere. People used to be so marvelous, making impossible dreams they made come true.

Colonel Reyes had had an inconclusive discussion with a fellow airman one time as to whether anything felt better than sexual intercourse. He was in contact on his radio now with that same comrade, who was back at the air base in Peru, and who was to tell him when Peru was officially at war with Ecuador.

Colonel Reyes had already activated the brain of the tremendous self-propelled weapon slung underneath his airplane. That was its first taste of life, but already it was madly in love with the radar dish atop the control tower at Guayaquil International Airport, a legitimate military target, since Ecuador kept ten of its own warplanes there. This amazing radar lover under the colonel's plane was like the great land tortoises of the Galápagos Islands to this extent: It had all the nourishment it needed inside its shell.

So the word came that it was all right for him to let the thing go.

So he let the thing go.

His friend on the ground asked him what it felt like to give something like that its freedom. He replied that he had at last found something which was more fun than sexual intercourse.

• • •

The young colonel's feelings at the moment of release had to be transcendental, had to be entirely products of that big brain of his, since the plane did not shudder or yaw or suddenly climb or dive when the rocket departed to consummate its love affair. It continued on exactly as before, with the automatic pilot compensating instantly for the sudden change in the plane's weight and aerodynamics.

As for effects of the release visible to Reyes: The rocket was much too high to leave a vapor trail, and its exhaust was clean, so that, to Reyes, it was a rod which quickly shrank to a dot and then to a speck and then to nothingness. It vanished so quickly that it was hard to believe that it had ever existed.

And that was that.

The only residue of the event in the stratosphere had to be in Reyes's big brain or nowhere. He was happy. He was humble. He was awed. He was drained.

•  •  •

Reyes wasn't crazy to feel that what he had done was analogous to the performance of a male during sexual intercourse. A computer over which he had no control, once he had turned it on, had determined the exact moment of release, and had delivered detailed instructions to the release machinery without any need of advice from him. He didn't know all that much about how the machinery worked anyway. Such knowledge was for specialists. In war, as in love, he was a fearless, happy-go-lucky adventurer.

The launching of the missile, in fact, was virtually identical with the role of male animals in the reproductive process.

Here was what the colonel could be counted on to do: deliver the goods in an instant.

Yes—and that rod which became a dot and then a speck and then nothingness so quickly was somebody else's responsibility now. All the action from now on would be on the receiving end.

He had done his part. He was sweetly sleepy now—and amused and proud.

•  •  •

And I worry now about skewing my story, since a few characters in it were genuinely insane, and giving the impression that everybody a million years ago was insane. That was not the case. I repeat: that was not the case.

Almost everybody was sane back then, and I gladly award Reyes that widespread encomium. The big problem, again, wasn't insanity, but that people's brains were much too big and untruthful to be practical.

•   •   •

No single human being could claim credit for that rocket, which was going to work so perfectly. It was the collective achievement of all who had ever put their big brains to work on the problem of how to capture and compress the diffuse violence of which nature was capable, and drop it in relatively small packages on their enemies.

I myself had had some highly personal experiences with dreams-come-true of that sort in Vietnam—which is to say, with mortars and hand grenades and artillery. Nature could never have been that predictably destructive in such small spaces without the help of humankind.

I have already told my story about the old woman I shot for throwing a hand grenade. There are plenty of others I could tell, but no explosion I saw or heard about in Vietnam could compare with what happened when that Peruvian rocket put the tip of its nose, that part of its body most richly supplied with exposed nerve endings, into that Ecuadorian radar dish.

•   •   •

No one is interested in sculpture these days. Who could handle a chisel or a welding torch with their flippers or their mouths?

If there were a monument out here in the islands, though, celebrating a key event in the past, that would be a good one: the moment of mating, right before the explosion, between that rocket and that radar dish.

Into the lava plinth beneath it these words might be incised, expressing the sentiments of all who had had a hand in the design and manufacture and sale and purchase and launch of the rocket, and of all to whom high explosives were a branch of the entertainment industry:

> . . . *'Tis a consummation*
> *Devoutly to be wish'd.*
> William Shakespeare (1564–1616)

# 35

TWENTY MINUTES before the rocket gave that French kiss to the radar dish, Captain Adolf von Kleist concluded that it was now safe for him to come down from the crow's nest of the *Bahía de Darwin*. The ship had been picked clean, and had fewer amenities and navigational aids, even, than had Her Majesty's Ship *Beagle* when that brave little wooden sailboat began her voyage around the world on December 27, 1831. The *Beagle* had had a compass, at least, and a sextant, and navigators who could imagine with considerable accuracy the position of their ship in the clockwork of the universe because of their knowledge of the stars. And the *Beagle*, moreover, had had oil lanterns and candles for the nighttime, and hammocks for the seamen, and mattresses and pillows for the officers. Anyone determined to spend the night on the *Bahía de Darwin* now would have to rest his or her weary head on nude steel, or perhaps do what Hisako Hiroguchi would do when she couldn't keep her eyes open any longer. Hisako would sit on the lid of the toilet off the main saloon, and lay her head on her arms, which were folded atop the washbasin in there.

• • •

I have likened the mob at the hotel to a tidal wave, whose crest swept past the bus, never to return again. I would say that the mob at the waterfront was more like a tornado. Now that ferocious whirlwind was moving inland in the twilight, and feeding on itself, since its members had themselves become worth robbing—carrying lobsters and wine and electronic gear and drapes and coat hangers and cigarettes and chairs and rolls of carpeting and towels and bedspreads, and on and on.

So the Captain clambered down from the crow's nest. The rungs bruised his bare and tender feet. He had the ship and the entire waterfront all to himself, as far as he could see. He went to his cabin first, since he was wearing only his undershorts. He hoped that the looters had left him a little something to wear. When he turned on the light switch in there, though, nothing happened—because all the light bulbs were gone.

There was electricity, anyway—since the ship still had her banks of storage batteries down in the engine room. The thing was: The light-bulb thieves had blacked out the engine room before the batteries and generators and starter motors could be stolen. So, in a sense, they had unwittingly done humanity a big favor. Thanks to them, the ship would still run. Without her navigational aids, she was as blind as Selena MacIntosh—but she was still the fastest ship in that part of the world, and she could slice water at top speed for twenty days without refueling, if necessary, provided nothing went wrong in the pitch-dark engine room.

As things would turn out, though: After only five days at sea, something would go very much wrong in the pitch-dark engine room.

•    •    •

The Captain certainly had no plans for putting out to sea as he groped about his cabin for more clothes to hide his nakedness. There wasn't even a handkerchief or a washcloth in there. Thus was he having his first taste of a textile shortage, which at the moment seemed merely inconvenient, but which would be acute during the thirty years of life still ahead of him. Cloth to protect his skin from sunburn in the daytime and from chills at night simply would not be available anymore. How he and the rest of the first colonists would come to envy Hisako's daughter Akiko for her coat of fur!

Everybody but Akiko, until Akiko herself had furry babies, would in the daytime have to wear fragile capes and hats made of feathers tied together with fish guts.

Quoth Mandarax to the contrary:

> *Man is a biped without feathers.*
> Plato (427?–347 B.C.)

The Captain remained calm as he searched his cabin. The shower in the head was dripping, and he turned it off tight. That much he could make right, anyway. That was how composed he was. As I have already said, his digestive system still had food to process. Even more important to his peace of mind, though, was that nobody was counting on him for anything. Those who had looted the ship almost all had numerous relatives in dire need, who were starting to roll their eyes and pat their bellies and point down their throats like the Kanka-bono girls.

The Captain was still in possession of his famous sense of humor, and freer than ever to indulge it. For whose sake was he now to pretend that life was a serious matter? There weren't even rats left on the ship. There had never been rats on the *Bahía de Darwin*, which was another lucky break for humankind. If rats had come ashore with the first human settlers on Santa Rosalia, there would have been nothing left for people to eat in six months or so.

And then, after that, the rats, after having eaten what was left of the people and each other, would themselves have died.

Quoth Mandarax:

> *Rats!*
> *They fought the dogs and killed the cats,*
> *And bit the babies in the cradles,*
> *And ate the cheeses out of the vats,*
> *And licked the soup from the cooks' own ladles,*
> *Split open the kegs of salted sprats,*
> *Made nests inside men's Sunday hats,*
> *And even spoiled the women's chats*
> *By drowning their speaking*
> *With shrieking and squeaking*
> *In fifty different sharps and flats.*
> Robert Browning (1812–1889)

The Captain's clever fingers, working in the blacked-out head, now encountered what would prove to be half a bottle of cognac sitting atop the tank of his toilet. This was the last bottle of any sort still aboard the ship, and its contents were the last substance to be found, from stem to stern and from crow's nest to keel, which a human being could metabolize. In saying that, of course, I exclude the possibility of cannibalism. I ignore the fact that the Captain himself was quite edible.

And just as the Captain's fingers got a firm grip on the bottle's neck in the darkness, something big and strong outside gave the

*Bahía de Darwin* an authoritative bump. Also: There were male voices from the boat deck, one deck below. The thing was: The tugboat crew which had delivered fuel and food to the Colombian freighter *San Mateo* was now preparing to haul away the *Bahía de Darwin*'s two lifeboats. They had cast off the ship's bowline, and the tug was nosing her bow into the estuary, so that the lifeboat on her starboard side could be lowered into the water.

So that the ship was now married to the South American mainland by a single line at her stern. Poetically speaking, that stern line is the white nylon umbilical cord of all modern humankind.

• • •

The Captain might as well have been my fellow ghost on the *Bahía de Darwin*. The men who took our lifeboats never even suspected that there was another soul aboard.

All alone again, except for me, he proceeded to get drunk. What could that matter now? The tugboat, with the lifeboats following obediently, had disappeared upstream. The *San Mateo*, all lit up like a Christmas tree, and with the radar dish atop her bridge revolving, had disappeared downstream, so that the Captain felt free to shout whatever he pleased from the bridge without attracting unfavorable attention. His hands on the ship's wheel, he called into the starlit evening, "Man overboard!" He was speaking of himself.

Expecting nothing to happen, he pressed the starter button for the port engine. From the bowels of the ship came the muffled, deep-purple rumble of a great diesel engine in perfect health. He pressed the other starter button, giving the gift of life to the engine's identical twin. These dependable, uncomplaining slaves had been born in Columbus, Indiana—not far from Indiana University, where Mary Hepburn had taken her master's degree in zoology.

Small world.

• • •

That the diesels still worked was to the Captain simply one more reason to make himself wild and stupid with cognac. He switched off the engines, and it was a good thing he did. If he had let them run long enough to get really hot, that temperature anomaly might have attracted the electronic attention of a Peruvian fighter-bomber in the stratosphere. In Vietnam, we had heat-sensing instruments so sensitive that could actually detect the presence of people, or at least big mammals of some kind, in the night—because their bodies were just a little bit warmer than their surroundings.

One time I called in an artillery barrage on a water buffalo. Usually it was people out there—trying to sneak up on us and kill us, if they could. What a life! I would have loved to put down all my weapons and become a fisherman instead.

• • •

And that was the sort of thing the Captain was thinking up there on the bridge: "What a life!" and so on. It was all very funny, except he didn't feel like laughing. He thought that life had now taken his measure, had found him not worth much of anything, and was now through with him. Little did he know!

He went out on the sun deck, which was aft of the bridge and the officers' cabins, his bare feet on bare steel. Now that the sun deck had been stripped of its carpeting, the plugged holes which were supposed to receive the mounts for weapons were plainly visible, even in starlight. I myself had welded four of the plates on the sun deck. Most of my work, and my finest work, however, was deep inside.

The Captain looked up at the stars, and his big brain told him that his planet was an insignificant speck of dust in the cosmos, and that he was a germ on that speck, and that nothing could matter less than what became of him. That was what those big brains used to do with their excess capacity: blather on like that. To what purpose? You won't catch anybody thinking thoughts like that today.

So then he saw a shooting star—a meteorite burning up on the edge of the atmosphere, up where Lieutenant Colonel Reyes in his space suit had just received word that Peru was officially at war with Ecuador. The shooting star cued the Captain's big brain to have him marvel yet again about how unprepared people were for meteorites striking the Earth's surface.

And then there was this tremendous explosion out at the airport, as the rocket and the radar dish honeymooned.

• • •

The hotel bus, all painted up outside with the blue-footed boobies and marine iguanas and penguins and flightless cormorants and so on, was at that moment parked in front of a hospital. The Captain's brother *Siegfried was about to go inside to get help for *James Wait, who had lost consciousness. *Wait's heart attack had necessitated this detour on the way to the airport, which had surely saved the lives of all on board.

The great bubble of the shock wave from that explosion was as dense as bricks. To those on the bus, it seemed that hospital itself had exploded. The windows and windshield of the bus were blown inward, but turned out to have been shatterproof. They had not turned to shrapnel. Mary and Hisako and Selena and *Kazakh and poor *Wait and the Kanka-bono girls and the Captain's brother were pelted with seeming kernels of white corn instead.

This would happen on the *Bahía de Darwin* as well. The windows would all be blown in, and white kernels would be underfoot everywhere.

The hospital, so full of light only moments before, was blacked out now, as was the whole city, and there were cries for help coming from inside. The engine of the bus was still running, thank God, and its headlights illuminated a narrow pathway through the debris up ahead. So *Siegfried, becoming more palsied by the second, still managed to drive away from there. What help could he or anybody else on the bus be to the survivors, if any, in the blasted hospital?

And the logic of the maze of rubble directed the creeping bus away from the center of the explosion, the airport, and toward the waterfront. The road across the marsh from the edge of the city to the deepwater wharves was in fact almost clear of wreckage, there was so little for the shock wave to knock down out there.

• • •

*Siegfried von Kleist drove to the waterfront because it was the path of least resistance. Only he could see where they were going. The others were still on the floor of the bus. Mary

Hepburn had dragged the unconscious *James Wait away from the Kanka-bono girls, so that he was lying flat on his back now, with her lap for a pillow. The big brains of the Kanka-bonos had shut down entirely, for want of even a wisp of a theory as to what was going on. Hisako Hiroguchi and Selena MacIntosh and *Kazakh were similarly immobilized.

And everybody was deaf, since the shock wave had done such violence to the bones in their inner ears, the tiniest bones in their bodies. Nor would any of them recover their sense of hearing entirely. With the exception of the Captain, the first colonists on Santa Rosalia would all be slightly deaf, so that a good deal of their conversations would consist, in one language or another, of "Eh?" and "Speak up" and so on.

This defect, fortunately, was not inheritable.

•   •   •

Like Andrew MacIntosh and Zenji Hiroguchi, they would never find out what hit them—unless there were answers to questions like that at the far end of the blue tunnel into the Afterlife. They would accept the Captain's theory that the explosion and another explosion still to come had been the impacts of white-hot boulders from outer space—but not wholeheartedly, since the Captain would prove to be laughably mistaken about so many things.

•   •   •

The Captain's palsied younger brother, his ears ringing, some of his hearing returning, stopped the bus on the wharf near the *Bahía de Darwin*. He had not expected her to be a haven. He was unsurprised to find her dark and apparently deserted, with her windows blown in, her lifeboats missing, and barely secured to the wharf by a single line at her stern. Her freed bow was some distance from the wharf, so that her gangplank dangled over water.

She had of course been looted, like the hotel. The wharf was littered with wrappings and cartons and other trash discarded by the scavengers.

*Siegfried did not expect to see his brother. He had heard that the Captain had left New York, but not that he had actually reached Guayaquil. If the Captain was somewhere in Guaya-quil, he was very likely dead or injured, or, in any case, in no position to be of much help to anyone. Nobody in Guayaquil at that point in history was in a position to be of much help to anyone else.

Quoth Mandarax:

> *Help yourself, and heaven will help you.*
> Jean de La Fontaine
> (1621–1695)

The most *Siegfried hoped to find was a peaceful stopping place in chaos. This he did. There did not seem to be anybody else around.

So he got out of the bus, to see if he couldn't somehow get the involuntary dancing movements caused by Huntington's chorea under control by doing exercises—jumping jacks and push-ups, and deep-knee bends and so on.

The moon was coming up.

And then he saw a human figure rising to its feet on the sun deck of the *Bahía de Darwin*.

It was his brother, but the Captain's face was in shadow, so *Siegfried did not recognize him.

*Siegfried had heard whispered stories about the ship's being haunted. He believed that he was beholding a ghost. He thought it was me. He thought he was seeing Leon Trout.

# 36

THE CAPTAIN recognized his brother, though, and he shouted down to him what I might have been tempted to shout, had I been a materialized ghost up there. He shouted this: "Welcome to 'the Nature Cruise of the Century'!"

• • •

The Captain, still holding on to his bottle, although it was empty now, came down to the main deck at the stern, so that he was nearly on a level with his brother, and *Siegfried, because he was so deaf, came as close as he could without falling into the narrow moat between them. That moat was bridged by the stern line, by that white umbilical cord.

"I'm deaf," said *Siegfried. "Are you deaf, too?"

"No," said the Captain. He had been much farther away than *Siegfried from the center of the explosion. He had a nosebleed, though, which he chose to find comical. He had bashed his nose when the shock wave knocked him down on the sun deck. The cognac had exacerbated his sense of humor to the point where everything was screamingly funny.

He thought that the exercises *Siegfried had done on the wharf were a lampoon on the dancing sickness they both might have inherited from their father. "I liked your imitation of Father," he said. The whole conversation was in German—the language of their infancy, the first language they had known.

"Adie!" said *Siegfried. "This isn't funny!"

"Everything is funny," said the Captain.

"Do you have any medicine? Do you have any food? Do you still have beds?" said *Siegfried.

The Captain replied with a quotation well known to Mandarax:

> *I owe much; I have nothing. I give the rest to the poor.*
> François Rabelais (1494–1553)

"You're drunk!" said *Siegfried.

"Why not?" the Captain asked. "I'm nothing but a clown." The random damage done to his brain by cognac made him terribly self-centered. He could give no thought to the suffering others must be doing in the dark and blasted city in the distance. "You know what one of my own crewmen said to me when I tried to keep him from stealing the compass, Ziggie?"

"No," said *Siegfried, and he started to dance again.

"'Out of the way, you clown!'" said the Captain, and he laughed and laughed. "He dared to say that to an admiral, Ziggie. I would have had him hanged from the yardarm, *hick*— if somebody hadn't stolen the, *hick*, yardarm, *hick*. At dawn, *hick*—if somebody hadn't stolen the dawn."

People still get the hiccups, incidentally. They still have no control over whether they do it or not. I often hear them hiccupping, involuntarily closing their glottises and inhaling spasmodically, as they lie on the broad white beaches or paddle around the blue lagoons. If anything, people hiccup more now than they did a million years ago. This has less to do with evolution, I think, than with the fact that so many of them gulp down raw fish without chewing them up sufficiently.

(PEOPLE)

And people still laugh about as much as they ever did, despite their shrunken brains. If a bunch of them are lying around on a beach, and one of them farts, everybody else laughs and laughs, just as people would have done a million years ago.

"H ICK," the Captain went on, "actually I have been vindi- cated, *hick*, *Siegfried," the Captain went on. "I have long said that we should expect to be hit by large meteorites from time to time. That has, *hick*, come to, *hick*, pass."

"It was the hospital that blew up," said *Siegfried. So it had seemed to him.

"No hospital ever blew up like that," said the Captain, and, to *Siegfried's dismay, he climbed up on the rail and prepared to jump to the wharf. It wasn't all that much of a jump, really— only about two meters across the moat, but the Captain was very drunk.

The Captain aviated successfully, crashing to his knees on the wharf. This cured his hiccups.

"Is there anybody else on the ship?" said *Siegfried.

"Nobody here but us chickens," said the Captain. He had no idea that he and *Siegfried were responsible for rescuing anybody but each other. Everybody on the bus was still on the floor. *Siegfried, incidentally, had entrusted Mary Hepburn with Mandarax, in case she had to communicate with Hisako Hiroguchi. Mandarax, as I've said, was useless as an interpreter for the Kanka-bonos.

The Captain put his arm across the quaking shoulders of *Siegfried, and said to him, "Don't be scared, little brother. We're from a long line of survivors. What's a little shower of meteorites to a von Kleist?"

"Adie—" said *Siegfried, "is there some way we can get the ship closer to the dock?" He thought the people on the bus might feel a little safer and surely less cramped on shipboard.

"Fuck the ship. Nothing left on her," said the Captain. "I think they even stole old Leon." Again—Leon was me.

"Adie—" said *Siegfried, "there are ten people on that bus, and one of them is having a heart attack."

The Captain squinted at the bus. "What makes them so invis- ible?" he said. His hiccups were gone again.

"They're all on the floor, and they're scared to death," said *Siegfried. "You've got to sober up. I can't look after them.

You're going to have to do whatever you can. I'm not in control of my own actions anymore, Adie. Of all the times for it to happen—I have Father's disease."

Time stopped, as far as the Captain was concerned. This was a familiar illusion for him. He could count on experiencing it several times a year—whenever he received news he could not joke about. He knew how to get time going again, which was to deny the bad news. "It isn't true," he said. "It cannot be."

"You think I dance for the fun of it?" said *Siegfried, and he was involuntarily dancing away from his brother.

He approached the Captain again, just as involuntarily, saying, "My life is over. It probably never should have been lived. At least I never reproduced, so that some poor woman might give birth to yet another monstrosity."

"I feel so helpless," said the Captain, and added wretchedly, "and so goddamn drunk. Jesus—I certainly expected no more responsibilities. I'm so drunk. I can't think. Tell me what to do, Ziggie."

He was too drunk to do much of anything, so he stood by, slack-jawed and goggle-eyed, while Mary Hepburn and Hisako and *Siegfried, whenever poor *Siegfried could stop dancing, hauled the stern of the ship right up to the wharf with the bus, and then parked the bus under the stern, so that it could be used as a ladder up to the lowest deck of the ship, which would have been unreachable otherwise.

And oh, yes, you could say, "Wasn't that ingenious of them?" and, "They could never have done that if they hadn't had great big brains," and, "You can bet nobody today could figure out how to do stuff like that," and so on. Then again, those people wouldn't have had to behave so resourcefully, wouldn't have been in such complicated difficulties, if the planet hadn't been made virtually uninhabitable by the creations and activities of other people's great big brains.

Quoth Mandarax:

> What's lost upon the roundabouts we pulls up on
> the swings!
>           Patrick Reginald Chalmers (1872–1942)

•  •  •

People expected the most trouble to come from the unconscious *James Wait. Actually, the most trouble would come
from the Captain, who was too drunk to be trusted as a link in
the human chain, who could only sit on the back seat of the bus
and rue how drunk he was.

His hiccups had returned.

Here is how they got *James Wait up on the ship: There was
enough extra stern line on the wharf for Mary Hepburn to make
a harness for him at the free end of the line. This was all her
idea, the harness. She was, after all, an experienced mountain-
eer. They laid him beside the bus with the harness on. Then
she and Hisako and *Siegfried got on the roof and hauled him
up as gently as possible. And then the three of them got him
over the rail and onto the main deck. They would later move
him up to the sun deck, where he would regain consciousness
briefly—long enough for him and Mary Hepburn to become
man and wife.

•  •  •

*Siegfried then came back down to tell the Captain that it was
his turn to get aboard. The Captain, knowing he was going to
make a fool of himself while trying to reach the roof, played for
time. Jumping while drunk was easy. Climbing anything the
least bit complicated was something else again. Why so many of
us a million years ago purposely knocked out major chunks of
our brains with alcohol from time to time remains an interesting mystery. It may be that we were trying to give evolution a
shove in the right direction—in the direction of smaller brains.

So the Captain, playing for time, and trying to sound judi-
cious and respectable, although he could scarcely stand up, said
to his brother, "I'm not so sure that man was well enough to
be moved."

*Siegfried was out of patience with him. He said, "That's too
damn bad, isn't it—because we just moved the poor bastard
anyway. Maybe we should have called a helicopter instead, and
had him flown to the bridal suite at the Waldorf-Astoria."

And those would be the last words the brothers von Kleist
would ever exchange, except for "Hup!" and "Allez oop!" and
"Whoops!" and so on, as the Captain tried and failed to get up
on the roof of the bus again and again.

But he finally did get up, although thoroughly humiliated. He was at least able to go from the roof to the ship without further assistance. And then *Siegfried told Mary to get on the ship with the rest of them, and to do what she could for *Wait, whom they believed to be Willard Flemming. She did as she was told, thinking it was a matter of manly pride for him to climb to the roof without assistance.

●    ●    ●

That left *Siegfried all alone on the wharf, looking up at the rest of them. And they expected him to join them, but that was not to be. He sat down in the driver's seat instead. Despite his limbs' jerking this way and that, he started up the engine. His plan was to head back for the city at top speed, and to kill himself by smashing into something.

Before he could put the bus in gear, he was stunned by the shock wave from yet another tremendous explosion. This one wasn't in or near the city. This one was downstream, and out in the virtually uninhabited marsh somewhere.

# 38

THE SECOND EXPLOSION was like the first one. A rocket had mated with a radar dish. The dish in this instance was atop the little Colombian freighter the *San Mateo*. The Peruvian pilot who gave the rocket the spark of life, Ricardo Cortez, imagined that he had caused it to fall in love with the radar dish of the *Bahía de Darwin*, who no longer had radar and so, as far as that particular sort of rocket was concerned, was without sex appeal.

Major Cortez had made what was called a million years ago "an honest mistake."

And let it be said, too, that Peru would never have ordered an attack on the *Bahía de Darwin* if "the Nature Cruise of the Century" had gone ahead as planned, with a shipload of celebrities. Peru would not have been that insensitive to world opinion. But the cancellation of the cruise made the ship an entirely different kettle of fish, so to speak, a potential troop carrier manned, any reasonable person might assume, by persons who were effectively begging to be blown up or napalmed or machine-gunned or whatever, which is to say "naval personnel."

• • •

So these Colombianos were out there in the marsh in the moonlight, headed for the open ocean and home, eating the first decent meal they had had in a week, and imagining that their radar dish was watching over them like a revolving Virgin Mary. She would never allow any harm to come to them. Little did they know.

What they were eating, incidentally, was an old dairy cow who wasn't able to give all that much milk anymore. That was what had been under the tarpaulin on the lighter which had provisioned the *San Mateo*: that dairy cow, still very much alive. And she had been hoisted aboard on the side away from the waterfront, so that people ashore couldn't see her. There were people ashore desperate enough to kill for her.

She was one hell of a lot of protein to be leaving Ecuador.

• • •

It was interesting how they hoisted her. They didn't use a sling or a cargo net. They made a rope crown for her, wrapped around and around her horns. They embedded the steel hook at the end of the cable of the crane in the tangled crown. And then the crane operator up above reeled in the cable so that the cow was soon dangling in thin air—in an upright position for the first time in her life, with her hind legs splayed, her udder exposed, and with her front legs thrust out horizontally, so that she had the general configuration of a kangaroo.

The evolutionary process which had produced this huge mammal had never anticipated that she might be in such a position, with the weight of her entire body depending from her neck. Her neck as she dangled was coming to resemble that of a blue-footed booby or swan, or flightless cormorant.

To certain sorts of big brains back in those days, her experience with aviation might have been something to laugh about. She was anything but graceful.

And when she was set down on the deck of the *San Mateo*, she was so severely injured that she could no longer stand. But that was to be expected, and perfectly acceptable. Long experience had shown sailors that cattle so treated could go on living for a week or more, would keep their own meat from rotting until it was time for them to be eaten. What had been done to that dairy cow was a shorter version of what used to be done to great land tortoises back in the days of sailing ships.

In either case, there was no need for refrigeration.

• • •

The happy Colombianos were chewing and swallowing some of that poor cow's meat when they were blown to bits by the latest advance in the evolution of high explosives, which was called "dagonite." Dagonite was the son, so to speak, of a considerably weaker explosive made by the same company, and called "glacco." Glacco begat dagonite, so to speak, and both were descendants of Greek fire and gunpowder and dynamite and cordite and TNT.

So it might be said that the Colombianos had treated the cow abominably, but that retribution had been swift and terrible, thanks largely to the big-brained inventors of dagonite.

•  •  •

In view of how badly the Colombianos had treated the cow, Major Ricardo Cortez, flying faster than sound, might be seen as a virtuous knight as in days of yore. And he felt that way about himself, too, although he knew nothing about the cow or what his rocket had hit. He radioed back to his superiors that the *Bahía de Darwin* was destroyed. He asked that his best friend, Lieutenant Colonel Reyes, who was back on the ground and who had turned a rocket loose on the airport that afternoon, be given this message in Spanish: *It is true.*

Reyes would understand that he was agreeing that letting the rocket go had been as elating as sexual intercourse. And he would never find out that he had not hit the *Bahía de Darwin*, and the friends and relatives of the Colombianos who were blown to hamburger in the estuary would never learn what became of them.

•  •  •

The rocket which hit the airport was surely a lot more effective in Darwinian terms than the one that hit the *San Mateo*. It killed thousands of people and birds and dogs and cats and rats and mice and so on, who would otherwise have reproduced their own kind.

The blast in the marsh killed only the fourteen crewmen and about five hundred rats on the ship, and a few hundred birds, and some crabs and fish and so on.

Mainly, though, it was an ineffectual assault on the very bottom of the food chain, the billions upon billions of microorganisms who, along with their own excrement and the corpses of their ancestors, comprised the muck of the marsh. The explosion didn't bother them much, since they weren't all that sensitive to sudden starts and stops. They could never have committed suicide in the manner as *Siegfried von Kleist, at the wheel of the bus, intended to commit suicide, with a sudden stop.

They were simply moved suddenly from one neighborhood to another one. They flew through the air, bringing a lot of the old neighborhood with them, and then came splattering down. Many of them even experienced great prosperity as a result of the explosion, feasting on what was left of the cow and the rats and the crew, and other higher life forms.

Quoth Mandarax:

*It is wonderful to see with how little nature will be satisfied.*
Michel Eyquem de Montaigne (1533–1592)

The detonation of dagonite, son of glacco, direct descendant of noble dynamite, caused a tidal wave in the estuary, which was six meters high when it swept the bus off the wharf at the Guayaquil waterfront and drowned Siegfried von Kleist, who wanted to die anyway.

More importantly: It snapped the white nylon umbilical cord which tied the future of humankind to the mainland.

The wave carried the *Bahía de Darwin* a kilometer upstream, then left her gently aground on a mudbank in the shallows there. She was illuminated not only by moonlight, but by sick, jazzy fires breaking out all over Guayaquil.

The Captain arrived on the bridge. He started the twin diesel engines in the darkness far below. He engaged her twin propellers, and the ship slid off the mudbank. She was free.

The Captain steered downstream, toward the open ocean.

Quoth Mandarax:

*The ship, a fragment detached from the earth, went on lonely and swift like a small planet.*
Joseph Conrad (1857–1924)

And the *Bahía de Darwin* wasn't just any ship. As far as humanity was concerned, she was the new Noah's ark.

# BOOK TWO

## And the Thing Became

# 1

THE THING BECAME a new white motorship at night, without charts or a compass or running lights, but nonetheless slitting the cold, deep ocean at her maximum velocity. In the opinion of humankind, she no longer existed. The *Bahía de Darwin* and not the *San Mateo*, in the opinion of humankind, had been blown to smithereens.

She was a ghost ship, out of sight of land and carrying the genes of her captain and seven of her ten passengers westward on an adventure which has lasted one million years so far.

I was the ghost of a ghost ship. I am the son of a big-brained science fiction writer, whose name was Kilgore Trout.

I was a deserter from the United States Marines.

I was given political asylum and then citizenship in Sweden, where I became a welder in a shipyard in Malmö. I was painlessly decapitated one day by a falling sheet of steel while working inside the hull of the *Bahía de Darwin*, at which time I refused to set foot in the blue tunnel leading into the Afterlife.

It has always been within my power to materialize, but I have done that only once, very early in the game—for a few wet and blustery moments during the storm my ship encountered in the North Atlantic during her voyage from Malmö to Guayaquil. I appeared in the crow's nest, and one Swedish member of the skeleton crew saw me up there. He had been drinking. My decapitated body was facing the stern, and my arms were upraised. In my hands I was holding my severed head as though it were a basketball.

• • •

So I was invisible as I stood next to Captain Adolf von Kleist on the bridge of the *Bahía de Darwin* as we awaited the end of our first night at sea after our hasty departure from Guayaquil. He had been awake all night, and was sober now, but had a terrible headache, which he had described to Mary Hepburn as ". . . a golden screw between my eyes."

He had other souvenirs of the previous evening's humiliating debauch—contusions and abrasions from the several falls he had taken while trying to get up on the roof of the bus. He would never have gotten that drunk if he had realized that he was going to be saddled with any responsibilities. He had already explained that to Mary, who had been up all night, too— nursing *James Wait on the sun deck, abaft of the officers' cabins.

*Wait had been put up there, with Mary's rolled-up blouse for a pillow, because the rest of the ship was so dark. At least there was starlight up there after the moon went down. The plan was to move him into a cabin when the sun came up, so he would not fry to death on the bare steel plates.

Everybody else was on the boat deck below. Selena MacIntosh was in the main saloon, using her dog for a pillow, and so were the six Kanka-bono girls. They were using each other for pillows. Hisako was in the head off the main saloon, and had fallen asleep while wedged between the toilet and the washbasin.

•   •   •

Mandarax, which Mary had turned over to the Captain, was in a drawer on the bridge. This was the only drawer on the whole ship with anything in it. It was slightly ajar, so that Mandarax had overheard and translated much of what had been said during the night. Thanks to a random setting, it translated everything into Kirghiz, including the Captain's plan of action, which went like this: They would go straight to the Galápagos island of Baltra, where there were docking facilities and an airfield and a small hospital. There was a powerful radio station there, so they would learn for certain what the two explosions had been, and how the rest of the world might be faring, in case a widespread shower of meteorites had taken place, or, as Mary had suggested, World War Three had begun.

Yes, and this plan might as well have been translated into Kirghiz, or some other language that practically nobody understood, because they were on a course which was going to cause them to miss the Galápagos Islands entirely.

His ignorance alone might have been enough to carry the ship far off course. But he compounded his mistakes during the first night, before he was sober, by changing course again

and again in order to steer for the probable impact points in
the ocean of shooting stars. His big brain, remember, had him
believing that a meteorite shower was going on. Every time he
saw a shooting star, he expected it to hit the ocean and cause a
tidal wave.

So he would steer for it in order to receive the wave on the
ship's sharp bow. When the sun came up, he could have been,
thanks to his big brain, simply anywhere, and headed for simply
anywhere.

· · ·

Mary Hepburn, meanwhile, somewhere between sleep and
wakefulness, next to *James Wait, was doing something people
don't have brains enough to do anymore. She was reliving the
past. She was a virgin again. She was in a sleeping bag. She was
being awakened in the faintest light of dawn, by the call of a
whippoorwill. She was camping in an Indiana state park—a
living museum, a patch of what the area used to be before
Europeans decreed that no plant or animal would be tolerated
which was not tamed and edible by humankind. When young
Mary stuck her head out of her cocoon, out of her sleeping bag,
she saw rotting logs and an undammed stream. She lay on an
aromatic mulch of eons of death and discard. There was plenty
to eat if you were a microorganism or could digest leaves, but
there was no hearty breakfast there for a human being of a million and thirty years ago.

It was early June. It was balmy.

The bird call was coming from a thicket of briars and sumac
fifty paces away. She was glad for this alarm clock, for it had
been her intention when she went to sleep to awake this early,
and to think of her sleeping bag as a cocoon, and to emerge
from it sinuously and voluptuously, as she was now doing, a
vivacious adult.

What joy!

What satisfaction!

It was perfect, for the girlfriend she had brought with her
slept on and on.

So she stole across the springy woodland floor to the thicket
to see this fellow early bird. What she saw instead was a tall,

skinny, earnest young man in a sailor suit. And it was he who was whistling the piercing call of a whippoorwill. This was Roy, her future husband.

•  •  •

She was annoyed and disoriented. The sailor suit so far inland was a particularly bizarre detail. She felt intruded upon, and that perhaps she should be frightened as well. But if this very strange person was going to come after her, he would have to get through a tangle of briars first. She had slept in her clothes, so she was fully dressed save for her stocking feet.

He had heard her coming. He had amazingly sharp ears. So did his father. It was a family trait. And he spoke first. "Hello," he said.

"Hello," she said. She would say later that she thought she was the only person in the garden of Eden, and then she came upon this creature in a sailor suit who was acting as though he already owned everything. And Roy would counter that she was the one, in fact, who acted as though she owned everything.

"What are you doing here?" she said.

"I didn't think people were supposed to sleep in this part of the park," he said. He was right about that, and Mary knew it. She and her friend were in violation of the rules of the living museum. They were in an area where only lower animals were supposed to be at night.

"You're a sailor?" she said.

And he said that, yes, he was—or had been until very recently. He had just been discharged from the Navy, and was hitchhiking around the country before going home, and found people were much more inclined to pick him up if he wore his uniform.

•  •  •

It would make no sense today for somebody to ask, as Mary asked Roy, "What are you doing here?" The reasons for being anywhere today are so invariably simple and obvious. Nobody has a tale as tangled as Roy's to tell: that he took his discharge in San Francisco, and cashed in his ticket, and bought a sleeping bag and hitchhiked to the Grand Canyon and Yellowstone National Park and some other places he had always wanted to see. He was especially fascinated by birds, and could talk to them in their own languages.

So he heard on a car radio that a pair of ivory-billed woodpeckers, a species believed to have been long extinct, had been sighted in this little state park in Indiana. He headed straight for there. The story would turn out to be a hoax. These big, beautiful inhabitants of primeval forests really were extinct, since human beings had destroyed all their natural habitats. No longer was there enough rotten wood and peace and quiet for them.

"They needed lots of peace and quiet," said Roy, "and so do I, and so do you, I guess, and I'm sorry if I disturbed you. I wasn't doing anything a bird wouldn't do."

Some automatic device clicked in her big brain, and her knees felt weak, and there was a chilly feeling in her stomach. She was in love with this man.

They don't make memories like that anymore.

*J*AMES WAIT interrupted Mary Hepburn's reverie with these words: "I love you so much. Please marry me. I'm so lone-some. I'm so scared."

"You save your strength, Mr. Flemming," she said. He had been proposing marriage intermittently all through the night.

"Give me your hand," he said.

"Every time I do, you won't give it back," she said.

"I promise I'll give it back," he said.

So she gave him her hand, and he gripped it feebly. He wasn't having any visions of the future or the past. He was little more than a fibrillating heart, just as Hisako Hiroguchi, wedged between the vibrating toilet and washbasin below, was little more than a fetus and a womb.

Hisako had nothing to live for but her unborn child, she thought.

• • •

People still hiccup as they always have, and they still find it very funny when somebody farts. And they still try to comfort those who are sick with soothing tones of voice. Mary's tone when she kept *James Wait company on the ship is a tone often heard today. With or without words, that tone conveys what a sick person wants to hear now, and what *Wait wanted to hear a million years ago.

Mary said things like this to *Wait in so many words, but her tone alone would have delivered the same messages: "We love you. You are not alone. Everything is going to be all right," and so on.

• • •

No comforter today, of course, has led a love life as compli-cated as Mary Hepburn's, and no sufferer today has led a love life as complicated as *James Wait's. Any human love story of today would have for its crisis the simplest of questions: whether the persons involved were in heat or not. Men and women now become helplessly interested in each other and the nubbins on their flippers and so on only twice a year—or, in times of fish shortages, only once a year. So much depends on fish.

Mary Hepburn and *James Wait could have their common sense wrecked by love, given the right set of circumstances, at almost any time.

There on the sun deck, just before the sun came up, *Wait was genuinely in love with Mary and Mary was genuinely in love with him—or, rather, with what he claimed to be. All through the night, she had called him "Mr. Flemming," and he had not asked her to call him by his first name. Why? Because he could not remember what his first name was supposed to be.

"I'll make you very rich," said *Wait.

"There, there," said Mary. "Now, now."

"Compound interest," he said.

"You save your strength, Mr. Flemming," she said.

"Please marry me," he said.

"We'll talk about that when we get to Baltra," she said. She had given him Baltra as something to live for. She had cooed and murmured to him all through the night about all the good things which were awaiting them on Baltra, as though it were a sort of paradise. There would be saints and angels to greet them on the dock there, with every kind of food and medicine.

He knew he was dying. "You'll be a very rich widow," he said.

"Let's not have any talk like that now," she said.

As for all the wealth she was going to inherit technically, since she really was going to marry him and then become his widow: The biggest-brained detectives in the world couldn't have begun to find a minor fraction of it. In community after community, he had created a prudent citizen who didn't exist, whose wealth was increasing steadily, even though the planet itself was growing ever poorer, and whose safety was guaranteed by the governments of the United States or Canada. His savings account in Guadalajara, Mexico, which was in pesos, had been wiped out by then.

If his wealth had continued to grow at the rate it was growing then, the *James Wait estate would now encompass the whole universe—galaxies, black holes, comets, clouds of asteroids and meteors and the Captain's meteorites and interstellar matter of every sort—simply everything.

Yes, and if the human population had continued to grow at the rate it was growing then, it would now outweigh the *James Wait estate, which is to say simply everything.

What impossible dreams of increase human beings used to have only yesterday, only a million years ago!

*WAIT HAD REPRODUCED, incidentally. Not only had he sent that antiques dealer down the blue tunnel into the Afterlife so long ago, he had also made possible the birth of an heir. By Darwinian standards, as both a murderer and a sire, he had done quite well, one would have to say.

He became a sire when he was only sixteen years old, the sexual prime of a human male a million years ago:

He was still in Midland City, Ohio, and it was a hot July afternoon, and he was mowing the lawn of a fabulously well-to-do automobile dealer and owner of local fast-food restaurants named Dwayne Hoover, who had a wife but no children. So Mr. Hoover was in Cincinnati on business, and Mrs. Hoover, whom *Wait had never seen, although he had mowed the lawn many times, was in the house. She was a recluse because, as *Wait had heard, she had a problem with alcohol and drugs prescribed by her doctor, and her big brain had simply become too erratic to be trusted in public.

*Wait was good-looking back then. His mother and father had also been good-looking. He was from a good-looking family. Despite the fact that it was so hot, *Wait would not take off his shirt—because he was so ashamed of all the scars he had from punishments inflicted by various foster parents. Later, when he was a prostitute on the island of Manhattan, his clients would find those scars, made by cigarettes and coat hangers and belt buckles and so on, very exciting.

*Wait was not looking for sexual opportunities. He had just about made up his mind to light out for Manhattan, and he did not want to do anything which might give the police an excuse for locking him up. He was well known to the police, who frequently questioned him about this or that burglary or whatever, although he had never committed an actual crime. The police were always watching him anyway. They would say to him things like "Sooner or later, Sonny, you're going to make a big mistake."

So Mrs. Hoover appeared in the front door in a skimpy bathing suit. There was a swimming pool out back. Her face was all raddled and addled, and her teeth were bad, but she still had a very beautiful figure. She asked him if he wouldn't like to come into the house, which was air-conditioned, and cool off with a glass of ice tea or lemonade.

The next thing *Wait knew, they were having sex in there, and she was saying they were two of a kind, both of them lost, and kissing his scars and so on.

Mrs. Hoover conceived, and gave birth to a son nine months later, which Mr. Hoover believed to be his own. It was a good-looking boy, who would grow up to be a good dancer and very musical, just like *Wait.

• • •

*Wait heard about the baby after he moved to Manhattan, but he could never consider it a relative. He would go years without thinking about it. And then his big brain would suddenly tell him for no good reason that somewhere in the world there was this young male walking around who wouldn't be in this world, if it weren't for him. It would make him feel creepy. That was much too big a result for such a little accident.

Why would he have wanted a son back then? It was the farthest thing from his mind.

• • •

The sexual prime for human males today, incidentally, comes at the age of six or so. When a six-year-old comes across a female in heat, there is no stopping him from engaging in sexual intercourse.

And I pity him, because I can still remember what I was like when I was sixteen. It was hell to be that excited. Then as now, orgasms gave no relief. Ten minutes after an orgasm, guess what? Nothing would do but that you have another one. And there was homework besides!

# 4

T HESE PEOPLE on the *Bahía de Darwin* weren't uncomfort-
ably hungry yet. Everybody's intestines, including those of
\*Kazakh, were still wringing the last of the digestible molecules
from what they had eaten the previous afternoon. Nobody was
consuming parts of his or her own body yet, the survival scheme
of the Galápagos tortoises. The Kanka-bonos certainly knew
what hunger was already. For the rest it would be a discovery.

And the only two people who had to keep their strength up,
and not just sleep all the time, were Mary Hepburn and the
Captain. The Kanka-bono girls understood nothing about the
ship or the ocean, and could make no sense of anything that
was said to them in any language but Kanka-bono. Hisako was
catatonic. Selena was blind, and \*Wait was dying. That left only
two people to steer the ship and care for \*Wait.

During the first night, those two would agree that Mary
should steer during the daytime, when the sun would tell her
unambiguously which way was east, from which they were fleeing, and which way was west, where the supposed peace and
plenty of Baltra lay. And the Captain would navigate by the
stars at night.

Whoever wasn't steering would have to keep \*Wait company,
and presumably would catch some sleep while doing so. These
were certainly long watches to stand. Then again, this was to
be a very brief ordeal, since, according to the Captain's calculations, Baltra was only about forty hours from Guayaquil.

If they had ever reached Baltra, which they never did, they
would have found it devastated and depopulated by yet another
airmailed package of dagonite.

· · ·

Human beings were so prolific back then that conventional
explosions like that had few if any long-term biological consequences. Even at the end of protracted wars, there still seemed to
be plenty of people around. Babies were always so plentiful that
serious efforts to reduce the population by means of violence

were doomed to failure. They no more left permanent injuries, except for the nuclear attacks on Hiroshima and Nagasaki, than did the *Bahía de Darwin* as it slit and roiled the trackless sea.

It was humanity's ability to heal so quickly, by means of babies, which encouraged so many people to think of explosions as show business, as highly theatrical forms of self-expression, and little more.

What humanity was about to lose, though, except for one tiny colony on Santa Rosalia, was what the trackless sea could never lose, so long as it was made of water: the ability to heal itself.

As far as humanity was concerned, all wounds were about to become very permanent. And high explosives weren't going to be a branch of show business anymore.

•   •   •

Yes, and if humanity had continued to heal its self-inflicted wounds by means of copulation, then the tale I have to tell about the Santa Rosalia Colony would be a tragicomedy starring the vain and incompetent Captain Adolf von Kleist. It would have spanned months rather than a million years, since the colonists would never have become colonists. They would have been marooned persons who were noticed and rescued in a little while.

Among them would have been a shamefaced Captain, solely responsible for their travail.

After only one night at sea, though, the Captain was still able to believe that all was well. It would soon be time for Mary Hepburn to relieve him at the wheel, at which time he would give her these instructions: "Keep the sun over the stern all morning, and over the bow all afternoon." And the Captain saw as his most pressing task the earning of his passengers' respect. They had seen him at his very worst. By the time they docked at Baltra, he hoped, they would have forgotten his drunkenness, and would be telling one and all that he had saved their lives.

That was another thing people used to be able to do, which they can't do anymore: enjoy in their heads events which hadn't happened yet and which might never occur. My mother was good at that. Someday my father would stop writing science fiction, and write something a whole lot of people wanted to read instead. And we would get a new house in a beautiful city, and nice clothes, and so on. She used to make me wonder why God had ever gone to all the trouble of creating reality.

Quoth Mandarax:

> *Imagination is as good as many voyages–and how much cheaper!*
>
>                    George William Curtis (1824–1892)

So there the Captain was, half naked on the bridge of the *Bahía de Darwin*, but in his head he was on the island of Manhattan, where most of his money and so many of his friends were anyway. He was going to get there somehow from Baltra, and buy himself a nice apartment on Park Avenue, and the hell with Ecuador.

•  •  •

Reality intruded now. A very real sun was coming up. There was one small trouble with the sun. The Captain had imagined all night that he was sailing due west, which meant that the sun would be rising squarely astern. This particular sun, however, was astern, all right, but also very much to starboard. So he turned the ship to port until the sun was where it was supposed to be. His big brain, which was responsible for the error he corrected, assured his soul that its mistake was minor and very recent, and had happened because the stars were dimmed by dawn. His big brain wanted the respect of his soul as much as he wanted the respect of his passengers. His brain had a life of its own, and the time would come when he would actually try to fire it for having misled him.

But that time was still five days away.

He still trusted it when he went aft to learn how "Willard Flemming" was, and to help Mary, according to plan, move him into the shade of the gangway between the officers' cabins. I do not put a star before the name of Willard Flemming, since there wasn't really such an individual—so he couldn't die.

And the Captain was so uninterested in Mary Hepburn as a person that he did not even know her last name. He thought it was Kaplan, the name over the pocket of her war-surplus fatigue blouse, which *Wait was using for a pillow now.

*Wait believed her last name to be Kaplan, too, no matter how often she corrected him. During the night he had said to her, "You Jews sure are survivors."

She had replied, "You're a survivor, too, Willard."

"Well," he had said, "I used to think I was one, Mrs. Kaplan. Now I'm not so sure. I guess everybody who isn't dead yet is a survivor."

"Now, now," she had said, "let's talk about something pleasant. Let's talk about Baltra."

But the blood supply to his brain must have been momentarily dependable then, because *Wait had continued to follow this line of reasoning. He'd even given a dry little laugh. He'd said, "There are all these people bragging about how they're survivors, as though that's something very special. But the only kind of person who can't say that is a corpse."

"There, there," she'd said.

•　•　•

When the Captain appeared before Mary and *Wait after sunrise, Mary had just consented to marry *Wait. He had worn her down. It was as though he had been begging for water all night, so that finally she was going to give him some. If he wanted betrothal so badly, and betrothal was all she had to give him, then she would give him some.

She did not expect, however, to have to honor that pledge almost immediately, or perhaps ever. She certainly liked all he had told her about himself. During the night, he had discovered that she was a cross-country skiing enthusiast. He had responded warmly that he was never happier than when he was on skis, with the clean snow all around, and the silence of the frozen lakes and forests. He had never been on skis in his life, but had once married and ruined the widow of the owner of a ski lodge in the White Mountains in New Hampshire. He courted her in the springtime, and left her a pauper before the green leaves turned orange and yellow and red and brown.

This wasn't a human being Mary was engaged to. She had a pastiche for a fiancé.

Not that it mattered much what she was engaged to, her big brain told her, since they certainly couldn't get married before they got to Baltra, and "Willard Flemming," if he was still alive, would have to go into intensive care immediately. There was plenty of time, she thought, for her to back out of the engagement.

So it did not seem a particularly serious matter when *Wait said to the Captain, "I have the most wonderful news. Mrs. Kaplan is going to marry me. I am the luckiest man in the world."

Fate now played a trick on Mary almost as quick and logical as my decapitation in the shipyard at Malmö. "You are in luck," said the Captain. "As captain of this ship in international waters, I am legally entitled to marry you. Dearly beloved, we are gathered here in the sight of God—" he began, and, two minutes later, he had made "Mary Kaplan" and "Willard Flemming" man and wife.

# 5

QUOTH MANDARAX:

*Oaths are but words, and words but wind.*
Samuel Butler (1612–1680)

And Mary Hepburn on Santa Rosalia would memorize that quotation from Mandarax, and hundreds of others. But as the years went by, she took her marriage to "Willard Flemming" more and more seriously, even though this second husband had died with a smile on his face about two minutes after the Captain pronounced them man and wife. She would say to furry Akiko when she was an old, old lady, bent over and toothless, "I thank God for sending me two good men." She meant Roy and "Willard Flemming." It was her way of saying, too, that she did not think much of the Captain, who was then an old, old man, and the father or grandfather of all the island's young people, save for Akiko.

•   •   •

Akiko was the only young person in the colony eager to hear stories, and particularly love stories, about life on the mainland. So that Mary would apologize to her for having so few first-person love stories to tell. Her parents had certainly been very much in love, she said, and Akiko enjoyed hearing about how they were still kissing and hugging each other right up to the end.

Mary could make Akiko laugh about the ridiculous love affair, if you could call it that, she had had with a widower named Robert Wojciehowitz, who was head of the English Department at Ilium High School before the school closed down. He was the only person besides Roy and "Willard Flemming" who had ever proposed marriage to her.

The story went like this:

Robert Wojciehowitz started calling her up and asking her for dates only two weeks after Roy was buried. She turned him

738

down, and let him know that it was certainly too early for her to start dating again.

She did everything she could to discourage him, but he came to see her one afternoon anyway, even though she had said she very much wished to be alone. He drove up to her house while she was mowing the lawn. He made her shut off the mower, and then he blurted out a marriage proposal.

Mary would describe his car to Akiko, and make Akiko laugh about it, even though Akiko had never seen and never would see any sort of automobile. Robert Wojciehowitz drove a Jaguar which used to be very beautiful, but which was now all scored and dented on the driver's side. The car was a gift from his wife while she was dying. Her name was *Doris, a name Akiko would give to one of her furry daughters, simply because of Mary's story.

*Doris Wojciehowitz had inherited a little money, and she bought the Jaguar for her husband as a way of thanking him for having been such a good husband. They had a grown son named Joseph, and he was a lout, and he wrecked the beautiful Jaguar while his mother was still alive. Joseph was sent to jail for a year—as a punishment for operating a motor vehicle while under the influence of alcohol.

There is our brain-shrinking old friend alcohol again.

Robert's marriage proposal took place on the only freshly mowed lawn in the neighborhood. All the other yards were being recaptured by wilderness, since everybody else had moved away. And the whole time Wojciehowitz was proposing, a big golden retriever was barking at them and pretending to be dangerous. This was Donald, the dog who had been such a comfort to Roy during the last months of his life. Even dogs had names back then. Donald was the dog. Robert was the man. And Donald was harmless. He had never bitten anybody. All he wanted was for someone to throw a stick for him, so he could bring it back, so somebody could throw a stick for him, so he could bring it back, and so on. Donald wasn't very smart, to say the least. He certainly wasn't going to write Beethoven's Ninth Symphony. When Donald slept, he would often whimper and his hind legs would shiver. He was dreaming of chasing sticks.

Robert was frightened of dogs—because he and his mother had been attacked by a Doberman pinscher when Robert was only five years old. Robert was all right with dogs as long as there was somebody around who knew how to control them. But whenever he was alone with one, no matter what size it was, he sweated and he trembled, and his hair stood on end. So he was extremely careful to avoid such situations.

But his marriage proposal so surprised Mary Hepburn that she burst into tears, something nobody does anymore. She was so embarrassed and confused that she apologized to him brokenly, and she ran into the house. She didn't want to be married to anybody but Roy. Even if Roy was dead, she still didn't want to be married to anybody but Roy.

So that left Robert all alone on the front lawn with Donald.

If Robert's big brain had been any good, it would have had him walk deliberately to his car, while telling Donald scornfully to shut up and go home, and so on. But it had him turn and run instead. His brain was so defective that it had him run right past his car, with Donald loping right behind him—and he crossed the street and climbed an apple tree in the front yard of an empty house belonging to a family which had moved to Alaska.

So Donald sat under the tree and barked up at him.

Robert was up there for an hour, afraid to come down, until Mary, wondering why Donald had been barking so monotonously for so long, came out of her house and rescued him.

When Robert came down, he was nauseated by fear and self-loathing. He actually threw up. After that, and he had spattered his own shoes and pants cuffs, he said snarlingly, "I am not a man. I am simply not a man. I will of course never bother you again. I will never bother any woman ever again."

And I retell this story of Mary's at this point because Captain Adolf von Kleist would hold the same low opinion of his worth after churning the ocean to a lather for five nights and days, and failing to find an island of any kind.

•   •   •

He was too far north—much too far north. So *we* were all too far north—much too far north. I wasn't hungry, of course, and neither was James Wait, who was frozen solid in the meat locker in the galley below. The galley, although stripped of light bulbs and without portholes, could still be illuminated, albeit hellishly, by the heating elements of its electric ovens and stoves.

Yes, and the plumbing was still working, too. There was plenty of water on tap everywhere, both hot and cold.

So nobody was thirsty, but everybody was surely ravenous. Kazakh, Selena's dog, was missing, and I put no star before her name, for Kazakh was dead. The Kanka-bono girls had stolen her while Selena slept, and choked her with their bare hands, and skinned and gutted her with no other tools than their teeth and fingernails. They had roasted her in an oven. Nobody else knew that they had done that yet.

She had been consuming her own substance anyway. By the time they killed her, she was skin and bones.

If she had made it to Santa Rosalia, she wouldn't have had much of a future—even in the unlikely event that there had been a male dog there. She had been neutered, after all. All she could have accomplished which might have outlasted her own lifetime would have been to give the furry Akiko, soon to be born, infantile memories of a dog. Under the best of circumstances, Kazakh would not have lived long enough for the other children born on the island to pet her, and to see her wag her tail and so on. They wouldn't have had her bark to remember, since Kazakh never barked.

# 6

I SAY NOW of Kazakh's untimely death, lest anyone should be moved to tears, "Oh, well—she wasn't going to write Beethoven's Ninth Symphony anyway."

I say the same thing about the death of James Wait: "Oh, well—he wasn't going to write Beethoven's Ninth Symphony anyway."

This wry comment on how little most of us were likely to accomplish in life, no matter how long we lived, isn't my own invention. I first heard it spoken in Swedish at a funeral while I was still alive. The corpse at that particular rite of passage was an obtuse and unpopular shipyard foreman named Per Olaf Rosenquist. He had died young, or what was thought to be young in those days, because he, like James Wait, had inherited a defective heart. I went to the funeral with a fellow welder named Hjalmar Arvid Boström, not that it can matter much what anybody's name was a million years ago. As we left the church, Boström said to me: "Oh, well—he wasn't going to write Beethoven's Ninth Symphony anyway."

I asked him if this black joke was original, and he said no, that he had heard it from his German grandfather, who had been an officer in charge of burying the dead on the Western Front during World War One. It was common for soldiers new to that sort of work to wax philosophical over this corpse or that one, into whose face he was about to shovel dirt, speculating about what he might have done if he hadn't died so young. There were many cynical things a veteran might say to such a thoughtful recruit, and one of those was: "Don't worry about it. He wasn't going to write Beethoven's Ninth Symphony anyway."

• • •

After I myself was buried young in Malmö, only six meters from Per Olaf Rosenquist, Hjalmar Arvid Boström said that about me, as he left the cemetery: "Oh, well—Leon wasn't going to write Beethoven's Ninth Symphony anyway."

Yes, and I was reminded of that comment when Captain von Kleist chided Mary for weeping about the death of the man they believed to be Willard Flemming. They had been out to sea for only twelve hours then, and the Captain still felt easily superior to her, and, for that matter, to practically everyone.

He said to her, while he told her how to hold the ship on its western course, "What a waste of time to cry about a total stranger. From what you tell me, he had no relatives and was no longer engaged in any useful work, so what is there to cry about?"

That might have been a good time for me to say as a disembodied voice, "He certainly wasn't going to write Beethoven's Ninth Symphony."

He made a sort of a joke now, but it didn't really sound like much of a joke. "As captain of this ship," he said, "I order you to cry only when there is something to cry about. There's nothing to cry about now."

"He was my husband," she said. "I choose to take that ceremony you performed very seriously. You can laugh if you want." Wait was right out back on the subject still. He hadn't been put in the freezer yet. "He gave a lot to this world, and he had a lot still to give, if only we could have saved him."

"What did this man give the world that was so wonderful?" asked the Captain.

"He knew more about windmills than anybody alive," she said. "He said we could close down the coal mines and the uranium mines—that windmills alone could make the coldest parts of the world as warm as Miami, Florida. He was also a composer."

"Really?" said the Captain.

"Yes," she said, "he wrote two symphonies." I found that piquant, in view of what I have just been saying, that Wait during his last night on earth should have claimed to have written two symphonies. Mary went on to say that when she got back home, she was going to go to Moose Jaw and find those symphonies, which had never been performed, and try to get an orchestra to give them a premiere.

"Willard was such a modest man," she said.

"So it would seem," said the Captain.

• • •

One hundred and eight hours later, the Captain would find himself in direct competition with the reputation of this modest paragon. "If only Willard were still alive," she said, "he would know exactly what to do."

The Captain had wholly lost his self-respect, and, although he had thirty more years to live, he would never get it back again. How is that for a real tragedy? He was abject in the face of Mary's mockery. "I am certainly open to suggestions," he said. "You have only to tell me what the wonderful Willard would have done, and that is what I will most gladly do."

He had by then fired his brain, and was navigating on the advice of his soul alone, turning the ship this way and then that way. An island the size of a handkerchief would have inspired the Captain to sob in gratitude. And, yes, yet again the sun, now dead ahead, now to port, now astern, now to starboard, was going down.

On the deck below, Selena MacIntosh was calling for her dog: "Kaaaaaaaa-zakh. Kaaaaaaa-zakh. Has anybody seen my dog?"

Mary yelled back, "She's not up here." And then, trying to imagine what Willard would have done, she came up with the idea that Mandarax, along with being a clock and translator and so on, might also be a radio. She told the Captain to try to call for help with it.

The Captain didn't know the instrument was a Mandarax. He thought it was a Gokubi, and he had a Gokubi in his hand-kerchief drawer, along with some cuff links and shirt studs and watches, in his house back in Quito. His brother had given it to him the previous Christmas, but he hadn't found it useful. To him, it was just another toy, and he knew this much about it: that it was certainly not a radio.

Now he weighed what he thought was a Gokubi in his hand, and he said to Mary, "I would give my right arm to have this piece of junk be a radio. I promise you, though, not even the saintly Willard Flemming could send or receive a message with a Gokubi."

"Maybe it's time you stopped being so absolutely certain about so much!" said Mary.

"That thought has occurred to me," he said.

"Then send an SOS," said Mary. "What harm can it do?"

"No harm, surely," said the Captain. "Mrs. Flemming, you are absolutely right. It can surely do no harm." He spoke into the tiny microphone of Mandarax, saying the international word for a ship in distress a million years ago: "Mayday, Mayday, Mayday," he intoned.

He then held the screen of Mandarax so that he and Mary might both read any reply which might appear there. As it happened, they had tapped into that part of the instrument's intellect, lacking in Gokubi, which knew so many quotations on every conceivable subject, including the month of May. On the little screen these utterly mystifying words appeared:

> *In depraved May, dogwood and chestnut, flowering Judas,*
> *To be eaten, to be divided, to be drunk*
> *Among whispers . . .*
>
> T. S. Eliot (1888–1965)

THE CAPTAIN AND MARY were able to believe for a moment that they had made contact with the outside world, although no response to an SOS could have come that fast and been so literary.

So the Captain called again, "Mayday! Mayday! This is the *Bahía de Darwin* calling, position unknown. Do you read me?"

To which Mandarax replied:

> *May will be fine next year as like as not:*
> *Oh ay, but then we shall be twenty-four.*
> A. E. Housman (1859–1936)

So then it was evident that the word *May* was triggering quotations from the instrument itself. The Captain puzzled over this. He still believed he had a Gokubi, but that it might be slightly more sophisticated than the one he had at home. Little did he know! He caught on that he was getting responses to the word "May." So then he tried "June."

And Mandarax replied:

> *June is bustin' out all over.*
> Oscar Hammerstein II
> (1895–1960)

"October! October!" cried the Captain.
And Mandarax replied:

> *The skies they were ashen and sober;*
> *The leaves they were crispèd and sere—*
> *The leaves they were withering and sere;*
> *It was night in the lonesome October*
> *Of my most immemorial year.*
> Edgar Allan Poe (1809–1849)

So that was that for Mandarax, which the Captain still believed to be a Gokubi. And Mary said that she might as well go back up into the crow's nest, to see what she could see.

Before she went up there, though, she had one more barb for the Captain. She asked him to name the island she might expect to see very soon. This was something he had done all through the third day at sea, naming islands which were just below the horizon and dead ahead, supposedly. "Keep your eyes peeled for San Cristóbal, or maybe Genovesa—depending on how far south we are," he had said, or, later in the day, "Ah! I know where we are now. At any moment we will be seeing Hood Island—the only nesting place in the world for the waved albatross, the largest bird in the archipelago." And so on.

Those albatrosses, incidentally, are still around today and still nesting on Hood. They have wingspreads as great as two meters, and remain as committed as ever to the future of aviation. They still think it's the coming thing.

•  •  •

As the fifth day drew to a close, though, the Captain remained silent when Mary asked him to name any island he believed to be nearby.

So she asked him again, and he told her this: "Mount Ararat."

•  •  •

When she got up into the crow's nest, though, I was surprised that she did not cry out in wonderment at what I mistook for a very queer weather phenomenon taking place right over the stern of the ship, and then trailing aft—over the wake. It seemed electrical in nature, although very silent, a close relative of ball lightning, maybe, or Saint Elmo's fire.

That former high school teacher looked right at it, but gave no sign that she found it at all out of the ordinary. And then I understood that only I could see it, and so knew it for what it was: the blue tunnel into the Afterlife. It had come after me again.

I had seen it three times before: at the moment of my decapitation, and then at the cemetery in Malmö, when Swedish clay was thumping wetly on the lid of my coffin and Hjalmar Arvid Boström, who certainly was never going to write Beethoven's Ninth Symphony, said of me, "Oh, well—he wasn't going to

write Beethoven's Ninth Symphony anyway." Its third appearance was when I myself was up in the crow's nest—during a
storm in the North Atlantic, in the sleet and spray, holding my
severed head on high as though it were a basketball.

The question the blue tunnel implies by appearing is one
only I can answer: Have I at last exhausted my curiosity as to
what life is all about? If so, I need only step inside what I liken
to a vacuum cleaner. If there is indeed suction within the blue
tunnel, which is filled with a light much like that cast off by the
electric stoves and ovens of the *Bahía de Darwin*, it does not
seem to trouble my late father, the science fiction writer Kilgore
Trout, who can stand right in the nozzle and chat with me.

• • •

The first thing Father said to me from above the stern of the
*Bahía de Darwin* was this: "Had enough of the ship of fools, my
boy? You come to Papa right now. Turn me down this time, and
you won't see me again for a million years."

A million years! My God—a million years! He wasn't fooling.
As bad a father as he had been, he had always kept his promises,
and he had never knowingly lied to me.

So I took one step in his direction, but not a second one. I
was like a female blue-footed booby at the start of a courtship
dance. As in a courtship dance, that uncertain first step was the
first tick of a clock, which would become irresistible. Already I
was changed, although I was still a long way from the nozzle.
The throbbing of the *Bahía de Darwin*'s engines became fainter
and the steel sun deck became transparent, so that I could see
into the main saloon below, where the Kanka-bono girls were
gnawing the bones of their innocent sister Kazakh.

That first step toward my father made me think this about
the Indian girls and Mary up in the crow's nest to my back,
and Hisako Hiroguchi and her fetus in the lavatory and the
demoralized Captain and the blind Selena on the bridge, and
the corpse in the walk-in freezer: "Why should I ever have cared
about these strangers, these slaves of fear and hunger? What do
they have to do with me?"

• • •

When I failed to take a second step in his direction, my father said, "Keep moving, Leon. No time to be coy."

"But I haven't completed my research," I protested. I had chosen to be a ghost because the job carried with it, as a fringe benefit, license to read minds, to learn the truth of people's pasts, to see through walls, to be many places all at once, to learn in depth how this or that situation had come to be structured as it was, and to have access to all human knowledge. "Father—" I said, "give me five more years."

"Five years!" he exclaimed. He mocked me with the three previous bargains I had made with him: "'Just one more day, Dad.' 'Just one more month, Daddy.' 'Just six more months, Pop.'"

"But I'm learning so much about what life is really like, how it really works, what it's really all about!" I said.

"Don't lie to me," he said. "Did I ever lie to you?"

"No, sir," I said.

"Then don't lie to me," he said.

"Are you a god now?" I said.

"No," he said. "I am still nothing but your father, Leon—but don't lie to me. For all your eavesdropping, you've accumulated nothing but information. You might as well be a collector of baseball cards or bottlecaps. For the sense you can make of all the information you have now, you might as well be Mandarax."

"Just five more years, Daddy, Dad, Father, Pa," I said.

"Not nearly enough time for you to learn what you hope to learn," he said. "And that, my boy, is why I give you my word of honor: If you send me away now, I won't be back for a million years.

"Leon! Leon! Leon!" he implored. "The more you learn about people, the more disgusted you'll become. I would have thought that your being sent by the wisest men in your country, supposedly, to fight a nearly endless, thankless, horrifying, and, finally, pointless war, would have given you sufficient insight into the nature of humanity to last you throughout all eternity!

"Need I tell you that these same wonderful animals, of which you apparently still want to learn more and more, are at this very moment proud as Punch to have weapons in place, all set to go at a moment's notice, guaranteed to kill everything?

"Need I tell you that this once beautiful and nourishing planet when viewed from the air now resembles the diseased organs of poor Roy Hepburn when exposed at his autopsy, and that the apparent cancers, growing for the sake of growth alone, and consuming all and poisoning all, are the cities of your beloved human beings?

"Need I tell you that these animals have made such a botch of things that they can no longer imagine decent lives for their own grandchildren, even, and will consider it a miracle if there is anything left to eat or enjoy by the year two thousand, now only fourteen years away?

"Like the people on this accursed ship, my boy, they are led by captains who have no charts or compasses, and who deal from minute to minute with no problem more substantial than how to protect their self-esteem."

• • •

As in life, he still needed a shave. As in life, he was still pale and haggard. As in life, he was still smoking a cigarette. And one reason, surely, that I found it hard to take another step in his direction was that I did not like him.

I had run away from home when I was sixteen because I was so ashamed of him.

If there had been an angel in the mouth of the blue tunnel, instead of my father, I might have skipped right in.

• • •

James Wait ran away from home because people were inflicting physical pain on him all the time. He might as well have gone straight from the delivery room to the Spanish Inquisition, so ingenious were some of the tortures the big brains of foster parents had devised for him. I ran away from a real parent who had never once in anger laid a hand on me.

But when I was too young to know any better, my father had made me his co-conspirator in driving my mother away forever. He had me jeering along with him at Mother for wanting to take a trip somewhere, to make some friends and have them over to dinner, to go to a movie or a restaurant sometime. I agreed with my father. I then believed that he was the greatest writer in the world, since that was all I could think to be proud of. We had no friends, and ours was the shabbiest house in the neighborhood, and we didn't even own a television set or an automobile. So why wouldn't I have defended him against my mother? To his credit, anyway, he never suggested that he might have greatness. When I was green in judgment, though, I found greatness implied in his insistence on doing nothing but writing and smoking all the time—and I mean all the time.

Oh, yes, and there was one other thing I could be proud of, and this really counted for something in Cohoes: My father had been a United States Marine.

When I got to be sixteen, though, I myself had arrived at the conclusion my mother and the neighbors had reached so long ago: that my father was a repellent failure, his work appearing only in the most disreputable publications, which paid him almost nothing. He was an insult to life itself, I thought, when he went on doing nothing with it but writing and smoking all the time—and I mean all the time.

I was then flunking every course but art at school. Nobody flunked art at Cohoes High School. That was simply impossible. And I ran away to find my mother, which I never did.

•   •   •

Father had published more than a hundred books and a thousand short stories, but in all my travels I met only one person who had ever heard of him. Encountering such a person after so long a search was so confusing to me emotionally, that I think I actually went crazy for a little while.

I never telephoned Father or dropped him so much as a postcard. I did not know he had died until I myself had died, and he appeared to me for the first time at the mouth of the blue tunnel into the Afterlife.

Yet I had honored him for the one thing I thought he had to be proud of still: I, too, had been a United States Marine. It was a family tradition.

And by golly if I haven't now become a writer, too, scribbling away like Father, without the slightest hint that there might actually be a reader somewhere. There isn't one. There can't be one.

•   •   •

So now we have both been like courting blue-footed boo-bies, doing what we had to do, whether there was anybody to notice—or, far more likely, not.

•  •  •

Now Father said to me from the nozzle, "You're just like your mother."

"In what way?" I said.

"You know what her favorite quotation was?" he said.

I certainly did, and so did Mandarax. It is the epigraph of this book.

•  •  •

"You believe that human beings are good animals, who will eventually solve all their problems and make earth into a Garden of Eden again."

"Could I see her, please?" I said. I knew she was somewhere at the other end of the tunnel, that she was dead. That was the first thing I had asked Father after I myself was dead: "Do you know what became of Mother?" I had searched everywhere for her, before joining the United States Marines.

"Is that Mother right behind you?" I said. The blue tunnel was in a restless state of peristalsis. Its squirms often afforded me glimpses deep into its interior. I saw this woman in there, that third time father appeared, and I thought it might be Mother—but no such luck.

"It's Naomi Tharp, Leon," the woman called out to me. She was the neighbor woman who, after my real mother left, did her best to be my mother for a little while. "It's Mrs. Tharp," she called. "You remember me, don't you, Leon? You come in here just like you used to come in through my kitchen door. Be a good boy now. You don't want to be left out there for another million years."

I took another step toward the nozzle. The *Bahía de Darwin* became a fantasia of cobwebs. The blue tunnel became as sub-stantial and sensible a means of transportation as the Malmö streetcar which used to take me to and from the shipyard every day.

But then, behind me, from up in the *Bahía de Darwin*'s gossa-mer crow's nest, I heard the dim spook which Mary had become shouting something over and over again. She was in agony of some sort, I thought. I could not make out her words, but her tone would have been appropriate if she had been shot in the stomach.

I had to know what she was saying, and so I took two steps backwards, and then turned and looked up at her. She was sobbing, she was laughing. She was bent over the rim of the steel bucket, so that her head was upside down as she shouted to the Captain on the bridge: "Land ho! Land ho! Praise God! Dear God! Land ho! Land ho!"

# 8

I T WAS SANTA ROSALIA which Mary Hepburn saw.

The Captain would of course steer for it at once, hoping to find it inhabited by people—or at least populated by animals he and the others could cook and eat.

What remained in question was whether I would be along to see what happened next. The price I would have to pay for satisfying my curiosity about the destinies of the people on the ship was unambiguous: to continue to haunt the earth, without a chance of parole, for a million years.

The decision was made for me by Mary Hepburn, by "Mrs. Flemming," whose joy in the crow's nest held my attention so long that when I looked back at the tunnel, the tunnel was gone.

•  •  •

I have now completed that sentence of one thousand millennia. I have paid in full my debt to society or whatever. I can expect to see the blue tunnel again at any time. I will of course skip into its mouth most gladly. Nothing ever happens around here anymore that I haven't seen or heard so many times before. Nobody, surely, is going to write Beethoven's Ninth Symphony—or tell a lie, or start a Third World War.

Mother was right: Even in the darkest times, there really was still hope for humankind.

•  •  •

On the afternoon of Monday, December 1, 1986, Captain Adolf von Kleist, whose ship was without a utile anchor, intentionally ran the *Bahía de Darwin* aground on a lava shoal which was close to shore. He believed that she could drag herself free, as she had done in Guayaquil, when it was time to sail again.

When did he plan to sail again? As soon as the larders were stocked with eggs and boobies and iguanas and penguins and cormorants and crabs, and anything else that was edible and easy to catch. When he had a food supply to match his stores of fuel and water, he could return at leisure to the mainland,

and seek a peaceful port which would take them in. He would rediscover the South American continent.

He switched off his faithful engines. That would be the end of their faithfulness. For reasons he was never able to determine, they would never start again.

This meant that the stoves and ovens and refrigerators would soon be out of business, too — as soon as the batteries ran down.

• • •

There were still ten meters of stern line, of white nylon umbilical cord, coiled by a cleat on the main deck. The Captain tied knots in this, and then he and Mary climbed down it to the shoal, and waded ashore to gather eggs and kill lower animals who had no fear of them. They would use Mary's blouse and James Wait's new shirt, which still had the price tag on it, for grocery bags.

They wrung the necks of boobies. They caught land iguanas by their tails, and beat them to death on black boulders. And it was during this carnage that Mary would scratch herself, and a fearless vampire finch would take its first sip of human blood.

• • •

The killers left the marine iguanas alone, believing them to be inedible. Two years would pass before their discovery that partially digested seaweed in the bellies of these creatures was not only a tasty hot meal, ready cooked, but a cure for vitamin and mineral deficiencies which had troubled them up to then. That would complete their diet. Some people, moreover, could digest this purée better than others, so that they were healthier and nicer looking—more desirable as sexual partners. So the Law of Natural Selection went to work, with the result, a million years later, that human beings can now digest seaweed for themselves, without the intervention of marine iguanas, which they leave alone.

That is such a much nicer arrangement for everyone.

People still kill fish, though, and, in times of fish shortages, they will still eat boobies, who still aren't afraid of them.

I could stay here another million years, and that still wouldn't be time enough, I'm sure, for the boobies to realize that people are dangerous. Yes, and as I've already said, they still dance and dance at mating time.

•  •  •

The people had quite a feast on the *Bahía de Darwin* that night. They ate on the sun deck, and the deck itself was the serving platter, and the Captain was the chef. There were roasted land iguanas stuffed with crabmeat and minced finches. There were roasted boobies stuffed with their own eggs and basted with melted penguin fat. It was perfectly delicious. Everybody was happy again.

And at first light the next morning, the Captain and Mary went ashore again, and took the Kanka-bono girls along. The girls could finally understand something which was going on. They all killed and killed, and hauled corpses and hauled corpses, until the ship's freezer contained, in addition to James Wait, enough birds and iguanas and eggs to last for a month, if necessary. Now they had not only plenty of fuel and water, but no end of food, and good food, too, as well.

Next the Captain would start the engines. He would head the ship due east at maximum velocity. There was no way he could miss South America or Central America or North America, the Captain told Mary, his sense of humor returning, ". . . unless we are unlucky enough to pass through the Panama Canal. But if we do go through the canal, I can virtually guarantee you that we will be in Europe or Africa by and by."

So he laughed, and she laughed. Everything was going to be all right after all. But then the engines wouldn't start.

B Y THE TIME the *Bahía de Darwin* slid beneath the dead calm ocean, which was in September of 1996, everybody but the Captain was calling her by a nickname given to her by Mary, which was "the *Walloping Window Blind*."

This disparaging title was taken from a song Mary learned from Mandarax, which went like this:

> *A capital ship for an ocean trip*
> *Was the* Walloping Window Blind.
> *No gale that blew dismayed her crew*
> *Or troubled the captain's mind.*
> *The man at the wheel was taught to feel*
> *Contempt for the wildest blow,*
> *And it often appeared, when the weather had cleared*
> *That he'd been in his bunk below.*
>
> Charles Carryl (1842–1920)

Hisako Hiroguchi and her furry daughter Akiko and Selena MacIntosh all called her "the *Walloping Window Blind*," and so did the Kanka-bono women, who loved the sound of the words without understanding them. And when the Kanka-bono women bore children, which they hadn't done yet, they would teach their young that they themselves had come from the mainland on a magic ship, since vanished, called "the *Walloping Window Blind*."

Akiko, who was fluent in Kanka-bono as well as English and Japanese, and who was the only non–Kanka-bono who could converse with the Kanka-bonos, would never find a satisfactory way to translate this into Kanka-bono: "the *Walloping Window Blind*."

The Kanka-bonos could no more understand it and its comical intent than could a modern person, if I were to whisper in his or her ear as he or she basked on a white sandy beach by a blue lagoon: "the *Walloping Window Blind*."

• • •

It was soon after the *Walloping Window Blind* went to the bottom that Mary began her artificial insemination program. She was then sixty-one. She was the sole sexual partner of the Captain, who was sixty-six, and whose sexual drive was no longer all that compelling. And he was determined not to reproduce, since he felt that there was still a good chance that he could pass on Huntington's chorea. Also, he was a racist, and so not at all drawn to Hisako or her furry daughter, and least of all to the Indian women who would ultimately bear his children.

Remember: These people were expecting to be rescued at any time, and had no way of knowing that they were the last hope for the human race. So that they engaged in sexual activities simply to pass some of the time pleasantly, to relieve an itch, or to make themselves sleepy, or what you will. So far as anybody knew, reproducing would actually be irresponsible, since Santa Rosalia was no place to raise children, and children would also place strains on the food supply.

Mary felt this as strongly as anyone before the *Walloping Window Blind* joined the Ecuadorian fleet of submarines: that it would be a tragedy if a child were born.

Her soul continued to feel that, but her big brain began to wonder, idly, so as not to spook her, if the sperm which the Captain squirted into her about twice a month could be transferred to a fertile woman somehow—with, hey presto, a resulting pregnancy. Akiko, who was only ten then, wasn't yet ovulating. But the Kanka-bono women, who ranged in age from fifteen to nineteen, surely were.

•   •   •

Mary's big brain told her what she had so often told her students: that there was no harm, and possibly a lot of good, in people's playing with all sorts of ideas in their heads, no matter how supposedly impossible or impractical or downright crazy they seemed to be. She reassured herself there on Santa Rosalia, as she had reassured the adolescents of Ilium, that mental games played with even the trashiest ideas had led to many of the most significant scientific insights of what she, a million years ago, called "modern times."

She consulted Mandarax about curiosity.

Quoth Mandarax:

*Curiosity is one of the permanent and certain characteristics of
a vigorous mind.*

Samuel Johnson (1709–1784)

What Mandarax didn't tell her, and what her big brain certainly wasn't going to tell her, was that, if she came up with
an idea for a novel experiment which had a chance of working,
her big brain would make her life a hell until she had actually
performed that experiment.

That, in my opinion, was the most diabolical aspect of those
old-time big brains: They would tell their owners, in effect,
"Here is a crazy thing we could actually do, probably, but we
would never do it, of course. It's just fun to think about."

And then, as though in trances, the people would really do
it—have slaves fight each other to the death in the Colosseum,
or burn people alive in the public square for holding opinions
which were locally unpopular, or build factories whose only
purpose was to kill people in industrial quantities, or to blow
up whole cities, and on and on.

• • •

Somewhere in Mandarax there should have been, but was
not, a warning to this effect: "In this era of big brains, anything
which can be done will be done—so hunker down."

The closest Mandarax came to saying anything like that was
a quotation from Thomas Carlyle (1795–1881):

*Doubt, of whatever kind, can be ended in Action alone.*

• • •

Mary's doubts about whether a woman could be impregnated
by another one on a desert island without any technical assistance led to her taking action. In a trancelike state, she found
herself visiting the camp of the Kanka-bono women on the other
side of the crater, having brought Akiko along as an interpreter.

And now I catch myself remembering my father when he was
still alive, when he was still an ink-stained wretch in Cohoes.
He was always hoping to sell something to the movies, so that
he wouldn't have to take odd jobs, and we could get a cook and
cleaning lady.

But no matter how much he might yearn for a movie sale, the crucial scenes in every one of his stories and books were events which nobody in his right mind would ever want to put into a movie—not if he wanted the movie to be popular.

So now I myself am telling a story whose crucial scene could never have been included in a popular movie of a million years ago. In it Mary Hepburn, as though hypnotized, dips her right index finger into herself and then into an eighteen-year-old Kanka-bono woman, making her pregnant.

Mary would later think of a joke she might make about the rash, inexplicable, irresponsible, plain crazy liberties she had taken with the bodies of not just one but all of the Kanka-bono teenagers. She was no longer on speaking terms, though, with the colonist who would have understood the joke, who was the Captain, so she had to keep it to herself. The joke, if articulated, would have gone like this:

"If only I had thought of doing this when I was still teaching at Ilium High School, I would be in a cozy New York State prison for women instead of on godforsaken Santa Rosalia now."

# *10*

WHEN THE SHIP went down, it took the bones of James Wait with it, all mixed up on the floor of the meat locker with the bones of reptiles and birds of a sort which are still around today. Only bones like Wait's are unclothed with flesh today.

He was some kind of male ape, evidently—who walked upright, and had an extraordinarily big brain whose purpose, one can guess, was to control his hands, which were cunningly articulated. He may have domesticated fire. He may have used tools.

He may have had a vocabulary of a dozen words or more.

•  •  •

When the ship went down, the Captain had the only beard on the island. One year after that, his son Kamikaze would be born. Thirteen years after that, the island would have its second beard, the beard of Kamikaze.

Quoth Mandarax:

> *There was an Old Man with a beard,*
> *Who said: "It is just as I feared!*
> *Two owls and a hen,*
> *Four larks and a wren*
> *Have all built their nests in my beard."*
> Edward Lear (1812–1888)

By the time the ship went down, when the colony was ten years old, the Captain had become a very boring person, without enough to think about, without enough to do. He spent much of his time in the neighborhood of the island's only water supply, which was a spring at the base of the crater. When people came to get water, he would receive them as though he were the kindly and knowledgeable master of the spring, its assistant and conservator. He would tell even the Kanka-bonos, who never understood a word he said, how the spring was that day—characterizing its dribbling from a crack in a rock as being

". . . very nervous today," or ". . . very cheerful today," or ". . . very lazy today," or whatever.

The dribbling was in fact quite steady, and had been for thousands of years before the colonists got there, and remains so, although people no longer have to depend on it, to the present day. Here was how it worked, and it didn't take a graduate of the United States Naval Academy to understand its mysteries: The crater was an enormous bowl which caught rainwater, which it hid from the sunshine beneath a very thick layer of volcanic debris. There was a slow leak in the bowl, which was the spring.

There was no way in which the Captain, with so much time on his hands, might have improved the spring. The water already dribbled most satisfactorily from a crack in a lava boulder, and was already caught in a natural basin ten centimeters below. That basin was and still is about the size of the washbasin in the lavatory off the main saloon of the *Walloping Window Blind*. If emptied, that basin, with or without encouragement from the Captain, would in twenty-three minutes and eleven seconds, as timed by Mandarax, be brimming full again.

How would I describe the declining years of the Captain? I would have to say that he felt quietly desperate. But he surely needn't have been marooned on Santa Rosalia in order to feel that way.

Quoth Mandarax:

> *The mass of men lead lives of quiet desperation.*
> Henry David Thoreau (1817–1862)

And why was quiet desperation such a widespread malady back then, and especially among men? Yet again I trot onstage the only real villain in my story: the oversize human brain.

• • •

Nobody leads a life of quiet desperation nowadays. The mass of men was quietly desperate a million years ago because the infernal computers inside their skulls were incapable of restraint or idleness; were forever demanding more challenging problems which life could not provide.

• • •

I have now described almost all of the events and circumstances crucial, in my opinion, to the miraculous survival of humankind to the present day. I remember them as though they were queerly shaped keys to many locked doors, the final door opening on perfect happiness.

One of those keys, surely, was the absence of tools on Santa Rosalia, save for feeble combinations of bones and twigs and rocks and fish guts—and bird guts.

If the Captain had had any decent tools, crowbars and picks and shovels and so on, he surely would have found a way, in the name of science and progress, to clog the spring, or to cause it to vomit the entire contents of the crater in only a week or two.

•  •  •

As for the balance the colonists established between themselves and their food supply: I have to say that that, too, was based on luck rather than intelligence.

Nature chose to be generous, so there was enough to eat. The birds on the other islands were having good years, and so sent emigrants from overpopulated rookeries to Santa Rosalia to take over the nests of those eaten by the people. There was no such natural replacement scheme for the marine iguanas, who were not long-distance swimmers. But the repulsiveness of those scrofulous reptiles and the contents of their intestines, inspired people to use them for nourishment only during dire shortages of almost any other sort of food.

The most satisfactory food, everybody agreed, was an egg cooked for hours on a nice flat rock in the sunshine. There was no fire on Santa Rosalia. After that came a fish stolen from a bird. After that came a bird itself. After that came the green pulp from inside a marine iguana.

Nature, in fact, was so bountiful that there was a reserve supply of food, of which the colonists were aware, but to which they never had to turn. There were seals and sea lions of all ages, none of them suspicious or ferocious, save for the males at mating time, lolling everywhere, making goo-goo eyes at passing human beings. They were edible as hell.

•  •  •

It just might have been fatal that the colonists killed off all the land iguanas almost immediately—but it turned out not to have been a disaster. It could have mattered a lot. It just happened that it didn't matter much at all. There have never been great land tortoises on Santa Rosalia, or the colonists probably would have exterminated them as well. But that wouldn't have mattered either.

Meanwhile, in other parts of the world, particularly in Africa, people were dying by the millions because they were unlucky. It hadn't rained for years and years. It used to rain a lot there, but now it looked as though it might never rain again.

At least the Africans had stopped reproducing. That much was good. That was some help. That meant that there was that much more of nothing to be spread around.

•   •   •

The Captain did not realize that any of the Kanka-bono women were pregnant until a month before the first one of them gave birth—gave birth, as it happened, to the first human male native to the island, who came to be known by the nickname the furry Akiko gave him, expressing her delight in his maleness, which was "Kamikaze," Japanese for "sacred wind."

•   •   •

The original colonists never became a family which included everyone. Subsequent generations, though, after the last of the old people died, would become a family which included everyone. It had a common language and a common religion and some common jokes and songs and dances and so on, almost everything Kanka-bono. And Kamikaze, when it was his turn to be an old, old man, became something the Captain had never been, which was a venerated patriarch. And Akiko became a venerated matriarch.

It went very fast—that formation from such random genetic materials of a perfectly cohesive human family. That was so nice to see. It almost made me love people just as they were back then, big brains and all.

# 11

THE CAPTAIN found out that a Kanka-bono woman was pregnant only very late in the game because nobody was about to tell him, certainly, but also because the Kanka-bono women hated him so much, mainly on racist grounds, that he hardly ever saw one. They came to his side of the crater for water only late at night, when he was usually sound asleep, just so they could avoid him. They would go on hating him that much right up to the end of his life, even though he was the father of all the children they loved so much.

But a month before Kamikaze was born, the Captain could not sleep on his and Mary's feather bed. His big brain made him itch and squirm with a scheme for digging down to the water supply from the top of the crater, and locating the leak, and thus gaining control of what nobody had any reason to complain about: the rate of flow of the spring.

This was an engineering project, incidentally, about as modest as the construction of the Great Pyramid of Khufu or the Panama Canal.

So the Captain got out of bed and went for a walk in the middle of the night. The moon was full and directly overhead. When he came to the spring, there were the six Kanka-bonos, patting the top of the water in the brimming basin as though it were a friendly animal, and sprinkling each other and so on. They were having so much fun, and they were especially happy because they were all going to have babies soon.

They stopped having fun as soon as they saw the Captain. They thought he was evil. But the Captain was also dismayed—because he was naked. He hadn't expected to run into anybody. He had not bothered to put on his iguana-skin breechclout. So now, after ten years on Santa Rosalia, the Kanka-bonos were getting their first look at his genitalia. They had to laugh, and then they couldn't stop laughing.

• • •

The Captain retreated to his dwelling, where Mary was fast asleep. He dismissed the laughter as simple-minded. He thought, too, that one of the women had a tumor or a parasite or an infection in her belly, and that, despite her merriment, she would probably die quite soon.

He mentioned this swelling to Mary the next morning, and she gave him a very strange smile.

"That's something to smile about?" he said.

"Was I smiling?" she said. "My goodness—it's certainly nothing to smile about."

"A swelling that big—" he said, "it can't be anything minor."

"I couldn't agree with you more," she said. "We will just have to watch and wait. What else can we do?"

"She was so cheerful," he marveled. "She didn't seem to mind at all—that awful swelling."

"As you've said so often," said Mary, "they aren't like us. They're very primitive in their thinking. They try to make the best of whatever happens. They figure they can't do much of anything about anything anyway, so they take life as it comes."

She had Mandarax there in bed with her. She and the furry Akiko, who was then only ten years old, were the only colonists who still found the instrument at all amusing. If it weren't for them, the Captain or Selena or Hisako, feeling mocked by its useless advice or inane wisdom or ponderous efforts to be humorous, would have pitched it into the ocean long ago.

The Captain, in fact, had felt personally insulted by Mandarax since it had come up with the poem about the ridiculous captain of the *Walloping Window Blind*.

So Mary was able to come up now with a comment concerning the supposed ignorance of the Kanka-bono woman, who was so happy despite the growth in her belly, to wit:

> *The happiest life consists in ignorance,*
> *Before you learn to grieve and to rejoice.*
> Sophocles (496–406 B.C.)

Mary was toying with him in a way which I, as a former fellow male of the Captain, was bound to think smug and mean-spirited. If I had been a woman in life, I might have felt differently. If I had been a woman, perhaps I would have been jubilant over Mary Hepburn's secret jeering at the limited role males played in reproduction back then, and which they still play today. That has not changed. There are still these big lunks who can be counted upon to squirt lively sperm in season.

Mary's secret jeering was about to become overt and nasty, too. After Kamikaze was born, and the Captain learned that this was his own son, he would stammer that he surely should have been consulted.

And Mary would reply: "You didn't have to carry that child for nine months, and then have it fight its way out from between your legs. You can't breast-feed it, even if you'd like to, which I somehow doubt. And nobody expects you to help raise it. The hope is, in fact, that you will have absolutely nothing to do with it!"

"Even so—" he protested.

"Oh, my God—" she said, "if we could have made a baby out of marine-iguana spit, don't you think we would have done that, and not even disturbed Your Majesty?"

## 12

A FTER SHE SAID THAT to the Captain, there was no way that their relationship could continue as before. A million years ago, there was a great deal of big-brained theorizing about how to keep human couples from breaking up, and there was at least one way Mary could have gone on living with the Captain for a little while longer anyway, if she had really wanted to. She could have told him that the Kanka-bono women had engaged in sexual intercourse with sea lions and fur seals. He would have believed it, not only because he held a low opinion of the women's morals, but because he could never even have suspected that artificial insemination had taken place. He would not have considered it possible, although the procedure, in fact, turned out to be child's play, as easy as pie.

Quoth Mandarax:

> *Something there is that doesn't love a wall.*
> Robert Frost (1874–1963)

To which I add:

> *Yes, but something there is which adores a mucous membrane.*
> Leon Trotsky Trout (1946–1,001,986)

So Mary might have saved the relationship with a lie, although there would still have been Kamikaze's blue eyes to explain. One person in twelve today, incidentally, has the Captain's blue eyes and his curly golden hair. Sometimes I will joke with such a specimen, saying, "*Guten morgen*, Herr von Kleist," or, "*Wie geht es Ihnen*, Freulein von Kleist?" That's about all the German I have.

It is more than enough today.

• • •

Should Mary Hepburn have saved her relationship with a lie? The question remains moot after all this time. They were never an ideal couple. They had been stuck with each other after

Selena and Hisako paired off and raised Akiko, and the Kanka-bono women moved to the far side of the crater, preserving the purity of their Kanka-bono beliefs and attitudes and ways.

One of the Kanka-bonos' customs, incidentally, was to keep their names a secret from anyone who wasn't a Kanka-bono. I was privy to their secrets, though, just as I was privy to everybody else's secrets, and there seems no harm in my now revealing that the first to have a baby by the Captain was Sinka, and the second to have a baby was Lor, and the third to have a baby was Lira, and the fourth to have a baby was Dirno, and the fifth to have a baby was Nanno, and the sixth to have a baby was Keel.

• • •

After Mary moved out on the Captain, and made a canopy and a feather bed of her own, she would say to Akiko that she was no lonelier then than she had been when she lived with the Captain. She had several specific complaints about the Captain, faults he might easily have remedied, if he himself had been at all interested in making their relationship viable.

"Both people have to work at a relationship," she advised Akiko. "If just one works on it, you might as well forget about it. It's just no good, and whichever one does all the work winds up the way I did, feeling like some kind of fool all the time. I was really happily married one time, Akiko, and would have been really happily married twice, if Willard hadn't died—so I know how it's supposed to work."

She enumerated the four most serious faults which the Captain might have remedied easily, but wouldn't, as follows:

1. When he spoke of what he would do after they were rescued, he never included her in his plans.
2. He made fun of Willard Flemming, although he knew how much this hurt her, doubting very much that he had written two symphonies or knew anything about windmills, or that he could even ski.
3. He complained constantly about the beeping sounds Mandarax made when she pressed the different buttons, although they could hardly be heard, and although he knew how rewarding it was for her to improve her mind, to

memorize famous quotations and to learn new languages
and so on.

4.  He would rather choke to death than ever say, "I love you."

"And those are just the four big ones," she said. So there was a
great deal of pent-up resentment coming out when Mary spoke
to the Captain as she did about marine-iguana spit.

•  •  •

I can't see that the breakup was tragic, since there were no
dependent children involved, and neither party found living
alone absolutely unendurable. Both were visited regularly by
Akiko, and then, after Kamikaze sprouted a beard, Akiko had
furry children of her own to bring along.

•  •  •

Mary was accorded no special status by the Kanka-bono
women, although she had made it possible for them to have
babies. They and then their children feared her as much as they
feared the Captain, believing her capable of doing great evil as
well as good.

And twenty years went by. Hisako and Selena had committed suicide by drowning eight years before. Akiko was now a
matronly thirty-nine years old, the mother of seven furry children by Kamikaze—two boys and five girls. She was fluent in
three languages without the help of Mandarax: English, Japanese, and Kanka-bono. Her children spoke only Kanka-bono,
except for two English words: *Grandpa* and *Grandma*. That was
what she had them call the Captain and Mary Hepburn. That
was what she herself called them.

•  •  •

One morning, at seven-thirty A.M. on May 9, 2016, according
to *Mandarax, Akiko woke *Mary, and told her that she should
go make her peace with the *Captain, who was so sick that he
would probably not last out the day. Akiko had visited him the
previous evening, and had sent her children home and stayed
and nursed him through the night, although there was very
little she could do for him.

So *Mary went, although she was no longer any spring chicken herself. She was eighty—and toothless. Her spine was shaped like a question mark, thanks, according to *Mandarax, to the ravages of osteoporosis. She didn't need *Mandarax to tell her it was osteoporosis. Her mother and grandmother's bones were made as weak as reeds by osteoporosis before they died. There is another hereditary defect unknown in the present day.

As for what was wrong with the *Captain, *Mandarax made the educated guess that he had Alzheimer's disease. The old poop couldn't look after himself anymore, and hardly knew where he was. He would have starved to death if Akiko hadn't brought him food every day and, one way or another, made sure he swallowed at least some of it. He was eighty-six.

Quoth *Mandarax:

> *Last scene of all,*
> *That ends this strange eventful history,*
> *Is second childishness and mere oblivion,*
> *Sans teeth, sans eyes, sans taste, sans everything.*
> William Shakespeare (1564–1616)

So *Mary, all stooped over, shuffled under the *Captain's feather canopy, which used to be her own as well. She had not been there for twenty years. The canopy had been renewed many times since her departure, and so, of course, had been the mangrove poles and stakes which held it up, and the feather bed. But the architecture was the same, with a view cut through living mangroves right down to the water, and framing the shoal on which the *Walloping Window Blind* had been run aground so long ago.

What had finally dragged that ship off the shoal, by the way, was an accumulation of rainwater and seawater in her stern. The seawater leaked in around the drive shaft of one of her mighty screws. She slid under during the night. Nobody actually saw her begin that last leg of "the Nature Cruise of the Century," three kilometers straight down to the locker of Davy Jones.

# 13

THAT WAS SURE SOME lugubriously historic shoal outside the *Captain's home! I was surprised that he wanted to look at it every day. It was down that same half-drowned hump that *Hisako Hiroguchi and the blind *Selena MacIntosh had waded hand in hand, seeking and finding together the blue tunnel into the Afterlife. *Selena was then forty-eight and still fertile. *Hisako was fifty-six, and had not ovulated for quite some time.

Akiko was still upset every time she saw the shoal. She couldn't help feeling responsible for the suicides of the two women who had raised her—even though *Mandarax had said it was surely *Hisako's intractable, monopolar, and probably inherited depression which had killed them both.

But there was the fact, inescapable for Akiko, that *Hisako and *Selena had killed themselves soon after Akiko set up housekeeping on her own.

She was then twenty-two. Kamikaze hadn't reached puberty yet, so he had nothing to do with it. She was simply living alone, and enjoying it quite a bit. She was well past the age when most people flew the nest, and I was all for her doing it. I had seen how much pain it caused her when *Hisako and *Selena continued to speak to her in baby talk long after she had become such a robust and capable woman. And yet she had put up with it for an awfully long time—because she was so grateful for all they had done for her when she was genuinely helpless.

On the day she left, they were still cutting up her booby meat for her, if you can believe it.

For a month after that, they still set a place for her at every meal, with the meat already all cut up, and they cooed at her and teased her gently even though she wasn't there anymore.

And then, one day, life just wasn't worth living anymore.

• • •

*Mary Hepburn, for all her ailments, was still self-sufficient when she went to see the *Captain on his deathbed. She still gathered and prepared her own food, and kept her home as neat as a pin. She was proud of this, and should have been. The *Captain was a burden on the community, which was to say a burden on Akiko. *Mary was surely not. She had often said that, if ever she felt that she was about to become a burden to anybody, she would follow Hisako and Selena down the shoal, and join her second husband on the ocean floor.

The contrast between her feet and those of the pampered *Captain were striking. Their feet certainly had very different stories to tell. His were white and soft. Hers were as tough and brown as the rock-climbing boots she had brought with her to Guayaquil so long ago.

So she said to this man to whom she hadn't spoken for twenty years, "They tell me you're very sick."

Actually, he was still quite handsome and well fleshed out. He was nice and clean, since Akiko bathed him every day, and shampooed and combed his beard and hair. The soap she used, which was made by the Kanka-bono women, was composed of ground-up bones and penguin fat.

One of the exasperating things about the *Captain's disease was that his body was still perfectly capable of taking care of itself. It was a lot stronger than *Mary's. It was his deteriorating big brain which was having him spend so much time in bed, and allowing him to soil himself and refuse to eat and so on.

Again: His condition wasn't peculiar to Santa Rosalia. Back on the mainland, millions of old people were as helpless as babies, and compassionate young adults like Akiko had to look after them. Thanks to sharks and killer whales, problems connected with aging are unimaginable in the present day.

• • •

"Who is this hag?" the *Captain asked Akiko. "I hate ugly women. This is the ugliest woman I ever saw."

"It's *Mary Hepburn—it's Mrs. Flemming, Grandpa," said Akiko. A tear skittered down her furry cheek. "It's Grandma," she said.

"Never saw her before in my life," he said. "Please get her out of here. I will close my eyes. When I open them again, I want her gone." He closed his eyes, and began counting out loud under his breath.

Akiko came over to *Mary and gripped her frail right arm. "Oh, Grandma—" she said, "I had no idea he would be like this."

And *Mary said to her loudly, "He's no worse than he ever was."

The *Captain went on counting.

From the neighborhood of the spring, half a kilometer distant, came a male cry of triumph and peals of female laughter. The male cry was a familiar one on the island. It was Kamikaze's customary announcement to one and all that he had caught a female of some sort, and that they were about to copulate. He was nineteen then, barely past his sexual prime, and, as the only virile male then on the island, was likely to copulate with anybody or anything at any time. This was another sorrow Akiko had to bear—the blatant infidelities of her mate. This was a truly saintly woman.

The female Kamikaze had caught by the spring was his own aunt Dirno, who was then beyond childbearing age. He didn't care. They were going to copulate anyway. He had even copulated with sea lions and fur seals when he was younger, until Akiko had persuaded him that, for her sake, if not his own, he could at least stop doing that.

No sea lion or fur seal got pregnant by Kamikaze, which in a way is a pity. If he had succeeded in impregnating one, the evolution of modern humankind might have taken a good deal less than a million years.

Then again: What was the hurry, after all?

•   •   •

The *Captain opened his eyes, and he said to *Mary, "Why aren't you gone?"

She said, "Oh, don't mind me. I'm just a woman you lived with for ten years."

At that moment, Lira, another of the Kanka-bono women, called to Akiko in Kanka-bono that Orlon, Akiko's four-year-old son, had broken his arm, and that Akiko was needed at home immediately. Lira wouldn't come any closer than that to the *Captain's home, which she believed to be infected with very bad magic.

So Akiko asked *Mary to keep watch over the *Captain while she went home. She promised to come back as soon as possible. "You be a good boy now," she said to the *Captain. "You promise?"

He promised, grumpily.

• • •

*Mary had brought along *Mandarax at the request of Akiko, in the hopes of using it to diagnose what had caused the *Captain to lapse into several deathlike comas during the past day and night.

But when she showed him the instrument, and before she could ask him the first question, he did a perfectly astonishing thing: He snatched it away from her, and he stood up as though there were nothing wrong with him. "I hate this little son of a bitch more than anything in the whole world," he said, and then he went tottering down to the shore and lurching out onto the shoal, up to his knees in water.

Poor *Mary pursued him, but she was certainly in no condition to restrain a man that big. She watched helplessly as he threw *Mandarax into what turned out to be about three meters of water on the slope of the shoal. The shoal sloped steeply, like the back of a marine iguana.

She could see where it was. There it was—the priceless heirloom she had promised to leave to Akiko when she died. So that game old lady went right in after it. She got one hand on it, too, but then a great white shark ate both her and Mandarax.

• • •

The *Captain had a lapse of memory, and so did not know what to make of the bloody water. He didn't even know what part of the world he was in. The most alarming thing to him was that he was being attacked by birds. These were harmless vampire finches going after his bedsores, some of the commonest birds on the island. But to him they were new and terrifying.

He slapped at them, and cried out for help. More and more finches kept coming, and he was so convinced that they meant to kill him that he jumped into the water, where he was eaten by a hammerhead shark. This animal had its eyes on the ends of stalks, a design perfected by the Law of Natural Selection many, many millions of years ago. It was a flawless part in the clockwork of the universe. There was no defect in it which might yet be modified. One thing it surely did not need was a bigger brain.

What was it going to do with a bigger brain? Compose Beethoven's Ninth Symphony?

Or perhaps write these lines:

> *All the world's a stage,*
> *And all the men and women merely players.*
> *They have their exits and their entrances;*
> *And one man in his time plays many parts . . . ?*
> William Shakespeare (1564–1616)

# 14

I HAVE WRITTEN these words in air—with the tip of the index finger of my left hand, which is also air. My mother was left-handed, and so am I. There are no left-handed human beings anymore. People exercise their flippers with perfect symmetry. Mother was a redhead, and so was Andrew MacIntosh, although their respective children, I and Selena, did not inherit their rusty tresses—nor has humankind, nor could humankind. There aren't any redheads anymore. I never knew an albino personally, but there aren't albinos anymore, either. Among the fur seals, albinos do still turn up from time to time. Their pelts would have been much prized for ladies' fur coats a million years ago, to be worn to the opera and charity balls.

Would the pelts of modern people have made nice fur coats for their ancestors in olden times? I don't see why not.

• • •

Does it trouble me to write so insubstantially, with air on air? Well—my words will be as enduring as anything my father wrote, or Shakespeare wrote, or Beethoven wrote, or Darwin wrote. It turns out that they all wrote with air on air, and I now pluck this thought of Darwin's from the balmy atmosphere:

*Progress has been much more general than retrogression.*

'Tis true, 'tis true.

• • •

When my tale began, it appeared that the earthling part of the clockwork of the universe was in terrible danger, since many of its parts, which is to say people, no longer fit in anywhere, and were damaging all the parts around them as well as themselves. I would have said back then that the damage was beyond repair.

Not so!

Thanks to certain modifications in the design of human beings, I see no reason why the earthling part of the clockwork can't go on ticking forever the way it is ticking now.

• • •

If some sort of supernatural beings, or flying-saucer people, those darlings of my father, brought humanity into harmony with itself and the rest of Nature, I did not catch them doing it. I am prepared to swear under oath that the Law of Natural Selection did the repair job without outside assistance of any kind.

It was the best fisherfolk who survived in the greatest numbers in the watery environment of the Galápagos Archipelago. Those with hands and feet most like flippers were the best swimmers. Prognathous jaws were better at catching and holding fish than hands could ever be. And any fisherperson, spending more and more time underwater, could surely catch more fish if he or she were more streamlined, more bulletlike—had a smaller skull.

• • •

So my story is told, except for the tacking on of a few not very important details I failed to cover elsewhere. I tack them on in no particular order, since I now must write in haste. Father and the blue tunnel will be coming for me at any time.

• • •

Do people still know that they are going to die sooner or later? No. Fortunately, in my humble opinion, they have forgotten that.

• • •

Did I myself reproduce when I was still alive? I got a high school girl pregnant by accident in Santa Fe shortly before I joined the United States Marines. Her father was the principal of her high school, and she and I didn't even like each other very much. We were just fooling around, as young people were bound to do. She had an abortion, for which her father paid. We never even found out if it would have been a daughter or a son.

That certainly taught me a lesson. After that, I always made sure that I or my partner was employing a birth-control device. I never married.

And I have to laugh now, thinking of what a loss of dignity and beauty it would be if a modern person were, before making love, to equip himself or herself with a typical birth-control device of a million years ago. Imagine, moreover, their having to do that with flippers instead of hands!

. . .

Have natural rafts of vegetable matter from anywhere arrived here in my time, with or without passengers? No. Have mainland species of any sort reached these islands since the *Bahía de Darwin* was run aground? No.

Then again, I've only been here for a million years—no time at all, really.

. . .

How did I get from Vietnam to Sweden?

After I shot the old woman who had killed my best friend and worst enemy with a hand grenade, and what was left of our platoon burned her village to the ground, I was hospitalized for what was called "nervous exhaustion." I was given tender, loving care. I was also visited by officers who impressed on me how important it was that I not tell anyone what had happened in the village. Only then did I learn that our platoon had killed fifty-nine villagers of all ages. Somebody had counted them afterwards.

While on a pass from the hospital, I contracted syphilis from a Saigon prostitute while drunk and also high on marijuana. But the first lesion of that disease, another one unknown in the present day, did not appear until I reached Bangkok, Thailand, where I was sent with many others for so-called "Rest and Recreation." This was a euphemism understood by one and all to mean more whores and drugs and alcohol. Prostitution was then a major earner of foreign currency in Thailand, second only to rice.

After that came rubber.

After that came teak.

After that came tin.

. . .

I did not want the Marine Corps to know that I had syphilis. If they found out about it, they would dock my pay during the time I was under treatment. The treatment period, moreover, would be tacked on to the year I was supposed to serve in Vietnam.

So I sought the services of a private physician in Bangkok. A fellow Marine there recommended a young Swedish doctor who treated cases like mine, who was doing research at the University of Medical Sciences there.

During my first visit, he questioned me about the war. I found myself telling him about what our platoon had done to the village and villagers. He wanted to know what I had felt, and I replied that the most terrible part of the experience to me was that I hadn't felt much of anything.

•   •   •

"Did you cry afterwards, or have trouble sleeping?" he said.

"No, sir," I said. "In fact, I was hospitalized because all I wanted to do was sleep."

I hadn't come close to crying. Whatever else I was, I wasn't a weeping Willy, a bleeding heart. And I wasn't much for crying even before the Marine Corps made a man out of me. I hadn't even cried when my redheaded, left-handed mother had walked out on Father and me.

But then that Swede found something to say which made me cry like a baby—at last, at last. He was as surprised as I was when I cried and cried.

Here is what he said: "I notice your name is Trout. Is there any chance that you are related to the wonderful science-fiction writer Kilgore Trout?"

This doctor was the only person I ever met outside of Cohoes, New York, who had heard of my father.

I had to come all the way to Bangkok, Thailand, to learn that in the eyes of one person, anyway, my desperately scribbling father had not lived in vain.

•   •   •

The doctor made me cry so much that I had to be sedated. When I woke up on a cot in his office an hour later, he was watching me. We were all alone.

"Feel better now?" he said.

"No," I said. "Or maybe. It's hard to tell."

"I've been thinking about your case while you slept," he said. "There is one very strong medicine I could prescribe, but I leave it up to you whether or not you want to try it. You should be fully aware of its side effects."

I thought he was talking about how resistant syphilis organisms had become to antibiotics, thanks to the Law of Natural Selection. My big brain was wrong again.

He said he had friends who could arrange to get me from Bangkok to Sweden, if I wanted to seek political asylum there.

"But I can't speak Swedish," I said.

"You'll learn," he said. "You'll learn, you'll learn."

# APPENDIX

## A "Special Message"
## to readers of the Franklin Library's
## signed first edition of "Slapstick"

WITH THIS BOOK, written by me at the age of fifty-three, I cease to be Kurt Vonnegut, Jr., and become what my father was—simply Kurt Vonnegut. Father died seventeen years ago, and conventional American practice suggests that I should have dropped the "Jr." then. There is something comical about being a "Junior." My children, I know, often refer to me as "Junior" when I'm not around.

For example: "Did you hear what Junior did last week?" Or, "What will Junior do next?" And so on.

Hi ho.

So I will now become more of a grown-up, more dignified. Let there be fewer stupid jokes at my expense.

• • •

My favorite song, "Ah! Sweet Mystery of Life," argues that it is love and love alone the world is seeking. The truth is, though, that, as a person grows old, he or she probably hankers more for dignity than for love.

My declining to be "Junior" anymore is surely an expression of that hankering.

And I submit that the human pursuit of dignity is far more comical than the pursuit of love. We are, after all, collateral relatives of the least poised and imposing of all mammals, the great apes. Hippopotami have an easier time seeming dignified than we do. And, giving our closest relatives their due—even the great apes have more seeming dignity than we do.

Giving my best friend his due—even my dog has more seeming dignity than I do.

This is because animals do not speak.

They do not reveal through language all the homely, mismatched embarrassing junk in their heads. Human beings, save for a few mutes and hermits, wreck their dignity every day with language, with putting their head junk on display.

Some of us even make permanent museums of our head junk, which we call "books." I, in fact, earn my living by creating such museums. Even if I were to shut up now, those museums would continue to mock my quest for dignity.

Being "Junior" has been the very least of my problems.

Hi ho.

•   •   •

"The Sermon on the Mount" increased the seeming dignity of its Author and of all mankind. So did *The Iliad* and *Hamlet* and *The Inferno*. Such examples are rare. It was for them that fancy bindings like this one were first designed.

So I am bemused by having my mind junk packaged this way. It belongs in cardboard bindings, mixed in higgledy-piggledy with sex books and science fiction and nurse stories and gothic novels—on racks in bus stations and PX's.

But here we are.

"If they could only see me now," as the saying goes.

And I laugh.

All I can say is that I worked very hard on this book. Word of honor: It was the best I could do.

Cheers—

K.V.
*1976*

## Address to
## the American Psychiatric Association,
## Philadelphia, October 5, 1988

A T THE TIME of the disgraceful Bush vs. Dukakis campaign for the Presidency of the United States of America (at which time the eventual winner was promising to protect rich light people everywhere from poor dark people everywhere), I was an invited speaker at a meeting of the American Psychiatric Association in Philadelphia. My inherited brain and voicebox said this to those assembled:

"I greet you with all possible respect. It is tough to make unhappy people happier unless they need something easily prescribed, such as food or shelter or sympathetic companionship — or liberty.

"You have honored my own trade, which is the telling of stories for money, some true, some false, by inviting my friend and colleague Elie Wiesel and then me to speak to you. You may be aware of the work of Dr. Nancy Andreasen at the University of Iowa Medical Center, who interviewed professional writers on the faculty of her university's famous Writers' Workshop in order to discover whether or not our neuroses were indistinguishable from those of the general population. Most of us, myself included, proved to be depressives from families of depressives.

"From that study I extrapolate this rough rule, a very approximate rule, to be sure: You cannot be a good writer of serious fiction if you are not depressed.

"A rule we used to be able to extrapolate from cultural history, one which doesn't seem to work anymore, is that an American writer had to be an alcoholic in order to win a Nobel Prize — Sinclair Lewis, Eugene O'Neill, John Steinbeck, the suicide Ernest Hemingway. That rule no longer works, in my opinion, because artistic sensibilities are no longer regarded in this country as being characteristic of females. I no longer have to arrive at this lectern drunk, having slugged somebody in a bar last night, in order to prove that I am not what was a loathsome creature not long ago, which is to say a homosexual.

"Elie Wiesel made his reputation with a book called *Night*, which is about the horrors of the Holocaust as witnessed by the boy he used to be. I made my reputation with a book called *Slaughterhouse-Five*, which is about a British and American response to that Holocaust, which was the firebombing of Dresden—as witnessed by the young American Infantry Private First Class I used to be. We both have German last names. So does the man who invited me here, Dr. Dichter. So do most of the famous pioneers in your profession. It would not surprise me if a plurality of us here, Jews and Gentiles alike, did not have ancestors who were citizens of the German or Austro-Hungarian Empire, which gave us so much great music and science and painting and theater, and whose remnants gave us a nightmare from which, in my opinion, there can never be an awakening.

"The Holocaust explains almost everything about why Elie Wiesel writes what he writes and is what he is. The firebombing of Dresden explains absolutely nothing about why I write what I write and am what I am. I am sure you are miles ahead of me in thinking of a thousand clinical reasons for this being true. I didn't give a damn about Dresden. I didn't know anybody there. I certainly hadn't had any good times there before they burned it down. I had seen some Dresden china back home in Indianapolis, but I thought then and still think now that it's mostly kitsch. There is another wonderful gift from German-speaking people, along with psychoanalysis and *The Magic Flute*: that priceless word *kitsch*.

"And Dresden china isn't made in Dresden anyway. It's made in Meissen. That's the town they should have burned down.

"I am only joking, of course. I will say anything to be funny, often in the most horrible situations, which is one reason two good women so far have been very sorry on occasion to have married me. Every great city is a world treasure, not a national treasure. So the destruction of any one of them is a planetary catastrophe.

"Before I was a soldier I was a journalist, and that's what I was in Dresden—a voyeur of strangers' miseries. I was outside the event. Elie Wiesel, seeing what he saw—and he was just a boy, and I was a young man—was the event itself. The firebombing of Dresden was quick, was surgical, as the military scientists like to say, fitting the Aristotelian ideal for a tragedy, taking place in less than twenty-four hours. The Holocaust ground on and on and on and on. The Germans wanted to keep me alive, on the theory that they might be able to trade me and my captured comrades for some of their own someday. The Germans, aided and abetted, of course, by like-minded Austrians and Hungarians and Slovaks and French and Ukrainians and Romanians and Bulgarians and so on, wanted Elie Wiesel and everyone he had ever known, and everyone remotely like him, to die, as his father would die, of malnutrition, overwork, despair, or cyanide.

"Elie Wiesel tried to keep his father alive. And failed. My own father, and most of the rest of my friends and loved ones, were safe and sound in Indianapolis. The proper prescription for the fatal depression which killed Elie Wiesel's father would have been food and rest and tender loving care rather than lithium, Thorazine, Prozac, or Tofranil.

"I hold a master's degree in anthropology from the University of Chicago. Students of that branch of poetry are taught to seek explanations for human comfort or discomfort—wars, wounds, spectacular diseases, and natural disasters aside—in culture, society, and history. And I have just named the villains in my books, which are never individuals. The villains again: culture, society, and history—none of them strikingly housebroken by lithium, Thorazine, Prozac, or Tofranil.

"Like most writers, I have at home the beginnings of many books which would not allow themselves to be written. About twenty years ago, a doctor prescribed Ritalin for me, to see if that wouldn't help me get over such humps. I realized right away that Ritalin was dehydrated concentrate of pure paranoia, and threw it away. But the book I was trying to make work was to be called *SS Psychiatrist*. This was about an MD who had been psychoanalyzed, and he was stationed at Auschwitz. His job was to treat the depression of those members of the staff who did not like what they were doing there. Talk therapy was all he or anybody had to offer back then. This was before the days of— Never mind.

"My point was, and maybe I can make it today without having to finish that book, that workers in the field of mental health at various times in different parts of the world must find themselves asked to make healthy people happier in cultures and societies which have gone insane.

"Let me hasten to say that the situation in our own country is nowhere near that dire. The goal here right now, it seems to me, is to train intelligent, well-educated people to speak stupidly so that they can be more popular. Look at Michael Dukakis. Look at George Bush.

"I think I was invited here mostly because of what happened to my dear son Mark Vonnegut, now Dr. Vonnegut. He had a very fancy crack-up, padded-cell stuff, straitjacket stuff, hallucinations, wrestling matches with nurses, and all that. He recovered and wrote a book about it called *The Eden Express*, which is about to be reissued in paperback by Dell, with a new Afterword by him. You should have hired him instead of me. He would have been a heck of a lot cheaper, and he knows what he is talking about.

"He speaks well. When he lectures to mental health specialists, he always asks a question at one point, calling for a show of hands. I might as well be his surrogate and ask the same question of you. A show of hands, please: How many of you have taken Thorazine? Thank you. Then he says, 'Those who haven't tried it really should. It won't hurt you, you know.'

"He was diagnosed, when I took him to a private laughing academy in British Columbia, where he had founded a commune, as schizophrenic. He sure looked schizophrenic to me, too. I never saw depressed people act anything like that. We mope. We sleep. I have to say that anybody who did what Mark did shortly after he was admitted, which was to jump up and get the light bulb in the ceiling of his padded cell, was anything but depressed.

"Anyway—Mark recovered sufficiently to write his book and graduate from Harvard Medical School. He is now a pediatrician in Boston, with a wife and two fine sons, and two fine automobiles. And then, not very long ago, most members of your profession decided that he and some others who had written books about recovering from schizophrenia had been misdiagnosed. No matter how jazzed up they appeared to be when sick, they were in fact depressives. Maybe so.

"Mark's first response to news of this rediagnosis was to say, 'What a wonderful diagnostic tool. We now know if a patient gets well, he or she definitely did not have schizophrenia.'

"But he, too, unfortunately, will say anything to be funny. A more sedate and responsible discussion by him of what was wrong with him can be found in the Afterword to the new edition of his book. I have a few copies of it, which I hope somebody here will have xeroxed, so that everyone who wants one can have one.

"He isn't as enthusiastic about megavitamins as he used to be, before he himself became a doctor. He still sees a whole lot more hope in biochemistry than in talk.

"Long before Mark went crazy, I thought mental illness was caused by chemicals, and said so in my stories. I've never in a story had an event or another person drive a character crazy. I thought madness had a chemical basis even when I was a boy, because a close friend of our family, a wise and kind and wryly sad man named Dr. Walter Bruetsch, who was head of the State's huge and scary hospital for the insane, used to say that his patients' problems were chemical, that little could be done for them until that chemistry was better understood.

"I believed him.

"So when my mother went crazy, long before my son went crazy, long before I had a son, and finally killed herself, I blamed chemicals, and I still do, although she had a terrible childhood. I can even name two of the chemicals: phenobarbital and booze. Those came from the outside, of course, the phenobarbs from our family doctor, who was trying to do something about her sleeplessness. When she died, I was a soldier, and my division was about to go overseas.

"We were able to keep her insanity a secret, since it became really elaborate only at home and between midnight and dawn. We were able to keep her suicide a secret thanks to a compassionate and possibly politically ambitious coroner.

"Why do people try so hard to keep such things a secret? Because news of them would make their children seem less attractive as marriage prospects. You now know a lot about my family. On the basis of that information, those of you with children contemplating marriage might be smart to tell them: Whatever you do, don't marry anybody named Vonnegut.

"Dr. Bruetsch couldn't have helped my mother, and he was the greatest expert on insanity in the whole State of Indiana.

Maybe he knew she was crazy. Maybe he didn't. If he did know
she was crazy after midnight, and he was very fond of her, he
must have felt as helpless as my father. There was not then an
Indianapolis chapter of Alcoholics Anonymous, which might
have helped. One would be founded by my father's only brother,
Alex, who was an alcoholic, in 1955 or so.

"There—I've told you another family secret, haven't I? About
Uncle Alex?

"Am I an alcoholic? I don't think so. My father wasn't one.
My only living sibling, my brother, isn't one.

"But I am surely a great admirer of Alcoholics Anonymous,
and Gamblers Anonymous, and Cocaine Freaks Anonymous,
and Shoppers Anonymous, and Gluttons Anonymous, and on
and on. And such groups gratify me as a person who studied
anthropology, since they give to Americans something as essential to health as vitamin C, something so many of us do not
have in this particular civilization: an extended family. Human
beings have almost always been supported and comforted and
disciplined and amused by stable lattices of many relatives and
friends until the Great American Experiment, which is an
experiment not only with liberty but with rootlessness, mobil-
ity, and impossibly tough-minded loneliness.

"I am a vain person, or I would not be up here, going 'Blah,
blah, blah.' I am not so vain, however, as to imagine that I have
told you anything you didn't already know—except for the
trivia about my mother, my Uncle Alex, and my son. You deal
with unhappy people hour after hour, day after day. I keep out
of their way as much as possible. I am able to follow the three
rules for a good life set down by the late writer Nelson Algren,
a fellow depressive, and another subject of the study of writers
made at the University of Iowa. The three rules are, of course:
Never eat at a place called Mom's, never play cards with a man
named Doc, and most important, never go to bed with anybody
who has more troubles than you do.

"All of you, I am sure, when writing a prescription for mildly
depressed patients, people nowhere as sick as my mother or my
son were, have had a thought on this order: 'I am so sorry to
have to put you on the outside of a pill. I would give anything
if I could put you inside the big, warm life-support system of an
extended family instead.'"

## A "Special Message" to readers of the Franklin Library's signed first edition of "Jailbird"

Two events in my life have impressed me so much that I have felt duty-bound to write something about them. One was the firebombing of Dresden. The other was a lunch in downtown Indianapolis some six months later with Powers Hapgood, the only aggressively altruistic Hoosier I ever met. I have now discharged both obligations.

I discharge the second at a time when we have a President, Jimmy Carter, who was elected because he claimed to be aggressively altruistic, to be unusually responsive to the teachings of Jesus Christ. Three years into his first term now, Mr. Carter has clearly determined that the beatitudes, except for the smile they imply, are too cumbersome to implement in the United States of America. The fault lies mainly with life itself, which is treacherous at best, but also with the economic system, an unnecessarily heartless and stupid engine that could be much improved.

Powers Hapgood, a labor organizer, believed that the American economic system was responsive to extortion schemes, to monopolies and the intimidation of legislators and law-enforcers and so on, and that the common people might make it their servant by themselves becoming more awesome—by forming themselves into great unions. If they were abused or cheated, they would strike. They would *en masse* punish or reward public servants at the polls.

This seems like such a childlike dream of glory now, since so many workers have been demoted or replaced by machines. The number of persons capable of wobbling the economy by withholding their skills grows smaller each year. And their unions become increasingly interesting to enthusiasts for extortion as a purely criminal enterprise. So the Powers Hapgoods of today must invent new schemes for helping ordinary citizens to survive. That much hasn't changed, anyway: Survival is still the issue. What is new is that an ordinary citizen is not much of a commodity anymore as a worker.

The economic system, which does nothing but dream in its own self-interest, may, in fact, be wondering how to turn most human beings into catfood or soldiers, since so few of them have any higher usefulness. It is time now for somebody somewhere, as I say, to come up with a better dream.

K.V.
*1979*

*Four excerpts from*
*"Fates Worse Than Death:*
*An Autobiographical Collage of the 1980s"*

THE FREE-SPEECH PROVISIONS of the First Amendment guarantee all of us not only benefits but pain. (As the physical fitness experts tell us, "No pain, no gain.") Much of what other Americans say or publish hurts me a lot, makes me want to throw up. Tough luck for me.

When Charlton Heston (a movie actor who once played Jesus with shaved armpits) tells me in TV commercials (public-service announcements?) about all the good work the National Rifle Association (to which Father and I both belonged when I was a kid) is doing, and how glad I should be that civilians can and do keep military weapons in their homes or vehicles or places of work, I feel exactly as though he were praising the germs of some loathsome disease, since guns in civilian hands, whether accidentally or on purpose, kill so many of us day after day.

(When I graduated from School Number Forty-three in Indianapolis, each member of our class had to make a public promise as to what he or she would try to do when an adult to make the world a better place. I was going to find a cure for some disease. Well—I sure don't need an electron microscope to identify an AK-47 or an Uzi.)

"A well-regulated Militia, being necessary to the security of a free State," sayeth Article II of the Bill of Rights, "the right of the people to keep and bear arms, shall not be infringed." Perfect! I wouldn't change a word of it. I only wish the NRA and its jellyfishy, well-paid supporters in legislatures both State and Federal would be careful to recite the whole of it, and then tell us how a heavily armed man, woman, or child, recruited by no official, led by no official, given no goals by any official, motivated or restrained only by his or her personality and perceptions of what is going on, can be considered a member of a well-regulated militia.

(To cut a Gordian knot here: I think a sick fantasy is at work, of a sort of Armageddon in which the bad people, poor, dark-skinned, illiterate, lazy, and drug-crazed, will one night attack the neat homes of the good white people who have worked hard for all they have, and have in addition given money and time to charity.)

I used to be very good with guns, was maybe the best shot in my company when I was a PFC. But I wouldn't have one of the motherfuckers in my house for anything.

I consider the discharge of firearms a low form of sport. Modern weapons are as easy to operate as cigarette lighters. Ask any woman who never worked one before, who went to the local gun shop and joined the NRA's idea of a well-regulated militia and then made Swiss cheese out of a faithless lover or mate. Whenever I hear of somebody that he is a good shot, I think to myself, "That is like saying he is a good man with a Zippo or Bic. Some athlete!"

George Bush, like Charlton Heston, is a lifetime member of the NRA. I am even more offended, though, by his failure to take notice of the most beautiful and noble and brilliant and poetical and sacred accomplishment by Americans to date. I am speaking about the exploration of the Solar System by the camera-bearing space probe *Voyager 2*. This gallant bird (so like Noah's dove) showed us all the outer planets and their moons! We no longer had to guess whether there was life on them or not, or whether our descendants might survive on them! (Forget it.) As *Voyager 2* departed the Solar System forever ("My work is done"), sending us dimmer and dimmer pictures of what we were and where we were, did our President invite us to love it and thank it and wish it well? No. He spoke passionately instead of the necessity of an Amendment to the Constitution (Article XXVII?) outlawing irreverent treatment of a piece of cloth, the American flag. Such an Amendment would be on a nutty par with the Roman Emperor Caligula's having his horse declared a Consul.

· · ·

When the American ad agency for Volkswagen asked me (along with several other fogbound futurologists) to compose a letter to Earthlings a century from now which would be used in a series of institutional ads in *Time* (no friends of mine), I wrote as follows:

"Ladies & Gentlemen of A.D. 2088:

"It has been suggested that you might welcome words of wisdom from the past, and that several of us in the twentieth century should send you some. Do you know this advice from Polonius in Shakespeare's *Hamlet*: 'This above all: to thine own self be true'? Or what about these instructions from St. John the Divine: 'Fear God, and give glory to Him; for the hour of His judgment has come'? The best advice from my own era for you or for just about anybody anytime, I guess, is a prayer first used by alcoholics who hoped to never take a drink again: 'God grant me the serenity to accept the things I cannot change, courage to change the things I can, and wisdom to know the difference.'

"Our century hasn't been as free with words of wisdom as some others, I think, because we were the first to get reliable information about the human situation: how many of us there were, how much food we could raise or gather, how fast we were reproducing, what made us sick, what made us die, how much damage we were doing to the air and water and topsoil on which most life forms depended, how violent and heartless nature can be, and on and on. Who could wax wise with so much bad news pouring in?

"For me, the most paralyzing news was that Nature was no conservationist. It needed no help from us in taking the planet apart and putting it back together some different way, not necessarily improving it from the viewpoint of living things. It set fire to forests with lightning bolts. It paved vast tracts of arable land with lava, which could no more support life than big-city parking lots. It had in the past sent glaciers down from the North Pole to grind up major portions of Asia, Europe, and North America. Nor was there any reason to think that it wouldn't do that again someday. At this very moment it is turning African farms to deserts, and can be expected to heave up tidal waves or shower down white-hot boulders from outer space at any time. It has not only exterminated exquisitely evolved species in a twinkling, but drained oceans and drowned continents as well. If people think Nature is their friend, then they sure don't need an enemy.

"Yes, and as you people a hundred years from now must know full well, and as your grandchildren will know even better: Nature is ruthless when it comes to matching the quantity of life in any given place at any given time to the quantity of nourishment available. So what have you and Nature done about overpopulation? Back here in 1988, we were seeing ourselves as a new sort of glacier, warm-blooded and clever, unstoppable, about to gobble up everything and then make love—and then double in size again.

"On second thought, I am not sure I could bear to hear what you and Nature may have done about too many people for too small a food supply.

"And here is a crazy idea I would like to try on you: Is it possible that we aimed rockets with hydrogen bomb warheads at each other, all set to go, in order to take our minds off the deeper problem—how cruelly Nature can be expected to treat us, Nature being Nature, in the by-and-by?

"Now that we can discuss the mess we are in with some precision, I hope you have stopped choosing abysmally ignorant optimists for positions of leadership. They were useful only so long as nobody had a clue as to what was really going on— during the past seven million years or so. In my time, they have been catastrophic as heads of sophisticated institutions with real work to do.

"The sort of leaders we need now are not those who promise ultimate victory over Nature through perseverance in living as we do right now, but those with the courage and intelligence to present to the world what appear to be Nature's stern but reasonable surrender terms:

1. Reduce and stabilize your population.
2. Stop poisoning the air, the water, and the topsoil.
3. Stop preparing for war and start dealing with your real problems.
4. Teach your kids, and yourselves, too, while you're at it, how to inhabit a small planet without helping to kill it.
5. Stop thinking science can fix anything if you give it a trillion dollars.
6. Stop thinking your grandchildren will be OK no matter how wasteful or destructive you may be, since they can go to a nice new planet on a spaceship. That is *really* mean and stupid.
7. And so on. Or else.

"Am I too pessimistic about life a hundred years from now? Maybe I have spent too much time with scientists and not enough time with speechwriters for politicians. For all I know, even bag ladies and bag gentlemen will have their own personal helicopters or rocket belts in A.D. 2088. Nobody will have to leave home to go to work or school, or even stop watching television. Everybody will sit around all day punching the keys of computer terminals connected to everything there is, and sip orange drink through straws like the astronauts."

•   •   •

As though I hadn't already given the world more than enough reasons to feel miserable, I sold this bouquet of sunbeams and bubbling laughter to *Lear's* magazine:

"In the children's fable *The White Deer*, by the late American humorist James Thurber, the Royal Astronomer in a medieval court reports that all the stars are going out. What has really happened is that the astronomer has grown old and is going blind. That was Thurber's condition, too, when he wrote his tale. He was making fun of a sort of old poop who imagined that life was ending not merely for himself but for the whole universe. Inspired by Thurber, then, I choose to call any old poop who writes a popular book saying that the world, or at least his own country, is done for, a 'Royal Astronomer' and his subject matter 'Royal Astronomy.'

"Since I myself have become an old poop at last, perhaps I, too, should write such a book. But it is hard for me to follow the standard formula for successful Royal Astronomy, a formula going back who knows how far, maybe to the invention of printing by the Chinese a couple of thousand years ago. The formula is, of course: 'Things aren't as good as they used to be. The young people don't know anything and don't want to know anything. We have entered a steep decline!'

"But have we? Back when I was a kid, lynchings of black people were reported almost every week, and always went unpunished. Apartheid was as sternly enforced in my hometown, which was Indianapolis, as it is in South Africa nowadays. Many great universities, including those in the Ivy League, rejected most of the Jews who applied for admission solely because of their

Jewishness, and had virtually no Jews and absolutely no blacks, God knows, on their faculties.

"I am going to ask a question—and President Reagan, please don't answer: Those were the *good old days*?

"When I was a kid during the Great Depression, when it was being demonstrated most painfully that prosperity was not a natural by-product of liberty, books by Royal Astronomers were as popular as they are today. They said, as most of them do today, that the country was falling apart because the young people were no longer required to read Plato and Aristotle and Marcus Aurelius and St. Augustine and Montaigne and the like, whose collective wisdom was the foundation of any decent and just and productive society.

"Back in the Great Depression, the Royal Astronomers used to say that a United States deprived of that wisdom was nothing but a United States of radio quiz shows and music straight out of the jungles of Darkest Africa. They say now that the same subtraction leaves us a United States of nothing but television quiz shows and rock and roll, which leads, they say, inexorably to dementia. But I find uncritical respect for most works by great thinkers of long ago unpleasant, because they almost all accepted as natural and ordinary the belief that females and minority races and the poor were on earth to be uncomplaining, hardworking, respectful, and loyal servants of white males, who did the important thinking and exercised leadership.

"Such wisdom is a foundation on which only white males can build. And there is a lot of it in the Holy Bible, I'm sorry to say.

"I went to a big luncheon last week for a vice-president of the filmmakers' union of the USSR, a kind and hopeful man as nearly as I could tell. Everybody was asking him about *glasnost* and all that. Would there really be more freedom in his country? And what about all the political prisoners still in the gulag and the mental hospitals? And what about the Jews who weren't allowed to emigrate? And so on.

"The experiment with more freedom and justice was just beginning, he said, but there were encouraging signs in the arts. All sorts of suppressed books and movies were being released. The demand was so great for writings previously taboo, he said, that there was a terrific paper shortage. Artists and intellectuals were elated. But most ordinary workers, to whom freedom of expression wasn't so important, were waiting to see if *glasnost* was somehow going to get them better food and shelter and clothing, and cars and appliances and other things of that sort, which, unfortunately, were not among the inevitable results of increased freedom.

"Alcoholism continues to make a lot of trouble over there, just as alcoholism and cocaine addiction are making a lot of trouble over here. Both are severe public-health problems not notably responsive to whether the sufferer is politically free or not.

"So what is going on over there is really a touching thing for us to watch and hear about, an honest effort to give the common people of a powerful nation more liberty than they or their ancestors have ever known. If the experiment goes on for any length of time—and just a few people could shut it down instantly—we can expect to see it dawn on the citizens of the Soviets that liberty, like virtue, is its own reward, which can be a disappointment. There as here and, in fact, almost everywhere on the planet, the great mass of human beings yearns for rewards that are more substantial.

"After that lunch I pondered my own country's continuing experiments with liberty, which have been going on for more than two centuries. The Soviet Union has been a Workers' Paradise only since 1922, coincidentally the same year I was born into this so-called Beacon of Liberty to the Rest of the World.

"And I said to the guest of honor, through an interpreter, that maybe the Soviet Union wasn't doing half badly, since in my own country slavery was perfectly legal for almost a hundred years after the signing of the Declaration of Independence. I said that even the saintly Thomas Jefferson owned slaves.

"I did not mention our genocide of Indians back in my great-grandfather's time. That would have been too much. I talk about that and think about that as little as possible. Thank God it isn't taught in school much.

"Our own country has a *glasnost* experiment going on, too, of course. It consists of making women and racial minorities the equals of white males, in terms of both the civility and respect to be accorded them and their rights under the law. This would seem an abomination to the ancient wise men whose works our young people are dangerously, supposedly, neglecting in favor of rock and roll.

"A proper reply by the American people to Royal Astronomers who denounce that neglect, it seems to me, would go something like this: 'Almost none of the ancient wise men believed in real equality, and neither do you—but we believe in it.'

"Is there nothing about the United States of my youth, aside from youth itself, that I miss sorely now? There is one thing I miss so much that I can hardly stand it, which is freedom from the certain knowledge that human beings will very soon have made this moist, blue-green planet uninhabitable by human beings. There is no stopping us. We will continue to breed like rabbits. We will continue to engage in technological nincompoopery with hideous side effects unforeseen. We will make only token repairs on our cities now collapsing. We will not clean up much of the poisonous mess that we ourselves have made.

"If flying-saucer creatures or angels or whatever were to come here in a hundred years, say, and find us gone like the dinosaurs, what might be a good message for humanity to leave for them, maybe carved in great big letters on a Grand Canyon wall?

"Here is this old poop's suggestion:

WE PROBABLY COULD HAVE SAVED OURSELVES,
BUT WERE TOO DAMNED LAZY TO TRY VERY HARD.

"We might well add this:

AND TOO DAMN CHEAP.

"So it's curtains not just for me as I grow old. It's curtains for everyone. How's that for full-strength Royal Astronomy?"

•  •  •

"MIT has played an important part in the history of my branch of the Vonnegut family. My father and grandfather took degrees in architecture here. My Uncle Pete flunked out of here. My only brother Bernard, nine years my senior, took a doctor's degree in chemistry here. Father and Grandfather became self-employed architects and partners. Uncle Pete became a building contractor, also self-employed. My brother knew early on that he would be a research scientist, and so could not be self-employed. If he was to have room enough and equipment enough to do what he did best, then he was going to have to work for somebody else. Who would that be?"

Such was what I considered a tantalizing beginning of a speech I gave at MIT back in 1985. (There have been times when I was nutty enough to believe that I might change the course of history a tiny bit, and this was one of them.) There in Kresge Auditorium I had a full house of young people who could do what the magician Merlin could only pretend to do in the Court of King Arthur, in Camelot. They could turn loose or rein in enormous forces (invisible as often as not) in the service or disservice of this or that enterprise (such as Star Wars).

"Most of you," I went on, "will soon face my brother's dilemma when he graduated from here. In order to survive and even prosper, most of you will have to make somebody else's technological dreams come true—along with your own, of course. You will have to form that mixture of dreams we call a partnership—or more romantically, a marriage.

"My brother got his doctorate in 1938, I think. If he had gone to work in Germany after that, he would have been helping to make Hitler's dreams come true. If he had gone to work in Italy, he would have been helping to make Mussolini's dreams come true. If he had gone to work in Japan, he would have been helping to make Tojo's dreams come true. If he had gone to work in the Soviet Union, he would have been helping to make Stalin's dreams come true. He went to work for a bottle manufacturer in Butler, Pennsylvania, instead. It can make quite a difference not just to you but to humanity: the sort of boss you choose, whose dreams you help come true.

"Hitler dreamed of killing Jews, Gypsies, Slavs, homosexuals, Communists, Jehovah's Witnesses, mental defectives, believers in democracy, and so on, in industrial quantities. It would have remained only a dream if it hadn't been for chemists as well educated as my brother, who supplied Hitler's executioners with the cyanide gas known as Cyklon-B. It would have remained only a dream if architects and engineers as capable as my father and grandfather hadn't designed extermination camps—the fences, the towers, the barracks, the railroad sidings, and the gas chambers and crematoria—for maximum ease of operation and efficiency. I recently visited two of those camps in Poland,

Auschwitz and Birkenau. They are technologically perfect. There is only one grade I could give their designers, and that grade is A-plus. They surely solved all the problems set for them.

"Yes, and that is the grade I would have to give to the technicians who have had a hand in the creation of the car bombs which are now exploding regularly in front of embassies and department stores and movie theaters and houses of worship of every kind. They surely solve the problems set for them. *Kablooey!* A-plus! A-plus!

"Which brings us to the differences between men and women. Feminists have won a few modest successes in the United States during the past two decades, so it has become almost obligatory to say that the differences between the two sexes have been exaggerated. But this much is clear to me: Generally speaking, women don't like immoral technology nearly as much as men do. This could be the result of some hormone deficiency. Whatever the reason, women, often taking their children with them, tend to outnumber men in demonstrations against schemes and devices which can kill people. In fact, the most effective doubter of the benefits of unbridled technological advancement so far was a woman, Mary Wollstonecraft Shelley, who died 134 years ago. She, of course, created the idea of the Monster of Frankenstein.

"And to show you how fruity, how feminine I have become in late middle age: If I were the President of MIT, I would hand pictures of Boris Karloff as the Monster of Frankenstein all over the institution. Why? To remind students and faculty that humanity now cowers in muted dread, expecting to be killed sooner or later by Monsters of Frankenstein. Such killing goes on right now, by the way, in many other parts of the world, often with our sponsorship—hour after hour, day after day.

"What should be done? You here at MIT should set an example for your colleagues everywhere by writing and then taking an oath based on the Hippocratic Oath, by which medical doctors have been bound for twenty-four centuries. Do I mean to say that no physician in all that time has violated that oath? Certainly not. But every doctor who has violated it has been correctly branded a scumbag. And why has the late Josef Mengele become the most monstrous of all the Nazis, in the opinion of most of us? He was a doctor, and he gleefully violated the Hippocratic Oath.

"If some of you elect to act on my suggestion, to write a new oath, you will of course have to examine the original, which is conventionally dated 460 years before the birth of Jesus Christ. So it is a musty old Greek document, much of it irrelevant to a physician's moral dilemmas in the present day. It is also a perfectly human document. No one has ever suggested that it came from a god in a vision or on clay tablets found on a mountaintop. A person or some people wrote it, inspired by nothing more than their own wishes to help rather than harm humankind. I assume that most of you, too, would rather help than harm humankind, and might welcome formal restraints on what a wicked boss might expect of you.

"The part of the Hippocratic Oath which needs the least editing, it seems to me, is this: 'The regimen I adopt shall be for the benefit of my patients, according to my ability and judgment, and not for their hurt or for any wrong. I will give no deadly drug to any, though it be asked of me, nor will I counsel such.' You could easily paraphrase this so as to include not just doctors but every sort of scientist, remembering that all sciences have their roots in the simple wish to make people safe and well.

"Your paraphrase might go like this: 'The regimen I adopt shall be for the benefit of all life on this planet, according to my own ability and judgment, and not for its hurt or for any wrong. I will create no deadly substance or device, though it be asked of me, nor will I counsel such.'

"That might make a good beginning for an oath everyone would gladly take upon graduation from MIT. And there is surely more than that you would gladly swear to. You could take it from there.

"I thank you for your attention."

What a flop! The applause was polite enough. (There were many Oriental faces out there. Who knows what *they* may have been thinking?) But nobody came up front afterward and said he or she was going to take a shot at writing an oath all technical people would be glad to take. There was nothing in the student paper the next week. It was all over. (If such a speech had been given at Cornell when I was a student there, I would have written an oath that very night whilst talking to myself. Then again, I had had lots of free time, since I was flunking practically everything.)

What makes the students of today so unresponsive? (Only this morning I, an old poop, got a letter asking me if I had any suggestions for a revision of the Pledge of Allegiance, and I answered by return mail: "I pledge allegiance to the Constitution of the United States of America, and the flag which is its symbol, with liberty and justice for all.") I'll tell you what makes the students so unresponsive. They know what I will never get through my head: that life is *unserious*. (Why not make Caligula's horse a Consul?)

Before my great speech to the MIT students I talked to some of them about Star Wars, Ronald Reagan's belief that laser beams and satellites and flypaper and who-knows-what could be linked together in such a way as to form an invisible dome no enemy missile could penetrate. They didn't think there was any way it could be made to operate, but they all wanted to work on it anyway. (Why *not* make Caligula's horse a Consul?)

*1991*

# Lecture at
## the Cathedral of St. John the Divine,
### New York, May 23, 1982

A ND GET A LOAD of this naive sermon I preached at the Cathedral of St. John the Divine in New York City:

"I will speak today about the worst imaginable consequences of doing without hydrogen bombs. This should be a relief. I am sure you are sick and tired of hearing how all living things sizzle and pop inside a radioactive fireball. We have known that for more than a third of this century—ever since we dropped an atom bomb on the yellow people of Hiroshima. *They* certainly sizzled and popped.

"After all is said and done, what was that sizzling and popping, despite the brilliant technology which caused it, but our old friend death? Let us not forget that St. Joan of Arc was made to sizzle and pop in old times with nothing more than firewood. She wound up dead. The people of Hiroshima wound up dead. Dead is dead.

"Scientists, for all their creativity, will never discover a method for making people deader than dead. So if some of you are worried about being hydrogen-bombed, you are merely fearing death. There is nothing new in that. If there weren't any hydrogen bombs, death would still be after you. And what is death but an absence of life? That is all it ever can be.

"Death is nothing. What is all this fuss about?

"Let us 'up the ante,' as gamblers say. Let us talk about fates *worse* than death. When the Reverend Jim Jones saw that his followers in Guyana were facing fates worse than death, he gave them Kool-Aid laced with cyanide. If our government sees that we are facing fates worse than death, it will shower our enemies with hydrogen bombs, and then we will be showered in turn. There will be plenty of Kool-Aid for everyone, in a manner of speaking, when the right time comes.

"What will the right time look like?

"I will not waste your time with trivial fates, which are only marginally worse than death. Suppose we were conquered by an enemy, for example, who didn't understand our wonderful economic system, and so Braniff airlines and International Harvester and so on all went bust, and millions of Americans who wanted to work couldn't find any jobs anywhere. Or suppose we were conquered by an enemy who was too cheap to take good care of children and old people. Or suppose we were conquered by an enemy who wouldn't spend money on anything but weapons for World War III. These are all tribulations we could live with, if we had to—although God forbid.

"But suppose we foolishly got rid of our nuclear weapons, our Kool-Aid, and an enemy came over here and crucified us. Crucifixion was the most painful thing the ancient Romans ever found to do to anyone. They knew as much about pain as we do about genocide. They sometimes crucified hundreds of people at one time. That is what they did to all the survivors of the army of Spartacus, which was composed mostly of escaped slaves. They crucified them all. There were several miles of crosses.

"If we were up on crosses, with nails through our feet and hands, wouldn't we wish that we still had hydrogen bombs, so that life could be ended everywhere? Absolutely.

"We know of one person who was crucified in olden times, who was supposedly as capable as we or the Russians are of ending life everywhere. But He chose to endure agony instead. All He said was, 'Forgive them, Father—they know not what they do.'

"He let life go on, as awful as it was for Him, because here we are, aren't we?

"But He was a special case. It is unfair to use Jesus Christ as an exemplar of how much pain and humiliation we ordinary human beings should put up with before calling for the end of everything.

"I don't believe that we *are* about to be crucified. No potential enemy we now face has anywhere near enough carpenters. Not even people at the Pentagon at budget time have mentioned crucifixion. I am sorry to have to put that idea into their heads. I will have only myself to blame if, a year from now, the Joint Chiefs of Staff testify under oath that we are on the brink of being crucified.

"But what if they said, instead, that we would be enslaved if we did not appropriate enough money for weaponry? That could be true. Despite our worldwide reputation for sloppy workmanship, wouldn't some enemy get a kick out of forcing us into involuntary servitude, buying and selling us like so many household appliances or farm machines or inflatable erotic toys?

"And slavery would surely be a fate worse than death. We can agree on that, I'm sure. We should send a message to the Pentagon: 'If Americans are about to become enslaved, it is Kool-Aid time.'

"They will know what we mean.

"Of course, at Kool-Aid time all higher forms of life on Earth, not just we and our enemies, will be killed. Even those beautiful and fearless and utterly stupid seabirds the defenseless blue-footed boobies of the Galápagos Islands will die, because we object to slavery.

"I have seen those birds, by the way—up close. I could have unscrewed their heads, if I had wanted to. I made a trip to the Galápagos Islands two months ago—in the company of, among other people, Paul Moore, Jr., the bishop of this very cathedral.

"That is the sort of company I keep these days—everything from bishops to blue-footed boobies. I have never seen a human slave, though. But my four great-grandfathers saw slaves. When they came to this country in search of justice and opportunity, there were millions of Americans who were slaves. The equation which links a strong defense posture to not being enslaved is laid down in that stirring fight song, much heard lately, 'Rule, Britannia.' I will sing the equation:

"'Rule, Britannia; Britannia, rule the waves—'

"That, of course, is a poetic demand for a Navy second to none. I now sing the next line, which explains why it is essential to have a Navy that good:

"'Britons never, never, never shall be slaves.'

"It may surprise some of you to learn what an old equation that is. The Scottish poet who wrote it, James Thomson, died in 1748—about a quarter of a century before there was such a country as the United States of America. Thomson promised Britons that they would never be slaves, at a time when the enslavement of persons with inferior weaponry was a respectable industry. Plenty of people were going to be slaves, and it would serve them right, too—but Britons would not be among them.

"So that isn't really a very nice song. It is about not being humiliated, which is all right. But it is also about humiliating others, which is not a moral thing to do. The humiliation of others should never be a national goal.

"There is one poet who should have been ashamed of himself.

"If the Soviet Union came over here and enslaved us, it wouldn't be the first time Americans were slaves. If we conquered the Russians and enslaved them, it wouldn't be the first time Russians were slaves.

"And the last time Americans were slaves, and the last time Russians were slaves, they displayed astonishing spiritual strengths and resourcefulness. They were good at loving one another. They trusted God. They discovered in the simplest, most natural satisfactions reasons to be glad to be alive. They were able to believe that better days were coming in the sweet by-and-by. And here is a fascinating statistic: They committed suicide less often than their masters did.

"So Americans and Russians can both stand slavery, if they have to—and still want life to go on and on.

"Could it be that slavery *isn't* a fate worse than death? After all, people are tough. Maybe we shouldn't send that message to the Pentagon—about slavery and Kool-Aid time.

"But suppose enemies came ashore in great numbers because we lacked the means to stop them, and they pushed us out of our homes and off our ancestral lands, and into swamps and deserts. Suppose that they even tried to destroy our religion, telling us that our Great God Jehovah, or whatever we wanted to call Him, was as ridiculous as a piece of junk jewelry.

"Again: This is a wringer millions of Americans have already been through—or are still going through. It is another catastrophe Americans can endure, if they have to—still, miraculously, maintaining some measure of dignity, or self-respect.

"As bad as life is for our Indians, they still like it better than death.

"So I haven't had much luck, have I, in identifying fates worse than death? Crucifixion is the only clear winner so far, and we aren't about to be crucified. We aren't about to be enslaved, either—to be treated the way white Americans used to treat black Americans. And no potential enemy that I have heard of wants to come over here to treat all of us the way we still treat American Indians.

"What other fates worse than death could I name? Life without petroleum?

"In melodramas of a century ago, a female's loss of virginity outside of holy wedlock was sometimes spoken of as a fate worse than death. I hope that isn't what the Pentagon or the Kremlin has in mind—but you never know.

"I would rather die for virginity than for petroleum, I think. It's more literary, somehow.

"I may be blinding myself to the racist aspects of hydrogen bombs, whose only function is to end everything. Perhaps there are tribulations that *white* people should not be asked to tolerate. But the Russians' slaves were white. The supposedly unenslavable Britons were enslaved by the Romans. Even proud Britons, if they were enslaved now, would have to say, 'Here we go again.' Armenians and Jews have certainly been treated hideously in modern as well as ancient times—and they have still wanted life to go on and on and on. About a third of our own white people were robbed and ruined and scorned after our Civil War. They still wanted life to go on and on and on.

"Have there ever been large numbers of human beings of any sort who have not, despite everything, done all they could to keep life going on and on and on?

"Soldiers.

"'Death before dishonor' was the motto of several military formations during the Civil War—on both sides. It may be the motto of the 82nd Airborne Division right now. A motto like that made a certain amount of sense, I suppose, when military death was what happened to the soldier on the right or the left of you—or in front of you, or in back of you. But military death now can easily mean the death of everything, including, as I have already said, the blue-footed boobies of the Galápagos Islands.

"The webbed feet of those birds really are the brightest blue, by the way. When two blue-footed boobies begin a courtship, they show each other what beautiful bright blue feet they have.

"If you go to the Galápagos Islands, and see all the strange creatures, you are bound to think what Charles Darwin thought when he went there: How much time Nature has in which to accomplish simply anything. If we desolate this planet, Nature can get life going again. All it takes is a few million years or so, the wink of an eye to Nature.

"Only humankind is running out of time.

"My guess is that we will not disarm, even though we should, and that we really will blow up everything by and by. History shows that human beings are vicious enough to commit every imaginable atrocity, including the construction of factories whose only purpose is to kill people and burn them up.

"It may be that we were put here on Earth to blow the place to smithereens. We may be Nature's way of creating new galaxies. We may be programmed to improve and improve our weapons, and to believe that death is better than dishonor.

"And then, one day, as disarmament rallies are being held all over the planet, *ka-blooey!* A new Milky Way is born.

"Perhaps we should be adoring instead of loathing our hydrogen bombs. They could be the eggs for new galaxies.

"What can save us? Divine intervention, certainly—and this is the place to ask for it. We might pray to be rescued from our inventiveness, just as the dinosaurs may have prayed to be rescued from their massiveness.

"But the inventiveness which we so regret now may also be giving us, along with the rockets and warheads, the means to achieve what has hitherto been an impossibility, the unity of mankind. I am talking mainly about television sets.

"Even in my own lifetime, it used to be necessary for a young soldier to get into fighting before he became disillusioned about war. His parents back home were equally ignorant, and believed him to be slaying monsters. But now, thanks to modern communications, the people of every industrialized nation are nauseated by the idea of war by the time they are ten years old. America's first generation of television viewers has gone to war and come home again—and we have never seen veterans like them before.

"What makes the Vietnam veterans so somehow spooky? We could describe them almost as being 'unwholesomely mature.' They have *never* had illusions about war. They are the first soldiers in history who knew even in childhood, from having heard and seen so many pictures of actual and restaged battles, that war is meaningless butchery of ordinary people like themselves.

"It used to be that veterans could shock their parents when they came home, as Ernest Hemingway did, by announcing that everything about war was repulsive and stupid and dehumanizing. But the parents of our Vietnam veterans were disillusioned about war, too, many of them having seen it firsthand before their children went overseas. Thanks to modern communications, Americans of all ages were dead sick of war even before we went into Vietnam.

"Thanks to modern communications, the poor, unlucky young people from the Soviet Union, now killing and dying in Afghanistan, were dead sick of war before they ever got there.

"Thanks to modern communications, the same must be true of the poor, unlucky young people from Argentina and Great Britain, now killing and dying in the Falkland Islands. The *New York Post* calls them 'Argies' and 'Brits.' Thanks to modern communications, we know that they are a good deal more marvelous and complicated than that, and that what is happening to them down there, on the rim of the Antarctic, is a lot more horrible and shameful than a soccer match.

"When I was a boy it was unusual for an American, or a person of any nationality for that matter, to know much about foreigners. Those who did were specialists—diplomats, explorers, journalists, anthropologists. And they usually knew a lot about just a few groups of foreigners, Eskimos maybe, or Arabs, or what have you. To them, as to the schoolchildren of Indianapolis, large areas of the globe were terra incognita.

"Now look what has happened. Thanks to modern communications, we have seen sights and heard sounds from virtually every square mile of landmass on this planet. Millions of us have actually visited more exotic places than had explorers during my childhood. Many of you have been to Timbuktu. Many of you have been to Katmandu. My dentist just got home from Fiji. He told me all about Fiji. If he had taken his fingers out of my mouth, I would have told him about the Galápagos Islands.

"So we now know for *certain* that there are no potential human enemies anywhere who are anything but human beings almost exactly like ourselves. They need food. How amazing.

They love their children. How amazing. They obey their leaders. How amazing. They think like their neighbors. How amazing.

"Thanks to modern communications, we now have something we never had before: reason to mourn deeply the death or wounding of any human being on any side in any war.

"It was because of rotten communications and malicious, racist ignorance that we were able to celebrate the killing of almost all the inhabitants in Hiroshima, Japan, thirty-seven years ago. We thought they were vermin. They thought we were vermin. They would have clapped their little yellow hands with glee and grinned with their crooked buckteeth if they could have incinerated everybody in Kansas City, say.

"Thanks to how much the people of the world now know about all the other people of the world, the fun of killing enemies has lost its zing. It has so lost its zing that no sane citizen of the Soviet Union, if we were to go to war with that society, would feel anything but horror if his country were to kill practically everybody in New York and Chicago and San Francisco. Killing enemies has so lost its zing that no sane citizen of the United States would feel anything but horror if our country were to kill practically everybody in Moscow and Leningrad and Kiev.

"Or in Nagasaki, Japan, for that matter.

"We have often heard it said that people would have to change, or we would go on having world wars. I bring you good news this morning: People have changed.

"We aren't so ignorant and bloodthirsty anymore.

"I dreamed last night of our descendants a thousand years from now, which is to say all of humanity. If you're at all into reproduction, as was the Emperor Charlemagne, you can pick up an awful lot of relatives in a thousand years. Every person in this cathedral who has a drop of white blood is a descendant of Charlemagne.

"A thousand years from now, if there are still human beings on Earth, every one of those human beings will be descended from us—and from everyone who has chosen to reproduce.

"In my dream, our descendants are numerous. Some of them are rich, some are poor, some are likable, some are insufferable.

"I ask them how humanity, against all odds, managed to keep going for another millennium. They tell me that they and their ancestors did it by preferring life over death for themselves and others at every opportunity, even at the expense of being dishonored. They endured all sorts of insults and humiliations and disappointments without committing either suicide or murder. They are also the people who do the insulting and humiliating and disappointing.

"I endear myself to them by suggesting a motto they might like to put on their belt buckles or T-shirts or whatever. They aren't all hippies, by the way. They aren't all Americans, either. They aren't even all white people.

"I give them a quotation from that great nineteenth-century moralist and robber baron, Jim Fisk, who may have contributed money to this cathedral.

"Jim Fisk uttered his famous words after a particularly disgraceful episode having to do with the Erie Railroad. Fisk himself had no choice but to find himself contemptible. He thought this over, and then he shrugged and said what we all must learn to say if we want to go on living much longer: 'Nothing is lost save honor.'

"I thank you for your attention."

## A "Special Message"
### to readers of the Franklin Library's
### signed first edition of "Galápagos"

M Y WIFE Jill Krementz and I went to the Galápagos Islands on a two-week cruise out of Guayaquil, Ecuador, in March of 1982. Our ship was the *Santa Cruz*, whose dimensions and amenities were a lot like those I have attributed to the fictitious *Bahía de Darwin* in this tale of mine. We were ferried between the ship and the islands in shallow-draft outboard motorboats with room for eighteen passengers, a boatman, and a trained guide. Each guide held a university degree in some natural science, and prevented our touching any animal or plant or stepping off narrow pathways. Each took part during the evenings in illustrated lectures on what we had seen ashore or were about to see.

It was very educational.

But Jill stopped going ashore and attending lectures quite early in the game. Instead, she finished writing a book based on her interviews of children whose parents had divorced. It would be published later that year under the title *How It Feels to Be Adopted*.

I was annoyed with Jill at the time. I was still insisting that seeing the archipelago was "a dream come true" for me, something I had longed to do since I was a boy, and so on. Three years later, I am now pleased to congratulate her for her honest response to the unpleasantness of the islands and the moral blankness of Nature in the raw. What were all those animals and plants ashore, after all, but clocks whose only purpose was to duplicate their repetitious, predictable selves? Why shouldn't Jill have preferred to stay on shipboard with the words of quicksilver human children? Those children could change their modes of adaptation to life a dozen times in the course of a single day, if necessary. The creatures on the islands might, if pressed relentlessly by outrageous fortune, make some trivial modification in their habits in twenty thousand years or so.

• • •

When I was a student at the University of Chicago a long time ago, Dan Boorstin, now Librarian of Congress, was a young history professor—and he said at a cocktail party one time, simply trying on an idea for size, that perhaps every major advance in scientific theory had considerable social consequences. He cited Darwin's Theory of Evolution and its undeniable influence on human behavior as an example.

This bright idea lived about as long as a June bug, like most of the bright ideas at that time and place. Nobody could think of any purely social consequences of Newton's Laws of Motion, or the Second Law of Thermodynamics, or, for that matter, Einstein's Theory of Relativity. Needless to say, the technological consequences of those theories were sensational, even catastrophic. But they altered people's notions of how best to act in harmony with Creation not at all.

Only the Theory of Evolution carried a seeming message to which human beings without scientific apparatus might respond at any time, if they were so inclined: "Prove by fucking or killing that you are Nature's favorite. Never mind mere human law."

And this planet now faces extinction of all life forms by human wars and human overpopulation, which are returns to Nature supposedly—which are thrilling suspensions of mere human law.

Stop thinking.
Stop planning.
Go crazy.
Let Mother Nature decide.

P.S. May the best man win.

K.V.

New York City

*1985*

CHRONOLOGY

NOTE ON THE TEXTS

NOTES

# *Chronology*

1922    Born Kurt Vonnegut Jr., November 11, in Indianapolis, Indiana, the third child of Kurt Vonnegut and Edith Sophia Lieber Vonnegut. (Both parents are the grandchildren of entrepreneurial German immigrants—merchants, manufacturers, and brewers—who settled in the American Midwest in the mid-1800s. Father, born in Indianapolis in 1884, is a practicing architect and graphic designer, the successor to his late father, Bernard Vonnegut, in the firm of Vonnegut, Bohn & Mueller. Mother, born in 1888, is the handsome, pleasure-loving daughter of former millionaire Albert Lieber, heir to the presidency of Indianapolis Brewing Co., now unemployed due to Prohibition. The Vonneguts were married in November 1913. Their first child, Bernard, was born in 1914, their second, Alice, in 1917.) Infant Kurt is brought from hospital to his parents' house, built in 1910 as a gift to his mother by Albert Lieber on his four-hundred-acre estate on the banks of the White River, six miles northwest of downtown Indianapolis.

1923    Spends the first of many "heavenly" childhood summers among father's extended family at the Vonnegut compound, a row of Victorian-era cottages on the eastern shore of Lake Maxinkuckee, in Culver, Indiana, ninety miles north of Indianapolis.

1924    Grandfather Lieber, short on savings and in need of ready cash, subdivides his White River estate and begins selling the land in parcels.

1927    In fall enters kindergarten at the Orchard School, a private day school (K–8) on the progressive model championed by John Dewey. Spends hours alone every day with the family's cook and housekeeper, Ida Young, the granddaughter of slaves, who, in the absence of a religious education from his nominally Unitarian parents, teaches him Bible stories.

1929    Grandfather Lieber, now bankrupt, is forced to sell the last of his subdivisions, and the Vonneguts, dispossessed by the sale, leave the White River house. They move into a large new brick residence, designed by father and built with borrowed

money, at 4365 North Illinois Street, near the intersection
with Forty-fifth Street, Indianapolis. After the Great Crash
of October, the mortgage payment on the property becomes increasingly difficult to meet.

1931    As the Depression deepens and new construction ceases,
Vonnegut, Bohn & Mueller struggles. Father sells invest-
ments and heirlooms to keep family solvent, and reluctantly dismisses Ida Young. ("She was humane and wise
and gave me decent moral instruction," Vonnegut will later
remember. "The compassionate, forgiving aspects of my
beliefs come from Ida Young.") Father's younger brother,
Alex Vonnegut, a Harvard-educated insurance salesman
and bon vivant, becomes Vonnegut's mentor and "ideal
grownup friend." ("He taught me something very important: that when things are going well, we should notice it.
He urged me to say out loud during such epiphanies, 'If
this isn't nice, *what is?*'") Vonnegut is withdrawn from private school and begins fourth grade at James Whitcomb
Riley Elementary, P.S. 43.

1934    Father, after years without an architectural commission,
closes his office, turns an attic room of the house into an
art studio, and begins to paint portraits, still lifes, and
landscapes. Mother takes night classes in creative writing
and attempts, unsuccessfully, to sell commercial short fiction to women's magazines. Vonnegut, age eleven, takes
a strong interest and vicarious pleasure in his parents' artistic pursuits. In September, Grandfather Lieber dies at
age seventy-one. The Vonneguts' share of his estate after
probate is less than eleven thousand dollars, and mother,
grieving, resentful, and obsessively insecure about the family's diminished social position, begins a long struggle with
alcohol abuse, insomnia, and depression. ("My mother was
addicted to being rich," Vonnegut will later write. "She was
tormented by withdrawal symptoms all through the Great
Depression.")

1936    Vonnegut enters Shortridge High School, the largest and
best equipped free public school in the state of Indiana.
Excels in English and public-speaking classes, and, after
dedicated application, the sciences. Joins the staff of the
Shortridge *Daily Echo*, a four-page broadsheet edited, set
up, and printed by students in the school's print shop, and
develops the habit of writing regularly, on deadline, for an

audience of his peers. (In his junior and senior years, he will be editor and chief writer of the paper's Tuesday edition.) Plays clarinet in school orchestra and marching band, and takes private lessons from Ernst Michaelis, first-chair clarinetist of the Indianapolis Symphony. Forms a book club for two with Uncle Alex and reads, mostly at Alex's suggestion, Robert Louis Stevenson, H. G. Wells, H. L. Mencken, Thorstein Veblen, George Bernard Shaw, and Mark Twain. Other enthusiasms include Ping-Pong, model trains, radio comedy, movies, and jazz, especially Benny Goodman and Artie Shaw. Begins smoking Pall Mall cigarettes, which will become a lifelong habit.

1940    At age eighteen his head is a mop of blond curls and he has attained his adult height of six foot two: "I was a real skinny, narrow-shouldered boy...a preposterous kind of flamingo." Graduates from Shortridge High, and, still living with his parents, enrolls at local Butler University. His vague ambition is to study journalism and, ultimately, write for one of Indianapolis's three daily papers.

1941    Disappointed in Butler, transfers to Cornell University, Ithaca, New York, in middle of freshman year. Following his father's orders and his scientist brother's example, shuns "frivolous" classes in the arts and humanities, focusing instead on chemistry and physics. ("I had no talent for science," Vonnegut will remember. "I did badly.") Neglects his studies, taking pleasure only in drilling with ROTC, drinking with his Delta Upsilon brothers, and writing jokes and news for the Cornell *Daily Sun*. In summer, father sells the big brick house and, with proceeds, builds a smaller one in Williams Creek, a new suburban development six miles north of Indianapolis.

1942    Vonnegut writes a regular column, "Well All Right," for the *Daily Sun*—"impudent editorializing" and "college-humor sort of stuff"—and is elected the paper's assistant managing editor. In the middle of the fall semester of his junior year, is placed on academic probation due to poor grades. Contracts viral pneumonia, withdraws from school, and goes home to recover.

1943    Against the pleas of his mother, enlists in the U.S. Army and in March begins basic training at Camp Atterbury, forty miles south of Indianapolis. Takes special classes in manning the 240-millimeter howitzer, the army's largest mobile fieldpiece. In summer joins the Army Specialized Training Program, and is sent first to the Carnegie Institute of Technology, Pittsburgh, and then to the University of Tennessee, Knoxville, for advanced studies in engineering ("thermodynamics, mechanics, the actual use of machine tools. . . . I did badly again").

1944    In March returns to Camp Atterbury and is assigned as private first class to Headquarters Company, 2nd Battalion, 423rd Regiment, 106th Infantry Division. Although he has no infantry training ("bayonets, grenades, and so on") he is made one of the battalion's six scouts. Assigned an "Army buddy," fellow scout Bernard V. O'Hare Jr., a Roman Catholic youth from Shenandoah, Pennsylvania, who will become a friend for life. Secures frequent Sunday passes, enjoying meals at his parents' house and movie dates with Jane Marie Cox, his sometimes high-school sweetheart. On May 14, while Vonnegut is home on a Mother's Day pass, mother, age fifty-five, commits suicide using barbiturates and alcohol. In October the 106th leaves Camp Atterbury and is staged at Camp Myles Standish, Taunton, Massachusetts. The division embarks at New York City on October 17 and, after three weeks' training in England, is deployed in the Ardennes on December 11. The Germans launch a surprise offensive against the American front on December 16, and three days later Vonnegut, O'Hare, and some sixty other infantrymen are separated from their battalion and taken prisoner near Schönberg, on the German-Belgian border. They are marched sixty miles to Limburg and on December 21 are warehoused, sixty men to a forty-man boxcar, on a railroad siding there. After more than a week, the stifling, fetid car is hauled by train to Stalag IV-B, a crowded German P.O.W. camp in Mühlberg, thirty miles north of Dresden.

1945    On New Year's Day the boxcar is opened, and Vonnegut and his fellow-prisoners are provided showers, bunks, and starvation rations of cold potato soup and brown bread. On January 10, Vonnegut, O'Hare, and about one hundred fifty other prisoners are transferred to a Dresden factory where, under observation by armed guards, they manufacture vitamin-enriched barley-malt syrup. Vonnegut, who has rudimentary German learned at home, is elected the group's foreman and interpreter. On February 13–14, the Allied air forces bomb Dresden, destroying much of the city and killing some twenty-five thousand people. Vonnegut, his fellow prisoners, and their guards find safety in the subterranean meat locker of a slaughterhouse. After the raid, the guards put the prisoners to work clearing corpses from basements and air-raid shelters and hauling them to mass funeral pyres in the Old Market. In late April, as U.S. forces advance on Leipzig, the prisoners and their guards evacuate Dresden and march fifty miles southeast toward Hellendorf, a hamlet near the border with Czechoslovakia. There, on the morning after the general surrender of May 7, the Germans abandon the prisoners and flee from the advancing Soviet Army. Vonnegut, O'Hare, and six others steal a horse and wagon and, over the following week, slowly make their way back to Dresden. Outside the city they meet the Soviet Army, which trucks them a hundred miles to the American lines at Halle. From Halle they are flown, on May 22, to Le Havre, France, for rest and recovery at Camp Lucky Strike, a U.S. repatriation facility. ("When I was captured I weighed 180 pounds," Vonnegut later remembered. "When I was liberated, I weighed 132. The Army fed me cheeseburgers and milkshakes and sent me home wearing an overcoat of baby fat.") On April 21, Vonnegut and O'Hare board a Liberty Ship, the SS *Lucretia Mott*, bound for Newport News, Virginia. Vonnegut returns to Camp Atterbury by train and serves three more weeks as a clerical typist; is promoted to corporal, awarded a Purple Heart, then honorably discharged in late July. Marries high-school sweetheart Jane Marie Cox, September 14, and honeymoons at a Vonnegut family cottage on Lake Maxinkuckee. Taking advantage of the G.I. Bill, Vonnegut applies, and in October is accepted, to the Master's program in anthropology at the University of Chicago. The newlyweds rent an inexpensive apartment near the campus, their home for the next two years. Vonnegut finds a part-time job as a police reporter for the City News Bureau, an independent news agency that provides local stories to Chicago's five dailies.

1946     Greatly enjoys his anthropology classes, especially those taught by Robert Redfield, whom Vonnegut will remember as "the most satisfying teacher in my life." Redfield's theory that human beings are hardwired for living in a

"Folk Society"—"a society where everyone knew every-body well, and associations were for life," where "there was little change" and "what one man believed was what all men believed," where every man felt himself to be part of a larger, supportive, coherent whole—quickly becomes central to Vonnegut's world view. ("We are full of chemicals which require us to belong to folk societies, or failing that, to feel lousy all the time," Vonnegut will later write. "We are chemically engineered to live in folk societies, just as fish are chemically engineered to live in clean water—and there are no folk societies for us anymore.")

1947 Son born, May 11, and named Mark Vonnegut in honor of Mark Twain. Master's thesis, "On the Fluctuations Between Good and Evil in Simple Tales," unanimously rejected by Chicago's anthropology faculty. Vonnegut leaves the program without a degree, fails to turn his part-time job into full-time newspaper work, and searches in vain for appropriate employment. Through the agency of his brother, Bernard, an atmospheric scientist at General Electric, Vonnegut is interviewed by the public-relations department at GE headquarters, in Schenectady, New York. Accepts position of publicist for research laboratory at ninety dollars a week, and moves with family to the village of Alplaus, five miles north of the GE complex. Joins the Alplaus Volunteer Fire Department, his window into community life, and reads George Orwell, whose work and moral example become a touchstone.

1949 Vonnegut enjoys the daily company of research scientists and is "easily excited and entertained" by their work, but despises the corporate hierarchy of GE and sees no room for advancement within the PR department. Devotes evenings and weekends to drafting his first short stories, one of which, "Report on the Barnhouse Effect," he submits to Knox Burger, chief fiction editor at *Collier's*, a general-interest mass-circulation magazine which, like its rival *The Saturday Evening Post*, publishes five stories a week. "Knox told me what was wrong with it, and how to fix it," Vonnegut will later remember. "I did what he said, and he bought the story for seven hundred and fifty dollars, six weeks' pay at GE. I wrote another, and he paid nine hundred and fifty. . . ." Daughter, Edith ("Edie") Vonnegut, born December 29.

1950      First published story, "Report on the Barnhouse Effect," in *Collier's*, February 11; it is adapted for NBC radio's *Dimension X* program (broadcast April 22) and chosen for inclusion in Robert A. Heinlein's anthology *Tomorrow, the Stars* (1952). Sells several more stories to *Collier's* and begins planning a satirical novel about a fully automated world where human labor and the dignity of work are rendered obsolete.

1951      Vonnegut rents a summer cottage in Provincetown, Massachusetts, and decides to resign from GE and move his family to Cape Cod. Having saved the equivalent of a year's salary in freelance income, he buys a small house at 10 Barnard Street, Osterville, on the south shore of the Cape, where he finishes his novel, *Player Piano*. At the recommendation of Knox Burger, places the book with New York agents Kenneth Littauer and Max Wilkinson, both formerly of *Collier's*. At Vonnegut's request, they submit it to Charles Scribner's Sons, the house of Hemingway and Fitzgerald, and have a contract by Christmas.

1952      *Player Piano* published in hardcover, August 18, in an edition of 7,600 copies. It receives few but respectful reviews. Continues to write short stories for *Collier's* and, with the help of Littauer & Wilkinson, Inc., begins placing work in *The Saturday Evening Post*, *Cosmopolitan*, and other top-paying magazines.

1953      *Player Piano* reprinted as a July/August selection of the Doubleday Science Fiction Book Club. Vonnegut becomes involved, as an advisor, fundraiser, volunteer, and actor, in the business and artistic affairs of two of Cape Cod's leading amateur theatrical companies, the Orleans Arena Theatre (summer-stock) and the Barnstable Comedy Club (a repertory company staging four plays a year).

1954      After several false starts abandons Prohibition-era social novel, "Upstairs and Downstairs," set in Indianapolis and inspired by the riches-to-rags career of grandfather Albert Lieber. Writes six chapters of a novel about "ice-nine," a synthetic form of ice that will not melt at room temperature, but soon sets the project aside. Second daughter and third child, Nanette ("Nanny") Vonnegut, born October 4. *Player Piano* reprinted in paperback by Bantam Books, under the title *Utopia 14*.

1955    In February, the Vonneguts leave the small house in Oster-
        ville for a large one at 9 Scudder Lane, in nearby West
        Barnstable. With his favorite market for stories failing (*Col-
        lier's* became a biweekly in 1953, and will cease publication
        in January 1957) and without ideas for a new novel, Von-
        negut takes a full-time job as copywriter in an industrial
        advertising agency. Commutes to Boston daily, and holds
        the job for about two years. Dabbles in playwriting, with
        an eye toward providing a show for the Orleans Arena
        Theatre.

1956    In January Vonnegut's father, recently retired from a sec-
        ond career in architecture and living alone in rural Brown
        County, Indiana, informs his family that he is dying of lung
        cancer. Vonnegut visits him a number of times before his
        death, on October 1, at age seventy-two.

1957    Makes stage adaptation of his short story "EPICAC" (*Col-
        lier's*, 1950) for an evening of one-acts at the Barnstable
        Comedy Club. (The cast features eight-year-old Edie Von-
        negut in the role of a talking computer.) With small in-
        heritance from his father, opens and manages Saab Cape
        Cod, the second Saab dealership in the United States, with
        a showroom and garage on Route 6A, just up the street
        from his house. At a Littauer & Wilkinson holiday party
        Vonnegut is asked by Knox Burger, now an editor for Dell
        Books, to write a science-fiction novel for his new line of
        mass-market paperback originals.

1958    Improvises an outline for his paperback novel, conceived
        as a satire on human grandeur in the form of a pulp-fiction
        "space opera." Writes the first draft with unaccustomed
        speed, then painstakingly revises. ("I *swooped* through that
        novel," Vonnegut will later recall. "All the others were
        *bashed out*, sentence by sentence.") Sister, Alice, a house-
        wife and amateur sculptor, dies of breast cancer in a New-
        ark, New Jersey, hospital, September 16, at age forty-one,
        with both of her brothers nearby. Only one day earlier her
        husband of fifteen years, James Carmalt Adams, had died
        when a commuter train taking him to Manhattan plunged
        off an open drawbridge into Newark Bay. Without hesita-
        tion Kurt and Jane Vonnegut take in Alice's four orphaned
        children—James Jr. (fourteen years old), Steven (eleven),
        Kurt (called "Tiger," nine), and toddler "Peter Boo" (twenty-
        one months). As Jane will later write, "Our tidy little fam-

ily of five had blown up into a wildly improbable gang of nine."

1959   The Vonneguts assume custody of the three older Adams boys, but after a protracted, bitter dispute with a childless Adams cousin, relinquish control of the youngest. (Allowing the boys to be split between distant and unlike households will be, according to Jane, "the most difficult decision" of the Vonneguts' marriage. "Peter Boo" is raised in Birmingham, Alabama, and until his teens will see little of his older brothers.) In October, Vonnegut's second novel, *The Sirens of Titan*, published in paperback by Dell in an edition of 175,000 copies. It is popular with readers but receives no reviews.

1960   *Penelope*, a two-act comedy about a war hero's unheroic homecoming, receives six performances at the Orleans Arena Theatre, September 5–10. *The Sirens of Titan* named a finalist for the Hugo Award for the year's best science-fiction novel, and Houghton Mifflin arranges to print 2,500 hardcover copies to meet demand from libraries. Vonnegut, having failed to make money for himself or his Swedish franchisers, closes Saab Cape Cod.

1961   In the ten years since the appearance of "Report on the Barnhouse Effect," Vonnegut has published more than three-dozen short stories in "slick" magazines and science-fiction pulps. In September Knox Burger, now at Fawcett Gold Medal Books, publishes *Canary in a Cat House*, a paperback collection of twelve of these stories. Burger also signs Vonnegut's third novel, *Mother Night*, the fictional memoirs of a German-American double agent during World War II. Vonnegut publishes "My Name Is Everyone" (*The Saturday Evening Post*, December 16), a short story evoking the backstage life of a community playhouse much like that of the Barnstable Comedy Club.

1962   In February *Mother Night* published as a paperback original by Fawcett Gold Medal in an edition of 175,000 copies. Vonnegut, returning to the "ice-nine" material of 1954, begins a new novel, *Cat's Cradle*, which Littauer sells to Holt, Rinehart & Winston. *Who Am I This Time?*, Vonnegut's stage adaptation of "My Name Is Everyone," presented by the Barnstable Comedy Club. (It will be revived two years later by the Cape Playhouse in Dennis, Massachusetts.)

1963    In June *Cat's Cradle* published in hardcover by Holt. Reviews are few but enthusiastic, and at Christmas Graham Greene, writing in the London *Spectator*, names it one of his three favorite novels of the year. In fall accepts year-long assignment as "the whole English department" at the Hopefield School, in East Sandwich, Massachusetts, a small private high school for students with emotional and learning problems.

1964    Responding to a changing editorial marketplace, stops writing short stories and begins contributing personal essays, book reviews, and other nonfiction pieces to periodicals including *The New York Times Book Review*, *Life*, *Esquire*, and the travel magazine *Venture*.

1965    In March *God Bless You, Mr. Rosewater*, a novel about a so-called fool and his money, published in hardcover by Holt, Rinehart & Winston to many if mixed reviews. Accepts last-minute invitation to teach fiction writing at the Writers' Workshop, Iowa City, on a two-year contract. Accompanied by Edie, who enrolls in nearby University High School, he lives on the first floor of a large brick Victorian house at 800 Van Buren Avenue, next door to the writer Andre Dubus. "I didn't get to know any literary people until [my] two years teaching at Iowa," he will later recall. "There at Iowa I was suddenly friends with Nelson Algren and José Donoso and Vance Bourjaily and Donald Justice . . . and was amazed. Suddenly writing seemed very important again. This was better than a transplant of monkey glands for a man my age." Enjoys teaching, and is good at it. His students include Loree Rackstraw, a future English professor and memoirist who becomes a friend and confidante for life. Begins work in earnest on a long-contemplated "Dresden novel," based on his experiences during World War II.

1966    In May is joined in Iowa by Jane and daughter Nanny. *Cat's Cradle* becomes a bestseller, especially among college-age readers, in its Dell paperback edition. *Player Piano* reprinted in hardcover by Holt, Rinehart & Winston, and *Mother Night* reprinted in hardcover by Harper & Row. Agent Kenneth Littauer dies, July, and Max Wilkinson, to Vonnegut's dismay, moves literary agency to Long Island and goes into semiretirement. In fall, Richard Yates rejoins the Iowa faculty and quickly becomes a lifelong friend.

Vonnegut's students for 1966–67 include the young and unpublished John Irving, Gail Godwin, and John Casey. In November, forty-year-old editor-publisher Seymour ("Sam") Lawrence—formerly of the Atlantic Monthly Press and Knopf, now launching his own imprint at Delacorte Press—offers Vonnegut a three-book contract. Vonnegut, with Wilkinson's consent, hires entertainment lawyer Donald C. Farber to handle the contract. (In 1977 Farber will become Vonnegut's sole agent and attorney.)

1967    Prepares first book for Sam Lawrence, a miscellany of previously published short works including eleven of the twelve stories in *Canary in a Cat House*, eleven uncollected and later stories, and two recent nonfiction pieces. To anchor the book with something new and substantial, writes "Welcome to the Monkey House," his first short story in nearly five years and the first not conceived for a magazine. In April awarded a fellowship from the John Simon Guggenheim Foundation, which finances a summer research trip to Dresden in the company of his Army buddy Bernard V. O'Hare. In May, ends two-year stay at the Iowa Writers' Workshop and returns with family to Barnstable to work on his Dresden novel.

1968    Collection *Welcome to the Monkey House* published by Delacorte/Seymour Lawrence, August, to mixed reviews. Vonnegut completes his Dresden novel, and Sam Lawrence, convinced of the book's sales potential, begins buying rights to earlier works for reissue as Delacorte hardcovers and Delta/Dell paperbacks. "Fortitude," a one-act teleplay commissioned by CBS for an unrealized comedy special, reshaped as a closet drama and published in the September issue of *Playboy*.

1969    On March 31, Vonnegut's Dresden novel, *Slaughterhouse-Five*, published by Delacorte/Seymour Lawrence to uniformly good and well-placed reviews, including the cover of *The New York Times Book Review*. The book spends sixteen weeks on the *Times* fiction list, peaking at number four, and creates an audience for his newly issued paperback backlist. Vonnegut begins a lucrative second career as a public speaker, especially on college campuses. Works on a new novel and teases the press with its title, *Breakfast of Champions*. In May, producer Lester M. Goldsmith options *Penelope*, Vonnegut's play of 1960, and begins planning

Off-Broadway premiere for the following fall. Vonnegut
spends most of the summer rewriting the play, giving it the
new title *Happy Birthday, Wanda June*.

1970    In early January, at the invitation of a private American
relief organization, visits the short-lived, war-torn African
republic of Biafra shortly before it surrenders to Nigeria,
from which it was attempting to secede. Publishes account
of the trip, "Biafra: A People Betrayed," in April issue of
*McCall's*. In May receives an Academy Award in Literature
from the American Academy of Arts and Letters. Interviewed by Harry Reasoner of CBS's *60 Minutes*, television's
most-watched program, for the broadcast of September 15.
(Reasoner introduces him as "the current idol of the country's sensitive and intelligent young people, [who] snap up
his books as fast as they're reissued. . . . His gentle fan-
tasies of peace and his dark humor are as current among
the young as was J. D. Salinger's work in the fifties and
Tolkien's in the sixties.") Accepts invitation to teach creative writing at Harvard University for the academic year
beginning in the fall. Commutes to Cambridge two days a
week from New York City, where, by arrangement with producer Lester Goldsmith, he lives as a "kept playwright" in a
Greenwich Village sublet. With director Michael Kane
and a cast starring Kevin McCarthy and Marsha Mason,
workshops the script of *Happy Birthday, Wanda June*
throughout September, tinkering with the show until its
first curtain. Play opens at the Theatre de Lys, Christopher
Street, on October 7; it receives mixed reviews and runs
forty-seven performances, closing on November 15. The
show moves to the Edison Theater, Broadway, on December 22. During production of *Wanda June* Vonnegut meets
and begins a relationship with the photojournalist Jill Krementz, born 1940.

1971    Son Mark, a self-described hippie and co-founder, with
friends from Swarthmore, of a commune at Lake Powell,
British Columbia, suffers a manic mental breakdown. On
February 14, Vonnegut commits him to the care of Hollywood Psychiatric Hospital in Vancouver, where he makes
a slow but steady recovery. Broadway production of *Wanda
June* closes March 14 after ninety-six performances. In
May, Vonnegut delivers the annual Blashfield Address to
the assembled National Institute of Arts and Letters and

American Academy of Arts and Letters. Awarded Master's degree in anthropology by the University of Chicago, which, at the department chair's suggestion, accepts *Cat's Cradle* in lieu of a formal dissertation. In June, book version of *Wanda June*, with a preface by the author and production photographs by Jill Krementz, published by Delacorte/ Seymour Lawrence. Resumes work on *Breakfast of Champions*. In December, Sony Pictures releases film version of *Happy Birthday, Wanda June*, directed by Mark Robson and starring Rod Steiger and Susannah York. ("It was one of the most embarrassing movies ever made," Vonnegut later writes, "and I am happy that it sank like a stone.") Grants WNET-New York and WGBH-Boston the option to develop a ninety-minute made-for-television "revue" based on scenes from his writings. The script, by David O'Dell, is revised by Vonnegut and titled *Between Time and Timbuktu, or Prometheus-5: A Space Fantasy*. Separates from Jane Marie Cox Vonnegut and rents a one-bedroom apartment at 349 East Fifty-fourth Street, between First Avenue and Second Avenue.

1972       On March 13 *Between Time and Timbuktu*, starring William Hickey, Kevin McCarthy, and the comedians Bob and Ray (Bob Elliott and Ray Goulding), broadcast nationally as an installment of public television's *NET Playhouse* series. In October, a book version of the teleplay—"based on materials by Kurt Vonnegut, Jr.," with a preface by the author and photographs by Krementz—published by Delacorte/Seymour Lawrence. On March 15 *Slaughterhouse-Five*, directed by George Roy Hill from a screenplay by Stephen Geller, released by Universal Studios. The film, starring Michael Sacks, Ron Leibman, and Valerie Perrine, delights Vonnegut, who finds the adaptation "flawless." In summer, Vonnegut and Krementz collaborate on an illustrated report from the Republican National Convention in Miami, published as the cover story of the November issue of *Harper's*. "The Big Space Fuck," Vonnegut's widely publicized "farewell" to the short-story form, published in *Again, Dangerous Visions*, an anthology of original science-fiction tales commissioned and edited by Harlan Ellison. Named vice president of PEN American Center, the U.S. branch of the international literary and human-rights organization, and remains active on PEN's behalf for the rest of his life.

1973    In April, *Breakfast of Champions*, embellished with more
        than a hundred felt-tip line drawings by the author, pub-
        lished by Delacorte/Seymour Lawrence to mixed reviews
        but strong sales. It dominates the *New York Times* fiction
        list for twenty-eight weeks, ten weeks in the number-one
        position. In May, speaks against state-sponsored censor-
        ship at the conference of International PEN in Stockholm,
        is inducted into the National Institute of Arts and Letters,
        and receives an honorary doctorate in the humanities from
        Indiana University, Bloomington. In September, begins
        one-year term as Distinguished Professor of English Prose
        at City University of New York, where his colleagues in-
        clude Joseph Heller, who becomes a close friend. In No-
        vember *Slaughterhouse-Five* declared obscene by the school
        board of Drake, North Dakota, which orders thirty-six
        copies of the novel burned in the high-school furnace and
        the teacher who assigned it dismissed; it is the first of more
        than a dozen such incidents of censorship during Von-
        negut's lifetime, all successfully challenged by the American
        Civil Liberties Union. Buys a three-story townhouse,
        built in 1862, at 228 East Forty-eighth Street, between
        Second Avenue and Third Avenue, which he shares with
        Jill Krementz. (The top floor of this whitewashed Turtle
        Bay brownstone becomes his office; the separate basement
        apartment, with its entry under the stoop, becomes her
        photography studio.) In December Jane Marie Cox Von-
        negut reluctantly agrees to a divorce.

1974    *Wampeters, Foma & Granfalloons (Opinions)*, a collection
        of twenty-five previously published short prose pieces,
        brought out by Delacorte/Seymour Lawrence, Septem-
        ber. This, the first of his "autobiographical collages" com-
        bining essays, articles, speeches, book reviews, and other
        writings, is the last of his works to be published by "Kurt
        Vonnegut, Jr."; subsequent works, and all reprints, will be
        published under the name "Kurt Vonnegut." In October
        visits Moscow with Krementz; their guide is Rita Rait, the
        translator of his books into Russian.

1975    Writes *Slapstick*, a comic novel about a brother and sister
        dedicated to wiping out "the peculiarly American disease
        called loneliness." In May begins four-year term as Vice
        President for Literature of the National Institute of Arts
        and Letters. Spends summer in a rented beachfront house

in East Hampton, Long Island, and begins search for a second home in the area. Uncle Alex dies, July 28, at age eighty-six. ("I am eternally grateful to him," Vonnegut writes in a tribute, "for my knack of finding in great books reason enough to feel honored to be alive, no matter what else might be going on.") In October, Mark Vonnegut publishes *The Eden Express*, a memoir of his madness, to good reviews and strong sales. The royalties will pay his way through Harvard Medical School.

1976    *Slapstick* published by Delacorte/Seymour Lawrence, October, to uniformly negative reviews, the worst Vonnegut will ever receive. ("The reviewers . . . actually asked critics who had praised me in the past to now admit in public how wrong they'd been," he later wrote. "I felt as though I were sleeping standing up in a boxcar in Germany again.") Sales, however, are strong: it is on the *New York Times* fiction list for twenty-four weeks, peaking at number four.

1977    At the request of George Plimpton, editor of *The Paris Review*, fashions a long autobiographical article in the form of one of the magazine's "Art of Fiction" interviews. Purchases a second home, a clapboard house dating from the 1740s, at 620 Sagg Main Street, Sagaponack, a village in Southampton, Long Island. Summer neighbors include Plimpton, Nelson Algren, Truman Capote, James Jones, and Irwin Shaw.

1978    Works on a new novel, *Jailbird*, the fictional memoirs of a good man who, through no wrongdoing of his own, becomes involved in several of the most shameful episodes in modern American political history.

1979    *Jailbird* published by Delacorte/Seymour Lawrence, September, to good reviews and strong sales. It is on the *New York Times* fiction list for thirty-one weeks, five weeks in the number-one position. In April, commemorates the centenary of the Mark Twain house in Hartford, Connecticut, with a speech in which he says that "we would not be known as a nation with a supple, amusing, and often beautiful language of its own, if it were not for the genius of Mark Twain." Throughout the summer a musical adaptation of *God Bless You, Mr. Rosewater*, with book and lyrics by Howard Ashman and music by Alan Menken, is developed by Ashman's WPA Theater company with Vonnegut's

"limited but noisy" involvement. The show, produced by
Edie Vonnegut, opens at the Entermedia Theatre, in the
East Village, on October 11. Despite good reviews, it closes
after only twelve performances, having failed to find a Broadway backer. Vonnegut marries Jill Krementz, November 24,
at Christ Church United Methodist, on Sixtieth Street at
Park Avenue.

1980    On January 27 Vonnegut, a self-described "Christ-wor-
shiping agnostic," delivers his first sermon, a lecture on
human dignity at the First Parish Unitarian Church, Cambridge, Massachusetts. Writes the text for *Sun Moon Star*,
a picture story with bold and simple full-color images by
the graphic designer Ivan Chermayeff. A retelling of the
Nativity as seen through the eyes of the infant Jesus, it is
published by Harper & Row as a Christmas gift book. First
solo art exhibition, featuring thirty felt-tip drawings on
vellum, at the Margo Feiden Galleries, Greenwich Village,
October 20–November 15.

1981    *Palm Sunday*, an "autobiographical collage" collecting short
nonfiction pieces written between 1974 and 1980, published by Delacorte/Seymour Lawrence, March. The title
piece is a sermon given on March 30, 1980, at St. Clement's Episcopal Church on West Forty-sixth Street. Vonnegut's text is John 12:1–8: "For the poor always ye have
with you . . ."

1982    Television adaptation of *Who Am I This Time?*, directed by
Jonathan Demme and starring Susan Sarandon and Christopher Walken, broadcast on PBS in its *American Playhouse*
series, February 2. Hires Janet Cosby, a Washington-based
lecture agent, to book his annual speaking tours—two
weeks in the spring, two weeks in the fall, a schedule he
will keep for most of the next two decades. *Deadeye Dick*,
a quickly written novel of guilt, self-punishment, and neutron bombs, published by Delacorte/Seymour Lawrence,
October, to mixed reviews. It is on the *New York Times*
fiction list for fourteen weeks, peaking at number ten. On
December 18, Vonnegut and Krementz adopt a three-day-
old girl and name her Lily Vonnegut.

1983    Begins work on a new novel, *Galápagos*, a fantasy about
the future of human evolution. Makes further drawings,
and begins to take himself seriously as a graphic artist,
though he doubts his technique.

1984    In January, unsuccessfully tries to interest art publisher
        Harry N. Abrams in bringing out a book of his drawings.
        On the evening of February 13, the thirty-ninth anniver-
        sary of the firebombing of Dresden, attempts suicide in his
        Manhattan home, apparently by overdosing on barbitu-
        rates and alcohol. Awakes in St. Vincent's Hospital, Green-
        wich Village, and is diagnosed, as he writes to a friend,
        "with acute (all but terminal) depression. . . . I was there
        for eighteen days, under lock and key. . . . I am no re-
        naissance man, but a manic depressive with a few lopsided
        gifts." Upon release returns to *Galápagos*, finishing the
        manuscript by Christmas Day.

1985    *Galápagos* published by Delacorte/Seymour Lawrence,
        October, to good reviews. It is on the *New York Times*
        fiction list for seventeen weeks, peaking at number five.
        Completes working draft of *Make Up Your Mind*, a sex
        farce for four actors. The play, his first since *Happy Birth-
        day, Wanda June*, is given a staged reading in East Hamp-
        ton. It is optioned by a Broadway producer but is not
        produced or published.

1986    Writes *Bluebeard*, the fictional memoirs of a seventy-one-
        year-old Abstract Expressionist painter whose work is loosely
        modeled on that of Barnett Newman. On December 19,
        Jane Marie Cox Vonnegut, now married to law-school
        professor and Defense Department spokesman Adam
        Yarmolinsky, dies of ovarian cancer. She leaves behind a
        memoir of her life with Vonnegut and their six children,
        published by Houghton Mifflin in October 1987 as *Angels
        Without Wings*.

1987    *Bluebeard* published by Delacorte/Seymour Lawrence,
        October, to mixed reviews. It is on the *New York Times*
        fiction list for eleven weeks, peaking at number eight.

1988    Works on new novel, *Hocus Pocus*, a commentary on "the
        way we live now" addressing, among much else, American
        trends in higher education, crime and punishment, po-
        litical correctness, social privilege, militarism, intolerance,
        and globalization.

1989    Sam Lawrence moves from Delacorte to Dutton and then
        to Houghton Mifflin, but Vonnegut declines to follow. Sells
        *Hocus Pocus* to G. P. Putnam's Sons, where his editor is
        Faith Sale. In October, at the request of the international

humanitarian organization CARE, travels to Mozambique to write about the country's decade-old civil war.

1990      "My Visit to Hell," Vonnegut's report on Mozambique, published in *Parade* magazine, January 7. The report is the journalistic centerpiece of his next "autobiographical collage," the assembling of which becomes a yearlong project. In May, gives anti-war speech in the form of an eye-witness account of the firebombing of Dresden at the National Air and Space Museum, Washington, D.C. Wartime buddy Bernard V. O'Hare, a longtime district attorney in Northampton County, Pennsylvania, dies, June 8. *Hocus Pocus* published by Putnam, September, to good reviews. It is on the *New York Times* fiction list for seven weeks, peaking at number four.

1991      Vonnegut and Krementz start divorce proceedings, and Vonnegut spends time at house in Sagaponack. *Fates Worse Than Death: An Autobiographical Collage of the 1980s* published by Putnam, September. The title piece is a sermon on humility, delivered at the Cathedral of St. John the Divine on May 23, 1982. Vonnegut accepts a commission from the New York Philomusica Ensemble for a new libretto to *L'Histoire du Soldat* (1918), Stravinsky's musical setting of a Russian fairy tale of World War I. Vonnegut bases his text on the case of Private Edward Donald Slovik, who, in 1945, became the first American soldier executed for desertion since the Civil War.

1992      Vonnegut and Krementz drop divorce proceedings. Named Humanist of the Year by the American Humanist Association, and accepts invitation to serve as Honorary President of the association until his death. ("We humanists try to behave as decently, as fairly, and as honorably as we can without any expectation of rewards or punishments in an afterlife," he says in his remarks of acceptance. "The Creator of the Universe has been to us unknowable so far. We serve as best we can the only abstraction with which we have some understanding, which is 'Community.'") Begins writing a new novel, which he claims will be his last.

1993      Sam Schacht, formerly of the Steppenwolf Theater Company, directs *Make Up Your Mind* in a limited Off-Broadway run at the New Group Theater, Forty-second Street, April 20–May 5. On May 6 the Philomusica Ensemble gives the world premiere of *L'Histoire du Soldat/An American Soldier's Tale* at Alice Tully Hall, Lincoln Center. Vonnegut approached by a former GE colleague, now a fundraising consultant in Lexington, Kentucky, to do a benefit reading for his client Midway College. Collaborates with Joe Petro III, an area printmaker, on a collectible limited-edition poster for the November 1st event. Delighted with Petro's result—a hand-pulled silkscreen print adapted from a felt-tip self-portrait—Vonnegut visits the thirty-seven-year-old artist in his Lexington studio. The two soon form a partnership, Origami Express, to produce signed and numbered limited-edition prints adapted from Vonnegut's drawings and calligraphy. This enduring collaboration solves most of Vonnegut's problems with technique, and helps him to become the graphic artist he has longed to be. (In 2004, after producing more than two hundred discrete Origami editions, Vonnegut will write: "One of the best things that ever happened to me, a one-in-a-billion opportunity to enjoy myself in perfect innocence, was my meeting Joe.")

1994    Sam Lawrence dies, January 5, at age sixty-seven. "That anything I have written is in print today is due to the efforts of one publisher," Vonnegut writes in tribute. "When [in 1966] I was broke and completely out of print, Sam bought rights to my books, for peanuts, from publishers who had given up on me. [He] thrust my books back into the myopic public eye and made my reputation." Invited by Daniel Simon, publisher-editor of the newly founded Seven Stories Press, to write an introduction to Nelson Algren's 1942 novel *Never Come Morning*. Struck by Simon's commitment to Algren's work and to publishing books on human rights, social justice, and progressive politics, he becomes an advisory editor to the small independent press.

1995    At the end of the year completes a draft of the novel *Timequake*, a fantasy on the subject of free will concerning "a sudden glitch in the space-time continuum" that, occurring on the eve of the millennium, forces mankind to relive, day by day and mistake by mistake, the entire 1990s. He is unhappy with the book and, to the dismay of Putnam, scraps it and begins again from scratch.

1996    On November 1 *Mother Night*, directed by Keith Gordon from a screenplay by Vonnegut's filmmaker friend Robert B.

Weide, released by Fine Line Features. Vonnegut finds the script "too faithful to the novel" but admires the performance of leading man Nick Nolte. In December completes a second version of *Timequake*—a fictional-autobiographical "stew" made up of excerpts from the earlier *Timequake*, humorous meditations on the creative process, and laments for the passing of the America of his youth.

1997    Brother, Bernard, dies, April 25, at age eighty-three; Vonnegut will write his obituary for year-end issue of *The New York Times Magazine*. *Timequake* published by Putnam, September, to admiring and elegiac reviews. It is on the *New York Times* fiction list for five weeks, peaking at number seven. Vonnegut sells the greater part of his personal and professional papers, including the various drafts of his fourteen published novels, to Lilly Library, Indiana University.

1998    With the news and features staff of WNYC-FM, develops a series of twenty-odd ninety-second radio skits, each a satirical "report on the Afterlife" in which Vonnegut, in a "controlled near-death state" chemically induced by Dr. Jack Kevorkian, interviews Sir Isaac Newton, Mary Shelley, Eugene V. Debs, or some other resident of Paradise. (The best of the skits are revised, expanded, and collected in an eighty-page book, *God Bless You, Dr. Kevorkian*, published in April 1999 by Seven Stories Press.) In October again visits Dresden and the slaughterhouse in which he survived the firebombing of 1945.

1999    Peter J. Reed, of the University of Minnesota, gathers the twenty-three short stories published in magazines in the 1950s and 1960s that did not appear in *Welcome to the Monkey House*, writes a critical preface to the collection, and asks Vonnegut for permission to publish. Vonnegut revises a couple of the less successful stories and writes an autobiographical introduction and "coda" to the volume. *Bagombo Snuff Box: Uncollected Short Fiction* published by Putnam, September, to respectful reviews and mild sales.

2000    On the evening of January 31 Vonnegut is hospitalized for smoke inhalation after successfully containing a fire in the third-floor office of his New York townhouse caused by a smoldering Pall Mall in an overturned ashtray. Pulled from the room by Lily and a neighbor, he lies unconscious for two days in Presbyterian Hospital and is dismissed after three weeks' recuperation. At the suggestion of his daughter Nanny, moves to a studio apartment near her home in Northampton, Massachusetts, where she and her family nurse him back to health. In spring invited by local Smith College to join the English faculty as writer-in-residence for the academic year 2000–01. Works with a handful of student fiction-writers and gives occasional public lectures and readings at the many college campuses throughout Western Massachusetts.

2001 In May begins writing a novel, each chapter a monologue by a famous middle-aged standup comedian who entertains America during the final weeks of mankind. Is shocked and creatively paralyzed by the events of September 11, and sets novel aside for more than a year.

2002 In response to threats posed to the First Amendment by the USA Patriot Act of 2001, lends his celebrity to public-service advertisements for the ACLU, stating "I am an American who knows the importance of being able to read and express any thought without fear." Gives Lilly Library drafts of his early short stories and the very few other literary manuscripts that survived the New York house fire. Writes foreword to the Seven Stories Press reissue of son Mark's *Eden Express*. In fall resumes work on novel, now titled "If God Were Alive Today," which develops as a topical satire on the Bush administration.

2003 In January is interviewed about the coming war in Iraq by Joel Bleifuss, editor of *In These Times*, a biweekly nonprofit news magazine headquartered in Chicago. Discovers easy rapport with Bleifuss, whose politics are "Midwestern progressive" in the tradition of Vonnegut's socialist heroes Eugene V. Debs and Powers Hapgood. Soon becomes a regular columnist and honorary senior editor at *In These Times*, contributing political opinion, personal essays, humor pieces, and drawings. Magazine column cannibalizes material developed for "If God Were Alive Today" and becomes the chief literary project of his remaining years.

2005 In October, *A Man Without a Country*, a collection of columns from *In These Times*, published by Seven Stories Press. A surprise bestseller, it is on the *New York Times* nonfiction list for six weeks, peaking at number nine.

2006        In June says to an interviewer: "Everything I've done is
            in print. I have fulfilled my destiny, such as it is, and have
            nothing more to say. So now I'm writing only little things —
            one line here, two lines there, sometimes a poem. And I do
            art. . . . I have reached what Nietzsche called 'the mel-
            ancholia of everything completed.'"

2007        In mid-March, falls from the steps of his townhouse on
            East Forty-eighth Street and hits his head on the pave-
            ment. Despite aggressive medical treatment, he never re-
            gains consciousness. Dies at Mount Sinai Hospital on the
            evening of April 11, at age eighty-four.

# Note on the Texts

This volume collects the four novels that Kurt Vonnegut published from 1976 to 1985: *Slapstick* (1976), *Jailbird* (1979), *Deadeye Dick* (1982), and *Galápagos* (1985). It also presents, in an appendix, a selection of nine short works of nonfiction that Vonnegut wrote from 1976 to 1990 that are thematically related to these four novels.

*Slapstick* was Vonnegut's eighth novel, published when the author was fifty-three. It was the first book that he wrote at 228 East Forty-eighth Street, New York City, the Turtle Bay townhouse that he had purchased in the fall of 1973 and that was his principal residence for the rest of his life. Conceived shortly after the publication of his previous novel, *Breakfast of Champions* (1973), *Slapstick* was drafted, under the working title "The Relatives," between the fall of 1974 and Christmas 1975. Vonnegut delivered the finished manuscript to his New York publisher, Seymour "Sam" Lawrence, in March 1976, and the novel was published, in hardcover, by Delacorte Press/Seymour Lawrence on October 1, 1976. (A substantial pre-publication excerpt had appeared in *Playboy*, September 1976, under the title "Slapstick, or Lonesome No More! The Strange Memoirs of the Final American President.") According to Vonnegut's bibliographers Asa B. Pieratt Jr. and Jerome Klinkowitz, the first printing was 85,000 copies. Two hundred fifty copies of the first printing were specially bound, autographed by Vonnegut, and sold by Delacorte as a slipcased "limited first edition." A British trade edition, offset from the Delacorte pages, was published in November 1976 by Jonathan Cape Ltd, London. In addition, in the fall of 1976 the Franklin Library, of Franklin Center, Pennsylvania, privately printed a specially designed "deluxe" edition of *Slapstick* for members of its Signed First Editions Society. Vonnegut did not revise the novel after its first printing, and the text of the 1976 Delacorte Press/Seymour Lawrence edition is used here. The drawings reproduced on pages 61, 107, 112, 115, and 133 are by the author.

*Jailbird* was drafted, under the working titles "Unacceptable Air" and "Mary Kathleen O'Looney," from the fall of 1976 to late 1978. Vonnegut delivered the finished manuscript to Sam Lawrence in February 1979, and the novel was published, in hardcover, by Delacorte Press/Seymour Lawrence on September 8, 1979. According to Pieratt and Klinkowitz, the first printing was 90,700 copies. Five hundred copies of the first printing were specially bound, autographed by Vonnegut, and sold by Delacorte as a slipcased "limited first edition." A

Book-of-the-Month Club edition was published simultaneously with the first Delacorte printing. (*Jailbird* and Philip Roth's *The Ghost Writer* were the club's dual Main Selection for September 1979.) A British trade edition, offset from the Delacorte pages, was published in October 1979 by Jonathan Cape. In addition, in the fall of 1979 the Franklin Library privately printed a specially designed "deluxe" edition of *Jailbird* for members of its Signed First Editions Society. Vonnegut did not revise the novel after its first printing, and the text of the 1979 Delacorte Press/Seymour Lawrence edition is used here.

*Deadeye Dick* was drafted, under the working title "Katmandu," in 1980–81. Vonnegut delivered the finished manuscript to Sam Lawrence in March 1982, and the novel was published, in hardcover, by Delacorte Press/Seymour Lawrence on October 19, 1982. According to Pieratt and Klinkowitz, the first printing was 100,000 copies. Three hundred copies of the first printing were specially bound, autographed by Vonnegut, and sold by Delacorte as a slipcased "limited first edition." Both a Literary Guild hardcover edition and a Quality Paperback Book Club edition were published simultaneously with the first Delacorte printing. A British trade edition, offset from the Delacorte pages, was published in February 1983 by Jonathan Cape. Vonnegut did not revise the novel after its first printing, and the text of the 1982 Delacorte Press/Seymour Lawrence edition is used here.

*Galápagos* was drafted in 1983–84, mainly in a two-room studio at 5 MacDougal Alley, in Greenwich Village, that Vonnegut rented for solitude's sake. Vonnegut delivered the finished manuscript to Sam Lawrence in February 1985, and the novel was published, in hardcover, by Delacorte Press/Seymour Lawrence on October 4, 1985. (A brief pre-publication excerpt had appeared in *Esquire*, August 1985, under the title "A Dream of the Future (Not Excluding Lobsters).") According to *Publishers Weekly*, the first printing was 85,000 copies. Both a Literary Guild hardcover edition and a Science Fiction Book Club hardcover edition were published simultaneously with the first Delacorte printing. A British trade edition, offset from the Delacorte pages, was published in the fall of 1985 by Jonathan Cape. In addition, in the fall of 1985 the Franklin Library privately printed a specially designed "deluxe" edition of *Jailbird* for members of its Signed First Editions Society. Vonnegut did not revise the novel after its first printing, and the text of the 1985 Delacorte Press/Seymour Lawrence edition is used here.

The publication history of the short nonfiction pieces collected in the Appendix is as follows:

"A 'Special Message' to readers of the Franklin Library's signed first edition of 'Slapstick'" originally appeared in the Franklin Library's deluxe edition of *Slapstick* (1976), the source of the text used here.

"Address to the American Psychiatric Association, Philadelphia, October 5, 1988" was first printed as part of Chapter 2 of Vonnegut's nonfiction collection *Fates Worse Than Death: An Autobiographical Collage of the 1980s*, published by G. P. Putnam's Sons in 1991, the source of the text used here.

"A 'Special Message' to readers of the Franklin Library's signed first edition of 'Jailbird'" originally appeared in the Franklin Library's deluxe edition of *Jailbird* (1979), the source of the text used here.

The first of the "Four excerpts from 'Fates Worse Than Death'" (beginning "The free-speech provisions of the First Amendment . . .") was first printed as part of Chapter 8 of *Fates Worse Than Death: An Autobiographical Collage of the 1980s,* published by G. P. Putnam's Sons in 1991, the source of the text used here.

The second of the "Four excerpts from 'Fates Worse Than Death'" (beginning "When the American ad agency for Volkswagen . . .") originally appeared, in slightly different form, in *Time* magazine, February 8, 1988, as the first in a series of "Letters to the Next Generation" commissioned as advertorials by Volkswagen of America, Inc. It was reprinted as part of Chapter 11 of *Fates Worse Than Death: An Autobiographical Collage of the 1980s*, published by G. P. Putnam's Sons in 1991, the source of the text used here.

The third of the "Four excerpts from 'Fates Worse Than Death'" (beginning "As though I hadn't already given the world more than enough reasons to feel miserable . . .") originally appeared, in somewhat different form, as "Light at the End of the Tunnel?," an essay published in *Lear's* magazine, November/December 1988. It was reprinted as part of Chapter 11 of *Fates Worse Than Death: An Autobiographical Collage of the 1980s*, published by G. P. Putnam's Sons in 1991, the source of the text used here.

The last of the "Four excerpts from 'Fates Worse Than Death'" (beginning "'MIT has played an important part in the history of my branch of the Vonnegut family . . .") is an excerpt from a speech delivered to the students and faculty of the Massachusetts Institute of Technology, Cambridge, Massachusetts, on October 22, 1988. It was first printed as the whole of Chapter 12 of *Fates Worse Than Death: An Autobiographical Collage of the 1980s*, published by G. P. Putnam's Sons in 1991, the source of the text used here.

"Lecture at the Cathedral of St. John the Divine, New York, May 23, 1982" originally appeared, in somewhat different form, as *Fates worse than Death*, a sixteen-page saddle-stitched pamphlet printed by Spokesman Books, the publishing division of the Bertrand Russell Peace Foundation Ltd., Nottingham, UK, in June 1982. It was reprinted as part of Chapter 15 of *Fates Worse Than Death: An*

*Autobiographical Collage of the 1980s*, published by G. P. Putnam's Sons in 1991, the source of the text used here.

"A 'Special Message' to readers of the Franklin Library's signed first edition of 'Galápagos'" originally appeared in the Franklin Library's deluxe edition of *Galápagos* (1985), the source of the text used here.

This volume presents the texts of the original printings chosen for inclusion, but does not attempt to reproduce nontextual features of their typographical design. The texts are presented without change, except for the correction of typographical errors. Spelling, punctuation, and capitalization are not altered, even when inconsistent or irregular. The following is a list of typographical errors corrected, cited by page and line number: 28.21, DuPonts,; 72.5, others'; 72.6, others'; 109.26, hypen; 136.11, parent's; 231.14, us that the; 258.29, Pride's; 322.38, penalities; 326.38, Haywood; 405.27, house a; 421.12–13, could have not; 458.2, I give; 459.24, carrying, Felix's; 468.28, become; 484.6, sec-before; 490.20, premiers; 553.28, certain; 571.34, Island; 594.2, Islands; 599.31, MacIntosh's; 601.8, chartered schooner; 606.17, translated them; 607.19, Treveranus; 645.17, not travel; 667.12, Island; 686.30, feel; 787.18, Andreassen.

# Notes

In the notes below, the reference numbers denote page and line of this volume (line counts include headings but not section breaks). No note is made for material included in standard desk-reference books. Biblical quotations are keyed to the King James Version. Quotations from Shakespeare are keyed to *The Riverside Shakespeare*, edited by G. Blakemore Evans (Boston: Houghton Mifflin, 1974). For reference to other studies, and for further biographical background than is contained in the Chronology, see William Rodney Allen, editor, *Conversations with Kurt Vonnegut* (Jackson: University Press of Mississippi, 1988); Asa B. Pieratt Jr., Julie Huffman-Klinkowitz, and Jerome Klinkowitz, *Kurt Vonnegut: A Comprehensive Bibliography* (Hamden, Conn.: Archon Books, 1987); Loree Rackstraw, *Love as Always, Kurt: Vonnegut as I Knew Him* (Cambridge, Mass.: Da Capo Press, 2009); John G. Rauch, "An Account of the Ancestry of Kurt Vonnegut, Jr., by an Ancient Friend of the Family," in *Summary* 1:2 (1971); Peter J. Reed and Marc Leeds, editors, *The Vonnegut Chronicles: Interviews and Essays* (Westport, Conn.: Greenwood Press, 1996); Charles J. Shields, *And So It Goes: Kurt Vonnegut: A Life* (New York: Henry Holt and Co., 2011); and Dan Wakefield, editor, *Kurt Vonnegut: Letters* (New York: Delacorte, 2012). See also the major collections of Vonnegut's nonfiction prose: *Wampeters, Foma & Granfalloons (Opinions)* (New York: Delacorte/Seymour Lawrence, 1974); *Palm Sunday: An Autobiographical Collage* (New York: Delacorte/Seymour Lawrence, 1981); *Fates Worse Than Death: An Autobiographical Collage of the 1980s* (New York: Putnam, 1991); and *A Man Without a Country* (New York: Seven Stories Press, 2005). For notes on Vonnegut's recurring fictional persons, places, and things, see Marc Leeds, *The Vonnegut Encyclopedia: An Authorized Compendium* (Westport, Conn.: Greenwood Press, 1994).

## SLAPSTICK

2.2    Arthur Stanley Jefferson and Norvell Hardy]    Birth names of the English music-hall performer Stan Laurel (1890–1965) and the American comic actor Oliver Hardy (1892–1957), who in 1926, through the agency of Hollywood producer Hal Roach, became the comedy team Laurel and Hardy, stars of some seventy film shorts and twenty-three feature films over the next two decades.

3.1     *"Call me but love . . . baptiz'd . . ."*]  *Romeo and Juliet*, II.ii.50.

8.16    Lake Maxinkuckee]  Two-thousand-acre lake in north-central Indiana.

11.3    "Turtle Bay"]  Neighborhood in Manhattan's Midtown East, extending between Forty-second and Fifty-third streets, and between Lexington Avenue and the East River. Its landmarks include the Chrysler Building and the United Nations Headquarters.

11.27–28    a couple of nice old Andy Gumps]  In the daily comic strip *The Gumps* (1917–59), created by the American cartoonist Sidney Smith (1877–1935), hapless Andy, head of the Gump family, was a tall, long-limbed "chinless wonder" with a push-broom mustache.

15.5    a joke by Mark Twain]  See Chapter IX of *A Tramp Abroad* (1880), in which the author attends a German production of Wagner's *Lohengrin*, during the choruses of which, he reports, "I lived over again all that I had suffered the time the orphan asylum burned down."

15.13    Renata Adler]  American journalist and fiction writer (b. 1938) who, at the time of the publication of *Slapstick*, was a staff writer at *The New Yorker* and the author of the best-selling novel *Speedboat* (1976).

15.15    Max Wilkinson]  Wilkinson (1904–1985), a partner, with Kenneth Littauer (1894–1968), in the Littauer & Wilkinson Literary Agency, was Vonnegut's agent from 1950 until 1977.

15.23    *Tosca*]  Italian opera (1900) by Giacomo Puccini (1858–1924). The first act is set in the basilica of Sant'Andrea della Valle, on the Piazza Vidoni, in Rome.

19.17    Americana Hotel]  Eighteen-hundred-room hotel on Seventh Avenue between Fifty-second and Fifty-third streets, built in 1962 by the Loews Hotel chain. In 1979 it was sold to the Sheraton Corporation and renamed the Sheraton New York.

24.2    Idiot's Delight]  Card game for one player, also known as Solitaire, or Patience.

35.10    Culver Military Academy]  Founded 1894, in Culver, Indiana, near Lake Maxinkuckee.

43.13    F.A.O. Schwarz]  "Carriage trade" retailer of children's toys and a New York City institution since 1870.

43.29    Parker House rolls]  Buttery, crusty dinner rolls, popularized by Boston's Parker House Hotel in the 1870s.

48.28     Great Stone Face] Natural rock formation on Mount
Cannon, in the White Mountains, near Franconia, New Hampshire,
that took the distinctive shape of a human profile. Widely called "The
Old Man of the Mountain," the formation was a tourist attraction and
unofficial state symbol from the early 1800s until its collapse, due to
erosion, on May 3, 2003.

55.15–16     intersection of Broadway and Forty-second Street] Times
Square.

63.3–4     "One sacred memory . . . is perhaps the best education."]   See the epilogue of *The Brothers Karamazov* (1880; trans.
Constance Garnett, 1912), in which Alyosha Karamazov tells the young
people gathered at their friend Ilyusha's funeral that "there is nothing
higher and stronger and more wholesome and good for life in the future than some good memory . . . People talk to you a great deal about
your education, but some good, sacred memory, preserved from childhood, is perhaps the best education."

73.12–13     "Angkor Wat."]   Twelfth-century C.E. temple among the
ruins at Angkor, the capital city of the Khmer empire, which flourished
in northeast Cambodia from the ninth to the twelfth century.

78.14     the era of Chester Alan Arthur]   Arthur (1829–1886) was the
twenty-first president of the United States (1881–85).

94.1–2     monument to the first use of anaesthetics]   The so-called
Ether Monument, erected in 1867 near the northwest corner of the
Boston Public Garden, is topped by a statue of a bearded Moorish
doctor in a robe and a turban holding an ether-soaked cloth to the face
of a swooning youth. A legend inscribed on the architectural base of
the statue reads: "To commemorate that the inhaling of ether causes
insensibility to pain. First proved to the world at the Mass. General
Hospital in Boston, October A.D. MDCCCXLVI."

94.23–30     "O! how thy worth . . . which thou deserv'st alone."]
From Shakespeare's Sonnet 39.

96.28     "'If you can do no good . . . Hippocrates.'"]   See Hippocrates (c. 460–c. 370 B.C.E.), in his *Epidemics* (c. 400 B.C.E.) I.xi:
"ἀσκέειν, περὶ τὰ νουσήματα, δύο, ὠφελέειν, ἢ μὴ βλάπτειν" ("The physician must have two special objects in view with regard to disease,
namely, to do good or to do no harm").

99.10     Clydesdale . . . "Budweiser"]   Since 1933, a hitch of Clydes-
dales drawing a beer wagon has been a trademark of Anheuser-Busch's
Budweiser brand.

100.29      Fu Manchu]    Fictional criminal mastermind, created in 1913 by the British writer Sax Rohmer (1883–1959), who figured into a long-running series of pulp stories and novels as well as into films, radio series, and comic strips. He was routinely described by his creator as "the Yellow Peril incarnate."

104.14–19      Eli Lilly Company . . . "tri-benzo-Deportamil."]    Founded in Indianapolis in 1876, Eli Lilly and Company is a global pharmaceutical manufacturer and distributor. The highly addictive sedative tri-benzo-Deportamil, however, is a Vonnegut invention.

111.19      "THE PAST IS PROLOGUE"]    This inscription, on the Pennsylvania Avenue side of the National Archives Building, actually reads "What Is Past Is Prologue," a variation on a line from Shakespeare's *The Tempest* ("What's past is prologue," II.i.253).

121.17–18      another club . . . on the very same premises]    The Century Association, at 7 West Forty-third Street, Manhattan, founded in 1847 as a club for "authors, artists, and amateurs of letters and the fine arts."

131.11      "I thought he was Newton McCoy,"]    See note below.

131.20–22      one of the few genuine extended families . . . since 1882]    During much of the late nineteenth century, the Hatfield family of West Virginia carried on a legendary feud with the McCoy family of eastern Kentucky across the Tug Fork of the Big Sandy River.

136.8–9      Century Association]    See note 121.17–18.

136.15      "Ol' Man River"]    Song by Jerome Kern, with lyrics by Oscar Hammerstein II, from the Broadway musical *Show Boat* (1927).

138.23–25      "'Take no thought . . . the evil thereof.'"]    Cf. Matthew 6:34.

144.11      Henry Martyn Robert]    Lieutenant H. M. Robert (1837–1923) of the U.S. Army published the first edition of his *Rules of Order* in 1876.

150.15–16      "Those who fail to learn from history are condemned to repeat it,"]    Cf. the Spanish-American philosopher George Santayana (1863–1952), in *Reason in Common Sense* (1905): "Those who cannot remember the past are condemned to repeat it."

## JAILBIRD

164.1      *Benjamin D. Hitz*]    Benjamin Dickson Hitz Jr. (1922–2009) and Vonnegut were classmates at Shortridge High School, Indianapolis, and lifelong correspondents.

165.1–8    Help the weak ones . . . NICOLA SACCO]    From a letter
addressed to "My dear Son and Companion," written in Charlestown
State Prison and dated August 18, 1927. It was published in *The Letters of
Sacco and Vanzetti*, edited by Marion Denman Frankfurter and Gardner
Jackson (New York: Viking, 1928), a volume consisting of the letters
that Nicola Sacco and Bartolomeo Vanzetti wrote during their years of
imprisonment in Boston-area jails (1920–27), transcripts of their court
testimony, and the editors' thirty-page account of the Sacco-Vanzetti
case. Vonnegut's own account of the case, based closely on that of Frankfurter and Jackson, can be found on pages 319–27 of the present volume.

167.2    KILGORE TROUT is back again.]    Vonnegut's fictional character Kilgore Trout previously appeared in the novels *God Bless You, Mr.
Rosewater* (1965), *Slaughterhouse-Five* (1969), and *Breakfast of Champions*
(1973).

167.8    John Dillinger]    Dillinger (1903–1934) and his gang robbed
a dozen banks in the Upper Midwest from June 1933 to June 1934. In
January 1934, he was arrested in Tucson, Arizona, and was later extra-
dited to Lake County Jail, Crown Point, Indiana. He escaped his jailors
on March 3, 1934, under uncertain circumstances, allegedly by threatening them with a pistol or a pistol-shaped object. On the evening of July
22, 1934, Dillinger was shot to death by three FBI agents upon leaving
the Biograph movie theater on Chicago's North Side.

168.8–9    Stegemeier's Restaurant in downtown Indianapo-
lis]    Stegemeier Bros., advertised as "The Most Popular Eating Place
in the City," offered a tavern, table service, and an all-day buffet from
the 1890s to the early 1950s.

168.35    CIO]    Congress of Industrial Organizations, a federation
of American trade unions founded in 1935. In 1955 it merged with its
older rival, the American Federation of Labor (founded in 1886), to
form the AFL-CIO.

168.35    His wife Mary]    Powers Hapgood married Mary A. Dono-
van (1886–1973) in 1927. A prominent writer, activist, and politician,
she was the Socialist Party candidate for governor of Indiana in 1940.

169.2    Norman Thomas]    Thomas (1884–1968) was a Presbyterian
minister, a prolific author, and a six-time Socialist Party candidate for
the presidency of the United States (1928–48).

169.12    Against stupidity even the gods contend in vain]    Cf. Friedrich Schiller (1759–1805), in his romantic tragedy *The Maid of Orleans*
(*Die Jungfrau von Orleans*, 1801): "*Mit der Dummheit kämpfen Götter
selbst vergebens.*"

169.16–17    Nietzsche's reply:]   Cf. Friedrich Nietzsche (1844–1900), in his philosophical work *The Antichrist* (*Der Antichrist*, 1895): "*Gegen die Langeweile kämpfen Götter selbst vergebens.*"

174.7    John L. Lewis's United Mine Workers]   Lewis (1880–1969) joined the United Mine Workers of America in 1906, and was elected the union's president in 1919. In 1938 he became the first elected president of the CIO (see note 168.35).

174.30    Sermon on the Mount]   See Matthew 5–7.

175.9–10    "Roy M. Cohn"]   Prominent lawyer (1927–1986) who, in 1951, as an assistant United States Attorney, participated in the prosecution of Julius and Ethel Rosenberg for espionage and, three years later, served as chief counsel to the Senate's Permanent Subcommittee on Investigations, assisting its chairman, Joseph R. McCarthy (R-Wis.), in staging sensational hearings into alleged communist infiltration of the U.S. Army.

176.4–5    day on which the atomic bomb was dropped on Hiroshima]   August 6, 1945.

191.18    "Watergate."]   See note 200.33–34.

197.19    "Ruben, Ruben."]   Traditional English children's song, sometimes called "Reuben and Rachel": "Reuben, Reuben, I've been thinking / What a queer world this would be / If the men were all transported / far beyond the Northern Sea."

198.16–22    *Sally in the garden . . . The cheeks of her ass went—*]   Variant on the traditional sea shanty "The Hog-Eyed Man," sung to the tune of "Reuben, Reuben" (see note above) and popular among the British and American troops during World War II.

199.16    *Crawdaddy*]   Monthly magazine, founded in 1966 by editor-critic Paul S. Williams (1948–2013), that chronicled the rock music scene through 1979.

199.22    Young Communist League]   Youth organization of the Communist Party USA.

199.26    nonaggression pact]   On August 23, 1939, shortly before its invasion of Poland, Nazi Germany signed a ten-year nonaggression pact with the Soviet Union. The agreement contained a secret protocol that divided Poland and the Baltic states into German and Soviet spheres of influence.

200.33–34    President's special burglars]   Vonnegut's "yeller and stomper" is E. Howard Hunt (1918–2007), a former CIA officer, and his "listener" G. Gordon Liddy (b. 1930), a former FBI agent who served as special counsel to the Committee to Re-Elect President Nixon in 1972. Hunt and Liddy planned and led the break-ins and wiretapping of the Democratic National Committee headquarters at the Watergate office complex in Washington, D.C. The apprehension of five burglars at the Watergate on the evening of June 17, 1972, precipitated the various political scandals collectively known as "Watergate," which ended in Nixon's resignation of the presidency on August 9, 1974, and the conviction of many of his closest aides. For their roles in Watergate, Hunt served thirty-three months in prison and Liddy fifty-two.

203.32    War Crimes Trials] Series of military tribunals held in Nuremberg, Germany, in 1945–46, in which lawyers for the Allied powers prosecuted Nazi leaders for crimes against humanity during World War II.

204.2    Heinrich Himmler] Himmler (1900–1945) became head of the SS (Protection Detachment) in 1929. Originally Hitler's Nazi party bodyguard, the SS under Himmler became the main instrument of state terror and genocide in the Third Reich, gaining control over the police, the secret police, and the concentration camps, and forming its own military force, known after 1940 as the Waffen (Armed) SS. Himmler committed suicide in British custody on May 23, 1945.

205.20    Siegfried Line] Allied name for the four-hundred-mile line of defensive fortifications built by Nazi Germany along its western frontier.

206.10–17    *How should I . . . At his heels a stone—*] See *Hamlet* IV.v.23–26, 29–32.

207.6–7    Hermann Göring] Göring (1893–1946), a World War I fighter ace, joined the Nazi party in 1922 and was commander of the Luftwaffe (German air force), 1935–45. He was designated as Hitler's successor in 1934, but was dismissed from all of his posts in April 1945 after Hitler learned that he was attempting to arrange a cease-fire. The highest-ranking Nazi to be tried at Nuremberg, he committed suicide by potassium cyanide on October 15, 1946, the night before his scheduled death by hanging.

207.26    *Wehrmacht*] The armed forces of Nazi Germany, 1935–45.

208.11–12    *chevalier* in the Légion d'honneur] The Legion of Honor is the premier French order of merit, established by Napoleon Bonaparte in 1802 to acknowledge outstanding military and civil service. Of the order's five levels, *chevalier* (or knight) is the lowest; its decoration is a five-pointed Maltese star affixed to a narrow solid red ribbon. Except on the day of presentation or on a state occasion, only the ribbon is worn in public, usually on the left breast.

209.10–11      *Männleinlaufen . . . Frauenkirche*]   The *Männleinlaufen* ("The running of the little men") is a mechanical clock with automata, built in 1506 for the façade of Nuremberg's *Frauenkirche* ("Church of Our Lady"), consecrated 1358. At noon daily, while the clock strikes twelve, the clockwork pageant that Vonnegut describes is performed for spectators gathered in the Nuremberg market square, onto which the church faces. The figures representing the seven electors circle the seated Charles IV three times, in an operation that takes more than four minutes to complete.

210.10      WAC]   Member of the Women's Army Corps, the women's branch of the U.S. Army, 1942–78.

210.17–18      drawing by Albrecht Dürer]   *"Betende Hände"* ("Praying Hands," c. 1508), drawing in black ink, gray wash, and opaque white on blue paper, now in the collection of the Albertina Museum, Vienna.

212.36–37      shooting to death of four antiwar protesters]   On May 4, 1970.

213.8      Spiro T. Agnew]   Agnew (1918–1996), the running mate of Richard Nixon in 1968, was the thirty-ninth vice president of the United States (1969–73). He resigned his office on October 10, 1973, after pleading no contest to tax evasion charges connected with bribes he had accepted while serving as governor of Maryland in 1967–69.

213.14      Henry Kissinger]   German-born American statesman and academic (b. 1923) who was National Security Advisor, 1969–75, and Secretary of State, 1973–77, to Presidents Nixon and Ford.

213.16      Richard M. Helms]   American intelligence officer (1913–2002) who served as director of the CIA from 1966 to 1973.

213.17–19      H. R. Haldeman and John D. Ehrlichman and Charles W. Colson and John N. Mitchell]   Haldeman (1926–1993) was White House Chief of Staff to President Nixon, 1969–73; Ehrlichman (1925–1999), Assistant to the President for Domestic Affairs, 1969–73; Colson (1931–2012), Special Counsel to the President, 1969–73; and Mitchell (1913–1988), Attorney General of the United States, 1969–72, and director of Nixon's 1968 and 1972 election campaigns. All four were indicted by a grand jury on March 1, 1974, for their roles in covering up the Watergate break-in. Haldeman, Ehrlichman, and Mitchell were convicted and spent eighteen to nineteen months in prison. Colson pled guilty to an obstruction-of-justice charge in connection with the failed prosecution of Daniel Ellsberg, who had given a secret government history of the Vietnam War (the "Pentagon Papers") to the press.

215.13    housemaid's knee]  Prepatellar bursitis, inflammation of the knee brought on by trauma or by frequent kneeling.

218.1–2    "Depart from me . . . angels."]  See Matthew 25:41.

218.30    Edith Piaf]  French *chanteuse* and cabaret performer (1915–1963), internationally known as "The Little Sparrow."

222.24    "Gilbert and Sullivan"]  Librettist W. S. Gilbert (1836–1911) and composer Arthur Sullivan (1842–1900), collaborators on fourteen comic operas (*H.M.S. Pinafore*, *The Pirates of Penzance*, *The Mikado*, etc.) first staged in London in 1871–96.

222.25    "Laurel and Hardy"]  See note 2.2.

222.26–27    "Leopold and Loeb."]  Nathan Leopold (1904–1971) and Richard Loeb (1905–1936) were precocious nineteen-year-old law students at the University of Chicago who, in 1924, kidnapped and murdered a fourteen-year-old acquaintance, Bobby Franks, in what they later described as an intellectual exercise in crime. The confessed murderers were defended by the celebrated trial attorney Clarence Darrow, who successfully argued for life imprisonment instead of execution.

226.5    Caryl Chessman]  In July 1948, Chessman (1921–1960), a drifter and petty criminal, was arrested in Los Angeles as the prime suspect in a string of apparently related robberies, rapes, and kidnappings. He forcefully but unsuccessfully defended himself at trial, and his case became a cause célèbre. During his twelve years on Death Row, he published four books, the first of which, *Cell 2455, Death Row: A Condemned Man's Own Story* (1954), was a bestseller. After eight stays of execution, he was put to death by cyanide gas in San Quentin State Prison on May 2, 1960.

229.30    "Non, Je ne Regrette Rien."]  Song (1956) by Charles Dumont, with lyrics by Michel Vaucaire, popularized by Edith Piaf (see note 218.30).

238.37    Down Home Records]  Independent label of the early 1950s, later a subsidiary of Verve Records, devoted mainly to LP reissues of early jazz recordings.

239.10    Maurice Chevalier]  Charming, elegant Parisian singer and entertainer (1888–1972) who, on the American stage, spoke English with a heavy French accent and usually wore a black tuxedo, a boutonniere, and a straw boater.

245.24 Mutt and Jeff] Pioneering daily comic strip (1907–82), created by Harry "Bud" Fisher (1885–1954) for the *San Francisco Chronicle*.
It was billed as the adventures of "two mismatched tinhorns": Augustus
Mutt, a gangly concocter of get-rich schemes, and his put-upon comic
foil, the small, dapper Jeff.

247.10 F.M.S.A.C.F.] Federal Minimum Security Adult Correctional Facility.

247.33 Waldorf Towers] The Waldorf-Astoria Hotel and Waldorf
Towers, exclusive New York City hotel and residential apartment complex on Park Avenue between Forty-ninth and Fiftieth streets.

249.38 *The Gulag Archipelago*] Three-volume nonfiction study of
the Soviet forced labor camp system, 1918–56, by the Russian novelist,
social critic, and Nobel laureate in literature Aleksandr Solzhenitsyn
(1918–2008). Written from 1958 to 1968, it was published in English
translation in 1974–78 and in the Soviet Union in 1989.

251.7 Fafner] In Richard Wagner's operatic cycle *Der Ring des
Nibelungen* (1848–74), Fafner is a giant who, after winning a fabulous
treasure from Wotan, king of the gods, magically becomes a dragon
that guards the hoard.

258.16 Diamond Jim Brady] James Buchanan "Diamond Jim"
Brady (1856–1917), American businessman, financier, and philanthropist, made his fortune in railroad supplies and stock market speculation
during the Gilded Age. A bachelor, he was known not only for his great
wealth but also for his appetite for food, drink, women, and New York
City nightlife.

258.19 Lillian Russell] American singer and actress (1860–1922)
and longtime companion of Diamond Jim Brady (see note above).

258.34 "Tudor City"] Planned community of apartment buildings
built in the 1920s and '30s in Manhattan's Midtown East, just south of
Turtle Bay. It extends from Forty-third Street to Fortieth Street, and
from Second Avenue to First Avenue.

268.37 George Grosz] German artist (1893–1959) best known for
his satirical drawings and caricatures of the Berlin demimonde in the
1920s.

280.9 Angkor Wat] See note 73.12–13.

281.25 Century Association] See note 121.17–18.

281.37 Hotel Royalton] Small hotel, built 1898, at 44 West Forty-
fourth Street, New York, just off Times Square.

288.14      Henry Morton Stanley and David Livingstone]   Stanley (1841–1904) was a journalist for the *New York Herald* who, in 1869, was sent to Zanzibar to discover the fate of David Livingstone (1813–1873), a renowned Scottish explorer and missionary who, three years earlier, had left for central Africa in search of the source of the Nile River. On November 10, 1871, Stanley found the explorer suffering from dysentery on the banks of Lake Tanganyika and reportedly greeted him with the question "Dr. Livingstone, I presume?" Stanley published *How I Found Livingstone: Travels, Adventures, and Discoveries in Central Africa, Including Four Months' Residence with Dr. Livingstone*, in 1872.

296.20      Cricket lighter]   Disposable plastic cigarette lighter, manufactured in the U.S. by Gillette from 1972 to 1984.

300.9       Luger]   German-made semi-automatic pistol, designed by Georg J. Luger in 1898 and used by the German military from 1904 through 1945.

301.1       *el calabozo*]   Southwestern American slang: jail, dungeon.

306.19      Stradivari's and the Amatis']   Antonio Stradivari (1644–1737) and the family of Nicolò Amati (1596–1684) were master violinmakers of Cremona, Italy.

313.1       *Love Story*]   Romantic feature film (1970) directed by Arthur Hiller from a screenplay by Erich Segal and starring Ryan O'Neal and Ali MacGraw.

313.6       Ray Milland]   Welsh-born American actor (1907–1986) who won an Oscar for his performance as the alcoholic writer Don Birman in Billy Wilder's film *The Lost Weekend* (1945).

313.23      S.S.]   See note 204.2.

313.23      Siege of Leningrad]   The German siege of Leningrad, from September 1941 to January 1944, was the longest of World War II and resulted in the death of approximately one million Soviet civilians from starvation and disease.

313.29      Martin Bormann]   Bormann (1900–1945) served as chief of staff to Rudolf Hess, the deputy leader of the Nazi party, from 1933 to 1941. He became head of the party chancellery in 1941 and grew increasingly powerful by controlling access to Hitler. He disappeared in Berlin in May 1945, and was sentenced to death in absentia by the International Military Tribunal at Nuremberg. Bormann's remains were discovered in Berlin in 1972 and identified by DNA testing in 1998.

858         NOTES

315.5    Adams House]   Undergraduate dormitory at Harvard College, built in 1932.

316.9    Buckeye]   Person from Ohio, the Buckeye State.

316.11–12    yellow-dog unions]   Employee associations, especially those of the 1920s and 1930s, that mimicked the behavior of independent trade unions but were secretly and illegally controlled by the employer.

316.22    "The Spirit of Seventy-six"]   Allusion to the famous oil painting (1875) by the Ohio-born artist Archibald Willard (1836–1918) depicting three citizen-soldiers of the American Revolution, two playing drums and the other the fife. The figure of the fife-player is notable for the large bloody bandage worn on his head like a crown.

319.26–27    "I seen Sacco's wife . . . sorry for the kids,"]   On November 16, 1925, a convict in the Dedham jail, where Sacco was then jailed, passed a note to a prison guard addressed to the editor of the Boston *American* newspaper. The note in its entirety read: "Dear Editor, I hear by confess to being in the shoe company crime at south Braintree on April 15 1920 and that Sacco and Vanzetti were not there. Celestino F. Madeiros." When defense attorney William Thompson asked Madeiros, then serving time for an unrelated murder, why he confessed to a second murder in which he was not a suspect, he replied, "I seen Sacco's wife come up here [to the Dedham jail] with the kids, and I felt sorry for the kids."

319.39–320.1    "Long live anarchy . . . Farewell, Mother,"]   Sacco's last words, as reported in the editors' preface to *The Letters of Sacco and Vanzetti* (see note 165.1–8).

320.10–16    "I wish to tell you . . . what some people are doing to me,"]   Vanzetti's last words, as reported in the editor's preface to *The Letters of Sacco and Vanzetti* (see note 165.1–8).

320.27–31    "In the immigration station . . . American shores."]   From "The Story of a Proletarian Life," an autobiographical essay written in Charlestown State Prison by Bartolomeo Vanzetti, translated from the Italian by Eugene Lyons, and published in Boston in 1923 by the Sacco–Vanzetti Defense Committee.

321.5–8    "Where was I to go? . . . sped by heedless of me."]   From "The Story of a Proletarian Life" (see note above).

322.24    Andrea Salsedo]   Italian-born American anarchist (1881–1920) and printer of the occasional radical pamphlet series *Plain Words*. On February 25, 1920, he was arrested in New York by the U.S. Justice Department's Bureau of Investigation (forerunner of the FBI) and died in a fall from a fourteenth-story window while in their custody eight weeks later, on May 3.

324.9–10     Webster Thayer]    Admitted to the bar in 1882, Thayer (1857–1933) was a judge of the Superior Court of Massachusetts from 1917 until his death at age seventy-five.

324.36     Al Capone]    Alphonse Gabriel "Al" Capone (1899–1947), also known as Scarface, was the leader of a Chicago-based Prohibition-era crime syndicate specializing in smuggling, bootlegging, and prostitution.

325.21–23     "Never in our full life . . . as now we do by accident."]    From Vanzetti's reported statement after receiving his death sentence, on April 9, 1927.

325.39     Robert Grant]    Grant (1852–1940), a graduate of Harvard College and Harvard Law School, was a popular novelist as well as a probate judge. He wrote about serving on the Sacco and Vanzetti review committee in *Fourscore: An Autobiography* (1934).

326.3     A. Lawrence Lowell]    Lowell (1856–1943), a legal scholar, was president of Harvard University from 1909 to 1933 and the principal author of the review committee's report.

326.4–5     Samuel W. Stratton]    Stratton (1861–1931), a former professor of physics and electricity at the University of Illinois and the University of Chicago, was president of the Massachusetts Institute of Technology from 1923 to 1930.

326.9–11     Romain Rolland . . . H. G. Wells]    All but Wells were Nobel laureates.

326.20–22     Two women claiming . . . cutting the baby in two]    See 1 Kings 3:16–28.

326.38     Edna St. Vincent Millay and John Dos Passos and Heywood Broun]    Millay (1892–1950) was a Pulitzer Prize–winning poet and feminist activist; Dos Passos (1896–1970) the author of the *U.S.A.* trilogy (1930–36) and other politically engaged American novels; and Broun (1888–1939) an American sportswriter and political columnist and a prominent spokesman for the U.S. Socialist Party.

327.19–20     DID YOU SEE . . . THE OTHER DAY?]    On April 19, 1927—ten days after Judge Thayer had sentenced Sacco and Vanzetti to death in the electric chair—James P. Richardson, a professor of law at Dartmouth College, wrote an unsolicited letter to Massachusetts governor Alvan T. Fuller. In it Richardson claimed that in the fall of 1924, shortly after Thayer had denied all motions for a new trial for

Sacco and Vanzetti, he had had a personal conversation with Thayer in which it was "very evident" that Thayer regarded the defendants "with a feeling which can only be described as abhorence." According to Richardson, Thayer asked, "Did you see what I did to those anarchist bastards the other day? I guess that will hold them for a while . . . Let them go to the Supreme Court now and see what they can get out of them." It was this letter that inspired Governor Fuller to appoint the committee of Grant, Lowell, and Stratton to review the conduct and fairness of the trial. The committee's appointment was announced on June 1, 1927, and its findings made public nine weeks later, on August 3.

332.25   *The Harvard Lampoon*]   Undergraduate humor monthly of Harvard College, founded 1876.

339.3   Diners Club magazine]   *Signature Magazine* (1953–87), the monthly magazine of Diners Club International, the first members-only credit card company.

340.23   bridge over the Rhine at Remagen]   The Ludendorff Bridge, a railroad bridge at Remagen, Germany, was captured by American troops on March 7, 1945.

342.15   Julie Nixon]   Younger daughter of Richard M. Nixon, born 1948.

346.32–33   "Come into my parlor . . . said the spider to the fly."]   See "The Spider and the Fly" (1829), cautionary tale in verse by the English poet Mary Howitt (1799–1888).

349.39   Mussolini-style desk]   The desk of Italian dictator Benito Mussolini (1883–1945) was conspicuously large and plain, almost the only item of furniture in his vast office at the Palazzo Venezia in Rome.

352.38   "Where there's life there's hope."]   Cf. Cicero (106–43 B.C.E.), *Epistulae ad Atticum* ("Letters to Atticus," 68–43 B.C.E.), Book IX.10: "*Ægroto, dum anima est, spes est.*"

353.38   Howard Hughes hired Mormons]   The financial empire of American business mogul Howard Hughes (1905–1976) was overseen in the last decade of Hughes's life by Frank William Gay, a member of the Church of Jesus Christ of Latter-day Saints, and his handpicked team of advisors, most of whom were fellow Mormons.

358.6   Carlyle]   The Carlyle Hotel (opened 1929), combination residential and luxury hotel on East Seventy-sixth Street, New York City.

361.2 Al Pacino] American actor (b. 1940) best known in the 1970s for playing Michael Corleone in the *Godfather* films.

361.3 Kevin McCarthy] American actor (1914–2010) who played lead roles in Vonnegut's stage comedy *Happy Birthday, Wanda June* (1970) and his television "revue" *Between Time and Timbuktu* (1972).

361.26–28 Isaac Bashevis Singer . . . Gunther Gebel-Williams] Singer (1902–1991), Polish-born Jewish-American writer in Yiddish; Mick Jagger (b. 1943), singer/frontman for the British rock band the Rolling Stones; Jane Fonda (b. 1937), actress and political activist; Gebel-Williams (1934–2001), animal trainer and performer for Ringling Bros. and Barnum & Bailey Circus, 1968–90.

361.29 Marlborough Gallery and Associated American Artists] Leading New York dealers in modern and contemporary art.

362.4–5 Saul Bellow and Mr. Singer] U.S.-Canadian novelist Bellow (1915–2005) was awarded the Nobel Prize in 1976, Isaac Bashevis Singer (see note 361.26–28) in 1978.

367.6–7 John Kenneth Galbraith . . . Flying Farfans] Galbraith (1908–2006), U.S.-Canadian economist, educator, diplomat, and author; Salvador Dalí (1904–1989), Spanish surrealist artist; Erica Jong (b. 1942), poet, teacher, and author of the best-selling novel *Fear of Flying* (1973); Liv Ullmann (b. 1938), Norwegian actress of stage and screen; the Flying Farfans, trapeze artists long associated with Ringling Bros. and Barnum & Bailey Circus.

367.9 Robert Redford] American film actor, producer, and director (b. 1936).

369.11 "Boris."] The BORIS Electronic Chess Computer, developed in 1978–81 by Arleen and Steve Chafitz, of Rockville, Maryland, was one of the earliest consumer computer chess games.

369.23 Putzi Hanfstaengl] Born in Germany, Ernst "Putzi" Hanfstaengl (1887–1975) graduated from Harvard College in 1909 and remained in the United States to run the New York office of the family art publishing firm. He returned to Germany in 1921 and met Hitler the following year. Hanfstaengl became a confidant and supporter of the Nazi leader and was appointed foreign press chief of the Nazi party in 1932, but gradually became estranged from Hitler. Fearing for his life, Hanfstaengl went into exile in England in 1937 and interned there at the outbreak of World War II. In 1942 he was sent to the United States, where he wrote confidential reports on Hitler and the Nazi leadership. His memoir *Unheard Witness* was published in 1957 and reprinted posthumously as *Hitler: The Missing Years*.

## DEADEYE DICK

378.1     Jill]   Jill Krementz, Vonnegut's second wife.

379.1–2     Who is Celia . . . That all her swains commend her?]   Cf. *The Two Gentlemen of Verona*, IV.ii.39–40: "Who is Silvia? what is she, / That all our swains commend her?"

381.13–15     *James Beard's American Cookery . . . The African Cookbook*]   Three best-selling cookbooks of the 1970s: *James Beard's American Cookery* (1972), by James Beard (1903–1985); *The Classic Italian Cook Book* (1973), by Marcella Hazan (1923–2013); *The African Cookbook* (1970), by Bea Sandler (Beatrice Pollock, 1907–1974).

381.19     Grand Hotel Oloffson]   The main building of what is now the Grand Hotel Oloffson was built in the 1890s as a compound for the Sams, a dynasty of Haitian businessmen and politicians with strong U.S. ties that produced two of the nation's presidents, Tirésias Simon Sam (1896–1902) and Vilbrun Guillaume Sam (February–July 1915). It was the murder of Guillaume Sam by a mob loyal to his political rival, the anti-American Dr. Rosalvo Bobo, that sparked the U.S. occupation of Haiti in 1915. During the occupation, which lasted through 1934, the Sam family compound was used as a U.S. military hospital. In 1935, the property was leased by the new Haitian government to a Norwegian entrepreneur, Walter Gustav Oloffson, who converted it into a forty-four-room hotel.

382.6–7     Al and Sue Seitz]   Al Seitz (1918–1982), of Queens, New York, purchased the Hotel Oloffson in 1960. In 1967 he married Suzanne "Sue" Laury (b. 1943), of Allentown, Pennsylvania, who became his business partner. After his death, Sue Seitz managed the hotel until 1987.

382.10     James Jones]   Among Jones's novels are *From Here to Eternity* (1951) and *The Thin Red Line* (1962). Jones married Gloria Mosolino (1928–2006) at the Hotel Oloffson in February 1957.

382.26–27     Cliff McCarthy]   Clifford T. McCarthy (1921–2003), a painter, photographer, and professor of art history, was born in Rockford, Illinois, and educated at Layton Art School, Milwaukee, Wisconsin, and the University of Wisconsin–Madison. He taught painting and art history at Ohio University, in Athens, from 1958 to 1991, and was host of Ohio Public Radio's "The Arts in Ohio" from 1991 to 1994.

382.27    John Rettig]    Rettig (1855–1932) was born in Cincinnati, Ohio, and studied painting under Frank Duveneck at the local Mc-Micken School of Art and Design. He worked in North Africa, Paris, and Rome before settling in the Netherlands, where he found an abiding subject in the fishing villages of northern Holland.

382.27    Frank Duveneck]    Duveneck (1848–1919) was born to German immigrants in Covington, Kentucky, and studied art in Cincinnati and at the Royal Academy of Munich. His first American show, in Boston in 1875, was such a success that three years later he opened a studio school in Germany for young American painters. In 1886 he married his accomplished student Elizabeth Boott (1846–1888). He returned to America after her death from pneumonia, and lived in Covington for the remainder of his life. To supplement his income, he taught painting at the McMicken School of Art and Design and its successor institution, the Art Academy of Cincinnati.

383.14    "The Minorite Church of Vienna"]    Vonnegut became familiar with Hitler's watercolor of the French Gothic *Minoritenkirche* (1910) when the German journalist Joachim C. Fest (1926–2006), who owned the painting, included a black-and-white reproduction of it in his best-selling biography *Hitler* (1973; English translation, 1974).

383.30    Frederic Courtland Penfield]    Penfield (1855–1922) was U.S. Ambassador to Austria-Hungary, 1913–17.

394.15    Liederkranz]    Semisoft smear-ripened cow's-milk cheese, ivory in color and with an edible yellow rind, developed in the 1880s by German immigrant cheese-makers as an American approximation of Europe's pungent, strong-smelling Limburger.

400.33    .30–06 Springfield rifle]    A bolt-action rifle with a five-round clip, the Springfield M1903 "thirty-aught-six" was the standard U.S. infantry weapon in World War I and saw limited service in World War II.

401.15    Iron Cross]    German military decoration for bravery in battle.

401.34–35    lifting of the Turkish siege of Vienna in 1683]    The Turkish siege of Vienna lasted from July 14 to September 12, 1683. It ended in the so-called Battle of Vienna, which broke the advance of the Ottoman forces into Europe and marked the beginning of the ascendency of the Austro-Hungarian Empire.

403.27    Sam Browne belt]    Wide leather belt supported by a matching strap across the right shoulder, named for General Samuel

Browne (1824–1901), the British Indian Army officer who popularized the device.

403.28    Hitler Youth]    *Hitlerjugend* (1926–45), a paramilitary Nazi youth organization. In 1936 membership became mandatory for all "Aryan" boys in Germany age ten to seventeen.

406.33    Carry me back to old Virginny]    Title of a minstrel song (c. 1878) by African American singer, songwriter, and performer James A. Bland (1854–1911).

412.17    Siege Perilous]    Vacant seat at King Arthur's Round Table reserved for the knight who retrieved the Holy Grail. Merlin put a spell on the chair, rendering it fatal to any unworthy who dared sit in it. It was eventually occupied by Galahad.

414.5–6    Nicholas Murray Butler]    American philosopher, diplomat, and educator (1862–1947) who was the twelfth president of Columbia University (1901–45) and, for his wide-ranging work with the Carnegie Endowment for International Peace, a recipient of the Nobel Peace Prize (1931).

414.7    Alexander Woollcott]    American playwright, drama critic, actor, broadcaster, and humorist (1887–1943) who was the model for Sheridan Whiteside, the title character of Kaufman and Hart's Broadway comedy *The Man Who Came to Dinner* (1939).

414.8    Cornelia Otis Skinner]    American actress, playwright, and monologist (1899–1979) who, with her Bryn Mawr classmate Emily Kimbrough, wrote the humorous autobiographical memoir *Our Hearts Were Young and Gay* (1942).

414.9    Gregor Piatigorsky]    Russian-born American cellist (1903–1976).

422.12    Garand . . . M-1]    The M-1 Garand semi-automatic rifle replaced the Springfield .30–06 bolt-action rifle as standard U.S. Army issue in 1936 and was used widely in World War II and the Korean War.

435.23    "Thou shalt not kill."]    Exodus 20:13.

440.3–4    "ink-stained wretches."]    Woollcott used the epithet repeatedly in his writings of the 1920s, especially his column "Second Thoughts on First Nights" in *The New York Times*.

443.26–27    Abraham Lincoln Brigade]    Collective name for the American volunteers who fought against Franco in the Spanish Civil War (1936–39).

451.1     *spuma di cioccolata*]   Italian: chocolate mousse.

453.24–25     Old Man River]   See note 136.15.

456.7     Eugene V. Debs]   Debs (1855–1926), an American politician and union leader, was a Democratic senator from Indiana (1885–89), organizer of the American Railway Union (1893–94), founder of the International Workers of the World (the Wobblies, 1905), and five-time presidential candidate of the Socialist Party (1900–1920).

456.8     Jane Addams]   Addams (1860–1935), a pioneer of the settlement house movement and an activist for workers' right, women's rights, and world peace, was the author of *Twenty Years at Hull House* (1910) and the first American woman to be a recipient of the Nobel Peace Prize (1931).

457.5     William Cowper]   English poet and hymnist (1731–1800).

457.8–11     God moves . . . upon the storm]   First verse of "Light Shining Out of Darkness," hymn (1774) by William Cowper (see note above).

461.12     Theatre de Lys]   Off-Broadway theatre at 121 Christopher Street, called the Theatre de Lys from 1953 until 1981, when it was renamed the Lucille Lortel Theatre. (Vonnegut's play *Happy Birthday, Wanda June* was staged there from October 7 through November 15, 1970.)

462.31–32     Edna St. Vincent Millay]   See note 326.38.

466.22     James Hilton]   Popular English novelist (1900–1954) whose bestsellers included *Lost Horizon* (1933), *Goodbye, Mr. Chips* (1934), and *Random Harvest* (1941).

466.33     Captain Kidd]   William Kidd (c. 1645–1701), Scottish pirate who, according to legend, left a buried treasure somewhere in Atlantic Canada or New England.

469.2     James Thurber]   American humorist (1894–1961) long associated with *The New Yorker*, known for his cartoons, short stories, memoirs, and comic writings.

469.5–6     *The Male Animal*]   Broadway comedy (1940) by James Thurber (see note above) and his Ohio State classmate, the writer, director, and actor Elliott Nugent (1896–1980).

481.38–39     Bendel's or Saks or Bloomingdale's]   Upscale retailers of women's fashions in New York City.

494.6     Joseph of Arimathea]   For the biblical figure, see Matthew 27:57–60, Mark 15:42–46, Luke 23:50–56, and John 19:38–42. For the figure of Arthurian legend, see Robert de Boron's twelfth-century French poem *Joseph d'Arimathe*.

494.18      Glastonbury]   Seventh-century abbey in Somerset, England, that, according to late medieval legend, was built on the site of an ancient church—the first Christian church in England—founded by Joseph of Arimathea (see note above).

502.7–9      'Velvet Fog,' . . . Mel Tormé]   According to his memoir *It Wasn't All Velvet* (1988), American jazz and pop singer Tormé (1925–1999), who possessed a warm and distinctive tenor voice, was given his enduring nickname in the late 1940s by New York City disc jockey Fred Robbins.

504.22      "Crucifixion in Rome"]   Oil on canvas (1888), measuring 8 × 10 1/16 inches, by John Rettig (see note 382.27). It was given to the Cincinnati Museum of Art in 1955 by the Friars Club of Cincinnati, a Roman Catholic service organization.

505.13      Volendam]   Fishing village in northern Holland, the subject of paintings by Rettig and by many other artists, including Renoir, Picasso, and Maurice Boitel.

506.4      Picasso's "Guernica"]   Mural-sized oil in black, white, and gray (1937) by the Spanish artist Pablo Picasso (1881–1973), conceived in response to the horrors of the Spanish Civil War, specifically the German bombing of the Basque village of Guernica on April 26, 1937.

509.23–26      Arjumand Banu Begum . . . Shah Jahan]   Arjumand Banu (1593–1631), better known by her epithet Mumtaz Mahal ("the chosen one of the palace"), was the second and favorite wife of Shah Jahan (1592–1662), fifth Mughal Emperor, 1628–58.

514.21      Pennwalt Biphetamine]   Schedule II stimulant (see note 521.8–18) containing equal amounts of amphetamine and dextroamphetamine, manufactured from the 1950s through the early 1980s by Pennwalt Chemical Company, of Philadelphia, Pennsylvania, and sold in a distinctive glossy-black capsule. Originally developed to treat narcolepsy, Biphetamine was widely prescribed as a weight-loss aid until banned by the U.S. Food and Drug Administration as too addictive.

516.34      Timex]   Inexpensive line of American wristwatches launched by the U.S. Time Company in 1950.

519.38      Henry Moore]   English sculptor (1898–1986) known for his semi-abstract human figures and large-scale abstract biomorphic forms.

520.2–7    Rabo Karabekian . . . 'The Temptation of Saint Anthony'] The fictional Rabo Karabekian (b. 1916) and his minimalist
painting *The Temptation of Saint Anthony* figure into Vonnegut's novel
*Breakfast of Champions* (1973). There the painting is described as being
"twenty feet wide and sixteen feet high. The field was *Hawaiian Avocado*, a green wall paint manufactured by the O'Hare Paint and Varnish
Company in Hellertown, Pennsylvania. The vertical stripe was day-glo
orange reflecting tape." Vonnegut's sketch of Karabekian's *Temptation*
from *Breakfast of Champions* is reproduced below.

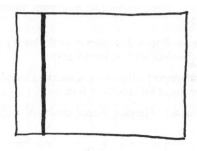

521.8–18    "Amphetamine has been . . . indistinguishable from
schizophrenia."] As required by the Controlled Substances Act of
the United States (1970), this notice from the U.S. Food and Drug
Administration is printed, under the rubric "Drug Abuse and Addiction," in the informational literature accompanying all "Schedule II"
prescription drugs sold in the United States. A Schedule II drug is
defined by the Controlled Substances Act as a legally manufactured
opiate, stimulant, depressant, or hallucinogen that has a high potential
for abuse and, if abused, may lead to severe psychological or physical
dependence.

521.13    sleep EEG] A "sleep electroencephalogram" is a test that
produces a graphic representation of the electrical activity of the brain
during sleep.

521.22–23    Darvon and Ritalin and methaqualone and Valium] Darvon (dextropropoxyphene) was a Schedule II opiate painkiller (see
note 521.8–18) manufactured by Eli Lilly and Company from 1953 until
2010, when it was banned by the U.S. Food and Drug Administration
as too addictive; Ritalin (methylphenidate) is a Schedule II stimulant
developed in 1955 by Ciba (now manufactured by Novartis) and widely
used to treat attention deficit disorder; methaqualone was a Schedule

II depressant sold by three successive manufacturers under the brand name Quaalude from 1951 until 1985, when it was banned by the FDA as too addictive; Valium (diazepam) is a benzodiazepine drug developed in 1963 by Hoffman–La Roche and widely used to treat general anxiety.

523.1–2    "The prodigal son . . . fatted calf!"]    See Luke 15:11–32.

525.6–7    remake of the movie *King Kong*]    The 1976 Dino De Laurentiis production, directed by John Guillerman and starring Jeff Bridges, Charles Grodin, and Jessica Lange.

532.4    Gleem]    Brand of fluoride toothpaste made since 1952 by Procter & Gamble.

535.8–11    one of Plato's dialogues . . . wild horse]    See *Phaedrus* IX.246a–254e (the so-called Chariot Allegory).

541.25    Barcalounger]    Reclining armchair made by the Barcalo Furniture Company of Buffalo, New York.

545.1    Blaupunkt]    German manufacturer of audio equipment, founded 1923.

555.17    Lafayette Escadrille]    Squadron of the French Air Service, 1916–18, composed mainly of American volunteer aviators.

556.9    M-16]    Assault rifle adopted by the U.S. military during the Vietnam War.

## GALÁPAGOS

560.1    *Hillis L. Howie*]    Howie, a teacher at the Orchard School, Indianapolis, when Vonnegut attended in 1928–32, directed Cottonwood Gulch, a southwestern American "summer camp on wheels," from 1926 to 1970. He and his assistants drove their charges from Indiana and Illinois to the wilderness of Arizona and New Mexico, where for six weeks they endeavored to, in the words of Howie's prospectus, "establish temporary camps in sagebrush, piñon, and big timber" and "investigate the fauna, flora, and geology of each territory." Vonnegut's father, a professional architect, designed six cabins and Howie's personal residence at Cottonwood Gulch Ranch, near Albuquerque, in exchange for his son's camp tuition.

560.4    Ben Hitz]    See note 164.1.

561.1–2    *In spite of everything . . . good at heart*]    From the entry for July 15, 1944, in *The Diary of a Young Girl*, by Anne Frank, translated from the Dutch by B. M. Mooyaart (Garden City, N.Y.: Doubleday, 1962).

567.3    James Wait]  Vonnegut's character shares the name of the title character of *The Nigger of the "Narcissus": A Tale of the Sea* (1897), short novel by the Anglo-Polish novelist Joseph Conrad (1857–1924).

567.20    Calle Diez de Agosto]  Street named for the date of Quito's principled but failed declaration of independence from Spain, on August 10, 1809. It was the gesture that sparked the revolutionary movement across South America, and put Quito (and, by extension, Ecuador) on the path to internationally recognized independence in 1830.

571.25–28    Charles Darwin . . . Her Majesty's ship *Beagle*]  While an undergraduate at Cambridge University, Darwin (1809–1882) became a favorite student of John Steven Henslow, one of the foremost naturalists of the day. At Henslow's recommendation, Darwin was invited by Robert FitzRoy, captain of HMS *Beagle*, to accompany him as an unpaid naturalist on a five-year survey of the coast of South America, from December 1831 to October 1836. Darwin's journal of his travels, *The Voyage of the Beagle*, was published in London in 1839.

571.35–572.12    "Nothing could be less inviting . . . most numerous."]  From a description of Chatham Island (modern San Cristóbal, the easternmost of the principal islands in the Galápagos Archipelago) in Chapter XVII of *The Voyage of the Beagle* (1839). Darwin explored Chatham Island from September 16 to 22, 1835.

572.29    *On the Origin of Species*]  Published in 1859, when Darwin was fifty years old.

574.34    Bishop of Panama]  Fray Tomás de Berlanga (1487–1551), fourth bishop of Panama (1534–37), was among the first party of Europeans to explore the Galápagos Archipelago, on March 10, 1535. In a letter to Charles V, Holy Roman Emperor and King of Spain, he described the archipelago as "dross, worthless, because it has not the power of raising a little grass, but only some thistles." He did, however, note the presence of phenomenally large saddleback land tortoises (*galápagos*), which, he remarked, might be a good source of meat for sailors.

578.27    *San Mateo*]  Spanish: Saint Matthew.

584.19    Antonio José de Sucre]  In 1822, as one of Simón Bolívar's revolutionary generals, Sucre helped liberate the city of Quito from Spain, paving the way for Ecuadorian independence in 1830.

594.11    Santa Rosalia]  The Galápagos island of Santa Rosalia is a Vonnegut fiction, named after Saint Rosalia of Palermo, Sicily

(1130–1166), a hermit who lived and died in a limestone cave in Mount Pellegrino. In his influential paper "Homage to Saint Rosalia; or, Why Are There So Many Kinds of Animals?" (1959), the Yale biologist G. Evelyn Hutchinson (1903–1991), a pioneer researcher in ecology and biodiversity, recounted his fruitful work studying the remarkably diverse but stable ecosystem of aquatic insects in an isolated pond at the foot of Mount Pellegrino, which was fed from waters flowing through Rosalia's cave. In a grateful aside, Hutchinson proposed that, for the purposes of his paper, "we take Santa Rosalia as the patroness of evolutionary studies," a fancy that has been widely adopted among Western biologists.

596.3–4    Jacqueline Kennedy Onassis]    Jacqueline "Jackie" Bouvier (1929–1994) married Massachusetts senator John F. Kennedy in 1953. A socialite and style icon, she was First Lady of the United States from 1961 until the president's death in 1963. In 1968 she married Aristotle Onassis, a Greek shipping magnate, who died in 1975. After 1975 she was a book editor, first for Viking Press, then for Doubleday.

607.19    Gottfried Treviranus]    German naturalist and botanist (1776–1837) who published the first volume of his multivolume masterwork, *Biologie*, in 1802.

607.29–32    *Sunset and evening star . . . out to sea*]    From "Crossing the Bar," by the English poet Alfred, Lord Tennyson, in his *Demeter and Other Poems* (1889).

608.33–36    *If I were hanged . . . O mother o' mine!*]    From "Mother o' Mine," by the English writer Rudyard Kipling, originally published as the untitled dedication to his novel *The Light That Failed* (1891).

609.2–7    *In the dark womb . . . some of her*]    From "C.L.M.," by English poet John Masefield, an elegy for his mother, Caroline Louisa (Parker) Masefield (1851–1884), in his *Ballads and Poems* (1910).

609.10–13    *Lord . . . the child she bears*]    From "The Mother's Hymn" (1861–62), by the American poet William Cullen Bryant, in his privately printed *Hymns* (1864).

609.17–18    *Honor thy father . . . thy God giveth thee*]    Exodus 20:12.

610.19–20    *Marriage: a community . . . making in all, two*]    From *The Devil's Dictionary* (1911), by American wit and short-story writer Ambrose Bierce (1842–c. 1914).

610.23–25    *Marriage from love . . . savour*]    From *Don Juan* (Canto III.v), by the English poet George Gordon, Lord Byron, first published in *Don Juan: Cantos III–V* (1821).

612.14      *Omoo*]   Polynesian word meaning "rover" or "wanderer"; also the title of an autobiographical novel by Herman Melville (1819–1891), *Omoo: A Narrative of Adventures in the South Seas* (1847).

624.35      Huntington's chorea]   Also called Huntington's disease: adult-onset hereditary disorder in which nerve cells in certain areas of the brain waste away.

635.24      Elaine's]   Bar and restaurant (1963–2011) at Second Avenue and Eighty-eighth Street, on Manhattan's Upper East Side, that catered to a largely literary crowd.

635.32–33      Rudolf Nureyev]   Celebrated Soviet-born dancer (1938–1993), a master of both ballet and modern dance.

644.8–9      Henry Kissinger, Mick Jagger, Paloma Picasso, William F. Buckley, Jr.]   Kissinger, see note 213.14; Jagger, see note 361.26–28; Paloma Picasso (b. 1949), French-Spanish jewelry designer, fashion icon, and entrepreneur, is the youngest daughter of Pablo Picasso (see note 506.4); William F. Buckley, Jr. (1925–2008), American writer, editor, and television personality who, in 1955, founded the conservative weekly *National Review*.

644.10      Walter Cronkite]   American journalist (1916–2009) who, as the anchorman of the daily *CBS Evening News* television broadcast for nearly twenty years (1962–81), earned the nickname "The Most Trusted Man in America."

644.35–36      president of Ecuador]   León Febres-Cordero (1931–2008) was president of Ecuador in 1984–88, not Vonnegut's fictional Dr. Sepúlveda de la Madrid.

646.2      *The Tonight Show*, starring Johnny Carson]   Comic entertainer Carson (1925–2005) was host of NBC television's *The Tonight Show*, a nightly talk and variety show, from 1962 to 1992.

646.14–15      *Ecstasy and Me . . .* Hedy Lamarr]   Lamarr (1914–2000), Austro-American screen actress and inventor, published an autobiography, *Ecstasy and Me: My Life as a Woman*, in 1966.

657.4      *Good Morning America*]   ABC television morning news and talk program, broadcast every weekday since November 1975.

658.12      finch which ate what woodpeckers would have eaten]   *Camarhynchus pallidus*, commonly called the woodpecker finch or carpenter finch.

658.19–20      *Geospiza difficilis*]   Commonly called the sharp-beaked ground finch or vampire finch.

662.1–2   *For of all sad words . . . "It might have been!"*]   From "Maud Muller" (1854), by the American poet John Greenleaf Whittier, first collected in *The Panorama and Other Poems* (1856).

667.3   Dom Pérignon]   Prestige champagne produced by the French winery Moët & Chandon, named after the Benedictine monk Pierre Pérignon (1638–1715), the first bottler of sparkling wine.

668.7–9   *A little neglect . . . the rider was lost*]   From "The Way to Wealth," the preface to the final edition of *Poor Richard's Almanack*, a pamphlet published serially, 1732–58, by Benjamin Franklin.

671.11   retinitis pigmentosa]   Inherited degenerative disease of the photoreceptors of the retina, often resulting in blindness.

677.26   Paul W. Tibbets]   Brigadier General Tibbets (1915–2007), commander and pilot of the B-29 Superfortress *Enola Gay*, dropped the atomic bomb on Hiroshima on August 6, 1945.

678.16   Carter Braxton]   Planter and business investor (1736–1797) who represented King William County in the Virginia House of Burgesses (1770–85) and was a Virginia delegate to the Continental Congress (1775–76).

683.20   Eleonore of Palatinate-Neuborg]   Eleonore (1655–1720), born Countess Palatine of Neuborg (Upper Normandy), married Leopold I (1640–1705), the Holy Roman Emperor, in 1676.

683.20–21   King Joseph the First]   Franz Joseph (1830–1916) was Emperor of Austria and King of Hungary from 1848 to 1916.

686.9   *All is well that ends well*]   English saying memorialized by the poet, playwright, and anthologist John Heywood in the second edition of his *Proverbs* (1546).

691.26   *Happy is the nation without a history*]   Epigram attributed to the Italian jurist and political philosopher Cesare Beccaria, author of the treatise *Dei delitti e delle penne* (*On Crimes and Punishments*, 1764).

693.11   *First comes fodder, then comes morality*]   "*Erst kommt das Fressen, dann kommt die Moral*," from Act II of *Die Dreigroschenoper* (*The Threepenny Opera*, 1928), play by Bertolt Brecht.

694.5–6   *Greater love . . . his life for his friends*]   John 15:13.

695.29–35   *It was the best of times . . . the other way*]   Opening words of *A Tale of Two Cities* (1859), novel by Charles Dickens.

699.12–15   *In works of labour . . . For idle hands to do*]   From "Against Idleness and Mischief" ("How doth the little busy bee / Improve each shining hour . . ."), in *Divine Songs Attempted in Easy Language, for the Use of Children* (1715), by the English hymnist and theologian Isaac Watts.

702.32–33    *'Tis a consummation / Devoutly to be wish'd*]    *Hamlet*, III.i.62–63.

704.29    *Man is a biped without feathers*]    From the apocryphal "Definitions" of Plato, a work widely thought to be posthumously compiled by Speusippus (408–339 B.C.E.), Plato's nephew and successor as head of the Academy.

705.16–26    *Rats! . . . sharps and flats*]    From "The Pied Piper of Hamelin," by the English poet Robert Browning, in his *Dramatic Lyrics* (1842).

710.7    *Help yourself, and heaven will help you*]    "*Aide-toi, le Ciel t'aidera*," moral of "Le Chartier embourbé" ("The Carter in the Mire"), by the French poet Jean de La Fontaine, in his *Fables*, Book VI (1668).

711.30    *I owe much . . . I give the rest to the poor*]    "*Je n'ai rien vaillant; je dois beaucoup; je donne le reste aux pauvres,*" apocryphal one-sentence will left by François Rabelais, French scholar, wit, and author of *Gargantua and Pantagruel* (1532–64).

714.35–36    *What's lost . . . the swings!*]    From "Roundabouts and Swings" (1915), by the Irish humorist Patrick R. Chalmers, in his *Pipes and Tabors: A Book of Light Verse* (1921).

715.34    Waldorf-Astoria]    See note 247.33.

718.33    Greek fire]    Incendiary liquid developed c. 675 C.E. by the Byzantine Empire. Its exact composition and means of production have been lost to history.

720.4    *It is wonderful . . . satisfied*]    "*Car c'est merveille combien peu il faut à nature pour se contenter,*" from "Apologie de Raimond Sebond," by the French essayist Michel de Montaigne, in *Essays* II.xii (1595).

720.22–23    *The ship . . . like a small planet*]    From Chapter 2 of *The Nigger of the "Narcissus"* (1897), by Joseph Conrad (see note 567.3).

735.5–6    *Imagination . . . much cheaper!*]    From the preface to *Prue and I* (1856), a fantastical series of autobiographical sketches by the American essayist and monologist George William Curtis.

738.3    *Oaths are but words, and words but wind*]    From *Hudibras* (II. ii.107), mock-heroic epic poem (1663–78) by Samuel Butler.

745.13–15    *In depraved May . . . Among whispers*]    From "Gerontion" (1920), by the Anglo-American poet T. S. Eliot, in his volume *Ara Vos Prec* (1920).

746.9–10    *May will be fine . . . twenty-four*]   From Number IX ("The chestnut casts his flambeaux, and the flowers . . ."), by the English poet A. E. Housman, in his *Last Poems* (1922).

746.19    *June is bustin' out all over*]   Title of a song from the musical *Carousel* (1945), book and lyrics by Oscar Hammerstein II, music by Richard Rodgers.

746.22–26    *The skies they were ashen . . . immemorial year*]   From "Ulalume" (1847), by the American writer Edgar Allan Poe, collected posthumously.

747.20    "Mount Ararat."]   Mountain in eastern Turkey identified with the "mountains of Ararat" where, according to Genesis, Noah's ark came to rest.

757.8–15    *A capital ship . . . in his bunk below*]   From "A Nautical Ballad; or, 'The Walloping Window Blind,'" by the American writer Charles E. Carryl, from *Davy and the Goblin; or, What Followed Reading "Alice's Adventures in Wonderland"* (1885), a fantasy novel for children.

759.1–2    *Curiosity . . . a vigorous mind*]   Cf. *The Rambler* No. 103, Tuesday, March 12, 1751, by the English essayist Samuel Johnson.

759.24    *Doubt . . . Action alone*]   From "Labour," Chapter 40 of *Past and Present* (1843), a study in "the condition of England" by the Scottish writer Thomas Carlyle.

761.18–22    *There was an old man . . . in my beard."*]   Untitled limerick, by Edward Lear, in his *Book of Nonsense* (1846).

762.25    *The mass of men lead lives of quiet desperation*]   From "Economy," Chapter 1 of *Walden; or, Life in the Woods* (1852), by the American essayist Henry David Thoreau.

766.30–31    *The happiest life . . . rejoice*]   From the *Ajax* of Sophocles (c. 450–430 B.C.E.), translated into English verse by Sir George Young (1885).

768.16    *Something there is that doesn't love a wall*]   From "Mending Wall," poem in blank verse by Robert Frost, in his *North of Boston* (1914).

768.25–26    *"Guten morgen . . . Wie geht es Ihnen . . . ?"*]   "Good morning . . . How are you?"

771.15–18    *Last scene of all . . . sans everything*]   *As You Like It*, II.vii.163–66.

776.9–12    *All the world's a stage . . . plays many parts*]   *As You Like It*, II.vii.139–42.

777.22    *Progress has been much more general than retrogression*]    From
"On the Development of the Intellectual and Moral Faculties," Chapter
2 of *The Descent of Man, and Selection in Relation to Sex* (1871), by Charles
Darwin.

APPENDIX

785.16    "Ah! Sweet Mystery of Life"]    Song by Victor Herbert,
with words by Rida Johnson Young, from the American operetta
*Naughty Marietta* (1910).

786.7    "The Sermon on the Mount"]    See note 174.30.

786.10    fancy bindings like this one]    The Franklin Library signed
first edition of *Slapstick* was bound in a full-leather case with 22-karat-
gold stamping and featured a gilt top stain, moiré-fabric endpapers,
and a satin ribbon marker.

786.14    PX's]    Post Exchange stores—that is, government-run
retail stores, usually built on military bases, for members of the U.S.
armed forces.

787.3    *American Psychiatric Association*]    Founded in 1844 as the
Association of Medical Superintendents of American Institutions for
the Insane, the American Psychiatric Association, based in Arlington,
Virginia, is the oldest and largest organization of mental-health profes-
sionals in the world.

787.4    Bush vs. Dukakis campaign]    Incumbent vice president
George Herbert Walker Bush (b. 1924) defeated Michael Dukakis (b.
1933), Democratic governor of Massachusetts, in the 1988 election for
U.S. president.

787.17    Elie Wiesel]    Eliezer "Elie" Wiesel (b. 1928) is a Romanian-
born writer who writes in Yiddish and in French. His autobiographical
book *Night* (*La Nuit*, 1958; English translation, 1960) is based on his
and his father's experiences in the Nazi concentration camps at Auschwitz and Buchenwald in 1944–45.

787.18    Dr. Nancy Andreasen]    Andreasen (b. 1938) is chair of psychology at the University of Iowa Medical School and director of the
Iowa Mental Health Clinical Research Center. Her thirty years of research
into the mental-health histories of writers and artists was published as *The
Creating Brain: The Neuroscience of Genius* (2005).

788.4–6    *Slaughterhouse-Five* . . . firebombing of Dresden]
*Slaughterhouse-Five* was published in 1969. As an American prisoner of

war in Germany, Vonnegut witnessed the Allied bombing of Dresden on February 13–14, 1945.

788.8    Dr. Dichter]   In 1988 Howard N. Dichter, M.D. (b. 1950), was director of Family Therapy at the Albert Einstein Medical Center, Philadelphia, and an organizer for the grassroots advocacy group the National Alliance for the Mentally Ill.

789.14–15    lithium, Thorazine, Prozac, or Trofanil]   Lithium compounds and the patented prescription drugs Thorazine (chlorpromazine), Prozac (fluoxetine), and Trofanil (imipramine) are widely used to treat bipolar disorder.

789.26    Ritalin]   See note 521.22–23.

790.7–10    Mark Vonnegut . . . *Eden Express*]   Vonnegut's son, Mark Vonnegut (b. 1947), is the author of *The Eden Express: A Personal Account of Schizophrenia* (New York: Praeger, 1975).

791.15    Walter Bruetsch]   Born in Germany and trained in Switzerland and Austria, Dr. Bruetsch (1896–1977) immigrated to Indianapolis in 1924 to head up the neuropathology department of the city's Central State Hospital.

791.23    phenobarbital]   Anticonvulsive depressant, once widely prescribed as a sleep aid.

792.28    Nelson Algren]   American writer (1909–1981) whose novel *The Man with the Golden Arm* (1949), a study in heroin addiction, won a National Book Award in 1950.

793.7–8    Powers Hapgood]   See pages 168–70 of the present volume.

795.9    Charlton Heston]   American actor and conservative political activist (1923–2008).

795.23    AK-47 . . . Uzi]   The AK-47 is a Soviet assault rife designed in 1947–48 by Mikhail Kalashnikov; the Uzi is an Israeli submachine gun designed in 1948 by Uziel Gal.

796.16    Zippo . . . Bic]   Brand-name American cigarette lighters of, respectively, the World War II and Vietnam eras.

796.17    George Bush]   After serving as vice president under Ronald Reagan (1981–89), George Herbert Walker Bush (b. 1924) was the forty-first president of the United States (1989–93).

796.22    *Voyager 2*]   Space probe launched by NASA on August 20, 1977, to study the outer planets and interstellar space.

796.30    Amendment to the Constitution . . . American flag]    In 1989–90, President George H. W. Bush unsuccessfully advocated a so-called flag-protection amendment to the U.S. Constitution, which would have made it a federal crime to burn or otherwise desecrate the flag of the United States.

796.33–34    Caligula's having his horse made a consul]    According to his contemporary the historian Suetonius, Caligula (reigned 37–41 C.E.) appointed his favorite horse, Incitatus (Latin meaning "swift"), a consul (or senator) of the Roman Empire. The veracity of the story, and whether it demonstrates Caligula's alleged insanity or his utter contempt for his consuls' advice, is a matter of historical debate.

797.5–6    'This above all . . . be true']    Hamlet, I.iii.78.

797.7–8    'Fear God . . . has come']    See Revelation 14:7.

797.10–12    'God grant me . . . wisdom to know the difference']    The so-called Serenity Prayer (c. 1943), attributed to the American Protestant theologian Reinhold Niebuhr (1892–1971) as adapted for use by Alcoholics Anonymous (founded 1935).

799.12    Lear's]    Monthly magazine (1988–94) founded, published, and edited by the feminist entrepreneur Frances Lear (1923–1996) for women over the age of thirty-five.

799.13    The White Deer]    Novel for children (1945) written and illustrated by James Thurber (see note 469.2).

800.28–29    vice president of the filmmakers' union of the USSR]    Estonian filmmaker Ilmar Taska (b. 1953), who was also a vice president of the short-lived not-for-profit American-Soviet Film Initiative (1987–88), an effort to coproduce documentaries for the American and Soviet markets.

800.30    glasnost]    Policy promoted by Soviet leader Mikhail Gorbachev (b. 1931) in the mid- to late 1980s that called for greater openness and freedom of discussion in Soviet society.

804.26    Boris Karloff]    English actor (1887–1969) who memorably portrayed Frankenstein's monster in the Hollywood version of Frankenstein (1931) and its sequels, Bride of Frankenstein (1935) and Son of Frankenstein (1939).

804.38–39    Josef Mengele]    Mengele (1911–1979) was a Nazi SS officer (see note 204.2) and the chief physician at the Auschwitz concentration camp, notorious for carrying out horrific medical experiments on live human subjects.

807.2     Cathedral of St. John the Divine]   Cathedral of the Episcopal Diocese of New York, designed in 1888 and still unfinished, and dedicated in 1899. It is one of the five largest Christian churches in the world.

807.27–29     Reverend Jim Jones . . . cyanide]   American religious leader James Warren "Jim" Jones (1931–1978) was the founder of the autocratic Peoples Temple Christian Church and Agricultural Project in Jonestown, Guyana. In November 1978, a party led by California congressman Leo Ryan visited Jonestown to investigate alleged human rights abuses at Jonestown reported by stateside families of Peoples Temple members. On November 18, after the departing Ryan and three U.S. journalists were murdered on a Guyana airstrip by Peoples Temple loyalists, Jones led Temple members in mass murder and suicide. A total of 909 persons, including Jones, took their lives or were killed at Jonestown, most by drinking cyanide-laced grape Flavor Aid.

808.16     Spartacus]   Gladiator (109–71 B.C.E.) and one of the leaders of a slave revolt against the Roman Empire (the so-called Third Servile War, 73–71 B.C.E.).

808.26–27     'Forgive them . . . what they do.']   See Luke 23:34.

809.20     Paul Moore, Jr.]   Episcopal clergyman (1919–2003) and bishop of New York, 1972–89.

809.27–28     'Rule, Britannia.']   British patriotic song originally written for *Alfred* (1740), a court masque with book and lyrics by the Scottish poet James Thomson (1700–1748) and music by the English theatrical composer Thomas Arne (1710–1778).

811.40     Charles Darwin]   See note 571.25–28.

815.12–19     Jim Fisk . . . 'Nothing is lost save honor.']   James "Big Jim" Fisk Jr. (1835–1872) was a stockbroker who conspired with fellow robber baron Jay Gould to wrest control of the Erie Railroad from the industrialist Cornelius Vanderbilt. Legend has it that when, after some twenty-six legal attempts, Gould at last admitted defeat, Fisk chuckled and then uttered his famous quip.

816.20–21     *How It Feels to Be Adopted*]   Nonfiction book for children, with text and photographs by Jill Krementz, published in 1982.

817.2     Dan Boorstin]   American academic and historian Daniel J. Boorstin (1914–2004) was Librarian of Congress from 1975 to 1987.

*This book is set in 10 point ITC Galliard, a*
*face designed for digital composition by Matthew Carter*
*and based on the sixteenth-century face Granjon. The paper*
*is acid-free lightweight opaque and meets the requirements for*
*permanence of the American National Standards Institute.*
*The binding material is Brillianta, a woven rayon cloth*
*made by Van Heek-Scholco Textielfabreiken, Holland.*
*Composition by Publishers' Design and Production Services, Inc.*
*Printing and binding by Edwards Brothers Malloy, Ann Arbor.*
*Designed by Bruce Campbell.*

# THE LIBRARY OF AMERICA SERIES

The Library of America fosters appreciation and pride in America's literary heritage by publishing, and keeping permanently in print, authoritative editions of America's best and most significant writing. An independent nonprofit organization, it was founded in 1979 with seed funding from the National Endowment for the Humanities and the Ford Foundation.

To subscribe to the series or to order individual copies, please visit www.loa.org or call (800) 964.5778.